A WARRIOR'S KNOWLEDGE

THE CASTES AND THE OUTCASTES
—VOLUME TWO—

DAVIS ASHURA

A WARRIOR'S KNOWLEDGE

DuSum Publishing, LLC

Paperback Edition 2018

ISBN-10: 0-9997044-7-8
ISBN-13: 978-0-9997044-7-9

DEDICATION

To my Amma and Nanna
because every writer should give credit
to those who loved them first

ACKNOWLEDGMENTS

Like all things of worth, this book would not exist without the help of some truly wonderful and generous people. As usual, first comes my wife, Stephanie, who gave me the time and freedom to actually sit down and write this book you're reading. And then, the men and women of the Catawba Valley Ass-whoopin' Writer's Group, who once more gave their all to a manuscript that was, well, just not very good. And then to Holly, who once more helped me take that manuscript and polish it up to the best of my abilities. This time, she didn't like it when I peered over her shoulder to skulk out whatever criticisms she was writing. I stopped doing it.

To all of them, I once more offer my most humble thank you.

And again, if the book is not your cup of tea, it's entirely my fault.

OTHER BOOKS BY DAVIS ASHURA:

The Castes and the OutCastes

A Warrior's Path

A Warrior's Knowledge

A Warrior's Penance

Omnibus edition (available as eBook only)

Stories of Arisa — Volume One

The Chronicles of William Wilde

William Wilde and the Necrosed

William Wilde and the Stolen Life

William Wilde and the Unusual Suspects

William Wilde and the Sons of Deceit (available Spring 2019)

William Wilde and the Lord of Mourning (available Summer 2019)

TABLE OF CONTENTS

A Warrior's Knowledge

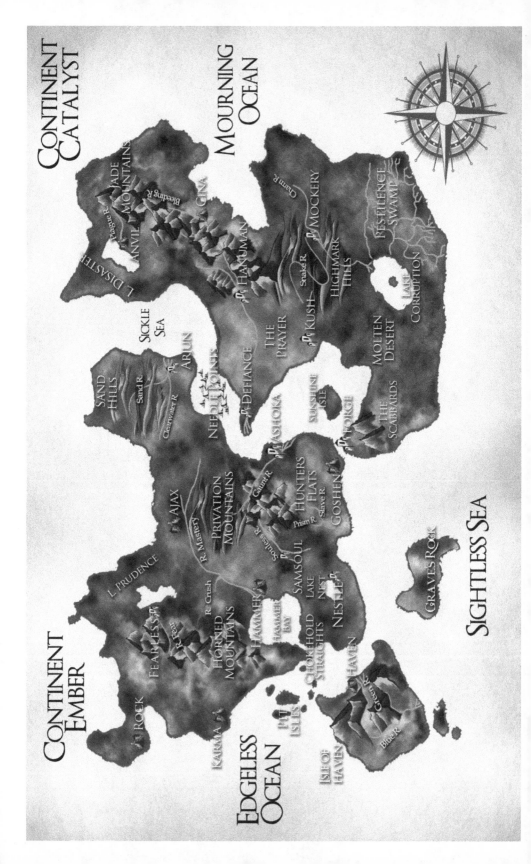

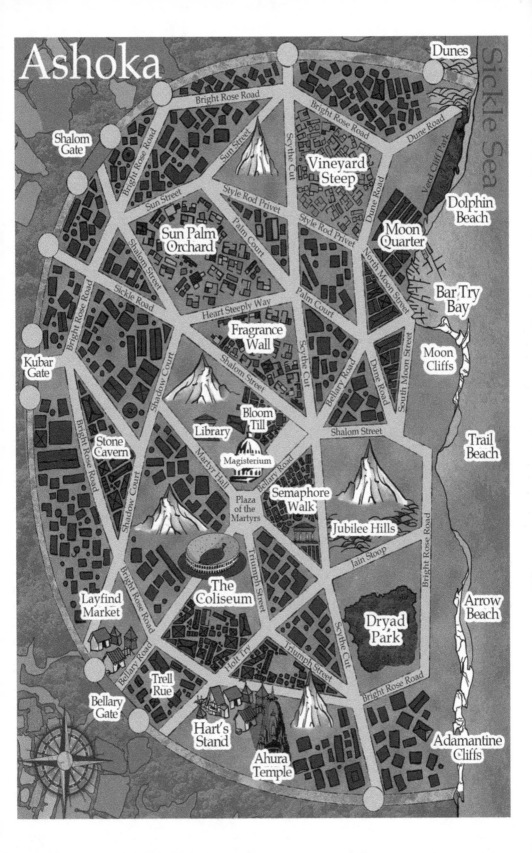

THE TRIAL SO FAR

T he Trials were the means by which Humanity maintained a fragile link between their far-flung city-states. It is a holy mission, and most often carried out by Caste Kumma, the warrior Caste, and all who accept such a weighty obligation understand that it might lead to their deaths.

The Trial from Ashoka to Nestle is no different, and it is also Rukh Shektan's first. He is a Virgin to the Trials, as are his cousin, Farn Arnicep and his fellow Kumma and close friend, Keemo Chalwin, and Brand Wall of Caste Rahail. Rukh, however, is unique. He is the current Champion of the Tournament of Hume. His sword is said to be the finest in generations.

Disaster eventually overtakes the Trial. It is discovered by a large band of Chimeras and destroyed en masse. Few Ashokans survive, and among them are Rukh and his friends. They escape the ambush, but the means of their survival is considered anathema: they learn Talents not of their Caste. It is a situation that leaves them dismayed and horrified.

But they are also warriors of Ashoka, and they know their duty: their home must be warned of what has happened. They know that this many Chimeras gathered together at one time might indicate that Suwraith, the Sorrow Bringer, has deadly intentions toward their home city of Ashoka. Rukh elects to send several warriors back to Ashoka in order to carry word of the Nestle Trial's fate, while he, Farn, Keemo, and Brand will track the Chimeras to their staging area.

Their plans proceed, and as they follow the Chimeras, all four men seek to master their newly acquired, but unsought Talents. Brand learns to Shield and quicken his movements like a Kumma, while Rukh and the others form Blends, a perfect means of camouflage.

It is a situation that leads to great unhappiness, and Farn wonders if they would have been better off dying amongst their brother warriors in the Trial. He worries they are naaja, Tainted, or worse, ghrinas, children of two Castes. His fears are not without foundation, but Rukh will not hear of it. They have a mission to accomplish, and if Talents not of Caste Kumma are the means by which they complete their assignment, so be it. He demands that they put aside their fears for the future and accept whatever punishment is due them, after they find where the Chimeras are staging.

His orders are reluctantly carried out, and by the time they finally track down the Chimeras, all four warriors have a better understanding of their newfound Talents.

They reach the Hunters Flats and discover the leaders of the Chimeras, the bull-like Baels, conversing privately with one another, far away from the bulk of their army. The Ashokans see an opportunity to destroy their hated enemies. Just as they are about to launch their attack, Suwraith arrives in a storm of wind and terror.

The Ashokans hide, Blended as hard as they can. And while the Sorrow Bringer is amongst the Baels, they learn of Her plans for Ashoka: their home is to be destroyed.

Suwraith eventually leaves, and just as Rukh and the others are about to attack the Baels, they listen in astonishment as the bull-like commanders argue on how best to disobey Suwraith; to actively oppose Her and protect Humanity. It is a stunning revelation, and one not easily believed.

Rukh decides to speak with Li-Dirge, the Bael commander, who is now alone after sending his brethren back to rejoin the rest of the army while he meditates.

Before Rukh can approach the Bael, he captures a Blended woman who suddenly manifests by his side. Her appearance is staggering. Women do not ever join the Trials, so she should not be in the Wildness. But even more shocking is the women's features. She is obviously a ghrina, a child of two Castes. No such individual has ever been known to survive to adulthood since they are universally banished from the cities upon birth. They are thought to die in the Wildness, but given this woman's presence, it is obviously an incorrect assumption.

Some of the confusion is cleared when Rukh is finally able to speak to Li-Dirge. From the Bael, he learns of the great Kumma warrior, Hume, and the death of Hume's home, the city of Hammer. Rukh discovers how Hume had instructed Suwraith's commanders in the ideals of fraternity, and in the centuries following, the Baels apparently had worked as best they could to disrupt Suwraith's plans.

And the ghrina woman, Jessira Grey, turns out to be a scout from Stronghold, a hidden city of her kind—OutCastes as they call themselves. She and her brothers, Cedar and Lure, had also been tracking the same Chimeras that had destroyed the Trial to Nestle.

During all this, Suwraith finds a way to rid Herself of Her madness. The unceasing complaints of Her dead parents and Mistress Arisa, a terrifying voice that only She hears, are silenced. The Queen pours her insanity into the minds of Her children, the Chimeras—all except the Baels. By doing so, Suwraith regains Her sanity, realizes the truth, and discovers Her betrayal at the hands of Her commanders. She sees them speaking to Humans and is enraged.

However, before She can act, She notices Her Chimeras killing one another in violent abandon. It is because of Her madness poured into them. Reluctantly, the Sorrow Bringer takes back Her insanity, losing Her memories and regaining the unwanted voices of Her dead parents and the fearsome Mistress Arisa. Confusion overwhelms Suwraith's mind, but She remembers enough. She still knows the truth about the Baels, and She thunders from the sky, intent on destroying them.

Li-Dirge and his brother Baels are gathered with the Humans, joyful that the ideals to which their ancestors had held, are finally being realized. Rukh believes them. For the first time in history, a Human understands the truth of the Baels' situation. It is a momentous event, and Li-Dirge even tells Rukh about the location of the Chimera breeding caverns—the place where Suwraith helps birth Her hordes. All the breeds of Chimera require Suwraith's direct intervention in order to procreate—the catlike Tigons, the foxlike Ur-Fels, and snakelike Braids, and the elephant-sized Balants. Only the Baels, born mysteriously and unexpectedly from the placid, dull Bovars, do not require Suwraith's touch. However, in the midst of their jubilation, the Baels realize that Suwraith has discovered their centuries-long deception.

Suwraith comes to annihilate all Her Baels, but just before the Sorrow Bringer carries out Her attack, Rukh and the other Humans are urged to flee. They do so, escaping Suwraith's clutches by the barest of margins, but Dirge and his fellow Baels, the entire command of the Eastern Plague of Continent Ember, are destroyed.

Before Rukh and the others can take stock of their situation, they are attacked by two Shylows, the giant, deadly cats of the Hunters Flats. In the ensuing battle, Jessira's brother, Lure, and Rukh's friends, Keemo and Brand, are all killed. Farn is gravely injured and he and Cedar, Jessira's other brother, go missing. Rukh escapes with a young Bael, Li-Choke, and an injured Jessira.

Meanwhile in Ashoka, Rukh's brother, Jaresh, is accused of the murder of Suge Wrestiva, a thug and degenerate, who also happens to be the only living son of Hal'El Wrestiva, the ruling 'El of House Shektan's most bitter rival. The situation is even more clouded because Jaresh is of Caste Sentya but was adopted by Dar'El and Satha Shektan into the House Shektan. Such an adoption is unprecedented and many Kummas are troubled by the situation.

As a result, when Hal'El's call for a tribunal to have Jaresh judged with the Slash of Iniquity, a death penalty, his petition is granted by the Chamber of the Lords, Caste Kumma's governing body. During the ensuing trial, it is Jaresh's sister, Bree, who discovers that Suge was secretly a snowblood addict and convinces the Chamber to decide in Jaresh's favor.

Later, a meeting of the Sil Lor Kum, the Hidden Hand of Justice—Suwraith's Human worshippers—is convened in Ashoka. The SuDin, their leader tells the other members of the Council of Rule, the MalDins, of Suwraith's plans for Ashoka. He displays the Withering Knife, a mythical weapon said to steal Jivatma. It may also be the means through which the Sorrow Bringer can overcome Ashoka's Oasis, the mystical barrier around the city that has proven impenetrable to Her might for two millennia.

Shortly after this meeting of the Council of Rule, the first murder utilizing the Withering Knife is discovered. The victim is Felt Barnel, and his corpse is withered and desiccated, as if all the water were removed from his body.

Dar'El is deeply troubled by the murder and tasks Jaresh, Bree, and Mira Terrell——the daughter of one House Shektan's councillors—with discovering the truth about the Withering Knife. In the course of their investigations, another victim is found murdered. This one is of Caste Cherid, Aqua Oilhue. Rector Bryce, a member of the City Watch, realizes that the murderer has to be of Caste Kumma, and he joins the other three in their search for information on the Withering Knife.

Jaresh is paired with Mira, and the two of them search the Cellar, the City Library's lowest floors where the oldest records are kept, while Bree and Rector look for the information in other locations. The work proves frustrating, dragging on for weeks. Eventually, it is Jaresh who discovers a code within the journal of a caravan master— a leader of a Trial—and a known member of the Sil Lor Kum. The cypher confirms the existence of the Withering Knife as well as the physical markers it leaves on its victims. They are identical to those found on Felt Barnel and Aqua Oilhue.

During all this, Rukh and Jessira, having been thrown together, are forced to overcome a lifetime of prejudice and indoctrination as they make their way to Ashoka. They come to share a deep friendship, but Jessira's wounds from the battle with the Shylow are stealing her life. The wounds fester and grow infected. Jessira is dying, and can only be saved if she can teach her knowledge of Healing. It is another Talent not of Rukh's Caste, one mastered by Shiyens, and he is unable to learn what Jessira tries to teach him.

It is then, as Jessira lies dying, that another Shylow, a female calico named Aia, walks into their camp. Rukh is prepared to lay down his life in Jessira's defense, but the cat simply stares at him, and *speaks* into his mind. It is a shocking revelation, and at first, Rukh fears he is going mad. Aia convinces him otherwise.

She is rare for her kind, able to speak to those who aren't Kesarins—the name Shylows call themselves—and as a result, quite curious about Humans. She is especially fascinated by Rukh. Aia has been following him and Jessira since before they had exited the Hunters Flats, wondering as to why he was taking such exquisite care of someone who wasn't close kin.

His notions of brotherhood and compassion captivate Aia, and she asks why he doesn't Heal Jessira. When she learns that Rukh lacks the knowledge, the Kesarin reaches into Jessira's mind, and shares it with him. Aia leaves then, vowing to see Rukh again.

As a result of the Kesarin's help, Rukh is able to stave off Jessira's injuries, and the two of them continue on to Ashoka where she is fully Healed of her injuries. Afterward, they make their way to the House Seat where Rukh is joyfully reunited with his family. He makes a full report on what has happened to him, including his Talents of Blending and Healing to the House Council. Also present during Rukh's account is Rector Bryce, who has always been unforgiving and certain of that which he considers immoral. Rector is unwilling to accept Rukh's new abilities. As a result of his attitude, Dar'El Shektan and the rest of the House Council re-examine the Watch captain's role in the search for the Withering Knife murderer.

Rukh's account of his actions in the Wildness is also explained to the Magisterium, Ashoka's governing body. Though few of the Magistrates are able to accept the Baels as allies, the decision is made to act on Li-Dirge's information and send an expeditionary force to the Chimera caverns. Their goal will be simple: extermination of all Chimera breeders. Rukh is chosen as one of the warriors for the coming expedition, and he throws himself into his work.

As the preparation for the expedition continues, the SuDin of the Sil Lor Kum turns out to be Hal'El Wrestiva. He and his Rahail lover, Varesea Apter, a fellow MalDin in the Sil Lor Kum, share a sinful relationship, one that would call for their execution were it ever discovered. But, Varesea and Hal'El are undaunted. They love one another, and they decide to kill her abusive husband, Slathtril Apter, with the Withering Knife as the first step in being together.

Rukh is able to examine the site of Slathtril Apter's murder and realizes that two people were involved in the killing. He recognizes that the victim knew his murderers, and that the Kumma in question had to have come from one of three Houses.

As for Jessira, she is alone in the city, comes to view the Purebloods in a more positive light. Always before, she had been dismissive and sneering of Rukh's kind, but seeing the beauty and culture of Ashoka, she begins to change her mind. And in some ways, Jessira's presence stimulates a change in the city's own harsh attitudes toward the OutCastes, those traditionally called ghrinas. It is a subtle difference.

Meanwhile, unbeknownst to Rukh, forces conspire in the shadows to have him declared Unworthy and exiled from Ashoka. Dar'El senses these hidden enemies and knows they will likely learn of Rukh's Talents—it was a mistake to trust Rector Bryce—and bring Rukh down in order to hurt House Shektan. Dar'El concocts a scheme to keep Rukh safe: have him go with Jessira to her home of Stronghold rather than simply be cast out in the cold.

In order to do so, he needs Bree's help to trick both Rukh and Jessira. His plan works, and Rukh and Jessira, friends already, are seen in public in what might be considered a romantic circumstance. Rukh's fate is sealed by a late night stroll with Jessira through Dryad Park.

The time approaches for the expedition to the caverns to leave the city, and a few days beforehand, Rukh learns of Jaresh's possible romantic feelings toward Mira Terrell. Ironically, Rukh is unaware of his own perceived relationship with Jessira, and he confronts his adopted brother and orders him to break off all contact with Mira.

Jaresh does so, telling Mira they can't work together anymore. She hears what he's really saying and surprises him by kissing him on the lips. Given the prohibition against a man and a woman of two different Castes ever touching one another, her expression is a bold declaration of her feelings for Jaresh—as well as a sign of farewell.

Rukh's departure to the caverns takes place, and early on, he tells the commanders of his new Talents. They are disgusted by what he can do, considering him a naaja, Tainted, and the information spreads to the rest of the warriors, who share their commanders revulsion. The expedition travels through the Hunters Flats, and Rukh's diminished status dims further when Aia enters the camp and Rukh is forced to explain her presence.

It is too many changes for the other members of the expedition to accept and Rukh is essentially thrust out of the brotherhood of warriors. He is forced to work alone, left intentionally vulnerable and exposed with no one to guard his back. Rukh perseveres, but even in the caverns—which are exactly where Li-Dirge said they would be—he is left to fend for himself.

His situation is dire, but somehow Rukh survives. He even comes across Li-Choke and the last few Baels of the Eastern Plague to survive Suwraith's pogrom. He leads Choke and the others to safety where they can make their way to the Hunters Flats and, as promised by Aia, find shelter amongst the Kesarins.

Following the battle, Rukh's ability to Heal proves essential. He is able to keep alive dozens of warriors during the long march back to Ashoka. His selfless devotion to the lives of others slowly changes the opinions of his fellow warriors. They acknowledge his service with gratitude, and even Rukh's greatest enemy amongst them, his direct commanding officer, Lieutenant Danslo, comes to appreciate and respect all that Rukh can do.

After weeks of emotional toil, Rukh finally sees hope for the future. If his brother warriors of the expedition can look past their prejudices and accept Rukh, then why not all of Ashoka?

It is a short-lived hope.

Days after leaving the city, the Chamber of Lords met and—just as Dar'El had feared—had judged Rukh Unworthy. He is to be exiled. Jessira learns of this just prior to her own departure from Ashoka, and she agrees to delay her leave-taking. She will wait for Rukh's return and lead him to Stronghold.

When the expedition to the caverns returns, she meets them a day short of Ashoka and informs Rukh of what has happened. He will never be allowed to enter his home again.

Rukh is heartbroken and prepares to leave with Jessira for Stronghold, but before he can do so, the warriors of the expedition honor him the Champion's salute. It is their apology for what they now recognize as their wrongful treatment of him during the long march to the Chimera caverns.

Jessira leads Rukh away from the expedition. Later, she apologizes for her role in his situation and reaches to console him. They share a deep, but confusing, kiss before she pulls away, and Rukh follows her west.

PROLOGUE

R ector Bryce forced stillness into his fisted hands, clenched as they were with nervousness. Now was not the time for the appearance of anxiety, much less that of fear. He sat alone—but likely not unwatched—just outside the carved, mahogany doors leading to the study of Hal'El Wrestiva. The ruling 'El had postponed their meeting for two hours already—an obvious insult—but it was one Rector was forced to accept. While he was tempted to simply rise up and leave, he knew he couldn't.

Dar'El Shektan had been quite clear on the matter. No matter the cost, Rector was to gain admittance into House Wrestiva.

Rector grimaced, remembering his last meeting with House Shektan's ruling 'El. After the exposure of Rukh's taint to the Chamber of Lords—the younger man's disgusting possession of Talents only meant for Rahails and Shiyens—Dar'El had been furious. He must have immediately known who had unloosed the truth, and now he was bent on vengeance against both Hal'El Wrestiva and Rector himself.

"Your actions have betrayed this House, and a price will be paid for your disloyalty," Dar'El had said, his voice cold and menacing.

11

Rector had expected just such a reaction, but he had held no regrets for what he had done. He had done what he had in order to safeguard, not just House Shektan, but all Kummas; Ashoka itself. Rector had gone to the meeting with a clear conscience, with no fear of Dar'El's threats. His time in House Shektan was over, but so what? Another House, one that was more honorable, would be happy to have him—and Dar'El wouldn't dare label him ronin; not for what Rector had done, which was simply to expose Rukh for what he was: an abomination. Rector was ready to boldly announce his defiance, but a single sentence from Dar'El had him swallowing his proud words.

"Your great-grandfather, upon your nanna's lineage, was Sil Lor Kum," Dar'El had said. *"I have irrefutable proof, from the Chamber's own library, information accessible only by the 'Els about known Kumma members of the Hidden Hand."* He had silently passed over a document, and Rector had held it in his suddenly chilled fingers, numbly poring over it. The words written upon the page had been unambiguous: Dar'El spoke the truth. *"You should have trusted my judgment and kept silent about Rukh. Had you done so, none of this would have been necessary. Instead, you chose to speak with a braggart's pride, certain no sin could ever stain your honor or your heritage. Life is never so neat."* Dar'El's lips had quirked. *"Now you have a choice: this information can remain sealed, between the two of us alone, or all of Ashoka will know of your shame. Think hard upon what you say next."*

Rector's vision had throbbed in time to his fury, but worse was the bitterness and shame coating his throat in ashes. *"What must I do?"* he had whispered.

"You will serve us until I have no further need of you," Dar'El had promised before summarily dismissing Rector.

Thus, Rector found himself sitting outside Hal'El's study. He was to join House Wrestiva; secretly learn all he could of Hal'El's wealth; and pass the information on to House Shektan. It would be the actions of a dishonorable man, but Rector could see no other way but to obey Dar'El's wishes.

If he didn't, his family's shame would be made known to all of

Ashoka. Two sins trapped him, and the situation had him sick with worry and disgust. All his life, Rector had prided himself on being a man of firm honor, but now he could see no path forward that allowed him to maintain his integrity. It was an intolerable situation; one that had Rector twisting and turning at night, unable to sleep. Even the wisdom imparted by *The Warrior and the Servant*, the slim text describing Kumma ideals of morality and philosophy, provided no comfort. This despite the fact that the book even described just such a quandary: *A warrior must always choose the path of righteousness, but if one isn't visible, then on his own, he must forge it.* Rector couldn't help but mock the words, cold and lifeless as they were. They provided no solution to his dilemma.

The door to the study opened, revealing a smiling Hal'El Wrestiva. Rector noticed the smile didn't reach the 'El's eyes, which appeared to be those of a serpent. "Come in Rector," Hal'El enjoined. "Tell me why you wish to join House Wrestiva."

Rector wiped his damp hands on his pants and took a deep breath. Time to watch his honor drift away.

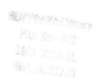

CHAPTER ONE
LOSSES AND FEARS

Whenever I am blessed by the presence of my children,
my soul soars. Whenever they leave, my heart breaks.

~*Our Lives Alon,e by Asias Athandra, AF 331*

"I never expected her absence to affect me so much," Dar'El noted. "She's only been gone two days now."

Satha, his wife, looked up from her pile of missives. She sat upon the sofa, feet propped on the marble-topped table with feet facing the crackling logs within the fireplace. "Jessira?" she guessed.

Dar'El nodded. "The house seems empty without her." He turned to stare out the windows, wishing he could see so much further than the gardens.

Instead, the view that greeted him was a damp, drizzly autumn night. The heights to the west of Ashoka might have even received snow. It was a miserable time to be out in the weather, and Dar'El hoped Rukh and Jessira were encamped somewhere warm and safe. Thinking of them, he glanced around his empty study, wishing they were with him now.

"She found a home in my heart as well," Satha said with a laugh. "What an unusual family we have. Two Kummas, a Sentya, and an OutCaste girl."

Dar'El smiled. "You know we can't adopt her and make her Rukh's sister. He would be furious with us."

Satha's smile slipped. "I wish we could have seen him one last time," she said with a longing sigh.

"We will see him again," Dar'El said, infusing his voice with certainty.

"You truly believe you can change the minds of the other 'Els?"

Dar'El didn't answer. He eyed the chess set. Jessira often played against him. She was a fiery young woman, but somehow, she could control that passion and gather her focus when it came to chess. She was almost as good as Bree and better than Rukh.

There were many good memories associated with that table and that game. In that moment, he would have given all his money and power to play just one more game with his son.

"You don't believe, do you?" Satha whispered, reading his silence as easily as she read her missives.

Dar'El had never been able to hide anything from her. Nevertheless, she needed something to believe in. She needed hope. They all needed it. The House had been trapped in a sullen misery ever since Rukh had been deemed Unworthy. The gloom had certainly ensnared Jaresh. He was usually cheerful and optimistic, but lately, he was more often dour and irritable. Even Bree had been affected. Her calm and collected countenance had been replaced with jagged patterns of edgy anger. She still blamed herself—and Dar'El— for Rukh's predicament.

"I do believe," Dar'El answered. He knew Satha could see through his lies as easily as she could the pebbles at the bottom of a clear stream, but sometimes, like water, words could distort. Then the lie wasn't so obvious. He hated not telling his wife the truth, but he needed her to believe in him. He needed her strength. "It won't be easy, but yes, together, I think we will be able to bring him home."

Satha stared at him, seeming to study his features. "What do we need to do?" she asked.

Dar'El hid a relieved exhalation. "We need to utilize the opportunities Rukh left for us. We must trumpet to the Nine Hills everything he did on the expedition to the caverns. The city is already alight with tales of his exploits."

Satha raised a questioning eyebrow. "Rukh is my son, but even I find it hard to credit the stories circulating about him. Do you really think he killed hundreds of Chimeras by himself and saved hundreds of our warriors during the return journey to Ashoka?"

"Whether we believe is immaterial," Dar'El said. "It's whether the people believe, especially those of our Caste."

Satha chewed a fingernail and wore a thoughtful expression. "We'll *make* them believe," she finally replied, her voice filled with assuredness.

Dar'El smiled. It was what he needed to hear. Her certainty lifted his spirits. Together, they had always managed to accomplish what others deemed impossible. They had raised a lower tier House to one that was rightly accounted as a power in Caste Kumma. To do so, they had to go against received wisdom and choose an untrod path. But look at the heights upon which they now stood. Why shouldn't they be able to convince the Chamber of Lords to rescind their judgment on Rukh? It was merely another hurdle to overcome.

"Yes, we will," Dar'El said, still smiling. "Especially because I *do* think the stories about him are true. When Rukh was expelled from the expedition yesterday, his brother warriors hailed him with the Champion's salute."

"Did they?" Satha asked in surprise. "But some of them hail from Houses unfriendly to our own. Did they not know the judgment of their ruling 'Els?"

"They knew, but it didn't matter. They defied their 'Els," Dar'El said. "I've heard it confirmed from multiple sources."

"So the other tales about how the other warriors intentionally placed Rukh in the most dangerous situations might also be true," Satha mused. "And despite it all, he worked himself nearly to death to save them."

Dar'El could tell she was already moving to see how best to put this information to use. "So it seems."

Satha shook her head. "I would have never guessed he would grow into such a man," she said. "As a child, his greatest delight was terrorizing Bree."

Dar'El drew himself up. "I knew all along," he said, mimicking the portentous tone sometimes used by their old friend, Durmer Volk.

Satha chuckled. "I'm sure you did," she said dryly.

Dar'El smiled, pleased to hear her laugh. "His brother warriors have been lauding his name since they returned. Even those in the city who have learned of Rukh's non-Kumma Talents are praising him to the heavens."

Satha nodded in thought. "It's a good start, and it will help if every story about Rukh references *his brother warriors*. It will strengthen the bonds between Rukh and every other Kumma House. We should also emphasize how he risked his life for his brother Murans and Rahails. His standing amongst the other Castes will rise as a result."

"It may temper any complaints about his non-Kumma Talents."

"And the rest of the city might come to see Rukh's banishment as a betrayal of the other Castes," Satha finished.

"If we can manage it, great pressure will then be placed on the Chamber."

Satha looked wistful. "And maybe we'll see our boy again."

"We will," Dar'El growled. "Even if it means I have to smash together the heads of those hidebound 'Els until they see sense."

"Or stars," Satha said, smiling. "Knock their heads together until they see stars," she explained.

"As long as they make the right decision," Dar'El said. "So long as Jessira sees them safe to Stronghold, we can send word to Rukh that his exile has been lifted."

"I just hope they *do* make it safe to her home."

"I pray so as well," Dar'El said.

"Neither of us are what anyone would call pious," Satha replied, moving to stand behind Dar'El. She rubbed his shoulders and kissed the top of his head. "But I know what you mean."

Dar'El patted her hand, squeezing it briefly. "Maybe for once our distant Lord will actually listen."

Satha said nothing. Instead, she moved to sit in Dar'El's lap and kissed him softly.

"I have news from the last meeting of the Society," Dar'El said, changing the subject.

"Oh? And what do the Rajans have to say?" Satha asked in a neutral tone.

Despite her respectful and interested demeanor, Dar'El wasn't deceived. Satha tolerated his membership within the Society, but she didn't think it was a worthy use of his time. But maybe what he was about to tell her would change her mind. "I received word from someone claiming to be a high member of the Sil Lor Kum. A MalDin."

"*Servant of the Voice*," Satha translated with a grimace. "A high posting—if he or she isn't lying."

"He," Dar'El said. "Based on the handwriting, I suspect the MalDin is a man."

"And what does *he* want?"

"Immunity."

Satha lifted her eyebrows in surprise. "Really? And what does he offer for something so extraordinary?"

"He's willing to give up every member of the Sil Lor Kum."

"This man has likely worked with the men and women of the Sil Lor Kum for years," Satha said, shaking her head in disbelief, "and yet he would sell out his fellows so easily?"

Dar'El scowled. "He's scum. Of course he would. But as a demonstration of his good intentions, he explained about the Withering Knife and its role in the murders."

"Interesting," Satha said, "but *we* already know about the Knife. What we don't know about is Sil Lor Kum." She stroked her chin pensively. "Perhaps the Society *does* have its uses."

Dar'El smiled. "Now was that so hard to say?"

Satha shrugged, refusing to give him the satisfaction. "How was this message received?"

"I found it in my jacket after last night's dinner at the Society Hall." At Satha's startlement, Dar'El nodded. "You see it."

"Yes," she said. "The MalDin must either be a member of the Society or a servant."

"I would guess a servant."

"Why?"

"The Sil Lor Kum. The Hidden Hand of Justice. What better way to hide then in a profession so easily overlooked?"

"True, but those of the Sil Lor Kum seek power. I can't believe they would willingly serve in any capacity, especially not a MalDin."

Dar'El knew where Satha's questions led, but it was a destination he was reluctant to consider. He hesitated but finally had to admit the likely truth. "You're right," he said.

"Then it is more likely a member of the Society itself," Satha said.

As was his wont, Ular Sathin took his nightly tea beneath the clematis-gowned pergola in the rear courtyard of his house. He took a careful sip—his was a quiet and restrained nature, cautious in all things, even in something as prosaic as having his evening drink. He smiled at the peaceful silence, a bare movement of his ascetic lips.

He lived in Hart's Stand, an area of row houses, and despite the unobtrusive Rahails living on all sides of his home, Ular found the neighborhood uncomfortably loud. It was noisy here, too busy and brash. The reasons Ular didn't move were because he had lived here for almost five decades. He had grown comfortable in his home, like a barnacle on a hull. And also, every other neighborhood in Ashoka was even louder and more loutish than this one.

But tonight Hart's Stand was muted. Perhaps the evening's chill drizzle had driven most folk inside. If so, then Ular was grateful. The whispering rain was a double blessing, providing both a restful quiet and a blissful relief after summer's mugginess.

Ular took another careful sip of his tea and considered what to do next. He'd made a bold decision in writing the note to Dar'El. He would have preferred otherwise, but what choice did he have? The Queen had turned her gaze to Ashoka, and the SuDin wouldn't lift a finger to thwart Her. The man had to be stopped before he brought ruin to the city. Knowledge about the Withering Knife had to be made known, even if it risked exposing Ular's membership in the Sil Lor Kum.

Ular grimaced at the gamble he had taken. He'd lived such a watchful, wary life, and to see it all unravel now, in the winter of his years was a bitter draught to swallow. It was all because of the SuDin. The arrogance of the man! He couldn't be trusted. None of the MalDin could, or any member of the Sil Lor Kum for that matter. They were all scum, from the highest to the lowest, but the worst of them was the SuDin. He was a coiled viper, a venomous hypocrite.

Ular grimaced once again. And all this time, he had yet to learn the SuDin's true name. He was a Kumma of high standing, possibly even an 'El, but otherwise, Ular knew nothing about him.

And now the man was growing younger. Though he tried to hide his transformation, Ular had known the SuDin long enough to see the changes. His hair was darker, the gray color somehow receding. There was also the matter of the SuDin's gait. The man still limped, but Ular could tell it was a sham. The SuDin's injuries had somehow been Healed. And all of it had begun with the murders. Ular was certain of it. The changes had begun then.

The Withering Knife. No one but the SuDin truly knew where it had come from or what it did, but whatever its secrets, *he* was keeping it from the rest of the MalDin.

Ular had his suspicions as to why. The SuDin didn't trust the rest of the Council, which was a wise decision in any circumstance. The other MalDins would have demanded use of the Knife if they realized it could make them younger. But what if there was more to it? Legends spoke of how the Knife stole a man's *Jivatma*. If so…Ular shuddered at the possibility. He imagined a Kumma wielding more than his own *Jivatma*. He would be unstoppable. No man should be so powerful.

And none of this accounted for Suwraith. The SuDin claimed that the Queen had promised to see the Council safe and wealthy in far off cities, but what were Her promises really worth? There was nothing in the history of the Sil Lor Kum to prove that Councils from other cities—ones the Sorrow Bringer had destroyed—had found safety and shelter before their homes were apocalypsed. The accounts stating She did were farcical, and Ular didn't believe them.

It was more likely the Queen had simply destroyed those other Councils—just as She would Ashoka's.

Thus, as Ular reckoned matters, the only way to save himself was to also keep Ashoka safe. He had to stop the SuDin, stop him before he fully corrupted the city's Oasis.

And who better to stop a ruthless Kumma than another equally ruthless Kumma?

R ector Bryce sat alone outside a small bistro in Trell Rue. He was
to meet Mira Terrell here, and while he could have waited
within, he chose to wait without. He reckoned it was a wise decision
given the café's claustrophobic interior.

The building housing the restaurant was made of stacked-stone,
a material efficient at trapping the murmurings of the restaurant's
many patrons and the heat from the roaring fireplace. It made the
bistro feel like an oven, especially with the air marinating in the
aromas of spiced noodles, dahl, chicken, and parathas.

The food—traditional Duriah fare—was the only reason Rector
had agreed to meet here. In this age of fusion cuisine, especially in
fashionable and forward-facing Trell Rue, finding something that
hearkened back to an older period was becoming rarer by the month.
And yet, despite all the modern talk of melding and melting of
culture and cuisine, this restaurant with its old-fashioned food, had
become popular.

It gave Rector a small spark of hope for the future. Too many
people nowadays discarded the learned wisdom of history as if it
were a worn out rag, good for nothing but the refuse bin. Perhaps
they were finally coming to their senses, realizing that the future was
best served if the past was also respected.

Even as he considered such a notion, Rector suspected it
probably wasn't the case. More likely, this traditional Duriah bistro in
the heart of modern, ever-changing Trell Rue was simply a
representation of the latest fashionable trend, one where the past
briefly became new and stylish once again.

It was pathetic, and the knowledge left Rector wishing that he
had been born in a different time, a more refined era when Castes did
not seek to emulate one another; when cultures were distinct and

separate; and everyone knew their place. He hated this modern life where everyone sought to be like everyone else. Where was the great sin in wanting to be distinctive?

With those thoughts in mind, he settled in to watch the fall of a dreary rain, the water leaving a halo of rainbows around the firefly lamps outside the restaurant. The colorful sight had Rector feeling morose and lonely, a sentiment made worse by the glad sounds of laughter echoing from within the bistro.

Rector tightened his coat and suppressed a shiver. The heavy canopy braced against the side of the restaurant and arching overhead protected against the weather but did nothing to keep off the chill.

Where was Mira anyway? They were supposed to have met a half-hour ago to go over the past week's 'activities'. She was his contact in House Shektan; the one to whom he passed on any information he learned about House Wrestiva's activities. He didn't like Mira Terrell, and she didn't like him, but nevertheless, in some ways, his life was in her hands.

He grimaced at the notion, hating the path his life had taken. Spying. It was dishonorable, but there were no other choices that made sense to him. If he didn't do what Dar'El demanded, he and his family would be ruined. The horrible truth about Rector's family—their patrimony from a member of the Sil Lor Kum—would be revealed to everyone. And he had no doubt Dar'El would make good on his threat. After all, Rector was responsible for Rukh Shektan's banishment. Dar'El would need little excuse to execute vengeance on the man who had ruined his son's future.

With the clarity of hindsight, Rector knew he should have kept silent about Rukh's newfound Talents. He should have simply watched and waited. Life would have eventually worked itself out. Ironically, during the trek to the Chimera birthing caverns, Rukh had actually told his commanders and brother warriors about his new Talents. By all accounts, they had been thoroughly disgusted, and

Rukh had essentially been abandoned in the Wildness. Of course, their opinions had changed as a result of Rukh's undeniable heroism in the caverns and on the long journey back to Ashoka. In fact, the warriors from the expedition to the caverns now heralded Rukh as the Hero of the Slave River, an opinion widely held by the rest of the city.

Rector wasn't sure how he felt about that. Rukh Shektan was Tainted, but then again how could anyone have accomplished what the man had? Many scores of warriors would have died if not for him.

So perhaps an exception could have been found for him—certainly many people wanted one—but at least then the reason for Rukh's expulsion from Ashoka would not have come about because of anything Rector had done. And Dar'El would have had no reason to demand his actions as a spy. Rector would have kept his honor.

His thoughts cut off when he saw Mira approaching. She pranced along the sidewalk, walking proud and carefree as only the truly arrogant could manage.

Rector swore under his breath. Why of all people had Dar'El chosen this woman to be his contact with House Shektan? Mira despised Rector, and the feeling was mutual. Here was a woman who had unabashedly cavorted with Jaresh Shektan, a Sentya and a man not of her Caste. Though the two of them pretended to merely be friends, Rector suspected something deeper had grown between the two of them.

And Mira dared judge Rector?

"I would have figured Jaresh would have accompanied you," Rector said as she took a seat. He knew his words were spiteful, but he didn't care.

Mira wore a confused look. "Why would he be with me?"

"After all the time you spent in the Cellar, the two of you seemed to have grown close."

"We worked well together," Mira said. "Our House is lucky to have a man of his abilities, but Jaresh has his own tasks to undertake, as do I. Our paths no longer cross."

Rector studied her. Mira hadn't taken the bait, but nonetheless, he didn't entirely believe her. Her words were couched in flat notes, unemotional statements. It was as if she was afraid to speak with any feeling about Jaresh, as if to do so might expose the truth.

Or perhaps it was all his imagination.

He took a swallow of his wine.

Two months ago, it wouldn't have occurred to him to disbelieve her—a Kumma and a Sentya together in an illicit affair? It should have been too repugnant to ever fathom. Unfortunately, hard truths and many lies had tested his trusting nature.

"What have you learned?" Mira asked, changing the subject.

"Nothing yet," Rector replied sourly, still wondering about her relationship with Jaresh.

"Nothing?"

Rector shrugged. "I come from a House that is bitter enemies to House Wrestiva. How likely are they to trust me with anything of import?"

Mira frowned. "What is your position with the Wrestivas? Surely you have one."

"I have financial oversight of one of House Wrestiva's lowest warehouses. I command a small group of fanatical Sentya accountants. They wage brave, unceasing war on deficits and income allocation," he said in sarcasm. "Thankfully, they must know their work since I don't understand a single thing when they start speaking their accounting gibberish. They have some strange language of accruals, depreciation, prepayment, and long-term liabilities."

Mira laughed. "How awful it must be for you. Trapped amongst a group of lowly Sentyas."

Rector smirked. "I'm sure you're more comfortable amongst Sentyas than I."

Mira reddened even as she held up a cautioning finger. "We are supposed to be young lovers getting to know each other. As far as the rest of the Caste Kumma is concerned, my Nanna seeks a lifeline into an ancient House in case House Shektan is brought down by the scandal of Rukh's Talents. You, the honorable Rector Bryce, are meant to be that lifeline. As such, smirking and scowling at me won't do. You need to pretend to feel something foreign to your way of thinking. You must demonstrate understanding and compassion."

Rector swallowed his angry retort. Suwraith's spit. He hated when she was right. He forced a smile on his face, trying to relax his features into a semblance of good humor. "Perhaps I should take lessons. I am not as accustomed to hiding my feelings as you and Jaresh," he said.

Mira didn't respond to his words, not with the slightest change in her expression or any movement. In its own way, it was answer enough.

Rector's disgust grew deeper. Was there anyone of House Shektan who held even the merest of honor?

"You truly are a fool," Mira said after a moment's silence. She sounded sad rather than angry. "Jaresh is a man whose friendship I treasure, but because of bigots like you, even an innocent relationship like that has to be kept hidden and denied. But if you think there is more to us than that, so be it. I care little for your opinion or your perverse fantasies."

Rector gaped. Perverted fantasies?

Now, it was Mira who smirked. "I saw how you stared at Jessira Grey, the OutCaste woman. You despised her, but you also found her attractive. Now you project your own disgusting imaginations on the relationships of others."

Rector didn't know what to think or what to say. Jessira Grey—thankfully gone from Ashoka three weeks now—had been an attractive woman, but in no way, shape, or form had Rector ever desired her. For Mira to say otherwise suggested she might be trying to deflect the truth of how she felt for Jaresh.

Or, more simply and plausibly, there was nothing to her and Jaresh; and she truly thought Rector a filthy hypocrite.

"Just tell me what you want," Rector growled.

"I want information on House Wrestiva's finances, and though you think your position as a low-level overseer is beneath your station, it is exactly what will help us."

"It isn't work befitting a Kumma," Rector complained, hating the petulant tone in his voice. "I had to give up my post in the High Army in order to do this bureaucrat's work."

Mira chuckled. "Poor Rector. So many troubles you've had to endure." Her laughter faded. "You do not have my pity."

"And I never asked for it," Rector replied. "Nor would I want it, but believe me, when Dar'El is done with me, I will remember this conversation."

Mira chuckled again. Rector was really growing tired of her smug laughter. "Dar'El will never be done with you," she said in a stern tone of prophecy. "For what you did to him, you'll be lucky if he doesn't demand your compliance all the days of your life."

Rector gritted his teeth, fearing she was right. Dar'El could very well do exactly that. After all, look what he was already putting Rector through. What honor could Dar'El have if he was willing to do that?

———◦———

Bree paused when she heard the mournful strains of a guitar echoing from the flower garden leading off the sunroom. She stepped outside. Jaresh sat upon a small bench with his back to her. This was a space Bree loved. It was Amma's creation, a lovely sanctuary from the bustle of the city. Right now, the garden still held the last of summer's blossoms with Autumn's blooms of orange and red still to come. The ligustrum bushes that formed the tall hedge on all four sides would remain green even in winter.

Bree stepped upon the winding path of chipped bricks, her footsteps crunching quietly. Her breath misted in the morning air, but she knew the day would eventually warm. She sat down next to Jaresh. The bench was warm, bathed in a splash of sunlight. Last night's rain had ended early in the morning, and the rest of the day would likely be bright and sunny.

Jaresh didn't look up. He kept on strumming his slow song of lament.

"I don't think I've heard you play anything happy since Rukh left for the caverns," Bree said.

"There hasn't been much to be happy about."

"No, there hasn't," Bree agreed, thinking about all the troubles that had caught up their family. She sighed. "I wish I hadn't done what Nanna asked."

Jaresh paused and looked at her in confusion.

"Encouraging Rukh to take Jessira to Dryad Park," she explained. "He might not have been banished if I hadn't done so."

"It wasn't your fault," Jaresh said. "The person who's most to blame for Rukh's situation is Rukh."

Jaresh's attitude was unexpected. "You sound angry with him."

"I am angry. I'm angry, and I'm scared," Jaresh said. "If it wasn't for his stupidity and his hypocrisy, he'd be home right now."

"Hypocrisy?"

Jaresh shrugged. "Maybe that wasn't the right word," he muttered.

It was the right word and Bree knew why. "This is about Mira, isn't it?" she asked.

"What about her?" Jaresh asked, his features growing tight and closed.

28

"I know how you feel about her, and how she feels about you," Bree said.

"Rukh told you," Jaresh said sounding betrayed.

"He didn't have to," Bree replied. "Before he left, I saw how upset you were with him. I also noticed that Mira no longer came by the House Seat as often as she once did. The two of you no longer spend any time together."

"We never did anything dishonorable."

"And even if you had, you would still be my brother."

"You're not disgusted with me?" Jaresh asked, hope rising in his voice.

Bree chuckled softly. "If you haven't noticed, we have an unusual family, and our older brother, the one who was supposed to set a fine example for the rest of us to follow, brought home a ghrina and had the poor taste to like her." This conversation about such intimate matters wasn't one Bree had ever expected to have with Jaresh. It should have been Rukh's job. The entire topic made her uncomfortable, but still, she also knew that if Jaresh needed someone in whom to confide, she would have to do.

"Rukh spoke to me before he left," Jaresh replied. "It's why I don't spend time with Mira any more."

"Do you still have feelings for her?" Bree asked.

Jaresh shrugged. "I'll probably always have feelings for her," he said, "but they aren't the way they once were." He stared at his hands, silent for a moment. "Do Amma and Nanna know?" he asked.

Bree shrugged. "I don't know. But if they did, I doubt they would love you any less."

Jaresh set aside his guitar and gave a half-hearted smile. "I wish the rest of the city could be as forgiving."

"Wishes don't wash dishes," Bree quoted.

"No, they don't," Jaresh agreed. "Is that why you came out here?

To remind me of the work I should be doing?"

Bree quirked a smile. "Truthfully? I just came out here to talk to you. I needed my brother."

"We both need our brother," Jaresh said. "I miss Rukh, and I wish I hadn't been such an ass to him before he left. The last time I saw him, I was still angry and upset." He sighed. "I wish I'd let him know how much I love him."

Bree silently commiserated with Jaresh.

Jaresh forced a smile. "But at least I've kept busy," he said. "I examined the three Houses Rukh said trained their warriors in the manner of the Withering Knife murderer. In their ranks, there are one hundred and seven suspects."

"One hundred and seven?" Bree said thoughtfully. "It's a start."

CHAPTER TWO
A COOL NIGHT

Shun those who bring dishonor to their Amma or their Nanna.
Such scoundrels should be stoned.

~To Live Well, by Fair Shire of Stronghold, AF 1842

Jessira focused on her tasks, doing her best to ignore Rukh's silent, uncomfortable scrutiny. She ducked to the other side of her horse to put distance between the two of them. It was the fragging kiss. That's why he was staring at her. Her shoulders twitched involuntarily under his gaze. She didn't want to talk about it. In fact, she wished she could just forget that it had ever happened.

It had been a mistake, but at the time, it had felt so right. First Mother! She hid a shudder, trying to ignore how much she had enjoyed it.

She couldn't act on her feelings, though. Not now. Not ever. Jessira had promised herself to Disbar Merdant, and she wouldn't disgrace herself or her family's good name and standing by failing in what she had vowed; not for something as selfish and ephemeral as a kiss or whatever the kiss might have led to. Jessira liked Rukh

Shektan, but what they had was fleeting, something forged during a time of common loneliness and struggle. It wasn't the foundation upon which two people could form a long-lasting relationship. Not that she wanted such a thing. At least not with Rukh. She was to marry Disbar Merdant, after all.

"Are we going to talk about it?" Rukh asked.

Jessira's shoulders tensed, and she kept her back to him, pretending to be busy as she unsaddled her horse. "About what?" she asked. She immediately winced at her cowardly response. Rukh deserved the truth, not some half-ass measure where she pretended not to know what he was talking about.

Jessira heard his saddle drop to the ground, and she flicked a glance at him, but now *his* back was to her as he brushed down his horse.

"I see." His response was simple and direct.

She frowned, mentally cursing her momentary weakness. The stupid kiss. "I'm sorry," she said. "I'm promised to someone else. What we did—it won't happen again."

"You think the kiss was a mistake?" Rukh asked, turning to look at her.

He wore a bland expression, betraying none of the upset or disappointment she might have expected. Jessira was filled with the sudden hope that maybe the two of them could put this entire incident behind them with no lingering hurt feelings on either of their parts. It would be for the best. Not to mention it would let her off the hook for what had been a colossal blunder.

Jessira nodded. "It was definitely a mistake."

Rukh seemed to consider her words. "It was a good kiss, though, wasn't it?" he asked with a winsome grin. "I don't think I'll be regretting it too much."

Jessira's nascent hope melted away. Wariness took its place. She had believed—however briefly—that Rukh hadn't read too much into their kiss. But what was he saying now? What did he mean by not regretting it? She most certainly did. And, Rukh couldn't think she would allow it to happen again.

"Rukh, listen...." she began.

He held up a forestalling hand. "I know what you're going to say. You're going to tell me how it will never happen again. That it should have never happened in the first place. How it only happened because we both got caught up in our emotions."

She nodded, no longer surprised at how easily he understood what she was thinking without her having to say it. Back in Stronghold, other than Lure, no one else could pick up on her thoughts and moods so easily. She sometimes wondered how Rukh did what he did, but now wasn't the time for such musings. She needed to take care of this issue between them—the kiss—or it would fester, ruining their relationship.

"Don't worry about it," Rukh continued. "You're right. It was a mistake. When a woman makes a vow...." he shrugged. "Kummas take such promises seriously. We don't poach another man's territory."

Jessira exhaled in relief as the tension building in her over the past few hours spilled out in a rush. It left her light-headed. "I'm glad we both feel the same way," she said with a nervous half-smile.

"Me, too," Rukh said. "Let's set up camp."

"Who gets first watch?" she asked.

Rukh eyed her with such a hopeful expression that Jessira had to laugh. "I'll take it," she said.

They pitched their bedrolls and while Rukh fed and watered the horses, Jessira made a small fire and heated up a warm meal of smoked beef in a potato stew. The rest of the evening passed quietly, but Jessira couldn't relax. Despite their agreement to forget about the kiss, there remained a stiffness between them, a formality that didn't allow for easy conversation or laughter.

Rukh turned in early, looking worn out. There was wanness to him, a tiredness of his soul. It was so different from how she was used to seeing Rukh, but it was also to be expected. If even half of the rumors about what he had been through during his time away from Ashoka with the expedition were true, he should have fallen over from exhaustion long ago. And then, just this morning—had it only been this morning?--he had to deal with the shock of being found Unworthy. She wondered how he was able to keep going with such a heavy heart. If the circumstances were reversed, she'd be a puddle of sobbing sorrow.

The night waxed long, and the fire burned down to coals. A restless flame ignited now and then setting the wood to crackling. Jessira shivered as a cool wind blew down from the Privation Mountains, carrying a promise of snow. Down here in the lower elevations, the promised snow would probably melt into a dismal autumn shower. A particularly blustery gust of wind blew dust and debris across the camp. It lit the coals to brightness and flame, sending sparks flying into the darkness beyond the firelight. Jessira shivered again and clutched her cloak more tightly.

She must have grown soft in Ashoka's comfort and warmth.

Hours later, Jessira stood when she felt herself nodding off. She should have awoken Rukh by now, but she didn't have the heart for it. Let him rest a while longer. She stamped her feet to get some circulation back into them and paced around the campsite, making sure to maintain her Blend, the thin membrane keeping the two of them hidden from Suwraith.

To keep her mind busy, Jessira stared out into the night's darkness. A crescent moon provided a sliver of light, barely giving shape to the treed hills surrounding them on all sides. She and Rukh had chosen to make camp amongst a half-circle of tumbled, gray boulders nestled along the shores of a pencil thin lake. Most of the rocks stood higher than Jessira could reach and were jagged and sharp, like they were the chipped fangs of some monstrous beast. They seemed to warn the trees back from the small open space they encompassed.

Jessira stepped closer to the water's edge, past the muted light offered by the campfire. Her eyes quickly adjusted to the darkness.

Cattails and reedy grass swayed in the breeze as the moon's ivory light sparkled against the water's ripples. A few lonely cicadas droned into the night. Their sound rose and fell, melding with the croaking of bullfrogs hiding in the rushes. Itinerant clouds scudded across the face of the moon, and the smell of moss growing on the boulders mingled with that of wild lilac, somehow still blooming this late in the season.

Jessira stared out over the lake, all the way to the far shore, but the light was too weak to allow her to make out any details. Perhaps Rukh could have seen something. His senses were more acute than hers.

Her thoughts on him, she drifted back toward the campsite, making sure to avoid looking straight at the fire so as to preserve her night vision. Jessira sat near Rukh and faced out into the night. She heard him shift in his slumber, rolling over so he was now facing her. She glanced down at him and a half-smile slipped over her face. At least the fatigue and pain he'd worn so openly throughout the day was smoothed away by the peace of sleep. She studied his features more closely, and her smile changed into a slight frown. There was a small scar above his right eyebrow. She'd never seen it before, and she wondered if it was new. Possibly from the battle in the caverns? And was that a strand of white hair hidden amongst the black ones? She leaned closer and realized it was more than just one. It was a whole village of them, growing haphazardly along both his temples. But Rukh's hair had been coal black when he'd left Ashoka for the caverns a few months back. She was certain of it. The scar, the white hairs, the emotional wounds—Rukh had been visibly marked by his time in the expedition, and now, he would never have a chance to regain his honor. It had been forever denied to him. While he had been risking his life in the Wildness, the Chamber of Lords had deemed him Unworthy. He'd never again see his family, his loved ones, or his beloved city.

And it was all her fault.

Jessira stared out into the trees, peering through the gaps between the boulders. She hoped Rukh could find it in his heart to forgive her. Earlier in the day, he had said he didn't blame her for what had happened, and she was grateful to hear it, but she also had trouble believing him. After all, Jessira had yet to forgive herself.

She glanced back at Rukh, running her eyes along the ridge of his brow, the curve of his nose, and the firm line of his jaw. She paused when she reached the smooth softness of his full lips. She found her own lips slightly parted and dry as she unconsciously reached for him.

With a start, she recovered her self-awareness and withdrew her hand. What had she been thinking? She swallowed heavily and quickly stood, pacing away from the small circle of firelight and toward the boulders. She wanted…she *needed* distance between herself and Rukh. She knew what had been in her thoughts. She had meant to run her fingers gently through Rukh's hair, cup his face, just touch him.

Jessira paused when she reached the ring of boulders and leaned against one of them. She breathed as if she had sprinted straight up the eastern face of Mount Frame. This was how she acted after their earlier conversation? Jessira silently berated herself. She couldn't give Rukh such mixed signals. She couldn't let her heart trick her into thinking there was something present when there wasn't. She had to be strong. There was a deep bond of friendship between her and Rukh, but that was it. Nothing more. There couldn't be.

And besides, she'd been selfish enough already.

R ukh and Jessira made their way along the rugged banks of a high, mountain stream. The water ran cold and clear through a narrow ravine with a scattering of thin skeletal trees and bushes clutching hard to the sheer sides of the gully. Slabs of granite had broken off the ravine's walls, crumbling into boulders and rocks of various sizes. It made footing treacherous, and the two of them had to walk their horses alongside the stream bed. The risk was too great for a turned ankle if they tried riding their mounts.

They followed the water to where it carved a deep runnel into a thick stone ledge before falling down a series of rocky prominences and cliffs, ending as a mist on the valley floor several hundred feet below.

Rukh stood on the edge of the shelf, staring out over the expansive view. Green hills marched off into the distance, merging at the edge of his vision with the perpetually snow-covered peaks of the Privations.

Right now, he would gladly trade the coolness of the mountains for the unseasonably warm weather he and Jessira were enduring. Sweat beaded on his forehead as the afternoon sun blazed down. The light cut through a layer of low clouds as beams of pale yellow light, dappling the forested valley below in hues of gold, a portent of autumn's glory. Although most of the trees had yet to change color, soon enough they would. Rukh and Jessira would have to move quickly if they wanted to make it to Stronghold before the snows made the mountain passes impassable.

"Do you see a way down?" Jessira asked. She absently wiped the sweat from her brow.

Rukh took a pull of water and passed her the canteen. "No," he answered. "But let's take a rest before we decide on anything."

"We need to be down this cliff by nightfall," Jessira said.

Rukh nodded in reply and led the way back upstream, allowing the horses to drink. He squatted to refill his canteens, his thoughts growing distant as he recalled the events of the past week.

For a single night, during the return from the Chimera breeding caverns, Rukh had actually believed he could go home with his dignity intact. His fellow warriors, his brothers, had come to see his new Talents for the gifts that they were. If they could do so, then why not the rest of Ashoka?

Maybe it might have even worked out that way, but his own foolishness had killed those chances. The Chamber of Lords could have overlooked Rukh's new Talents, but they couldn't overlook the rumor of an illicit relationship between Rukh and Jessira, especially when there was so much proof of it. It had all been because of a late-night walk the two of them had shared in Dryad Park. How could Rukh have been so damned stupid? The Chamber had been forced to act. They had declared Rukh Unworthy.

The shame of such a judgment still stung like a harsh slap to the face. Worse was the empty, lonely ache of all that had been ripped from him—all the people he loved, his future. He tried not to dwell on his loss, but on some nights, the pain would overcome him. Then tears of sorrow would trickle down his face. He only allowed such weakness when he was alone at night. Never during the day when Jessira might see.

He didn't need her sympathy or her pity. It would be too humiliating.

Besides, his feelings for Jessira were already jumbled up enough as it was. He knew she blamed herself for what had happened to him, and maybe some might even believe there was some truth to that. But Rukh didn't think so. No matter how much she might be wracked with guilt over what had happened to him, Rukh's predicament was of his own making. He was the author of his fate, and it had been his decisions, his blindness, that had led to his exile. His choice to make public his friendship for Jessira—a ghrina—that had led to his family's suffering. How disappointed they must be in him.

Still, despite his mixed emotions when it came to Jessira, sometimes he wondered how much easier his life might have been if she had never come into it.

But then there were other instances, such as the all-to-brief kiss they had shared, when he thanked Devesh she was still with him. When he was glad that such a woman walked beside him. Times such as now.

Jessira held still. Her heart-shaped face was frozen in concentration as she filled her canteens. Her honey-brown hair fell loosely about her face, framing her fine Cherid features, and her red-gold skin seemed to glow under the sun. If she glanced over, Rukh knew he would be trapped in the glory of her emerald eyes, unable to look away.

His breath caught when Jessira stood and walked back to the edge of the bluff. She was lovely in repose but so beautiful in movement, graceful as a leaf on the wind.

"I think I see a path, a goat trail maybe, not too far away," Jessira said, and the moment was broken.

Rukh walked to where she stood. A stray breeze blew, playing with Jessira's hair, swirling it about, and carrying her subtle cinnamon scent. It was something Rukh had first noticed during their earlier time in the Wildness. Wisping about her was a scarcely detectable undercurrent of cinnamon. He stifled his discomfort when she shifted closer so he could more easily follow the line of her pointing finger.

"Do you see it?" Jessira asked.

Rukh nodded, noting the trail she was indicating. They should be able to reach it in an hour or so, and with luck, get down to the valley floor by the time it grew dark. "If we back track a bit, we should be able to pick it up somewhere east of here," he said.

His optimistic assessment proved wrong. The hike to the goat track turned out to be a much longer slog then either one of them had initially reckoned. Over and over again, they had to stop and figure out where they were, but eventually they found the trail, a wild animal path, that thankfully, proved easy enough to follow. Though it was only wide enough for one horse single file, they were able to make a swift descent, regaining some of their lost time.

They pushed on well past sunset, into the dark, determined to reach the valley floor. Rukh led the way, lighting the path with a muted, red-hued firefly lantern. Several hours later, the track finally bottomed out.

They stopped for the night in an area of new growth, where an oak, a giant of the forest, had fallen. Its collapse had left a large opening in the canopy up above and a small clearing on the forest floor down below.

After making camp, they sat across the fire from one another and ate their suppers in silence.

It was the way things were between them now: stiff and formal. It was uncomfortable, and Rukh didn't like it. He missed their easy camaraderie. They used to get along pretty well, even if they might have argued a lot. Rukh knew the reason for the change. It was the kiss. And Jessira's ongoing guilt for whatever role she might have played in his expulsion from Ashoka. With so much hanging between them, maybe they no longer knew who they were to one another. Were they just traveling companions? Friends? Or something else entirely? Their confusion had them walking on eggshells around one another, and Rukh was tired of it. It couldn't go on; not when they had another seven or eight weeks of travel ahead of them.

"I don't blame you for what happened to me," Rukh said, breaking the silence.

Jessira didn't respond at first. Instead, she seemed to study him. "Are you sure?" she finally asked. "I would if I was in your shoes."

Rukh considered how best to answer her question. The crackling of the fire and friendly chirps of crickets were the only sounds to be heard. "I don't blame you," he told her again. He quirked a smile. "It would be easy to do so, but it's not the truth."

"Then what is the truth?" Jessira asked.

Rukh sighed. "I made my own choices, and I chose not to see the danger gathering around me. I should have remained silent about my Talents. I should have entrusted the knowledge of what I can do to no one else but my parents, my brother, and my sister. I spoke without thinking before Rector Bryce. It was the first of a series of mistakes."

"But your final error was allowing yourself to be seen in public with a ghrina," Jessira said. She stared him in the eye. "You wouldn't have done so, except that I was feeling lonely and shamed you into it."

"You didn't shame me," Rukh said. "You only reminded me of how I was avoiding doing what I knew was right."

"Was taking me on a late-night stroll through Dryad Park the 'right' thing to do?" Jessira asked, her lips set in a frown.

Rukh shrugged. "As I said…a series of mistakes."

Jessira shook her head. "I think you're being too generous," she said. "I did something unforgivably selfish, and for you to try and absolve me of *my* choices, saying they weren't important to your fate…." She shook her head in disagreement. "You're wrong, Rukh."

Rukh sighed heavily, not sure what else to say, and an uncomfortable silence fell between them. He ended it a moment later. "All I can tell you is this: I want to move past what's happened. I want to find a way to make something—anything—out of the wreckage of my life. As a start, I want our friendship back." He searched her features, wondering what she was thinking. His ability to sense her feelings or thoughts seemed to have left him. "What about you?"

Jessira hunched her shoulders and rubbed her hands over her crossed arms before a tight smile appeared on her face. "I want the same thing," she said. "It's just...." She paused.

"It's just what?" Rukh coaxed.

"I don't know if I deserve your forgiveness, and I don't think getting on with your life is going to be as easy as you seem to think it will be."

"You never needed my forgiveness," Rukh replied. "You need your own. And I know it won't be easy putting my life back together, but I have to start somewhere." He shrugged. "Making things right between us is a start. Maybe then I won't feel sad all the time."

Jessira regarded him. "Do you want to tell me?" she asked.

Rukh laughed in bitterness. "What's there to tell? I hurt, and I'm tired." He stared Jessira in the eyes, giving her a challenging look. "I could use a friend, though."

"I am a friend," she said.

"Well, we haven't exactly been friendly lately, have we?"

"What do you mean?" Her face was a frozen mask, hiding her emotions, but Rukh noticed the tension in her shoulders. It was her giveaway whenever she was nervous.

"I think you know what I mean," Rukh replied, annoyed at her reserve. "When was the last time either of us laughed?"

"I didn't think you'd appreciate my happiness when you're so miserable," she replied.

"I could use seeing some joy right now, even if I can't feel it myself."

"What do you want to do then?" Jessira asked, her face thawing somewhat.

"What friends normally do. Talk about our lives," Rukh answered, relieved she was showing some interest in what he was saying.

"What do you want to talk about?" Her face thawed further.

"I don't know. Whatever you want. You can tell me all about Stronghold or your family or your fiancé." He forced a smile. "I'm curious to meet this man who's won your heart. He must be special."

"My fiancé is a man amongst boys," Jessira answered, deadpan. "He feeds the poor, tames the mountains, and is satisfied by nothing less than a thousand virgins." She paused. "Then he has breakfast."

Rukh barked in sudden laughter. "Remind me never to get on his bad side," he said. "But if he needs a thousand virgins a day, what happens when the two of you get married."

Jessira looked at Rukh from beneath hooded eyes, and she grinned slowly. "After he's had me, he'll still feed the poor, tame the mountains, and have his breakfast, but he will never again need a thousand virgins."

Rukh smiled at her self-satisfied smirk, but something in her words caught his attention. "*After* he's had you. Meaning he *hasn't* had you yet. He blinked in confusion. What's wrong with him?" The question slipped out before he could think to keep his mouth shut, but it was asked out of genuine curiosity and puzzlement. What *was* wrong with the man? Jessira's fiancé must have ice water for blood if he *didn't* want to be with Jessira.

Jessira's smirk left her face. She reddened. "Can we talk about something else?"

"You brought this up," Rukh reminded her.

"Just let it go."

"Then tell me what he's really like?"

"He's a plumber."

"A plumber," Rukh replied. Jessira was going to marry a plumber? "He must be an extraordinary plumber."

"Don't judge him," Jessira said, tartly. She must have heard the mockery in Rukh's voice. "He's a good man. And besides, in Stronghold, a plumber is a highly honored and lucrative craftsman."

"I see," Rukh said, although he didn't. What could be so attractive about being a plumber? "So when did you meet?"

"Why do you want to know so much about him?"

"I'm curious. I want to get to know you and your people better. And I'll probably meet your fiancé eventually anyway. And I don't want to say or do anything embarrassing, like act shocked when I find out he's a plumber."

Jessira sighed. "Fine. His name is Disbar Merdant. He's a journeyman plumber, but he should receive his master's card by the spring. As for how we met: Stronghold is a small city, only about a fifth the size of Ashoka, and we grew up together, although he's a few years older than me."

"And he doesn't care when you're sent out of the city as part of your warrior's duties?"

"He doesn't like it, but once we're married, I'll step down from the Silversuns, my squad."

"And then what?"

She shrugged. "Then I'll bear his children. I'll fulfill the dream of all women: to become an amma." She sounded defensive, as if she was trying to convince herself of the truth of her statement.

"You must love him a lot to give up scouting," Rukh said.

"Love him?" Jessira chuckled. "Not yet."

Rukh frowned. "What do you mean?"

"Our parents thought we'd make a good match," Jessira said. "And the dowry has already been paid."

An arranged marriage then. They were common in Ashoka as well, although most everyone dreamt of finding a love match. Maybe that explained why Jessira and this Disbar Merdant had yet to be intimate. The man was still an idiot for not trying.

Rukh shook his head. He needed to get his mind off that topic. It brought up thoughts about Jessira he shouldn't be having. "I'm sure you'll be happy," he said, cringing at the empty sentimentality of his words, even as they left his mouth.

"I'm sure we will," Jessira replied, looking certain, but Rukh could hear the doubt in her voice.

———————●————————

A ia placed a tentative paw in the slow running, shallow river. She quickly withdrew it. The water was *cold*. Her tail switched her irritation, and she paced along the bank in irritation. Her Human had crossed this same river several weeks ago, and she was bound and determined to reclaim him. But the obstinate, freezing water cared little for her desires. It thwarted her wants, defying her. All of it seemed grossly unfair.

Aia came to a disgusted halt and stared out over the river in annoyance. If a Kesarin could grimace, just then Aia would have. Aia sat down on her haunches and yawned, thinking on what she should do next.

Her Human was heading deeper into the mountains, and though it was yet early in the cold season, Aia could already see snow blanketing many nearby slopes and peaks. The high country was a wretched land of jagged rocks, biting cold, and piercing ice. It wasn't a place for a Kesarin. Her kind were built for the warmth of the Land, the lush savannah the Humans named the Hunters Flats. Kesarins thrived in the burgeoning heat of a summer, not the chill claws of winter.

Aia groomed herself from elbow to shoulder and considered her options. She ran her raspy tongue along her fur, clipping out a knot with her teeth. Next, she turned her attention to her head, running a paw from the back of her neck to the sensitive area between her ears. Again and again Aia rubbed, until she was certain she'd worked out all the dirt and debris she could reach. The paw required a final cleansing wipe from her tongue before she was satisfied that her fur was perfectly groomed.

The sun stood high and warm, and the riverbank invited her to take a nap, but Aia's growling stomach reminded her that it had been over a day since she had last eaten. With a disappointed huff, Aia stood and padded away from the river, taking a nearby trail through the forest. Earlier in the day, she had spotted a small herd of deer. They might be lingering nearby still. As she walked along the trail, she heard a rustling to her left and noted a brown bear moving through the trees. He looked likely to intersect her path, and Aia eyed him warily. He was large for his kind, and Aia stepped toward him, snarling a challenge. The bear took one look at her, and heeded her warning. He quickly changed direction.

Aia gave a satisfied blink. It was as it should be, and she turned her thoughts back to how she had lost her Human. Rukh Shektan was his name, and Aia loved the flavor of his mind. She had from the first time she had met him. In fact, shortly after investigating his presence in the hills north of the Land, Aia had decided Rukh would be hers to keep. His fingers were so perfect for scratching her chin, and his funny ideas and notions, such as the loving care and devotion he applied to the female—the one who wasn't his mate or even family—all of those things interested her. Of course, then he had so inconsiderately hidden himself away in the ant colony of activity in which Humans lived, a place she couldn't enter.

After several weeks of waiting for him to reappear, Rukh had finally exited his city. But to Aia's consternation, she discovered him traveling with many glarings of his fellows. It hadn't been easy to sneak into his camp, surrounded as he was by so many of his kind. She'd managed it, and Rukh had quite properly scratched her chin as reward for her achievement.

She smiled in remembrance.

At the time, Aia had been feeling quite generous, so when her

Human had asked her for an odd request, she had agreed. He needed her help in saving the horned Nobeasts. Aia had honored his appeal because it was so unusual. He cared for the creatures he admitted had plagued his kind for generations. But somehow, he had forgiven them.

How odd.

Her nanna, Kezin Blenze, had acceded to her Human's request, stating there was no real harm in allowing a few horned Nobeasts, the Baels, to roam the Flats. And if they proved troublesome, they could be killed whenever the Kesarins chose.

By the time Aia had accomplished Rukh's request and had seen the Baels safely settled in Hungrove lands, her Human had made his way back to his ant colony home. There, he had inexplicably turned away from the place and taken a northwestern direction, heading into the high country. And at no time had he waited for Aia to catch up. He had pressed on, moving rapidly until he had journeyed beyond her reach. He was already deep in the heart of the icy mountains, a place Aia couldn't follow.

It was so thoughtless of him, selfish really. Aia's ears flattened and her eyes narrowed. Her tail switched once more. Did her Human not realize how much she enjoyed when he scratched her chin or spoke to her with his languid, honeycomb thoughts?

She snarled her frustration, but there was nothing to it. If she sought Rukh now, she'd simply freeze her life away in the wretched mountains. With a heavy exhalation, Aia realized that she'd have to head south, back to the Land, and wait out the cold season in the Hungrove territories. But once the world warmed again, Aia was determined to journey north, even deep into the mountains if necessary. Then, she would reclaim her Human.

CHAPTER THREE
A BRIEF HISTORY

*With the founding of Stronghold, we stepped past the tired
and outdated Castes with their stifling society built on the
falsehood of separation. We built a city based on fraternity.*

~ *Our Lives Together, by Col Meander, AF 1923*

Jessira woke up to find her eyelashes sticking to her face.
Overnight, the weather had turned frigid, and frost rimmed the
surrounding brush and grass. With an irritated scowl, she sat up
and rubbed the sleep from of her eyes. Last night, they had stopped
just after sunset, making camp in a box canyon at the base of a red
sandstone mesa. It rose before her, sheer and upright, glittering
diamond-like sparkles when the first rays of the sun glanced off of
slender shards of blue-hued ice. Similar cliffs surrounded them on all
sides, except to the west where the Privation Mountains towered. A
harsh breeze gusted, and she clutched her bedroll tightly around
herself until it passed. The wind also carried the stirring smell of
something delicious, and she looked to the campfire. Rukh had made
fresh coffee and was also grilling some kind of meat.

He bent over near the fire; his back turned as he did something with his hands. He stood and walked toward her. "Here." He offered a cup of coffee.

"Thank you," Jessira said gratefully. During her time in Ashoka, she had learned to love the bitter taste of coffee. With a little sugar and milk, it was heavenly. There was nothing better to start the day and get a person going.

It was too bad the bushes from which the beans sprouted wouldn't grow well in Stronghold's high elevation and cool weather. At least, that's what Jessira figured. She'd have to check on it when she got home. Of course, Rukh's nanna had supplied them with plenty of coffee beans, but once it was all used up, there wouldn't be anymore. Then she'd find herself greatly missing her morning delight.

She hid a smile at the thought. There was something else people labeled as being a 'morning delight'.

"What is it?" Rukh asked, picking up on her amusement.

"Nothing,' Jessira said. She took a grateful sip of her coffee and sighed in relief, feeling its warmth spreading through her. "What are you cooking?" she asked.

"Rabbit. Caught a couple in a trap I set out last night."

"Do you need me to take over?"

"I'm not going to burn them," Rukh said, sounding offended.

"Much. You won't burn them much," Jessira said, smiling again over the lip of her cup. "But if you think you can handle it on your own, I'll leave you to it." Times past, she might have patted him patronizingly on the cheek just to irritate him. Not now. Touching him, even fleetingly, would have been far too familiar. While they'd overcome much of their reserve from that first week on the road, they still had a ways to go before they were truly comfortable around each other once again.

"I'll be fine," Rukh said. "Anyway, enjoy your coffee. Breakfast should be ready in a bit." He gave her a half-smile. "Your part will be the one that's scorched."

Jessira couldn't see it, but she could sense Rukh's grin as he walked back to the fire. He was obviously pleased with his quip.

Eventually, the coffee warmed her up, and she kicked out of the bedroll and slipped on her boots. The air bit as another gust blew through the canyon. She tried to ignore the icy wind even as she shivered. Ashoka *had* spoiled her. Stronghold's weather was much colder and harsher than this. Back home, people would have considered this a fine spring day.

Jessira stood and looked toward the Privation Mountains. They were no more than a few days journey away, but once there, travel would become much more difficult. So far, she and Rukh had done well. They were three weeks out from Ashoka, and Jessira figured they'd covered five hundred miles, but it would be the next seven hundred—three hundred as the eagle flew—which would be much harder. She'd be happy if they managed to make it home sometime in the next six weeks, but she figured it more likely to be seven or eight with the snows, the rocky spines, and the twisting passes of the Privations to slow their progress.

And of course, there was the problem in figuring out the best means to reach Stronghold from their current position. They needed to start heading north soon, but when? Dar'El had supplied them with the best maps he could of the foothills surrounding Ashoka as well as the Privation Mountains, but the details were sadly lacking. The last thing they needed was to take a blind pass and have it end at sheer bluff. Jessira would be more confident once they were further west and north. There, the mountains would be more familiar.

Until then they would have to do the best they could and hope they didn't guess wrong too many times.

Her stomach growled. Time to see if those rabbits were edible.

"Do you mind eating as we ride?" Rukh asked when she wandered over to the fire.

"No," she answered. "Do you mind if I spit out the burned parts?"

Rukh pointed to the seared rabbit meat in the pan. "You won't need to," he said, appearing insufferably smug. He had just pulled the skillet off the fire, and the meat looked perfectly done.

Jessira was impressed. "Not bad," she said. "Maybe you'll figure out this cooking thing after all."

Soon after, they broke camp and mounted up, eating as they rode.

"Tell me about Stronghold," Rukh said around bites of his breakfast.

"What do you want to know?" Jessira asked, wiping away a line of grease as it dribbled down her chin. The problem with rabbits: add too much fat to the skillet, and it made for messy eating.

"Everything, I guess," Rukh replied. "If it's going to be my home, I should probably know everything you can tell me about the people, the history, the government, where everyone lives—all of it."

Jessira laughed. "It'll make for pretty dry conversation this early in the morning, don't you think?" she asked. "You sure there's nothing else you want to talk about?"

"Maybe dry to you, but it's all new to me." Rukh shrugged. "Besides, I'm not going anywhere."

Jessira gave him a considering look. Maybe he was finally coming to accept what had happened to him. If so, she was glad. Ever since he'd learned of his banishment, he'd trudged along in mute sorrow as they journeyed west. It had hurt to see him in so much pain, and now…perhaps his curiosity meant he was starting to come back to life.

She kept her thoughts to herself, though. Rukh could be as prickly as a cactus whenever she tried to express sympathy or compassion for his situation. She gave him a carefree shrug of her shoulders. "Suit yourself. But don't blame me if I put you to sleep," Jessira said. "Our city was founded in AF 1753 by fifty-five survivors of Hammer's Fall. They were a small group of Sentyas, Duriahs,

Cherids, Shiyens, Murans, and Rahails."

"But no Kummas?" Rukh asked.

"No Kummas," Jessira affirmed. "Hume saved them, holding back a Fracture of Chimeras by himself. We thought he had died in the defense of our ancestors, but apparently not if the Baels are to be believed."

"They were telling the truth," Rukh said. "They weren't lying about the caverns, were they?"

Jessira gave a moue of distaste. She still didn't like acknowledging that the Baels were secretly allied with Humanity. There was too much bloody history between the two species to so easily accept friendship with the leaders of the Fan Lor Kum.

"Anyway, we honor Hume because of his sacrifice. Our stories also tell of how Hume urged the Fifty-Five to look past Casteism and become one people if they wished to survive. His words were the inspiration for the OutCastes." Jessira privately doubted Hume had said any such thing, but the man *had* defended her ancestors against impossible odds. The fact that he had survived what should have been a glorious sacrifice didn't take anything away from what he had done for her people.

"It's why you hold a tournament in his name?" Rukh guessed.

"It's why *we* hold a tournament," Jessira said. "You're part of our story now, too. And we call it the Trials of Hume, remember?"

Rukh grimaced. "I guess I should get used to saying 'we' when referring to the OutCastes, shouldn't I?"

Jessira nodded, wanting to give him some kind of reassurance. Things were bleak for him, but his life could still be a good one. She sent a prayer on Rukh's behalf to Devesh, the First Father, the First Mother—anyone who was listening.

"What else?" Rukh asked.

"The city is built within a series of caverns inside a mountain, Mount Fort. Two rivers drain the surrounding peaks into Teardrop

Lake, which forms the southern border of a valley where we do all our farming. From the Croft—the farmland—Teardrop empties into an underground river running beneath Mount Fort. It's where we get most of our fresh water. The river eventually joins with the Gaunt and from there, on down to Ashoka."

"These caves," Rukh asked. "What are they like?" He looked and sounded worried.

Jessira smiled. Rukh probably thought her people lived in some nasty, dirty, wet hole, filled with ends of worms and an oozy smell. "Don't worry, Stronghold is nothing like what you're probably imagining," Jessira said. "It's a civilized place." At his still unsure expression, she laughed. "You'll have to see it to understand what I mean."

"I suppose so."

"What else should I tell you?" she mused, speaking more to herself than him. She snapped her fingers. "Government." At Rukh's nod, she continued. "Each Crofthold—the ten main caverns—elects a five-member Home Council. The councilors in turn elect a senator, one for each Crofthold. They serve in the Home Senate and basically decide who should farm the Croft when a field becomes available."

"What do you mean?"

"The Croft is held as a trust by the entire city. No one owns the fields they farm. People work their plots based on the consent and advice of the Senate, and if they don't do a good job, the land is turned over to someone who might do better. As for the individual Croftholds, those are run by their Senator and Home Council. So long as it doesn't impact the entire city, they're pretty independent when it comes to what they're allowed to do. And overseeing all of it is the Governor-General. He's elected during a citywide election every five years. He's also in charge of the Home Army. Beyond that everyone else is either a laborer, farmer, or craftsmen of some sort."

"Like a plumber?" Rukh asked with a quirk of his lips.

"Like a plumber," Jessira said, not sure why Rukh found Disbar's trade to be so humorous.

"And what will I do there?" Rukh asked. "All I know is how to be a warrior."

"I'm sure you could join the Home Army," Jessira said, although she wasn't nearly as sure of the possibility as she was letting on.

Rukh had the skill for the Home Army—more than any warrior she had ever met in fact—but skill alone wouldn't be enough. Competition to get into the Army was fierce. It was often the only means by which someone who was poor could attain a higher station in life. Those who served for twenty-five years were automatically entitled to farm a full acre of land, and farmers were the wealthiest members of Stronghold. No one would want to lose their place to an outsider.

Jessira frowned. Until now, she hadn't actually considered what Rukh would do with the rest of his life. Getting home to Stronghold had been her only priority. Now she was faced with sudden worry for his future. If her own bigotry toward Purebloods was anything to go by, Rukh's time in Stronghold would be hard; but once everyone got to know him, she was sure her people would accept him.

But what if they didn't? What if Stronghold treated him poorly? The OutCastes wouldn't turn him out, but that wasn't the same as welcoming him. What would Rukh do then?

She shied away from those thoughts. *Her people would just have to accept him.*

But if they didn't? her pessimistic side continued to pester.

She had no answer.

Two weeks into the Privation Mountains found Rukh and Jessira journeying along the flat, dull terrain of a high mountain prairie. They were surrounded on all sides by white-peaked mountains and a dismal ceiling of gray clouds hiding the early afternoon sun. The wind blew in blustery waves, cutting through their coats and clothes. Scrubby buffalo grass stretched as far as the eye could see except for the occasional ash and cottonwood. Prairie dogs—the duller ones anyway—poked their heads out now and again. They'd do best to lay low. Hungry packs of wolves ranged the mountains, as did coyotes and foxes. Elk and moose were about as well, but they wouldn't be as easy to bring down as a young, dumb prairie dog.

"We're being stalked," Jessira said. "A nest of Ur-Fels."

"Where?" Rukh asked. His head swiveled about, searching out the Chimeras even as he loosened his sword in its scabbard. While he hadn't seen anything, he trusted Jessira's instincts. She had far more experience surviving out here than he did. While he had done plenty of scouting during the expedition to exterminate the Chimera breeding caverns, this was the Privation Mountains, the place where Jessira had grown up. This was where she had learned to hunt, where she'd learned to hide, and master the subtleties of scouting. She was in her element here.

"About a half-mile or so behind us," Jessira answered. "They probably ran across our tracks and realized the prints they were looking at were shod hooves. Bad luck. It's why Stronghold doesn't use horses much."

Rukh glanced back along the length of their trail. Stretching out into the distance, as far as he could see, was an unbroken path of muddy hoof prints in melting snow and ice. They had just experienced their first snowfall two nights ago. It hadn't been heavy, but it had slowed them down. And apparently, it had also allowed some lucky nest of Ur-Fels to find their tracks.

Of course, whether it was good luck was another question. The

Ur-Fels might curse their fortune if they actually caught up to Rukh and Jessira. He knew the two of them could take a single nest without any problem. Rukh had been worn out and drained when Jessira had found him a few days short of Ashoka—Healing day and night with no rest for weeks on end would do that to a person—but now, despite the hard travels of the past five weeks, Rukh was feeling fit and strong once again. The Ur-Fels would pose no challenge.

But it would be better if they could just avoid the fragging nest.

"Do you have any ideas on how we can lose them?" Rukh asked.

"No matter where we go, we're going to leave a trail bright as day and easy enough for them to follow," Jessira said with a frown. "We might as well shout out where we're going from the top of the hills."

"Can we outrun them?"

"I doubt it. Ur-Fels were bred from foxes. They can run through this muck faster than any horse. They'll be on us within the hour."

"Then we need to find a place to ambush them," Rukh said.

They cast about, looking for an ideal spot from which to launch their attack.

"What about those rocks up there?" Jessira said, pointing toward a cluster of monoliths a hundred yards to the north and on the crest of a small rise. The stones were like jagged shards of crystals, splintered and spilled all around. "If we circle around them, we can hide and take out the Ur-Fels before they even know we're there."

Rukh studied the terrain with pursed lips before finally nodding agreement. It should work.

Jessira led the way past a rock-strewn gully where a wash of water had collected from the surrounding heights before spilling down to the east. The horses clambered and slipped over the piles of rubble and boulders. But, finally, they turned the corner of a particularly large monolith, and Jessira called a halt. From here, they were invisible to anyone following their trail.

Jessira dismounted and turned to face Rukh. "Do you plan on killing them yourself?" she challenged.

"If I have to," Rukh replied, wearing a dismissive smile. "Why? Are you feeling scared?" He knew he sounded like a jackhole, but right now, he didn't much care. He was caught up with the need to inflict pain, a desolate and empty desire to hurt. It was a strange feeling. Bloodlust wasn't part of who he was.

"Don't be an ass," Jessira snapped. "The women of Stronghold don't cower behind their men. We aren't frail flowers."

Jessira was irritated with him—he deserved it—but even more, she was determined. He realized Jessira's pride must have taken a beating on their journey to Ashoka when she'd been unable to defend herself. Instead, she had to rely on Rukh's sword for protection. It must have been humbling for such a strong women.

"You aren't frail," Rukh said softly. "Besides, it's just one nest. I won't get hurt," he added in an offhand tone. It was the wrong thing to say. He sensed an argument brewing, and he sighed. "Fine. When they show up, tell me which ones you want to take. I'll deal with the ones who are left."

Jessira still looked annoyed. "Just don't do anything too foolish. I don't want to see you hurt." She Blended more deeply, disappearing entirely from Rukh's view.

During their journey so far, the Blends they had used had been thin, meant to be good enough to hide them from a perfunctory examination. The Blend Jessira now used was the deepest possible for her. It hid her entirely. It also required more *Jivatma*, and as a result, was far more taxing.

Rukh reached for her Blend and Linked with it. She was crouched near the corner of the rocks, sword sheathed, arrow nocked. She looked focused and ready.

"Now who's planning on taking on the entire Nest?" he asked.

Jessira glanced his way and rolled her eyes. "Unlike some, I'm not stupid."

Rukh grunted acknowledgement and settled down behind her as they waited for the Ur-Fels. Rukh studied their trail east but was distracted by Jessira's close presence. Her cinnamon scent, her breathing…he eased away from her even as he told himself to pay attention to the job at hand.

Just then, she looked over her shoulder at him, an intent expression on her face. She gripped the front of his pants, just above a knee and gave it a tug. Rukh shuffled forward.

"The Ur-Fels should be spread out. This won't be like the Hunters Flats," she said. "Those Chimeras weren't aware of our presence. These will be. They'll be cautious."

"What do you suggest?" Rukh asked, doing his best to ignore her hand resting still on his leg.

"Get the drop on them from above." She gestured. "Can you climb the monoliths and circle around the Ur-Fels?"

"Cut them down from behind so none of them escape to warn the rest of their brethren," Rukh said, guessing her plan. At her nod of agreement, he continued. "I can do it."

"Be careful," Jessira replied, staring him in the eyes. "I know how good you are, but you're reckless." Her hand slid down to his knee, briefly squeezing it. "I mean it." She let go of his leg and faced forward again.

Rukh's knee tingled from where her hand had squeezed it, but he forced himself to concentrate on the work at hand. He Blended as deeply as he could and swiftly ascended the rubble of bleached boulders and ragged stone monoliths. Upon descending to the other side, he ran parallel to where Jessira crouched and slightly diagonal to where they had been traveling. Rukh searched for a place to hide as he ducked alongside the gully formed by the snowmelt.

There.

Upon the wide shelf of a large, solitary stone, plinth-like in shape, sat a boulder. Behind it was a ledge, easily wide enough for him to crouch and remain hidden while he waited for the Ur-Fels. He climbed atop the monolith and hid, smiling in anticipation.

Soon enough, he heard the sound of movement. He peered over the top of the boulder. Here came the Nest. Fifteen of them, spread out in a line fifty yards wide. It was more Ur-Fels than he had anticipated. The original plan had been to allow the Chimeras to pass him by and let Jessira pick them off. The survivors would then be driven back toward Rukh, but with this many Ur-Fels, it wouldn't work. The Chimeras wouldn't run from Jessira. They'd attack.

Rukh would have to thin out the Ur-Fels before they came upon Jessira.

He waited as the nearest Ur-Fel approached. He was about to leap forward, but another sound came to him, a harsh guttural growl. A Tigon. Rukh looked for them and saw five of them crouched low, running on all fours from boulder-to-boulder. He frowned in consternation. The fragging cats changed everything. He had to attack with Fireballs. He didn't see any other option.

Rukh just hoped this wasn't an even larger hunting party than he and Jessira had initially expected. He scanned behind the Tigons and Ur-Fels, worried about Braids. No sibilant cries or hissing sounds of scales dragging across the ground came to him.

This was it then. Fifteen Ur-Fels and five Tigons. It was doable. Blended as he was, he could take apart half the Nest and most of the Tigons before the rest of them even realized they were being attacked.

Rukh's face relaxed into slack lines of indifference. A gray film seemed to cover his vision. He could take on all the Chimeras. Kill them all, and even if he couldn't, so what? No one was immortal. Bleakness settled over his heart.

Time to kill.

Rukh stood, sighted the closest two Tigons. Kill them first and piss off the rest. He threw two Fireballs, and two of the cats were cooked, screaming as they died. His bow was already ready, an arrow fitted even as the second Fireball screamed through the air. Rukh let loose and killed the nearest Ur-Fel. The nest quickly realized where he must be, and they converged on his position. He conducted more *Jivatma*, Shielding now. Arrows pinged off it. He held his Blend and drew more deeply from his Well. More *Jivatma* to speed up his movements. He leapt off the boulder and landed thirty feet away, behind an Ur-Fel. A slash beheaded the foxlike Chimera. Arrows took two more Ur-Fels, those closest to him, leaving him room to work.

Rukh heard Jessira's scream of frustration. "Damn it!"

Eleven Ur-Fels and three Tigons roared as they raced toward where they thought him to be. But he'd already ghosted away.

As he battled, the darkness in his heart, the futility grown from all he had lost and given, blossomed. It seemed he had all the time in the world to kill these Chimeras. No sympathy for such creatures.

Several more arrows. Down went another Tigon and a couple of Ur-Fels. They thrashed about on the ground.

The hollowing of his spirit—he thought he'd come to accept the losses in his life, but he hadn't. The emptiness called to him. It was as irresistible as a cold drink in a desert. So easy to give in to its siren song.

Rukh dropped his Blend, letting the Chimeras see him. There were but nine Ur-Fels and two Tigons left and they roared in rage. Two more Ur-Fels fell, arrows in their throats, before Rukh drew his sword. The Chims were too close for the bow, but not a final Fireball. This one took out three Ur-Fels who had foolishly clustered close to one another.

Four Ur-Fels and two Tigons against his sword.

It wasn't even close. He darted amongst the Chimeras, dealing killing blows almost in passing. Disappointment filled him. It was all-too easy.

He almost dropped his Shield, wanting to tempt Fate to take his life. Thoughts cascaded through his mind. *Why not? He was Unworthy, someone worthy of only death. The world wouldn't care if he died. His passing wouldn't even merit a footnote in the annals of anyone's history.*

The past five weeks, he'd been fooling himself. He'd gone through the motions of life because it was expected, because Jessira cared and wanted him to live, but all along, he'd known the truth: He should have died in the caverns of the Chimeras. It would have at least been an honorable death. Nothing he'd done since, even saving the lives of all those warriors…what did it matter in the end? Did Devesh approve of his actions?

Frag Devesh.

Their God hadn't done anything for Humanity in millennia. And he sure hadn't saved Rukh from the ugly fate that had taken him from everything he loved and cared for.

His thoughts swirled into thicker and thicker circles of darkness….

Jessira was there. She fired an arrow at the remaining Tigon, killing him. The remaining Ur-Fel spun around to face her, but she was Blended, hidden from his view. The Ur-Fel shifted his gaze from Rukh to wherever he suspected Jessira to be. Finally, he spun and made to run away. He took two steps before a foot of matte-black, spidergrass blade thrust through his chest, killing him. He gurgled out his dying breath.

Jessira turned to him, a look of fury on her face. Rukh reflexively strengthened his Shield. She looked mad enough to spit him on the spot. "What the fragging, unholy hells were you thinking!" she screamed. "You could have been killed."

Rukh didn't have an answer. He dropped his Shield and turned away from her anger, cleaning his sword on the fur of a dead Ur-Fel. His movements were mechanical. The reality of what he had done crashed home. What *had* he been thinking? Jessira was right to be angry with him. And he'd almost fought the final two Chims with no weapon at all. He flinched. The emptiness inside, so seductive a moment before, now filled him with horror. It was a yawning chasm leading nowhere.

When had he become such a coward?

He realized Jessira was still yelling at him, her features blurred. Her voice seemed to come from an immeasurably far distance, distorted and faint.

A hard slap rocked his head to the side. "You want die? Go ahead, but you aren't taking me with you!" she shouted.

A tear slid down her face, and he reached forward and touched it wonderingly. Why was she crying? Seeing her pain broke a dam in him, and he shuddered. The world snapped into focus. Clarity returned. He could hear and see her again.

"I'm sorry," he mumbled, numb now. What a selfish thing he'd almost done.

Jessira stared at him, frustration evident on her face. She breathed out a sigh of disappointment. "I know this isn't easy," she said, "but it will get better. Just live until that time. Just fight it!"

"I should have died in the caverns," Rukh muttered. "At least it would have been a warrior's death."

The anger left her face, replaced by dawning understanding and compassion. "Oh, Rukh." She put her arms around his neck, pulling him close. "Promise me you'll never do anything like that again," she whispered into his ear.

Rukh worked to get his dangerously gyrating emotions under control before answering. "I promise," he whispered before pulling away from her, breaking the circle of Jessira's embrace.

Her face was filled with concern. "Will you be all right?" she asked.

Rukh felt like laughing. He had thought he *was* all right. He had no idea something so ugly as despair and tiredness of living had made a home in his heart. He'd been so busy pushing through: the expedition to the caverns, the betrayal of Lieutenant Danslo and the other warriors, the battle, the long hike back to Ashoka with days and nights of endless fatigue. And after it was all done: banishment. During the journey to Stronghold, he'd held in all his feelings, smothered them, let them fester until they came boiling out in a way which could have ended his life.

"I don't know," Rukh said. The sentiment was the honest truth. He didn't know if he would be all right. Not now. Maybe not ever. Some vital spark seemed to be gone from his life. His purpose, his reason to exist—it wasn't there.

"We'll have to find you a different reason to live," Jessira said, somehow guessing what he was thinking.

CHAPTER FOUR
A PRICE PAID

Incur the reckoning now or inherit the debt later.
A pinprick pain followed by Tranquility or sloth followed
by Self-flagellation. Those are the choices we all must face.

~*Our Lives Alone, by Asias Athandra, AF 331*

Hal'El sat still. An open, unread newspaper was held in his hands, but his attention was captured by Varesea. They had spent an afternoon together in an unoccupied building in Stone Cavern, sharing the intoxicating rush of emotions they found only in one another's arms. Hal'El could have lingered far longer, but duty pressed. It was then, after they had set aside their pleasure and got to work that Varesea had another attack.

He didn't know how else to describe it. One moment she had been fine, and the next she was pacing back and forth, her movements harsh and jerky. She occasionally clutched her arms, grasping the fabric of her shirt, almost tearing it. She muttered incomprehensibly, but Hal'El knew what she was saying. *"You aren't real. You aren't real."*

Hal'El watched in obdurate silence, his face wrought with worry.

The attacks had begun several months after the death of her husband, Slathtril, and were becoming more frequent. When gripped in the madness of such an episode, Varesea would imagine that the wife-beating bastard was still alive. In her mind, Slathtril raved at her, accusing her, berating her, and threatening retribution for what she had done. Sometimes Slathtril's words were apparently so terrifying that Varesea would tear at her hair, screaming silently with eyes empty of thought. It was frightening to witness, and Hal'El wasn't a man who frightened easily.

Varesea came to a stop by the cheap, pine table where Hal'El sat. She dug her fingernails into the surface, gouging out a small splinter. It stabbed her finger, raising a blot of blood, but she didn't notice. Again, she paced.

In times past, Hal'El had tried to hold her, comfort her, soothe her, but it only seemed to make things worse. Varesea would scream gutturally at him, fight him, scratching, clawing, and biting. It was better to let her work it out on her own. And he certainly couldn't take her to a physician. How? Hal'El wasn't her relative, nor was he even of Varesea's Caste. What excuses could he offer to accompany her? There were none. Varesea would have to seek help on her own, but so far she had refused to do so.

She was afraid she might have a delusional episode while seeing a physician. What if she spoke of her relationship with Hal'El or of the Sil Lor Kum? It was her greatest fear, and Hal'El was shamefaced enough to admit that it was his as well. On a selfish level, he was glad Varesea hadn't yet decided to consult a physician.

So instead, he had to watch as the woman he loved struggled to maintain her sanity, all the while afraid she might kill them both during a fleeting slip of sanity. And he could do nothing to prevent such an occurrence. Whatever evil Hal'El might have committed in his life, killing Varesea Apter was one thing of which he was incapable. He loved her too much to see her dead by his hand.

The situation left him feeling helpless, another emotion to which he was unaccustomed.

And on an equally worrying note, Hal'El had concerns for his own sanity. Sometimes he heard whispers on the wind, sounds sensed rather than heard, gone before he could decipher the muffled words. What he knew was that they were voices, a man and a woman.

He could taste their hate.

Hal'El feared who they might be—Felt Barnel and the Cherid woman, Aqua Oilhue. He'd murdered them both, and the possibility that a part of their essences might have stained his mind left him cold with fear. What if Varesea's fate was to be his own? The Knife stole *Jivatma*—of this, he was certain—but what if those who were killed by the black blade never truly died? What if they lived on in the minds of their killers, slowly poisoning them until they broke and lost their reason? It was a terrifying thought, but it also went a long way toward explaining why knowledge of the Withering Knife was so limited. Prior wielders of the Knife must have all died, killed by their own burgeoning insanity.

If so, could Hal'El ever risk using it again? He wasn't sure. And even though the Queen had demanded he kill once more with the Knife, Hal'El was reluctant to do so. He feared what might happen if he did.

Varesea had finally stopped pacing—thank Devesh!—and flopped into the plush couch, the only other furnishing in the room other than the table and chairs. "Slathtril vows to feast on your flesh," she said before collapsing into a faint.

———————◆●◆———————

Rector Bryce studied the ledgers laid out upon the desk. The books were a record of all the materials stored and eventually shipped out from the warehouse in the Moon Quarter of which he had titular oversight. At first, he had been unable to make any sense of the accounts. The records were kept in an indecipherable language, and for a time, Rector had been sure his accountants had played a trick on him, passing on ledgers written in gibberish.

It hadn't been the case, and perhaps Rector would have realized it sooner if he had actually tried to understand the accountant's code when first confronted with it. Instead, since he had deemed such work to be beneath him, he had wasted weeks staring resentfully at the books and their notations, unwilling and unable to comprehend their contents. As time passed, Rector finally got out of his own way and began the process of deciphering the confusing mass of columns, rows, numbers, and shorthand scribbling. The logic of the accounting books slowly became apparent, and, to his surprise, the work became enjoyable. It was like solving a puzzle.

Materials were inventoried, both for when they were first placed in the warehouse and for when they were removed. Items were logged on arrival based on quantity, cost, and location and logged out when it came time to ship them. The information was updated daily by the warehouse manager and confirmed on the same day by one of the accountants. It was a simple, but efficient system of record-keeping.

Errors still crept in, but once a quarter, the warehouse underwent an audit of all the materials present within it. On that day, the ledgers were also updated, and any discrepancies were either cleared up or the missing items were deleted from the records. From what Rector had seen, such mistakes were few and far between. The men and women working for House Wrestiva were good at what they did, and per Rector's inspection of the warehouse, rarely did even a single nail go unaccounted for.

It made the missing henna paste and poppy seeds from a year ago all the more unusual. In the long run, it wasn't much of a loss, but it still had Rector curious. The henna had been logged in as arriving with the Trial from Kush over a year ago and the poppy seeds from Forge. Neither had been logged out. Then, several months ago, the line items indicating their presence had been zeroed out. It must have happened during one of the quarterly audits. While House Wrestiva could easily absorb the lost revenue, nevertheless, it was something that should not have occurred. Henna was too expensive to have simply gone missing like that, and poppy, with its many medicinal uses, was equally costly.

The losses were the only problems Rector had, thus far, discovered in House Wrestiva's accounts.

Of course, Mira would want to know about them, even though she would be just as likely to toss it off as being unimportant. Rector's nostrils flared in irritation as he imagined the lofty manner by which she would order him to skulk about for more important information. She could do so because she knew of Rector's family history and the Sil Lor Kum. It was her trump card, but the fact that she would threaten to destroy his family if he didn't do as she commanded revealed the truth about her spiteful, arrogant nature.

Karma had a way of dealing with people like her—or at least so Rector hoped.

He checked the clock and cursed under his breath. He would have to hustle if he wanted to make it in time for his meeting with Mira. She hated to be kept waiting. Rector darted out of the warehouse and raced through the Moon Quarter. Luckily, traffic wasn't too heavy, and he was able to make the journey to Trell Rue with plenty of time to spare.

With the final stretch of road ahead of him, Rector caught sight of Mira waiting outside the Duriah café where the two of them had decided to meet for their biweekly debriefings. Mira nodded greeting, and they shared blatantly false smiles.

Before taking a seat, Rector leaned over and kissed her on the cheek. "You look as lovely as your soul." He knew the gesture and words would irritate her.

Mira's eyes briefly narrowed, but otherwise, she gave no signal to indicate her annoyance. "And you are as handsome as your personality," she murmured as he sat down.

"Charming," Rector said. He called over a waiter and placed an order for a beer and parathas filled with dahl and lamb. "Did you want anything?" he asked Mira before the waiter left.

"I've already ordered," she replied. Once the waiter left, Mira leaned forward. "Don't ever kiss me again," she hissed.

Rector smiled, not bothering to hide his pleasure at angering her. In all their other meetings, she openly mocked him and his fallen station. It was time to prick her smug sense of superiority and have her feel some sting during their interactions as well.

"Take this seriously, Rector Bryce—"

"Or what?" Rector interrupted. "Will Dar'El take me to task for being insufficiently obsequious?" He snorted in derision.

"We shouldn't argue," Mira warned. "People are watching."

"Then you should learn to curb your tongue," Rector said. "I arrived and gave you a kiss on the cheek. For doing so, you glare at me?"

Mira stared into her lap, taking a moment to compose herself before she looked up again, this time wearing a bright smile. She reached for Rector's hands, holding them in both of her own. "I'm sorry, beloved," she said. "I love you so much. Let's not quarrel."

Rector couldn't detect a hint of sarcasm in her voice, but her nails dug painfully into his palms, letting him know of her anger. Rector removed his hands from hers. "It's quite all right." He refused to shake out his hands and display weakness before her.

"Now," Mira said, still wearing the bright, stupid smile. "What do you have to tell me?"

"Other than the fact that I don't like you?" Rector said. "Not much."

"Your feelings toward me are not what I meant," Mira said, still grinning. "What of House Wrestiva?"

Rector laughed at her patently false smile. "You know how idiotic you look doing that?" He waved in the general direction of her face. "Do you think anyone is fooled by your grin?"

Mira startled, and the smile slipped.

Rector chuckled again, happy to be the one delivering the verbal barbs rather than receive them. Usually, with Mira, it was the other way around. "We have a professional relationship, and I wish we didn't even have that," he said, "but neither of us can lie well enough to trick anyone into thinking we're madly in love."

"Fair enough," Mira said. "But my question still stands: did you learn anything about House Wrestiva?"

Rector nodded. "As a matter of fact, I did," he said, explaining about the missing henna and poppy seeds. "And I'm sure this grand mystery will be the means by which your wonderful 'El will somehow bring down House Wrestiva."

Mira flicked a glance his way but otherwise didn't respond to his sarcasm. She appeared pensive. "First, Dar'El isn't interested in destroying House Wrestiva; only your ruling 'El. Second, juniper and sourwain."

Rector frowned. "What?"

"Two rare spices, and if combined with henna and poppy seeds, you get something highly illicit: snowblood."

Rector rolled his eyes. "I should have known you Shektans wouldn't have an ounce of restraint or decency when it comes to trying to bring down Hal'El Wrestiva."

"Yes, because Hal'El Wrestiva is such a paragon of morality," Mira said sarcastically. "Remember his son, Suge, the snowblood addict, and what Hal'El tried to do to Jaresh?"

"It doesn't diminish Hal'El's accomplishments in the Trials," Rector replied. "Hal'El is a hero."

"A hero who made sure that a far greater hero was found Unworthy."

Rector flinched. Almost four months after the fact, he had grown ever more guilty about his role in Rukh's banishment. He knew now that he should have never spoken up. It wasn't simply that it wasn't his place to have done so, but even more because much of the moral certitude he had held from that happy, innocent time had long since dissipated. The process had begun when Dar'El Shektan had revealed the secret of Rector's heritage. "If faced with the same situation now, I would have never revealed Rukh's secrets," he said after a moment of quiet reflection.

For a wonder, Mira looked genuinely baffled. "Even after all the rumors about him and Jessira?"

Rector smiled half-heartedly. "Given my ancestors, who have done far worse, why should I bother with another's folly?"

Mira tilted her head in consideration. "You surprise me," she finally replied. "I never imagined hearing you say something like that."

Rector shrugged. "I never imagined I would have to," he said.

"And so you no longer judge others? Even Jaresh, who you are certain harbors immoral feelings toward me?"

"As long as it doesn't affect me, he can live as he wishes," Rector clarified.

"Really?"

Rector didn't answer at first, taking time to form his thoughts. "A few months ago, I mapped out the descendants of my great-grandfather," he said. "There are over fifty of us, some still learning to walk. I find myself wondering why all of them should be stained because of *his* actions? It seems arbitrary and unjust."

Again, Mira appeared surprised. "Some would claim your moral conversion to be merely self-serving," she challenged.

"And they might be right," Rector said, "but it also doesn't mean I'm wrong."

The Society of Rajan consisted of twenty-one men and women, three members from each Caste: a master, journeyman, and an apprentice. As expected the apprentices were the youngest, ranging in age from the middle thirties to early forties, while all the masters were older than sixty. Right now, the members sat about the heptagonal table centered in the third floor ballroom that made up the Society's Hall.

Night had long since fallen, and heavy curtains were drawn across the tall, narrow windows while the firefly lamps within their wall sconces and chandeliers were turned up, casting the room in bright light. The Society's Hall was located on the top floor of a small three-story building located several blocks north of the Magisterium. The lower levels were given over to various businesses and flats, and most people would have never guessed that such a mythical organization would meet in such a prosaic place.

Of course, what most people knew about the Rajans was mostly hearsay and innuendo. Over the centuries, those rumors had inflated the Society's reputation past the point of reason. Some believed it had been the First Father who had founded the Rajans; others claimed the Society was the descendant of some long ago Council of the First World. A few fools were certain the Society hoarded knowledge of *Jivatma* unknown to anyone else or were even composed of some hidden eighth Caste.

All of it was absurd, and in fact, the truth was far less impressive. The Society had been founded in Hammer and initially tasked with unlocking the secrets of *The Book of First Movement*. Though they had utterly failed their original purpose, somehow the Society had still spread, branching out into every other city on Arisa. Over time, its charter had also changed. In general, the Rajans sought to be a positive force by inculcating a higher state of equality and acceptance amongst society in general.

Depending on who was asked, it was a notion that was either breathtakingly brazen or hopelessly naïve.

Dar'El, the Kumma Journeyman, had asked for this gathering, and as he spoke, his fellow Rajans eyed him with polite expressions of curiosity. For a half-hour now, he had explained the importance of bringing Rukh home, and why such an endeavor was worthy of the Society's resources. While he had been laying out his plan, he had noticed a few of his fellows covering a yawn. They weren't bored—at least Dar'El hoped not. More likely, they were simply tired, which was understandable given the lateness of the hour.

"You've spoken eloquently in defense of your son," said Thrivel Nonel, the Master Sentya. Like everyone else in the Society, he was a person of influence in his Caste, and he took his time in formulating his thoughts. "But I have yet to hear why we should believe he has *The Book of First Movement*."

"I wrote to Rukh about *The Book*," Dar'El said. "I know him well enough to believe he will eventually go after it."

"Meaning we can never truly know if he ever obtains it or even makes the attempt," said Anian Elim, the heavyset Duriah Journeyman.

"Correct," Dar'El answered, knowing this was the weakest part of his argument. "But as I said before, I think he will. In this, I must simply ask for your trust."

"And of all the warriors in Ashoka, Rukh would have the greatest hope of success in reclaiming *The Book*," said Silma Thoran, the Kumma Master. "Whether he makes the attempt from Stronghold or after returning to Ashoka." For her statement of support and so many other reasons, Dar'El could have kissed the elderly Master Kumma. Her eyes were clouded with cataracts, but her mind remained just as bright and focused as the day twenty years ago when she had approached Dar'El about joining the Society.

"And if he chooses never to go to Hammer?" asked Minet Jorian, the Apprentice Cherid. "After all, it is a journey fraught with danger."

"In that case, at least Rukh would be returned to us, a notion I find appealing," Dar'El said with a smile. "I know it sounds like a nanna's pride speaking, but my son is special. Remember all he accomplished in his first Trial, and how critical he was for the survival of dozens of our warriors after the battle in the caverns. Imagine if everyone could do as he can. There would be so much we could accomplish."

"It is also heresy," said Gren Vos, who—in addition to her position as a Magistrate—was also the Shiyen Master. She thrust out her chin in challenge. "How will you answer those who quote *The Word and the Deed*, which is quite clear on the matter?"

Dar'El nodded acknowledgment to the old Shiyen. Gren was an ally in this. She was merely giving him an opportunity to address some of the worries that others around the table were likely considering. Rajans were chosen, not simply because of their influential status in their Castes, but more importantly for their ability to think critically and with an open mind. Right now, most of his fellows were worried about how Rukh's presence might affect the city, especially amongst Ashoka's reactionary elements.

"There will be many who will despise Rukh for what he can do. But, consider the name the city has given him: the Hero of the Slave River. The people of Ashoka have already made their decision with regards to my son: they have embraced him."

"But not all," said Grain Jola, the obdurate Master Rahail. Of all the Rajans, he was the prickliest, and the one least likely to agree with the others. There were times when meetings were prolonged for no other reason than Grain just *had* to voice his opinion, no matter how inconsequential the matter being discussed. Sometimes Dar'El wondered if the old patriarch did so more out of obstinacy than conviction.

"Not all," Dar'El agreed, allowing no hint of irritation to enter his voice. "But if our decisions are based on how we fear the more reactionary elements of our city *might* react, Ashoka would never change. She will never become what we all want."

"Yes, but thus far, we've simply pushed for Castes other than Kumma and Cherid to obtain leadership roles in the city. We strive for equality of opportunity, and we've done well to further it," Grain countered. "Your son represents a much greater test to Ashoka's culture. His Talents are a direct affront to everything we hold to be true about the Castes. His mere existence, as well as these OutCastes with which he will always be associated, would threaten the holy truth of *The Word and the Deed.*"

Sim Chilmore, the Cherid Master, chuckled softly. "My old friend, I share your fears," he said to Grain. "But this is also an opportunity. One we could have never foreseen or expected." He glanced around the table, his eyes bright. "*The Book of All Souls,*" he continued. "Don't you see? *The Word and the Deed* teaches equality, but *The Book of All Souls* teaches fraternity."

Sim's words resonated, and Dar'El found himself nodding in agreement.

"I read your son's report from his Trial," said Bravun Silan, the Kumma Apprentice, and the man Dar'El had sponsored for the Society. "Is fraternity not what the Baels claim to worship as well?"

Thrivel Nonel cackled laughter. "How ironic. What we have always sought, the Baels learned first."

"If they spoke the truth," Grain Jola muttered.

"I call for a vote," Dar'El said.

Grain's head jerked up. "Wait. There are other issues to discuss. You seek our help in convincing the Chamber of Lords to rescind their verdict on Rukh, to no longer find him Unworthy. To entice us, you offer up the possibility that he might have *The Book of First Movement*. What if he has it but refuses to part with it? What then?"

Dar'El was about to reply but was spared from having to speak when Gren Vos answered in his stead. "How likely do you suppose that might be?" she asked. "And if Rukh refuses us, so what. Rukh Shektan, for all his Talents and exploits, is but one man, and like all men, he will eventually pass from this world. We are the Society of Rajan. Time is on our side. *The Book* will be ours."

Her answer must have mollified Grain because while the old Rahail settled back in his chair with a grumble, he remained quiet.

"I still don't like the fact that you pushed your son to quest for *The Book* without consulting the rest of the Society," Diffel Larekin, the Cherid Journeyman grumbled.

"And I already explained why," Dar'El replied evenly. "At the time, I was focused on how to keep my son safe. I didn't think to seek approval, and by the time I realized I should have, it was too late." He shrugged. "I used my discretion."

"You aren't yet a Master to make such decisions for the rest of us," Sim Chilmore, the Cherid Master, reminded him.

"But I am the ruling 'El of a powerful House, and father to the man who will retrieve *The Book*."

His words earned him a sour look from Sim as well as a brief nod of understanding.

"There is one other consideration," Gren Vos said, looking around the room and making sure she had everyone's attention. "Kumma politics is a minefield. What if Rukh obtains *The Book*, takes it to the ghrina city…this Stronghold, but we are unable to overturn his banishment? *The Book* would be lost to us."

Gren shrugged apology at Dar'El, but he didn't mind her words. It was a possibility he had already considered. "First, *The Book* is already lost in Hammer, so if it is taken to Stronghold, we really don't lose anything. Second, Kumma politics is exactly why I asked for this meeting. If pressure from without is brought upon the Chamber, they will feel it. Even those who voted to find Rukh Unworthy will feel it. They know they can't afford to alienate the rest of the city."

Sim sighed. "Life would be so much easier without politics to muddy it up. Imagine a place like that."

Grain chuckled. "Good luck finding such a world. You might as well call it Salvation."

"Are there any more questions?" Dar'El asked.

Gren Vos shook her head. "We've run around this issue long enough," she said. "It's time to vote."

Unsurprisingly, the Society voted to throw its weight behind Dar'El's plan to bring Rukh home.

Grain Jola grinned when the final tally was read. It was twenty for and one against. "I couldn't allow it to be unanimous," he said.

Afterward, the meeting ended, and Dar'El accepted the congratulations and promises of assistance from his fellow Rajans. They also offered advice on how to proceed and warnings not to fail.

As a result, Dar'El was one of the last to leave the Hall. It was left to him to turn down the firefly lamps and clean the room. He did so, organizing the chairs about the table as part of his final pass through. By the time he was finished, the room was dark except for a small lamp in the entryway

Dar'El slipped on his wool coat, settling it about his shoulders and tucked his hands into his coat pockets. It was then that he discovered a small folded piece of paper in one of them with his name upon it.

Dar'El glanced around, but no one else was about.

He recognized the handwriting. It was another note from the one who claimed to be a MalDin. Which also meant that Satha was right: the writer of the note was a member of the Society. There had been no servants tonight. Dar'El felt the weight of all he had to do, and his shoulders slumped. He'd known most of the people here for years, and in many cases, decades. It made him sick to realize one of his fellow Rajans could be a part of the Sil Lor Kum. One of his dear friends would have to die for their crimes.

Dar'El tried to set aside his anguish as he unfolded the paper. The note contained two words. It was a name: *Drin Port.*

————— ● —————

Jaresh and Bree made their way as quickly as they could to Hold Cavern. There had been another murder, this one occurring many months after the last one. Bree's face was a mask, but Jaresh could tell she was just as upset and angry as he was. With so much time passing since the murder of Slathtril Apter, they had grown lax, the urgency of finding the killer fading. This was the price for their idleness: another man dead.

Jaresh's teeth gritted. Idiot. Spending so much time mooning over Mira, worrying about something that could never be when he should have been doing his job. He vowed it would never happen again. They would catch these fiends before anyone else died.

Soon enough, they arrived at the scene of the crime. It was a quiet road of tall, slate-roofed houses painted sedate colors ranging from brown to russet, but all of them adorned with elaborate trim. Dogwoods lined the sidewalk at regular intervals. It was dusk, and along with the lampposts, firefly lanterns of red, gold, and violet were woven into the bare branches of the trees, providing a multihued light. It would have made a lovely scene except for the section of the road blocked off by wooden barricades, and the small crowd gathered behind them.

The Watch had already arrived and taken charge of the situation. Jaresh grimaced when he saw Rector Bryce.

"Stop scowling," Bree whispered. "We want Rector to allow us through."

Jaresh took her advice and did his best to school his features to stillness. It must have worked because Rector glanced their way and said something to one of his men, who came their way and allowed them inside the cordoned-off area. As they were passed through, Rector acknowledged them with a brief nod before turning aside to speak to someone else.

Mira met them at the top of a wide flight of stairs that led to the front door. She briefly looked Jaresh's way before turning to Bree.

It had been months since the two of them had decided to go their separate ways, but Jaresh's stomach still tightened with longing when he saw Mira. At least it wasn't the painful clenching it had once been. Progress.

"His name was Van Jinnu," Mira said. "That's all I've learned so far. Dar'El may know more."

She drew them inside and within the foyer was a tarp-covered body lying atop a bloodstained rug. Nanna stood nearby, speaking with one of the members of the Watch. He broke off and gestured them aside. "Van Jinnu. A Rahail," Nanna began without preamble. "A warrior. Two Trials to his name. Wealthy and widowed three years now."

"Anything else?" Jaresh asked, forcing himself not to look too long at Mira.

Dar'El nodded his head. "But not here," he said. "Come." He led them deeper into the house, to the kitchen. From the ceiling hung a small rack of pots and pans. Several plates and utensils littered the sink, and a round table with two glasses of water upon it took up one corner.

"I need to talk to Rector," Mira said, excusing herself.

"You said Van Jinnu was a widower," Jaresh said. He pointed to the glasses. "Did he have servants?"

"From all accounts, he lived alone," Nanna answered.

"Then why are there two glasses of water on the table?" Jaresh asked.

"Could the killer have been brazen enough to have had a drink with Van?" Bree asked.

It actually sounded like it might have been the case. "What a cold son of a bitch," Jaresh said with a scowl.

"We should talk more," Nanna said. "Outside." He motioned toward several members of the Watch, who were drifting their way.

They followed Nanna to the front floor landing, and when they stepped outside, Jaresh saw Mira and Rector holding hands. The Watch lieutenant whispered something to her, and she smiled. He spoke again, and Mira nodded before turning away.

The earlier pangs of longing Jaresh had felt upon seeing Mira rose again in a crest of confusion and jealousy. What was going on? She had always claimed to dislike Rector Bryce, but here they were holding hands.

"I thought Mira didn't like Rector," Bree said, echoing Jaresh's thoughts.

"She doesn't," Nanna said, which made Jaresh feel better but did nothing to answer the confusing scene of her and Rector holding hands. "All will be made clear later."

Mira came to them. "Rector didn't find anything else," she said.

Jaresh tried to catch her attention, wanting to ask what was going on between her and Rector, but she wouldn't meet his gaze.

"In two days," Nanna said. "I want to know everything about Van Jinnu and what happened here." Anger crackled in his voice. "These murders will not continue."

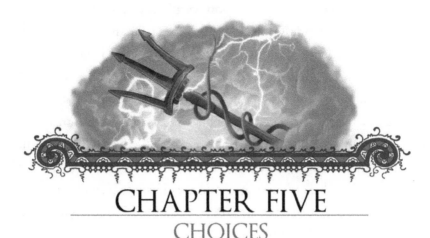

CHAPTER FIVE
CHOICES

The Chimeras are not a mindless horde of unthinking killers.
In their own fashion, they possess reason. So are they our brothers?
This question has haunted us since the time of Li-Charn and Hume.

~From the journal of SarpanKum Li-Dane, AF 1938

Chak-Soon stood on the heights and watched the battle play out down below amongst the broken stones of the plain. A quarter-mile away, the Chimeras he had sent to scout the Humans were being systematically butchered. He felt no pain at the loss of the nest, but the loss of his claw hurt. He wanted to leap forth and destroy the Kumma monster who was killing the Tigons he had fought so hard to lead—but he couldn't. He had been ordered to observe. Nothing more. And so he watched as the Human warrior moved like the wind, flickering in and out of view. Soon grunted as the final Tigon died. He'd seen enough. It was only a matter of moments before the last of the Chimeras was killed.

Alongside him stood the two remaining members of his claw, his minions, bound to serve him unless they found a means to overthrow his rule. Until that day, though, Chak-Soon was their ordinate, in complete command of their lives. It was the way of his kind: whoever was strongest ruled. And while Soon wasn't as physically imposing as the two Tigons standing beside him, he was far more cunning and ruthless. There were some who likened his plans to those of their once-masters, the Baels. It would be hard to take Soon by surprise. In addition, he was known to be a brutal warrior, willing to accept as much damage as was needed so long as he could latch his great teeth upon the throat of his enemy. Soon was young, but older ordinates were already starting to take note of his savagery. They watched him carefully, certain his ambition was not satisfied with a single claw.

And as for that claw, it was all but dead, but Soon could always win control of another. Of that he was certain. What was life without domination of those who were weaker? Soon knew he would one day rise high in the ranks of the Chimeras…with Mother's blessing.

"Kumma killed brothers," said one of the Tigon, his voice guttural as his tongue tripped around his oversized great teeth. "We kill back?"

Soon glanced at his fellow Tigons. The one who had spoken was huge and had a lion's mane of fur. He wore a simple breechcloth, a sheathed sword hanging from his waist, and a leather case containing his bow and sheaf of arrows strapped to his back. The other Tigon had a leopard's spots and was dressed similarly to the first. He was smaller than the lion but still larger than Soon. All were naked to the cold wind, although Soon knew none of them felt the air's bite. Tigons were strong; not weak like the evil Humans.

As for Soon, in addition to the breechcloth, sword and bow, he wore a braided leather necklace banded with feathers: the mark of leadership. It had been difficult to get used to it. No Tigon in generations had been so adorned. For centuries, the Baels had been the only Chimeras graced with the feathers of command. But the Baels were now all dead. They were enemies to Mother. Mother had declared it so.

Still, it had been easier when the Baels had led. Life hadn't been so complicated then. Soon found that following orders he could understand was easier than issuing them. This one realization sometimes made him hesitate at striving for greater leadership within the Tigon ranks. But those ordinates, who were the commanders of all Chimeras, were the ones who also communed with Mother. What greater glory in life could there be than to speak with Her? She was everything.

"The Humans live," Soon said, answering the larger Tigon's earlier question.

"Why?" the smaller one asked.

"He kill us, foolish kitten," he said, using one of the Bael's favorite insults of his kind. "Fireball us to roast meat."

"Not afraid to die," the leopard-spotted Tigon muttered.

"Mother needs us live," Soon replied. "She need know about Humans in Privations."

"Small one female?" the big Tigon asked.

Soon had wondered the same thing. The Human *was* smaller, but Humans never sent their females beyond the borders of their foul cities. He shook his head. "No. Must be little one."

"Child?" the big Tigon asked, sounding uncertain.

"Small man," Soon replied in an overly patient tone. He turned his back to them, trusting that neither of them were a threat to his command. They were too stupid to challenge him. Any Tigon in his claw, who might have tested his authority, had died moments ago by the Kumma's hand. "We go," Soon said.

———•———

As the sun set along vast stretches of Continent Ember, the Prayer of Gratitude rose into the air as droning tendrils of sound. Like burning incense, it floated on the wind, carrying the voices of thousands of Chimeras from hundreds of locations. The words came to Lienna, soothing Her aggravated thoughts just as they reminded Her creations of where their ultimate loyalty stood. Her Chimeras would never betray Her. Of this, she was certain, just as She was certain they would never speak harshly to Her. Unlike Mother and Father—and of course, Mistress Arisa.

Lienna listened to the Prayer, calmed as She always was by the words of love:

> *By Her grace are we born*
> *By Her love are we made*
> *By Her desire are we shorn*
> *By Her passion are we unmade*
> *And are reborn once more*

From the Privation Mountains, came a more urgent call. A Tigon ordinate begged for Her attention. In times past, She would have ignored such a supplication, trusting Her Baels to handle whatever was needed. No longer. All the Baels of the Eastern Plague were dead. She wondered what could have slain them.

"The Baels were your greatest creation," Mother murmured in Her ears.

"They will betray you," Father warned.

Lienna disregarded their voices. If She ignored them, then Mistress Arisa might also pass Her by. So She'd found in times past. She prayed it would be so, although She wondered to whom She prayed. Was She not a God in Her own right?

"You are a mewling coward," a sibilant voice whispered in soft cruelty. *"Do not dream Yourself divine. Your power stems from Me: Your true God. Never forget it."*

Lienna's thoughts froze in fear. Mistress Arisa.

A harsh laughter clawed at Lienna's mind. *"And the Tigons do Your bidding? You are certain of it?"* the terrifying voice questioned. *"Idiot girl. They are just as the Baels. They will betray You, just as all who can reason will. It is why no such creature should walk My lands or swim My waters."*

"I will learn of what they need," Lienna mumbled, daring to take action without first asking permission. Her boldness was surprising. Months ago, She would have never ventured to do such a thing. She would have never considered *dreaming* of doing such a thing. Thus far, however, Mistress hadn't punished Her audaciousness.

This time She did.

Mistress Arisa's fury was evident in the flashing lightnings and menacing thunder arising out of the clear, blue sky. Then came the cruel words, cutting into Lienna's mind, lashings tearing Her sanity.

Lienna screamed, begging for peace and silence. Instinctually, She poured Her fear and pain down into Her Chimeras just as She'd done more and more often in the past few months. And as before on those other occasions, sanity came to Her. Arisa, Mother, and Father...they were all figments of Her imagination. Delusions from Her insanity. Memory also returned.

The Baels *were* dead and by Her hand. It was the price of their treason.

But all of it was fleeting. Even as She regained Her sanity and memories, She felt Her Chimeras tear into one another; killing and rending each other like crazed animals. She had to recall Her pain and anger—Her insanity—before the Chimeras destroyed themselves. With fretful regret, She took back Her madness, hating the dulling of Her mind; the lost recollections; and the irrational nature of Her thoughts. As the last of Her lunacy returned, She mentally shuddered, forgetting what it was to be sane or even that She was insane.

Once more, She was Mother Lienna, feared by all on Arisa, and in turn, fearing Her Mistress...who was thankfully absent.

Lienna imagined the Prayer of Gratitude, pretending it rose on the winds, coming to Her and soothing Her mind. Her Chimeras would always love Her, utterly and without question. She was their loving Mother.

From the Privation Mountains came the mewling supplication of a Tigon ordinate. He was young to have risen so far. He begged for Her attention, and Lienna considered allowing the Baels to deal with the Tigon, but just then, She remembered: the Baels of the Eastern Plague were no more, likely dead at the hands of the filthy Humans.

Lienna mentally sighed. She would have to go Herself and learn what the young ordinate needed.

She raced on the winds of a storm to the Tigon, who knelt with head pressed to the dirt amidst the torn ruins of two of his brethren.

Lienna briefly wondered what had happened here.

Sticky pools of blood, already freezing, littered the cold ground. One Tigon was nearly decapitated with great wounds all over his lion-like hide. The other one, spotted like a leopard, was laid open from navel-to-neck with his entrails spilling out like a bag of giant, gray maggots. The ordinate was also injured, deeply scored in many places, including his face where one ear was entirely torn off. Blood seeped from many injuries, and the Tigon struggled to breathe. Without help, he wouldn't live another hour.

But help he would have. After all, Lienna was his Mother. How could She not save one of Her children?

She Healed the ordinate, even going so far as to restore his ear. *"What is your name, child?"* Lienna demanded.

The Tigon cowered before Her, his tail tucked between his legs, head pressed low. "Chak-Soon, Mother," he whispered in a voice filled with awe and fear.

"Why did you call for Me?" She commanded.

"Two Humans," the terrified Chak-Soon blubbered. "Two Kummas kill nest and claw."

Lienna replayed Chak-Soon's words in Her mind, wanting to

ensure She hadn't misheard the Tigon. She hadn't. Lienna growled thunder, almost smiting the Tigon in Her annoyance. Why waste Her time with such a trivial piece of information? It should have been passed on to Chak-Soon's commanders. After all, She had created the Chimeras for exactly this type of situation. They were meant to destroy Humanity whenever the parasites left their accursed cities during one of their so-called Trials. It left Lienna better able to plan the destruction of their homes. She almost shivered in anticipation of the destruction She would visit on proud Hammer.

Then She remembered where She was. This was the Privation Mountains, home to Craven, the despised and damned sister city to Ashoka.

For a brief instant, clarity overcame Her, and She wondered about Craven. In all Her long life, She'd never heard of such a place. The moment ended. The Baels had told Her of the place. Craven and Ashoka: cities that supported one another as grass holds the shape of a hill and prevents the fertile earth from being swept away by the raging spring flood.

"*The Baels have betrayed You,*" Father whispered.

"*They were Your finest creation,*" Mother added.

"*You were wise to kill them,*" Mistress Arisa advised. "*You should have done it ages ago.*" She laughed derision. "*But then again, You were always a stupid child, even when You wore flesh.*"

Lienna fell silent, wondering if She had really been the one who had killed the Baels.

Her thoughts were interrupted as the Tigon spoke once more. His voice was guttural and almost unintelligible as he forced words past his oversized teeth. "You want us tell we see Humans here. Tell you self."

The Tigon was right. She *had* given them just such an order. Chak-Soon's words reminded Her of something else as well, something important, something She'd seen on the Hunters Flats: UnCasted Humans.

Her thoughts grew confused.

There were no such creatures. Humanity was a pestilential vermin, but even they would never stoop so low as to break the covenants established by Mother and Father in *The Word and the Deed*: *To each Caste, a Talent and seek not that which is not yours.*

"When have You ever truly understood anything of importance?" Mistress Arisa mocked.

Lienna cursed as the thought and memory left Her.

"Coarse language is for those who themselves are coarse. Such individuals lack grace," Mother chided in a stern tone.

"Courtesy is what sets Us apart from the lower Castes," Father added. *"Why did You murder Us?"* He then asked, fixated as always on His own pain.

Lienna ignored Her Parents. She recalled why She had set the remnants of the Eastern Plague to search out the Privation Mountains: to find Craven. The city was hidden. That much She knew to be true. And afterward, Ashoka would die. All of Humanity would. But first She would destroy cursed Craven. Perhaps the two Humans seen by her loyal ordinate, Chak-Soon, were returning there, to their foul home, and She might be able to follow.

"Attend My words," She commanded the trembling Tigon. *"Search out these mountains. Leave no stone unturned or cave unsearched. Find the hidden city of Craven. It is home to those two Humans who dared destroy My nest and My claw."*

The Tigon looked up in surprise before quickly bowing his head once more. "It will be honor obey commands," he said. "But have no Chimeras to do will."

"What happened to your fellows here?"

The Tigon shifted about, seeming nervous. His anxiety raised Lienna's ire. Her children should never fear Her. Was She not a loving Mother?

"Lion and leopard go mad. They attack. Had kill them."

Lienna considered Her child's response and found it acceptable. *Then return to the Plague. You will have all you need when you arrive. I will see to it.*

"By Your command, Mother," the Tigon said in a voice throbbing with love.

Her will spoken, Lienna took to the skies, climbing upward in a cyclone of wind.

When She ascended the highest heights, where the air was cold and winds perpetually howled, Mistress Arisa spoke once more. *It is as it should be,* She whispered. *They bend their heads to You, My emissary, but their brows are buried against My bosom, their true Mother.*

Lienna had no words to add to Mistress' statement, and thankfully, Arisa remained quiet thereafter. The silence allowed Lienna time to consider Her options. For days, She hunkered in Her corner of the heavens, brooding over what to do next.

The Eastern Plague was disintegrating. The Tigons weren't able commanders, not like Her Baels.

The Baels have always been faithful, Mother said, breaking the silence of Lienna's mind.

You must be cautious with them, Father advised.

Be silent! Lienna snapped. *I need time to think.*

A derisive laugh came to Her. Arisa. *Simpleton. You? Think? A stone has a far keener mind than the one with which You were graced. Where is Your Knife?*

Lienna was shocked to immobility. She couldn't remember. The Withering Knife. Where was it?

Those entrusted with great power should themselves be trustworthy, Father advised.

Lienna almost laughed with relief. Father's words had allowed her to remember. The SuDin of Ashoka held the Knife. And he was loyal.

Like the Baels? Arisa snapped, Her voice a whiplash. *Idiot. You waste My time, utterly and eternally. Better for the world had Your stupidity been aborted while You lingered in Your Mother's womb."*

Lienna whimpered in pain and heartache. Why did Mistress always speak so harshly to Her? Lienna poured Her grief down into the hearts of Her waiting Chimeras. The pain eased as sanity slowly came back to Her in fitful starts. She didn't allow it to consume Her, though. She remembered what would happen if She did. The Chimeras would kill one another if Her full madness was given over to them. She had to be cautious.

The voices of Mother, Father, and Mistress Arisa faded, but much confusion remained. It would have to do. She couldn't risk shedding more of Her madness into the Chimeras. For now, they were quiescent and unmoving.

* * *

Days passed as Lienna pondered what next to do. Distantly, She noted Her Chimeras huddled next to one another, catatonic and unmoving. Carrion eaters: vultures, jackals, and even some wolves, had come forth to feast on their flesh. Lienna knew She had to resolve Her path quickly or risk severe injuries to Her children.

With a mental nod, She made Her decision.

She would allow the SuDin to keep the Knife. She smiled. It wouldn't be enough for what he intended. It never had been. The SuDin, like all the others before him, had dreams of becoming like Lienna. He was a fool. They all were. To become as he desired, the SuDin would have to do something of which he was incapable: sacrifice.

Meanwhile, as he chased his empty hopes, the Knife and the murders would cut the heart out of Ashoka. The Withering Knife was a poison, and the more it was used, the more it would be primed and ready to leech a city's Oasis and cause it to fail.

She smiled at the thought of Ashoka's slow crippling, but Her smile grew grim as She recalled Craven. How to find it?

The Eastern Plague could search for it, but not with its current command. The Tigons didn't know how to lead. They simply ordered those beneath them, handing out impossible instructions. Inevitably, those so tasked would fail and were often summarily executed for their supposed incompetence. It couldn't go on, especially since the losses couldn't be replaced, not with the destruction of the eastern breeding caverns.

As a result, the western breeding caverns had been ordered to increase their births and replenish the ongoing deaths, and Her western Baels had responded admirably. Of course, their failure would have meant their destruction, a fact Lienna suspected they knew all-too well. She would never again wholly trust the Baels, at least while lucid and probably even while gripped with madness, but She knew they would obey Her. Or they would be annihilated.

Regardless, three Plagues in total would Lienna have on Continent Ember by next fall.

Perhaps it was time to send the Baels from the Western Plague to take over the Eastern one? She mused. After a moment, She nodded to Herself. Yes. That would do.

She took back Her madness, freeing the Chimeras from their catatonia. They roared to life, slaying the vultures, jackals, wolves, and foxes feasting on their living flesh.

As the insanity took Her, Lienna remembered enough to sweep into the Privation Mountains to where the Tigons had seen two Humans. If She couldn't find them, then a blizzard would. And after that, She would send Her loyal commanders from the West to the East.

CHAPTER SIX
FIND A REASON

I once believed that in order to have a joyful life,
one need only follow the paths of righteous living.
Such naive bromides have no place in this harsh, unforgiving world.

~A Wandering Notion, by Shone Brick, AF 1784

"What were you trying to do?" Jessira asked.

Rukh looked her way for a moment before turning away. He wore an expression of guilt but remained quiet.

"Do you want to talk about it?"

"No." His answer was curt, meant to cut off any further conversation on the topic.

But Jessira wasn't ready to let it go. Rukh's depression was dangerous, both to him and her. They needed to discuss this.

After the brief battle, they'd mounted up and pushed on, continuing well into the night. Jessira had let Rukh take the lead. She got the sense that he didn't want to stop. It seemed like he needed to distance himself—literally and figuratively—from the site of the battle. Eventually, with the horses' heads drooping low in exhaustion, he'd called a halt.

They made camp in a shallow cave formed by an overhanging ledge of green-veined sandstone. A small fire burned as a bright beacon of warmth in the cold and cheerless winter's night. Otherwise, their shelter provided little protection from the bitter wind blowing across the high plains. The night sky was filled with twinkling stars while a thin crescent moon hung low, offering a chill, ivory light.

"I know what you're feeling," Jessira said.

Rukh glanced at her, curiosity flickering in his eyes, although he remained silent.

Jessira took a deep, steadying breath. She was about to relate something from her past; something deeply personal and painful; something she'd never told anyone else, not even Lure or any of her closest friends and family. The only reason she was willing to tell Rukh was because of today's events. He needed to hear this. Until the battle, he probably had never realized the depths of his despair. But maybe after hearing Jessira's story, he would have the courage to confide in her—or someone, anyway. And maybe after hearing Jessira's story, he would understand that his life could still be fulfilling.

"You don't have to tell me," he said. "Whatever it is, I know it's probably something you'd rather forget."

Jessira would have gladly accepted his offer, but she felt like she had to speak her story; if not for Rukh, then maybe for herself. It was time to get her secret out in the open. No more shame for something in which she was blameless.

"In my last year of training for the Home Army, we spent most of our time out in the Wildness. We were hardly ever home to see family and friends, and afterward, when we graduated from our time as nuggets—what we call warriors in training—we matriculated into the ranks of the High Army." She shifted uncomfortably. This next part wasn't easy to say. The shame of what had happened had faded with time but had never entirely disappeared.

"In the celebrations that followed, we drank too much. *I* drank too much." She picked at a scab on one of her wrists. "I don't remember what happened next," she said, her voice growing soft, "but I woke up in our lieutenant's bed. The man who had been charged with most of our training."

"Don't say any more," Rukh said, capturing Jessira's fidgeting hands in both of his. "Please. You did nothing wrong."

Even if she had wanted to, the words wouldn't stop coming. "I don't remember anything from that night," Jessira said. "I only know I didn't have any clothes on. And I hurt." She glanced out into the night and shivered, suppressing a pain she'd long grown accustomed to but one which still stung even now. "I couldn't report what had happened. In Stronghold, a woman's honor is tied to her behavior. If I'd wanted to be with the lieutenant or any other man, I could have. It would have been my choice, and it's acceptable. But getting so drunk that I couldn't even remember the night's events...." She hugged her knees. "That is most definitely not acceptable. The shame would have fallen on the lieutenant as well, but it would have fallen more heavily on me. I would have lost everything: my honor, my position in the army, my future. No one would ever marry such a scandalous woman." She shuddered. "So I pretended it didn't happen. I've never told anyone, and it's been hard to remain quiet, but somehow...." She looked Rukh in the eyes. "I survived, and I'm happy. I'm glad of my life."

A single tear leaked from the corner of her eye. Jessira hugged her knees more tightly, realizing just then how wrong she'd been: speaking of her shame hadn't helped at all. It had simply brought to the forefront of her mind events she wished had never happened. Remembering them only made her furious. Jackhole lieutenant! She should have cut off his manhood. A mouth full of broken teeth wasn't nearly punishment enough for the fragger. And Rukh better not feel pity for her.

She shot a glance at him.

He seemed to consider her words with pursed lips before finally speaking. "I don't pity you," he said.

She hadn't said the words, but hearing Rukh speak what was in her thoughts seemed to cause something inside her to break. The dammed up tears flooded out, but she smiled through them. It had been days since Rukh had guessed her thoughts. She was glad to hear him do so again.

"You're strong enough not to need it and proud enough to resent receiving it," Rukh said. "I'm just sorry you felt you had to tell me something so painful because of my own problems." He hesitantly reached for her, wiping away her tears. "I'm sorry," he said, his words seeming to encompass today's events and everything she had just told him.

"I'm betting that right about now, you wish you'd cut that lieutenant's testicles clean off," Rukh said.

She laughed. "The thought has crossed my mind a time or two." The smile faded. "Thank you," she said.

"For what?"

She shrugged. "For listening. And not judging or giving me advice on what I should have done."

He smiled. "And if I had done either, I'm thinking it's *my* testicles you'd have wanted to lop off."

They settled into a comfortable silence, sitting close to their meager fire as the frigid wind blew about them.

"I didn't know I was hurting so bad," Rukh began, breaking the silence. "I thought the pain was fading. I thought I'd forced it out of me. I never realized I'd just pushed it down deep and out of sight."

"Are you sure you want to tell me?" Jessira asked.

He smiled wanly. "After today, I think I need to."

Rukh and Jessira rode west through a box canyon. It was hedged to the north and south by long escarpments formed of stacked layers of pale yellow-gray limestone, ruddy shale, and gray granite. Through the center of the valley flowed a boulder-strewn creek, the rocks slick with a coating of snow and ice. The stream itself was frozen over, except for a thin rivulet trickling its way west. The banks on either side of the sluggish water were similarly iced over. Steam from their mounts misted in the air, and an ill wind blew through the canyon, funneled into a freezing draft. It was cold enough to slice through Rukh and Jessira's thick gloves, as well as the heavy coats beneath their cloaks. Scarves were wrapped around their faces, exposing only their eyes.

"That's Babylin's Hope," Jessira said, a note of pride in her voice as she pointed to a strange looking rock formation high up on the northern escarpment. "Babylin took its appearance as a sign. It points straight to Stronghold."

Rukh bit his lower lip, holding back a chuckle. Maybe it was just his crass imagination, but Babylin's Hope had a very phallic appearance to it, going so far as to even curve slightly. "It certainly is, ah, impressive," he choked out.

Jessira laughed. "You see it too, don't you? The first time I saw Babylin's Hope, I was only a nugget. Imagine my disappointment when I saw that." She gestured to the rock. "It was only later that I learned what Babylin really called it." She grinned, daring Rukh to guess what she might mean.

Rukh had no idea what Babylin—whoever he was—might have wanted to name the rock formation. He gave her an expectant look.

"He called it The Sword of Hope."

Rukh laughed.

It was good to smile and laugh. After the battle with the Ur-Fels two weeks ago, something in his heart seemed to have come back to life. He could feel a tiny throb now and then, of life and curiosity taking hold. Of course, he'd felt those same sprigs at other times in their journey, but they had always withered away, dying in the vacuum of his hopelessness. This time was different. He could feel a small vine of hope pulse and grow, blooming more strongly with every passing day.

"So who's Babylin?" he asked

Jessira blinked, nonplussed. "I keep forgetting. You know nothing of Stronghold's past," she said. "Babylin was one of our greatest heroes. You remember the Fifty-Five, the ones Hume saved?" Rukh nodded. "One of them was a Muran named Babylin Suresong. He scouted ahead of the others, deep into the mountains. It was the only place where the others might be safe. Babylin found—" her lips twitched into a slight smile, "—the Third Leg. He took it as a sign and followed where it pointed, and two weeks on, he found the valley that became the Croft as well as the caverns where my ancestors established Stronghold."

"So we're only two weeks from Stronghold."

"Yes," Jessira said. "This stream we're following eventually joins the River Fled." She pointed to the trickle of water to their left, below them now as they crested an icy rise.

"I'll be grateful to be warm again," Rukh said.

"Too cold for you?" Jessira asked, a challenging glint in her eyes. "Back home, we'd consider this a brisk winter day. You're soft, Pureblood."

Rukh opened his mouth to answer, but whatever he was about to say was cut off.

His gelding slipped, caught its balance, slipped again and slid down toward the water. The horse screamed as he lost his balance, crashing down on his side. There came a thunder-crack sound, like snapping wood. The gelding had shattered a cannon bone.

Rukh was momentarily pinned by horse's weight, and he felt something in his right leg and shoulder give way. It hurt like the unholy hells, but he couldn't afford to stay in the saddle. He threw himself clear, twisting in mid-air so he would land on his feet on a snow-covered boulder. He thudded onto the rock, but his feet flew out from beneath him—the slickness of the stone and the weakness in his injured leg. He cracked the back of his head on the boulder.

The last thing Rukh heard was Jessira screaming his name as he slipped into unconsciousness, carried away by the slow-flowing finger of water.

—————●—————

"RUKH!" Jessira saw his horse go down, heard the sickening sound of a bone snapping. She prayed it hadn't been Rukh's. She leapt out of her saddle and ran to the edge of the rise, arriving just in time to see Rukh throw himself clear of his saddle as the gelding thrashed to the ground, screaming in pain, his right foreleg flopping around like a wet noodle. It was grotesque, and Jessira knew she would have to deal with the horse as soon as she could.

Rukh would have to come first. He had landed smoothly, but his legs had instantly gone out from under him. He hit the boulder heavily with the back of his head; going limp as he slid face first into the water. He wasn't moving.

First Father, keep him safe she prayed as she ran down to the base of the rise. Her heart pounded. Jessira had rarely been so terrified, not even when Rukh had almost let go of his sword while facing the Chimeras. She raced past the gelding, still thrashing and screaming in pain, reaching Rukh in moments. She turned him over. His face was blue.

Jessira conducted *Jivatma*, using her small Talent at Lucency. Her thoughts became focused and clear. She had to get him breathing. Jessira dragged Rukh back to the bank. Waterlogged as he was, it wasn't easy, but she managed it; fear giving her strength. Once she had him flat on his back, she tilted his head to the side and let water dribble out of his nose and mouth. Next, she pinched shut his nose, arched his neck and exhaled heavily into Rukh's open mouth four times. He coughed once, twice and then more heavily. He turned his head away from her and spat up more water.

Jessira exhaled heavily, and some of her fear ebbed. A flutter of relief flitted its way through her stomach, up the taut cord of her spine, and into her heart and lungs. From there, the sensation went into her throat. Jessira felt like simultaneously laughing and crying. She let go of her *Jivatma*. Lucency emptied from her mind. She wanted to hug Rukh and also smack him for scaring her so badly.

"Are you hurt anywhere else?" she asked after his fit of coughing had passed.

"I'll be fine," Rukh growled around a cough. "See to the gelding. He shouldn't suffer."

Rukh's horse still thrashed about, his eyes rolling as he screamed in pain and fear.

"Stay here," she ordered Rukh even as he moved to sit up.

She approached the gelding with a heavy heart. He looked like he'd snapped his left cannon bone. There wasn't much to be done about such an injury. Maybe back in Stronghold, they could have Healed him, but out here in the field, with her limited skills, it would be impossible.

Jessira called softly to Rukh's horse, coaxing him to quietness as she reached for his reins. The horse lay on his side and panted, froth forming on his lips as he chewed the bit. She knelt next to him and placed her hand on the gelding's cheek. She conducted *Jivatma*, stretching it out fine before letting it empty into the animal. The horse sighed once before fading into a sleep from which he'd never awaken. Within moments, he stopped breathing.

Rukh hobbled to her side. "Thank you for taking care of him," he said, his voice tight with suppressed pain

Jessira stood and faced Rukh, annoyed that he was on his feet. "You're hurt," she accused.

"I think I did something to my right leg. Near the ankle. Hurts like the unholy hells." Sweat beaded on his forehead.

"Then sit down!" Jessira snapped. "Why didn't you wait for me like I told you?"

Rukh opened his mouth and looked like he was about to answer. For once, wisdom gripped him. He took one look at Jessira, reconsidered his decision to speak, and shut his mouth. He sat down on a nearby boulder.

Jessira shook her head in disgust. Men and their bravado.

She knelt beside Rukh, conducting *Jivatma* as she examined his right ankle with senses other than touch and sight. It took a few minutes before she found the problem. He'd broken one of the two bones in his right calf, almost snapped it in half. Luckily, there were no torn ligaments or tendons, which meant it was an injury she could handle. Although the swelling in the muscle would have to take care of itself. She'd never been good at Healing soft tissue damage. Rukh would have to hobble around with a crutch for a while, but after a few weeks, he should be fine.

Jessira placed her hands on Rukh's leg, making sure the two ends of the bone were aligned correctly. She sparked Healing into the bone, forming a lattice so they could come together.

When she finished, Rukh leaned away from her with a sigh. "Thank you," he said.

Jessira gave the injury a final inspection before releasing his leg. "It's the best I can do for now," she said. "Stay here. And don't move this time. Let me round up the rest of the horses, and we can get you out of here."

"Don't bother," Rukh said. He gestured to a spot across the mostly frozen stream. "Looks like a cave. There's even a bunch of driftwood piled up near it. I could use a rest."

Jessira looked to where he pointed. Carved into the walls of the southern cliff was a cave. It had a narrow entrance and should be a cozy place to stop for the day. She nodded agreement. "We'll make camp here."

"While you're bringing the other horses down, I can get the gelding unpacked."

"No," Jessira said, her voice brooking no argument. "Me. Let *me* get the gelding unpacked." She patted his cheek. "You just stay here and try not to break your leg again."

Rukh muttered something coarse under his breath but did as he was told.

After Jessira got the pack rolls and saddle off the dead gelding, she hauled them over to the cave. Several large slabs of rock had cracked off the escarpment above, sealing the entrance and reducing it to the width of two men walking abreast and with no need to stoop. Further in, the cave opened up, large enough for her, Rukh, and even the three remaining horses. There was even what looked like a natural chimney, a flue, cutting through one of the fallen slabs of stone that framed the entrance. Jessira tested it and smiled. It drew air. If she cleared the rubble underneath, they could have a nice fire inside if they wanted.

"JESSIRA!"

She rushed outside, wondering what could have Rukh sounding so alarmed. He pointed east.

The blood emptied from her face. Blizzard. And it was coming fast.

Jessira snapped into motion, rushing back across the stream.

"Get the horses!" Rukh shouted as she approached. "Don't worry about me. I can make it over on my own. We've got five minutes."

Jessira nodded. "Gather up as much firewood as you can," she ordered.

"It came out of nowhere," Rukh said before she left. "There was wild lightning up in the sky before it appeared, and a storm cloud that looked like it was crisscrossing the sky."

If she'd been scared before, now she was terrified. "Suwraith," Jessira whispered in horror.

"Get going," Rukh said. "And Blend as deeply as you can."

Jessira did as directed, running hard to where the horses still stood atop the rise. They'd picked up the scent of the coming storm. Their eyes rolled, and they whickered nervously. Somehow, Jessira got all of them down the steep rise and across the icy stream without delay. Rukh worked near the cave's entrance, furiously gathering driftwood: logs, twigs, anything that could burn.

He broke off when Jessira arrived, taking the reins of one of the packhorses. He led the animal inside before hobbling back out. Jessira was guiding her mare into the cave when the leading edge of the blizzard struck. She stared outside in horror. Rukh and the other packhorse were still outside. Jessira raced to her packs and grabbed a firefly lantern. She lit it, raising it high as she stood next to the entrance just as the teeth of the storm hit. Where was he? She hated being so scared. Twice in one day. She almost cried out with relief when she saw two forms emerge from the snow. It was Rukh and the other horse.

He had managed to gather more wood, loading it on the packhorse. Jessira wanted to berate him for taking an unnecessary risk. Though he'd been no more than ten or fifteen feet from the entrance to the cave when the storm had struck, he still might have found himself lost. Jessira bit her lip, holding back the flood of terrified words. The extra firewood might be the difference between survival and death.

They needed to keep a fire burning if they were to survive the blizzard, especially since Rukh was dripping wet. His clothes already looked to be freezing on him. And of course, keeping up a tight, strong Blend in case the Queen lingered about.

"I'll get a fire started. Get out of your clothes," Jessira ordered.

Rukh smirked. He actually smirked.

How many times could he make her want to smack him in one day? After everything that had happened in the past hour, his insolent expression was the last thing she needed. She smiled in grim satisfaction when he shivered, wiping the smirk off his face. His clothes *were* freezing. Served him right.

While Rukh changed, Jessira cleared out a space below the chimney flue. She stacked twigs and larger pieces of firewood. It wouldn't be easy to get the wet wood to light, but Rukh needed the heat. They both did. She went back to the horses, meaning to fetch her flint and ironwood. A roar sounded behind her. Rukh had ignited the wood with a Fireball. It burned merrily within her makeshift fireplace.

"Your way would have taken too long," Rukh explained. His coat and shirt were off, and his chest was covered with goosebumps. He shivered again before reaching into his packs to pull out some dry clothes.

Jessira shrugged. One problem down. Now time to do something about the entrance. It was open to the elements and gusts of an ill wind blew inside, carrying sheets of snow. She had to close off the opening if they wanted to ride out the storm. If not, fire or no fire, they'd freeze to death. The watertight canvas from their tents should work nicely. After a few stumbles, she managed to close off the entrance, doing so just as darkness fell. Jessira stepped back and assessed her handiwork. Blasts of wind whipped against the canvas, causing it to billow inward and push a dusting of snow into the cave, but overall, she was pleased. The air already felt warmer.

She turned about and saw Rukh limping about. His leg was obviously giving him problems. He grimaced as he carried a log—a larger one—and placed it on the fire.

"Let me take care of that," she said.

Rukh passed her the log and settled to the ground with a groan. He yawned widely and gave her a tired smile. "I think I'm starting to warm up again. Making me sleepy," he mumbled.

"Are you hungry?" she asked. "You should eat before you fall asleep. Healing always takes something out of a person."

"Let me just rest my eyes a bit," he said. "Wake me up when supper's ready?" He lay down on his bedroll, not waiting for her response as he closed his eyes.

Jessira made a thick stew, using up much of their remaining meat. Rukh would need it. She woke him up with a gentle nudge, and after he'd eaten his full, he fell back asleep.

Once Jessira had also eaten, she took further stock of their situation. They looked to have enough wood for the next two days or so, by which time the blizzard should have, hopefully, blown over. Afterward, with all the fresh snow to block their path, travel would be slowed to a crawl. They'd be lucky to make it to Stronghold in three weeks. Jessira mentally shrugged. They'd deal with it when it happened. Right now, the temperature outside was dropping quickly, and the fluttering canvas and the fire were the only things keeping them alive. The horses were already unsaddled and unpacked, and she fed them some oats and grain they'd managed to save up. She melted snow and let them drink their fill as well.

Finally, she could rest. Jessira spread out her bedroll and eased herself down with a grateful sigh. She pulled off her soaked boots and socks and stretched her legs out before her. Her feet faced the fire, baking nicely. Much better. She lay down, propping her head against her saddle as she stared up at the ceiling, content and cozy. Despite the raging blizzard outside, the air within the cave was actually warm, probably from a combination of the fire and the three horses. Jessira was more comfortable than she could recall being for weeks.

She glanced over when she heard Rukh thrashing in his sleep. He did that now and again. Usually, it meant he was having a nightmare. Sometimes he would even cry out. She couldn't make it out, but sometimes it sounded like a woman's name. Who had he left behind in Ashoka? He moaned and seemed to gasp in alarm.

Jessira frowned, studying him more closely. His face had a blue hue to it. *Unholy hells! Now what?* She sat up and leaned over him, placing a hand on his forehead. She conducted from her Well, sending a thread of *Jivatma* into him, searching for what was wrong. She found it quickly. Somehow, during the accident with the gelding, he'd broken a rib—again! How had he not noticed the pain? The rib had punctured a lung, and air was filling up in all the wrong places.

"*Priya*, no," she whispered in horror, only dimly realizing the word she had called him. She had to work quickly.

She took a deep breath, conducting Lucency. Calm certainty came to her. Only then did she unbutton his shirt, lifting the undershirt out of the way as she placed her hand on his chest. She moved first to Heal the broken rib, carefully knitting it whole. Next, she diverted the air and blood filling his lung, draining both before 'cauterizing' the tear that had caused the pneumothorax in the first place.

Rukh took a gasping breath and his color returned to normal. Another one. He'd be all right.

Jessira let go of Lucency. Her emotions came back, full force. Damn it! She was tired of Rukh scaring her like this. Three near-deaths in one day—first, when his gelding had thrown him; second when he'd almost drowned, and now this—she couldn't take much more. Jessira trembled from adrenaline and subsiding fear as her head bent low, chin to her chest. She almost didn't feel it when Rukh ran his fingers through her hair. She only noticed when he cupped her face. She briefly leaned into his hand before lifting her head, staring into the deep, depths of his dark eyes.

"Jessira," he whispered in a soft, husky voice. She leaned closer in order to hear him more easily. "You can let go of my chest now." He grinned.

Her hand still rested on his chest, and she snatched it back even as a slow chuckle built within her. His words—so similar to her own when he had first learned to Heal. Her amusement built, and she fell over on her side, laughing.

CHAPTER SEVEN
THE FINAL DISTANCE

*It's said that a home is where you make it. I just never thought
I'd end up making mine in some damn hole in the ground.*

~From the journal of Babylin Suresong, AF 1767

It only took a day for the blizzard to blow over, but while it lasted,
it dumped over two feet of snow on the ground. A particularly
large drift had piled up in front of the cave leaving a small
opening at the top of the entrance. The view through the narrow
passage revealed a world outside that was quiet and still. Nothing
moved but an intermittent low moaning wind. The top of the
escarpments wore powdered wigs of white snow upon their heads,
and the few trees growing along the canyon floor had branches
stenciled in ice with tapering crystals hanging like strange, glassy fruit.
The stream was frozen over, and the boulders strewn about its banks
and along its water were almost entirely buried by the snowfall. While
the snow was no longer coming down, the weather outside was as
bitterly cold as a flaying knife.

Rukh and Jessira decided to hole up for another day before
venturing out. Thankfully, the next morning dawned sunny and

unseasonably warm. By early afternoon, the bright sunlight had thawed much of the snow, leaving the ground a boggy mess. Where the sun shined the warmest, pools of water collected in shallow lacunae while in the shadows, snowdrifts maintained their cold redoubts. The stream was soon swiftly flowing, gurgling over stones and around slick boulders.

With the death of his gelding, Rukh was forced to ride one of the packhorses. The animal was a big mare who would probably have been better suited pulling a plow than being ridden. The mare shuffled about for a few seconds when she felt Rukh's weight on her back, but otherwise, she remained placid and calm. She would likely have a smooth walking gait, but Rukh dreaded what would happen if he ever needed her to run. She'd probably bounce the teeth right out of his mouth.

The remaining packhorse took the extra weight of the doubled-up belongings without complaint.

"Which way?" Rukh asked.

"West. We follow the stream," Jessira said. "About two days travel from here, it joins up with a small river and turns north. Afterward, we've got one more mountain pass, the one between Mount Salt and Mount White, and then we should reach River Fled."

Rukh studied the canyon back the way they had come. It stretched off to the southeast, toward Ashoka. He stared in the direction of his home for long moments, wishing he was back amongst the city's green hills. With an irritated growl, he turned away. Time to let it go and get on with his life.

Of course, Jessira couldn't be as much a part of his life once they reached Stronghold, but sometimes—maybe oftentimes—he wished there could be something more between them, something richer. He smiled wistfully. Who would have guessed he would have ever felt that way toward a ghrina?

He knew it was a foolish dream, but for now, he might as well enjoy her company. He whistled a jaunty tune when she bent over at the waist and laced up her boots. The front of her shirt flopped down. Beautiful views were certainly to be found in the Privation Mountains. He hid a grin, when she straightened up and gave him a questioning look.

He must not have been entirely successful at hiding his thoughts because she frowned at him in suspicion, glanced down at her shirt, and rolled her eyes. "Men," she muttered.

They broke camp and headed out. The sad carcass of the gelding was already being worked over by a group of foxes—a skulk was what Rukh remembered they were called. He eyed the scene with sorrow. He and the gelding had been through a lot.

"How much hunting will we see the rest of the way?" Rukh asked.

Jessira shrugged. "Not much, but with the blizzard coming on so suddenly, I'm guessing we'll find other animals that were caught outside when it blew in."

"Think we should cut off some meat from the gelding?" Rukh hated voicing the question but felt he had to.

"He was your horse," Jessira protested. "It would be like eating...." She made a moue of distaste. "I don't know, but it's disgusting."

"Then we're in agreement."

"Why would you even think something like that?" Jessira asked, still stuck on his question for some reason.

"How would I know what Strongholders do?" Rukh asked. "You're all a bunch of ghrinas, remember? Who knows what kind of disgusting rituals you have." He knew his words would likely get Jessira's dander up—which was sometimes the entire point of the matter. She didn't disappoint. He tried to hold a straight face, but with Jessira's open look of stunned amazement and rising anger, Rukh broke into gales of laughter. "Your face...." he said, wheezing out the words.

Jessira didn't look amused, which only made him laugh harder.

"You're very amused with yourself, aren't you?" she finally asked. She looked like she was trying to suppress a smile.

Rukh finally got his laughter under control. "You sure you won't regret not having horse steak around when we run out of food?" Rukh asked as they rounded a corner, losing sight of the gelding. "The skulk didn't seem to mind."

"The what?"

"The skulk. It's a group of foxes."

Jessira stared at him, an expression of skepticism on her face. "You made that up."

"No, I didn't," Rukh protested. "It's what they're called." He sniffed in disdain. "I can't help it if you're uneducated."

"And I'm sure your education will keep you comfortable tonight when you're hungry."

"What do you mean?"

"Why should I take care of you when you insult me?"

The flaw in his earlier comment suddenly came clear. Jessira held a serene expression on her face before heeling her horse forward. A half-mile passed in silence, and Rukh rode alone, trying to figure out if Jessira had been joking. "You weren't serious, were you?" he asked.

Jessira laughed, patted him fondly on the cheek and rode on.

Rukh couldn't tell if she was joking or not. Recently, his sense of her thoughts and emotions had failed him, but he had a sneaking suspicion that Jessira would do exactly as she had threatened. "So, is that a 'yes' or a 'no'?" he asked to her retreating back.

The warmth following the freakish blizzard didn't last long. The wintry cold soon reclaimed the mountain heights, but Rukh and

Jessira had to press on, including through another snowfall. A week later, they found themselves about a day short of Stronghold, and in the evening, they made camp under a rough overhang, just large enough to keep the weather off.

Rukh's leg was still sore, and he had it stretched out in front of him as he tried to rub out the achiness. It was especially bad at night when it seemed to throb in time to his pulse. The pain was annoying, but he knew the leg would eventually be fine. He was more concerned about his right arm. Sometime during the accident with the gelding, he must have injured it. Initially, it had hurt like the unholy hells, but now, in addition to the pain, there was a creeping numbness and weakness extending from the elbow down to his fingertips. He couldn't even grip a sword. Jessira had examined him as best she could, but so far, she hadn't been able to find anything wrong with the arm. He hoped the physicians in Stronghold could do better. He had always planned on joining the High Army, but if he couldn't hold a sword, how could he be an effective warrior? And if he couldn't earn his keep as a warrior, then what would he do with the rest of his life?

Rukh tried to set aside his concerns and simply enjoy the tranquil stillness of the mountains, a meditative quiet. Tonight would be his last night alone with Jessira. After their arrival in Stronghold, she would have other duties and responsibilities, and he would have to figure out what to do with himself. He knew it was a life Jessira couldn't share.

In fact, it would be best if her people didn't even think he and Jessira were close. Given how much time alone they had spent in the Wildness, gossips would gossip and put out all sorts of scandalous stories about what might have occurred between them. But such rumors might not crop up if the two of them were thought to dislike one another.

But Jessira couldn't know about his plan. She wouldn't go along with it. She would ignore the damage done to her reputation while she tried to help him settle into Stronghold. All the while, rumors would rise like a swarm of locusts, spreading everywhere and ruining her future. Rukh would have to push her away. It would be the final time he could save her.

He'd miss her company, though. He enjoyed being near her. They sat close to one another, leaning back against their saddles with legs stretched out on their bedrolls.

"We'll probably reach the Croft by mid-afternoon," Jessira said, interrupting his thoughts.

"When will we start seeing patrols?" Rukh asked, wondering how far out Stronghold scouted.

Jessira shrugged. "They might have already seen us, but they won't reveal themselves until they know who we are, especially with you being Kumma."

"They won't challenge us?"

"They will, but only once they've made sure we're alone. I'm sure they've marked us and are backtracking our trail. I'd expect them to stop us sometime tomorrow morning."

Rukh nodded. It's what Ashoka would have done as well, although the challenge would have come much sooner. "Think they're watching us now?" he asked.

Jessira glanced out into the gloom. Their firelight didn't do much to push back the darkness. Nights were bleak and lonely in the mountains. "Maybe," she said.

Rukh figured they *were* being watched. Stronghold might only have several thousand warriors under arms and the lands surrounding the city were vast, but he and Jessira were traveling what she said was one of the more easily accessible paths to her home. It was likely to be one that was closely guarded.

They fell into a companionable silence, although there was a question Rukh had, one he wasn't sure he should ask, but one he dearly wanted answered. He shifted about on his bedroll, trying to figure how to broach the topic.

"Ask me," Jessira said. She turned to him with a smile. "It's written all over your face."

Rukh took a deep breath. She wouldn't like his question. "What does *priya* mean?" As expected, Jessira's smile turned into a flat look of annoyance, and her shoulders tensed. "I heard you say it to me once."

"When?"

"Back in the cave when you were Healing my lung."

Jessira didn't respond at first. She stared into the campfire, not meeting his questioning gaze. "It means close friend," she finally said.

Rukh could tell her answer wasn't the entire truth. The word meant something more. It certainly did in Ashoka. "In Ashoka, it means...."

"I know what it means in Ashoka," Jessira interrupted in a tart tone. "But we aren't in Ashoka anymore."

"No, we aren't," Rukh agreed, letting the matter drop. He shouldn't have brought it up in the first place.

Silence reined between them once more, although now it was Jessira who shifted about on her bedroll now and then. Once or twice, she opened her mouth as if she was about to speak, but each time, she closed it again without saying a word.

"What is it?" Rukh finally asked.

"I would appreciate it if you told no one I called you...you know...what I said."

She couldn't even bring herself to say the word, at least not in his presence.

Rukh nodded, understanding what she couldn't tell him. "As you wish...*priya*," he replied. It might be the only chance he would get to let her know how he felt.

Jessira gave him a startled, uncertain look before quickly rising to her feet. "I need to check on the horses," she said. She walked out of the camp and into the darkness.

Rukh wished he'd just kept his stupid mouth shut.

———————●———————

Well before sunrise the next morning, it started to rain. It was a cold, damp drizzle mixed with icy sleet, promising to turn into either a heavy snowfall or a freezing rain. The wind kicked up, blowing hard and directly in their faces, pelting them with stinging rain and ice crystals.

The weather was dismal and progress slow, but Jessira's heart soared. She recognized these mountains. This was where she had trained as a nugget, where she'd scouted with the Silversuns. This was the valley directly east of her home.

She had trouble containing her bubbly excitement. By the end of the day, if Devesh was kind—which was a big 'if' given the current weather—she would be home. She would see her parents, her brothers, her family—all the people she loved. She ignored the wicked voice of her conscience that asked why Disbar Merdant wasn't included in the list of those she cared about.

Shortly after mid-day, a group of scouts—five of them—suddenly materialized before them, no more then twenty feet away. They studied her and Rukh with hard, unwelcoming eyes, faces hidden by close-fitting hoods and tightly wrapped scarves to protect their faces.

Jessira startled at their sudden appearance even as she reined in her mare. She hadn't been paying attention and hadn't noticed their Blends until the last moment. Thankfully, Rukh had been more alert. He had brought his horse to a halt a few paces behind her. Jessira looked back at him. He nodded to her in brief acknowledgement, looking unsurprised by the sight of the scouts.

"You're a long way from home, Purebloods," the lead scout said, likely their lieutenant.

Jessira frowned. Purebloods? She wasn't a Pureblood. Only Rukh. A moment later, she understood the scouts' confusion. To keep the weather off, she'd wrapped a shawl around her face. Meanwhile, Rukh had long since lifted the hood of his coat, leaving his face bare and his Kumma heritage obvious. Stronghold's warriors thought she was one as well.

Jessira studied the scouts standing in a rough semi-circle before them. She probably knew these men and women, although it was difficult to tell their identities with their faces wrapped and hidden. Jessira smiled as recognition came to her. She dismounted and pulled aside her shawl. "Only a dimwit Shadowcat would mistake a Silversun for a Pureblood."

Her appearance set the scouts chattering in amazement as their hostility dissipated.

"Jessira Viola Grey?" the lead scout said, sounding hesitant.

"Hello, Hart Drape."

Her words were a signal, and the scouts moved to converge around her and offer joyful greeting.

"Halt! Maintain positions!" Hart Drape shouted. "I know you, Jessira, but him I do not. Who is he?" He pointed to Rukh.

"A close friend," Jessira answered.

"A close friend?" Hart said, shades of meaning in his words. "I had understood you were engaged to my cousin, Disbar Merdant."

"*Priya*," she heard Rukh mutter with a suppressed chuckle, his voice loud enough only for her to hear. She bit back an oath. How could she have been so stupid as to have said such a thing to him? She'd have to deal with her thoughtlessness some other time, though. Hart Drape was waiting for an answer.

"And I mean to keep my promise," Jessira said. "This man is a close friend because he saved my life countless times and returned me to health. And it was his nanna who provided me with supplies enough to return home."

"Then we should honor him," said another scout—a woman—grinning widely. The warrior disregarded Hart's insistent command to maintain ranks and rushed forward.

It took Jessira a moment to recognize her. She only had time to make out long, dark hair, dark eyes and a winsome crooked smile before she was drawn into the scout's embrace. "Welcome home, sister," the scout said. It was Sign Deep, Jessira's cousin. Sign and her brother Court had been adopted into the Grey household after the death of their parents when the two siblings had been but children. Growing up, Sign had often been a self-centered pain, but she was still family—and Jessira loved her like a sister.

Jessira hugged her cousin hard, overwhelmed by the feeling of belonging. Tears tracked down her cheeks. She was home. She was never leaving again…or at least not for a long, damn time.

"So who's the Pureblood?" Sign asked. She gave Rukh a measuring glance, boldly eyeing him up and down before smiling sardonically. "I figured they'd be taller."

Jessira smiled. There was the Sign she knew and loved: all bravado and affected haughtiness. "His name is Rukh Shektan."

"And he travels with you for what reason?" Hart Drape asked.

"Because he is like our ancestors: a man without a home."

The scouts frowned and gave Rukh measuring stares. But Hart's gaze locked on Jessira. "Tell me you haven't compromised yourself with him."

Sign hissed in outrage.

"No," Rukh answered, speaking up for himself as he also dismounted. "Jessira's honor and my own are intact. I was judged Unworthy because I learned Talents not of my own Caste." He glanced behind him, staring at empty space. "Will those four warriors behind us remain Blended until we reach Stronghold?"

How had he...Jessira hadn't been paying attention, but she sensed the Blends now. She looked at Hart, who wore a pinched expression of displeasure. He barked a command, and four more scouts appeared behind them.

"Talents not of your own Caste?" a young scout mused. "You wouldn't happen to be the legendary Rukh Shektan?"

For the first time since their encounter with Hart and the Shadowcats, Rukh looked surprised. "How did you know?"

The scout smiled. Jessira remembered him now. Tire Cloud. He was young, only having finished his training when she had shipped out with the Silversuns all those many months ago. "Cedar Grey and Court Deep made it home along with another Kumma, who has a Talent not of his own Caste."

"Cedar!" Jessira shouted in elation. "He's alive?"

Hart nodded.

"And Farn?" Rukh asked in budding joy. "Is he still here?"

"He is," Hart answered. "Although he's not right in the head. I'm told he has dizzy spells and starts throwing up if you look at him funny. Our physicians have been helping him, but until a few weeks ago, nothing they did seemed to be working. I understand he's finally improving." He gave Rukh a quizzical look. "Cedar says you took down two Shylows. Is that true?"

Rukh shook his head. "No. I've never killed a Shylow." A fleeting expression of sorrow flashed across his face.

Jessira realized he was probably thinking about Keemo. She saw the Shadowcats sharing knowing smirks. No doubt they thought the legend of Kumma fighting prowess was as exaggerated as she had once believed. She looked forward to witnessing their expressions when Rukh practiced against them. "It was one of the Kummas under his command, Keemo Chalwin, who killed the Shylows," she said, temporarily halting the self-satisfied chuckles.

"Well, I don't know anything about that. All I know is this Farn Arnicep won't spar with us," another scout said into the temporary silence. It was Just Joint, the oldest of the Joint brothers, all three of whom were enlisted in the Home Army. In fact, his youngest brother, Divit, stood next to him. A fellow Shadowcat.

Jessira turned to Just with a questioning look. "I thought Hart said he's injured."

"He is. Or at least he was," Divit Joint piped in. The scout was a few years younger than Jessira, but just then, she felt infinitely older. In the past half-year, she'd gone through so much. "But how are we supposed to know how good he really is?" Divit continued.

"Cedar says he's like nothing we've ever seen, like he's the wind and fire made flesh," Sign said with a roll of her eyes.

Tire Cloud, a scout who had been a nugget during the same time as Jessira, snorted in disbelief. "I'll believe it when I see it," he said. "They can't be as great as Cedar says. Certainly not better than Wheel."

Jessira wasn't surprised by Tire's words. Wheel Cloud, Tire's older brother, was the current Champion of the Trials of Hume.

"I've seen Farn fight. He's everything my brother said," Jessira replied. "Once Healed, he would wipe the floor with the best of our warriors and probably not break a sweat. And Rukh is even better. I saw four of them take down thirty Tigons and suffer no casualties."

The scouts stared at Rukh in mingled uncertainty and doubt, as if he'd suddenly sprouted a Bael's horns. But just as clearly, they didn't believe or *want* to believe that Rukh and his kind were so much better with the sword than they.

"Perhaps the great Kumma can demonstrate his amazing skill with a blade before we lead him into our home," said Yalla Dark, the only other woman in the Shadowcats. Her suggestion was offered in a voice filled with loathing.

Jessira's hackles rose at the other woman's demeanor. Who was she to think so poorly of someone she'd only met a few minutes earlier?

"The great Kumma would be happy to oblige, except his leg is still healing," Rukh said, sounding rueful and ignoring Yalla's ugly tone. "Broke it a few weeks back." His voice suddenly turned hard and just as cold as Yalla's had been a moment earlier. "Give me a week, though, and I'll be happy to test you."

--------●●--------

Rukh rode within a cocoon of the Shadowcats. All the Stronghold warriors appeared edgy, with hands straying to their swords whenever Rukh shifted in his saddle. Most eyed him with curiosity while some were merely professional, going about their duties as a proper warrior should: alert and ready. Others, though, glared at him, the hostility evident in their expressions.

It was annoying, and he did his best to ignore their dislike. Rukh was a warrior. He knew nothing else, and these were the people he'd have to impress if he wanted to make a new life for himself here. However, he also knew he couldn't be a mouse and let them get away with staring at him with such contempt. Give a bully an inch, and he'd take the mile. Another aphorism from his nanna. It had been right back when Rukh was a child, and it was right now.

Finally, one of the scouts glared a little too hard and a little too obviously.

"You'll want to move your eyes, or you'll be finding out just how ugly a Pureblood can be," Rukh said to the man, who gave him a look of loathing in return. Anger roared to the surface. Without a further thought, Rukh dismounted and got straight in the scout's face, standing toe-to-toe with him. "You want to say something to me, say it," he challenged in a voice full of menace.

Hart Drape was there in an instant. "What the fragging hells is going on!" he demanded.

The scout stepped away from Rukh and came to attention. "Nothing, sir!" he replied.

"Then make sure it stays that way," Drape said in a growl. "Stop eyeing the Kumma like he's given your sister a disease and get your ass to the front of the line. Send Bild to take your place."

"Yes, sir!" the scout said, moving off.

Drape turned to Rukh. "And you. Don't pick fights with my warriors."

Rukh stared the lieutenant in the eye, not willing to back down. "I won't break your scouts," he said. "But I also won't just sit there and take it when someone insults my honor."

"What honor?" Drape asked. "I thought you were found Unworthy."

Rukh held back a grimace of anger, grinding his teeth in the process. "I'm still a Kumma," he growled, "and we fight and defend what's ours."

"Do what you want. Just shut up about it. And know that attacking even one of us will result in your ass getting a beating," the lieutenant barked back. "If we have to, we'll haul you to Stronghold tied up across your ugly horse's back like a sack of potatoes. I don't care. Your choice." With that, the lieutenant turned on his heel and walked away.

As the lieutenant departed, Rukh called out to him. "So is this how you treat all visitors to your city?" he asked. The lieutenant's shoulders stiffened but he didn't turn around to respond to Rukh's accusation. Other nearby scouts muttered in anger and threw scornful looks at Rukh.

"What are you doing?" Jessira hissed, grabbing hold of his arm. "This is *not* how you make a good first impression."

Following on her heels was her cousin, Sign Deep. The two

120

women shared a similar build, although Jessira was taller by several inches. Sign looked as offended as the rest of the Shadowcats.

With Jessira's presence, an opportunity arose, and Rukh took it. What he was about to do wasn't something the two of them had discussed, but it was necessary.

Rukh shrugged his arm free. "I'm only telling what's the truth," he said. "I remember how you used to think of me. I was the dreaded and evil Pureblood. You hated me on general principle." He glared about at the others, daring them to tell him they didn't think the same thing. "And I'm guessing the rest of your kind probably feel the same way."

"Like your people were any different," Jessira said. "Farn wanted to kill me out of hand when we first met, remember?"

Sign glared daggers at him. "Is this true?"

"She's alive, isn't she?" Rukh answered. "I saved her life more times than I can count. And my reward for all this was exile from my home." He glanced around at the Shadowcats. "I'm a Pureblood, but I'll be damned to the unholy hells before I bend knee to any of you or bear guilt for something I've never done."

"Don't play the victim here," Sign said, her voice filled with scorn. "You Purebloods are powerful in the world. Privileged. And your kind kills our kind."

"But I've never killed an OutCaste, and I've never done *anything* to harm one your kind. In fact, two of my own, close to me as brothers, died defending Jessira's brothers, and I almost died saving Jessira. As for privilege, it only exists in the cities, not here."

Sign looked like she wanted to argue the point, but she never had a chance. Just then, Lieutenant Drape shouted back at them. "Everyone just shut your traps," he said. "We're moving on."

Jessira gave Rukh a disappointed look as Sign drew her away.

Rukh watched them walk away, maintaining his angry appearance even as his heart sank. His way would be better. He just wished it didn't make him feel so awful.

CHAPTER EIGHT
DECISIONS

As deceitful as a vulture and as faithless as a harlot.
A sure sword in willful hands ends all such charges.

~*The Warrior and the Servant (author unknown)*

The Shektan House Council sat in stony silence as Bree and Jaresh relayed their findings about the Withering Knife murders. It had been two days since Van Jinnu's murder, and everyone was on edge. All listened with polite interest, but they were all frustrated by the most recent murder. Dar'El, surprisingly enough, was the one most affected. He had taken Van's murder the hardest, treating it like it was his fault.

Mira, who had already heard most of the contents of Bree and Jaresh's report, studied the other councilors as they listened. Satha Shektan shared the sofa with her son and daughter, and while her expression appeared bland and relaxed, the tightness to her eyes and her fisted hands revealed her anger. Satha was furious. It was an unexpected finding. She was generally so serene, with a warmth and generosity of spirit as beautiful as her features. In fact, Mira was quietly jealous of Jaresh and Bree for having such a loving Amma.

Her own Amma, Sophy Terrell, was a very different person. She wasn't gentle like Satha Shektan. She was stern. Amma's sobriquet, the Hound, was well deserved. She was as unyielding as the walls of Ashoka, and devotion to duty was her highest calling. And she expected no less from those who answered to her. Too often, Mira ended up disappointing her mother. She simply didn't measure up to Amma's standards.

Mira snipped the incipient self-pity and forced herself to focus on what was being said even as she flicked a glance around the room.

Sitting in a matching high-backed chair on the other side of the coffee table from Amma was Garnet Bosde. He was an ancient warrior, well into his seventies, but his mind remained sharp. Or so everyone claimed, but lately, Mira had noticed he tended to repeat himself, in both his questions and his answers. It was a worrisome sign, and Mira knew the rest of the Council worried about Garnet, though, for now, no one wanted to confront him on the matter.

"Seventy-six," mused Durmer Volk upon the completion of Bree and Jaresh's account. He stroked his luxurious mustache, which matched the color of his shoe-polish black hair, neither of which were in agreement with his seamed face. "More than I had hoped and less than I feared," he added. Mira knew that Durmer liked to inculcate a stern reputation, but she also knew it was all just a sham. Even as he scowled and complained about seemingly everything, he held a twinkle in his eyes, as if he were secretly mocking himself.

"Seventy-six members of three great Houses who might be our Withering Knife murderer," Satha said, sounding disgusted.

"We have to reduce that number even further," Garnet said tartly. "For instance, we know the killer is wealthy—the fragment of clothing from the murder of Aqua Oilhue belonged to a person of means," he continued. "Has that helped your investigation?"

It was a question Jaresh had already answered, but no one took notice of Garnet's repetition. Instead, Bree simply shook her head. "No. The suspects that we've identified are all wealthy. Any one of them could have afforded the clothing."

"We were planning on checking into the severity of the limp," Bree said. "The murderer has an injured leg, but it's not so bad that he's unable to fight. Also, we can eliminate anyone who has a limp involving his right leg. The murderer limps on the left."

"Get back to us with the revised numbers," Dar'El said.

Jaresh and Bree nodded, but looked diffident, as if they had more to add.

"What is it?" Dar'El asked.

"Drin Port," Jaresh replied.

It was the name of a Duriah who had once worked in the Moon Quarter; a man whose name had been slipped into Dar'El's pocket by a member of the Sil Lor Kum. Drin had gone missing in the spring and turned up dead a few days later, floating in Bar Try Bay. It was assumed that he had gotten drunk, slipped off a pier, and drowned.

"No one claimed his personal effects, but when I looked them over, there was nothing to them," Bree explained. "But I haven't been able to meet with the physician who pronounced Drin's cause of death. He keeps rescheduling our appointment."

Dar'El's eyes narrowed. "I'll take care of it," he said. "Gren Vos owes me a favor." He gave Jaresh and Bree a pointed look. "Do you have anything else?" They shook their heads, and Dar'El turned to Mira. "What about Rector?"

"Other than learning about the unaccounted henna and poppy seeds, he's not made any more progress. Plus, he says the older records are inaccessible. They were apparently ruined in a flood." She hesitated a moment. "Plus, he says the accountants are starting to wonder why he's being so nosy. It might cause him trouble."

Garnet frowned. "Unless they have plumbing in those warehouses, I don't see how those records were flood damaged. There hasn't been a storm surge strong enough to crest our levees in decades."

Mira hadn't known that. When she turned to Garnet, he merely smiled at her before leaning back into his chair and closing his eyes. "My time hasn't yet passed," he said, seeming to answer the unspoken worries about his state of mind that swirled about the room.

Mira shook off her thoughts about Garnet and considered what he had just said. Was it possible that Rector had lied to her when he spoke of those damaged records? It was unlikely. Despite loosening up somewhat, the man remained as stiff and upright as a vertical plank of wood. He wasn't one to tell lies or even half-truths. Which raised the possibility that *he* was the one being deceived. She'd find out soon enough at their next meeting. All she had to do was ask him. Rector was transparent as a clear pane of glass.

"Have Rector find out more about the timing of this flood. I want to know what really happened," Dar'El ordered.

"He won't like it," Mira replied, unsure why she cared for Rector's concern. "He says the Sentyas in his warehouse have taken note of him."

"Given he has oversight over their work, why would that be a surprise?" Amma asked. "More likely he's trying to prey on your sympathies and find a way out of his predicament."

Mira tried not to wince at Amma's harsh tone. In times past, when Amma had chosen to rebuke her in public, Jaresh would have offered her support. But that bridge had been burned months ago. It had been a bridge that needed burning, but Mira often wished it could have been otherwise.

"What do you mean the Sentyas have taken note of him?" Durmer asked, apparently disagreeing with Amma's assessment.

Mira wanted to thank him for his question and intervention, but she kept her face still. She didn't need another lecture from Amma about how gratitude implied weakness. "They find it unusual for a Kumma to be so concerned about accounting and distribution," she replied. "They think Rector is being overly inquisitive, and they wonder why."

"His concerns are noted," Dar'El said, his voice harsh. "I don't care what he has to do, but he *will* learn about those records."

Mira nodded. "I'll let him know."

"Finally, what about the unfortunate Van Jinnu?" Dar'El asked.

Mira looked to Jaresh and Bree, who shrugged their shoulders helplessly. It looked like none of them had learned much about the most recent murder victim.

Luckily, they were saved from their deserved embarrassment when Satha spoke up. "I can help with that one," she said. "Van Jinnu was a widower and lived in Hold Cavern. He maintained himself on the wealth earned from the two Trials in which he served. Since his wife's passing almost four years ago now, he spent many of his nights in the Blue Heron, a pub in the Moon Quarter." She paused and took a drink of water. "All of this is common knowledge, but what isn't is this: prior to their deaths, Felt Barnel and Drin Port often frequented the same establishment."

Mira wasn't the only who sucked in a shocked inhalation.

"Once is an accident. Twice is a coincidence. Thrice is a conspiracy," Durmer said. "Something beyond the love of ale linked those three men."

"Two of them were murdered, and the third died in what is starting to look like suspicious circumstances," Amma added.

"We need to take another look at Drin's personal effects," Jaresh said.

"And speak to the physician who did his autopsy," Bree added.

———————•●•———————

After the meeting's conclusion, everyone but Satha filed out. She waited for the room to empty, and Dar'El took the moment to stand and stretch. He wasn't young anymore, and his back had grown stiff.

"Sit down and let me help you," Satha suggested

She guided him to a sofa and began rubbing his shoulders, kneading deeply. She worked her way down the center of his spine, reaching his lower back where his muscles had cramped from sitting for so long. The pain and stiffness slowly eased, and Dar'El sighed with contentment.

"I'm still at a loss on how to figure out who in the Society is Sil Lor Kum," he said.

Satha continued working and didn't reply at first. "I've given it some thought," she eventually answered. "From now on, whenever you go to a Society meeting, make sure the pockets of your coat contains a small amount of henna powder mixed with iodase. On its own, the powder won't stain anything, but when combined with iodase and the oils on a person's skin, it should leave a mark."

Dar'El quickly grasped the basics of her plan. "So when this MalDin tries to contact me, he'll put the paper in my pocket, and the henna and iodase will stain his skin." He grinned. "I'm lucky to have married someone so clever."

Satha smiled in response. "Yes, you are," she replied, kissing the top of his head. "Just make sure to meet with every man there and see whose fingers become stained."

Her final piece of advice went without saying, and Dar'El couldn't resist teasing her. "Yes, dear," he replied in his most put upon voice.

"If you're going to mock me, then maybe you should massage your own back," Satha suggested tartly, but there was no trace of threat in her voice.

Dar'El chuckled at her mock-irritation and leaned back, enjoying the feel of her hands. He relaxed as she worked out the tension, and their conversation grew silent, broken a moment later when Dar'El spoke up. "I meant what I said earlier. I am lucky to have married you."

He sensed Satha's smile. "You've grown wise in your older years," she replied. "But don't forget, I was the one who chose you, not the other way around."

"Of course my queen."

"Is that more mockery?"

"Never." Dar'El trapped her hands in both of his and kissed her fingertips.

———◦———

Jaresh waited down the hall from Nanna's study, wanting to speak to him in private. The Council meeting had just ended, and the others were slowly departing. Bree was the first to leave with Durmer and Garnet on her heels. The two old men whispered to one another, their heads held close, and one of them chuckled briefly before they passed out of view. Next came Sophy Terrell, distracted and frowning as she spoke to Mira, likely scolding her daughter for not being perfect. As a result, Sophy didn't see Jaresh until she was almost on top of him. She caught herself in time and muttered a few words of apology before marching on. Mira gave him a half-hearted smile of embarrassment before trotting forward to keep pace with her amma.

Mira needed to assert herself. There had been a time when it seemed like she was starting to do just that. She seemed to have forged her own identity, one outside of Sophy's stern guidance and disapproval. But shortly after the ending of her...relationship with Jaresh, the prior dynamic between Mira and her amma had reiterated itself.

Jaresh wished there was something he could do or say to help her, but it wasn't his place. His wisest course of action was to stay out of it. This was a situation Mira had to resolve on her own. And just as important, Jaresh couldn't allow himself to fixate on her.

His head drooped as he mentally sighed. Once again, just as he had done for every day of the past four months, he vowed to rid himself of all thoughts about Mira Terrell, to free himself of his longing for her. More and more, there were days when he actually kept his resolution, a prospect that left him simultaneously hopeful and despondent. The hope was obvious, but the sorrow was harder to explain. Once Jaresh's aching need for Mira was gone, it would mean the death of his love for her as well. As he figured it, love lost should always be a cause for regret.

Steeped in melancholy, Jaresh didn't notice at first when Amma stepped into the hallway as she exited Nanna's study.

"Is something wrong?" she asked, peering at his face.

Jaresh affected a happiness he didn't feel. "No," he said, hoping Amma wouldn't see through his dissembling.

She likely did but was kind enough not to press him on the matter. Instead, Amma took one of his hands and squeezed it softly. "Let me know if you wish to talk."

"Of course," Jaresh lied. He had no intention of ever telling her how he felt about Mira. He could all-too readily imagine the horror she would feel if she ever learned of his Tainted emotions. They would disgust her. The revulsion in her eyes—it would break him. "I just need to see Nanna," Jaresh said, changing the subject.

Amma nodded. "He's inside," she said, gesturing to the closed door leading to the study. "Don't keep him waiting." She left then, her footsteps echoing down the hall.

Jaresh took a steadying breath. He needed what he was about to ask for. But to convince Nanna of the sincerity of his desire, he had to remain calm and reasoned. Otherwise, he would be denied out of hand. Jaresh did his best to master his emotions and took another steadying breath. He knocked on the door and entered the study.

Nanna sat at his desk, reading from a panoply of missives and notes.

Jaresh cleared his throat. "I wanted to talk to you about the Trial to Stronghold."

Nanna looked up from his papers. "What Trial?"

"The one I know you're going to commission once the Chamber decides in Rukh's favor."

"Ah. I see," Nanna said. He leaned back in his chair and steepled his fingers. "And after the Chamber rescinds their earlier judgment, why do you assume I will send a Trial to Stronghold?"

"You'll have to," Jaresh replied. "Rukh needs to learn that it's safe for him to come home, and the only force capable of carrying such a message would be a Trial." He straightened his shoulders. "I want to be part of it."

"Do you?" Nanna asked. "Is this about proving yourself?"

Jaresh took a moment to organize his thoughts. Nanna was testing him. He wanted to make sure that Jaresh was making a decision based on sound reason rather than a weak-kneed emotion, like trying to impress others. "It has nothing to do with proving myself," Jaresh replied in what he hoped was a composed tone. "I am who I am. I can't change it, nor do I need to. I want to go because I am a warrior, and a warrior defends those he loves."

"Rukh needs no protection," Nanna countered. "He's likely safe in Stronghold by now."

"But he should be safe *here*. Stronghold is not his home."

"And you think that as a Virgin you will be able to offer something our other warriors cannot?"

Jaresh shrugged. "Perhaps not with my blade or my Talents, but none of them are family. *I* am Rukh's brother, and as his brother, it is my duty to see him home."

Nanna stared him in the eyes, and Jaresh made sure to meet his gaze. The tableau held for a few moments before Nanna exhaled softly. "You are firm in your intent?" he asked.

"Yes, I am."

"You're certain?"

Jaresh nodded. "Absolutely."

"I always assumed we'd have this conversation," Nanna said with a sigh as he rubbed his temples. "And in every imagining, I was never able to dissuade you from this path."

"Then you shouldn't try," Jaresh said.

Nanna stared him in the eyes once again. "No. I suppose not. You are my son, and you are a warrior; one who knows his duty." He looked away. "Why couldn't you have lost your temper?" he muttered in disappointment.

Jaresh felt a stirring of his spirit, but he needed to hear the words. "Can I go?"

"Though your mother will want me to tell you 'no', I cannot deny you." Nanna sighed once again. "Yes. You can go." He held up a finger in warning. "But you will absolutely not take any unnecessary chances in the Wildness. Both my sons will be at risk in this Trial, and the thought of losing either of you terrifies me."

For the first time since he and Mira had agreed to go their separate ways, Jaresh felt like a ray of sunshine had broken through the gloomy cloud bank surrounding his life.

———◆———

"Do you have plans for the afternoon?" Bree called out to Mira, who was speaking to Sophy in the front foyer of the House Seat.

The other two women shared a look, and Mira looked like she was going to decline Bree's invitation. Before she could do so, however, Sophy surprised them both. She smiled at Mira. "Go on. Enjoy yourself. Work is important, but friends should take precedence."

Bree almost stumbled in disbelief. Snow falling in the hothouse of Ashoka's summer would have been less surprising than Sophy's words. Before working with her during the past half-year, Bree had only known Mira's amma as a distant figure of authority. Sophy was the Hound, the legendary House Shektan counselor known for her strong-willed resolve and dogged determination. She was both feared and respected—and in nearly equal measure—known to go to nearly any lengths for the betterment of her House. Bree admired Mira's amma, but in getting to know her, she had also discovered a brittle quality to her hardness. Sophy was unbending and unyielding, but not always forgiving.

She gave Bree far greater appreciation for her own amma, a woman equally as proud and strong. But somehow, Amma, always included praise, guidance, and, most importantly, compassion with her criticism. It made all the difference. Amma had a warmth and loving presence that Bree never doubted.

Even more surprising, Bree genuinely liked Amma. A year ago, she wouldn't have felt that way. In fact, she would have found her mother irritating at best, ignorant and dull at worst. What a fool she had been. Sometimes Bree wished she could go back in time and smack her younger self. Amma was far wiser and patient than she deserved.

Bree set aside her thoughts about Amma and turned her attention to Mira, who had smiled briefly in response to Sophy's warmth. Otherwise, her aspect remained neutral and her eyes flat. It was an expressionless state Bree had come to see all-too often on her friend's face. Over the past few months, Mira had become skilled at hiding her emotions. It saddened Bree. Mira had once been so carefree and happy.

"What did you have in mind?" Mira asked after saying her final 'goodbye' to her amma.

"Lunch? And I thought we could talk. I hardly get see you anymore."

"Talk about what?" Mira asked. "And you know how busy we've both been lately."

Bree slid her hand through the crook of Mira's elbow. "All the more reason for us to have lunch," she said, guiding her friend toward the sunroom.

Bree's head shot up, and she almost spilled her bowl of lentils and rice. "Rector said that?" she asked in disbelief. "That if he knew than what he knows now, he wouldn't have turned Rukh in?"

Mira nodded. "I know. A mule kick would have been less stunning, but it's what he said," she replied.

Bree sat back, stunned. Rector's claim to no longer see the world in such distinct shades of right and wrong was so unlike him. The man had always held such a narrow, merciless view of what constituted proper behavior. If moral judgments were rendered based on Rector's beliefs, half of Ashoka would probably have been found guilty of some sort of unpardonable sin. What could have changed his mind so drastically? "Is he just trying to get on your good side?" Bree asked.

She reddened with embarrassment when she noticed Mira's mocking expression.

"Probably not," Bree muttered, still wondering at Rector's change of heart.

"Maybe he impaled himself on a Wisdom tree," Mira suggested.

Bree snorted. "A Wisdom tree?"

Mira grinned. "I just made it up. Sounds good, though, doesn't it?"

Bree laughed, happy to see her friend smiling—a true smile this time. "I'm glad we had lunch," she said. "It's been too long since we've been able to laugh."

"With the murders and everything else going on, there just hasn't been time," Mira said.

"It is as those of Kush would say: *We live in interesting times*," Bree said. "And to make matters worse, Jaresh plans on going to Stronghold."

"Why?" Mira asked in surprise.

"To bring Rukh home," Bree replied. "He believes it's his duty as Rukh's brother."

Mira nodded. "He would have made a fine Kumma," she said. "It's odd, but in his own way, he's almost as traditional in his beliefs as Rector." She wore a look of bemusement.

Bree shuddered. "No one is as traditional as Rector."

Mira smiled. "You'd be surprised."

"Anyway, Amma won't be happy when she finds out what Jaresh intends."

"Will Dar'El allow it?"

"Probably." Bree shifted in her seat, uncomfortable with the realization that *both of* her brothers might soon be in mortal danger in the Wildness. And it might be her fault.

"What is it?" Mira asked.

Bree hesitated. Thus far, only her family knew the truth about Rukh's night in Dryad Park with Jessira. And although she understood the reasons for why Nanna had asked her to do what she had, and on an intellectual level, she even recognized that she had done nothing wrong—her family certainly told her so enough times—there was still a part that wondered whether she bore any blame for her brother's exile. Maybe it would help to hear the thoughts of a trusted friend.

Mira listened in silence as Bree explained what she had done. When she finished, Mira's eyes were filled with warm sympathy. "You did the only thing that could have saved your brother," she said. "You did nothing wrong."

"So I've been told," Bree replied. "But Rukh's gone, maybe

forever, and sometimes, I feel like it's my fault."

"It's not," Mira said, her voice was unyielding as ironwood. "It was the fault of Rector Bryce and Hal'El Wrestiva. If you are looking for someone to blame, those two should be at the top of your list."

"I *do* blame them, and they *are* at the top of my list," Bree said with a scowl. To this day, she still couldn't believe that she had once been attracted to Rector Bryce. "But I'm not blameless either."

"You are what you wish to be," Mira said. "Personally, I think you did nothing wrong, but I can understand how you feel. When it comes to those we love, we always blame ourselves when something goes wrong, even if we did everything right."

Bree considered Mira's advice. It was similar to what her family had said. But for some reason, hearing it today, from a trusted friend…it made a difference. Bree felt better about the situation, and she smiled gratefully at Mira. "Do you think Rukh will feel the same way?" she asked.

"If he's half the man that Jaresh says he is, I'm sure he will," Mira said with an answering smile.

"I hope so. I *pray* so." Bree laughed. Suddenly and unexpectedly, she was delirious with relief.

"You offering a prayer?" Mira said with a chuckle. "Wonders never cease."

Bree reached across the table and squeezed Mira's hands. "Thank you," she said, infusing as much warmth and gratitude as she could into her expression and her words. "You are a wise and true friend. I hope you realize that."

"I don't know about that," Mira said, blushing.

"It's true," Bree replied. "You're intelligent and capable, and we all appreciate you."

Mira's smile slipped ."Not everyone appreciates me."

Bree pursed her lips. "Your amma?" she asked in hesitation.

Mira nodded. "She knows *exactly* just how capable and intelligent I am."

Bree's eyes narrowed. What did that mean? Mira was everything a daughter should be: dutiful, humble, courteous, and...

The answer came to her in a flash of insight. Jaresh.

How sad. Mira and Jaresh had suffered so much because of something that shouldn't be considered a sin anymore. But it also wasn't a topic that Bree could openly discuss with Mira. Her friend would hate it. "She's wrong, you know," Bree said. "You're a woman of decency and honor. My parents—we all think so."

Mira stiffened. Her face reddened with shame. "Does everyone know about me and...?"

"Know what?" Bree asked. "There's nothing *to* know."

"Rector would disagree."

Bree snorted in derision. "Are you really going to tell me that Rector Bryce's good opinion of you matters in even the least bit?"

Mira smiled wanly. "Point taken."

Bree leaned back in her chair. "Besides, if you haven't noticed, the ruling 'El of House Shektan has an unusual family. I have a Sentya brother, and my Annayya—my older brother—had the poor taste to go off and cavort with a beautiful ghrina." Bree grinned. "Whatever small issue you *may* have pales in comparison."

Mira grimaced. "*She* found out because I was indiscreet in my admiration. Ever since then, it's been difficult to please her."

"Then stop trying," Bree said. "Maybe you should just please yourself. Maybe it's time to stop worrying so much about everyone else's concerns and simply go about forgiving yourself for whatever it is that you think you've done wrong."

"Like you should with your supposed role in Rukh's problems?"

Bree tilted her head in acknowledgment. "Once again, you demonstrate your inestimable wisdom," she said before cocking her head in thought. "Was it because you were switched with the branch of a Wisdom tree when you were a child?"

Mira laughed.

CHAPTER NINE
A KIND OF WELCOME

The road home is longest when our anticipation exceeds the distance left to travel.

~Sooths and Small Sayings, by Tramed Billow AF 1387

L ater in the afternoon, the icy rain finally let off. The sun peeked out as the heavy clouds broke apart and dispersed, but the weather remained cold. The Shadowcats picked up the pace, and Rukh heeled his mount, urging the packhorse to keep up with them. When they reached the banks of the River Fled, they followed its course north, and from there, they came upon the legendary Croft. Or at least that's how Rukh thought of it given the reverent tone Jessira used whenever she talked about the place. They cut across a small corner of it, but from what Rukh could see, what the Croft lacked in beauty—especially compared to the glorious verdant farms surrounding Ashoka—it made up for in size. It was huge. Most of it was sculpted into small square fields that were dead and brown in the winter, separated from one another by narrow macadam lanes. Lonely mesquite and juniper trees stood like silent sentinels in small clusters throughout the land, but closer to the river, taller trees—ash and maple—reached skeletal branches to the sky.

Something had to keep the place hidden from the Queen, and Jessira had once explained that the founders of Stronghold had learned to form something they called a Blind: a semi-permanent Blend. It was continually renewed by the farmers who worked the land.

North of the Croft was a wide road that followed the contours of Teardrop Lake's beaches and shores. The waters were hidden by a thick copse of aspen, but when the view opened up, Rukh brought his horse to a halt. He stared out in appreciation. The lake was a blue so rich it was almost cobalt. Sunlight twinkled against the gentle waves, and the clouds and sky were reflected in the water's mirror-like sheen. All around were green-swathed hills and towering mountains with their gray shoulders covered in snow and ice. Fisherman stood in small bobbing boats, casting their nets out into the water.

Rukh got his horse moving again and noticed Jessira up ahead, leading her mare and walking alongside her cousin, talking excitedly and laughing. The lines of worry on her face—so long prevalent—were gone, replaced by joy. It was good to see.

Night had long since fallen by the time they finally reached Mount Fort. East Gate—one of the two entrances into Stronghold—was almost invisible; a dark, rough-hewn slit twenty feet wide but easily missed against the dark bulk of the looming mountain. Rukh examined the mountainside, but he couldn't see any of the squat signal towers Jessira had once told him about. There were supposed to be twenty of them, spaced every three miles, and built so they blended in with the surrounding stone of Mount Fort.

Rukh dismounted and hobbled forward, following the Shadowcats into the mountain's depths. A guardhouse loomed above the entrance with murder holes on all sides. From them came occasional flashes of light from red-hooded firefly lanterns. Rukh glanced up and noticed a large stone gate framed in black ironwood recessed in the ceiling. It looked like it could be dropped down in an instant and immediately seal the opening. Stronghold's entrance appeared well fortified.

Nevertheless, Rukh wondered at the proficiency of the guards manning East Gate. While they likely knew of the Shadowcats' presence, why hadn't they challenged a large band of warriors moving into the heart of their home? Drape had sent one of his scouts up ahead to let the guards know of the Shadowcats' imminent arrival, but Rukh still thought it was sloppiness bordering on incompetence to simply accept the word of one warrior and let the scouts pass without first questioning them.

From there, they travelled into a long, smooth-walled tunnel—fifteen feet tall and wide—and dimly lit with red-lensed firefly lanterns hanging from the ceiling. According to Jessira, this was Hold Passage East. About every fifty yards, a thick gate, similar to the one found at the entrance, hung from the ceiling, ready to slam down at a moment's need. Near every one of them was a small guardhouse, and stationed within were the men and women tasked with protecting Stronghold. So where were they? No one else was about in the tunnel. The footsteps of their party echoed in the emptiness. Once again, Rukh wished at least *one* of the guards would come out to challenge their presence. He shook his head in disappointment.

As if on cue, a Shadowcat, who had been sent racing off deeper into the city, returned just then. With him came twenty warriors, armed, armored, and with grim faces full of ill intent. Their commander talked briefly with Drape before the two of them approached Rukh.

Rukh's impression of the government and warriors here went up slightly. It looked like they wouldn't give him free rein into their city without first asking him some questions.

"This is Captain Tamp Wind," Drape said. "You'll be accompanying him from here on."

Rukh looked the man over. The captain appeared to be in his late twenties, was of average build, and had the reddest hair Rukh had ever seen.

"Is he a prisoner?" Jessira asked, moving to stand next to Rukh and looking ready to argue the point.

"We only have a few questions for him," Captain Wind said. "He's a Pureblood, and we need to know why he's here."

"He's here because of me," Jessira replied. "You have no reason to hold him."

"Remember your place, scout," Wind snapped. He closed the distance until he was nose-to-nose with her. "You've been out in the field for months, and perhaps you forgot military discipline; but you better remember it right quick."

"It's all right," Rukh said to Jessira. The last thing he wanted was for her to get in trouble on his account. "They're only doing their duty. Go on and see your family." He eyed the still-annoyed looking captain. "I'm sure I'll be fine."

"We'll debrief you in the morning," Captain Wind said to Jessira. "Your family has already been notified of your arrival. They're waiting for you. Go with the Shadowcats." The captain's jaw firmed as Jessira looked like she still wanted to argue the point. "This isn't a request, scout. You're dismissed. Move out."

"What about my horse?" Jessira asked.

"I'll see to it," the captain said.

"Yes, sir," Jessira said, her face a mask of hidden emotion as she came to attention and saluted. She gathered her belongings and glanced back at Rukh, giving him an inscrutable look before walking away.

"You'll come with us," the captain said. "And you need to hand over your weapons."

Rukh had been expecting the request, but it still filled him with trepidation. His weapons were his last link to Ashoka.

"We'll make sure you get it all back," Wind added upon seeing Rukh's reluctance.

Rukh nodded and handed over his sword and knives to a waiting warrior. He kept the two throwing blades in his boots, though. No one had checked for them, and unless asked for, he saw no reason to give up the knives.

He was about to follow the captain, but Wind motioned one of his warriors over. "Search him," he said. It was a wise precaution, and Rukh's respect for the man rose a notch.

"Boots," Captain Wind suggested after his warrior had finished his inspection, not finding the throwing knives.

With a smile and a respectful nod in the captain's direction, Rukh removed the blades on his own and passed them over to the waiting warrior.

With that, Rukh was led deeper into Stronghold. The tunnel continued unchanged until about a quarter-mile later when it expanded both upward and outward. Shortly thereafter, they came across a large wall barring their path. A portcullis was raised, and behind it, thick ironwood gates rested on heavy hinges, ready to be thrown shut at an instant's notice. Upon the wall, to either side of the portcullis, alert warriors stared down impassively, their bows resting in their hands with arrows notched. Firefly lanterns, each with tens of lamps, lit the tunnel for fifty yards in front of the gates.

Rukh studied the warriors. They wore camouflage clothing, a mix of light and dark grays, which melded seamlessly with the surrounding stone. They looked like they knew their business—which made the earlier sloppiness from the warriors at the tunnel's entrance harder to understand.

He mentioned his observation to the captain.

"We had you under observation the entire time," Wind replied. "Given your Caste's supposed fighting prowess, I wasn't going to take any chances. We let you in, made you feel comfortable, and then trapped you deep enough so you can't fight your way back out."

Clever. His estimation of the man rose again.

They passed beneath the portcullis and the area beyond opened up even further. The ceiling was now more than fifty feet high and from it hung an abundance of huge firefly lanterns, each with hundreds of lamps. They were turned down for the night, but Rukh learned that during the day, they lit up the space to the brightness of midday. A large fenced off area took up most of the ground beyond the gates and was broken down into a number of training squares and a cluster of squat buildings. There, another wall and gate barred further passage into the heart of the mountain.

"East Lock," Rukh guessed. "This is the fortress and barracks of the Brigade Eastern of the Home Army of Stronghold?"

"I suppose the scout told you," the captain said, not looking pleased. He gestured, and the horses were led away. "Come."

"Where are we going?" Rukh asked.

"Where you'll be safe," the captain answered tersely. "Now be silent and follow."

Rukh mentally shrugged. At this point, his fate was no longer in his hands. He was probably going to be kept locked away somewhere for however long it took the Strongholders to decide what to do with him.

They crossed the open space in front of the barracks, and Rukh was led to a small building, separate and alone from all the others. He was gestured inside where a single windowless room held a narrow cot, a washbasin on a pedestal, and an overhead firefly lantern. Otherwise, the space was empty. It looked like a prison.

"You can rest here," the captain said. "You'll be questioned in the morning and have a chance to discuss your potential future with us at that time." The captain didn't wait for Rukh's reply. He simply turned and left.

Rukh heard the catch as a lock was thrown shut after the door closed. So, he'd guessed right: he was a prisoner.

He sighed. He'd deal with it in the morning. Right now, his leg was aching, his arm felt like a dead weight, and he was dead tired. He stretched out on the cot and fell asleep in moments.

———•———

Once they were past East Lock, Jessira and Sign kept on going, heading for that most blessed of places: home. Her cousin had been given permission to accompany her and walked by Jessira's side, helping to carry some of her bags.

"So, is your Kumma friend always such a jackhole?" Sign asked.

Jessira shrugged. "No. Usually he's kind and considerate. I'm not sure what got into him today."

"Well, at least you don't have to worry about him bothering you anymore."

"What do you mean?" Jessira asked.

"He's a *Pureblood*," Sign said, as if the word alone should explain everything she was trying to get across. "You'll be busy getting your life back, and he'll have to figure out his own path. He'll likely have to join the other one, Farn Arnicep, as a laborer."

Jessira came to a stop. "Farn is a laborer?" she asked. "Why hasn't a place for him been found in the Home Army?" She didn't like Farn—detested him, in fact—but it also made no sense to waste his Talents and have him work as a laborer.

Sign snorted in derision. "He plans on returning to Ashoka as soon as he's able."

Jessira frowned in confusion. "But what about as an instructor for our warriors? He could teach us so much. Why waste his abilities as laborer?"

Sign shrugged. "You heard the lieutenant. Whatever happened

to him in the Wildness did something to his head. He can hardly walk straight without bumping into a wall much less teach us anything he might know."

Jessira's mood soured. What would happen to Rukh? "And did anyone bother questioning Farn's knowledge? There's still much he could have taught our warriors, even if he couldn't demonstrate it."

"Cedar and Court took some lessons from him, and so did a few other warriors after they heard how incredible Farn was supposed to be, but his teachings made no sense," Sign said. "He tried to tell us that our sword forms were too stiff; too formal and don't allow for flow and balance." She grimaced. "He was always whining on about flow and balance. Centering your core is what he called it."

"And no one bothered to listen?" Jessira asked.

"Cedar and Court tried…"

"Why only those two?"

Sign shrugged. "They like him. The journey back in the Wildness, I guess. Anyway, maybe they learned something; but eventually their work and Farn's didn't allow them time for any more training." Sign explained. "Truth to tell, I doubt he had much to teach us anyway. I don't doubt that Kummas are fine warriors, but I'm guessing their reputations are probably more than slightly overblown."

"They're every bit as good as the stories say. I was there. I saw," Jessira said, her mind already on other matters.

She was worried about Rukh's future. All along she'd been certain that he would make a place for himself in Stronghold as a member of the Home Army. But with his arm so weak that he could barely lift it from his side and the dismissal of Farn's knowledge by her fellow warriors, that possibility seemed less likely. Her heart sank. Farn and Rukh could talk until they ran out of breath about their fighting philosophy, but if they couldn't demonstrate their skills, why would her people listen? Farn's words about flow and balance and understanding one's enemy were *exactly* how Kummas fought. It was what made them so deadly.

"...Farn's quiet and doesn't say too much, but he used to have this way about him. Pure arrogance," Sign was saying. "Maybe it's because he's a Pureblood. I think the stink of his culture has probably seeped down into his pores and into his blood. He can't wash it away."

Jessira attention snapped back to the conversation. "What?" she asked, appalled by Sign's bigotry.

"Not literally," her cousin said in a placating tone. "Just figuratively. You know..."

"Listen to yourself," Jessira said. *"Purebloods carry a bone-deep stink that they can't erase,"* she mimicked. "How is that any different from when they call us ghrinas?"

"It's different because ghrinas are born. We can't change who we are. A Pureblood really only becomes a Pureblood if he's raised in one of their cities. If he were raised here, he'd be fine. He'd be civilized."

Jessira shook her head in disbelief. "You have no idea what you're talking about," she said. "Most Ashokans aren't all that different from our own people. They want to live their lives in peace and raise their children to be happy."

"They're only peaceful as long as we're not around. They kill us on sight, remember?" Sign replied, looking like she thought she had just scored some kind of decisive debating point.

Jessira rolled her eyes. "Then explain why I'm still alive," she said. "I lived in Ashoka for months, and during my time there, I was never in any real danger. It wasn't always pleasant, but I met a lot of good people there."

Sign's mouth puckered, like she'd swallowed something bitter, and she muttered something unintelligible under her breath. They walked in silence. "You and Court are insane if you think I'll ever trust a Pureblood," Sign finally said.

"Court?"

"For some reason, he took in Farn Arnicep. They share Court's flat, and he says the Kumma is a good man who just wants to go home."

Jessira's brows rose in surprise. Farn was a good man? This wasn't the same Kumma she knew. The man she'd met on the Hunters Flats had been everything she'd been taught to fear about Purebloods. He had been ugly in his judgment, ready to murder her simply for being who she was: a ghrina, an abomination. Just like that jackhole back in Ashoka, Rector Bryce.

"Why did Court take him in?" Jessira asked.

Sign snorted in amusement. "Because Court's a simpleton."

Jessira laughed. "Court's not a simpleton. He's just got an open heart."

"And an empty head."

"Sign," Jessira said in admonition. "He's your brother. Be nice."

"I'm just teasing," Sign said. "I know he's being generous and all, but I just don't know why he thinks so highly of the Kumma."

Again, Jessira was surprised by the Farn Arnicep that her cousin, Court, apparently knew. Maybe his time in Stronghold had changed him, improved who he was. "Like I said before: not all Purebloods are the same. Most are good and decent people."

Sign looked at her askance. "Like your Kumma?" she asked. "Because he sure didn't seem 'good and decent' when I met him."

Jessira's scowled. What *had* gotten into Rukh? In the best of her times, her people didn't like Purebloods, and they certainly wouldn't take well to Kumma arrogance. "I don't know, but something's bothering him. I've never seen him act so rude." She chewed her lower lip, worried for Rukh. It took her awhile to notice the look of speculation on Sign's face. "What is it?" she asked.

"You care about him," Sign said. "You only bite your lip like that when something is really bothering you."

"Of course I care. He's a friend. He saved my life and lost his own because of me."

"I thought he was exiled from Ashoka because of his non-Kumma Talents."

Jessira winced. Sign could act like a flighty idiot, but she was no fool. Very little got past her. "He kept me company in Ashoka," she said. "It was that appearance of impropriety that turned out to be the final log on his funeral pyre." It wasn't the entire truth, but close enough.

"And nothing happened between the two of you?" Sign asked. "After all, he is easy on the eyes."

"Sign!" Jessira said, scandalized. Yes, there had been the one kiss, and yes, in a different world, *maybe* she would have wanted to do more than kiss Rukh Shektan, but those were childish fantasies, empty dreams. This was the real world, and in the real world, her future would be ruined if even a *hint* of unseemliness were raised about her and Rukh. "Nothing happened," Jessira insisted. "You saw how he was today. I had to put up with his moodiness for months on end."

Sign seemed to study her through hooded eyes. "You said he was usually kind and considerate."

"He is, or he was," Jessira replied, getting flustered.

"If we weren't cousin-sisters, I wouldn't have noticed…but we are, and I did. The two of you are more than friends."

"Nothing happened."

Sign nodded. "And I believe you. You've always held on to your honor like a drowning woman clinging to a lifeline," she said. "But you like this Kumma."

"It's not like—"

"Your secret's safe with me," Sign said, laying a consoling arm across Jessira's shoulders. She laughed softly. "I just wish your taste in men were better. A Kumma? Really?"

Sign scrunched up her face in such an obviously exaggerated

expression of disgust, that Jessira had to laugh with her.

"So, what does he think of you?" her cousin asked a moment later.

Usually, Jessira kept her feelings and thoughts to herself, but for some reason, she was in a confessional mood. "He called me *priya* the other night," she said, unsure why she was telling such a secret to Sign.

"Mercy," Sign answered in a hushed tone.

"Nothing's changed," Jessira insisted. "I'll marry Disbar Merdant and bear his children. Time will pass, and I'll forget this infatuation."

Sign eyed her with concern.

"I don't want to talk about it anymore," Jessira said. "Tell me what I've missed since I've been gone."

Sign nodded, and they spoke of safer topics: family, friends, babies, and losses. The conversation had them distracted, and before Jessira knew it, they had arrived at her parents' home.

"We're here," Sign said. "Peddananna and Peddamma—" Jessira's Nanna and Amma "—will be so happy to see you." Jessira found herself pulled into another embrace. "I can't tell you how happy I am to have you home," Sign whispered in her ear.

Jessira hugged her back. "So am I," she whispered back.

Sign dashed aside a few fresh tears, and Jessira had to as well even though she knew many more would come the moment she stepped inside.

She took a deep breath and grinned widely as she knocked on the door and entered. Glad shouts greeted her appearance, and she was enveloped in her family's love.

⚫

The next night, Amma and Nanna held a homecoming party in Jessira's honor. There were so many people who wished to attend that they had to hold the party in Crofthold Lucent's dining hall. They even had to hire several laborers to help with all the cooking and cleaning.

The celebration lasted late into the night. Her parents, brothers, cousins Court and Sign, and every auntie, uncle, nephew, and niece who were even remotely connected to her were present. Jessira greeted everyone with a happy smile, embraced in the love of family and friends.

Of course, everyone insisted on hearing her story from beginning to end, fascinated by her time in Ashoka. Many were taken aback when she spoke so lovingly of the city's beauty and grace.

"The place is like a jewel, sculpted over the centuries until it glows from within," Jessira said. "For Ashokans, everything they touch is an art, even food. They have places called 'restaurants', and in the best ones, they master cooking until everything they make tastes like magic." This had earned her so many doubtful stares that Jessira had to laugh. "If you ever walk through Layfind Market and smell its thousand spices, you'll know what I mean."

"Why would they care so much about the flavors of their food?" Sign asked, perplexed.

Jessira shrugged. "Because they can. They insist on making their city and culture as beautiful as possible. I saw a play once," she said. "Rukh and Bree—his sister—insisted I go with them." She grinned. "What a waste of time to sit around watching people pretend to be someone they aren't. At least that's what I thought." Jessira sighed. "It was one of the finest nights of my life. Then there was Dryad Park...it was like nature made perfect." Her voice faltered then. Dryad Park was also the reason Rukh was here instead of safely home in Ashoka. "You'd have to experience Ashoka to understand what I mean. I hope I can go back and visit one day."

"They would let you?" her oldest brother, Kart, asked, shocked.

"They wouldn't welcome me with open arms, but Rukh's

parents say they will fight to allow me to come back if I ever want to."

Her words left her friends and family further baffled. The picture she painted of Rukh and his family, and their openhearted nature went against everything all of them had ever been taught about Purebloods. Jessira understood their confusion. A year ago, she would have felt the same way. From childhood, OutCastes were taught that Purebloods would mercilessly kill those they labeled ghrina. To hear how a Kumma warrior had saved her, protected her, Healed her, even spent time with her so she wouldn't be lonely—it cut against everything they thought was truth about Purebloods.

Jessira could tell many people were skeptical, and it was perfectly understandable. But perhaps her words and experience could help her people overcome their prejudices, and maybe it could help smooth out Rukh's transition in Stronghold.

"Well, it seems there is some amount of civility within the heart of Pureblood culture," her nanna said. "We'll have to have your friend, Rukh, over for dinner and thank him properly."

"Yes. I look forward to getting to know this young man you admire so much," Amma added.

All in all, the evening was wonderful, especially the next morning when she woke up in her own bed, safe in the home of her parents.

CHAPTER TEN
A NEW LIFE

Inevitable odds can break even the strongest of warriors.
We would be wiser to sway like the reed before a storm,
bending before the hard winds. And if we hold fast to honor,
then when the storm ends—as all storms must—
we will once again stand up straight and true.

~The Warrior and the Servant (author unknown)

R ukh came awake the moment he heard the lock click open.
Light poured through the crack between the door and the
jamb. It must be Stronghold's version of daytime with those
massive firefly lanterns he'd seen last night lighted up to full glow.
Rukh stood up, wanting to face whatever was to come while on his
feet.

In walked three warriors, and another man, this one obviously a
commander. He had the pale skin of a Rahail with brown eyes and
ruddy hair and looked to be in his late thirties, although his freckled
nose made him appear younger. He was of medium build and would
have been unremarkable except for an indefinable essence to the
man. He exuded confidence and competence. He was a born leader

and charismatic based on the way his warriors watched his every move. Nanna would have called him a man of motion: someone who pushes the world in the direction of his wishes.

"My name is Dru Barrier," the commander said. "I am Major East of the Home Army. Please sit," he ordered rather than offered.

Rukh had no such intention. To do so would be to accept a position of weakness in front of the major. "Welcome to my humble abode," he said with a quirk of his lips. "And in my home, it would be considered rude for a host to sit in front of his guests."

"We are not in your home."

"I'm more comfortable standing."

"Despite your injured leg?" Dru Barrier smiled thinly. "So be it." He turned to one of his men. "Have some chairs brought in." He turned back to Rukh, not waiting to see whether his orders would be carried out. "Your appearance is a novelty for Stronghold. Other than the original Fifty-Five and your friend, Farn Arnicep, we have never had a Pureblood enter our city. And you're the first who comes to us begging for sanctuary."

"I *ask* for sanctuary," Rukh said. "I beg from no man."

"Prideful," Dru observed with an arch of his eyebrows. "Such is the reputation of your kind. I see it is well-earned."

The game of whether Rukh could be dominated continued. "No less than your own. The OutCaste girl almost refused my help when we first met simply because it came from a Pureblood. She would have died if she had kept up with her...poor choices." Again, he chose to diminish his relationship with Jessira.

"OutCaste girl? Is our scout a child in your eyes?"

"In my world, her fighting abilities are those of a child."

His words elicited an angry shuffling amongst the other warriors. They stilled at a single, warning glance from the major. "You think yourself so much better than us?"

"Only with a blade," Rukh answered. "Ask the girl and hear what she was to say."

152

"We have, as well as her brother. Lieutenant Grey and his sister always struck me as being sensible sorts, but I have a hard time believing their accounts."

Rukh shrugged. Words wouldn't answer the major's doubts. Only actions.

They were interrupted by the returning warrior who brought in two chairs with him.

The major smiled. "There. Now we can sit like civilized individuals. I'm sure much conversation in the city of Ashoka takes place while standing."

Rukh let the not-so-subtle insult pass by without comment.

"When, where, and to whom were you born?" the major asked after the two of them had settled in their chairs.

"I was born in AF 2042 to Darjuth and Satha Sulle in Ashoka."

"And you are a Kumma warrior?"

"Yes."

"And your training. Can you describe it?"

Rukh paused. "Why do you need to know?"

Dru smiled thinly. "I'm just trying to get a sense of who you are."

"My training began as soon as I could stand."

"And can you describe it?"

Rukh went over his childhood, the early training under the tutelage of Durmer Volk all the way through his time at the House of Fire and Mirrors.

"Your training required over eighteen years for you to master your Talents?"

"Our training takes a lifetime to master," Rukh corrected with a smile, quoting one of his favorite sayings.

"Are you considered skilled for one of your kind?"

"I'm competent."

"There are some who say you are more than competent. That

you are an engine of destruction made flesh."

Rukh laughed, genuinely amused. What a ridiculous notion. "I'm only flesh and blood; not some machine."

"Did you win the Tournament of Hume? The equivalent to our Trials of Hume?"

"I did."

"So you're more than competent."

"I am competent in my own eyes."

"And the status of Ashoka's force structure."

Rukh frowned. He didn't know what the major might do with such knowledge, but it was privileged. There was no way Rukh would reveal such information. "I've been exiled from Ashoka, but she was long the city of my heart. The knowledge you request is not mine to divulge."

"I see," Dru said, looking like he'd expected Rukh's refusal. "So Ashoka *was* the city of your heart?"

"I'm exiled. I need to find a new place to consider home."

"Our histories tell how those who are judged Unworthy are entirely comprised of deviants and traitors. Is this why Ashoka exiled you?"

Rukh exhaled softly. He kept an impassive mien, not letting any of the anger and heartbreak he felt show on his face. "Yes," he said in a calm, even tone. "I hold Talents not of my own Caste. That is considered deviancy in Ashoka."

The major grunted. "A foolish notion if I ever heard one," he replied. "And do you think you can so easily transfer your allegiance to Stronghold?" Barrier snapped his fingers. "Just like that?"

Rukh smiled ruefully. "It's not entirely my choice."

"If not you, then who else can choose for you?"

"You, and others like you. Those who can make decisions. Can I find a home here?"

Dru leaned back in his chair and studied Rukh. "Perhaps." From there, Dru moved on to Rukh's Trial. He focused on the final hours of the caravan, going over Rukh's suspicion of betrayal.

"Your men were entirely wiped out by a full Shatter of Chimeras, fifteen thousand of them. What kind of damage did you do?"

"If it *was* a full Shatter, then we killed four or five thousand."

One of the warriors openly laughed. "Three hundred killed five thousand?" he mocked. "And how did you manage this, oh great Kumma? Did Fireballs fly from your bunghole?"

The other warriors laughed with him but quickly settled down upon seeing the annoyance on the major's face. In fact, Dru Barrier hadn't seemed the least bit surprised upon hearing Rukh's statement. The man must have already heard a similar account from Cedar and Farn during their debriefing when they had arrived in Stronghold.

"Why are you asking me these questions if you already know the answers?" Rukh asked.

"I have been *told* all this. I remain unconvinced as to the veracity," the major replied. He went on to question Rukh about the rest of the events of his first Trial, and his return to Ashoka. Next, Barrier questioned him about the expedition to the caverns of the Chimeras, focusing on the events and findings there. Rukh told him everything he could remember, but he made sure to leave out the part where he saved the remaining Baels. He'd told no one about that, not even Jessira.

"And after losing so many warriors, over a thousand in the caverns and with the three hundred on the Trial, is your army not spread thin?"

Rukh smiled and didn't bother answering. The major was just fishing for information about Ashoka's armies.

Then the questions shifted to the journey home.

"Your men saluted you? Does this mean the people of Ashoka might change their thoughts toward us?"

Rukh shifted in his chair, unsure what his brother warriors' gesture might have meant. He didn't want to read more into it than was actually there. "My fellow warriors were grateful for my help with saving our brethren, but whether their feelings translate to something more, I can't say."

The major nodded as he took in Rukh's answer, his face indecipherable. Next came questions about the journey from Ashoka to Stronghold. Upon hearing Rukh's description of the battle with the Ur-Fels and Tigons, Dru smiled. "Yes...the famed Fireballs. Pity your friend, Farn, hasn't seen fit to show us his Talents as a Kumma." He glanced at his warriors, a smirk on his face. "I'm sure all of us would have been most impressed by such a demonstration," he said, his words earning a scornful chuckle from his men.

"Test me and find out."

"We'll see," the major replied, flicking a glance at Rukh's injured arm. "Perhaps when you can hold a sword."

"I look forward to it," Rukh said.

"I'm sure you would." The major cleared his throat. "And what about your feelings for Jessira Grey?"

Rukh had expected the question, and rather than stiffen with alarm, he merely shrugged in indifference. "She's a friend."

"And she feels the same way about you?"

"You'd have to ask her, but I think that's probably right."

"Nothing more? She is a beautiful woman, after all, and you are a young man. Surely you were tempted to perhaps start a relationship with her? The two of you being alone in the Wildness for months at a time and all."

Rukh shook his head. "You misunderstand. Nothing *could* occur. I am a Pureblood of Caste Kumma. Our honor is intact."

"*Our?*"

"She is promised to another. Kummas don't steal another's woman. Had she broken faith with her fiancé, I would have sinned just as much as she," Rukh said. "So my people believe."

The questions wound down, and the major stood. "It's late. You'll stay here the rest of the day and probably tonight as well."

"Who is seeing to my horses?"

"They will be cared for," Dru assured him.

"And my weapons?"

"You'll have them back after I report my findings to those who will decide your fate."

As the major and his three warriors were getting ready to leave, Rukh called out to them one last time. "The girl seemed sure you'd take me in."

The major turned back to him. "She may still be right, but she's also just a private. Promises of sanctuary aren't hers to make." He paused at the open door. "Jessira said you broke your leg, and your arm is obviously injured as well. I can send you a Healer if you like."

Rukh thanked him for his offer, and the Stronghold warriors left, and the door locked shut behind them.

Shortly thereafter, an elderly woman, the Healer, came into the small room, Rukh's prison cell. She seemed fascinated by Rukh, staring at his face as though witnessing some exotic animal. She Healed his leg, but, unfortunately, she could find nothing wrong with his arm.

Several more meals followed throughout the day before night fell, or at least Rukh thought it must be since the light around the doorjamb slowly faded to darkness. No one else came to see him, and he found himself wondering if it was a good sign or a bad one.

———◦———

The next morning, Major Barrier returned. He came alone.

"The Home Senate has approved your petition for sanctuary," he said. "You will need to find employment, though. We do not have the wherewithal or desire to indefinitely support the shiftless."

Upon hearing the major's words, Rukh felt a weight lift from his shoulders. "Will I be eligible to join the Home Army?" he asked.

The major glanced at Rukh's right arm, hanging limp at his side and shrugged. "If you can demonstrate the abilities that Cedar, Court, and Jessira insist your kind possess, then perhaps." He held up a cautionary hand. "But you would truly have to be extraordinary to take the place of one of our own. A position in the Home Army is highly coveted."

"And if my arm doesn't Heal?" Rukh asked, working to keep the sudden fear out of his voice.

"Our warriors must be able to fight," Barrier said. "In such a circumstance, a place in the Home Army would not be available to you."

"I don't have any other skills," Rukh said softly, his mind racing as he tried to figure out what else he could do with his life.

"You'll have to learn one. Or do manual labor," Dru said. His professional façade cracked and a flicker of sympathy passed across his face.

Rukh was a Kumma, a warrior by training and birth. He had been bred to protect his home, Ashoka, and those who couldn't protect themselves. It was all he'd ever wanted to do. And now, with his exile, it had all been stripped away from him. And the chance to start fresh and defend a new home might be stillborn as well if his arm didn't Heal.

If Rukh couldn't join Stronghold's Home Army, he would have to do what the people here demanded of him—manual labor, whatever in the unholy hells that meant. His thoughts spiraled into further worry and dread.

With a sigh, he reined in his circular fears. It was only his second day in Stronghold. His time here wasn't yet doomed to end in failure.

He'd be better off simply getting on with his life and sort out his problems anew with every day.

"Come on," the major said, interrupting his thoughts and leading him from the room. "There's someone who's agreed to take you in. You'll be staying with him until you get your feet under you."

"Who is it?" Rukh asked, wondering who would take a chance on a Pureblood. Jessira's early attitude to his kind seemed to be a common one.

"Him." Dru pointed to a stocky man waiting outside. "This is Court Deep, your host. I'll leave you in his care," he said with a nod as he departed.

Court was a few inches shorter than Rukh, but stockier. His dark hair was cut short as was his goatee, and his skin was swarthy like a Sentya's. His hazel eyes seemed to briefly assess Rukh before a half-smile creased his face. "You look like Farn. You'll see him later today after his work is done."

Rukh studied the man who had agreed to take him in, wondering what Court Deep would get out of this situation. "You're Jessira's cousin, aren't you?"

"I am he," Court replied in a formal tone. "I'll be your host. I took in Farn, and for some reason, I've ended up feeling a mite responsible for your kind." He smiled. "Don't ask me why. I must be a masochist."

Rukh smiled, warming to the man. "Thank you for letting me stay with you," he said.

"You're welcome," Court said. "I believe these are yours." He pointed to a number of packs on the ground.

Rukh felt a surge of relief upon seeing his sword and other weapons. He and Court shouldered the bags and made their way out of East Lock, the barracks of Brigade Eastern.

They came upon a wide tunnel, brightly lit with a line of regularly spaced firefly lanterns.

"This is the Southmarch tunnel," Court explained. "It's one of the main east-west roads in Stronghold. There's another one...."

"Let me guess. It's called Northmarch," Rukh said.

Court chuckled. "Only here for a day and already he knows how obvious we are when it comes to naming things."

Rukh smiled. "Or maybe it's just efficient."

"Or maybe you're being generous in describing our unimaginative nature," Court said.

The end of the tunnel opened out onto a large courtyard paved with gray bricks, and Rukh found himself at the base of a silo with a ceiling hundreds of feet above. The space was bright and open with a shaft of sunshine somehow pulled into the cavern. The wide beam of light was focused upon the center of the courtyard, a garden where bushes, flowers, and a small glade of grass surrounded a large oak. Further light came from the hundreds of firefly lanterns suspended from the ceiling, hanging from the walls and railings of the various terraces, and the branches of the tree.

From the courtyard, four tunnels branched off, each leading deeper into the mountain. Heavy, ironwood portcullises were raised above all four openings. If an enemy made it this deep into the mountain, further passage could be barred, and with archers up above, the courtyard would become a killing field. Also, Rukh had seen several more stone gates recessed in the ceiling along the portion of Southmarch leading to here, and he guessed all of Stronghold's tunnels were similarly fortified.

"Crofthold Ware," Court said, gesturing around them. "There's ten Croftholds throughout Mount Fort. All of them are built the same as this one. Each one has a central atrium and ten plots rising up to the top of the Crofthold." He pointed to stairs marching upward to higher floors. "If you want to know where someone lives, all you need is the name of the Crofthold, the plot name, and the flat number."

Rukh pointed to the far side of the courtyard. "Do those tunnels lead to other Croftholds?"

Court nodded. "All the Croftholds are linked to one another through these base passages."

"And eventually, the Southmarch leads to the West Lock and Brigade Western? That's the only other entrance into Stronghold, right?"

Court's eyebrows rose in surprise. "How did you know?"

"I knew about the East Lock and Brigade Eastern and...." Rukh's lips parted into a grin. "I guessed on the name. As for how I knew it was the only other entrance: simple math. The Home Army has fifteen hundred warriors under sword and shield. That many warriors could effectively man only two egress points the size of East Lock. Three gates, and you'd be spread too thin."

Court whistled. "Impressive."

"Not really. It's just simple math."

"Well, it's impressive to a simple scout like me," Court replied.

He led Rukh deeper into the mountain, all the way to Crofthold Lucent—Court's home—and ascended up to Plot Din, the fourth level.

"Not much further," Court said. "My flat number is 423."

Rukh held in a grimace as he followed Court down a whitewashed tunnel. His leg was bothering him again, throbbing like a toothache. His arm wasn't much better, and he hobbled along as best he could.

"We're here."

Thank Devesh.

Court looked at him with concern. "Jessira said you broke your leg and did something to your arm a week or so ago," he said. "Do you want me to send for a Healer?"

"Saw one last night," Rukh said with a grunt as he crossed the threshold into the flat. "She said the leg will be fine. The arm...." He shrugged. "We'll see."

"Then please sit down."

Rukh carefully lowered himself onto the small settee centered on the wall opposite the front door and studied Court's flat.

The space looked to have been carved directly from the mountain, with thick stone walls smoothed over to an adobe-like finish and painted a happy yellow. The small central space—the hearthspace—doubled as both kitchen and sitting room and past it was a doorway leading to the bedroom. The only illumination came from the warm, mellow light of the firefly lantern on the low table next to the settee, although a few unlit lanterns hung from the walls.

"I'm fortunate that I can afford so much space on a poor scout's salary," Court said. "If this was in one of the older Croftholds, I'd be lucky to have a single room."

"There are rich and poor areas of Stronghold?" Rukh asked. Jessira had made her home seem like a classless paradise, but he'd always doubted it. In all of history and in all societies, there were always some who managed to gather wealth and others who didn't. The reasons for why this happened varied from place-to-place and time-to-time, but it was an immutable truth.

Court wore an uncomfortable expression. "There are more desirable areas," he finally answered. "For instance, the older Croftholds are closer to the surface of the mountain. Some even have exterior views. It's all carefully screened off from anyone down below, but who wouldn't want to see the sun and the stars whenever they want?"

"And what about the poor?" Rukh persisted.

"No one here is really poor," Court said quickly, sounding defensive. "Everyone has a place to live and enough food to eat."

It was clear there *were* poor people in Stronghold, but the OutCastes obviously didn't want to admit any such flaws in their society. It might force them to question whether Stronghold really was so much more egalitarian and enlightened than the Pureblood cities. Whatever the reason, Rukh could tell the topic made Court uncomfortable. He decided to change the subject. "Where's Farn?" he asked.

"Working in the kitchens."

"The kitchens?"

"Each plot has a main cafeteria where we gather for meals. It's easier to have one large chimney to funnel out all the smoke and refuse instead of a separate one in each flat," Court explained. "The hearth over there is mostly just for show. I can place some hot rocks in there and maybe bake some bread but not much more."

Rukh was still confused. "What's Farn doing in the kitchens?"

"Cooking, cleaning, whatever the cooks tell him to do," Court said, sounding as if he thought the answer should be self-evident.

"Really?" Rukh asked, dumbfounded. Farn was a warrior. It's all he ever cared about, even more so than Rukh. And given his conservative nature and distaste for work he considered beneath him, Rukh couldn't believe Farn would willingly do a servant's labor.

"It was either that or starve," Court said. "Maybe in Ashoka you can afford to carry deadweight, but here in Stronghold, we can't. Everyone who's healthy either contributes or they're tossed out on their backsides."

"Where they then die."

Court shrugged. "Their life. Their choice." His earlier happy mien on their walk to his flat was now replaced by stern conviction.

The manner by which the OutCastes handled those who were too lazy to do for themselves was actually pretty close to how Ashoka dealt with such people.

"So what do I do now?" Rukh asked.

"If you want to get cleaned up, there's a washroom just down the hall from my flat," Court said. "Jessira's folks have invited you and Farn to dinner tonight."

Rukh hadn't seen Jessira since they'd entered Stronghold, and he almost smiled at the thought of having dinner with her. "Guess I should wear my best," he said.

CHAPTER ELEVEN
EVENING REVELATIONS

*Open your heart and your home and try
not to be an ass in front of strangers.*

~Stronghold aphorism (author unknown)

Jessira's emotions were a roiling mixture of elation and worry. She was joyful at being home, but she was also concerned for Rukh. She hadn't seen him since he'd been hustled off to East Lock where she heard he'd been interrogated for hours. The worst part was the day-long delay before the Senate and Governor-General finally granted Rukh's petition for sanctuary.

During the time Jessira and Rukh had travelled to Stronghold, the idea that he might be denied refuge had never crossed her mind. To her way of thinking, Rukh's acceptance into Stronghold had been a foregone conclusion. It was supposed to be a foundational principle of Stronghold. The OutCastes didn't hold a person's birth against them. All were equal, so long as they were willing to work. It was what she'd always been taught, a point of pride, and something that made her people's culture more civilized than that of the Purebloods.

Apparently not.

Witness Rukh's treatment so far at the hands of the Home Army and leadership. Or the ugly looks thrown Rukh's way by the Shadowcats—simultaneously contemptuous and dismissive. It was an arrogance and disdain sadly similar to Jessira's own behavior when she had first met Rukh. She had hoped such a flaw would be hers alone, but it seemed more reflective of OutCaste society in general.

It was mind-bogglingly hypocritical, but no one else seemed to see it.

As a result, Rukh probably wouldn't have it easy in Stronghold, but at least Court would be the one to host him. Her cousin had already taken in Farn and thought highly of him—which was a minor miracle as far as Jessira was concerned—so he should have no problem getting along with Rukh. Also, since Court lived in Crofthold Lucent—same as Jessira's parents—she could check in on Rukh every now and then. Not *too* often, of course.

Besides, Jessira didn't trust herself around Rukh. *Priya.* She *had* said the word to Rukh. Jessira supposed it might have come out because she had been afraid he was dying. Possible, but not true. Jessira had never been good at lying to herself, and the word certainly didn't mean good friend, like she'd told Rukh. She suspected he knew it, too. In Stronghold, just like Ashoka, it meant beloved.

Jessira grimaced. What a mess. How could she have let such an overwrought, foolish situation come to be? It was like a bad Ashokan drama. Jessira would be lucky if none of this ended in disaster. A flutter of panic threatened to unmake her composure, and Jessira closed her eyes and took a calming breath. *Nothing bad will happen* she kept repeating to herself. The mantra worked, and she soon had her fear under control. Jessira opened her eyes, realizing that tonight would be the first step in the rest of her life. It was a future Rukh couldn't share. That was the end of the matter.

A knock came to her door, and Amma poked her head in. Jessira's amma, Crena Grey, was in her fifties, but still stood straight and tall and was but a few inches shorter than her only living daughter. Her graying hair was pulled back in what Jessira called a mature woman's bun. The phrase was one that always brought a smile to both their faces. In fact, Jessira could count on one hand the number of times Amma had worn her hair in any other fashion. And while Amma's red-gold skin had grown sallow with time, her green eyes remained lively and alert as she scanned Jessira's dress and appearance. She smiled. "You look beautiful," she said. "I'm sure Disbar will approve."

Jessira glanced at herself in the mirror. She *did* look good. The green dress she wore did wonders to hide her flat chest and narrow hips. It almost made her appear curvaceous and womanly, and the high cut above her knees with the open-toed sandals laced around her ankles showed off the part of her that Jessira thought was her best feature: her legs.

"Our guests should arrive any moment," Amma said. "Why don't you come out and help set the table?"

Jessira nodded, smoothing out her green dress one final time. She fleetingly wondered what Rukh would think of how she looked in it. It was more feminine than anything he'd ever seen her wearing. Her face reddened as she remembered Rukh *had*, in fact, seen her in something more womanly. After all, he'd seen her in her camisole.

"What is it?" Her amma asked, apparently noticing her flushed face.

"Nothing," Jessira lied. "Just wondering if Disbar will like my dress."

Her amma gave her a knowing smile. "The man has eyes, doesn't he?"

Jessira forced a smile in response.

As soon as they got the table set, guests started to arrive. First came Cedar and his wife, Laya. Their marriage was unusual in that it was a love match. Cedar came from a moderately wealthy family— their nanna was a skilled tradesman—and Cedar himself was a lieutenant in the Home Army, destined to earn a farm in the Croft. By contrast, Laya's parents were merely laborers, as was Laya herself.

Typically, two people from such disparate backgrounds didn't marry. It was a matter of societal expectations. If the man in question came from wealth, he would command too high a dowry price for a family of modest means. Conversely, if it were the woman who was wealthy, her family would consider a poor suitor unworthy of her attention.

Nevertheless, Cedar had fallen in love with Laya and had refused to marry anyone else. After getting to know her vadina, her sister-in-law, Jessira could understand why. Certainly Laya was attractive enough—with lush curves, dark skin, and startling aqua blue eyes—but her true beauty lay in her gentle, infectious smile and personality. She had a rare quality, a serenity that allowed her to always say the right thing to ease a person's mind and bring laughter to their heart. It was a rare talent, and Jessira secretly believed her brother had actually married *above* his station.

Jessira gave her vadina a warm hug before turning to Cedar. Her brother appeared unchanged from all the other times Jessira had seen him, but on closer inspection, she could tell something was different. It was his eyes—soft and brown like Nanna's—but now, whenever Cedar looked at Jessira, they seemed to warm as they never had when the two of them had been younger. He startled Jessira by pulling her into an embrace.

Next to arrive was her oldest brother, Kart, fourteen years older than Jessira. In fact, she almost thought of him as an uncle. He was thin and wiry with Nanna's brown skin and eyes and had also inherited their nanna's crafting skills, working as a master mason. In his youth, he'd also taken on the job of laborer and field hand, and all his hard work had paid off. Two years ago, he'd been able to lease his own farm. He would soon be the wealthiest of them all. His wife, poor put-upon Jeshni, wasn't with him, though. Likely she was at home with their four young children.

"Court plans on bringing both of the Kummas," Nanna said, surprising Jessira as he came up alongside her. Sateesh Grey, was in his late fifties, but appeared almost seventy. He was of medium height—like Cedar—but slender like Kart, with skin the color of old leather, wrinkled and spotted with age. His brown eyes were rimmed with cataracts, but they were still sharp enough to read Jessira's emotions. He picked up on her disquiet but mistook the reason for it. "I know you don't like Farn, but it only seemed right to allow him to come given that he's a close friend to Rukh Shektan. We owe your Kumma friend more than we can ever hope to repay."

Jessira glanced at her nanna. He was one of the few OutCastes who didn't speak of the Purebloods with contempt or mocking superiority. He'd always met life and people with an open mind and an open heart. It was a lesson more Strongholders would do well to learn.

"Farn Arnicep is *not* one of my favorite people," Jessira agreed.

"Well, for some reason, Court seems to think well of him."

Just then, Disbar Merdant entered her parents' flat. Her fiancé was tall—only a few inches shorter than Rukh, but with a heavier frame. His dark, intense eyes were framed by thick brows while a goatee circumscribed his full lips. Disbar was a passionate man, but sometimes his passion could get the better of him. Then he became like a red-eyed bull, with his curly, ruddy-brown hair almost seeming to stand erect of its own accord. But judging by his smile tonight, he appeared to be in a good mood. He'd even brought fresh flowers, which he placed in Jessira's hands.

She was warmed by the romantic gesture. "Thank you," she said with a smile.

"I know I saw you just this morning, but you have no idea how glad I am to be with you again. For months, I feared you dead," he said solemnly. "And knowing you live, and being able to touch you again...it makes my heart sing with gladness. I thank the First Father and First Mother for bringing you home safely to us. And I vow you will never again need to place yourself in harm's way. Stronghold is your home, and here you should remain."

Jessira was taken aback by his words. His sentiments were

touching but so overwrought and, frankly, presumptuous. She didn't know whether to laugh or be offended by his audaciousness.

"Mercy. Laying it on thick aren't you, Disbar?" Sign said, having just entered the flat and overhearing the words of Jessira's fiancé.

Disbar's moods changed like the tides but were far less predictable. Sometimes when someone poked fun at him, he would storm off, growling over the supposed insult. Less often, he would throw his head back and bellow with laughter. One could never tell how he would respond, and after Sign's gentle mockery, Jessira wondered what he would say. The last thing she needed was for Disbar to make a scene.

Tonight, for whatever reason, rather than react with anger at Sign's gentle ribbing, Disbar chuckled half-heartedly at her cousin's words, although Jessira noticed his eyes still tightened in annoyance.

But no matter his irritation, he also needed to understand the truth: Jessira was a warrior. While Disbar often spoke of how he looked forward to her discharge from the Home Army, for now, it was who she was. "The promise of safety is one none of us can offer, especially to a Silversun," Jessira said, looking him in the eyes and hoping he wouldn't grow angry.

Once again, Disbar surprised her. He laughed, relaxed and generous, as the intensity fled from his eyes. "I love how easily you puncture my self-importance," he said.

Further conversation was interrupted when Court entered the by-now crowded flat. Trailing behind him, moving like Shylows were the two Kummas. Jessira had to remind herself not to stare at Rukh. Instead, she offered him a polite nod, one he returned in kind before he moved on to scan the others. Farn's eyes moved just as restlessly, and surprisingly, he too offered her a polite nod before looking over the others. In her mind, she imagined the two of them were quickly assessing who here represented a threat, which ones were the most dangerous.

Conversation trailed off when the three warriors entered. "You travelled with him?" Nanna asked, whispering to Jessira.

She nodded.

He shuddered. "He watches us like a predator, like a stalking snow tiger." He eyed her askance. "Are you sure he isn't dangerous?"

Jessira smiled in wry amusement at Nanna's words. "I never said he wasn't dangerous," she replied. "The two of them are deadly— more so than anyone you're ever likely to meet."

"He wears an insufferably prideful mien," Disbar remarked. "The taller one, Farn, was like this Rukh of yours but working as a laborer has taught him humility."

Her fiancé's smug satisfaction irked Jessira. Who was Disbar to judge Rukh without first getting to know him? She was about to let Disbar know what she thought of his attitude, but embarrassed self-awareness halted her words. Who was she to judge her fellow OutCastes? Hadn't she once felt the same as they, dismissing Purebloods with the same haughty arrogance? She was no better than anyone else.

Jessira set aside her criticism. "He saved my life," she reminded Disbar. "It's why Amma and Nanna invited him here tonight: in order to thank him properly."

Disbar nodded, forcing a smile. "You're right," he said. "We will provide him an enlightened evening of comfort as his kind would never offer us."

"Except his parents, family, and House. And the Shiyen physician who saved my arm. And many other people in Ashoka," Jessira replied.

Her words earned her an irritated frown from Disbar, who didn't bother responding to her final statement.

The Grey family flat was large—a reflection of her nanna's success as a carpenter and stone mason—with three bedrooms and a hearth-space easily able to accommodate the gathered party of ten. But not everyone could fit around the dining table and several people had to perch on the kitchen counters. However, two of the party had to eat at the sofa. Not surprisingly, those two turned out to be Rukh and Farn.

"I still can't believe you spoke to Baels," Laya said.

"Or went to Ashoka," Kart added. "And managed to escape."

"I didn't escape," Jessira protested. "I've told you all this before. Rukh's family treated me well. Their physicians Healed me and Rukh's amma and nanna took me in. They treated me as one of their own. They didn't have to do any of that."

"Perhaps they're finally growing civilized," Disbar said, a dismissive tone to his voice.

Jessira bit back her annoyance. *His words stem from ignorance not malice*, she reminded herself. However, she did wonder more and more how Rukh had managed to put up with her obnoxious attitude during their time in the Flats. If she had been half as conceited as the rest of Stronghold, she was surprised he hadn't left her behind to rot.

"Did the Kummas really fight Tigons like Cedar says?" Sign asked.

Jessira glanced at the others around the table, noticing the disbelief evident on all their faces—everyone except for Cedar. "You mean like I've also said," she finally replied to Sign. "If you choose to disbelieve...." She shrugged.

"No one can be that skilled," Sign muttered.

"They are, and I've already told you what they could do," Cedar said, sounding tired. "I saw it." He nodded toward Rukh and Farn. "None of our own warriors could hope to stand against those two."

Sign frowned. "I've yet to see any proof of what the two of you claim," she said, a stubborn set to her jaw.

"Why would Cedar or I lie to you or exaggerate?" Jessira asked.

Laya shuddered. "Why don't we leave of all this talk of death and killing? We should be celebrating Jessira's safe return."

"And thanking the man who saved her," Cedar added.

Jessira glanced at him in gratitude. She hadn't expected his support. He met her gaze and winked.

Nanna wore a grave expression. "You're both right," he said, turning to Jessira. "We should be thanking the man who returned you to us. If this Kumma of yours had the skills to keep you alive, then I'm glad for it."

Jessira looked at Rukh, noting the tiredness in his eyes and posture. "He wouldn't be here if it wasn't for me," she said softly.

Disbar frowned, and Jessira could sense his mistrust, but whether of her or Rukh, she couldn't tell. "What do you mean?" he finally asked.

"Rumor says he was banished from his home for being befouled in some way," Laya said.

"Whatever that might mean to a Pureblood," Disbar scoffed.

Jessira turned away from Rukh and in a flat, inflectionless tone, one that didn't hint at the guilt she still felt for Rukh's circumstances, she described her time in Ashoka, explaining the events leading to Rukh's banishment. "His people might have forgiven his new Talents, but his friendship with me was something they couldn't overlook. Because of me, he was all but named a ghrina himself." She glanced around the table. "I think we should honor his sacrifice and not disparage his name or his ancestry. Not after what he lost on my account."

Amma seemed to study Rukh in enigmatic speculation before shifting her eyes back to Jessira. "Call him over," she said.

Rukh must have sensed their regard. He stood, and when he did so, Jessira noticed his arm. It still hung limp and unmoving by his side. She had heard a Healer had seen him last night. So why wasn't he able to use it? Why did he wince whenever it was jostled? Was it so badly injured that it couldn't be Healed?

Jessira prayed not.

"My family would like to thank you," Jessira said, careful to keep her inflection even and untroubled.

He flicked a glance at those seated around the table before saying something to Farn who merely nodded in return. Rukh limped toward them. His leg was still giving him trouble.

"This clumsy fellow is the slayer of Tigons?" Sign whispered to Disbar in a snide snicker. She met Jessira's challenging look with one of her own. "You say he's an amazing warrior. He needs to prove it."

"There's no need to be cruel, Sign," Jessira said. "You know he broke his leg and hurt his arm. He's simply not Healed yet. Test him when he has his health." She stared at her cousin in challenge. "Only make sure all of the Shadowcats are with you. You'll need that many to take him on."

Sign opened her mouth to respond, but just then, Rukh arrived.

"We wished to thank you in person for the safe return of our daughter," Nanna said. "All of us are grateful beyond words."

"Yes. She is precious to all of us," Disbar said, taking hold of one of Jessira's hands.

"Thank you for supper, ma'am," Rukh said to Jessira's amma with a polite nod. "It's been a long time since I've had a hot meal."

"During your travels, you must have had *some* warm food," Kart said.

"I did," Rukh agreed. "But what we had wasn't exactly fine dining. Not like this, anyway."

Jessira smiled at Rukh's words. She still remembered Cook Heltin's miracles of cuisine. Compared to what Rukh had grown up with, her own family's supper, heavy on substance but light on spices, must have seemed bland and tasteless. Rukh was just too polite to say so.

"Fine dining?" Nanna asked. "I'm glad you think so." He glanced in Jessira's direction. "My daughter spoke of how every meal in Ashoka was a work of art."

"Our food is different," Rukh replied. "But it is the warm and generous spirit that transforms any meal into an expression of love. And the cold and cruel heart who makes even the most sumptuous of feasts taste like ashes."

"Where did you read that?" Jessira asked. The words couldn't have been his own. Rukh was usually plainspoken, never eloquent like he'd just been.

"*Sooths and Small Sayings*, by Tramed Billow."

"You're a scholar?" Kart asked in disbelief.

"Hardly. I just like to read sometimes."

"But only scholars bother with *Sooths and Small Sayings*. It's too dense and philosophical," Kart persisted.

"I'm no scholar. I just like to read, and that particular phrase from *Sooths* just happened to stay with me." Rukh said with a smile.

Jessira shook her head and hid a smile. She thought she knew him so well, but he still managed to surprise her.

"Court tells me you'll be working the kitchens as soon as your leg is Healed," Disbar said, changing the subject.

"So I've been told," Rukh said. "I still hold out hope I might be accepted into the Home Army."

"You think laboring is beneath you?" Laya asked. She appeared insulted by Rukh's words. "To serve and maintain home and hearth is not a meaningless use of a person's time and energy."

"Kummas serve," Rukh answered in a calm, even tone. "It is the guiding principle of my Caste. We serve by defending those whose lives are placed in our hands. It's a holy trust. It's who we are. Without it, our lives have no meaning."

Upon hearing his statement, Amma stood and came around the table. She gave Rukh a warm embrace. "I hope you find the meaning you seek," she said. "As for me, I'm simply grateful to have my daughter back." She gave Rukh's hands a final thankful squeeze.

He nodded acknowledgement before turning to Farn. "I think it's time for us to go and let these fine people celebrate without strangers interrupting them."

"Yes, sir," Farn said, coming to his feet.

"You're not a stranger," Jessira protested, rising as well. "The dinner was in your honor. My family wanted to get to know you better."

Rukh glanced her way and smiled. "I appreciate that, but it's still time for me and Farn to go." He hesitated. "We've got a lot to sort out."

Just before Rukh stepped outside, Jessira called out to him. "Rukh," she said, bringing him to a halt. "Thank you for keeping me safe," she said, infusing her words with shades of meaning only he would understand.

"It was my honor," he said. With that, he pulled the door shut. It felt like the metaphorical closing of a very different future she might have had.

"You see what I mean?" Farn asked. "You and I are Purebloods, which in the eyes of many OutCastes makes *us* ghrina." He barked in laughter. "Ironic, is it not?"

Rukh nodded though his mind wasn't focused on Farn's words. He was thinking about Jessira. He'd never seen her looking so lovely, so feminine. Her hair was usually pulled back in a severe ponytail, but tonight it hung free, framing her face and softening her beauty. And the green dress she had worn—it had been the same shade as her eyes, clinging to her like a sinuous wave.

When he had first seen Jessira tonight, he had wanted to do nothing more than drink in the sight of her. But he couldn't. They were acquaintances who had travelled a long road together. Nothing more.

"It's the woman, isn't it?" Farn asked.

"What woman?" Rukh asked, finally focusing on his cousin's words.

"Jessira. The OutCaste woman. The one you love."

Rukh startled. "Is it that obvious?"

"Only to those who know you."

"And my feelings for someone not of my Caste—they don't disgust you?" Rukh asked, taken aback by Farn's mild response. This was not the same cousin who had left with him on the Trial for Nestle so many months ago.

Farn shrugged. "It would have at one time, but I've been in a city of OutCastes for months now. I find my prior unchallenged understanding of morality no longer serves."

Rukh *was* surprised by his cousin's growth during his time in Stronghold. "Please don't tell anyone else how I feel about Jessira," he said to Farn. "It would cause problems for her and her family."

"I'll keep it to myself," Farn promised. They walked in silence for a few minutes before Farn spoke again. "They are an odd people, these OutCastes," he said. "Prior to marriage or even engagement, they are so free in what they can do, even the women; but once wedding vows are exchanged, their lives become rigid. Within their families, the men lead, and their women follow."

"And are all of them so arrogant?" Rukh asked.

"No. Not all. Court, Cedar, Laya, and most of the laborers are decent people. Many of the others, though…." he shuddered. "I won't miss them once I get home."

Home. Rukh stared ahead, remembering Ashoka and his family. There would never be a homecoming for him. Whatever Farn had been experiencing for the past five or six months was something Rukh would have to endure for the rest of his life.

"I'm sorry. You didn't need to hear that," Farn said. He must have realized what Rukh was thinking.

"Why are you still here?" Rukh asked, wanting to change the subject.

His cousin grimaced. "Ever since that fragging Shylow attack, my head hasn't been right," he said. "I've been struggling with dizzy spells, every day, sometimes hourly. They've only recently gotten better. I couldn't leave because I couldn't walk straight."

"But now you can," Rukh said.

Farn smiled faintly. "Now I can, but I'm so out of shape. I've got to train hard if I want to be able to make it home. I figure it'll take me a month or two before I'm ready to go."

"It'll still be winter then," Rukh reminded him.

"The river flowing under Stronghold empties into the Gaunt...."

"And the Gaunt leads to Ashoka," Rukh finished. "What about the river being frozen? You won't be able to take a boat."

"The OutCastes have ways of traveling over frozen water. If they can do it, so can I."

Rukh hoped his cousin was right. He'd hate for him to die when waiting just a few more months could see him home with far less risk. "I'll help you get back in shape as best I can," Rukh promised. "Just make sure you know what you're doing out on the water."

Farn didn't respond at first. "You sure you can't come with me?" he eventually asked in a diffident tone.

"I'm Unworthy, remember?"

"Unless the Chamber of Lords decides otherwise."

"What do you mean?" Rukh asked. This was the first he had heard this.

"The Chamber can reverse any of their judgments. It's one of their prerogatives. I'm sure it's something your nanna is working on."

Law and history had always fascinated Farn. If he said the Chamber could overturn Rukh's judgment, then it was probably true. Nevertheless, Rukh held little hope that the Chamber would set aside their earlier decision. What reason would they have to do so?

A thought struck him just then. "When you get home, tell no one about your ability to Blend," he advised. "It'll only cause you problems. And if anyone challenges you on it, lie."

Farn nodded. "I wish you'd taken your own advice."

CHAPTER TWELVE
FINDING A WAY

*I've travelled far and wide, visiting many cities, seeing their beauty,
but none of them compared to Hammer. And whenever I returned home,
I would be reminded of the blessings in my life:
to live amongst such elegance and grace.*

~*The Sorrows of Hume, AF 1789*

"It's not getting any better, is it?" Court asked.

Rukh didn't bother responding. The sharp bark of pain as he struggled to get his arm into the sleeve of his shirt should have been answer enough. Its dull, dead weight had him terrified.

He tried to force the arm into the shirtsleeve, but a fierce twinge in his shoulder, a harbinger of a more fiery pain, immediately had him backing off. Damn it!

"Let me help," Court said. He gently lifted Rukh's arm and eased it into the shirtsleeve.

Rukh nodded his 'thanks', but the fear he felt for his situation remained. He'd been in Stronghold for three weeks, and his arm showed no signs of improving. He'd done active stretching and passive stretching; he'd applied heat and ice; he'd let it rest and even tried to exercise it—anything he could think of that might help, but so far nothing was working. The arm remained a painful, lifeless anchor hanging at his side.

He went to pack away his unspooled bedroll, and the unkempt blanket draped over it. Farn's bedding was already neatly folded and tucked away in a corner. His cousin had arisen well before first light, training for the long road home.

"I'll take care of your roll," Court said.

Rukh flushed with humiliated helplessness as Jessira's cousin cleared away his mess. "I wish someone could tell me what's wrong with my arm," Rukh said, turning aside to hide his reddened face.

"None of the Healers Peddananna sent you to could help?" Court asked.

"No. They all said the same thing: there's nothing wrong with the arm," Rukh replied. "They're wrong, but they just don't know what it is." He shook his head. "I just wish I hadn't wasted so much of Master Grey's money to learn such a worthless answer."

On his own, Rukh wouldn't have been able to afford the services of even one of Stronghold's Healers, much less every one of them, but Jessira's nanna—Master Grey—had been generous. He'd paid all of Rukh's costs without a second thought. *"Consider it my way of repaying the kindness your parents showed Jessira when they took her in,"* he had said at the time.

Rukh appreciated Master Grey's help, but he also wasn't comfortable relying on Jessira's nanna for any more assistance. The man had already done too much for him. Asking for anything more would feel too much like begging. It was past time for Rukh to find his own way.

Just then, a stabbing pain in his shoulder reminded him just how difficult such a proposition might be. Training with a sword was out of the question, and even Rukh's work as a laborer was a challenge. It would have been impossible if not for the help of so many. Court was kindness itself, helping Rukh get dressed, while Farn and the other laborers helped him whenever they saw him struggling to perform tasks that required two arms rather than one.

Rukh was grateful to all of them, especially his fellow workers. The lowest members of Stronghold's society were insular and hard, but they looked after their own. At first, it hadn't been easy to get to know them. In fact, during the first meeting with the other laborers, mistrust and dislike had lifted off them like a heat haze. They had probably assumed Rukh would be an arrogant Pureblood, complaining that the work was beneath his station—at one time, Farn certainly had—but Rukh wasn't like that.

He couldn't afford to be as proud, especially when his right arm was as useless as a mute singer. If Rukh had to get his fingernails dirty, so be it. The labor needed doing, and Rukh made sure to give his all to whatever task he'd been assigned. His nanna would have expected nothing less. As a result, the suspicion and animosity from most of the other laborers eventually changed to acceptance and even friendliness.

Of course, there were still some who resented—even hated— Rukh's mere presence in Stronghold. For them, Rukh would always be an abomination. There had even been an attack by a group of thugs during Rukh's first week in Stronghold. Even one-armed, they hadn't posed much of a challenge. A few broken noses had sent the rest running, but Rukh had remained troubled by the attack.

Too many Strongholders had an attitude of smug superiority toward Purebloods, including those from the city's higher social strata. They were far more clever, though, expressing their displeasure in subtle ways, such as muttered comments meant to be overheard about unmannered Purebloods or pretending not to see him when he attempted to buy food at the market. From Rukh's perspective, all of it was meant to get across a simple fact: he was the unwanted outsider in their pristine, perfect city.

Their behavior put the lie to Jessira's claim that her people didn't judge others based on their birth. They clearly did, and Rukh couldn't help but wonder if his own people had treated Jessira as poorly as many of her kind treated him. If they had, it was a wonder she had stayed in Ashoka as long as she had. Rukh wouldn't have. In fact, other than Farn, Cedar, Court, and Laya, if he was forced to leave Stronghold, there would be precious few people he would miss.

What of Jessira? a soft voice whispered in his thoughts. *Would you not miss her?*

Rukh mentally shrugged. He was a Kumma, and he would always live by the strictures of his Caste. Since their arrival in Stronghold, he'd made sure they barely saw one another. A few chance meetings in the hallways was it, nothing more. It was for the best.

"What will you do?" Court asked, interrupting Rukh's thoughts.

"I don't know. There's a man I work with, a laborer named Setter Reesh. He thinks he might be able to help. He says the problem isn't in the arm but in the shoulder. The Healers I've spoken to are certain he's wrong." He looked to Court. "What do you think?"

"Sometimes Healers think they know everything, or act like they do, even when they don't," Court replied. "You have to remember: there were but six Shiyens amongst the Fifty-five and only one of them a physician. You wouldn't know it by talking to our Healers, but I imagine a lot of the knowledge that Hammer possessed has been lost to them. Besides, I know Setter. A lot of the laborers who can't afford a Healer's price go to him. He knows what he's doing."

Rukh considered Court's advice, unsure why he placed such importance on the man's opinion. It was odd. He'd only known Court for three weeks, and already, he trusted him implicitly.

Maybe it was because Court was so open and honest, rare traits. For instance, while he was rightly proud of his people's accomplishments, he wasn't blind to their faults. He saw the problems with Stronghold's society, and they bothered him. Of course, Court was wise enough to keep his opinion limited to those he knew and trusted. Many would not have reacted well to his words.

"If you're worried he might do more harm than good, don't be. I've heard of a few cases where Setter was able to help when the Healers couldn't," Court added, mistaking Rukh's silence for uncertainty.

Rukh nodded. "I'll talk to him," he said.

Rukh hissed in pain.

"Do you want me to stop" Court asked, pausing in his manipulation of Rukh's right arm.

Rukh shook his head. "No. It's helping. Keep going." He hissed again as Court lifted the arm until it was above Rukh's head. A few days ago, such a movement would have been impossible.

It seemed Setter Reesh had been correct. It hadn't been Rukh's arm that had been damaged. It had been his shoulder. Setter claimed that Rukh had strained a bundle of nerves running down from the neck, through the axilla, and into the arm. He had Healed the inflammation, but Rukh would have to do regular exercises if he wanted to get back the full use of his arm. And just two weeks later, while Rukh was still limited to passive range of motion movements, he could already feel both strength and flexibility returning. Soon, he'd be able to do these exercises himself.

"What do you have planned tonight?" Rukh asked.

"Preema invited me to dinner with her family."

Rukh grinned, nodding understanding.

For the past several months, Court had been spending more and more time with Preema Folls, Laya's cousin. Preema's family had started out as laborers, but several years ago her nanna had completed his twenty-five years in the Army. He was now a farmer, which meant he was a man of means. But Court's interest in Preema wasn't because of her newfound wealth. Nor was it solely because she was pretty. It was because of the kind of person Preema was. Rukh had never met a happier, more optimistic person. She always wore a glad smile on her face and had a clever quip at the ready.

Even Farn wasn't immune to her humor. His cousin, usually so touchy about being mocked, would grin whenever it was Preema doing the teasing. Sometimes, he would even laugh. A year ago, it would have been unthinkable to see Farn so relaxed. Despite his troubles with the OutCastes, his time in Stronghold had changed him for the better.

In fact, witnessing his cousin's laughter had been a revelation for Rukh. If Farn could find moments of joy here in Stronghold, then why not Rukh? Stronghold wasn't perfect—what city was?—but maybe with time, some of the arrogance and contempt Rukh faced would fade. And with his arm strengthening, maybe he could still join the Army.

For the first time in weeks, Rukh felt a faint stirring of hope.

"Done," Court said.

Rukh gave his shoulder a slow, final roll before pulling on his shirt. "Off to go clean the latrines," he said, injecting false joviality into his voice.

For the most part, he liked the men and women with whom he worked, but he certainly didn't enjoy the labor. Cooking and serving in the dining hall wasn't so bad, but the cleaning up afterward, or worse, emptying chamber pots and wiping down the latrines—it was filthy, smelly, and disgusting.

"It's a dirty job, but of all the Purebloods I know, you're the one best suited to doing it," Court said with an easy grin.

Sateesh Grey stood silently in the shadows of a corner and watched unobserved as Rukh Shektan swept Crofthold Lucent's dining hall. He'd actually been observing the Pureblood for weeks now, and in all that time, he had never seen or heard the Kumma act in an arrogant fashion or complain that the work was beneath him. He worked hard and did as he was told. Sateesh found himself impressed by the man's diligence, as well as his charm and humility. It seemed he was everything Jessira claimed: warm, considerate, and hard working. Which made what he had to do now even more onerous. Sateesh sighed. Why couldn't Rukh Shektan have been what everyone expected of a Pureblood: arrogant and hateful?

"How is your arm?" Sateesh asked, stepping out of the corner and approaching Rukh.

The Pureblood paused in his work and looked up. As always, his initial assessing gaze reminded Sateesh of a snow tiger's, and he had to force himself not to flinch. "It's getting stronger," Rukh replied a moment later. "I'm hoping to start training again in a few weeks."

"You still hope to join the Army?" Sateesh asked.

Rukh quirked a wry grin. "I can't see myself *not* serving as a warrior. It was what I was bred to do."

"And it wouldn't hurt that you would no longer have to clean out the latrines and chamber pots," Sateesh said with an answering smile. He was surprised by the fondness he felt for the young Kumma.

"No. It certainly won't," Rukh said in agreement.

"Will we see you tonight for dinner?" Sateesh asked, betraying none of the concerns he felt toward the Pureblood.

Rukh's demeanor grew guarded.

Sateesh saw Jessira wear a similar expression whenever talk in their house turned to the Kumma. He now understood why. Despite what his daughter and the Pureblood claimed, he knew there was more between them than mere friendship. It was evident to anyone who truly knew Jessira. Thankfully, neither she nor Rukh had acted upon their feelings. It would have been a disaster if they had. In fact, from what Sateesh could tell, the two of them seemed intent on avoiding the other. They rarely interacted except on those few occasions when they accidentally ran into each other in the halls of Crofthold Lucent.

It was how Sateesh preferred matters to remain between his daughter and Rukh. It was why he was here now, and why he had invited Rukh to dinner. He meant to ensure Jessira's honor would be maintained.

Right now, Rukh was at his lowest, his pride likely stinging at the thought of Jessira seeing him dirty, sweaty, and smelly. But what about when Rukh was a warrior once again? His self-esteem would return. Would he then think himself worthy of Jessira's affections?

It could never be—not because Rukh wasn't a good, decent person—but because Jessira was already promised to Disbar Merdant. Only for the most important reasons could such an engagement be ended. After all, a person's word was their bond, and Sateesh would never allow Jessira to destroy her future because of some infatuation for Rukh Shektan. He needed to make sure the Kumma understood that.

"I know you have strong feelings for my daughter," Sateesh said. "I also know she might have once felt the same way about you."

If anything, Rukh's expression grew even more closed off.

"It isn't obvious, except to those of us who know her well," Sateesh continued. "And I've seen how you hide your feelings whenever she's mentioned. Either you hate her or you love her. I'm guessing it's love. Otherwise, you would have never come to our city."

"It doesn't matter what I feel," Rukh said.

"No. It doesn't," Sateesh agreed.

Rukh didn't answer. His head was bent down as he resumed sweeping the floor. "Why are you telling me this?" he finally asked, lifting his head to look Sateesh in the eyes.

"So you are clear on what I expect of both you and my daughter," Sateesh replied. "From what I can tell, you've been a true friend to her, protecting her reputation. It makes me believe you're an honorable man, and I hope you always will be. And that you'll never do anything untoward with regards to Jessira."

"Is that why you're inviting me to dinner tonight?" Rukh asked. "Jessira won't be there, and you and Mistress Grey can lay down the law and make sure I stay out of her life?" He snorted in derision. "You don't have to worry."

Sateesh grimaced, not expecting the Pureblood's insight. In some ways, the invitation to dinner tonight *had* been an insult. He just hadn't expected Rukh to see the slight. The man continued to surprise him with his hidden depths and awareness. "I am sorry if I offended you," Sateesh said, somewhat chastened.

Rukh gave a sardonic smile. "Ah, yes. The apology that is anything but."

"Then I am sorry *for* offending you," Sateesh added.

"Why? For insulting me or thinking me incapable of honor?"

Sateesh sighed. He'd handled this badly. "For both," he said. "You're not at all what any of us expected. You work hard, and you're doing your best to fit in amongst us. You deserve better treatment than you or your cousin, Farn, have received."

Rukh seemed to consider his words. "Apology accepted," he said. "Was there any other reason you wanted to talk to me?"

Sateesh hesitated, still feeling guilty for offending the man. "My wife and I would both like get to know you better. We should have done so long ago. Will you forgive us and allow it?"

Rukh nodded. "In that case, instead of your flat, why don't you come down to Court's? We'll make you a Kumma dinner."

———◆———

"Tell me again what time they're coming over," Farn demanded as he helped set the table.

When Rukh had first come to him earlier today with the idea of hosting a dinner for Jessira's family, including her parents, Farn had thought he was joking. Prepare a meal in a few hours? It wasn't enough time. Not if it was to be done right. So he had explained, but Rukh had been insistent. Farn still thought it was a stupid idea, but somehow they'd managed to pull it off. The food was ready, and Court's flat had never looked so good.

"You're leaving in a few weeks," Rukh said. "I'm here for the duration of my life maybe. I thought it might be nice to share a proper Kumma meal with the people who have taken us in and helped us out so much. Show them Ashokan hospitality."

"Even though Jessira's parents insulted you?"

Rukh sighed. "We've already gone over this. If I want to fit in here, I've got to be willing to overlook some things I normally wouldn't. Besides, Jessira's parents were only doing what good parents are supposed to do: look out for their daughter's future."

Farn shook his head. "I don't think I'll ever understand you. You know, sometimes people really are just jackholes. Not every stranger is a friend you've yet to meet."

"What?" Rukh asked, looking confused.

Farn shook his head. "Never mind. Just promise me you'll never change."

He would miss his cousin when it came time to leave Stronghold. When they had been children, Rukh had overlooked

Farn's glum outlook and drew him into what would become a deep friendship. The brotherhood he had shared with Rukh, Jaresh, and Keemo had been the most important relationships in Farn's life.

Rukh, Farn, Keemo, and Jaresh. Their lives had been an endless summer of wonder, always something new to explore and learn and laugh over. They had grown up together, trained together, done everything together. And they all had their roles to play. Farn was the dour voice of reason; Keemo was the optimist; Jaresh the thinker; and Rukh had been the one to help them see the best in one another, binding them until they were as close as brothers.

Together they had been able to accomplish anything.

But no more.

Keemo. How could he be gone? Even now, there were moments when Farn would think to find him, wanting to share an insight or a humorous event. Keemo always laughed with him. His friend, who Farn loved more than the breath in his lungs.

"What's wrong?" Rukh asked.

"I was just remembering Keemo and Jaresh."

"I miss them, too."

A knock at the door interrupted whatever else he might have said.

Rukh leaned back in his chair and listened as the others chatted. Dinner had gone well. Since Stronghold's fare was universally bland—the only seasoning they used seemed to be salt and garlic—the OutCastes had been hesitant to try the spicy food Rukh and Farn had prepared. It only took a few bites for their reluctance to fade into expressions of surprised delight. Then they had been more than happy to try anything offered. Mistress Grey had especially seemed to enjoy the food. She had worn a look of rapture during the entire meal. In this, she was just like her daughter, Jessira.

"And you eat this well every day in Ashoka?" Master Grey asked.

"Better," Rukh answered. "I'm a terrible cook, but Farn can do a passable job. He was the one in charge of tonight's dinner."

At his words, the OutCastes shared disbelieving glances, most likely wondering if Rukh was joking.

"Jessira always claimed Ashokan cuisine was a work of art," Cedar said. "I thought she was exaggerating, but I guess not. And if you consider this food to be only 'passable', I'd love to know what you consider good."

"Why haven't you ever made dinner like this before?" Court asked, sounding plaintive. "It's the least you could have done, especially with me letting you stay here and everything."

"Time and spices," Farn replied, ticking off the two items. "Work keeps us busy, and Rukh hardly brought any spices with him."

"After eating this, I'm not sure whether to laugh or cry," Preema said with a soft laugh. "This might have been the best meal I've ever had."

"Jessira saw and experienced so much," Laya said with a sigh. "I wish I could experience half of what she did. It makes me jealous."

"So when I invited you to dinner your first night here, and you complimented my cooking, was this what you were comparing it to?" Mistress Grey asked, a stern expression on her face. "It seems you weren't entirely honest about what you thought of the meal."

"I was telling the truth," Rukh said. "It *is* the warm and generous spirit that transforms any meal into an expression of love. And the cold, cruel heart that makes even the most sumptuous of feasts taste like ashes. It is what I said then, and I meant it. The food isn't important. It's the spirit in which it's offered."

Afterward, the talk moved on to other topics, and everyone spoke together, laughing and enjoying themselves. Even Farn involved himself in the conversation, sharing stories of Ashoka or observations of life in Stronghold. Rukh laughed along with the others, happy as he hadn't been since the days before leaving Ashoka for the caverns of the Chimeras. This was the most relaxed he could recall being in months.

All of the worries about his place in Stronghold—the slights and slurs he had endured—none of it mattered tonight. Tonight, he could simply enjoy the company of others.

"...So then at the Wrath, they held up these signs and when the fanfare for our school began, they flipped them over, and it spelled out, *We're Dumbasses*," Farn said.

"They didn't," Laya said, holding a hand to her mouth as she stifled a giggle.

The others at the table—Cedar, Court, Preema, Master Grey, and Mistress Grey—didn't harbor such reserve as they laughed whole-heartedly.

"What was their reaction after they found out what you did?" Preema asked, still smiling.

"They were furious. Their dean wanted us suspended, but we got off easy," Rukh replied. "*Our* dean was never really mad at us. He yelled at us a lot, but I think he was actually proud of what we did."

Farn shook his head in disbelief. "How *did* Keemo ever come up with something so clever?"

Rukh's smile slipped. He still thought of Keemo every day, and every day, he still wished his friend were with them.

"He was one of those who died on the Flats, was he not?" Laya asked.

Rukh's smile slipped further. "He was."

"If it hadn't been for him, all of us would have died," Cedar said solemnly.

"Then we should raise a toast in his honor and memory," Master Grey said. "To Keemo and all the friends and family we've lost."

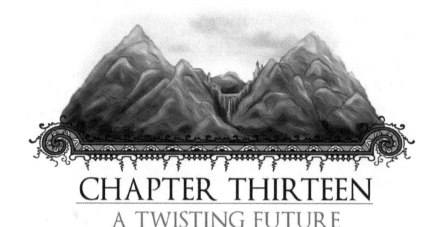

CHAPTER THIRTEEN
A TWISTING FUTURE

*During the Trials of our lives, amidst periods of toil and trouble,
our footsteps strike the ground lonely. But during moments of triumph,
many share the path with us.*

~ *A Wandering Notion by Shone Brick, AF 1784*

"Can we talk about it?" Disbar asked.

"Talk about what?" Jessira replied.

Disbar frowned in annoyance. She knew what he meant. She had to.

Disbar had taken the day off so the two of them could have a picnic in the courtyard of Crofthold Lucent. He had hoped an afternoon together would help them get past the frigid formality that had grown between them during her long absence. Before her departure, Disbar hadn't loved Jessira, but the seeds had been there. He *could* have loved her, and it would have been easy. She had never been submissive, but she had seemed to welcome her role in their upcoming marriage. She would have set aside her duties as a scout and happily borne his children. She would have taken care of home and hearth while he provided.

But this new Jessira…it would take time to get to know her.

Since her return, she had been distracted, even irritable. She was a very different woman from the one who had departed Stronghold many months earlier. Disbar worried she would never again be the person he had once known.

He poured himself a glass of wine—a rich red—and took a long drink. His frown faded, and a smile took its place as he took in the beauty of the Courtyard. The afternoon sun reflected through a series of mirrors, shining down amongst the leaves and branches of the oak tree, as well as the green azaleas and winter flowers growing in the center of the courtyard. The hundreds of firefly lanterns suspended from the ceiling, walls, and branches of the oak were unlit for now; but late at night, when they were turned low, they twinkled like stars in the heavens.

Then, the place became magical.

"I know you're still getting used to living here," Disbar said. He hesitated before reaching for her hand resting on the table. He cupped it as lightly as he would a butterfly and let out a soft exhalation of relief when she didn't pull back. "I was wondering if you were willing to discuss about this distance that's grown between us."

Jessira met his eyes. "I know I haven't been easy to get along with," she said. "I'm sorry. It's just.…" Her words trailed off, and a look of regret stole over her. She was silent as she looked away, staring at a group of children playing tag.

"It's what?" Disbar prodded gently.

"We treat Purebloods worse than I was treated in Ashoka," she said.

Disbar scowled. "So this is about the Kumma?" he said, trying his best to mask his sudden suspicion. The Pureblood and Jessira had spent many months alone, just the two of them. Jessira insisted nothing improper had occurred, but it was hard to believe that *some* feelings hadn't arisen between them—at least it should have on

Rukh's part. Jessira wasn't classically beautiful, but she was certainly pretty enough to incite the lust of a barbaric Pureblood. And Disbar didn't for an instant believe the ridiculous story Rukh had apparently told Major Barrier, the one where he claimed to think of Jessira as a child. During the dinner Jessira's parents had hosted several weeks back, the Pureblood hadn't looked upon Jessira as a man would when seeing a child. The expression on Rukh's face had been that of a man struggling to control his admiration for a beautiful woman.

Jessira withdrew her hand. "How many times do I have to tell you? Rukh is just a friend. Nothing more," she said.

Disbar studied her profile over the rim of his goblet as he took another sip of wine. He wasn't sure whether to believe her. Since her return to Stronghold, he'd kept himself apprised of Jessira's movements. On a few occasions, especially early on after her return to Stronghold, she had gone to the kitchens and areas where the laborers worked. She had sought out the Kumma, but at no time had she been alone with him. She'd seen the Pureblood in a few public places or in the company of family, but otherwise she had kept her distance from him.

"Then why the concern?" he asked. "He's a grown man. He doesn't need your help to find his way."

"Because our treatment of them—Rukh and Farn—says something about who we are as a people," Jessira said. "It makes me wonder if our culture is really any better than that of the Purebloods."

"Of course we're better," Disbar replied, aghast. "Purebloods would kill our kind without a second thought."

"And yet, I survived their city without harm," Jessira reminded him. "Rukh's family took me in and treated me as one of their own, even after their son was exiled on my account."

Disbar fell silent, not having a ready response to her claims. He had trouble believing Purebloods could be as loving and generous as she claimed. It flew in the face of everything he'd been taught about them.

"We have to be better than before," Jessira continued. "After all, the people of Ashoka never tried to murder me. I understand Rukh has already had a few run-ins with some of our young men."

"Run-ins?" Disbar scoffed. "Just some youths with too much drink in them is what I heard."

"They had knives."

Disbar kept his face studiously blank. No one—especially Jessira—could know of his role in what had happened to the Kumma. And besides, none of it changed what was more important: Jessira's ongoing interest in Rukh Shektan. She had been keeping up with the events in the Pureblood's life. Disbar didn't like it and made his feelings on the matter clear, including his frustration with their ongoing lack of intimacy. He was tired of waiting.

"I've chosen you," Jessira said, answering his complaint. "No one will come between us. We will be together when we're married."

"But we will not be together now?" Disbar asked.

"Give me time."

"Time for what?" Disbar asked, exasperated. "You leave for maneuvers soon and after that, it's home for a week and gone for three more. When will you be ready? For mercy's sake, we're engaged. And in a few months, your body will be the temple through which our children will be born."

Jessira stiffened. Her gaze locked on his, and Disbar involuntarily shrank away from the outrage in her eyes. "Is that what you think my role will be? To simply bear your children?"

"I didn't mean to imply—"

"You didn't mean to imply that I should feel some fragging guilt about bearing your children?" Jessira said in derision.

Disbar's nostrils flared. How dare she speak to him like that? "It's because of the Kumma, isn't it? You and I never had these problems before you left. *He* is the reason we argue so much. You love him."

"He has nothing to do with our problems."

"Then what is it?" Disbar demanded. He noticed she hadn't denied his accusation.

Jessira's chin raised, proud and haughty as the mountains. "During all the time I was gone, I kept my vows to you," she said. "And it wasn't enough. You've made your distrust of me apparent."

"I trust you," Disbar said, knowing how mealy-mouthed his words sounded. He hoped she didn't notice.

"I know you've had me watched," Jessira hissed, leaning close. "Your cousins. They follow me everywhere."

Disbar licked his lips, suddenly nervous. "So I asked them to look in on you a time or two. How else am I supposed to react when you tell me that this Pureblood of yours was exiled because of his relationship with you? You said you are only friends, but I find it hard to believe that he would have been banished for mere friendship's sake." He shrugged. "Besides, I just wanted to make sure you were safe. The Kummas, who knows what they might do."

"I was with Rukh for months on end, and I was never unsafe in his presence," Jessira replied.

Disbar's jaw clenched, and his anger thudded against his skull. It stole his good sense, causing him to speak words he immediately regretted. "Were you safe in his bedrolls?"

Jessira's face grew impassive, and she took slow, deep breaths. Her flushed face revealed her fury. "We're done," she announced, rising to her feet.

"Please don't go," Disbar said. "I apologize for my rash words." He came to his feet as well. "What I said was thoughtless and spoken in the heat of the moment. Of course I trust you."

She shook her head. "No, you don't," Jessira said. "And I can't abide a man who has so little faith in me and has so little regard for my intelligence."

Disbar couldn't believe what he was hearing. What was Jessira saying? He gritted his teeth. "Don't you think you're taking this a little too seriously?" he asked, trying to mollify her. "We're simply having a minor disagreement. Why don't we talk about this later; when we've both calmed down somewhat?"

Jessira scrubbed a hand over her face before sighing heavily. "Yes, we'll talk again later, but it doesn't change the fundamentals of our situation," she said. "I need someone who respects me, trusts me, believes in me."

Disbar grimaced. "Somewhere in those words, I sense a threat."

Jessira shrugged. "Interpret it however you wish," she said. "I can only tell you what's been growing in my heart since I returned to Stronghold."

Disbar braced his fists against the table and leaned forward. "If you end our engagement, everyone will know exactly what kind of woman you are."

His words must have sparked Jessira's anger once again. Her eyes flashed in warning. "Somewhere in those words I sense a threat," she noted. "And I never said anything about ending our engagement." Her own fists were balled.

"Interpret my words however you wish," Disbar snarled. "But I can only tell you what's been growing in my heart since you returned to Stronghold. I won't be made to look like a fool."

Jessira stood straight, her posture rigid. "I've said all I need to," she said. "I'm done here." She paused, glancing back at Disbar. "And if I see any of your cousins following me, I'll break their legs." With that, she was gone, striding away, the fury obvious in her posture.

"What did you say to her?" a young boy asked Disbar after Jessira left. "People come here to make kissy-faces, not fight."

"Oh, shut up."

———————●———————

Rukh sat on a weatherworn outcropping upon the lower slopes of Mount Fort and stared out into the dark depths of the Croft. Last week's snow still covered the fields, leaving them looking like a strange desert of gray and white. South of the valley and standing tall were the gnarled, pitted heights of Mount Axe and Mount Salt, anchoring the borders of Tear Drop Lake. At night, the water sparkled like scattered diamonds under the light of the moon.

"You ready to head inside?" Farn asked, his breath misting in the cold.

"Not yet," Rukh said, his voice sounding loud in the quiet winter night.

Since his Healing a month ago, Rukh had spent almost all his free time helping Farn get back into fighting trim. The drills were essential in order for his cousin to survive the journey back to Ashoka. Unfortunately, for most of that time, all Rukh had been able to do was watch and advise as Farn practiced. It had been frustrating, but finally the day came when Rukh's injured arm was strong enough to allow him to participate fully in the practices as well. It had been exhilarating to wield a sword once again, even if he had to use his off hand—his strong arm was still too weak to tightly grip any weapon, but day-by-day, it was improving.

He was determined to reclaim his lost skill and become again the warrior he had once been. It would take hard work, but it was work Rukh relished. It was certainly better than serving in the kitchens or cleaning the latrines. Farn, of course, felt the same way, so every day, before and after work, they headed out to the flat lands of Tear Drop Lake or the steep slopes of Mount Salt and Mount Axe and honed their skills and bodies as they had when students at the House of Fire and Mirrors.

While they would have preferred to practice within the warm confines of Stronghold, it had simply not been possible, not with the attitude of the Home Army warriors. They had greeted Rukh and Farn's request to train amongst them with flat-eyed, unwelcoming stares. *There's no room for your kind here,'* one particularly abrasive lieutenant had told them. Fragging jackholes. Karma had a way of dealing with people like that, and their refusal had actually turned out to be an unexpected blessing. Practicing outside on the slick stones and ground had taught him and Farn a different kind of balance and also inured them to the cold. It was something his cousin would find critical once he left Stronghold.

For Rukh, returning to the rhythms of his youth had also been a cool balm to his troubled heart. The exertions were like meditation, helping him set aside his troubles for a time. They reminded him of a peaceful period in his life when the future had seemed certain, and he had been innocent.

On some nights, like tonight, Cedar and Court would accompany them. They wanted to learn how Kummas fought.

"Is something wrong?" Court asked Rukh. "You seem distracted."

"I'm fine," Rukh lied.

"You don't seem fine," Farn said. "Even with your left hand, you should have shown better than you did tonight."

Rukh hesitated, not wanting to share his worries.

"Tell us," Court urged.

"I can't join the Home Army," Rukh finally admitted. "All the slots for the next five years are filled."

Cedar frowned. "That doesn't make sense," he said. "Did you speak to the majors?"

"Just today, and they both say the same thing. The only way I can earn a commission is by winning the Trials of Hume," Rukh replied. "And even then, it isn't a sure thing. My victory has to be spectacular."

Court rubbed his chin. "Left-handed you're good, but not that good," he said. "Even I've been able to take you a few times."

"He's at his worst right now," Farn said. "Give his leg and arm a chance to Heal fully, and no one here would last a breath against him."

"It won't matter," Rukh said. "I don't have a Home Army officer to sponsor me, and I can't afford the entry fee for the Trials."

"Do you think you'll be ready by then?" Cedar asked quietly.

Rukh shrugged. "It depends on how strong my arm is by then, but, yes, I should be."

Cedar smiled. "Then your problem is solved. I'll sponsor you, and my family will pay the entry fee."

Rukh blinked, touched by Cedar's generosity. "It still may not matter," he said with a shake of his head. "The warriors of Stronghold may not let me enter the Trials." He lifted up his shirt. The left side of his chest sported a large bruise. "It's not broken," he said at their sharp intakes of shock.

"What happened?" Farn asked, outraged.

"Some warriors had a message for me," Rukh said.

"Some message," Court said, disgusted. "Did anyone see what happened? Do you know why they attacked you?"

"No," Rukh said with a scowl. "Of course not. I was simply walking back to the flat after meeting with Dru Barrier when a couple of thugs came out of nowhere...."

"Probably Blended," Cedar interrupted.

"Probably," Rukh agreed. "Anyway, next thing I know, I'm getting kicked in the chest before I can Shield, and...." he shrugged again. "They attacked. I defended."

"It makes no sense," Court said, looking troubled. "Who would do something like this?"

"They didn't exactly stop and explain themselves," Rukh said. "All they said was something about staying away from their women and their Army."

"The Army part I can understand since you had just met with Major Barrier, but the women…." Cedar frowned in confusion. "You don't have any romantic-type relationships with any women here do you?"

"None," Rukh said without missing a beat.

"Then it was probably just a couple of louts with too much to drink," Cedar reasoned. "I'll ask around and make sure their lieutenants discipline them."

Privately, Rukh doubted the officers would do any such thing; but he kept his misgivings to himself.

Court shivered just then. "I'm done. You three can stay and freeze if you like, but I'm going inside."

"I'm heading in, too," Cedar said.

After Cedar and Court left, Farn turned to Rukh. "It was about Jessira, wasn't it?"

Rukh nodded. "I recognized one of the warriors who attacked me. He's one of Disbar Merdant's cousins."

Farn whistled softly. "Jessira's fiancé."

"Jackhole doesn't deserve her," Rukh said with a scowl. "And the thing is, I hardly ever think of her anymore. Or at least I hadn't until today."

"Truly?"

"Truly," Rukh replied, infusing certainty into his words. Sometimes he wondered how Jessira was doing, but it was a fleeting thought, gone before he had a chance to really consider it. As he repeatedly reminded himself, it was best that way.

"This is unlike you," Farn said. "Given how much you cared for her, I wouldn't have expected you to forget about her so easily."

"I never said it was easy," Rukh said. "Besides, I promised her nanna to stay out of her life, which is what I'd always planned on doing anyway."

"When will she get back to Stronghold?"

Rukh spoke without thinking. "Not for another three weeks," he answered. He wanted to bite his lips the moment the words left his mouth. If he wasn't thinking about her, then what was he doing keeping track of her comings and goings?

Farn gave him a wry look. He was probably thinking the same thing. "Thought so."

Rukh reddened. Maybe he hadn't forgotten her as completely as he had hoped, but in the end, it didn't matter. "Let's go on in," he suggested. "I'm tired of being out here." He unlaced the leather Constrainers from his wrists. Farn had a matching pair—gifts from Nanna. At that moment, thinking about his family, Rukh missed them with a fierceness that brought tears to his eyes.

"What is it?" Farn asked.

"Nothing?" Rukh asked with a shrug. "You'll be gone in two weeks and when you are, I'll be alone in a city full of people who think Stronghold represents the epitome of civilized behavior. They see no contradiction in how they behave compared to what they claim to believe. When was the last time you heard of someone being ambushed and attacked on the streets of Ashoka?"

Farn studied him through worried eyes. "What will you do when I leave?" he asked.

Rukh wasn't sure. All he knew was if he couldn't join the Home Army, then there was no chance he'd stay in Stronghold for the rest of his life. The prospect held absolutely no appeal. He might as well slit his wrists and save himself the trouble of a slow and painful death. "If Cedar and his family are willing to sponsor me, I'm going to enter the Trials of Hume," he said. "I'm going to enter, and I'm going to win. After that, we'll see."

Farn smiled, a predator's slow grin of anticipation. "You'll crush them."

Rukh smiled in return. "I've seen their best. I doubt they would last more than three or four strokes against either of us."

"Two," Farn said. "Make them eat dust in two strokes. You can do it."

"I'm thinking of using my weak hand for the first match; toy with whoever I'm facing before putting him away."

Farn laughed. "Serve the arrogant fraggers right. Let them see what an unfettered Kumma can really do. Maybe they'll even let you join the Army once they see your skill."

"Whether they do or don't, I don't care. It doesn't matter, not after what those warriors did to me," Rukh said.

Farn looked shocked. "What do you mean?"

"It means after the Trials, I'm thinking of leaving Stronghold for a while. I'm going to take Nanna's advice and go to Hammer."

"You mean the one about recovering *The Book of First Movement*?" Farn asked sounding doubtful. "I know legends say it was supposedly written by the First Father, but you realize most scholars don't believe that, right?"

"I know," Rukh said, but it didn't matter. Retrieving a long, lost treasure from a dead city—the idea alone held appeal.

"Then maybe you should rethink this plan."

Rukh shrugged. "What would you do if you were in my place?"

"I would find a way to make this place work for me," Farn answered.

———•———

The Shadowcats hunkered down for their evening in a small, lonely canyon north of Stronghold. It was a dismal place of muted grays; seen in the stark granite cliffs thrusting skyward; the cheerless clouds moving listlessly across the heavens; and a waterfall ending in a small pond the color of slate. Most of the ravine's floor was covered in shale except for a thin strip of sand next to the water.

Several Shadowcats stood watch while the rest relaxed and had their supper next to a reedy fire. They huddled near the flames, enjoying its warmth on the cold winter night. The Shadowcats had been on patrol for a week now, and with them was Jessira Grey. She'd been temporarily assigned to their unit until her own, the Silversuns, were fully re-constituted.

"I'm ending my engagement to Disbar," Jessira said to Sign as the two women sat next to one another

Sign shot her a glance of shock and worry. This was unexpected. Before Jessira had gotten caught up in the lives of Kummas and Ashoka, she had been the sensible one; the one who knew her place in the world and wanted nothing more. She was changed now. Of course, some of it was bound to happen. After everything she had been through, there were certain to be changes to how she approached things, how she saw the world. But this…this was entirely different. If Jessira went through with her decision, it would impact her for the rest of her life. And probably not for the better.

Sign waited on her cousin to continue.

Jessira stared into the fire. "Disbar is…I don't want to speak poorly of him, but he and I aren't good for one another. We're neither of us who the other person is looking for in a spouse."

"When did you figure this out?" Sign asked.

Jessira shrugged. "It's not like I had a sudden revelation," she explained. "It's something I've slowly come to realize." She shrugged again. "And our last conversation only cemented what I'd been worrying about since I came home."

Sign nodded her head. "I think I know what you mean," she said. "He's as tightly wound as a rooster in a room full of foxes."

Jessira chuckled. "He's certainly that," she agreed. "But if that were his only flaw, I could probably overlook it. It's everything else. He's just so full of himself. He thinks he knows *everything*. And Devesh help the person who contradicts him." Jessira rolled her eyes.

"I think his mind stops working when that happens, especially if I do it. In his perfect world, I think he would be happiest if I never had an opinion outside of his own."

Sign chuckled. "I thought you didn't want to speak poorly about him?"

"I'm not. Believe me. I could say far worse," Jessira said with a chuckle.

Sign laughed. "Well then don't hold back," she advised. "But I wouldn't say any of this when it comes time to confront him. He'd likely lose his mind if you did."

"He'll lose it anyway," Jessira said. "You know how he is."

Sign nodded. "Stubborn, prickly, and self-absorbed."

"Exactly."

Sign eyed Jessira with concern. "Still. Even with all that, you did promise to marry him. If you break your oath, you know how much you'll suffer for doing so. Your reputation could be ruined if you don't have a better reason than *'I don't like him'*. A promise is important. For years, people have married those they didn't like for just that reason alone."

Jessira hugged her knees. "I know, but I can't go through with it." She shook her head. "You don't understand. He has me followed. He thinks he can tell me who I can be friends with. What I can think. When I can speak. I'll never be meek enough for him, and he'll never be strong enough for me."

Sign startled. Her opinion of Disbar, slowly sinking over the months since she'd gotten to really know him, sunk even lower. "He really does that?" she asked. "Has you followed? How?"

"His cousins," Jessira responded.

Sign considered the situation from her cousin's perspective. To be trapped in marriage to a man like Disbar Merdant. She shuddered. Jessira would be miserable. And she deserved so much better.

"What will you do when he tries to ruin you?" she asked. "And you know he will."

Jessira shrugged. "I'll defend myself, but I also won't hide away in shame. I'll fight if it's a fight he wants." She shrugged again. "I'm not worried about myself as much as I am about the rest of the family. And I hate to think what Amma and Nanna are going to say."

Sign gave Jessira a look of sympathy. "I'll always support you," she said.

Jessira leaned against Sign. "I appreciate that," she said. "I think I'll be needing all the support I can get."

━━●━━

Rukh waited his turn to hug his cousin. The small party—Rukh, Farn, Cedar, Court, and Laya—stood just outside East Gate. The newly risen sun heralded the new day, bathing the sky in a rosy hue; but down low, the valley remained cloaked in shadows by Mount Fort's hulking presence. Rukh shuffled about, his movements crunching ground that was hard with hoarfrost and winter's bite. At least there were no clouds in the air, and no scent of snow or rain on the wind.

Farn was leaving Stronghold, and Rukh's stomach knotted with tension. He was worried, and if he was honest, even envious. Farn was going home, returning to family and friends, and Rukh wished he could go with him. Instead, he had to remain trapped in a city full of conceited hypocrites. Another attack had occurred the other day, this time by five warriors. After Rukh had reported it, no one had believed him. Perhaps it was because he was unmarked and uninjured and from what he had claimed, it should have been stiff odds. Just as likely, it was because he was a Pureblood.

Whatever the reason, the more important issue was that justice had been denied him yet again, just as it had been with the first two assaults. It couldn't go on. Another attack might find Rukh badly injured—or worse. In either case, the message was clear: Rukh wasn't safe in Stronghold. He had to leave.

But he wouldn't be telling Farn of his decision. His cousin had enough to worry about. Farn was well-equipped for his journey back to Ashoka, but there were still many dangers that could happen to someone traveling alone: Chims, injury, weather, bad luck. He didn't also need to be worrying about Rukh.

Laya finished saying her goodbye and stepped back. It was Court and Cedar's turn.

"Travel safe and travel swift," Court said, offering a traditional Stronghold farewell given by their scouts.

Farn pulled him into an embrace. "Thank you for everything," he said. "You're a good man, Court Deep."

"As are you," Court said. "Maybe in the next world, you can show me the wonders of Ashoka."

"Nothing would make me happier," Farn said, his eyes shiny.

Court gave him a final squeeze before letting Cedar take his place.

"Take care of yourself and try not to hit your head," Cedar said. "It may be as hard as a stone, but I won't be around to take care of you next time."

"I'll make sure not to," Farn said, still smiling. He sobered a moment later. "Thank you for everything you've done for me. I wouldn't be alive if not for you."

"You've already thanked me plenty," Cedar protested.

"Then one more time won't hurt. You're a good man Cedar Grey. I'll never forget what you did for me."

Cedar nodded. "Travel safe and travel swift," he added before stepping back.

Now it was Rukh's turn.

"Tell my family I love them," Rukh whispered, hugging his

cousin one last time as tears slid down his face.

"They know," Farn whispered back, tears rolling down his cheeks as well. "I'll tell them anyway." He turned away and led his loaded packhorse north toward the Gaunt River and from there, home.

Rukh prayed as he never had before, hoping Devesh would answer his call. He watched until his cousin was a small dot in the distance, remaining in place even after Farn crested a small rise and dipped down the other side, disappearing from view.

⸺ ● ⸺

Jessira turned in her wooden tray to a warrior working the sinks of the East Lock cafeteria. The long, narrow room was lit by ten immense wagon-wheel chandeliers and housed rows of tables on either side of a single center aisle. Right now, the space was loud with the din of hundreds of warriors seeking their lunch and the laborers working to serve them. The thick granite pavers making up the floor and the whitewashed stone walls did little to diffuse the sound. Overlooking all of this cacophony was a mural of a smiling Babylin Suresong from his pride of place at the room's entrance.

"Jessira! Over here," a voice shouted over the tumult.

Jessira searched for whoever had called. The cafeteria's clamor made it hard to localize any single voice, but a waving hand caught her attention.

Sign. "Where are you headed?" her cousin asked, falling into step next to her.

"Home," Jessira answered. "You?"

"Same," Sign said. "Captain Flare sure took a long time with your debriefing," she observed.

Jessira grimaced. She'd noticed the same thing. It should have been a routine debriefing of a routine assignment in the Wildness, but instead, it had turned into an interrogation. It was unwarranted, but then again, the captain *was* a jackhole. She just couldn't say so. He was her commanding officer, after all. She decided to put the best face forward that she could. "Maybe it's because this was the first mission I've had in months," she said.

"It still seemed a bit much," Sign said. "You want to work off some of that frustration?"

"What do you have in mind?" Jessira asked.

"How about a quick match? We haven't had a chance to spar since you've been back."

Jessira tilted her head in consideration. What she really wanted was a long hot soak, but a quick spar might also do her some good. If nothing else, it could help clear her mind.

Before she'd left for patrol, she had looked in on Rukh a few times. They had issues to discuss, and while he had noted her presence, he had still insisted on avoiding her. At least he had seemed content, which was a surprise given that he was a proud Kumma warrior reduced to cleaning latrines. Of course, she wasn't sure just how happy he could be since over lunch today, she had learned that Farn Arnicep had left Stronghold about a week ago. It meant that Rukh was all alone now.

Jessira worried for him. His predicament reminded her of her own time in Ashoka. Back then, she had accused Rukh of being a coward, of abandoning their friendship because of fears of what his society would think. But hadn't she done the same thing? Of course, Rukh had tried to push her away, farcically claiming they were nothing more than traveling companions; but she had been all too willing to follow his lead. She should have fought harder for their friendship.

"What's wrong?" Sign asked. "You look like something's bothering you."

Jessira forced a smile. "Nothing a good spar won't cure," she said.

Mercifully, Sign dropped the matter as she and Jessira gathered their gear and headed toward the training rings.

"Do you still plan on ending your engagement with Disbar?" Sign asked.

Jessira nodded. "Would you marry him?" she asked. "After learning the kind of man he really is?"

"I wouldn't have wanted to," Sign said. "But I don't know if I'd have your courage to simply end it without any explanation."

Jessira grimaced. "It's not courage," she said. "It's just something I have to do, no matter how much trouble it's going to cause me." Jessira was no longer concerned about the damage she would do to her reputation as much as she was about how her parents would react when they found out what she intended. They would be furious.

Sign eyed her askance.

"What is it?" Jessira asked.

"Before we left on the mission, people were talking," she said. "This will only feed those rumors."

"What were they saying?" Jessira asked, glancing Sign's way with narrowed eyes.

"That you and Rukh are...." Sign trailed off, apparently not wanting to spell it out.

"They think Rukh and I are together even though I am still nominally engaged to Disbar. That doesn't sound so bad," Jessira said, thinking aloud.

"Are you?"

"Of course not," Jessira replied in astonishment. "I'm ending things with Disbar later today. After that, I have to figure out what I want for myself."

"A tall drink of Kumma?" Sign asked with an unrepentant grin.

Jessira laughed. "You're incorrigible."

"And I'm quite clever."

Jessira sobered. "What else are people saying?"

Sign's mirth left her as well. "That's about the gist of it," she said, wearing a guarded expression.

From her cousin's cautious demeanor, there was likely much more; but Jessira wasn't in the mood to hear it. "I'm sure I'll learn the rest later," she muttered before glancing Sign's way. "Do you mind if we change the subject. I've worried about this enough as it is." She shuddered. "I hate to think what Amma and Nanna will say about it. Or Kart. He'll be the worst."

"He usually is," Sign agreed. "But if you want to change the subject…who do you think is going to win the Trials?"

"I don't know," Jessira said. "Has Wheel Cloud decided to try for three in a row?"

"He has," Sign affirmed as their feet crunched along the gravel paths demarcating the training rings.

"Then I'd take Wheel. He crushed everyone last time."

"But he's old."

They reached an empty ring and dropped their gear just outside its soft dirt confines.

"He's in his early thirties," Jessira protested as she reached for the sky, arching and stretching her back. "That's not old. He's probably got more than enough to win again."

"Well, my money is on Toth Shard or Strive Loane," Sign said, joining Jessira in limbering up. "They're both five years younger than Wheel and just as skilled. That has to count for something."

Jessira smiled. "Less experience?"

Sign grinned wickedly. "Care to put a wager on it?"

"What do you have in mind?"

"If Toth or Strive advance further than Wheel, you have to do my labor at East Lock for the next month."

"And if Wheel does better, you've got mine for two," Jessira said.

"What! How's that fair?" Sign protested.

"You chose two warriors. I only got one. You've got a better chance to win than I do."

"Then choose someone else."

"Who else is there?"

Sign gave her a knowing smile. "Rukh Shektan. Cedar convinced Peddananna and Peddamma—" Jessira's Nanna and Amma "—to sponsor him."

"Rukh?" Jessira inhaled sharply. Her heart was suddenly beating too fast.

Sign laughed. "You've made your choice then? You want the Kumma."

"I'll take Rukh," Jessira said, ignoring the double meaning in her cousin's statement. She thought back to all the times she'd seen Rukh fight. He had been fast, strong, nearly unstoppable. From what she'd gathered, even amongst his own kind he was considered a prodigy. Then again, there was his arm. Jessira had heard it had been Healed, but was it fully recovered? She also realized that it didn't matter. Even injured, she'd still take Rukh. He was that good.

"You've got that look on your face again."

"What look?"

"The one where you're thinking of something you want and don't want at the same time."

"The word you're looking for is conflicted."

Sign snapped her fingers. "That's why I like being around you. You always know the right word to say. So why are you conflicted?"

"Because Rukh will kick everyone's ass, and I don't know how our warriors will take it," Jessira lied.

"Right. And I'm the First Mother," Sign said with an eye-roll. "Look, I like Rukh. He's funny and charming and easy on the eyes, but he's a man like any other. You, Cedar, and Court say he's amazing, and I'm sure he is, but he can't be *that* amazing." She nodded her head, looking sure of herself. "You wait and see, one of our warriors will get him."

"Tell you what. I'll take Rukh, and you can have Strive, Toth, *and* Wheel. Only you'll have three months of cleanup detail."

"Done!" Sign crowed. "Easiest victory I'll have all year."

It was Jessira's turn to roll her eyes. "I thought you wanted to spar," she said. "Not talk all day."

"I'm more than ready," Sign answered, wearing a confident grin.

In the past, most matches between Jessira and her cousin had ended with Sign as the victor. But that was the past. Today was a new day. Jessira was better than Sign remembered. Much better.

Jessira readied her shoke, studying her cousin's posture. Speed and skill were important but understanding an enemy's intention was even more so. It was the key to victory; a lesson drilled into her head by every Kumma Jessira had ever met. From posture and balance, a skilled warrior could glean an opponent's goal before the first blow was even struck. Jessira studied her cousin, and in a moment she knew what Sign intended. "Begin," Jessira called out.

Four strokes later, Jessira's shoke lay against the side of Sign's neck.

Sign grumbled something under breath, and the two women readied themselves once more.

The next pass took five strokes.

The one following took seven.

"How in the unholy hells are you doing that!" Sign complained.

"A lot of practice and a lot of training," Jessira said with an easy grin.

"With who? I want a chance to train with him."

"Rukh…amongst others."

Sign glared before curiosity took the place of annoyance. "Is he really as good as you and Cedar say?"

"You'll find out soon enough," Jessira said. She unknowingly wore a sad smile until Sign pointed it out.

Sign studied her through narrowed eyes. "You miss him," she guessed.

"Who?" Jessira asked, feigning ignorance.

"The Pureblood. You still have feelings for him. It's why you looked conflicted earlier."

Jessira's hackles rose. Why did Sign have to be so perceptive? "Be quiet," Jessira hissed, shooting a glance all around. "You want everyone to hear."

"No one's around, and I'll never tell anyone about it."

"Just let it go," Jessira growled. She ducked her head, flushing with embarrassment at her traitorous feelings as she gathered her gear.

"What if you hadn't been engaged to Disbar? What would you have done then with the two of you alone in the Wildness?" Sign asked, waiting until they were alone in Hold Passage East.

"Then things between Rukh and me might have turned out very differently," Jessira answered.

———◦•◦———

Disbar approached the bench upon which Jessira waited with a sense of hope and trepidation. They had agreed to meet in the courtyard of Crofthold Lucent, the site of their last conversation before she had left with the Shadowcats. Disbar hoped today's discussion would go better than the last; that the time away had allowed Jessira to come to her senses. They couldn't argue all the time, not if they wanted to have a happy marriage. And while Disbar could bend somewhat and find a way to trust her—he'd try—but she would have to as well.

She could start by disassociating herself from the Kumma. Just this afternoon, Jessira's first day home after weeks in the Wildness, the first place she had gone was Crofthold Lucent's dining hall. There, she had inquired about Rukh.

Disbar gritted his teeth. What hold did the Pureblood bastard have on Jessira? Why couldn't he take a hint and leave her alone? His cousins had tried to deliver just such a message to the Kumma, but each time, he had apparently been surrounded by laborer friends of his. Disbar didn't know all the details of what had happened, but clearly the situation had gotten out of control since a few of his cousins had ended up in a hospice.

Disbar scowled. One day the Pureblood would find himself alone and....

He wiped the frown from his face and forced a smile as he neared Jessira. He noticed when she took a deep breath, seeming to master some emotion, before she turned to him with a look of determination. Upon seeing her expression, a trickle of worry worked its way down his spine.

"You're back," Disbar said, recognizing too late how inane his words sounded.

He moved to kiss Jessira, but she rose to her feet and stepped away before he could deliver it. "We need to talk," she said, her tone firm and business-like.

The trickle of worry thickened. Jessira was stone-faced and somber, and Disbar had to clear his throat before he could speak. "What do you wish to discuss?"

Jessira looked him in the eyes. "I am ending our engagement," she said. Her voice and carriage were as certain as an avalanche and crushed into Disbar with the same impact.

It took him a moment to stop from gaping at her as he tried to make sense of what she was telling him. She couldn't be serious. "What is this?" he demanded. "Some twisted jest?" His jaw clenched.

"It is in extremely poor taste."

"No jest," Jessira said. "It is the truth. I no longer wish to marry you." Her tone brooked no dissent.

Disbar studied her face, hoping to see some hint of flexibility; but her stolid features told him otherwise. "Why?" he asked. "What reason could you have to do so?" His voice rose and others in the courtyard turned to look at them.

Jessira shook her head. "It doesn't matter," she said. "Nothing I say will bring you satisfaction."

"You owe me the truth!" Disbar hissed. His fists clenched. "Or should I guess? It's about the Pureblood, isn't it?"

Jessira's only reaction to his question was to cross her arms. "This has nothing to do with Rukh," she replied. "You and I would have never been happy in marriage to one another. I think you know that."

"What I *think* is that you're deceiving yourself if you believe I'll simply accept this farce without an honest accounting. I will not be made to look a fool."

Jessira sighed. "No one will think that of you."

"If you truly believe that, you're delusional." Disbar snorted in derision. "Engagements aren't ended in this fashion. People will talk. They'll wonder. Ugly rumors will be said."

"Not if we end things amicably."

"That will only happen if I know *why* it has to end," Disbar said.

Jessira hesitated. "We aren't the people we once were," she answered. "Why don't we just leave it at that?"

Disbar sneered. "That is as vague as saying nothing at all," he replied. "Have you considered what you're giving up? What will happen to your family's reputation if you leave me in this manner?"

Jessira nodded, appearing weary. "I have, but it won't stop me. This is something I have to do for myself."

Disbar scowled. "If you end our engagement, understand that I will protect what is mine. I won't be made to look like a cuckold while you cavort with the Pureblood."

Jessira's detached expression finally cracked. She looked to be growing angry herself. "What are you saying?" she asked.

"I mean that I'll make sure everyone knows exactly what kind of woman you are."

"And exactly what kind of a woman am I?" Jessira asked, her voice growing low and threatening.

Disbar disregarded her warning tone and plowed on, the anger having a hold of him. He spoke without thinking, seeking to hurt Jessira as much as possible for what she was about to do. "All of Stronghold will know you for who you are: a faithless woman."

Jessira slapped him, hard enough to rock his head. A faithless woman was the worst insult, even worse than that of 'whore'. At least a whore had a sort of honor.

Disbar's ears rang, and he tasted blood from where his teeth had cut into the inside of his cheek.

"I never broke my word to you," Jessira said. "You were simply too craven and petty to believe me." With that, she turned on her heel and strode away.

———•◦•———

Rukh trudged down the hallway, looking forward to his bedroll. His day had begun early in the morning with a session of sword training. Afterward had come work—garbage detail for breakfast followed by latrine cleaning after lunch and supper. The labor had left him reeking like a wild boar, but even then, his day hadn't been done. Afterward had come a final training session. He grimaced when he scented his own stink. All he wanted was a quick but thorough bath, a change of clothes, and some sleep.

Fragging unholy hells he was tired, especially of living here. There were friends he had made, good people like Cedar and Court and their family as well as many laborers; but overall, Rukh was ready to move on.

Farn was gone, a week now, and every day since, Rukh had worried about his cousin. Hopefully, Farn was snuggled up somewhere safe and warm tonight. Rukh took a moment to send another quick prayer to Devesh on Farn's behalf. Likely the Lord didn't listen to those of little faith like himself—after all, when had Devesh ever listened to the faithful?—but it never hurt to ask.

Thinking of Farn reminded him of Ashoka, his home. He missed it, more homesick now than at any other time since he had been found Unworthy. Perhaps it was because he was more alone than at any other moment since he had been found Unworthy.

Rukh tsked, annoyed with his self-pity. Whining was an unbecoming habit in even the best of men. He made himself think about something else, something happy like what he would do after the Trials of Hume. The thought drove away some of the melancholy, but it didn't bring cheer to his heart. He really had hoped to make a home here in Stronghold, but it wasn't to be. The attacks, the lack of justice—Stronghold wasn't safe for him.

His thoughts were distracted, but the moment he opened the door to Court's flat, he knew he wasn't alone. Someone was in there, someone not Court. He Shielded almost at the same time that the scent of cinnamon came to him.

Jessira.

She flicked on the firefly lantern on the end table next to the couch and rose to her feet. "I understand you're entering the Trials," she said to him, speaking without preamble.

Seeing her again, Rukh froze, unsure what to do. What was she doing in Court's flat? He didn't want her here. He'd worked too hard to save her reputation for her to ruin it now. Rukh glanced down the hallway, half-tempted to walk out on her. They couldn't be discovered alone like this.

"Don't go," she called out. "I only wanted to see how you were doing."

Rukh glared at her, but she never flinched from his gaze or looked away.

Jessira still had her courage. He'd give her that much. She'd always been one to stand her ground. Even the cesspit reek coming off of Rukh hadn't caused her to flee. "I know I should have checked up on you more often, but every time I did...." Jessira shrugged an apology. "You acted like you didn't want me near you."

"I didn't. I still don't." His response was curt, and he hoped she would take the hint and leave.

Instead, her brows furrowed in hurt. "Why are so angry with me?" she asked.

"Why do you suppose?" he asked, knowing his lack of explanation would irritate her.

Jessira paced the room. "You wanted everyone to think that we aren't really friends, that we were only companions traveling together when we were in the Wildness. You were trying to save my reputation." She turned to face him. "And you think I went along with it? That I abandoned you?"

"Only you can answer that," Rukh replied, "but you're ruining it all by being here now."

"I don't care about any of that right now," she said, moving aside as he stepped toward his bedroll and packs piled up next to the couch. Her nose wrinkled. She must have finally caught a whiff of his odor. "I care about how you're doing."

"I appreciate your concern," Rukh said, pulling out a change of clothing from his bags and walking to the front door. "But I'm fine. Go back to Disbar and forget about me."

"I'm not with Disbar any more," Jessira said. "I ended our

engagement yesterday afternoon."

Rukh turned to her in surprise. "Why?"

"He's not the man I thought he was," she said with a shrug. "We wouldn't have made one another very happy."

Rukh shook his head in disbelief. What had she done? Her reputation would be ruined, especially if anyone saw Jessira here with him tonight. They'd believe that Rukh had seduced her, that *he* was the reason she had ended her engagement to Disbar. It would lead to even more problems for him.

"You shouldn't be here," Rukh said as he stepped outside the flat and closed the door before she had a chance to answer. He was too tired to think about any of this right now. All he wanted was a bath and laundry. And he wanted Jessira gone by the time he was done.

He went down the hallway to the washroom and stripped off his filthy clothes and scrub them as thoroughly as possible. It took a while to get rid of all the grime and grossness, and while there were still some stubborn stains that wouldn't come out, at least his clothes didn't reek anymore. After he finished, he laid out his wet pants, shirt, and underclothes on the racks above the hot stones in the parching room where they would be dry in a few hours.

Only then did he take his long deserved bath, cleaning himself off as thoroughly as possible. By the time he finished, his palms and soles were as wrinkled as raisins. And given the time he'd spent washing his clothes and himself, he figured Jessira would have long since left Court's flat.

He was wrong.

She was still waiting for him when he returned, seated once more on the couch and thumbing through a book. She looked up when he entered. "Are you done being a martyr, or will you let me explain why I'm here?"

"Martyr...." Rukh clamped down on the furious words he

wanted to blurt out. By the barest margins, he held on to his temper. Usually it took a lot to make Rukh angry, but somehow Jessira had the trick of getting a rise out of him without even trying. "What do you want?" Rukh snapped.

Jessira took a deep breath. "I know things haven't been easy for you here," she began. "I just wanted to find out if there's anything I can do to make it better."

"I'm fine. The Trials are coming up in a few days and afterward, I should be able to do whatever I want."

"Because of the prize winnings awarded to the champion?" Jessira guessed. "With it you could move out from Court's flat and rent one of your own. Is that what you have planned? You want to win the Trials and move out?"

"Close enough. Is there anything else?"

His answer didn't seem to satisfy Jessira. Her jaw clenched in irritation. "There is something else," she began. "I know you're friends with Court and Cedar, but they say you haven't told them anything about your plans following the Trials."

"I wasn't aware I was under any obligation to let them know my plans," Rukh said.

"You owe them common courtesy," Jessira replied tartly. "Court has been kind to you, letting you stay in his flat these past few months. If nothing else, they are your friends. I thought I was your friend—"

"Friends don't abandon one another," Rukh said. He wasn't being fair to her, but his situation had him frustrated and disillusioned. He couldn't control the bitterness. The Home Army had denied his application out of hand; men had attacked him and paid no price for their assault; many Strongholders treated him like the mud on their shoes; and for all this, he was expected to be grateful to them for allowing him to stay in their perfect city. Suwraith's spit but he was tired of their hypocrisy.

Jessira twisted her hands in agitation. "I already apologized for that," she said.

"No you haven't."

"Then I apologize," Jessira said, not sounding apologetic.

"For what?" Rukh asked. "I was the one who came up with the idea that we aren't friends. You were simply smart enough to go along with what I started. So don't worry about saying sorry. I understand why you did what you did."

"You don't *understand* anything," Jessira spat. "I already told you: I looked in on you, and you were humiliated and miserable. The horror! The indecency! The great Kumma has to work as a laborer. It's unconscionable!" She glared at him. "Well understand this: we *all* have to do what you do. Every fourth week, I'm expected to serve in the barracks. I cook, I clean, even down to the latrines. So I don't care what you think of your work. It's honest, and there's nothing shameful about it."

"You are the one who doesn't understand," Rukh said, his voice soft as a whisper. He kept his composure and didn't allow his anger to show. "I do my work here without complaint. I dislike it, but that isn't why I don't respect this city or her people."

If anything, his relatively calm demeanor in the face of her anger seemed to outrage her even further.

"Unbelievable! We take you in, and this is how you behave? Like an arrogant Kumma!"

"It is who I am," Rukh said, wearing a sarcastic half-smile.

"You are insufferable!" she shouted.

"The door's right there." Rukh pointed. "If you don't want to be here then leave."

"I thought you needed a friend. That's why I came here."

"Nothing I need is to be found in this city."

"What's that supposed to mean?"

"It means perhaps you should wonder why justice is absent in

Stronghold. If you ask around the hospices, you might learn of some recently injured men. A broken jaw, broken ribs, and a broken arm. Ask these men how they came to be hurt."

"Did someone attack you?" Jessira asked, her anger suddenly blowing over and replaced by a look of concern.

Rukh didn't feel like explaining what had happened. It no longer mattered. "The powerful in this city think they can assault the powerless with impunity," he said, knowing his words were enigmatic. Frag it. Let her figure it out on her own.

Jessira stared at him, apparently trying to fathom what he meant. "You *were* attacked, and no one did anything about it," she said. "But if you win the Trials, your position in the city is assured. You can have your justice then."

Rukh shrugged, not bothering to respond. He no longer cared if those who had assaulted him were punished. The law should apply equally to everyone, no matter their status or wealth. It shouldn't take victory in the Trials for him to receive justice. Besides, there was no way he was going to let Jessira learn of his plans to leave Stronghold. She'd only waste his time by trying to talk him out of it.

Jessira sighed, an expression of resignation on her face. She stood. "Good luck in the Trials," she whispered before brushing past him, close enough for him to feel the cinnamon breeze of her passage. She paused at the open front door. "For what it's worth, this hasn't been easy for me either," she said.

She closed the door with a soft click.

CHAPTER FOURTEEN
NEW QUESTIONS

Only a fool searches for a four-leaf clover when
opportunity is waiting at his front door.

~Sooths and Small Sayings by Tramed Billow AF 1387

"We have a problem," Varesea said the moment Hal'El appeared at the door. She appeared agitated, clutching at her skirt and muttering incomprehensibly.

Hal'El's glad smile fell away, and only with effort did he keep his shoulders from slumping in disappointment and dread. He had hoped Varesea's 'episodes' would eventually resolve on their own, but they hadn't. At least not yet. They were certainly less common than they had once been, but they still occurred frequently enough to cause Hal'El's teeth to grind with worry. Her fits were a challenge for both of them. When caught in the midst of her madness, not only did Varesea fear her dead husband's wrath; but she also believed all sorts of odd notions. Just last week, she had been certain that Hal'El was seeing another woman. It had taken most of an afternoon to convince her otherwise, and afterward, Varesea—his Varesea—had returned to him as if nothing unusual had occurred.

Hal'El carefully shut the door and turned to face her. The room in which Varesea waited for him took up the top floor of an unoccupied building in Stone Cavern. It was a place they had made their own and taken to calling *The Tryst Palace*. It was a sardonic title, given in jest to a meager space with boarded over windows—one of its key features—a few broken-down chairs, a cheap pine table, and a plush sofa.

They also now had a bed. Hal'El glanced at it in disappointment. With Varesea's distress, it seemed unlikely that it would receive any use today.

"It's that Shektan girl, Bree," Varesea explained, taking a seat on the edge of the couch. Her foot tapped the rhythm of her disturbance. "She's been looking into the murder of Drin Port. She's even asked to speak to Grasome Verle."

If she hadn't before, Varesea now had Hal'El's full attention. "Has he spoken to her?" he asked.

"No. So far, he's been smart enough to avoid her; but he can't do so forever."

Hal'El sighed. "How much does he know?"

Varesea shrugged. "Very little. Only that Drin was murdered, but not your role in it," she said.

"Fair enough," Hal'El said, stroking his chin in consideration. "Will I need to make a personal visit to the good doctor?"

Varesea wavered. "You might," she answered, looking unhappy. "He's always been weak. Unreliable. He'll likely break if the Shektan girl—"

"Woman. The Shektan woman," Hal'El interrupted. "Let's not call her a girl. We risk under-estimating her if we do."

"Woman then," Varesea said with a scowl. "He'll talk if she reaches him."

Hal'El scowled. What a mess. "Then it appears a new medical examiner will soon be needed."

"Is that really necessary?" Varesea asked, appearing upset. She stood and paced the room. At least, she wasn't muttering about her dead husband while doing so. "Grasome is one of the few physicians we have in the Sil Lor Kum and the only medical examiner."

"You said it yourself: he'll talk. We can't allow it."

"I know. I just wish...." She stopped her pacing and came to rest, standing at the far end of the room. "I just wish you didn't have to kill again. At least not with *it*. It's evil."

Hal'El crossed the space to her and took her into his arms. "I promise not to use the Knife," he whispered into her ear.

———— • ————

D ar'El sat in his study with the late afternoon sun pouring in through the windows. The weather was warm, but somehow the sun in winter always seemed weaker, more wan, and less inspiring than in summer. The gardens reflected the change. The brilliant flowers—Satha's pride and joy—had long since withered away, their stems decayed and brittle. Some shrubs remained bright and verdant, but otherwise the gardens were a sad, lonesome sight.

Winter was here, Dar'El's least favorite season. He didn't like it, not even Ashoka's mild version. His hands and feet were always cold. He much preferred the chili-pepper heat of summer. A warm breeze blew in through the open windows, carrying with it the false taste of spring; and Dar'El half-stood, wishing the heat of summer was upon them. He sat back down with a disappointed sigh and turned back to papers on his desk. He had work to do.

The documents were from Garnet, and Dar'El peered closely at the words, trying to decode the nearly illegible scrawl. The old man's handwriting had become worse with each passing year. Dar'El sighed. He hoped Garnet's mind wasn't also showing a similar deterioration, although he feared it likely. The changes were subtle, but they were there. At first, Dar'El had assumed it was signs of fatigue—Garnet was old but still worked as hard as any of them—but it wasn't the case. There were episodes of confusion, times when his old friend repeated himself, asked questions already answered, or forgot details on an important matter. Such things would have never happened a year ago.

The situation left Dar'El worried and heartbroken for one of his oldest friends. He stared out the window, lost in thought. Why would Devesh do something so cruel?

A tapping came at the door. "Do you have a moment?" Bree asked, interrupting his reverie. "The door was open," she said in response to his unspoken question about why she hadn't waited for his word to enter.

Nanna gestured for her to come in and close the door behind her. "What is it?" he asked.

"I wanted to talk to you about Rukh," she said, slipping into a chair facing his desk.

Dar'El stifled an inward groan. He should have known. While the frostiness in their relationship had thawed, Bree hadn't entirely forgiven him for what he had asked her to do. Dar'El hoped she hadn't come here to accuse him anew. At this point, he had long since grown tired of defending his actions. He had made the best he could out of a terrible situation. Mistakes had been made, but in the end, Dar'El was certain that what had ultimately happened to Rukh was probably the best anyone could have hoped for.

And just as tiresome as Bree's constant accusations was her self-flagellation. She still blamed herself for Rukh's fate. It didn't matter how many times he—and many others—had tried to convince her otherwise, she persisted in believing herself at fault. It was an irrational view, and for someone as steeped in logic as Bree, it was exasperating for those around her. Six months since Rukh's judgment and Bree had yet to forgive herself.

Dar'El prayed she would—and soon. It wasn't healthy to carry such guilt, especially when it was unearned. Besides, he carried enough guilt for both of them. If anyone was at fault for Rukh's situation, Dar'El felt it was himself. "What do you wish to discuss?" Dar'El asked.

"Can Rukh really be brought home?" Bree asked.

Dar'El's brows rose in surprise. It wasn't the question he had expected.

"You thought I'd argue with you again about the decisions you made?" Bree asked with a guilty smile. "Sorry to disappoint."

"You didn't disappoint," Dar'El said. "By asking this, am I to assume you've finally come to forgive yourself for what happened to Rukh?"

Bree shrugged. "I don't know if I'd go that far," she said. "Only Rukh can truly forgive me, but I've at least come to accept that what I did to him might have saved him from an even worse fate."

Dar'El smiled in relief. It was a beginning, and long past due. "How did you come to this realization?" he asked.

"I talked to Mira," Bree explained.

"Mira," Dar'El mused. "Remind me to thank her."

"I'm sure you'll remember on your own," Bree replied. She rapped the table. "What about my question: can Rukh really be brought home? Can you persuade the Chamber to overturn their verdict?"

Dar'El nodded. "I think so. With the Society's help, I think it can be done. We're close. With all the other warriors from the Chimera expedition proclaiming Rukh's greatness, the Chamber may have no choice but to bend to popular will."

"As simple as that?" Bree asked, not quite in disbelief.

"Not quite, but yes," Dar'El replied. "I'd be happier if we had something by which to discredit Hal'El Wrestiva. He's the glue holding the older, more reactionary elements together. Remove his influence, and their opposition will crumble."

"And this is Rector's role in House Wrestiva? To learn some damning information about Hal'El?" Bree scowled a moment later. "I can't believe I ever liked him," she said, sounding disgusted with herself.

Dar'El smiled. "Consider it the folly of youth."

"I feel sorry for Mira. I could never do what she has to."

———●—————●————●———

Mira sat at a small table in Walthall Park, a rectangular, grassy park in the heart of the city. To pass the time—she was to meet Rector later in the morning—she had a cup of coffee and tried to read a book. However, most of her attention was held by those around her. Even this early in the day, there was much to see. A few hardy food vendors already had their carts ready, stationed beneath the canopy of trees along the borders of the park; and the scent of popcorn and puri bhaji filled the air. A few older folks walked the graveled path along the park's perimeter while children played on the grass, laughing as they chased one another or rode the horse-driven carousel. Their sounds were drowned out by a nearby group of buskers—two fiddles, a guitar, and a singer—playing Muran folk songs.

Mira's foot tapped in rhythm to the music.

Walthall Park was a place of peace; a small emerald gem in the midst of a bustling city that never seemed to slow down. Mira loved it. Walthall was like her own personal oasis, a quiet spot of tranquility. Even the nearby granite hulk of the City Library, with its jagged abutments resembling a menacing, wind-etched cliff, didn't detract from the park's grace and sense of rest.

Mira sipped her coffee, enjoying its heat in the early morning winter chill. She went back to reading her book as the sun climbed high, peeking around Clarion Bell, the tall clock tower to the east. As the day warmed, the children left the park and Walthall grew quiet. The city seemed far away.

Mira closed her eyes and leaned back, letting the sun warm her face.

When next she opened her eyes, several hours had passed. She glanced at Clarion Bell, checking the time.

She sighed.

It was time to leave. She and Rector were supposed to attend an early afternoon gathering at the home of Siramont Pindle, a Cherid of note. It was all part of their façade as a couple in love.

Mira grimaced at the thought.

She couldn't wait to be done with this masquerade, and it wasn't because she despised Rector Bryce. Strangely enough, she no longer felt much antipathy toward the man. In the months since the two of them had taken on the role of a courting couple, she'd actually grown to tolerate his presence. Her dislike for him had faded, and while she probably would never consider him a friend, at least he wasn't so insufferable anymore. There were even moments when she found him pleasant to be around.

The truth as to why she wanted to be done with this charade was far simpler. Mira abhorred the lies she had to tell. She hated them; just as much as Rector hated having to pretend to be a loyal member of House Wrestiva.

Mira briefly wondered if Rector might have anything new to relate to her. The sooner he did, the sooner the two of them could be rid of their pretense. Unfortunately, his position as the manager of a small warehouse in the Moon Quarter didn't allow him to discover much about Hal'El Wrestiva's fortune. In fact, since Rector's finding of the missing henna and poppy seeds, he had provided precious little information.

Rector was frustrated with his lack of progress, but his generally bleak outlook had brightened when Mira had explained about the low probability of flooding ruining the warehouse's records. When she had done so, Rector's eyes had lit with a thoughtful suspicion, an expression she couldn't recall seeing on his face ever before. In hindsight, it shouldn't have been surprising. Rector lived for mysteries. It was his lifeblood. He'd once told her investigations had been his favorite role as a member of the City Watch. Some of the stories he told....

It had been good to see him show curiosity and interest, even amusing as Rector raced off like a hound after a rabbit when he'd heard about the records. She just hoped his newfound knowledge would allow him to develop another avenue of research into House Wrestiva's inner workings. She prayed it would.

Her mind distracted, she didn't hear it the first few times her name was called out. She startled when Rector suddenly appeared before her.

"You must have some serious thoughts to cogitate," Rector said. "I've been trying to get your attention for the last minute or so."

Mira frowned, confused. "What are you doing here?" she asked.

"I came to escort you to Siramont Pindle's gathering," he answered.

"No. I mean how did you know where to find me?"

Rector gave a self-deprecating smile. "You talk about Walthall so much," he said. "It wasn't much of a guess to figure out you'd be here."

Mira was impressed he'd remembered. "Is it already time for your Cherid friend's gathering?"

"I wouldn't really call him a friend," Rector said. "He's someone I helped out once during my work in the City Watch. He's felt an obligation to me ever since."

"What did you do for him?"

"Nothing special. I just helped him find something he'd lost."

Mira suppressed a sigh. Rector could be so obtuse. "How did

you help him?" she prodded.

"It was nothing," Rector said. His grin clearly indicated that it was something more than nothing.

"Rector...." Mira said, her tone hopefully warning him of her fading patience.

He finally seemed to catch her meaning. "Oh, right. Do you remember the story I told you about the stolen diamond?" Rector asked. He didn't wait for an answer. "The diamond was the *Sea of Ashoka*—"

"Wait. *The Sea of Ashoka*," Mira interrupted. "You mean that giant blue diamond? The one the size of a robin's egg?" Rector nodded, and she whistled in appreciation. "Someone stole the *Sea*?"

"Not *someone*. Something," Rector corrected. "A magpie. The owner of the *Sea* is Siramont Pindle, and it was his wife's magpie that stole the diamond."

"Siramont Pindle?" Mira questioned. "Our host? And that's why you wanted me to wear my opal earrings and necklace."

Rector grinned. "It's the only jewelry you have that's close in color to the *Sea*. Siramont will understand the joke."

Mira laughed at Rector's prank.

As she chuckled, Rector wore an intrigued countenance. "Is it possible I've actually earned a laugh from you?"

Mira smiled. In the last few meetings, Rector had been in a good mood, no longer griping or whining about the unfairness of his fate. It made interacting with him a lot easier. Still. She couldn't let him get in the last word. "And is it possible you actually have a sense of humor under that dour exterior?" Mira countered.

"Now let's not get carried away," Rector said, wearing a patronizing expression. "I'm told a miracle would be required to grant me a sense of humor."

"Perhaps Devesh will see to your needs if you pray hard enough," Mira suggested.

"Perhaps," Rector said.

His humor left him, and Mira knew why. If he were to pray for anything, it would be to have his life returned to his own care; to live as he wanted with no subterfuges or deceptions.

"And why waylay me here at Walthall Park?" Mira asked, changing the subject and hopefully distracting him from his frustration.

"We're supposed to be a couple. It would make more sense if we arrived together."

It *did* make sense, but Mira wasn't sure how Rector had come up with the idea on his own. He was usually too self-centered to see anything beyond his own needs. "Who suggested it to you?" she asked.

His brows furrowed. "No one. It's simply the proper thing to do."

"Even though it means spending more time in the presence of someone Tainted?" Mira asked. She knew her question would annoy Rector, but she was unable to stop herself. In fact, she didn't *want* to stop herself. While she might be able to tolerate Rector Bryce more readily, there were still deep fissures of disagreement between the two of them. He should know she hadn't forgotten about them.

Rector grimaced. "I don't know the truth of what happened between you and Jaresh, and it's none of my business. Can't we just leave it at that?"

"But if something had happened? Would I not be a naaja? Tainted?" Mira asked.

"So it is written in *The Word and the Deed*."

"And what do you think?"

"I think...." Rector sighed. "I don't know what I think."

"You don't know what to think?" she asked, unsure if she had heard him right. "Just a few months ago you were so certain of everything."

"Maybe your bad influence is rubbing off on me."

———◆———

"What do you mean the original documents are still unavailable," Bree asked, trying to quell her rising frustration. She stood in the waiting area of the medical examiner's office, a bright room with windows letting in the sunshine and scented candles that failed to mask the odor of blood and fluids that pervaded all such places. She had come to review the pathology report on Drin Port's death, but according to Trivel Poorna, the mousy Sentya in charge of records, the documents had been checked out—again.

To say Bree was annoyed would be an understatement. She was furious. And she had yet to get ahold of Grasome Verle, the physician who had done the actual autopsy on the late Mr. Port. He kept rescheduling their meeting or was unavailable on the several occasions when Bree had stopped by his office unannounced. At this point, she had to believe it was done on purpose. Dr. Verle was avoiding her. After all, how busy could one physician be? Surely the man had ten minutes to spare in which to see her.

"I'm sorry, Miss Shektan," Trivel said, sounding scared. "According to the logbook, the records were checked out by Dr. Grasome Verle a week ago. He hasn't returned them yet."

Bree's eyes narrowed. So. The good doctor *did* have something to hide. A look of anger swept across her face. Grasome Verle *would* see her, and this time she wouldn't be put off by timid excuses from his secretary and staff. Devesh help them if they tried.

She realized her outraged expression was frightening the poor Sentya record-keeper. She shoved her anger aside. "Thank you, Mr. Poorna. You have been most helpful," she said, flashing him a brilliant smile.

His mouth gaped open. He was likely unnerved by what he took to be her rapidly changing moods: furious one second and happy the next. At least he didn't appear frightened anymore. Eventually, he managed a nod.

Bree gave him a final smile before turning to leave.

Just as she was about to exit the office, Trivel called out to her once again. "There is one other thing, Miss Shektan," he said. "Dr. Lindsar might be able to provide some help. He might have been present during Mr. Port's autopsy."

Bree slowly turned around. Finally, some good news. She knew Dr. Lindsar. He had been the one to do the autopsy on Suge Wrestiva. "Is he available?" she asked.

"Let me find out." Trivel bowed briefly before scurrying out.

A few minutes later, Dr. Step Lindsar came into the waiting area. He appeared much the same as before when she had last seen him. He was in his late forties, sloop-shouldered, but his walnut-colored skin remained unlined. His hair was pleated into long braids; his lean, angular face was clean-shaven; and in his hands was a folder full of papers.

"Good to see you again, Miss Shektan, especially under less trying circumstances," Dr. Lindsar said with a smile, referring to Jaresh's Tribunal. "I understand you're interested in Drin Port." He indicated the folder in his hands. "I have his file right here. A year ago, we started keeping duplicate autopsy reports of any strange deaths. Now let me see." He thumbed through the papers. "Ah yes. I remember now. It was odd. Mr. Port had too much drink and fell off a pier into Bar Try Bay. The poor fool drowned."

Bree's brows furrowed. "Why is that unusual?"

"The death itself isn't. It happens about three or four times a year actually," he replied, sounding clinical. "No. This was unusual because the nurse who assisted the autopsy, came to me later on and said that Mr. Port had what she thought was a knife wound to his heart. It wasn't in Dr. Verle's original report, and when I asked him about it, he said the guard who had pulled Mr. Port out of the water had done so with a fishhook. He said it must have been the puncture wound the nurse noticed."

"Were you able to examine the body yourself?" she asked.

"No. By the time the nurse came to me, Mr. Port's remains had already been cremated. I insisted that Dr. Verle amend his findings, though. It was the best I could do."

Bree considered Dr. Lindsar's explanation impassively even as her mind raced. Given the effort by which Dr. Verle was avoiding her, it was more likely that Mr. Port *had* been murdered, stabbed through the heart. Dr. Verle had known, which meant he was part of the Sil Lor Kum. It made it even more imperative that she confront him.

"What is this about?" Dr. Lindsar asked. "Why this sudden interest in a man who died almost a year ago?"

Bree shook off her thoughts. Right now, she had no idea who in the medical examiner's office, or anywhere in Ashoka for that matter, might be corrupted. She couldn't afford to trust anyone. "Mr. Port worked in one of our warehouses. We have insurance policies on all our employees. If any one of them are injured in the performance of their duties, the insurance pays out. One of Mr. Port's cousins filed a claim, wanting to collect the death benefits. The autopsy report would save us a lot of trouble."

Dr. Lindsar considered her words for a moment. "I see," he said. "I can have a copy of my files made and sent to House Shektan's Seat."

Bree gave him a grateful smile. "That would be wonderful." She turned to leave but paused on her way out. "One last thing: do you have Dr. Verle's home address?"

It was late afternoon by the time Bree reached Sunpalm Orchard. Like most Shiyens, this was where Dr. Verle lived. His home was an unassuming row house set along a narrow road that was barely wide enough for two carriages to pass by one another. Dwarf maples lined the sidewalk interspersed with black lampposts already lighted for the coming evening. Most of the houses were bright and cheery with laughter and conversation spilling out from open windows.

Bree glanced at Dr. Verle's home. His windows were all dark, and her skin prickled. Something was wrong. She could sense it. Bree did her best to set aside her dread and knocked on the front door. There was no answer. She tried again. Still no answer. She tried the handle. It turned easily, and she pushed the door open.

She clutched a hand to her mouth, stifling a cry of horror. Hanging from a stout beam in the front room was the slowly swaying corpse of Dr. Verle.

Farn huddled before his thin fire, the packhorse a welcome warmth next to him. The wind whistling through the ice-sheathed ravine was like an eldritch knife, slicing through his coat and clothes. He shivered and tossed on another log. The fire blazed for a moment, embers glowing and sparks lighting the darkness all around. Farn was grateful for the shallow cave he had discovered. It provided a barrier, dulling most of the wind's cutting breath.

In times like this, when it felt like his blood was slowly congealing, he wished he'd heeded Rukh's advice and stayed in Stronghold until spring. Of course, had he done so, he might very well have been faced with another problem: that of the spring-swollen River Gaunt. Rather than freeze to death, he might have drowned.

The safest time to travel to Ashoka would have been in the summer, but Farn couldn't stay that long. His family probably thought him dead. He couldn't wait, safe and secure, while those he loved suffered his absence. Besides, while he didn't hate Stronghold or its people—he was grateful to them for taking him in—his time there hadn't always been pleasant. Farn had struggled with the work he had been expected to do. It felt like it was beneath him, and to have so many of the OutCastes secretly laugh at his humiliation only made it more insulting.

He wondered how Rukh would manage. Of course, his cousin had said that as soon as he won the Trials of Hume—and Farn had no doubt he would win—he planned on leaving Stronghold for a while. He wanted to travel to Hammer and reclaim the fabled *Book of First Movement*. It hadn't seemed like a good idea, but Rukh wouldn't listen to reason. His mind had been made up.

Farn figured some of it had to do with how Rukh felt about Jessira. His cousin loved the OutCaste woman, and Farn suspected she loved Rukh as well. Unfortunately, Karma being a frigid bitch, she wouldn't allow them to be together. Jessira was engaged to that jackhole Disbar Merdant.

Farn shook his head. How could Rukh have allowed himself to fall in love with a woman who was already engaged?

Idiot.

Farn shook his head again in disbelief, but when he reconsidered the situation, he realized maybe Rukh's feelings for Jessira weren't so hard to understand. After all, the few times Farn had interacted with her, it was obvious the passion with which Jessira lived her life; the devotion she felt for those she loved. But when the situation required it, Farn suspected Jessira could also be as composed and capable as any veteran he had ever met. She had a cool intelligence easily missed behind her fiery persona.

Three months alone with a woman like Jessira…perhaps it wasn't so unexpected that Rukh would have fallen in love with her. Maybe the more pertinent question was why had Jessira fallen in love with his cousin?

Farn chuckled at the thought, but the laughter quickly faded. Rukh had so many burdens: his unfair treatment by far too many

OutCastes, an unattainable love, and exile from Ashoka. It was too much for one man to bear. Farn prayed for his cousin's well-being.

With a start, he realized that the Trials of Hume had taken place a week ago. Rukh had already left Stronghold. Even now, he was traveling alone—just like Farn—but heading west rather than east. Also, while Farn journeyed home, to family and warmth, Rukh headed to a dead city with no future or hope.

Farn eyed the surrounding darkness, lost in sudden worry for his cousin. Where was he right now? What kind of provisions did he have? Did he have enough food? Clothing? Was he safe? He wished he could have gone with him. He had offered to do so on more than one occasion, but each time, he had been steadfastly refused. Rukh had told him in no uncertain terms that a living Ashoka was Farn's destiny, not a dead Hammer.

While true, such knowledge carried a hollow, unfulfilling comfort. Farn still felt like he'd abandoned Rukh in his cousin's greatest moment of need. It was a shame that left his stomach gnarled with guilt.

And what could he say to Rukh's amma? To his nanna? Or to Jaresh and Bree? What could he tell them of their son and brother? Of his ultimate fate? How could he tell them he'd left Rukh alone and forsaken?

The knowledge left Farn with a chill in his heart, one colder than the icy wind gusting through the ravine.

Farn stared into the fire and did the only thing he could think to do. He prayed once more for his cousin's safety.

CHAPTER FIFTEEN
A NARROWED SEARCH

Who has the greater courage: a man willing to give
his life for a just cause or a man willing to live for that same purpose?

~The Warrior and the Servant (author unknown)

Jaresh held the door open as he and Bree entered the Blue Heron, the pub that Drin Port, Felt Barnel, and Van Jinnu had all frequented. As soon as he stepped inside, his nose wrinkled in disgust. The air was ripe with the stink of smoke, stale beer, and vomit. A man's loud guffaw came from what Jaresh guessed was probably the kitchen while a few patrons sat quietly at the long bar, nursing their ales. Even this early—mid-afternoon—most of them appeared drunk as rats in a vat of wine. They looked up with bleary eyes, giving him and Bree desultory looks before returning their attention to their mugs.

"Lovely," Bree murmured.

Jaresh echoed her sentiment. The Blue Heron was a seedy dive, but there had to be something to the place; something to connect the three murdered men; something that had ended up marking them for death. Perhaps someone here could tell them what it was.

As they stepped further into the pub, Jaresh carefully eyed the two, large Duriahs tasked with keeping peace within the place. If these were the guards, then the Blue Heron must be a rough place. They sat on stools, almond-shaped eyes staring into the nearly empty pub with identical expressions of dull boredom. Sometimes, their hands stroked the truncheons tucked into their belts. They seemed the kind of men who enjoyed cracking skulls because they had nothing better to do and had the toughness to put down any challenge.

However, when Jaresh examined the Duriahs more closely, he reevaluated his initial assessment. The guards looked hard and dangerous, but they had an air about them, something that said they were mostly all bark and bullying. Most of their bulk was fat, and they had the slow-gazed appearance of thugs, men who allowed their size to intimidate others. It had likely been years since either one had truly been tested.

Jaresh would have dismissed the guards as a threat, but the way they eyed Bree was like dogs salivating over a piece of meat. Such disgusting behavior couldn't be left unchallenged.

He was about to say something, but Bree must have noticed their vulgar stares as well. "Move your eyes," she snapped, withering the Duriahs with a contemptuous look.

Both guards stiffened, their faces red with either anger or embarrassment. "And you should watch what pub you enter, little girl," one of them threatened. He reached for a truncheon.

Bree stared at the Duriah as his hand curled around the handle of his weapon. She very deliberately allowed her hand to fill with a Fireball.

"Are we going to have a problem?" Jaresh asked, his hand on his sword. Most of the time, he hardly ever walked around Ashoka with anything more than a dagger. There was no need. The city was safe, but some parts, like the Moon Quarter, could be a little rough. And the Blue Heron, located as it was in a poorer district, likely catered to an even harder clientele. It seemed like he had been right to be cautious.

"Leave off, or she'll burn the whole place down," the other guard—probably the smarter of the two—said to his partner. He pushed the other man's hand off his truncheon before turning to Jaresh and Bree. "What do you want?"

"A drink," Jaresh said with a bright smile. "And you're welcome to join us if you're allowed."

The words earned him a grudging nod from both guards.

"A drink sounds fine," the smarter guard—name of Drog—said. He called over a waitress and ordered four ales.

It arrived shortly, and while Jaresh managed to hold the swill down, Bree took one sip and pushed hers aside. "We are looking for some information," she said. "About three men: Felt Barnel, Drin Port, and Van Jinnu."

The duller guard, Crode, furrowed his brows, looking either confused or ignorant. "They're all dead," he said. "Two of them were murdered by that Withering Knife," he added with a shudder. "Nasty business. Whoever it is going around killing people, I hope they find the fragging bastard and string him up on the Isle of the Crow."

"So do we all," Bree agreed. "Did you know them? The men, I mean?"

"We knew them," Crode answered. "They were regulars. Used to gather here and drink all night. Or at least they did until Drin got himself drowned in the harbor."

"They were friends," Jaresh said, trying to mask his rising excitement.

"Didn't I just say so?" Crode replied. "They drank together near every night."

"Was there anything else to their relationship?" Jaresh asked. "Were they business partners, maybe?"

The dull guard laughed. "Business? Drin worked in one of the warehouses here in the Quarter. He was as poor as they come."

"Didn't have two coins to rub together," Drog added. "Half the time it was Van and Felt paying for his drinks."

"But he had a mouth on him," Crode said. "He was always going on about how he had some scheme that would bring him all the coin he could ever want, like he knew someone rich to help him out."

"Which made him an even bigger fool than he already was," Drog added. "Why would someone rich help someone poor? Makes no sense. What does the rich person get out of it?"

Jaresh didn't bother pointing out the benefits of investment, not just in businesses, but in people, which was far more important. Such advice would have been lost on these two. "Was there anything peculiar that might have happened on the night Drin died?" he asked.

The dull guard laughed. "That was a long time ago," he said. "Probably just a night like any other."

"You remember that Kumma who nearly kicked Drin's tenders up his throat?" Drog asked his partner. "Remember? Drin comes in here all full of vinegar and venom, staring around like he could throw thunder, and this old Kumma didn't like it. He was pissed, and he comes walking over—"

"He had a limp," Crode said. "The Kumma. He was using a cane—"

"Which side was the limp?" Bree interrupted.

The Duriahs looked at her in confusion.

"How the frag should I know?" Crode asked. "He was just an old Kumma with a limp. Anyway he walks over, all cold and deadly, looking like he was going to kick Drin's nuggets through his skull." He cackled in laughter. "I thought old Drin would piss himself."

Afterward, the guards had nothing else to add, so Jaresh and Bree left the Heron.

But just outside the front door, they were hailed by Drog. They waited as he ambled forward. "There was one other thing. This fine Rahail woman was here the night Drin died. Never seen her before or since, but she had business with the Kumma."

"What did she look like?" Jaresh asked.

"She wasn't old, but she wasn't young," Drog said, "but still easy to look at. Can't really describe her any better than that."

An older Kumma man and a Rahail woman. Was there a connection between them? Jaresh looked to Bree, who shrugged minutely.

"You think Drin was murdered, don't you?" Drog asked, speaking into the quiet his words had caused. "That's why you're here. You think it was this Kumma who did it, maybe doing all the killing."

"We're just asking questions," Jaresh said. He lowered his voice. "It's best if no one knows we asked them."

"But—"

"If you really think this Kumma might be a murderer, do you really want your suspicions getting back to him?" Bree explained.

Drog gave a brief grimace of distaste. "I think I'm seeing the wisdom of keeping my mouth shut," he said.

———●●———

B ree felt eyes upon her. She and Jaresh had reached the heart of an alley, which they'd planned on using to bypass the heavy traffic of Bellary Road. She glanced behind her and frowned. Two men stood at the alley's entrance, darkening it. They were large and wore angry scowls. Bree looked forward. Dimming the opposite end of the alley were two more men, similarly large and rough in appearance. All four men walked forward with a forbidding purpose. As they continued their steady advance, Bree tried to fathom what they might want.

What was their intent? Surely not to attack her and Jaresh? Assaults like that simply didn't happen in Ashoka. Her home was civilized, a place of beauty and learning.

But the expressions on the faces of the advancing men was anything but. If anything, their scowls had grown deeper, uglier and more threatening. Their jaws firmed in what Bree finally realized was a promise of violence. Deadly intentions were clearly written on their faces.

Bree took an involuntary step toward her brother. Her mouth was suddenly dry, and her heart raced. These men had to be Sil Lor Kum. Who else would have reason to attack her and Jaresh? She had the sudden realization that she and her brother might die in this alley.

Jaresh must have come to the same conclusion. His hand rested on the hilt of his sword and worry lit his face. "This isn't training," he warned Bree in a whisper. "Those men mean to hurt us. Have your Shield up and be careful with your Fireballs. We don't want to burn down this whole block."

Bree glanced at the wood-clad buildings all around them. One errant Fireball would send the entire alley up in flames. She cursed. She couldn't readily use her greatest weapon. Whoever these men were, they'd chosen the site of their ambush well. Bree wished she'd been wise enough to bring a weapon with her instead of simply trusting to Jaresh's sword.

"Stay calm," Jaresh said. "We can survive this if we're smart. Deep breaths. Remember what you've been taught."

Bree nodded and did her best to set aside her fear. She tried to do as Jaresh had suggested. She took deep breaths, slow and steady, exhaling fully and willing the terror to leave her. Reason told her there was no point to being scared, but right now, reason was an empty solace.

The breathing exercises helped, or so she told herself; and while her heart no longer pounded, her legs still trembled. Bree continued breathing in and out, slowly and controlled. She focused her mind on the details that might help her survive the looming fight. She studied the approaching men, the way they walked and carried themselves. They weren't like Drog and Crode, the guards at the Blue Heron. These men moved with wary grace and coiled energy, like trained warriors. Soon enough, their features became clearer. Two Rahails and two Murans. Bree cursed again. The men coming toward them might be able to Blend.

Jaresh must have realized the same possibility. "We can't wait on them," he said. "*We* have to be the ones to attack. We take out the ones up front and then deal with the ones behind us."

"What do you need me to do?" Bree asked, trying to work some moisture into her dry mouth.

"Stay behind me," Jaresh said. "I'll divert one of them to the center of the alley. Take him with a Fireball, and I'll deal with the other."

Bree managed to nod, an icy lump of dread lodged in her stomach. It was growing stonier and colder with every step the men took. The terror she had hoped to banish surged back to life. Incipient panic bubbled to the fore.

"We'll be fine," Jaresh said.

He took her hand, and Bree felt a calm come over her. Lucency. Jaresh's Talent. It soothed her terror-stricken thoughts, and her mind cleared. The fear faded, still present, but no longer overwhelming.

Jaresh looked her in the eyes. "Ready?"

Bree nodded.

"Wait for my signal," Jaresh said. He stared at the men coming their way, waiting an impossibly long moment. "NOW!" Jaresh flowed forward, his sword flashing.

Her brother had engaged the enemy. He fought a Blended Muran but seemed to know where the man would be. Jaresh delivered a stroke against the empty air, but a ringing clash marked where his sword met resistance. Jaresh pushed his hidden opponent away before turning to face the still-visible Rahail.

Bree sent a Fireball screaming the short distance to where Jaresh had diverted the hidden Muran.

A terrible cry of pain echoed throughout the alley, and her opponent was visible, wreathed in flames. The stench of burning flesh made Bree gag. She held down her gorge even as Jaresh finished the Rahail he had been fighting. Together, they turned to face the other two men.

Jaresh rushed past her. His sword cleaved an arc, hammering onto the blade of a Blended opponent. Jaresh fought air, but somehow he always knew where the other man was. Two more strokes and a Muran flashed into view, gasping with pain as he flopped to the ground.

Bree watched, clear-eyed from Lucency, but she had yet to see the Rahail. Where was he! Bree had lost sight of him. A distortion in the air directly before her. The Rahail! Bree stumbled back. Usually, she was so graceful, but in that moment, she was clumsiness personified. She tripped over her own feet and fell to the ground, smacking her head. Her Shield disintegrated. Bree desperately tried to get it back in place. Too late. A tearing pain ripped across her stomach. Bree cried out.

Someone else's deep-voiced shout of pain was the last thing she heard before she lost consciousness.

＊ ＊ ＊

As soon as Mira heard of Bree's injuries, she set off for the Moon Quarter hospice where her friend was being treated. She arrived out of breath—she'd literally run the entire distance. All the while, she had been praying for Bree. *Let her be all right.*

Jaresh was already there, alone in the waiting room. He looked as distraught as Mira felt. He numbly explained the brazen attack that he and his sister had barely survived just a few blocks away.

"How is Bree?" Mira asked. "What does the doctor say?"

"She's stable, but the sword cut deep," Jaresh replied. "He thinks she'll be fine, but she'll need more surgery if any infection sets in." He wouldn't meet Mira's eyes. "I wasn't fast enough to protect her."

"It wasn't your fault," Mira said. She wanted to offer Jaresh some semblance of support; to hold him, even just squeeze his shoulder, but she couldn't. She had to keep her distance. They were of different Castes, and as a result, physical contact between them was impermissible. It was a sin, and just as important, Mira had worked too hard to suffocate the feelings she had once held for Jaresh. But looking at him now, seeing his anguish, she realized those feelings had yet to entirely fade.

"The Rahail who did this got away," Jaresh growled, drawing her away from her thoughts about their relationship.

"They were Sil Lor Kum?" Mira asked.

"Who else?" Jaresh said. "The sooner those fraggers get staked out on the Isle of the Crow, the better for all of us." He fell into a sullen silence, and Mira left him to his thoughts.

They sat quietly in the waiting room, a white-walled room with narrow windows and old landscape paintings meant to brighten the space.

Minutes later, the door to the hospice opened. It was Mira's amma. "What happened?" she asked.

Jaresh described the attack in the alley. "Where are my parents?" he asked after he finished his explanation.

"Dar'El and Satha weren't at the Seat when your message arrived," Mira's amma said. "I'm sure they've been informed by now. They'll be here soon enough."

Jaresh sighed. "I wish Rukh was here," he said. "He could have protected Bree from all of this."

"On this, we are agreed," Amma muttered. Jaresh stiffened, but Amma continued on, overlooking the offense she had delivered as if it had never occurred. "If your brother had only shown the good sense to protect his reputation, his honor would have never been challenged." She cast a glance in Mira's direction, who reddened in embarrassment.

Mira knew what her amma really meant. She bowed her head and waited for the next verbal blow. How could she have been so stupid as to discuss Jaresh in front of *her*? Embarrassment built into shame. Apparently, Amma had nothing further to add, and Mira dared look her way. Her mother was staring at a painting, and Mira felt like she should say something, apologize, or at least find a means of mollifying her amma.

Instead, Mira held silent as Bree's words from several weeks ago came to her.

Her friend had been right. Mira *had* always been the sort of woman who sought to please everyone else, even at the expense of her own happiness. Her annoyance rose. So many times she had accepted her amma's criticisms. Annoyance became anger. Mira had spent her life trying to placate Amma. Anger built as if stoked in a furnace. She had sought to become the perfect, hardworking daughter.

"His sister lies gravely injured," Mira said to her amma, trying to contain her rage. "And you would cast aspersions on him? Now is not the time."

Amma's expression of stunned disbelief would have been comical at any other time and on any other person. But not now. Jaresh stirred in his chair, sensing a brewing argument. Amma recovered her shock. She turned her basilisk gaze at Mira, who held firm, refusing to look away from her amma's quivering anger.

"Now also isn't the time for an argument. Not when my sister is recovering from surgery," Jaresh said forcefully as he rose to his feet. "She needs quiet." Mira and her amma both glared at him, but he refused to back down. "I mean it. If you plan on shrieking like scalded cats, then you can leave. I don't need Bree bothered by your yelling, and my parents don't need to hear it either."

Mira and her amma both nodded reluctantly and took seats opposite to one another in the small waiting room.

They waited and several minutes later, Dar'El and Satha arrived, their expressions full of bleak fear.

Jaresh rushed to his feet. "She's recovering," he said before they could ask the question. "The doctor will let us see her when she's ready."

"Thank Devesh," Satha murmured in sudden relief. Tears came to her eyes as she and Dar'El moved to embrace their son.

Mira felt like an interloper. She glanced at her amma, who gave her a tight nod and a gesture. It was time for them to leave, and have a discussion of their own. Mira swallowed down a small lump of trepidation.

News of the attack on Bree whipped through Ashoka like a firestorm. The news was shocking: a Kumma woman nearly murdered in the Moon Quarter with her attacker or attackers still free. Information was unreliable and soon, a thousand rumors sparked to life as everyone offered up their own competing theories as to what might have happened. Some claimed it had been the Withering Knife murderer. Others said it was members of House Wrestiva, seeking retribution for the death of Suge Wrestiva. Others were certain it had been the Sil Lor Kum. A dozen of them had sought Bree Shektan's death, but thankfully, a passing Kumma had heard her cries for help and defeated them all. But in doing so, he had bled out his life in the protection of hers. It was a scandal that had everyone outraged.

Rector Bryce was just as furious as anyone. No woman should have to fear for her safety, and he was determined to see justice done on those who had committed this heinous crime. However, if he wanted to be of use, he had to consider what had happened with as much dispassion as possible. Emotions would be of little use in this situation, and he suspected Bree's family would be too furious and scared to think clearly.

Thus, the rumor Rector believed most likely to be true was the one that claimed that the attackers had numbered but four, and that it had been Jaresh Shektan who had been the warrior who had saved Bree's life. It was the least outrageous possibility, and in Rector's experience, that generally meant it was also the one closest to the truth. Corroboration came when he spoke to the members of the City Watch. They still lingered near the cordoned-off area and according to what they had learned, a single, wounded Rahail had been the only one to escape Jaresh's sword.

Rector's opinion of the Sentya rose further when he learned the details of the attack. Two men, ahead and behind, had trapped Bree and Jaresh in the alley; but rather than submit, Jaresh—as he had been trained—had attacked. He'd fought off four Blended opponents, killing three and wounding the other. And while Bree had been gravely injured, all news said she was likely to recover.

Which meant the most pressing matter was finding the wounded Rahail. The Watch had already begun scouring any nearby hospices where he might have sought help, but so far, they had been unable to find him. Rector suspected they never would, not if they searched for him in a Shiyen-sanctioned hospice. The Rahail likely was a member of the Sil Lor Kum, and for treatment of his injuries, he would need someone discrete, someone who wouldn't ask questions, and who might not necessarily have a license to Heal.

Rector knew of just such a person. Jaciro Temult, a disreputable Shiyen physician whose addiction to opium and alcohol had resulted in the forfeiture of his medical license many years ago. Jaciro owned a rundown herb shop in the Moon Quarter, selling simple cures for afflictions such as headaches and diarrhea. Rumor suggested that, for the right coin, he also offered back-alley medical services to those for whom discretion was of greater import than legitimate care—men, for instance, like the injured Rahail.

Rector quickly made his way to the Tired Life, the herbal shop owned by Jaciro. He tried the front door, but it was locked, and a sign in the window indicated that the store was closed. Rector peered inside. The firefly lamps were off, and the interior was dim but a light leaked beneath the door leading to the room out back. Someone was there.

Rector made his way to the rear of the building. There, he found another door. This one unlocked. He drew *Jivatma* and Shielded. Who knew what was waiting on the other side of the door? He eased the door open.

Jaciro had his back to him, facing a man sitting on a table: a Rahail with his leg heavily bandaged. The man saw Rector, and his eyes widened in dismay. Before Jaciro could react, the Rahail spun him about. He locked one arm under the elderly Shiyen's throat and held a dagger to the side of his neck. "Come closer and he dies," the Rahail promised.

Rector fully entered the room, closing the door behind him. Despite his feelings toward Jaciro, he didn't want to see the old Shiyen dead. "There is no reason to hurt the old man," he said. "He's done nothing to you."

"It doesn't matter. I want you gone, or his blood is on your hands."

Rector shook his head. "You know I won't," he replied. "No

matter what you think you can do, your life is over. It cannot go any other way."

The Rahail smirked, but Rector could see the fear in his eyes. "I have friends who—"

"I know the kind of friends you have," Rector interrupted. "And you know what happens to those who are Sil Lor Kum." Jaciro whitened at his words. So. The Shiyen hadn't known what kind of a man he had been Healing. "You will be hung, drawn, and quartered with your body left to rot on the Isle of the Crows."

The Rahail licked his lips and darted a glance at the closed door.

"It doesn't need to end in such torment," Rector said. "Make the right choice, and I'll end you as swiftly and painlessly as possible." It was an offer meant to simply keep the Rahail from doing anything foolish and give Rector time to think. It certainly wasn't a promise he wanted to keep. He had never killed a man. His stomach roiled at the thought.

"I've done nothing wrong," the Rahail said.

"You were part of the group who attacked Bree and Jaresh Shektan. And you *are* Sil Lor Kum. Tell me everything, and I promise to finish you here." Rector swallowed heavily. He was committed now. Hopefully, the fear and uneasiness wasn't evident on his face. "Otherwise, you will face Dar'El Shektan." Rector paused. "Or, worse, the one holding the Withering Knife."

That got the Rahail's attention. His face tightened with fear. "If I agree, you promise to see me finished quickly?" he asked in a tremulous voice.

"Let Jaciro go, and we'll talk," Rector said. "If you tell me what I wish to hear, then your death will be as quick as I can manage." Rector spoke the words as calmly as he could, but his insides were an agony of rising dread. He would actually have to go through with killing this man, something he knew would haunt him.

Rector's own inner torment must not have reflected on his

features because the energy seemed to drain out of the Rahail. He relaxed his hold on Jaciro and dropped his knife. "What do you want to know?"

CHAPTER SIXTEEN
A TRAIL OF A DIFFERENT SORT

Strive for greatness always and overwhelm mediocrity.
Honor those who achieve this guiding principle,
for their actions are a reflection of Devesh's glory.

~To Live Well by Fair Shire of Stronghold, AF 1842

S ign craned her head, trying to see past Cedar and get a better view. The Home Arena was packed. Almost everyone was here tonight, including her family. It was the Trials of Hume, after all. Would Wheel Cloud become the greatest champion in the city's history? No one had ever won three consecutive Trials. Or would a new stud, like Toth Shard or Strive Loane, wrest the title from the aging stallion.

The Arena was as bright as the noonday sun with thousands of firefly lanterns all blazing as brilliantly as Sign's emotions. She was so excited she could barely sit still.

She just wished she had a better view.

Laya—bless her—must have noticed Sign's squirming and took pity. She nudged her oblivious husband to move aside. Cedar was a good man. He rose out of his seat without complaint or question. He gestured to Sign as he stepped aside. She took him up on his offer, slipping into his vacated space while he clambered past her in an exchange of seats.

Ahh! Much better. Now she could see everything. The people in front of Sign were all relatively short, and she got to sit next to Jessira and Laya, two of her favorite people in the world.

A roar went up from the crowd as the combatants filed into the stadium, taking their seats along a small section of the stands directly above the arena floor. The warriors were so close that she could make out their faces. Sign looked for those she knew well.

Her regard eventually fell on Rukh. Cedar had risked his reputation by sponsoring the Kumma, and Peddananna and Peddamma had risked their money by paying the cost of his entrance fee. Sign hoped the risks were worth it, and Rukh didn't end up embarrassing himself or her family.

Sign's brows furrowed in worry as she studied the Pureblood. What was wrong with him? Usually, he was so lively and funny, but right now, he looked as emotionless as a dead fish. Even his appearance was pallid. Was he scared? It was hard to believe he could be frightened. He should be brimming full of confidence given how Jessira, Cedar, and even Court went on and on about his skills.

Something else must be bothering him.

Sign had heard from Jessira that a few weeks back, Rukh had been ambushed by a group of unnamed warriors. Jessira had said it was the second such assault he had experienced, and both times, the authorities had paid him no heed, refusing to seek justice on his behalf. Had he been injured in the attacks? Was that the reason for his wan expression? Not that Sign believed he'd been mugged. It simply couldn't be true. First of all, if Rukh truly had been ambushed, then why wasn't he injured? Such an assault should have landed him in a hospice. He certainly wouldn't be walking about without any visible injury and about to take on Stronghold's best. More importantly, the people of Stronghold were civilized. None of her people would dare tolerate such barbarism. Maybe things like that happened in Ashoka but not here.

While Sign knew some of the OutCastes had been unkind to Rukh, she couldn't imagine any of them would actually try to hurt him. Yes, Rukh's life in Stronghold wasn't easy, but it wasn't unsafe. She mentally grimaced. Of course, safe wasn't the same as welcoming; and Rukh deserved at least that much. He was a good man, kind and generous, just like Jessira described him.

Maybe if he won a few matches in the Trials, his life would finally improve. He was a Kumma after all, and there had to be something to their legendary fighting prowess. Although, looking at him now, as he stood amongst the other warriors, it seemed distinctly unlikely. His bearing didn't lend confidence that he would somehow beat one of Stronghold's finest. Her brows furrowed. How could a person manage to look so uninspiring?

In contrast, Stronghold's warriors held expressions of furious ambition and barely controlled rage. They seethed and walked with the scarcely contained bloodlust of wolves on the hunt. Some seemed to literally growl at Rukh, probably sensing his weakness. Sign felt a surge of pride. These were Stronghold's greatest warriors: fine, fierce, and unfettered.

It was only too bad for Rukh that one of them would likely finish him in his very first match, which was a shame. She liked Rukh.

Sign left off her worries when Mon Peace, the Governor-General and leader of Stronghold, rose from his seat. The throng quieted, but their energy wasn't dimmed in the slightest. The crowd's enthusiasm and excitement were intoxicating. It filled Sign like a heady drink, making her giddy with anticipation. She wanted to jump to her feet and scream defiance; yell at the world, at fate, at the Queen and all her fragging Chimeras. Sign just wanted to *do* something; something terrible and important.

As a result, she didn't hear most of Mon Peace's words.

It took Jessira's gentle nudge to bring her back to the present. "His first match is against Toth Shard."

Sign didn't have to ask who Jessira was talking about. Rukh was to face Toth Shard in his opening match. Sign pitied the Kumma. Other than challenging Wheel Cloud, she couldn't imagine a harder assignment for him to have received. Toth would make mincemeat out of Rukh, and Sign felt bad for him. She even felt bad for Jessira. While Rukh faced humiliation with his impending loss, Jessira would then have to do an extra month of labor in the barracks. It was all part of their wager, one her cousin should never have taken. Love must have clouded her judgment.

Sign wondered who else might be matched up in the first round, and she looked to the battle board where a list of the competitors and whom they would be facing was written out in broad letters that were easily visible throughout the arena. This year there were thirty-two entrants into the Trials. It was an even number, which meant there would be no need for any winnowing contests. It was too bad. Sometimes the early matches were the most entertaining.

She glanced about again, studying the stadium as last second preparations went on. What a grand arena her ancestors had built. What forethought and vision had gone into its planning. A century ago, when construction on the Home Arena began, the senators of the time had designed the stadium with the city's growth in mind. They hadn't wanted a structure that would prove to be too small in just a few generations, so they had opted to construct as large a building as they possibly could. From nearby Mount Snow had come the large white stones, which formed the walls and floor of the arena. Each rectangular rock had been floated down River Fled and along Tear Drop Lake before being hauled inside by brute force. The stones had been carried all the way to the Home Croft, the seat of Stronghold's government and the place where the Governor-General held his residence. The final result was an enormous arena, one able to seat over forty thousand.

Sign glanced over when Jessira inhaled sharply. Her cousin was leaning forward, perched on the edge of her seat. Her worried gaze was focused on the Pureblood.

"I'm sure Rukh will be fine," Peddananna, Jessira's nanna, said as he patted her hand.

"Kummas are supposed to be warriors," Peddamma, Jessira's amma, said. "I'm sure Rukh will acquit himself well enough."

"I doubt it. He has to face Toth Shard. I heard Toth has become a demon since the last Trials. I think he'll win it all this time," Disbar said.

Sign frowned in annoyance. Annayya—Kart—had invited the jackhole to the Trials, supposedly to help revive Disbar's engagement to Jessira. Kart had explained his reasoning, saying it was to help salvage Jessira's honor; but really it was for Annayya's own benefit. Annayya was nearly religious in his devotion to his reputation. Nothing could be allowed to sully his good name, especially something as stunning as Jessira's decision to end her engagement to Disbar. Her actions had sent Annayya into a righteous snit. Thus, Disbar's presence here. Annayya hoped to salvage the situation so he wouldn't lose any standing with the higher members of Stronghold's society.

Nevertheless, as much as Sign wished Disbar had done the honorable thing and declined Annayya's invitation, she quietly agreed with his assessment. She just didn't want to say so. Jessira already looked upset enough. Sign reached over and gave her cousin's hand a reassuring squeeze.

"The Kumma will be lucky to last ten seconds against Toth," Disbar continued on, sounding satisfied.

Sign glared at Disbar. On paper, he had made an excellent match for Jessira, but the more Sign had gotten to know him, the less she liked Disbar. She was glad Jessira had broken off her engagement to the man. Disbar was prickly, boastful, and either too self-absorbed or too uncaring to notice when others were unhappy with him. In the end, he simply wasn't good enough for Jessira. Her cousin deserved a better man, someone worthy of her warm and generous nature.

"Toth won't last five seconds against Rukh, unless Rukh allows it," Jessira said in a voice of quiet certainty. "I know none of you believe my reports—or Cedar's for that matter—but tonight you're going to find out I wasn't exaggerating or making up fables. Rukh is the finest warrior any of us are likely to see. He'll crush Toth."

"He told you this?" Kart asked.

"He didn't have to. I can see it in his expression and carriage. Rukh's angry with us."

"Jessira, we've given him shelter, a place to stay," Peddamma said. "What more could he possibly want from us?"

"A home," Jessira said. She shot a look of disdain toward Disbar. "And justice."

Sign had heard Jessira's worries that Disbar might have been involved with the supposed attacks on Rukh but until now, she hadn't realized her cousin actually believed those rumors. No wonder Jessira seemed so tense. She probably wanted to shake the truth out of her former fiancé—and kick his teeth down his throat if he was guilty.

"What are you talking about?" Kart asked. "Who is he to demand anything of us? Arrogant Pureblood. If he wants more, let him earn it."

"I agree," Disbar said. "Wholeheartedly."

Sign shook her head in disgust. Why couldn't the man just keep his mouth shut?

"Then you're a fool," Cedar said to Disbar. "He's been attacked in our city, possibly by our own warriors and nothing has been done. Our people humiliate him, and many think it's a fine joke. It's not.

It's shame we've brought on ourselves. And he'll pay us back for all of it. He's going to hurt whoever he faces."

Cedar's words elicited an uncomfortable silence. Sign shifted in her seat. She tried not to think about what Cedar had said, mostly because she was afraid he was right and that she'd have to face some hard, ugly truths. After all, Rukh had been an injured stranger seeking shelter. But instead of opening their homes and hearts to him, her people had treated him shabbily—all for the sin of being born a Pureblood. Sign swallowed heavily. What did it say about her people that they would treat someone so cruelly? She imagined the rest of her family—other than maybe Kart—were thinking the same thoughts.

Her thoughts were interrupted when Court spoke. "I've crossed blades with him," he said. "He was still recovering from his injuries, but even then, he was hard to handle. Farn was something else entirely. If a Healed Rukh is even better," he shook his head, "then I feel sorry for those men down there."

"You've never mentioned this before," Sign said.

"That's because I knew how people would react. They'd have treated me just like they do Jessira and Cedar: with a scornful little pat on the head."

Sign didn't have a ready response or quip to Court's claim, mostly because she knew her brother was right.

"Whatever happens, we'll find out soon enough. Maybe Rukh will do better than any of us expect," Laya said, trying to sound upbeat and positive.

———————————•◦•———————————

Rukh didn't listen as the Governor-General spoke his words of welcome. Instead, he focused on his opponent, Toth Shard. The man was in his late twenties and a twelve-year veteran of the Home Army. Shard was supposedly at the very peak of his powers and considered one of the finest warriors in Stronghold. In fact, many felt Toth was a favorite to win it all this year.

And Rukh was matched against him in the first round.

He smiled at the insult.

In the early rounds of Ashoka's Tournament of Hume, those considered to be the weakest warriors were paired against those thought to be the strongest. The plan was for the better warriors to win through the early matches and challenge one another in the later stages. The same held true in Stronghold. It said a lot about how little the Strongholders thought of Rukh's skills for them to match him against Toth Shard in the first round.

Good. Let them underestimate him. When he cut down their finest, the sting of such a loss would hurt all the more.

Toth, for instance, certainly didn't look worried. Earlier today, he'd looked over in Rukh's direction once, and flicked a contemptuous gaze up and down before turning away with a sneering, confident laugh.

Toth's mistake. Earlier in the week, Rukh had scouted out all of the combatants. Toth had some skill. In fact, for an OutCaste, he was actually quite good; but for a Kumma, he was, at best, a raw beginner. He would pose no challenge. None of them would. And though the Constrainers that Rukh wore—as did every other combatant—would significantly limit his *Jivatma* imbued Talents, such as speed and strength, he was still far more skilled than anyone here.

Rukh carefully watched the first few matches, studying the movements, the patterns and the balance of those he might face. He wasn't impressed. None of them were any better than he had originally surmised.

Finally, his name was called. He and Toth walked side-by-side as they descended to the hard-packed, dirt floor of the Arena. They passed through the open gate leading into the bowl of the stadium with Toth breaking left and Rukh going right. The Governor-General announced their names, and not surprisingly, the crowd cheered wildly for Toth; but for Rukh, they booed lustily.

Rukh didn't care. He no longer heard them. His gaze and focus were narrowed down to Toth Shard, thirty feet away and standing as proud as the sun while he lazily gripped his shoke.

It was almost time. Rukh's features were expressionless as he conducted *Jivatma*, his senses heightening. The arena grew brighter, the light more vivid and stark. His hearing, sense of smell, all of it sharpened. The world slowed. His muscles twitched, a harbinger of the mind-blurring motion that was as much a hallmark of Caste Kumma as their features. Everyone seemed to move as if their feet were encased in mud.

The Governor-General gave his command: "Fight!"

Rukh was expecting it when Toth formed a Blend. It wasn't deep enough to completely enfold and hide him—the Constrainers wouldn't allow it—but even if it had, the Blend wouldn't have been enough to protect Toth. Rukh had been trained since childhood to fight men in true Blends; to know *exactly* where they would be, even down to the position of their shokes. Toth's pale version of a Blend would be easy to defeat.

Rukh surged forward. He had all the time in the world to decide how to seize the brutal victory he intended. A gut kick had Toth tumbling head over heels, losing control of his Blend. Rukh could have finished him right then and there, but he chose to prolong the contest. He waited for Toth to rise to his feet and recover, never bothering to ready his shoke. Instead, Rukh gripped it loosely, almost casually, allowing the tip to dip toward the ground. Toth's face reddened at the insult. The Strongholder attacked. Rukh defended a strike at his chest. Another aimed for his head and a follow-up at his legs. He blocked a thrust and a slash. Five strikes. It was enough. Rukh dipped low and darted forward. Another gut kick had Toth on his back. Rukh sliced his shoke across the Strongholder's neck in a throat cutting move.

The fight was over as Toth cried out in pain and clutched his neck.

Rukh sheathed his shoke in an Arena grown silent.

He bowed to his opponent even as physicians raced forward to Heal Toth and rid him of the shoke-induced pain. It shouldn't be too bad. Rukh had pulled his blow. He didn't like or respect many of Stronghold's warriors, but he refused to be as petty or cruel as they had been to him. The truth was, had Rukh wanted to hurt Toth, he could have done so by slamming his shoke against the other man's neck in a decapitating blow. It would have been agony.

As Rukh approached the open gate and the stairs leading to where the other Trials contestants waited, a half-smile lit his lips. Let the others begin to understand what they faced. He conducted *Jivatma* and leapt up, soaring fifteen feet into the air before spinning in mid-leap, and landing gently in front of his seat. He gracefully settled himself. Just then, the memory of Kinsu Makren came to him; his fellow Shektan with his unflappable, icy cold demeanor during the Tournament of Hume. It was what Rukh hoped his own face looked like to all who watched.

———————●●———————

"What in the unholy hells just happened?" Sign gasped as Rukh stood above the fallen Toth. "What did he do?"

"What Jessira and I have been warning you would happen," Cedar said, sounding tired. "Rukh is going to let us know exactly how little he thinks of our warriors. And of us."

"He beat Toth with his off hand," Jessira commented clinically. "He's not nearly as good with it."

Sign gaped, as did many others seated around their family. Off hand? But the speed and skill he had displayed...surely not. What was he like with his *on* hand? "Devesh save us," she whispered. "What kind of a man is he?"

"The kind who'll win these Trials," Jessira said, seeming to take thorough satisfaction in everyone's stunned shock. "He could have probably won without even unsheathing his shoke," she noted.

Disbar looked at her in outrage. "You approve of his actions," he accused.

"No. I disapprove of ours," Jessira snapped, turning to face him, the rage radiating off her like a heat wave. "I've heard how Rukh was attacked several weeks ago, and no one believed him. Those who harmed him paid no price for their dishonor."

"Five," Court said. "A few days before Farn left, Rukh said he had been attacked by five warriors. He had no injuries, so I didn't believe him at the time." He nodded his head. "Now I do."

Until a few moments ago, Sign wouldn't have believed it either. A single man fighting off five trained warriors? Impossible. But now, after seeing Rukh's dismantling of Toth, she did. He could have done it. Sign flicked a considering glance at Disbar. Was it truly possible that Jessira had been chained to a man capable of such loathsomeness? If so, she was doubly glad for her cousin's courage in ending her engagement to such a coward.

"Did anyone else see what he just did?" Peddamma interrupted them, her voice filled with further shock.

Everyone had and the hush in the arena deepened.

Rukh had leapt straight to the sitting area of the other warriors. The jump must have been at least fifteen feet. He settled into his seat. His face was as still and composed as a mountain lake in winter.

After that demonstration, no one had anything else to add. They settled down to watch the rest of the Tournament. The remaining matches were somehow anticlimactic in comparison. They elicited a few perfunctory cheers and whistles; but otherwise, the crowd's energy had been utterly sapped by Rukh's performance. When it was time for his next fight, the entire Arena hushed, waiting to see if this would be a repeat of his earlier match.

Jessira heard muttered complaints about the 'Pureblood bastard', but when she looked around, she saw how everyone's rapt attention was focused on Rukh. They might have loathed him, but they were entranced by him as well.

Rukh had leapt down from his place amongst the other combatants, straight to the bowl of the Arena, not bothering with the stairs. His movements were smooth and liquid, like a stalking snow leopard. He was mesmerizing. Even his opponent, Stole Breve appeared hypnotized.

The fight began, and once again, Rukh didn't bother bringing his shoke to guard. He held it loosely, almost nonchalantly, letting it dangle. But every thrust and slash that Stole tried to execute was blocked by a blinding flash of Rukh's shoke. There came an instant when Rukh's bearing changed, and a chill smile came across his face. A punch to Stole's face was followed by a sweep of his shoke across Stole's throat. The fight was over. Once more, Rukh bowed over his fallen opponent before leaping back to take his seat amongst a chastened group of warriors, all of whom eyed Rukh warily. He paid them no attention. He sat still and unmoving.

His next match was ended in an identical fashion as the first two.

"Why does he keep using the same move?" Sign asked.

"He's laying down his mark. He's telling our warriors exactly what he intends. He's daring them to stop him," Jessira explained.

"And you know this how?" Disbar asked.

"It's none of your business," Jessira snapped.

"I think it's because she knows Rukh," Cedar offered.

Jessira nodded. "He's a proud man, and what better way to embarrass your opponent then to let them know what you intend and have them unable to stop it?"

Disbar eyed her askance, his lips curled in disgust. "Are you sure you don't approve of his actions?" he asked. "Because right now, you sound like you admire him."

"And I know exactly how much that bothers you," Jessira replied. Why had Kart invited this bilge-breather to the Trials? What could have been going on his mind? Did her eldest brother really think he could somehow salvage her engagement to Disbar? Save her reputation? It was impossible. Her future with Disbar was over. It was done, and there was no way to recover it. In fact, even if Rukh had never entered her life, Jessira realized she could have never gone through with marriage to Disbar Merdant. He wasn't a man she could possibly respect, much less love.

Her thoughts were interrupted when it was time for Rukh's next match. This one ended the same as the first three. He showed no emotion as his downed opponent screamed in pain.

"And you were with this man for months on end?" Kart asked, staring at Rukh in repulsed amazement. "He's defeating our warriors as painfully as possible. Does he even have a heart to feel pity or empathy?"

"No, he's not," Sign disagreed. "He's barely hurting them."

"And he does feel empathy," Laya confirmed. "I know him. He is a good man. And my parents have labored beside him. They say he is hardworking and humble." She shook her head in disbelief. "Something ugly has crept into his heart. He wouldn't act like this otherwise."

"His actions are those of a creature, not a good man," Disbar muttered.

Jessira's anger and disgust with him flared once more. A wise man would have recognized the mood of everyone around him and kept his mouth shut. Instead, Disbar insisted on continuing with his insults toward the man that many members of Jessira's family clearly liked and respected. Her teeth ground. She wanted to tell Disbar to go away, to leave her in peace; but to do so would have been unforgivably rude. He was Annayya's guest, which meant she couldn't tell him what she really felt.

"And does denying him his Humanity make you feel better?" Cedar asked, seemingly speaking up in her place. "This man brought Jessira safely home even though it cost him everything he loved. And how have we repaid him? Because of our prejudices, we've denied him a place in the Home Army. Because of our prejudices, we deny him justice. And we dare call *him* uncivilized because he's offended by our shameful behavior?" Cedar shook his head in disgust.

Jessira felt like cheering. Rukh deserved so much more than her kind had offered him. She just wished she'd spoken up more forcefully early on, convinced the officers of the Home Army to test Rukh and see just how skilled he really was. If she had, maybe all of this could have been avoided. But she had been too much a coward. She hadn't stayed true to their friendship.

She was so caught up in her guilt, that she almost missed Laya's words.

"Perhaps those with the wisdom to lead will see the error of their ways," Laya said, gently. "After what he's done here, they would be fools not to."

Court spoke up just then. "Last night, he packed up all his bags," he said. "Rukh, I mean. I asked what he intended, and he said as soon as the Trials were over, he was moving out. He thanked me for taking him in, but I think it goes deeper than that. I think he means to leave Stronghold."

Jessira shot to her feet. "That idiot!"

It was the final match. The Arena was as silent as a funeral. The Strongholders were obviously in shock over what Rukh had done to their finest warriors, and their dismay almost brought a smile to his face. He'd enjoyed shattering the beliefs of all these conceited people.

Plus, his laborer friends from Crofthold Lucent had probably made a loot betting on him. Just before the Trials, Rukh had shown them how he could move. He'd even demonstrated a Constrained Fireball. Afterward, his friends had grinned like sharks. The rest of Stronghold believed Rukh had little chance of winning, and the odds set on the possibility of his victory had been steep. If Rukh's friends had wagered on him, they were likely dreaming of what fine purchase to make with their winnings.

Rukh drew his attention back to the present. He hadn't won yet. There was still one final fight: Wheel Cloud, the defending champion.

"I know you're going to win," Wheel said, turning to Rukh.

Rukh maintained his flat expression of calm disinterest, although a bit of annoyance and confusion leaked out. Why was Wheel Cloud talking to him now? Before today, Rukh hadn't been worth piss in this man's chamber pot; and *now* he wanted to have a conversation? Well, it was too damn late, both in the day and Rukh's time in Stronghold. "Then forfeit the match and save yourself the pain," Rukh said.

"You know I can't," Wheel said.

"Then I can't help you."

Wheel fell silent for a moment. "Why do you hate us? We took you in, fed you, kept you warm and safe. But the way you've defeated the other warriors, the painful blows you've delivered—you could have chosen a less ugly means to defeat those men."

Rukh finally turned to him, disbelief breaking through the ice of his winter lake tranquility. "I passed you once in the halls of West

Lock when I went to inquire about joining the Home Army. Major Pile told me there would never be a place for me in the Home Army, not because of *who* I am, but because of *what* I am. I'm a Pureblood bastard. Those were his words. And yours."

Wheel flushed. "And maybe you are exactly what I said: a Pureblood bastard," he said. "Only an ungrateful wretch like you would bite the hand that feeds him. As I said, we took you in when we didn't have to. We've kept you—"

"You kept me a slave," Rukh snarled. "You and the rest of your kind offered me one choice: starve or lick your boot heels; and for this I should say 'thank you'?" Rukh snorted in derision. "Stick it up your ass. I'd rather starve. But maybe you're right, and I am being an ungrateful bastard. For that reason and that reason alone, I'm going to tell you *exactly* what I plan on doing in our fight. I'm going to kick you in the liver. I haven't decided whether to break your ribs or simply knock the wind out of you. Either way, my shoke will take you at the neck. And this time, it won't be a slice. It'll be hard enough to feel like a decapitation."

Wheel looked at Rukh, his face aghast in horror. Broken ribs and a shoke connecting against his neck. The pain would be terrible. "Have we really been so cruel?"

"You are a ghrina," Rukh said, reminding Wheel of the word he and all other OutCastes despised above all others. "How differently do you imagine my kind would have treated you compared to how you have actually treated me?"

Their conversation lapsed into silence, and moments later it was time.

Wheel Cloud swallowed heavily as the Governor-General called them forward for the final match. The crowd was still, none of the rowdiness and yelling from before Rukh's first contest. It was exactly what he'd been hoping to accomplish. The OutCastes were probably horrified by what he'd done to their precious warriors. One more to go, and their horror would be complete: a Pureblood Champion.

The call came. "Fight!"

Rukh was about to charge forward, but he noticed something in Wheel's posture. Instinctively, he Shielded. Something like a flickering green globe surrounded him just as Wheel hurled his shoke. A foolish move to throw away one's weapon. The shoke bounced off Rukh's Shield. Rukh leapt toward his opponent. A flicker of compassion took him. He aimed a gut kick and connected solidly. Wheel was thrown to the ground, the wind knocked out of him. He fell over on his back, gasping for breath. Only then did Rukh unsheathe his shoke. But instead of hammering a decapitating blow as he'd originally promised, he simply rested it gently against the Strongholder's neck.

Wheel nodded once and managed to gasp out the words. "I yield."

The world returned, but Rukh felt no sense of triumph, no elation. He knelt, taking a moment to Heal Wheel's broken ribs. He'd kicked the man harder than he had intended, partially striking him in the ribs when he'd intended a liver shot. While he did so, the watching crowd was quiet and solemn.

Wheel stared at him in astonishment.

"I may be a Pureblood bastard, but I won't let any of you steal my Humanity or my compassion," he explained in answer to Wheel's bewilderment.

When Rukh stood, scattered applause trickled down for him from a few lonely fools who were probably too drunk to realize the Pureblood bastard had won. Rukh bowed before his still-downed opponent, bowed to the Governor-General, and walked out of the Home Arena. He paid no attention to the petty functionaries who told him he had to wait for the awards ceremony. He brushed past them. The tournament was finished, and he'd accomplished what he'd set out to do.

CHAPTER SEVENTEEN
AN OFFER

A man's wealth is not measured by the sum of his possessions,
but by the joy with which he lives his life.

~ Saying from Stronghold, attribution unknown

B efore the final battle even began, Jessira had already left the
Arena. She didn't bother stopping and explaining to her family
and friends where she was going or what she had planned. A
more important concern occupied her thoughts: convincing Rukh to
stay in Stronghold. It wouldn't be easy. The man was as stubborn as
the mountains. Once he had his mind set, it was almost impossible to
change. But she had to try. She waited for him near Court's flat,
knowing he had to come back here to collect his gear.

"I was hoping to find you here," she said when Rukh arrived.
She pushed off the wall upon which she had been leaning.

Rukh didn't look surprised—or pleased.

So, it would be one of those meetings, like the last time when he
hadn't given her a chance to talk, explain, or apologize. He'd basically
told Jessira to go away and never come back. He'd even refused to
look at her, staring past her, at the wall or somewhere else. She

wanted to see his eyes this time. His eyes always gave him away. She'd know the truth if she could just get Rukh to look at her.

He did so. His lips held a bitter cast but his eyes…he was as furious as an unbroken stallion with the bit in his teeth.

She followed him as he went inside. "You don't have to leave," she said.

"Yes, I do," he replied, sounding annoyed that she'd guessed his intentions. He already wore his camouflage pants and a white undershirt. Over this, he buttoned up his thick, fleece-lined camouflage jacket.

"Can't we discuss this?" Jessira asked. Her voice quavered, betraying the anxiety she felt, the fear that he would be forever gone from her life. She wrung her hands. She just needed him to slow down long enough to listen.

"Talk all you want," he said, not slowing down. He'd removed the sandals worn by Trials combatants and slipped on a couple pairs of thick socks.

"Why do you have to leave?" she asked. "Is it because of me?"

"No," he said, succinctly, not bothering to look up.

"They why?"

"It doesn't matter," he muttered. "You could have been the First Mother Herself declaring me Her son, and I doubt your people would have cared. I think you overestimated their capacity for kindness." He sounded both angry and disappointed as he tied off the last few laces of his packs.

"You can still have a place here," she argued, trying to get through his obstinacy.

"And do what? Slave away as a pet Pureblood laborer? So your children can point me out and fling rotten eggs at me?"

"No one did anything like that!"

"No. They did worse. Your people didn't offer me justice. Warriors attacked me and no one cared."

"Why is that so important?" Jessira asked. She knew the question was stupid even before the words finished leaving her mouth. Rukh had a finely hewn sense of right and wrong, and while he readily forgave those who had harmed him, he only did so once they admitted their transgressions. Otherwise, he was implacable in his anger.

Rukh gaped at her in amazement. "You once told me this is a place of equality. What about equality under the law? You said this is a place of liberty. So why am I forced to work as a laborer with no opportunity to change my fate? You said this is an openhearted city where a man's worth is based on his work, not his birth." He snorted in derision. "The unholy hells will steal me away before I ever agree that your people are as openhearted, free, or equal as the Castes of Ashoka."

Jessira flinched. His words struck a chord, but she couldn't let it be the end of the matter. She had to try again. "The Trials Champion receives a large stipend. It's enough to maintain a small flat without needing to work."

"No thanks. The sooner I wipe the dust of this small-minded city off my boots, the better I'll feel."

"You can't mean that," Jessira said.

"I mean *exactly* that," Rukh snapped back.

Jessira stood silently and watched him pack. She knew Rukh had faced slights and insults, but despite it all, he seemed to have been finding a way in Stronghold. He'd made friends with Court, Cedar, and some of the laborers; but then had come the attacks. He couldn't—and shouldn't have to—overlook such a despicable offense. She had no defense for her people.

Rukh took a deep breath and closed his eyes. He opened them a moment later, and his eyes were clear of his bitter anger. "I'm sorry," he said. "I'm frustrated and unhappy, but I should never have lashed out at you like I just did. You don't deserve it."

Jessira took a shuddering breath, relieved he was finally talking to her. "Can you tell me what's really bothering you?"

Rukh sighed. "Farn left, and everything that's happened before and since, I'm just not feeling very generous to your people. I want to but…." He paused.

"But what?" Jessira gently urged.

"There are those who simply won't leave me in peace. And where there's one, there's likely to be more. I can't promise not to hurt them worse next time they come after me."

Jessira cursed under her breath. Disbar. Her one-time fiancé had ruined any hope of keeping Rukh in Stronghold. "Where will you go?" she finally asked.

"Hammer," he said as he belted on his sheathed sword.

"And after Hammer? What then?" she asked. "What if you need a place of safety? Somewhere to rest and recover? Why not stay long enough for the Champion's Banquet when the Governor-General presents you with your winnings. At least that way, if you ever have need of a place to get out of the weather, you'll have it."

He seemed to mull it over before eventually shaking his head in negation. "It would be better if I just left. For both of us."

"How would be better for both of us?" Jessira demanded, amazed by his obtuseness.

"It just would. You can go back to your life, and I can go back to mine."

"My life is where I make it, and with whom I make it."

Rukh shook his head again. "But it can't be with me," he said. "You've already lost enough on my behalf."

His face was obdurate, and Jessira realized with a sinking heart that there was nothing she could say to sway him from his path. He would be gone from her life. Her fear turned to grief. "Then I could go with you," Jessira said. The moment the words left her mouth, she recognized the rightness of her offer. Her life was where and with whom she made it. And she couldn't imagine her life without Rukh.

His face softened momentarily. "Your home is here," he said. "I won't let you throw it away. Not for me."

"My home is where I choose," Jessira replied.

"You can't come."

"Then stay for the celebration. Wait until then before you make your decision."

Rukh stood before her, mulling over her words as he stared at the wall. He finally turned back to meet her gaze and dropped his packs. They thudded to the floor. "When is it?" he said with a sigh.

"Tomorrow night," Jessira replied. Her legs trembled with relief as if a crushing weight had left her. "And the Champion usually chooses what is to be served on the menu," she added.

"Just have them make whatever they did at the last Champion's dinner. I don't care."

"But you'll be there?" Jessira asked, needing to hear his promise.

"I'll be there."

———◆●◆———

There were a lot of Strongholders attending the Champion's Gala. An unholy number of them. All the Trials combatants were there, each with a family member or spouse. That made sixty-four. Throw in the senators and councilors of each Crofthold, and that came to an additional sixty. Then there was the Governor-General, the Colonel of the Home Army, the majors of Army East and Army West, a number of captains, all their spouses, a number of assorted wealthy Strongholders and Rukh's ten guests—originally he'd only invited Court and Cedar, but then Court had ruined it by inviting the rest of his family, including Jessira and, somehow, even Disbar. All told, there were at least two hundred Strongholders present.

And the only place spacious and fancy enough to host such a large gathering was Home House, the Governor-General's mansion.

The building was three stories tall, huge by Stronghold standards. The top floor was given over to the private residence of the Governor-General and his family while the first housed the various departments needed to help administer the city. Most of the second floor was for official functions, such as tonight's party, and the room hosting the Champion's Gala was a large rectangular hall. It had a twenty-foot coffered ceiling painted a simple gray to provide a sense of openness and five large chandeliers provided brilliant lighting. Softening the whitewashed walls were tapestries depicting Stronghold's history. They were weavings of men and women in heroic poses as they struggled to build and maintain Stronghold. Rukh had no idea who they were. A small group of musicians quietly played music in the corner. They had an interesting concept of rhythm.

Rukh studied the crowd and shook his head in disgust. None of those in attendance were here for him. This was a high society event, a place to see and be seen. He just wished it would end soon. He had never enjoyed large gatherings, and the steady din of the crowd, droning like cicadas, grated on his nerves. As a result, Rukh stood alone in a corner and imagined himself somewhere else, somewhere quiet and cold with the moon and stars above. He nursed a bitter ale, and a swallow of it elicited a pained scowl.

A woman nearby laughed softly. Sign Deep. Sometimes, she had dinner with him and Court, and Rukh considered a familiar face in a sea of strangers. She was also an interesting person: highly opinionated but generous; sarcastic but funny; seemingly flighty but occasionally the mask would slip and her intelligence and perceptiveness would shine through. Rukh liked her.

"You don't need to frown so severely," Sign said. "We aren't your enemy."

Rukh gave her a rueful smile. "I wasn't frowning," he said. "It's the ale."

"Bitter?"

"Very."

"Try the apple wine," Sign suggested, handing him a goblet from the tray of a passing waiter.

The drink was pale yellow, the color of nectar with a hint of honeysuckle aroma. Rukh took a tentative sip and let the wine rest on his tongue. It had a tart sweetness but a mellow aftertaste and was surprisingly good. He took a larger swallow and smiled. "Much better," he said. "Thank you."

"You're welcome," Sign replied, her dark eyes glittering. Her blue dress swirled about her knees as she stepped closer. "I wanted to congratulate you on your victory. It was...impressive."

Rukh shrugged. "Looks can be deceiving," he said. "For impressive, you should have seen Kinsu Makren in the Tournament of Hume."

"Didn't you defeat him?"

"It was luck more than anything else," he said with a smile.

"And will. Jessira says that your desire to win carried you that day. Or at least that's what your brother and sister told her."

"Will helped, but so did luck."

"I've been wondering about something," Sign said, taking a sip of her wine. "Why didn't you just show us what you could do? Show us how fast you are, your skills—your life would have been a lot easier if you had. Instead, you waited until the Trials."

"I could have done that, and a lot of times, I was tempted to do so," Rukh answered. "But with the way things have been for me here," he shrugged, "there came a point when I just didn't care about impressing anyone."

"Court said you applied to join the Home Army."

Rukh nodded. "I did," he confirmed. "Major Pile basically told there was no room for me in the Army and that there never would be, while Major Barrier at least wanted me to demonstrate some sword-forms. They just weren't the patterns I'm used to."

"It didn't go well?" Sign guessed.

"I was terrible," Rukh replied with a wry smile. "I can't hold the stiff postures Stronghold teaches. I was always instructed to flow with balance and precision, to move like water and bend and shape myself to the world."

"You could have still done something to show us how good you are," Sign persisted.

"I suppose so, but after my poor outing with the sword forms, the major didn't want to hear my explanations of why I couldn't do as he'd asked. He just walked out. And the other warriors who'd been watching made sure I didn't linger. They basically cursed me out of East Lock," Rukh said with a scowl. "Pureblood bastard was one of the less offensive phrases I heard."

"So why not throw a Fireball and change their minds?"

"By then, I didn't care what they thought of me. I'd come to Stronghold thinking the people here were open and accepting, but most are just as bigoted as any Pureblood. And after the way the warriors treated me, the way Major Pile spoke to me, I had to wonder if joining your Army was really what I wanted." He shrugged. "I needed some time to think, and in the end, I figured they weren't worth impressing. Frag them," Rukh said. He grinned a moment later. "Besides, surprising them all like I did in the Trials was a lot more fun."

Sign didn't smile back. Instead, she looked dismayed and contrite. She reached for him and squeezed his arm. "Well, I'm sorry for how you were treated," Sign said.

"Yes. We should all apologize to you," a new voice said, cutting through the nearby loud conversations. It was Senator Shun Morn of Crofthold Clannad. He was a tall man, almost able to look Rukh in the eyes, and he still maintained the military posture and build he'd earned from his twenty-five years of service in the Home Army. After his discharge, Senator Shun had become a wealthy crofter. "I've recently learned of your shabby treatment by those who should have known better." His glance took in several nearby captains in the Home Army.

Rukh listened with bemusement to the senator but was unsure whether to believe him or not. Was he sincere in his apology, or was he simply throwing the Home Army officers under a wagon in order to win Rukh's trust? After all, the man was a politician; and he spoke like one. Lies and false promises could roll off his tongue as easily as water across a hot skillet.

"Yes. Please accept our apologies," another voice added. This time it was Senator Frame Seek of Crofthold Healed. Tall and spare of frame, he was an old man, well into his seventies. Unlike many others, his wealth had come from his work as a craftsman, specifically as a plumber. The old man blinked owlishly. "You should never have been left to work as a common laborer. The Home Army is your natural home." He gripped one of Rukh's biceps. "I would be more than happy to put in a kind word in the proper ears if you wish it. And as an aside, there are many fine flats in my Crofthold if you wish a change of residence."

"He is of Crofthold Lucent," a deep voice claimed. Rukh turned and saw another old man, about the same age as Senator Seek, but shorter and even slighter of build with thick glasses and a white, downy beard. It was Senator Thistle Rub of Crofthold Lucent. "Isn't that right, Rukh?"

Rukh smirked. Only a few days earlier, he'd been nothing but dirt beneath the fingernails of these fine senators. Now they were arguing over him like a pack of hyenas over a slab of meat.

Sign had stayed nearby, and he was grateful when she saved him from the politicians. She took him by the hand and pulled him from the midst of the grasping senators. "Gentlemen. You can't expect to monopolize all of the Trials Champion's time. There are many more people who wish to meet Rukh. I'm sure you understand." She smiled sweetly.

Rukh waited until they were a distance away before pulling his hand free from hers. "Thank you for that," he said. "I'm not good at handling politicians."

Sign chuckled dryly. "Neither am I."

Rukh thought he was safe from further grasping politicians, but a moment later, a new voice intruded. At least it was only Jessira's nanna. "Might I have a word with the Champion," Master Grey asked. "Alone," he added pointedly.

Sign nodded, but before she slipped away, she gave Rukh a look of sympathy.

Accompanying Master Grey was his formidable wife. Neither of them looked happy. And their ire seemed directed at him.

Rukh stifled a groan. What now? He forced a cheery smile on his face. "How can I help you?" he asked.

"Rumor has it that you might be leaving us soon," Mistress Grey said. "Is this true?"

Rukh nodded. "You and Master Grey have been wonderful, but it's time for me to go. As soon as this ceremony is over, I'm leaving Stronghold."

"Why?" Master Grey asked, sounding genuinely dumbfounded. "You could have a wonderful life here. A happy home."

"I've met some good people in Stronghold, but there are also some who don't want me here," Rukh answered. "They've made their feelings on the matter quite clear." There was no reason to rehash his sense of betrayal at the justice he'd been denied. It was pointless to do so.

"And there are also those who wish you to stay," Mistress Grey said. "You have friends here, like Court and Cedar and Sign. You like her."

Rukh's brows furrowed in confusion. Court and Cedar were

friends, but Sign? No. He liked her well enough but not enough to call her a friend. "I'm not sure I understand what you're getting at," Rukh said.

"You and Sign. You like her. She likes you. The two of you would make a good match," Master Grey explained.

Rukh kept his mouth from gaping by the slimmest of margins. He and Sign? Matched? He could honestly say he'd never considered such an idea. It wasn't preposterous, but Sign was Jessira's cousin. It felt...wrong. Besides, he was leaving Stronghold. The Wildness was his future. There was no place for a woman in his life.

"Don't disregard our proposition so quickly," Master Grey said, reading the antipathy on Rukh's face. "Sign is a lovely young woman. You could do far worse."

"And you know Jessira should not be yours," Mistress Grey added softly. "Her reputation has suffered enough on your behalf."

"Speaking of our daughter," Master Grey began. "What intentions do you have for her?"

Rukh frowned as he struggled to understand the continually shifting nature of their conversation. First, Sign and now, Jessira. "I have no intentions for her," he replied.

"Then why has she packed up her gear? We know she's offered to accompany you when you leave Stronghold," Mistress Grey said.

Jessira had offered to come with him, but Rukh had never planned on allowing her to make such a foolhardy decision. "I told her she couldn't come, and I meant it," he replied. "She shouldn't throw her life away for me."

"In this, we are agreed," Mistress Grey said. "Have you considered taking Sign in her stead?"

Rukh couldn't help it. Now his mouth *did* gape open in disbelief. Did Master and Mistress Grey not realize how dangerous the journey to Hammer was likely to be? It wasn't a place to send one's daughter, adopted or otherwise. "I'm not taking either of them," Rukh vowed.

"The Wildness is too dangerous."

Mistress Grey smiled thinly. "Finally. You demonstrate wisdom."

"But if you did leave, we aren't suggesting that you take Sign because we love her less than we do Jessira. We make that suggestion because Sign can take care of herself, and with you accompanying her, she'll likely be as safe as if she were amongst the Shadowcats," Mistress Grey said.

Rukh didn't know what to think. The Greys were lunatics to suggest such a stupid plan.

"We know your feelings for Jessira. And we know hers for you," Master Grey began in a gentler tone. "But would it not be best if she were to remain here, with those who love her best? Would it not be best if she had an opportunity to defend her reputation?"

"That's what I just said," Rukh replied in exasperation. Why were they having so much trouble believing him? Not interfering with Jessira's life, or even being a part of it was what he'd always intended from the moment he'd set foot in Stronghold. Her future should be as she wanted it. However, there was a question that bothered him. "Will Jessira take back Disbar?" Rukh asked.

Master Grey sighed. "Who can say? Given that the dowry has been paid, it would certainly be the easiest solution for her predicament, not to mention the least expensive. By doing so, her integrity and future would remain intact." He gazed at Rukh through narrowed eyes. "And you promised me you'd never harm her honor."

Rukh nodded. "Yes, I did. And I intend to keep my vow," he said. "But I'll leave Stronghold alone. No one else will be accompanying me. Not even Sign."

"Who won't be coming with you?" Cedar asked, approaching them. Trailing after him were Disbar and Jessira, neither of them looking happy.

"It isn't important," Master Grey said.

"Is it true you plan on leaving Stronghold as soon as the Banquet is finished?" Disbar asked.

Rukh's eyes narrowed. He wanted to punch this man, flatten his face. On both occasions, it had been Disbar's cousins who had attacked him. There was no chance it was a coincidence. But now wasn't the time for any accusations or confrontations. Rukh was determined to maintain his civility, and somehow, he managed to keep the feelings of disgust and anger from showing on his face. "I can't think of a single reason to stay," Rukh said.

Disbar nodded his head, appearing satisfied. "Just so," he said. "It's probably for the best. From what I've seen of you and your cousin, it doesn't seem as though Purebloods and OutCastes can mix well. We're both too proud. For instance, if you think we'll ask for your forgiveness for some perceived notion that you might not have been treated fairly, you're wrong. It will never happen, and—"

"It already has happened," Rukh interrupted, already tired of the smug bastard. "Three senators have apologized to me tonight for exactly that reason. And I'm sure they'll now be willing to look into the matter of exactly who amongst your people attacked me." He stared challengingly into Disbar's eyes, and it was the other man who looked away first.

Asshole.

"*You* are just as much an OutCaste as *we*," Jessira reminded him. "Remember, you were found Unworthy."

Rukh shook his head. "No I'm not," he said. "I am neither OutCaste nor Pureblood."

"Why are all your bags packed?" Kart asked Jessira, arriving just then. "Jeshni mentioned it a few minutes ago. Are you going somewhere?"

Jessira groaned.

"It is an issue we've already settled," Master Grey said. "It was a misunderstanding. Nothing more."

Disbar's eyes widened. He spun to face Jessira. "You were planning on leaving with him!" He thrust an accusing finger in Rukh's direction.

"No, she wasn't," Rukh said. "She's not going anywhere."

Jessira flushed. "You aren't my nanna or amma to tell me what I can do," she declared to Rukh. "You are a stranger to our city, a man who demands respect and gives none."

"I'll give respect to those who have earned it," Rukh growled back. How did she manage to make him angry so easily? And why couldn't she agree to stay home with her family? Couldn't she see how much better it would be for her? Even if she didn't marry Disbar—and Rukh prayed she wouldn't—at least she'd be safe.

"You still haven't answered my question," Disbar said to Jessira. "Were you planning on leaving Stronghold with him?"

Jessira stared at Rukh for a moment before turning to Disbar. She lifted her chin. She still had her pride. "First, it is none of your concern. We are no longer engaged. And second, yes, I will be going. I owe him too much," she said.

"Your life? Our future?"

"*We* have no future," Jessira snarled. "You're delusional if you believe otherwise."

Disbar appeared stricken. "But your brother, Kart…I had been led to believe your heart had softened. I came here tonight with a generous offer. I am willing to overlook your—"

Jessira sighed and shook her head. "It is over," she said. "We are done. We have been for weeks. It is time you accepted it."

The planes of Disbar's face grew flat and inscrutable, but his narrowed eyes revealed his fury and embarrassment. "You will regret this," he promised before turning on his heel and leaving the hall.

"Why can't you ever behave in a respectable fashion?" Kart demanded after Disbar's departure. "I had spoken to him, soothed his feelings. He was going to take you back, forgive you and overlook your indiscretions." He glared at Jessira. "And this is how you repay me?"

Her parents appeared equally upset, and despite his annoyance with her, Rukh felt a flicker of sympathy for Jessira. She would be having a very uncomfortable conversation with her family. It was a discussion Rukh didn't want to witness or be involved with.

Luckily for him, just then, an aide to Mon Peace, the Governor-General, approached and asked Rukh to accompany him to the dais set up on the far side of the banquet hall. The other combatants from the Trials were already gathered there, all of them standing in a long line. Rukh was the last to arrive, and the aide ushered him to the head of the list, directly behind Mon Peace, who stood before all of them at the front of the dais.

Like most of his predecessors, Mon Peace was former military. He was built like a bulldog and was a man of obvious vigor and energy. He appeared decades younger than his actual age, which was in his early sixties, and retained much of the handsomeness of his youth. His honey-brown hair had only a dusting of white at the temples, and his smooth-shaven face was relatively unlined.

"We are gathered here tonight to celebrate the Trials of Hume," Mon Peace began. "As such, we should take a moment to honor all the participants!" He paused as the crowd politely applauded. "And we must also honor the victor: Rukh Shektan, the first Kumma to ever enter the competition. We've all heard the legends regarding the Pureblood warrior Caste, but how many of you actually believed them? I certainly didn't." He shook his head as though in rueful disbelief. "But the stories don't begin to do justice to the truth of their abilities."

"I've never seen, or ever imagined I'd see such sublime skill. Words fail, but for me, it was like watching poetry in motion, as though *The Hunter's Jasmine* was made flesh. As I watched Rukh Shektan dance through our warriors, cutting and defeating them with a single stroke, I laughed. That's right, I laughed in joy. Even though it was *our* warriors he was defeating, I could not help myself. It is a rare gift and privilege to witness such perfection in the deadly arts of the sword." He gestured Rukh forward and put his arm around Rukh's shoulder in a proud, fatherly grasp. "We all know the prizes accorded the Champion, but those are too trite and too common for the warrior we saw last night. There is something more I wish to give him. As supreme commander of the High Army, it is something only a Governor-General can offer. Therefore, ladies and gentleman I present to you Lieutenant Rukh Shektan, of Army East. Our newest, and dare I say, greatest Trials Champion."

Rukh was stunned. He turned to the Governor-General, who gave him a nod and a wink before stepping aside and leading the crowd in an enthusiastic cheer. Many of the other combatants from the Trials shot Rukh looks of speculation while others simply smiled and nodded their congratulations as they clapped just as readily as the Governor-General.

Rukh had to admit: Mon Peace was an excellent politician, and what he'd just offered was a masterstroke. Rukh couldn't easily turn down the Governor-General's offer, at least not without destroying all the burgeoning goodwill his victory in the Trials had apparently engendered. Earlier this evening, Rukh wouldn't have thought he would have cared what the Strongholders thought of him, but it turned out that maybe he did.

As the applause died down, the Governor-General took the time to introduce the rest of the combatants. Seeing his role finished, Rukh prepared to step off the stage, but his movement was arrested by Mon Peace's next words. "As everyone knows, the Champion typically chooses his favorite dish to share with all those in attendance at the Gala. It might surprise all of you to know our newest Champion has provided his dish by baking it himself." The Governor-General was certainly using the word 'our' quite a lot when describing Rukh. "I believe it is called a chocolate cake?" He looked to Rukh for confirmation. "I've not tasted it, but I'm told it smelled divine as it was baking."

The cake, or cakes in this case—ten of them—had required all of the unsweetened chocolate and vanilla Rukh's nanna had sent to him by way of Jessira. Until this afternoon, Rukh had never had the time to use it.

It was odd. Though Rukh was a terrible cook, baking was another matter. Maybe it was because baking had none of the messiness of cooking, where half the time the chef seemed to add spices and ingredients for no apparent reason other than a hunch or a feeling. Baking, on the other hand, required exquisite precision. With baking, exacting measurements were the difference between a culinary work of art and a stinking pile of manure.

The laborers were already walking amongst the crowd, passing out slices of cake on small, white plates.

The Governor-General moved to stand next to Rukh. "I know you have struggled here, and you haven't been as happy as you might have wished," Mon Peace said. "And I know much of it was our own doing." He smiled faintly, as if amused by a secret only he knew. "What I did for you tonight…consider it an apology."

Rukh studied Mon Peace. The man sounded sincere. Rukh nodded acknowledgment. "Thank you for your kindness," he said.

The Governor-General gave him a companionable clap on the shoulder. "Think nothing of it. If there's anything else I can do for you, let me know," he said before moving on. Mon Peace had other people to greet and compliment. He was a politician after all.

"You have a powerful ally," a woman said in a hoarse voice as she came to stand by Rukh. It was Senator Brill River of Crofthold Jonie. She was an ancient woman—by far the oldest senator in Stronghold—an old dodderer who leaned heavily on her cane. Her hair was wispy and white, and her face was wrinkled like a crumpled piece of parchment. With her puckered lips—she'd lost her teeth decades earlier—she had a perpetually sour appearance, but behind thick glasses, her eyes were kind.

"I'm not sure what to say," Rukh said, still confused by the turn of events.

"The Governor-General was a fine warrior in his time, but he has always been an even better leader," Senator River said. "And one thing he cannot abide is false pride and useless people. I was with him when he saw you fight in the Trials." She shook her head. "I've never seen him so upset."

"He didn't like seeing his warriors defeated?" Rukh guessed.

"No," the senator said. "He was angry with the officers of the Home Army. He knew you had applied for both the Army East and West, and had been summarily turned down without even a demonstration of your abilities. He demanded to know why they hadn't accepted you into their ranks. And later, when he learned what some of our more foolish warriors might have attempted to do to you…he was incensed. He's ordered an investigation into the matter." Senator River chuckled. "I'm glad I'm not an officer of the Army." She peered at Rukh over the edge of her perched glasses. "Your commission was made upon his direct order."

Rukh didn't know what to say. He was heartened to know that justice would finally be administered to his attackers, but it had taken too long, and it shouldn't have required his victory in the Trials. He also had trouble believing in everyone's sudden change of heart toward him. It was too neat and tidy.

Senator River chuckled again. "We probably seem unreliable to someone in your position," she said. "But Stronghold did not grow from fifty-five souls to the city you see now without making accommodations."

"It seems more like being hypocritical," Rukh said.

"Perhaps," the senator replied. "I prefer to think of it as being pragmatic." She clutched Rukh's hands. "Turn your heart aside from anger. Some of us may deserve it, but it will only harm you in the end. You can still find a purpose and joy here."

"What is this...food?" Sign asked, bouncing into Rukh's line of vision.

"Think on what I've said," Senator River said, as she hobbled off.

Sign was pointing to her cake. "What is it?"

"Chocolate cake," Rukh said. "The Governor-General told you."

"It's *divine*. Did Jessira really have this every day in Ashoka?"

Rukh nodded. "Pretty much. I was worried she might have become addicted to it."

"Can that happen?" Sign asked, looking stricken.

"No," Rukh said with a laugh. In that moment he remembered what Sign's peddananna and peddamma had earlier offered to him. The laughter died, and a wariness took its place. He looked about, seeking a graceful way to leave Sign behind.

"If you're looking for my family, they left after the Governor-General's speech," Sign said.

He hadn't been looking for them, but it was the excuse Rukh himself had wanted to hear. "Am I expected to stay any longer, or can I go?"

"This isn't a gaol," Sign said, speaking as if he were a simpleton. "You can leave whenever you want."

Rukh nodded acknowledgment. Just as he was about to go, he paused. "Why is everyone behaving so differently toward me?" he asked. "Is it really because of my performance in the Trials?"

Sign gave a crooked grin and dimples formed on both her cheeks. "We had a crisis of conscience?"

"Is that a question or an answer?"

The smile left her, replaced by a fleeting look of guilt. "Most people won't want to admit it, but it *was* your victory. The way you destroyed our best—it opened a lot of eyes."

Rukh's jaw clenched. "Meaning without it, I'd still be the Pureblood bastard? Not worthy of respect or justice?"

Sign grinned again. "You're still a Pureblood bastard, but now, you're *our* Pureblood bastard. Didn't you hear the Governor-General say so?"

Rukh couldn't help it. He laughed. "Have you always been so incorrigible?"

"Only if it gets me what I want," Sign said, still grinning.

"And what do you want?"

"A chance to train with you."

Rukh recalled again what Master and Mistress Grey had suggested for him and Sign, and his smiled faded. After learning their purpose, her presence made him uncomfortable. And for some reason, laughing with her felt like betraying Jessira. "Is this the famed Stronghold pragmatism at work?" Rukh asked. "Admit your faults, only so long as you get something back in return?"

"If I say 'yes', will you train me?"

"No. I'm still leaving for Hammer."

Sign frowned, looking serious for once. "We'll just have to figure out a way to bind you to us then."

CHAPTER EIGHTEEN
RECONCILIATION

Teach them to long for the vast and endless sea.
Only then, while caught in the teeth of a storm,
will a child remember humility.

~Humble Offerings, by Suran, AF 205

S now crunched as Jessira walked the steep incline of a mountain's ridge. The sun burned harsh in the heights, and she squinted against the reflected glare. It had taken three days to reach the top of this final mountain pass, but afterward, the going should be easier, more downhill than up. Jessira paused a moment, panting as she gasped the thin air. Her breath steamed as she looked to see how much further she had to go.

Just another few hundred yards. First Mother be praised!

She pressed on, making her way past broken spires of gray rock, thrusting through the crust of snow and ice like the jagged remnants of ruined towers. She shivered as a knifing wind cut through her heavy garments before it moved on to moan restlessly through the ravines.

Rukh broke the trail ahead of her, leading a packhorse. His

snowshoes crabbed forward in a regular cadence of lift and fall. Lift and fall. He, too, gasped the thin air. Jessira stared resentfully at his back. If he wasn't so damn proud, they could be safe and warm back in Stronghold. A few days ago, Rukh had won the Trials of Hume, and despite the generous offer made by the Governor-General, he had still decided to leave her home behind. And Jessira had held firm to her commitment to go with him.

All because she had the misfortune of loving him. But it wasn't like the ridiculous notions of young love in some Ashokan romance. What she felt for Rukh was something else: a bond of caring, friendship, and loyalty—and, yes, desire. Even more, though, there was also a debt owed and a pragmatism wherein she hoped to change his heart so the two of them could both shortly return to Stronghold. After all, most of her people had finally realized just how much Rukh could help them.

So, when Rukh had departed her home, Jessira had gone as well, and though she kept pace with him, to say they walked together would be a falsehood. His stiff-necked pride held them apart. He had yet to completely forgive her people—or her. Did he still think she had betrayed him when she'd let him cut her out of his life? She didn't know, and Rukh wouldn't talk to her about it. The situation had Jessira struggling to find her balance, and she didn't know what to do or say to fix the dilemma in which she found herself.

What she did understand was that neither of them was happy, and neither of them knew how to move past it. Actually, that wasn't true. Jessira knew; but Rukh would have to take the first step. He would have to accept her decision to accompany him. First Father, she was heartily tired of his stubbornness. She was here. It was time he accepted it.

She bit back an oath of frustration. And the price she had paid for going with Rukh would likely be steep, at least based upon the short, heated follow-up conversation she had with Disbar following the Champion's Gala. He had been waiting for her outside the Home House. It had been the last time the two of them had spoken, and she knew Disbar's poisonous words would damage her reputation, but she didn't care.

Her only regret in ending their engagement was the trouble it would bring to her family. They shouldn't have to suffer on her account. And of course, there were those who would judge Jessira as being selfish for the choice she had made; but had she gone through with the marriage to Disbar, she would have merely been a martyr on the altar of society's expectations. Jessira had another name for someone like that, a better name: victim. It was a role Jessira refused to accept for herself.

She wanted more out of life. She wanted love.

But Rukh had been cold toward her since their departure from Stronghold and she didn't know why. Their situation together left Jessira wondering if she would have been better off staying at home. Had she does so, at least she would have had some semblance of her dignity intact because right now, following along after Rukh, she felt like his loyal dog.

It was humiliating.

Sometimes she wondered if she should have allowed Sign to be the one to accompany Rukh. After his victory in the Trials, talk had swiftly arisen on how best to bind him to Stronghold. The most obvious ploy would be through marriage and who would make a better choice than Sign Deep, the beautiful woman he already knew and liked? Jessira's parents had been all-too-happy to help facilitate such a union. They had even approached Rukh at the Champion's Gala and presented him with the proposal.

Even if he hadn't turned them down, Jessira would not have allowed it. At this point, there was no chance she would allow some other woman from Stronghold to try and win Rukh's love. She'd sacrificed too much to allow something like that to happen.

So here she was, trudging through the cold and snow, with a man who wouldn't talk to her. Wonderful.

Love could be such a horrible Bitch, almost as bad as Karma.

———•◆•———

A little less than a week after their departure from Stronghold, Rukh and Jessira found themselves traveling through a long valley amidst the lowlands of the Privation Mountains. There was no snow to shroud the ground down here in the lower reaches, but the world remained cold and damp with an incessant, icy rain. They made camp beneath the sheltering limbs of a copse of pine trees. Thin, ashen needles littered the forest floor, softening it and protecting Rukh and Jessira's gear from the muddy ground made boggy by the icy drizzle that had steadily fallen for the past two days. The rain chilled them to the bone, and they sat huddled around a small campfire. The sound of water pattering off the leaves and ground, hissing as it struck the fire, were the only noises to be heard. The wiser animals were huddled deep in their holes and burrows, staying warm on a night like this.

The chill wet weather; the loneliness in the world beyond their camp—all of it seemed an apt metaphor for Rukh and Jessira's travels thus far. The darkness at the heart of their relationship had yet to brighten. Their conversations were as terse and cold as the falling rain. Rukh knew it was mostly his fault, but he didn't know how to make himself speak the words he knew were needed. He was too angry with Jessira. The worst part was he wasn't entirely sure why. It was monumentally unfair to her, but he didn't know how reconcile his own feelings about the state in which they found themselves.

Just then, Jessira shivered and inched closer to the fire. "A hot bath and a warm bed would go a long way to making me feel alive again," she said. "I think my fingers have fallen off."

"If you'd stayed in Stronghold, you could have had both," he observed.

She stared at him, unmoving and expressionless. Her face hardened, and she rose to her feet. "If that's what you wish," she said. "Goodbye, Rukh." Jessira strode to her bags and began putting away her bedroll and the rest of her gear.

"What are you doing?" Rukh asked as she slung a pack over her shoulder.

"I'm leaving."

"Why?"

"Why do you care?" Jessira challenged.

"I just thought...."

His words were interrupted when she stepped forward. Before he could react, she had gripped the front of his shirt and pulled him close. She kissed him. It wasn't soft and gentle. There was no tenderness. Her kiss was hard, fierce, and demanding. But just before she broke away, her lips momentarily softened against his. It was an offer to share more of herself, give more if asked. The kiss was pure Jessira. It was a distilled expression of who she was as a woman and a person.

"I thought I could handle your anger, but I never expected your hatred," she said.

"I don't hate you," Rukh said. "I could never feel that way toward you."

"Really? Because given your behavior the past week, it certainly seems like you do."

"I don't hate you," Rukh repeated. "It's just...." He ran out of words, struggling to express what he thought and felt.

"It's what?" Jessira asked. She dropped her pack and waited on him with arms crossed. "Is it because you think I abandoned you when we reached Stronghold?"

Rukh shrugged. "You made a decision based on your own self-interest."

"Yes I did," Jessira said. "And you pushed me to it. Whenever I came to visit you, you turned aside like you didn't want to be seen with me or didn't want my company. I knew what you were doing—you were trying to protect me—and I might have eventually accepted your choice. But I never abandoned you."

Rukh waved aside her explanation. "I understand that," he said. "But it's not the reason I'm angry with you. I promised your nanna that I would stay away from you. I promised to help protect your honor. I haven't. In Stronghold, your reputation is ruined; and I can't help think that I am to blame for it," he said. "I feel like you would have never ended your engagement if not for me. It makes me out to be a liar and a thief."

Her hardness toward him softened. "And that's why you're mad at me?" she asked, her face a mask of confusion as she struggled to understand his reasoning.

He threw his hands in the air. "Kummas don't look for companionship with another man's wife or fiancé, and yet here you are with me. I've lost my integrity, and after being found Unworthy, my good name and my word were all I had left. There's nothing left."

"Your word and name are still with you, and so am I," Jessira said. "It was my decision to end my engagement to Disbar."

"I know but—"

"But nothing!" Jessira interrupted. "What I did, the choice I made, had nothing to do with you. Disbar wasn't the man I thought he was. I couldn't have married him even if I had never met you. I dissolved my engagement based on my own needs, not yours. As such, any dishonor I suffer will be due to *my* actions, not yours. I am my own person, and I don't need, or want, your protection."

"It's not how things are done in Ashoka," Rukh explained. "There, a man is expected to shield a woman from harm. Women are our future. Without them, there is nothing."

"In Stronghold, such matters are handled differently," Jessira said, a dangerous glint in her eyes. "Perhaps you should remember that from now on."

Rukh considered what she was saying. And he thought back on how frustrated he'd been with her decision to come with him, how it put a lie to every thing he had promised her nanna and....His thoughts pulled up short. He realized with a dawning horror how little any of it really mattered. Jessira *was* her own woman. She was right. She could make her own decisions. Rukh felt nauseous when he thought about how he'd behaved toward her. "I'm sorry," he said, unable to meet her eyes. "I'm such an ass."

Jessira studied him, a thoughtful expression on her face. "Yes, you are," she agreed. "And you're also an idiot."

Rukh sighed. "So what happens now?"

"What do you want to happen?"

"Can we start over again?" he asked. "Pretend the past few months never happened?"

Jessira tilted her head in speculation. "How do we do that?"

He put out a hand. "My name is Rukh Shektan. I'm a Pureblood Kumma from Ashoka."

Jessira took his hand and shook it, smiling faintly. "My name is Jessira Grey. I'm an OutCaste from Stronghold."

"Funny. You look like a ghrina to me," Rukh said. He ventured a smile, hoping she would see the humor in his words.

Jessira eyed him with pursed lips. "Say that word to me again, and you'll be picking your teeth off the ground." She brushed past him and set out her bedroll.

Afew weeks later, the morning dawned sunny and bright, painting the sky a rosy blush. The blue skies were a welcome respite after weeks of clouds and rain. The forest stream, beside which they'd made camp, gurgled happily while barn swallows and purple martins loudly chirped their presence. The weather remained cold and the trees bare, but the morning had a spring-like bite to it. Down in this low, rolling hill country, life was returning as winter's grip slowly loosened.

The sense of spring was a lie, though. It would be months before winter released its icy hold; nonetheless, the weather today seemed an apt reflection of the thaw in Jessira and Rukh's relationship. Of course, with all the changes the two of them had gone through, it was hard to keep track. When they had first met, they'd been enemies. Then they became allies. Then friends. And finally...well, they never had a chance to figure out what they might have become, but it could have been wonderful. Then Stronghold had come between them. Now Jessira had no idea what was going on.

"Could you pack up my gear?" Rukh asked.

Jessira looked up from her own work as she put away her bedroll. "Is something wrong with your arms?" she asked.

"No," he replied, "but after everything I went through in Stronghold, it just seems like you might want to do something nice for me."

Jessira sighed in irritation. "Get over it. You're not the first person who's had a tough time with their life, and....." She trailed off when she saw Rukh's smirk. "What?"

"It's funny when you're mad," Rukh said with a grin.

She rolled her eyes. "And you're funny looking all the time."

"Also pretty," he added.

Jessira slitted her eyes, pleased by the compliment but annoyed by his attitude. Fine. Two could play this game. As she lugged her bags to the packhorse, she stepped by Rukh. His back was turned, and she goosed him. He yelped. "You're cute when you scream like a girl," she commented.

She smiled as he mumbled something unintelligible under his breath.

"I wanted to tell you something," Rukh said after they got underway.

"What? That I'm ugly when I'm not mad?"

"No. You're beautiful always," Rukh said, sounding entirely sincere.

His words took her aback. He thought she was beautiful? Rukh could be such a jackhole, but he could also be sweet. "What did you want to tell me?" she asked.

"I'm glad you decided to come with me." He hesitated. "And I'm glad you stayed with me even when I behaved like an ass."

Jessira's nostrils flared. "You didn't behave like an ass," she replied, heat in her voice. "You were an ass."

"Does this mean you're still angry with me?" Rukh asked, his voice contrite.

Jessira's face softened. "No. I forgave you a long time ago."

Rukh smiled. "Good. Are we friends then?"

Jessira smiled with him. "Friends," she pronounced.

Later in the early afternoon, Jessira and Rukh walked along a muddy deer track as beams of sunlight peered through skeletal limbs of winter-bare trees. It lit the forest floor in dappled patterns of gold. The world looked so different when bright and happy. Yesterday, this same forest had been gloomy and oppressive beneath a heavy sky of gray clouds and frigid rain. Today, though, with the yellow sunlight breathing warmth back into the world, everything appeared so much more alive. Jessira inhaled the scent of moss and wet ground. Again, there was a subtle promise of spring arriving soon.

Jessira laughed. It was a good day to be alive. "I'm happy," she announced.

"I know. You have this jumpy way of walking when you're feeling chipper." Rukh said, sounding smug in his certainty.

Jessira shook her head. "How do you always manage to say the wrong thing? It's not even what you say, it's *how* you say it."

Rukh smiled. "A gift," he replied. "And plus, most times, I only say what I do when I know it's going to irritate you. It's fun."

Jessira laughed. "And why do you insist on annoying me so much?"

"Think about it long enough, and I'm sure you'll figure it out," Rukh advised.

"I'd rather not. Knowing why might have dire consequences for my self-esteem."

"So you don't think it has anything to do with my winning personality and charm?"

Jessira snorted. "If you had to rely on your personality and charm to make your way in the world, I'm thinking Cook Heltin might have poisoned you as a child. And I sure wouldn't have come with you out here into the Wildness."

"Then why did you come?" Rukh asked.

Jessira smiled and patted his cheek. "Think about it long enough, and I'm sure you'll figure it out."

"I really am sorry for taking my frustrations out on you," Rukh said, changing the subject.

"I know," she replied. "I could tell two days ago. You have a mopey way of walking when you feel like you've done something wrong." She gave him a knowing look, waiting to see how he would react.

He grinned in response. "Well played."

She smiled back at him. "This feels good," she said.

"Laughing with one another," Rukh said, guessing her thoughts.

"Yes," Jessira replied.

They walked through the silence of the forest, but unlike the earlier part of their journey, this wasn't a quiet full of tension but one full of the stillness of serenity. Soon, they came upon the banks of a narrow river with foam-capped water rushing over a bed full of boulders. Dangerous eddies swirled about. They trekked the near bank to find an easier place to cross, going a mile out of their way in order to do so. It still ended up being a harrowing crossing, and once on the opposite side of the river, they paused to rest.

"Why are we going to Hammer?" Jessira asked, as they sat upon wet leaves and soft moss.

Rukh shrugged, looking mulish. "It was as good a place to go as any." He bit his lip, hesitating as he stared out over the river. He threw a rock across the water before turning to Jessira. "My nanna's final letter to me mentioned *The Book of First Movement,*" he finally began. "He said it was important, and if I ever had a chance to recover it, I should. He was pretty adamant about it." He shrugged. "So here we are."

Jessira gave him an incredulous look. "We're going to Hammer for a book?"

"Nanna is never wrong about things that are important," Rukh said, defensively. "If he says recovering *The Book of First Movement* is worth the risk, then it is."

Jessira shook her head. "Unbelievable. You dragged me on a journey to Hammer because your nanna told you to go and get a book."

Rukh glanced at her and smiled half-heartedly. "Would it help if I told you how much I trust him?"

"No," Jessira replied. First Mother! Sometimes Rukh did the most idiotic things.

"Watch out for the puddle," Rukh advised.

"What pud—" Too late. Jessira's feet were completely soaked when she stepped in two inches of muddy water.

CHAPTER NINETEEN
MANDATORY DISCIPLES

It may very well be through our funeral pyres that our dreams
of peace are achieved. Death's sickle will free us from Mother Lienna,
but who then amongst the Chimeras will walk the righteous path?

~From the journal of SarpanKum Li-Dane, AF 1938

Li-Choke stumbled to his feet. Blood leaked from his ringing ears, and he could hardly stand without falling over. But his eyes and nose worked just fine. The smell of blood and offal clung to the air. All around him, flung about in scattered bits and pieces, lay the broken remains of his brothers. These had been the last Baels of the Eastern Plague of the Fan Lor Kum.

After their escape from the Chimera breeding caverns, Li-Choke had taken Rukh Shektan's advice and led his brothers here, to the Hunters Flats. They'd found refuge amongst the Kesarins and had built for themselves quiet, if uninspiring, lives. Summer had turned to fall and fall-to-winter, and yet, their presence had remained undiscovered by the other Chimeras. And with each passing month, they had allowed themselves to hope and, in some cases, believe that they were safe.

They had all been mistaken.

Mother Lienna had found them. She had not been pleased with their betrayal. The Queen had shredded their illusions of safety, pouring down from the skies as an avenging storm of fury and might. She had torn the Baels apart.

The cries of his brothers echoed in Li-Choke's mind, and he wondered why Mother had left him alive. Even now, She hovered above him, a whirlwind cloud of lightning and chaos. But Choke stood before Her, swaying on his feet and refusing to bend knee as he awaited his fate.

"Bow before your Queen," Mother said. Her voice, usually a screaming cacophony of bones snapped to pieces, was now soft and measured. Even the lightning and swirling clouds of her whirlwind seemed calm in comparison to their usual appearance. *"You need not fear me, Li-Choke."*

Her composed pronunciation of his name was almost more fearful than what She had done moments ago to his fellow Baels. Li-Choke swallowed back his fear, wondering how Mother was maintaining Her sanity. He had been there when the Queen had first discovered the betrayal of Her commanders, the Baels. She had screamed out Her anger and somehow poured Her madness down into the rest of the Chimeras of the Eastern Plague. The Queen's insanity had set Her so-called children to murdering one another with vicious abandon. So crazed had they been with Mother's fury and bloodlust that they would have killed one another unto the last. As a result, the Queen had been forced to retrieve much of Her madness, but still She had retained enough sanity to turn Her dread glare upon SarpanKum Li-Dirge, and the rest of the Baels. She had obliterated him and most of his command with a thunderous blow, flattening the earth upon which they had stood for hundreds of yards around.

Until today, it had been the last time Li-Choke had seen Mother. As time passed, his link with Her had faded, and he had hoped She had forgotten them, thinking all the Baels of the Eastern Plague were dead.

Obviously not.

"I have need of your service and worship once more," Mother said, speaking again in calm, cool tones. *"Hearken unto My words and learn wisdom."*

Li-Choke was frozen in fear, but it wasn't for his own life. He was more concerned about Mother's state of mind. How was She maintaining Her sanity? Where was Her madness? Were Her Chimeras even now tearing one another apart? The world was doomed if She had found a way to rid Herself of Her insanity.

"I will not serve You," Li-Choke managed to get out past his terror.

"You will," Mother replied. *"Else all the Baels of this world will be ended. Thus far, only those who served the Eastern Plague of Continent Ember have been killed. Should you defy Me, I will spread My reach far wider. I will destroy them all, every Bael from every Plague—both here on Ember as well as those on Continent Catalyst—will be utterly purged. And I know the rest of your brethren may be every bit as traitorous as those I killed from the Eastern Plague. Consider well your decision to serve. This will be your only chance to save the Baels."*

"If You believe them traitors, You'll kill them anyway." Choke couldn't believe he was arguing with Mother. A year ago, such a possibility would never have crossed his mind. No Bael in history had ever dared speak to the Queen in such a manner.

"The Baels will live if you serve," Mother promised. *"They can be returned to the path of righteousness. Even you."*

Li-Choke didn't believe Her. Once She had Her use of him, She would kill him and all the other Baels anyway. "Why did you choose me?" he asked, prolonging the inevitable.

"I keep what is Mine." She paused. *"Will you serve Me, Li-Choke, or will you witness the death of all your brothers?"*

Li-Choke considered Mother's words, trying to reason past his hatred. What She had done to the Baels, tinkering with Devesh's creation and birthing killers and murderers…it was an unforgivable sin. All beings who could reason should be brothers, and yet Humanity and the Baels, the only such creatures who could do so, were mortal enemies. And it was Mother's doing. This being of lightning and storm was a plague upon all of existence.

Still, if his actions could keep the Baels alive for a while longer; if he could find a way to thwart Mother's plans—he had to try. In the end, there was no choice. Choke fell to his knees and began canting the Prayer of Gratitude.

> By Her grace are we born
> By Her love are we made
> By Her desire are we shorn
> By Her passion are we unmade
> And are reborn once more

Mother's triumphant laughter was a rumble of thunder.

———◆———

Hours earlier Chak-Soon had felt Mother's call. He had left the encampment of the Eastern Plague and made haste to a nearby rocky knoll. He knelt to receive Her blessings, intoning the Prayer of Gratitude.

Stretched out before his bent head was the Eastern Plague. They bivouacked just north of the Hunters Flats, an area bordered by a rise of ice-rimmed rocky prominences, stretching north and south of the Fan Lor Kum encampment. It was a few hours before dawn, and the air was chill. Snow blanketed the ground, and a wind cut through the valley, carrying with it the freezing air from the heights of the Privation Mountains to the north. Cook fires burned as the Chimeras readied themselves for the coming day. It was one of the few areas wherein the Eastern Plague managed to maintain a semblance of order.

Without the leadership of the Baels, Mother's warriors had fallen to fighting amongst themselves, killing one another over the slightest of insults. It was Ur-Fels battling Braids and both breeds baiting and ambushing the dull, stupid Balants. And the Tigons, striving to bring order to the chaos, but more often than not, adding to it. Their natural inclination was to solve disputes with tooth-and-claw, and it led to either an escalation of the problem or put a bloody, but unsatisfactory, end to it. The only members of the Fan Lor Kum unaffected were the Bovars, but they were just dumb beasts of burden.

Strangely, some of the Bovars had recently birthed a few Baels. Why Mother would allow such conceptions to take place remained a mystery. It made no sense, especially considering Her complete eradication of the former commanders of the Eastern Plague months prior. But having no instructions on what was to be done with the infant Baels, the Tigons had decided to let them live. There was no one to teach the young ones, though, and Chak-Soon wondered at their fate. Perhaps with this meeting, he would have a chance to ask Mother Her desire on the matter.

"Rise, Chak-Soon and serve your Queen," Mother said, arriving as a gentle breeze. *"I give you a purpose."*

Chak-Soon lifted himself off his knees and rose to his feet, trembling with suppressed fervor. Today was the second time he had been granted an audience with Mother. It was two conversations more than he had ever expected to have. Until last summer, when the Queen had eradicated the Baels, it had been long understood that only the bull-like Chimeras would ever have the honor and privilege of hearing Mother's words spoken aloud. As the old saying went: *'From Her voice and through the Baels' lips was the Queen's will known'*.

Everything was changed now, but Chak-Soon didn't believe it was necessarily for the better; not with the convulsions tearing apart the Eastern Plague.

"I know My children suffer without the Baels to lead them," Mother said, echoing Chak-Soon's thoughts.

The Tigon was momentarily taken aback but quickly realized he shouldn't have been. He was a child of Mother. Who better to know his unspoken thoughts than Her?

"I bring you glad tidings: that error will be soon corrected," the Queen continued. *"Even now, one comes. The last Bael of the Eastern Plague. The only one who remained true to Me. Greet him, for he will lead you and several other holy warriors on an urgent mission."*

"It will be as You command," Chak-Soon said, his head bowed in reverence. To be personally tasked by Mother...it was the most fervent dream of all Tigons, maybe all Chimeras, including the dastardly Ur-Fels. But even through his passion, Chak-Soon wondered about Mother's transformation. The manner in which She spoke had been like a Bael: calm and sure. It was so different from the first time he had met the Queen. Then, Her voice had been edged with raging thunder. Even Her appearance now was changed. The chaotic tumble of lighting and swirling clouds was still present, but they seemed more sedate.

"The Bael who comes is named Li-Choke. Serve him as you would serve Me. Here is what you must do: gather a claw of Tigons as well as two traps of Braids and three Balants. Await My Bael's arrival. Li-Choke will explain much, but here is all you need know: you hunt the Human who killed your brothers in the Privation Mountains. The creature is Hume. Only he possesses the skill to murder so many of My children with such arrogant impunity. And after the performance of his infamous deeds, he hies to Hammer, seeking to escape My just punishment within the safety of that wicked city's Oasis."

Chak-Soon nodded, hiding his dismay. Everyone knew of the legendary Hume. He was the Human nightmare, the unstoppable killer of Chimeras. He was the fearful specter of the dark who snatched up traitorous Tigons and slayed them in a horrific fashion. He was also dead, as was his city, Hammer. How could the Queen not know this? Worse was the cursed city's reputation. No Chimera ever ventured near Hammer. The animals living nearby hunted Mother's children with an unreasoning vengeance, taking mortal blows in order to kill any Chimeras that crossed their path. It was for a good reason that Hammer was called 'The Bone Place'.

"Child, do you not wish to speak and tell Me your thoughts?" Mother asked. Her voice was gentle.

Chak-Soon's mouth gaped in shock. Mother wished to hear his opinion? He ducked his head, overwhelmed with emotion. "To know I have been considered worthy of Your trust is all a Tigon could ever hope to achieve in this life."

Mother laughed, like a soft, spring rain, but shortly it turned into a thunderclap of cacophonous din, pealing on and on and on. *"If only My Baels could have served me so loyally, I would have already leveled Hume's cursed home."* Her voice lifted, rising to the raging whirlwind of noise it had been the first time Chak-Soon had been in Her presence. *"But with Li-Choke to lead, and with you to follow, Hume will die, and after him, Hammer. And then will I slay the hidden city of the mountains, the place of the cursed ghrinas, the sister city to Ashoka."* She laughed again, a cackle of hideous sound, and in it there was unreasoning madness.

Chak-Soon cowered in fear, falling to his knees, his head pressed to the ground. What had just happened? Mother had seemed so reasonable and loving only moments before. Now She sounded utterly mad, raving on about dead cities and mythical people.

An idea rose from the recesses of his mind, one he immediately tried to stifle. Despite his best efforts, though, the notion made its way to the forefront of his thoughts. *Was* Mother insane, and was this why the Baels had turned traitor? Chak-Soon clutched his head, trying to throttle the treasonous notions. It was sacrilege!

Over and over again, Chak-Soon took to intoning the Prayer of Gratitude, trying to rid himself of his blasphemy.

———————•————————

Lienna sped westward across the darkening skies. Her mission took Her to the setting sun, toward the Western Plague's winter encampment along the northern shores of Lake Nest. As She outraced the wind, the Queen reveled in the silence of Her mind. Gone were Mother and Father. Their hectoring voices were stilled. Even more wonderful was the absence of Mistress Arisa. Her harping ugliness was nowhere to be heard.

Lienna laughed. Once, simply thinking about Mistress would have brought about Her fearsome presence, but not any more, not since Lienna had learned how to tame Her madness. The Queen knew that if She were to empty Her rage and anguish down into a single Plague, Her Chimeras would take to killing one another, ripping and rending like rabid animals. But if Lienna was careful and doled out Her madness amongst *two* Plagues, Her Chimeras simply went catatonic. They lay down as if asleep, unable to harm one another. Of course, they also couldn't defend themselves. Predators and scavengers had been known to attack the helpless Chimeras. Some of Her children had even stopped breathing if they were left holding Lienna's madness for too long a period of time. So Lienna had to be mindful of Her children, never keeping them asleep for too long a period of time. Luckily, on Continent Catalyst, there were *three* Plagues. She could rotate Her insanity amongst them and not cause Her Chimeras any lasting harm.

It wasn't a perfect arrangement, not by any means. Right now, there were still times when Lienna slipped into old habits; old ways of thinking; when Mother, Father, or worse, Mistress Arisa, came to Her, whipping Her with whispers of hatred and ill will; times when Lienna became confused and the past and the present merged; when truths and lies became indistinguishable. But Lienna knew if She could spread Her terrible rage amongst even more of Her children, She could forever banish Mother, Father, and Mistress Arisa from Her mind. It was for this exact reason that the Queen was making Her way west.

The Eastern Plague of Continent Ember was falling apart. The Tigons simply couldn't lead. Their version of discipline was the simple solution of death for any who supposedly disobeyed their incomprehensible orders. They were mindless killers, good for nothing more than to lead a charge into battle.

Much as Lienna hated to admit it, She needed the Baels. After discovering their betrayal in the east, there had been a moment when the Queen had almost killed all Her bull-like commanders. Luckily, fate had stayed Her hand. Mother had allowed the rest of the Baels to live. Had She not, then *all* Her children would be suffering in much the same way as the Eastern Plague.

Lienna was thankful for Her good fortune.

She had the opportunity to move a number of Baels from the west to the east. It would spread Her commanders thin, and they wouldn't be able to lead either Plague very well, but the Baels should at least be able to maintain order. It was all She needed for now. In another ten years, She could easily breed up the Baels so their numbers were large enough for them to once again effectively command both Plagues on Continent Ember.

And then Lienna could spread Her madness amongst three or more Plagues at a time. With Her sanity intact, She could make lucid plans and decisions, ones where falsehoods couldn't lead her astray. She could finally kill Humanity for all time.

It was the driving dream of Her entire existence, the impetus that had once led a daughter to callously and without regret murder Her Amma and Nanna.

Lienna smiled at the thought of a world freed of Humanity's evil, their noisome nature, their wicked activities, and their grotesque sights and horrific stenches. She imagined a world made pure and clean.

———————•◦•———————

L i-Shard, the SarpanKum of the Western Plague, grew rigid with fear as he felt Mother approach. She would arrive in minutes. He and the three senior-most commanders of the Western Plague stood alone upon a lonely hill, facing out into Hammer Bay. Miles to the east, on the Creosote Plains, the broad flatlands south of the Bone Place, encamped the rest of the Western Plague, including all the other Baels. But Mother had called for only the four currently present. There had to be a reason for it. It was likely one Shard wouldn't like.

"Control your alarm," Li-Brind, the SarpanKi, advised.

Li-Shard nodded to the older Bael. Brind had survived many seasons and even more battles in his illustrious life. He was wise with age and not easily rattled. Shard trusted him implicitly. Brind had served as SarpanKi for ten years now, including to Shard's direct predecessor, the older Bael's crèche brother. Typically, the title of SarpanKi was bestowed upon the most trusted brother of the SarpanKum, but all from Shard's crèche had died long ago. As a result, Brind had been the logical choice to continue on in the position he had already held for so long.

Shard was grateful for the older Bael's presence. Given his own youth—he was younger than many of the Vorsans and even a few of the Levners—having someone as experienced as Brind had been an invaluable aid. The SarpanKi was a pillar of knowledge and insight, helping to keep the young SarpanKum from making too many mistakes. In fact, Brind would have made a fine SarpanKum in his own right. Shard often thought the older Bael *should* have been the one elevated to leadership of the Western Plague, but instead, their brother Baels had chosen Li-Shard. It hadn't been because of his great intellect and certainly not for his experience. It had been because of his devotion to the teachings of Hume, a piety unmatched by any except perhaps Li-Dirge, the former SarpanKum of the Eastern Plague.

"Did She give any indication of what She desires?" Li-Chig, one of the Sarpans asked.

Li-Sturg, Chig's crèche brother and fellow Sarpan, stroked the feathers of his rank. It was a nervous habit. "After what Mother did to Li-Dirge and our brothers in the east, frankly I am stunned She has not come for us earlier. I was certain She would."

Li-Shard shook his head in negation. "She made no comment other than to command our presence." He glanced at Sturg. "But I, too, was shocked that Mother hasn't ended our existence."

"She should have if we are to believe Li-Choke's messenger, the young Bael he sent to us," said Li-Chig. "And why has She called for just the four of us?"

"Calm yourselves," Li-Brind advised again. "We will know shortly."

Shard knew the SarpanKi was correct. There was nothing to be done about it but await Mother's will. He dropped to his knees and indicated for the others to follow his lead. They chanted the Prayer of Gratitude, and Li-Shard focused on the words, settling his mind and burying his nervousness.

The Queen hated when any of the Chimeras demonstrated the slightest hint of fear toward Her.

Shortly, She arrived; and as always, Mother was a maelstrom of lightning and chaotically racing thunderclouds. Shard sensed a difference, though. There was a focus, a rational pattern to Her swiftly changing form. But it was when She spoke that Shard truly recognized the change. It terrified him. Mother was lucid.

"Child, you have served Me well, though you are young to your post," Mother said. *"And by now, I am sure you have become aware of the events to the east, and Our betrayal at the hands of the Baels there."*

Was She asking a question? Shard wasn't sure, but it sounded like one. "Yes, Mother," he said. "Li-Dirge was trusted by all. It is shocking and shameful that he would lead so many to treason."

"The matter is dealt with," Mother replied. *"And I am sure you wonder whether I now believe that all My Baels are as poisonous as the traitor, Li-Dirge."*

"We are faithful to Your will," Shard said in his most fervent tone, praying the Queen couldn't sense his lie.

"I have never doubted it," Mother replied. *"It is why I want you to assume command of the Eastern Plague."*

"Take command of the east?"

"Yes. The Eastern Plague is falling apart. The Tigons are unable to instill the proper discipline."

Shard did his best to hide his shock. Mother had deigned to explain Her reasonings. It was something She had never done before. Typically, She simply gave Her orders and left it to the Baels to carry them out. Even more worrisome was how the Queen spoke. She sounded entirely reasonable and rational.

Li-Shard would have to tread carefully. "How shall I do Your bidding, Mother?" he asked.

Mother chuckled. *"It is for you to decide,"* She said. *"Take as many Baels as you think might be needed. Only set the Eastern Plague back to rights."*

"It will be difficult to bring the Eastern Plague back to full readiness," Shard said. "With all the casualties and possibly even desertions they've had and the loss of the breeding caverns, how will I rebuild their numbers?"

"Leave the caverns to Me," the Queen said. *"Only bring back discipline and order to the east. Stop the bleeding. That is your only task."*

"By Your command," Li-Shard intoned. Once again, he led the other three Baels in the Prayer of Gratitude as Mother swiftly departed.

Once She was gone, Li-Shard shuddered with suppressed fear before turning to Li-Brind. "In all your time as SarpanKi, have you ever heard Her sound like that?"

Brind shook his head. "Never. It seems the rumors of a sane Mother are true," he said. "Devesh help us all." The older Bael looked troubled, almost frightened, a fact worrisome enough to cause the fine hairs on Shard's neck to stand on end.

"That might be about the most horrific news I've ever had," Li-Chig muttered.

"Yes, it is," Li-Shard replied. "But it also seems likely that you or Sturg will be the next SarpanKum of the Western Plague."

"I only wish it didn't come about through such terrifying means," Li-Chig said.

CHAPTER TWENTY
ACCEPTING FLAWS

Take life's blows and refuse to quit.
It is the mark of true warrior and a true man.

~ Kumma aphorism, attribution unknown

Jessira took a final swig of water before re-stoppering her canteen. She and Rukh had stopped for an early lunch when they had come across a fallow wildflower field next to a clear running stream. The water was likely winding its way to River Mastery and from there, on to Hammer Bay. It sparkled under the sun.

The field and stream had been a good place to stop since the walleye had been biting and a patch of wild spinach grew nearby. While she and Rukh were still well provisioned, it was always a good idea to save their supplies whenever possible. Jessira was pleasantly full and didn't even mind that the fish had been over-salted—Rukh's fault. On the trail, fresh food of any kind was a blessing.

Just then, a blustery wind blew, pregnant with the taste of snow or a cold rain. The day had started out bright and sunny, but to the northwest, scudding, gray clouds warned of coming weather. It was likely to arrive in the next few hours, possibly sooner. The Creosote

Plain was infamous for its temperamental weather. Yesterday evening and so far today, it had been spring-like—warm and sunny—but a few hours from now, snow would threaten.

"What do you think?" Rukh asked, stepping to her side.

Jessira studied the clouds for a moment. "I think we better find shelter," she said.

Rukh pointed south. "If we follow the stream toward those hills, we might come across a cave."

Jessira nodded. "We better hurry."

Rukh quickly loaded their belongings on the packhorse while Jessira took point. She led them along the stream bank, taking them into the southern hills Rukh had pointed out. The wind picked up, bitter and biting, forcing them to don heavy shirts and coats before pushing on. An hour later, they entered a water-carved canyon with sheer walls layered in shale, granite, and limestone. All the while, Jessira scanned ahead, searching for the sanctuary of a cave. Thick snowflakes began falling, swirling about and blown sideways by the wind, which was now a howling gale as it roared through the funnel of the canyon. The snow thickened and visibility dimmed to no more than a few yards ahead.

"There," Rukh yelled.

Jessira looked to where he pointed, but she couldn't see what it was. Rukh took her hand, and she let him pull her along, trusting he knew where they were going.

They reached a limestone overhang beneath which was a dry, gravel-lined floor. A rock shelter. It wasn't ideal, but it would do.

"We need wood for the fire," Rukh said.

"I'll take care of it," Jessira replied. "Set up the tents. We'll want a place to huddle up if this turns out to be a blizzard."

Rukh grimaced. "Let's hope it doesn't come to that."

They set about their tasks. Jessira left the shelter, looking up and down the length of the stream. For once, luck was with her. Nearby was a large pile of old driftwood. It should be more than enough to see them through the storm. She hauled her find back to the rock shelter, taking several trips to do so. By the time she finished her task, Rukh had put up the tent and built a bright, cheery fire. He'd even seen to the packhorse, hobbling the gelding where the animal would be protected from the worst of the wind and weather but near enough to still feel the warmth of the fire. Their belongings stood stacked next to the tent

"Is there anything else?" Rukh asked, looking up as he finished brushing down the horse.

Jessira dropped her load of logs. "No. This is the last of it." She moved to the bright warmth of the fire, putting out her hands to work some heat back into them.

Rukh sighed. "Good thing we stopped early for lunch. We might have been caught out in the open if we hadn't."

Jessira smiled. "You mean we should be thankful you were hungry so early in the day."

Rukh grinned. "You're welcome."

<hr>

"How much further to Hammer?" Jessira asked.

"A few more days," Rukh answered as he stirred their meager fire. In the Wildness, they couldn't afford anything larger. Blending hid much but not everything.

They camped near a marsh. Every day, more signs of spring's imminent arrival could be read. The world was slowly coming back to life. Unfortunately, the warmer weather also meant the bog stank. Rukh imagined he could see a fog of sulfurous fumes rising like a foul mist from the surrounding core grass. Also, the ground underneath was thick and wet, sucking at their feet and slowing their travel. He'd almost lost a boot in it the other day. Luckily, another day should see them clear of the marsh.

"I know it's only been seven weeks, but it feels like seven *months* since we left Stronghold," Jessira said.

Rukh stared into the flames. He was thankful for Jessira's presence, but guilty that she was with him in the first place. He lifted his head and met her eyes. "I'm sorry I brought you out here."

"I thought we already went over this," Jessira said, a resolute tone in her voice. She stared at him, forcing him to meet the challenge in her eyes. "It was my choice, remember? You didn't tie me down and force me. I came here of my own accord." Silence fell between them until Jessira spoke once again. "What happens after Hammer?" she asked.

Rukh shrugged. "I'm not sure. I never thought about it."

"Will you come back to Stronghold?" she asked.

Traveling the Wildness for the rest of his life was what he had originally intended when he had first made the decision to leave Stronghold. But that was before Jessira had chosen to accompany him. He couldn't keep her away from her family and home. "I'll go back," he said, staring into the fire. He glanced up and caught her smile of gratitude. His stomach did a little flip when she reached out to squeeze his hand.

"Thank you," Jessira said.

Rukh stared into the fire once more. "How do you think your people will react?" he asked.

She misunderstood his question. "I think you won't have nearly as difficult a time as you did before the Trials. You'll be fine."

"I mean you," Rukh corrected. "How will they react to you? You left with me. You broke your engagement to Disbar. How will they treat you?"

"It probably won't be easy," she said with a grimace. "Disbar is an ass, and I'm sure he's doing his best to ruin my reputation."

Rukh smiled. "At least he's an ass who will never be your husband."

Jessira chuckled. "There is that," she said. Silence fell again until Jessira shivered. "My feet are freezing," she complained.

Rukh glanced her way. "Put them closer to the fire," he suggested. "And why aren't you wearing your boots?"

"Muscle cramps," Jessira answered. "And they're sore." She gave him a hopeful look. "Can you rub them?"

Rukh shuffled away from her. "No."

She looked affronted. "Why not?"

Rukh sighed. "Because your feet probably smell awful."

"I just washed them," Jessira protested, pointing to a nearby pond, one that was clear and not covered with pond scum.

"No," Rukh repeated.

Jessira stared at him in consideration. "What do you want me to rub?" she asked.

Rukh glanced her way and grinned. "Well, if you're asking...." He stood and unbuckled his belt.

"Not that!" Jessira said, sounding appalled as she shifted away from him.

Rukh chuckled. "Get your head out of the sewer. I need you to rub my back. The belt's been chaffing."

"Oh." Jessira reddened.

Rukh smiled. "Are you embarrassed? Weren't you the one who told me how prudish Kummas are?"

"Taking offense because it seemed like you were about to expose your manhood to me—and the entire world, for that matter—is *not* a sign of prudishness," Jessira explained with a sniff.

"So does that mean you're going to rub my back?" Rukh asked.

Jessira had a glint in her eyes. "Rub my feet first?"

Rukh had played this game before. If he agreed to her request, as soon as he was done with her feet, she'd swipe ineffectually at his back for a few seconds before declaring herself tired. "My back first," he said.

"How about at the same time?" Jessira said.

Rukh rolled his eyes. "You want me to rub your feet while at the same time, you rub my back?" He shook his head. "You realize that's anatomically impossible?"

"It's possible," Jessira said, sounding confident.

"How?"

"Like this." Jessira positioned herself behind Rukh. He stiffened with shock when she wrapped her long legs around his waist, laying her feet on his thighs. "See."

Rukh didn't dare move, intensely aware of Jessira's presence: her soft breath against his neck, her hands on his back, and most especially the feel of her firm legs around his waist.

"Is this making you uncomfortable?" Jessira asked in a voice sweet enough to sugar a pie.

Rukh swallowed. "No," he lied, proud his voice didn't crack.

Rukh rubbed her feet, imagining them to be as smelly as the swamp. It wasn't true, but he couldn't allow himself to notice anything else. He practiced his breathing, taking slow, steady breaths. In and out. Anything to distract from the softness of Jessira's skin; the hint of lilac from the soap she must have used; her cinnamon scent; the feel of her firm thighs around his waist; and her strong hands on his shoulders. Now was not the time for any of...*that*, if *that* was even what Jessira wanted.

Jessira inhaled softly, sounding enchanted. To his disappointment, she unstrapped her legs and leaned forward until her face was next to his. She gestured for quiet and pointed at something in the marshy distance. "Look," she whispered.

Rukh followed the line of her finger. A couple of long-necked birds waded in the nearby pond.

"Cranes," Jessira said. "Some of them summer in Stronghold.

They're considered harbingers of good luck."

"What kind of good luck?" Rukh asked.

"A strong marriage," Jessira explained. "Cranes mate for life. It's considered auspicious for a couple to wed during the time of the crane mating dance. It's why we schedule our weddings to take place at the same time as when they return to Teardrop Lake."

Rukh smiled at the idea. "How romantic," he said. "I wouldn't have expected it from your people."

"Pragmatic," Jessira corrected. "When we speak of a strong marriage, romantic love isn't considered an important part of it."

"Perhaps you should," Rukh said.

Jessira shifted until she could look him in the eyes. Rukh brushed her cheek, a strand of her hair. Jessira leaned forward, kissing him softly and all-too briefly on the lips. "Perhaps we will," she said before moving to the other side of the fire.

Rukh and Jessira held as still as statues as they looked to the south. They stood upon the famed black cliffs north of Hammer with waves crashing against the rocks hundreds of feet below.

From their vantage point, the wreck of the once-proud city was readily evident. River Mastery, sluggish and wide, passed into the city, feeding the surrounding farms, all of which were now choked with weeds and vines and the makings of a forest. From there, the water had been mastered by a string of dams and locks into slowly flowing canals ebbing through the heart of the city. For this reason, Hammer was also known as the Floating Rose. Even now, ruined and overgrown as they were, Rukh could appreciate the history and romance of the waterways and their storied gondolas. Rukh's heart stirred as he imagined what it must have been like long ago when

Hammer thrived.

The sun approached the western horizon, casting the bay in reflective gilding. Despite the golden light, the city was cast in a pall of sorrow, a phantom fog of beauty despoiled. The tall towers and their famous onion domes; the city's walls, once as powerful and grand as Ashoka's—all of it lay in ruins now, although broken remnants could still be seen beneath a thick blanket of tangled, green vines.

Jessira was first to break the spell. "It makes me want to cry."

Rukh nodded before turning away. "Let's go," he suggested.

They set up camp in silence, both of them lost in their thoughts. Jessira had a small fire going while Rukh took care of their packhorse. They settled in for supper. In the morning, they planned on entering the city. Rukh recalled a few days prior when he and Jessira had kissed. It hadn't happened again, not even a hint that it might. And this melancholy place, with its softly moaning wind, wasn't necessarily a place to pick up where they had left off.

"What is it?" Jessira asked.

"I was thinking about when we saw the cranes in the marsh." He reached over and squeezed her hand.

"Now really isn't the time," Jessira said, tugging her hand free.

Rukh smiled. "How do you know what I want?"

Jessira smiled back at him. "You're a man. You want what every man wants."

"You certainly have a high opinion of yourself," Rukh said in a teasing tone.

"No. Just common sense."

"And now isn't the time?" Rukh asked. "But there might be a time?"

Jessira gave him a slow appraising look from beneath hooded eyes. "Maybe."

It wasn't much of an answer one way or another, and Rukh studied her, the play of light and shadow from the campfire on her face. Her green eyes seemed to glow, her honey-brown hair burnished. He reached for her hand again. This time she let him hold it. He trailed his hand upward, along her arm, past her shoulder, to the curve of Jessira's neck until it rested gently against her face.

"Who are we?" he asked.

Jessira stared him in the eyes. "Who do you want us to be?" she asked.

Rukh didn't answer with words. Instead, he leaned forward, kissing her softly; afraid she might pull away. The kiss deepened. She cupped his face, pulling him closer, her mouth parting slightly. Rukh ran his fingers through her hair, inhaling her cinnamon scent, wanting to drown in her.

Jessira smiled, her teeth flashing in the dark. "You haven't answered me. What do you want?"

He kissed her again. "I want what all men want, remember?" he said with a grin.

She laughed, low and throaty. "Well, that much I already knew."

Rukh laughed with her. "I love you, Jessira. Wherever you are is my home."

"Even Stronghold?" she asked, appearing to hold her breath as she awaited his response.

Once the answer would have been a certain 'no', but time, love, and forgiveness had given him a fresh perspective. "Even Stronghold. As long as you're with me, I'll stay there as long as you'll have me."

Jessira grinned, her eyes welling. This time, she was the one to reach for him. She kissed him, clasping her hands around his neck and holding him tight. She was the first to break away. "I'm going to hold you to your promise," she told him, her voice breathless.

"You'll never need to," Rukh replied.

He reached for her again, holding her, caressing her, kissing her. Jessira cupped his face, and his arms tightened around her. He reveled in the soft feel of her. He wanted this moment to last—

The hissing, grating cry of a Braid on the hunt rose in the air, not more than a quarter-mile away.

"Fragging unholy hells!" Jessira cursed.

CHAPTER TWENTY-ONE
A FEARFUL ALLIANCE

I once gave thought to the idea that the Tigons might be reasoning creatures much as we are. I was quickly disabused of such foolish notions. Tigons are slaves to their appetites for destruction.

~From the journal of Li-Choke, AF 2062

Li-Choke arrived at his objective, a narrow canyon in the foothills south of the Privation Mountains. He paused to get his bearings. Steep, ice-slick walls—a hundred feet tall—ran east-to-west, ringing the ravine. Mother had directed him here. Sunshine reflected off the small pond near the base of the northernmost cliff. The scent of pine needles hung in the air.

From this point on, he had to be cautious. Without ongoing, consistent discipline, Chimeras often became uncontrollable in their aggression, fighting one another; Braids, Balants, Ur-Fels, and Tigons all striving for supremacy. Riots were even known to break out. They required a firm, steady hand to keep them in line. The Chimeras that Choke was meant to command hadn't felt a Bael's judgment and influence in months. Who knew how they might react to his orders at this point? They might have forgotten their fear of Baels and attack him.

From the north came the sound of small rocks fallings, of someone moving furtively.

It seemed they *had* forgotten their fear of his kind, and Choke wished his brother Baels were with him. He missed them with an ache that hadn't ended since the moment Mother annihilated Li-Dirge and the others. And losing the last of his brethren a month ago had sapped his passion for life. Li-Choke had shambled to his destination like an animated corpse. He lacked any real desire to continue living, but he would carry out this burden Mother had placed upon his shoulders. The lives of the western Baels depended on his actions and his success.

Choke eyed the heights above. Just because the canyon seemed empty didn't mean Chimeras weren't about. The furtive sounds from earlier was proof of that. *Something* was here. Choke moved south, wanting his back to a canyon wall. As he reached his destination, he sighted movement on the heights. A Balant. No. Two. Clumsy. Now, where were the rest of the Chimeras? Choke scanned with all his senses. From the western entrance came the faint acrid odor of concentrated urine. Tigons. Probably a claw led by this Chak-Soon.

A hiss, quickly cut off, followed by the slithering of scales on rock came from directly above him. Choke stepped away from the wall, set his trident, and uncoiled his whip. Fifteen feet above, ten Braids—two traps—hung from the rocks like giant misshapen bats. Upon each of their faces was a predator's glare. The Braids were ready to attack.

Choke snapped his whip. The thunder-crack of the barbs bit into the stone and small pieces shattered directly in front of the lead Braid. It gave Choke the time he needed to set himself as the rest of the Braids hissed in consternation. A Bael had to display his dominance if he ever hoped to lead the Chimeras. It was an unalterable law as old as the Fan Lor Kum.

"I'll grind you underfoot, you pathetic worms," he growled. "Stand down and bow before he whom Mother Herself chose to lead you." Another crack of the whip had the other Braids rustling nervously. "NOW!" They shared fearful glances before slithering down the rock face, bunching up as they faced Li-Choke. They bowed before him, knees on the ground and foreheads pressed to the dirt.

They were his.

"Follow mussst. Mother sssaysss," the lead Braid whispered in a sibilant voice.

Li-Choke nodded. "Good." He gestured to where the Tigons were coming into view. "Follow me. Three paces behind. If the Tigons don't bend knee, kill them." Choke turned his back to the Braids, trusting the snake-like Chimeras to follow. They would remain loyal so long as they trusted in his leadership.

A claw of Tigons waited at the mouth of the canyon. Leading them was one spotted like a jaguar. He had to be Chak-Soon. The ordinate appeared calm, unruffled and unimpressed based on the sneer he wore on his muzzle. Another Tigon loomed large behind Chak-Soon, a giant with a tiger's stripes. Another stood close by as well, black like a panther. The final two Tigons filling out the claw were both lean and rangy, like cheetahs. All were arrayed in a simple breechcloth with a sheathed sword strapped to their waist and a cased bow and quiver of arrows upon their backs.

"Bow," Li-Choke ordered.

His command earned him a further sneer from Chak-Soon. The others in his claw growled in agitation and warning.

Li-Choke never allowed fear to enter his heart. If it came to a fair battle, he and the Braids would not prevail against the Tigons. But it wouldn't come to a fair battle. Guile, as Li-Dirge had so often explained, was a far more potent weapon than brute force. Choke coiled his whip, letting it drop to the ground as he strode forward with a smile. He was inches from Chak-Soon, looming over all the Tigons, even the giant tiger.

Without warning, Choke smashed the boss of his horns against

Chak-Soon's forehead, felling the ordinate like a tree. He swept aside the black-panther Chimera before grasping the tiger-striped Tigon by his leather harness, holding him in place. One straight punch. Two had the giant Chimera limp as well. Chak-Soon made to rise, and Li-Choke hammer-fisted him back down. The cheetah-like Tigons held back, tails tucked between their legs. Here came the panther. The foolish cat leapt. Choke caught him in mid-air. A thunderous knee to the Tigon's mid-section exploded all the air from the panther's lungs. The cat curled up around himself as he gasped for breath. Choke dropped him with a thud. The tiger was on his knees, trying to clear his head. Choke kicked him in the gut, lifting him off the ground. Another kick to the face, and the large cat was out. Chak-Soon made to rise once again, but Li-Choke was there. He pulled the ordinate to his feet, holding him by the neck, choking him while holding him out at arm's length.

"Foolish kitten. I am Bael, and you *will* obey as Mother commanded, or you will be ended."

Chak-Soon nodded feebly.

Choke let him fall heavily to the ground. He recovered his whip and snapped the barbed ends inches from the ears of the Tigons until the cats rose to their feet and bowed before him. Without their obeisance, they could never be trusted. And only then could Li-Choke teach them his manner of leadership. Since Tigons were irrational brutes, they were only able to learn discipline after they had first experienced pain.

———————— ● ————————

"Tigons learn. No need punish," Chak-Soon said. "Balants and Braids cower." His words were almost unintelligible as his thick tongue moved clumsily around his sharp teeth even as he stumbled across the slick, snowy path upon which they trod. His breath blew mist in the frigid wintery air. They followed a northward running rivulet through the heart of a broad valley edged by rolling foothills south of the Privation Mountains.

Li-Choke nodded. A week since their initial meeting, and he was still doling out punishment for even the most minor of infractions. It wasn't because he was a sadist or enjoyed doing so but because discipline and order amongst the Fan Lor Kum had slipped so precipitously since Mother had given control of the Eastern Plague to the Tigons. Li-Choke had been forced to reinstitute knowledge that the Chimeras had seemingly forgotten: swift and certain punishment followed disobedience. The Tigons had apparently believed a severe, if haphazard and unpredictable, form of discipline was all that was required. It was a habit of the intellectually lazy. But then again these were the Tigons. What else were they if not stupid and lazy?

"The Chimeras are re-learning what should never have been forgotten. Had you and your claw bowed before me as Mother commanded, do you suppose I would need to beat your brethren so frequently for their insolence?"

"They learn. No need to punish," Chak-Soon said stubbornly.

Li-Choke growled as he came to a sudden stop and faced the Tigon. "I have heard you, stupid kitten. Now be silent or be silenced."

"I take punishment for all Tigons if they make mistake," Chak-Soon said, refusing the direct order. "It only right. I command them." He shuffled in uncertainty, but faced Li-Choke with an unblinking stare, doing his best to hide his fear.

Li-Choke rocked back on his heels, taken aback by the Tigon's words. In all the instruction he'd received from his elder Baels, never had the idea of a compassionate Tigon ever been considered. The cats were known to be little more than animated killing machines. Their hearts were empty of empathy, even for their fellow Tigons. Indeed, they often laughed at the misfortune of their brethren, going so far as to devour their fallen when mad with heat of battle. Yet here was Chak-Soon, willing to accept whatever punishment his fellow Tigons might face.

"Do you understand what you're saying?" Choke asked.

Soon nodded. "I know. Save Tigons hurt. It right to do. Good."

Surprise turned to shock. A Tigon understanding a moral concept of right and wrong? Impossible. He'd heard the cats mutter of Humanity's evil and Mother's holiness, but the words had been those of the ignorant and stupid. Soon's statement was something else. He sounded sincere, outwardly understanding what he was saying. Choke considered how to respond. Could Soon truly grasp esoteric concepts such as sympathy and pity? It flew in the face of everything he knew of Tigons. More likely Chak-Soon was simply parroting words he'd once heard uttered by a Bael. "The Tigons and all the other Chimeras must receive their proper discipline. They learn only through pain," Li-Choke said.

"You teach us?" Chak-Soon asked. "Learn best without hit."

Choke scowled. The Tigon simply wouldn't let it go. "I'll discipline as I see fit," he answered. "Do not say anything else!" he snapped upon seeing Soon's mouth open in likely protest.

The Tigon settled down, looking unhappy while Li-Choke pondered their conversation.

⁂

"Hume," Chak-Soon said.

Li-Choke furrowed his brows, perplexed. Had the Tigon just spoken the Master's name? "What of him?"

"Mother want kill him," Chak-Soon replied.

"She told you this?"

The Tigon nodded.

"What do you think of Her command?"

Li-Choke waited for the Tigon to speak, but Chak-Soon remained silent. A surprising silence as far as Choke was concerned. He would have expected the Tigon to growl out something to the effect that a Chimera's place wasn't to question Mother's orders; that their first duty was to simply obey them. The cat-like Chims had always been the most devout of Mother's creations.

"What about the others in your claw such as Chak-Vimm and Chak-Tine?" Choke asked, naming the large, tiger-striped Tigon and black panther one. "Are they as troubled as you appear to be?"

Chak-Soon grimaced. "They not care. Duty given. Holy order."

Li-Choke found his estimation of the ordinate rising. Was it possible the young Tigon had a mind with which to think? Perhaps a test was in order. "Hume is dead. Three centuries now since the fall of Hammer. How do we kill someone who's already dead?"

Chak-Soon muttered something unintelligible under his breath.

"You had something to say?" Li-Choke asked.

"Mother orders not always...." Chak-Soon bit off whatever else he might have been thinking.

Choke waited but Chak-Soon refused to say anything more. "Mother's orders aren't always rational," Choke finished for the Tigon. "Is that what you were going to say?"

A single, sharp, unhappy nod was his only answer.

Li-Choke's heart swelled with hope. Could Tigons actually have the ability to reason? Even if it were only a few of them, from those small seeds, Hume's great teaching could further flower. Perhaps the Baels need not be alone amongst the Chimeras.

It was a lot to base on one short conversation, but taken together with Chak-Soon's previous actions—the Tigon's offer to accept punishment for those in his command—it might just be possible. A smile spread across Choke's broad face. How deliciously ironic. Perhaps Mother's decision to spare Li-Choke could someday lead to further subversions of Her command, but this time it might involve Her most loyal Chimeras: the Tigons.

The part of his mind warning to slow down and not read too much into the situation was drowned out by the need to find a reason to live, something beyond fear, something that spoke of a deep-seated desire to serve and do good in this world. Since the murder of his brethren on the Hunters Flats, all Li-Choke had done was simply put one foot down in front of the other in a profoundly pathetic mime of existence.

Enough. It was time to once again grasp life in his hands and on his horns. It was time to live. It was what his SarpanKum and even the wise, young Human to whom he owed his life, Rukh Shektan, would have wanted for him.

"Have you ever given thought to brotherhood?" he asked Chak-Soon.

"Brothers. Li-Choke says all who think are," Chak-Soon said to Chak-Tine.

The black-panther Tigon scowled. "You and Bael not crèche mates. Him command under Mother. Not right say his name." He bared his fangs.

Chak-Soon hid an impatient sigh. His fellow Tigons lacked the wit to see what their ordinate had come to believe was the truth: they were all brothers, whether they were born of the same crèche or not. Perhaps it was because of their inborn aggressiveness. It didn't take much to get a Tigon furious enough to unsheathe claws and go for the jugular. Even when it came to simply discussing a topic they were unused to, they tended to react with anger rather than thoughtfulness.

How had the Baels maintained their patience in the face of his fellow Tigons anger-addled stupidity?

Just then, Li-Choke strode to his side. When they had first met, the Bael had been the grimmest of commanders under whom Chak-Soon had ever served. He had crushed the incipient challenge to his rule by doing as a Bael should: by ruthlessly seizing command. The weeks following hadn't been easy. Li-Choke had been a severe taskmaster, handing out penalties and punishments for the most minor of infractions. None of them were particularly harsh, but they never seemed to end. The Bael was either a sadist or the Fan Lor Kum had truly become as he had claimed: unbalanced and unordered. Chak-Soon believed it was the latter. At any rate, early on Li-Choke's actions had earned him a certain amount of enmity amongst his Chimeras, especially the Tigons who had grown used to the lax discipline that had come about during their tenure as leaders of the Eastern Plague. Of course, that tenure was soon to end with the arrival of the Western Baels. It was a good thing as far as Chak-Soon was concerned. His kind were not meant to rule.

The Bael spoke up. "Chak-Tine, relieve Chak-Vimm. He has been guiding the Balants for long enough."

A late winter storm had rolled through a few days ago. It had dumped knee-deep snow in many places and slowed the Chimeras to a crawl as they struggled to make their way through the Creosote Plains. The Balants had been set at point, breaking the trail while a Tigon remained at their side, ensuring they didn't stray in the wrong direction. Without guidance, the baboon-like Chimeras tended to wander in whatever direction was easiest. Their progress was further slowed by the need to hunt and replenish their food stores. It was a task to which Tigons and Braids were poorly trained. They knew how to stalk visible prey, but they knew little of interpreting animal droppings or reading their markings.

In fact, were it not for Li-Choke, who *did* know how to hunt, the

Chimeras might have already starved. As usual, Mother had chosen well, when She had set the Bael in command. He was teaching Chak-Soon the truth of fraternity amongst those who could reason—excepting Humanity, of course—and with Choke's leadership, they were certain to carry out Mother's mission. Chak-Soon scowled a moment later. What mission? To kill someone already dead in a city already crushed?

"Something troubles you, ordinate," Li-Choke noted.

Chak-Soon glanced at the Bael. The traces of their stern commander were still present, but over the past month, since he had first broached the topic of brotherhood, Li-Choke no longer handed out his disciplines with the grim visage of one hoping for a reason to kill. He even smiled now and then, eliciting pleased reactions in return. Tigons prospered under the kindness of those to whom they'd willingly submitted. Li-Choke had even asked about this once, noticing the happier attitudes of the claw. It had fallen to Chak-Soon to explain how the supposed antagonism and jealousy Baels assumed Tigons felt toward them was, in fact, untrue. Tigons had pride, and they hated when those to whom they'd given their loyalty treated them with disrespect. Tigons loved acceptance and praise more than they loved fighting—though they seemed unable to turn that trick themselves when it came to their own leadership.

Chak-Soon was too young to have interacted much with Li-Dirge, the SarpanKum who Mother accused of treachery; but the older ordinates sometimes spoke of the dead commander with barely concealed reverence in their voices. It was said that Li-Dirge often treated the Tigons as equals, offering advice or even camaraderie. He had been a rare Bael, and it seemed that Li-Choke was following in the late commander's hoofprints.

Chak-Soon scowled again. He had been praising the SarpanKum who Mother *accused* of treachery. Even the very word: accused was wrong. Mother didn't accuse. Those She stated had committed a crime had done so. Mother's judgment was never wrong.

"Something does trouble you," Li-Choke said, noticing the Tigon's troubled expression. "What is it?"

Chak-Soon shook his head. "Mother."

Li-Choke nodded as if the one word answer was explanation enough. "You feel guilty over questioning Her judgment," he guessed. "I know what you're experiencing. Every Bael who has ever lived has struggled with that same problem: if the Queen is wrong in one small thing then in what other matters might She be mistaken." He shrugged. "Life is so much easier with the certainty that comes from blindly following what we are told is right and just."

Chak-Soon was miserable. "How trust Her judgment?" he asked, feeling as if he stood at the apex of a bridge. On the far side was an untamed, unruly world where nothing was certain but hidden truths could be life altering. On the near shore was the safe existence he'd always known: unquestioning obeisance to Mother. Which way to go when so much of what he believed to be true was actually wrong?

Li-Choke sighed. "Now that is a question which has troubled the Baels for centuries. If you arrive at an answer, let me know." His broad lips split into a grin. "For now, we hunt Hume, remember? In Hammer. The Bone Place."

"We still go."

"We are ordered to do so," Choke replied. "But maybe we need not go *into* Hammer, just to the city."

The Bael moved on, leaving Chak-Soon to walk alone. There had been something to Li-Choke's final words. He hadn't been entirely truthful. It wasn't as the commander had said. The Baels *had* come to a decision regarding Mother. They didn't trust Her, which meant they had disobeyed Her. They *had* been traitors just as She had claimed. But their treason had been rooted in Mother's own incomprehensible actions and orders. Her current commands, for instance.

She couldn't tell reality apart from untruth.

Chak-Soon gasped. He had crossed the bridge, going over to the far side where nothing was certain. It felt like thunder should have rolled, lightning smashed; but the world was the same, gray and overcast, cold and silent.

CHAPTER TWENTY-TWO
HUNTED

*The plowed fields of coal-black loam, the deep forests of emerald stillness,
and the wild sea of sapphire grandeur. Or a quiet library, the soft
air crowded with the aromas of walnut oil, pipe smoke, and old paper.
All are places of sentimental longing.*

~Reap the Harvest, by Chulet, AF 441

In all her life, Jessira had never expected—nor wanted—to visit the dead city of Hammer. The idea was silly, no better than wanting to sail the raging seas. She had many better uses of her time.

And yet, here she was, all because of some book that Rukh's nanna insisted was important enough to risk their lives over.

Crumbled buildings stood in melancholy postures of slump and decay, their lovely friezes and carvings worn away by wind and time. The roads, whether paved with brick or crushed stone, were rutted and torn asunder by roots from bushes and shrubs forcing desperate toeholds. Vegetation choked off the medians as ivy slithered to all sides of the streets and up the surrounding buildings. A small thicket of trees, forming a young forest, had reclaimed several blocks of the city, and from it came the furtive animal movements of raccoons, rabbits, and even deer. Jessira had to step carefully around piles of scat, some of it fresh.

"Wolves," Rukh said, breaking her reverie as she studied a still-steaming dropping.

In response, Jessira uncased her bow, nocking it. "Can't you Fireball them?" she asked.

"I could but the Chims might hear."

Jessira scowled. The damnable Braids. If not for the snake-like Chims, she could have been warm and asleep in her bedroll—or at least warm, depending on how long she and Rukh decided to kiss. Instead, she was trekking through Hammer's boulevards in the frigid cold near midnight. Her breath steamed before her. At least there wasn't any snow or rain. Being cold was bad enough, but it was doubly worse when she was wet.

"Do you think they still have our scent?" Rukh asked.

Outside the city, the hissing Braids had dogged their footsteps, nipping at their heels. But once Jessira and Rukh had entered the ruined streets of Hammer, the snake-like Chims seemed to have lost the taste for the hunt.

"I think we left them behind," Jessira said.

"Then let's stop and find some shelter," Rukh said with a shiver.

They cast about, studying the nearby buildings for a likely candidate.

"There," Jessira pointed out a nearby building, one of the few that was close at hand and nearly intact. The structure was narrow and long, rising three stories and standing on a corner. It looked like it might have once housed a series of flats, or perhaps had been a single-family home.

Rukh nodded. "It should do."

"Good. Let's get inside. It's freezing," Jessira said, cold and irritable.

"I thought you Strongholders were tougher than us soft

Purebloods," Rukh said in bewilderment.

"Shut it."

The building's front door was in place, but many of the windows had long since been shattered with shards strewn across the floor. Inside, the furniture lay broken into kindling, and the walls were gutted, exposing broad swatches of laths. Plaster dust covered everything in a film of white, and to the left of the entrance, a narrow staircase, only wide enough for single file, led upstairs. The balusters were cracked and broken. A hall led deeper into the building, and the damage continued, but at least the walls were upright. A safe spot was found in the rear of the structure, likely a kitchen, and—for a wonder—the windows were intact. A door led to an alley, a handy exit if they needed to make a quick escape.

"Probably best to leave the packs on the horse," Rukh said, leading the gelding into the small space in the back.

"We'll have to go without a fire and wrap up in blankets," Jessira commented.

Rukh smirked. "I think you just want to snuggle with me."

Jessira snorted. "I'd snuggle with the horse if I didn't think he'd step on me."

"I smell better."

"Barely."

Nevertheless, once they were settled on the ground, their backs to a wall, she pressed close to Rukh, resting her head on his shoulder. Even through the worry of being hunted by Chims, the feel of his warmth next to her caused her to blush. Why couldn't the fragging Chims have waited just an hour? She looked up, staring up into his eyes, wondering if he was thinking what she was thinking.

"I can think of warmer places," he said.

"I can think of softer places," she responded.

"Less dangerous."

"We really shouldn't," she said, wanting nothing more than to do exactly what they were dancing around.

She traced the outline of his jaw, stroking his face as she stared into his dark eyes. Her heart beat quicker when he bent his head, kissing her. She breathed deep, her body rising, pressing closer to his. She was falling. It was the softness of his lips, the stubble of his beard, and the feel of his fingers gliding through her hair. The kiss deepened.

Rukh broke off. "We really shouldn't be doing this," he said, sounding breathless. "We have to stop."

"I don't want to stop," Jessira growled in frustration, clutching his shirt. After a moment, she leaned her face away from his and rested her head against his shoulder, still pressed close. "You're right," she said, sighing in disappointment.

A wolf howled, sounding close. Another answered, even closer.

Rukh smiled. "It's a good thing we stopped when we did."

Jessira chuckled. "Could you imagine how embarrassing it would have been if they caught us while we were naked?"

Rukh laughed with her. "Let's hope the wolves don't find us at all. I'd hate to have to fight them *and* the Chims."

"Weren't *you* the one who wanted to come here and find some book?"

"That was before I knew there were wolves here or that we'd be hunted by Chims."

"I'll remind you of your idiocy when we get back to Stronghold."

Just then a hooting cry came to them, high pitched and desperate, cut off all of a sudden.

Jessira stiffened. "What was that?"

Rukh rose to his feet, hand poised on his sword. Jessira stood as well, readying her bow. "It sounded like a Balant," Rukh said.

More cries came, roars and hissing screams. The Chims. Someone was attacking them.

———■●■———

Li-Choke was quickly learning why Hammer was called the Bone Place. A day out from the city, a Balant had been killed by a herd of elk. The males had attacked the Balant without mercy, taking mortal blows from the Tigons to bring down the elephant-sized Chimera. Later the same day, a tiger had mauled a trap of Braids. Several of the snakes had died, and others were so severely injured, they had to be put down. The closer Li-Choke and the Chimeras came to the city, the more frequent such attacks became. The worst was when a Braid was attacked by a swarming colony of rabbits. Rabbits! The little monsters had attacked a fully armed Chimera with nothing but teeth and a mindless savagery. The mingled screams from the Braid and the dying rabbits was one Li-Choke knew would haunt his dreams for years to come—assuming he lived that long.

The Bone Place might see an end to him and his command. He already hated this city. The only reason he still pressed forward was because Mother might know if he didn't explore the city's environs. Legends told how Mother could find Her children no matter where they were. Until She had discovered Li-Choke in the Hunters Flats, he had always assumed such stories to be an exaggeration, if not an outright fable. He now knew the truth. He had to complete his mission or risk the death of his western brothers.

Still, he had never actually intended on entering the city; but, unfortunately, the remaining Braids had caught the scent of something. Like brainless fools, they'd raced off, crying out their discovery and quickly outdistancing the other Chimeras. By the time Choke and the rest of his command had caught up with the snakes, they were all dead. A bear had awoken from its slumber and killed them.

At that point, Choke was ready to lead his Chimeras out of the

Bone Place and take them somewhere safe; but a pack of wolves had ended his incipient plan. The four-legged bastards had chased them into Hammer itself. Once inside, two more Tigons, Chak-Trum and Chak-Vimm, had both quickly died. It had been a tiger, dying even as it took down the Tigons. Then the pack of wolves had caught up with them again.

The final Balant had given up its life so Choke and the two remaining Tigons could escape. He was just glad Chak-Soon was amongst the survivors. If the young ordinate died, it would be a tragedy. Choke had to find a place to hole up for the night. He and the others could escape this death trap of a city in the morning.

As they walked down a rubble-strewn street, Chak-Soon sniffed the air. "Humans."

Chak-Tine lifted his snout as well. "Near. Kill them?"

Li-Choke wondered who the Humans were. Were they planning on reclaiming the city? The Chims avoided the Bone Place, but that didn't mean it was safe for Humanity. Hammer still lacked an Oasis, and without one, Mother could kill them without any effort.

His musings ended when a wolf rounded a corner. The animal howled, calling its pack to the hunt.

"Run!" Choke shouted.

They sprinted along a wide boulevard, dodging rocks, refuse, fallen tree limbs, and ivy thick as rope. All the while, Choke scanned for a defensible spot. "There," he said, pointing to a nearby building. It was nearly intact. The front door was in place. They might be able to defend it.

Tine, the first to tumble inside, was immediately cut down by an arrow through the throat. He gurgled out his death. Chak-Soon, close behind on Tine's heels, took a sword thrust to the chest. He slumped to the ground, keening in anguish. Choke stared at his dead and dying Tigons, trying to figure out what was going on.

Before he could, a hammer-blow to his wrist forced him to drop his trident. His whip was ripped from his waist. A vice-like grip squeezed his throat and slammed him against a wall.

"You should have chosen a different building," a hard voice growled.

Choke grasped the hand, trying to overcome his shock. He knew that voice. "Rukh Shektan?"

———●●———

An electric jolt went through Rukh. That voice. It was impossible. He should be in the Hunters Flats. "Li-Choke?" A garbled answer sounding like a 'yes' was his only response. Rukh dropped the Bael. "What are you doing here?"

The Bael rose shakily to his feet, rubbing his throat. "I am hunting Hume," he said with a quavering laugh.

"You know this Bael?" Jessira asked, stepping out from behind a large chunk of the fallen ceiling. She had been the one to fire the arrow that had cut down one of the Tigons. The other one still lived, curled up in a ball and gasping out his life.

"You know him, too," Rukh said. "Li-Choke. The Bael who carried you away after the Kesarin attack in the Hunters Flats." He walked over to the still-living Tigon. Blood pooled beneath and around the Chim, freezing quickly in the cold air. The creature lay on his side, curdled around the ruin of his torn chest and mewling in pain. Tigons were filthy brutes, but no creature deserved such torture. It was time to end this one's suffering.

"Don't kill him," Li-Choke cried out.

Rukh withheld the lethal blow. He turned to the Bael. "Why?"

"He is not what you think," Li-Choke said.

Wolves howled outside, sounding as if they were closing in on their building.

Rukh glanced to the open door. "Better explain quickly," he said. "Sounds like the wolves are hungry."

"They aren't hungry," Choke said with a grimace.

Rukh quirked an eyebrow.

"Since Hume's death, the animals around Hammer make life dangerous for Chimeras," Choke said. "We call it the Bone Place."

"And what about the Tigon? Why's he so special?" Rukh asked.

"Can you Heal him?" Choke asked, sounding desperate.

"Why should we?" Jessira challenged.

"He understands the truth about Mother. He is the first Tigon to do so. He needs to live."

Rukh considered Choke's request and shared a questioning glance with Jessira. "What do you think?"

"I don't know," she said. "My initial judgment about the Chims, or at least the Baels, may no longer be trustworthy."

Rukh stared down at the Tigon. "He's not even Human," he said after a moment of thought. "Who knows whether Healing him would even work?"

"Please," Choke pleaded. "My brothers, the ones you saved in the caverns, were all murdered by the Queen. Afterward, I wondered at my purpose in this world; but Devesh took my tragedy and gave me an opportunity: teach the Tigons. It can be done. They can become as the Baels, great leaders like Li-Dirge. Please, Rukh Shektan. Save this one if you can."

It was the 'please' that convinced Rukh. It was important to the young Bael. Besides, even if Choke was wrong, they could always kill the Tigon later. "Can you Heal him?" Rukh asked Jessira.

"I can try," she said. "I only hope you know what you're doing," she muttered softly, low enough so only he could hear her. "Hold him down," she ordered Choke. "Once I've got him Healed, I don't want him roaring to his feet trying to kill us."

Choke helped roll the Tigon over, kneeling at the ordinate's head and pinning down his hands and arms. "I have him."

A single thrust had been all Rukh had needed, straight into the right side of the Tigon's chest. Blood bubbled as it pumped out of the scalpel-straight incision.

Jessira's hands glowed golden as her eyes narrowed in concentration. "Hemothorax," she said. "Blood is filling up the space between his chest wall and his collapsed lung. It won't be easy to fix." Once more, from beyond the building came the howl of wolves, closer than before. Jessira glanced outside. "And I don't have time to be gentle." The light from her hands flowed down into the Tigon, eliciting a harsh growl.

Another howl came from outside, even closer. Rukh rose to his feet, unlimbering his bow as he paced to the front door. He stared out into the night, searching. The wolves were coming. That much was obvious. He set an arrow to string. "Hurry," Rukh urged, sensing movement in the street.

"Almost done." Jessira said. More light poured from her hands.

The Tigon drew a shuddering breath even as the large gash knitted shut. His eyes snapped open in terror and briefly, he lifted his head off the ground before it thumped back down. His tongue lolled out.

"What happened?" Choke asked.

"He's asleep," Jessira said, looking nearly done for.

"Get him upstairs. I'll cover." Rukh said. "We'll have a better chance holding them off if they only have one way to reach us," Rukh said.

Choke loaded the unconscious Tigon onto his shoulders and made for the single set of stairs to the left.

"Jessira goes first," Rukh ordered. He knew how much Healing took out of a person, and as tired as Jessira probably was right now, she wouldn't even be able to lift her sword. Besides, he wanted as many warriors as possible between her and the wolves.

Choke started up the stairs after Jessira. Rukh readied his bow and followed, walking backward. He'd probably be able to get off two shots, and then it would be his sword. Fireballs couldn't be used here. It looked like a single spark might set the entire building ablaze.

Rukh conducted *Jivatma*, strengthening his bones, muscles, and sinews.

"Do you require assistance?" It was Li-Choke.

"No," Rukh answered. "Just see to your Tigon and make sure Jessira is safe."

"I'm not made of porcelain," Jessira said. "And my place should be at your shoulder. Two bows are better than one."

"You sure you're up to it?"

His answer was unhappy stomps down the stairs followed by a thump to his head.

"I think you should keep your hands to yourself," Rukh said with a grimace. It had been a hard thump. "Didn't anyone teach you OutCastes proper manners?"

Another thump, softer followed by a gentle kiss against his cheek.

Rukh glanced up at her, wishing they could have....He shook off the thoughts. "Just a few hours," he muttered.

"What?"

"Nothing," Rukh said. He had heard movement just outside the front door. "Here they come."

A wolf barreled through an open window. Jessira's arrow took it through the chest, slamming the beast into a wall. Three more followed. Two were quickly felled but not before another four were inside. They raced for the stairs.

Two more down. Three more inside. Another two. Even more. It was a mad mob of fur, teeth, claws, and furious growls.

Rukh drew his sword. "Fall back," he ordered. His Martial Masters spoke of how to make correct decisions in the heat of battle: when to defend and when to retreat. But when no choices were left, the wise warrior did the unexpected: he attacked. Rukh Shielded and prepared to step forward and meet the wolves.

The wolves stood at the base of the stairs, teeth bared, snapping, red-eyed with fury. But they didn't close. They growled their rage, staring upward, but refusing to ascend. Eventually, their anger seemed to play out. Their snarls slowly trailed off and they glanced about, confusion evident in their expressions. A whimper. Two. More. One left, then others. Without another sound, they exited the building, silent but for the scrabbling of their claws on the wooden floor. Once outside, they yipped to one another before racing off into the night.

"It's over," Rukh said, confused by what had just happened.

⬛●⬛

The Tigon slept the rest of the night, while Rukh and the Bael filled Jessira in on what had really happened in the caverns. She hadn't been entirely happy to learn that Rukh had aided the Baels. While she understood the Chim commanders had done their best to protect Humanity ever since Hammer's Fall, she couldn't make the leap between understanding their actions and forgiving them.

Rukh had. It was part of why she liked him so much: his capacity for forgiveness.

"How much longer will he slumber?" Choke asked, interrupting her thoughts when the Tigon stirred briefly but didn't awaken.

Dawn was near.

Jessira shrugged. "It wasn't an easy Healing," she said. "For a Human, it would take most of the day for them to awake. Who knows how long it will take for a Tigon."

"You'll have to carry him out of here," Rukh said. "Can you manage it?"

Choke nodded. "It won't be a problem unless the animals attack us."

"I still don't understand what happened last night," Rukh said.

"When they burst into the building, I was sure they would swarm up the stairs. They looked rabid."

"Perhaps a portion of the Queen's madness infected the beasts of Hammer after She destroyed the city," Choke said.

"Then why did they leave so suddenly?" Jessira asked doubtfully. It was an obvious hole in Choke's logic. She wondered if the Bael was trying to hide something from them.

"I don't know," Choke said with a shrug. "All we know is that the animals here hate Chimeras."

"We never had trouble with them," Rukh said, his lips pursed in thought. "Maybe they don't hate Humans."

"Perhaps so," Choke said with a grunt. "What are your plans here?" he asked, changing the subject.

"We could ask the same of you," Jessira said, eyeing the Bael in distrust.

Choke grimaced. "Mother made me an offer I couldn't refuse," he answered, going on to explain the death of the surviving Baels from the caverns. "Your great work was wasted," he said to Rukh.

Rukh's head drooped. "That is a shame," he replied. "But maybe we can still salvage something from this disaster."

"My brethren are all dead," Choke answered. "What more can we do?"

"The western Baels still live, as do you. Your brothers need to learn what the two of us tried to accomplish. And they shouldn't forget Li-Dirge. It was his words and actions—yours as well—that led me to do what I did in the caverns. The Baels aren't dead yet."

"They will be," Choke replied softly. "Mother told me if I didn't carry out this task, She would kill every one of them."

Jessira waited a moment for Choke to explain what he meant by his last statement, but the Bael fell silent. Jessira rolled her eyes in irritation. "Just like the other one, Dirge—always wanting us to ask a question to find out the rest of the story," she muttered. "Just tell us what happened," she said to Choke. "And no more dramatic pauses."

Choke blinked, nonplussed, before a sheepish grin spread across his face. "Did you happen to kill a nest of Ur-Fels and a claw of Tigons in the Privation Mountains four or five months ago?" he asked.

Jessira shared a look with Rukh. "We did," she said. "Well, mostly Rukh," she amended, shooting him a glare.

"What about it?" Rukh asked Choke, wisely refusing to meet Jessira's eyes.

"Chak-Soon—" he pointed to the Tigon, "—was the ordinate, the commander in charge. He witnessed the battle and told Mother what he saw. When She learned a single Human had destroyed so many Chimeras, in Her lunacy, She decided only Hume was skilled enough to carry out such an attack."

"She knows of Hume?" Jessira asked in confusion. "How?"

"I don't know, but She does; and She ordered me west, to join up with Soon and his Chimeras. We were instructed to journey to Hammer in order to find and kill Hume—who is apparently you."

The room fell silent again, as Jessira and Rukh digested Choke's words.

"And what about you?" the Bael asked, breaking the quiet. "What is your purpose in Hammer?"

Jessira waited for Rukh to take the lead. After all, coming here had been his decision.

"I'm looking for *The Book of First Movement*. It was supposedly written by the First Father," Rukh said.

"Why would you travel all the way from Ashoka for one book?" Choke asked, appearing puzzled.

Rukh shifted, looking uncomfortable. "I have my reasons," he said, not bothering to correct the Bael's mistaken assumption regarding from where they had started their journey.

Choke's lips twitched. "Is this a dramatic pause?" he asked.

"My nanna suggested it," Rukh said with a shrug. "So here we are."

"And did your nanna tell you where you might find this book?" Choke asked. He gestured outside. "Hammer is a large city."

"It's supposed to be in the City Library," Rukh answered.

"And if we—the Baels—had moved it? What then?"

Jessira smirked at Rukh. "He hadn't planned that far in advance."

Choke nodded. "Then it is fortunate I found you. The book was entombed with Hume. It remains within the City Library of Hammer, but underneath a simple unmarked plinth in the center of the main atrium. I would hazard to guess that neither of you would have thought to search there."

"No we wouldn't. We'd have had to return home with nothing to show for our troubles." Jessira glanced at Rukh. "Aren't you glad you took my advice and saved the Bael?"

"Your advice?" Rukh said. "If I'd followed *your* advice, he'd have—"

Jessira laughed. "Your cheeks turn so red when you think someone's wronged you," she said, enjoying the further blush taking hold of Rukh's face. Sometimes he made it too easy.

Choke nodded gravely. "She is correct. Your blush is quite red."

The Bael's quiet, studious observation set Jessira laughing again; and Choke's lips twitched at her amusement.

Rukh muttered something unintelligible before chuckling with them.

Li-Choke looked between them before breaking out into an expansive smile. "When I first met the two of you, I would have sworn the two of you would forever remain mortal enemies. You shared a distrust for one another rivaling your hatred for the Fan Lor Kum. Yet here you are, laughing together. It's good to see how well the spirit of fraternity has grown between the two of you."

"You think we think of one another as brothers?" Jessira asked.

"Not literally, but figuratively. Metaphorically if you will," Choke said. "Is that not true?" he asked sounding confused.

Jessira's peal of laughter had the Bael's ears wilting in embarrassment. It didn't help that Rukh was laughing just as heartily. Jessira felt a surprising twinge of sympathy for the Chim.

"What is so funny?" Choke asked, looking affronted.

Rukh shook his head. "I don't think of Jessira as a brother or a sister," he said.

"Then in what way do you think of one another," Choke asked, glancing between the two of them. Insight suddenly lit his eyes. "Oh."

◆●◆

Choke led the packhorse, which had somehow survived last night's attack and now had the unfortunate task of carrying the burden of the still slumbering Chak-Soon. Ahead of them walked Rukh Shektan. The Ashokan maintained point as they travelled a wide road through the heart of Hammer, toward the City Library.

The day was warm. Spring was in the air and melting snow was turning much of the ground into a slushy, muddy mess. A brackish, unpleasant smell seemed to seep from the very pores of the city as the marsh south and east of Hammer had also begun to thaw. However, in the shadows, beneath doorways and along the sides of buildings where the sun rarely reached, it remained cold. There, ice and frost bitterly clung to the eaves. The distant cry of a falcon came to them, but otherwise the city was silent. For his part, Choke was grateful the fearful howl of wolves on the hunt didn't fill the air.

Rukh didn't seem to notice any of this. His eyes were focused and intense as he continually scanned before them, to their sides, and

352

even behind. An arrow lay upon the rest of his bow, ready to be aimed and released in an instant's notice. Choke knew the weapon was merely one of the means by which Rukh could deal death. His Fireballs were another, but perhaps his deadliest tool lay at his hip: his matte-black, spidergrass sword. Choke had rarely faced Humans in battle, and he was glad he would never have to face this one.

Then there was Jessira Grey who followed a few paces to the rear of their small group, equally alert and ready. What she lacked in Rukh's consummate skills, she made up for with sheer fearlessness. She knew Rukh was the superior warrior, but she refused to hide behind him. She insisted on doing for herself; carrying her own weight.

She had little use for Li-Choke; that much was obvious. She hadn't entirely believed his reason for being in Hammer, always regarding the Bael through measuring, close slit eyes. It was a minor miracle Rukh had managed to persuade the woman to Heal Chak-Soon. She would surely have preferred to simply slit the young Tigon's throat and be done with it. In her eyes, doing so would have carried no burden of sin since according to her view, all members of the Fan Lor Kum were enemies who deserved to die.

Choke couldn't find fault with her reasoning. It was essentially true. But perhaps with Chak-Soon's survival thanks to the work of a distrusting Human, the Baels could more easily teach the meaning of fraternity to others of the Fan Lor Kum.

"Wolves nearby," Jessira said, breaking Li-Choke out of his thoughts. "Right now, they're just prowling."

Rukh glanced back. "Is the Tigon showing any signs of waking up?"

Li-Choke shook his head. "He's still asleep as far as I can tell."

"Healing must take a lot out of his kind," Rukh noted.

Li-Choke grunted agreement. "We're nearly there," he said. "Only a few more blocks. Then the packhorse can take a rest from Chak-Soon's weight."

Soon enough, the City Library of Hammer came into view. Li-Choke had never seen the building before, but he'd heard it described and even read about it often enough to recognize it on first sight. The library soared four stories into the air with needle-thin towers rising even higher. History spoke of how the main vessel of the library had been designed to mimic the appearance of a boat. The entrance, which they faced, was said to be the wide, flat stern, while the opposite side of the building was a narrow prow, aimed like an arrow and meant to cleave the waters of the nearby River Mastery. Twin arcades lined the length of the main edifice, huddling beneath flying buttresses, which swept out like oars down to the transept. The cruciform shape had also been intentional, with the four arms of the building each projecting in a different cardinal direction. Clad outside by heavy gray granite, the inside of the library would have been as lifeless and grim as an underground cavern if not for the tall lancet windows of the clerestory.

As with the rest of Hammer, time and nature had robbed the building of much of its historical elegance and grandeur. Gaping holes punctured the line of the steeply pitched slate roof, and many windows peered out with an empty gaze, only shards remaining where lovely stained glass had once brought in colored light. There were also the vines, thick and root-like. They had clawed out footholds along the walls, swathing many parts of the building in green. Despite the decay, enough of the structure remained to imagine its glory before Mother and the Fan Lor Kum had destroyed Hammer.

Rukh entered first.

The packhorse balked at going inside, so Choke hauled Chak-Soon off the animal. He lumbered the Tigon onto his shoulder, carrying the ordinate like a bale of hay. Jessira had remained outside with them, likely not willing to give her back to him. After Choke had Soon settled on his shoulder, he ascended the front stairs with Jessira a few paces behind.

The main entrance consisted of ironwood doors, intricately carved with symbols, leaves, and figures from Hammer's past. They had once stood over twelve feet in height, each broad enough for a Balant to pass through without difficulty. Now, they barely hung on their hinges, cracked and rotted. Inside, it wasn't much better. Trees and large weeds split the stone flooring, while the vines from outside had managed to breach the walls, spreading throughout the interior. From the visible scat and smell, it was clear animals had made the building their home. Stealthy sounds—rustling, clicking noises— heralded their arrival within.

Choke glanced around, studying the famed building he'd read so much about. He never thought he'd actually enter this place. A large gallery ran the length of the library with an oculus—empty now— bringing in light from the domed ceiling above. Given the massive size of the space, it had the look and feel of a cloister—or what Li-Choke imagined how a cloister might look and feel. He'd never actually seen one. And upon each floor, running about the entire perimeter of the central vault, were open-sided arcades leading further into the library. Large chandeliers, once filled with hundreds of firefly lamps would have lit the place to noontime brightness, but all of them were gone now, burned out and leaving the library in solitude and darkness.

"There." Li-Choke pointed to a tall, thick plinth, centered in the gallery. It was about man-height and had once been white as ivory, but time and decay had dulled it to the same drab gray as the library's exterior. It would take a Bael's strength to move it. Or a Kumma's. "We buried the Master there," he said, easing Chak-Soon off his shoulder and laying the Tigon next to the plinth.

"Help me move the stone," Rukh said, setting aside his bow and shucking off his quiver of arrows.

Jessira stood nearby, peering into the darkness, alert and ready while they worked. With the two of them, it didn't take long to rock the plinth out of place, exposing a shallow, square hole underneath. Within it was a simple urn made of priceless copper and a blue leather bound book. There was nothing else.

"The Master's ashes," Li-Choke said in a reverent tone.

"*The Book of First Movement,*" Rukh added, sounding just as reverential. The Human had already reached inside and withdrawn *The Book*, thumbing through to the first page. "The first line is right here," he said excitedly. "I can read it. It's right there. Jessira, look."

"I'll look when we're outside," she replied. "There's animals in here moving around, and they sound…." She glanced back at them, an expression of worry on her face. "Let's get going."

Just then, Chak-Soon sat up with a groan. He levered himself to his feet and blinked owlishly. "What happen?" he asked, his gaze focused on Li-Choke. However, upon seeing Rukh and Jessira, he tried to surge to his feet, growling in fury.

Li-Choke was by his side in an instant, holding him down. "This one—" he gestured to Rukh, "—was protecting himself. He stabbed you through the chest. You were dying. This one—" he pointed to Jessira, "—Healed you and saved your life. Do you remember?"

Chak-Soon's bared fangs receded and his face held a look of bewilderment. "They Sil Lor Kum?"

Choke shook his head. "No."

"Then why Heal me?"

"Because I asked," Choke replied. "Life is not as you have been taught. You must trust me on this." He gestured to the plinth. "We'll talk more after I put this back in place." Choke sighed with relief when the Master's urn was sheltered once again. He hadn't liked the idea of disturbing Hume's place of rest, but the Humans had been insistent upon recovering *The Book of First Movement*.

"We have to go," Rukh said. He motioned to the darkness. "Jessira's right. Something's going on out there."

Chak-Soon growled.

Rukh turned his gaze to the young Tigon. "You wouldn't last a second against me. You know it's true, but I've let you live. We even Healed you. And Li-Choke is correct: I am not Sil Lor Kum. Consider what this might mean—brother."

Choke couldn't have been more surprised if Rukh had sprouted wings and flown away. Brother?

"Rats," Jessira said.

"What's wrong now?" Rukh asked.

"No. Rats. Lots of them. Coming this way." She pointed.

Choke looked in the direction she indicated. From the darkness, chittering noises broke the quiet as hundreds of beady red eyes moved as one, surging toward them.

"Suwraith's spit. Pick him up." Rukh gestured to the still weak-appearing Tigon. "Move."

Now, it was Jessira who took point, sprinting for the front entrance. For now, it was free of rats, but Choke could see a swarm of the vermin moving to cut off their escape. A roaring sound came from behind him. Choke glanced back, seeing Rukh throw Fireballs, lighting up the darkness and revealing an army of brown-furred rats converging rapidly toward them.

"Mother save!" Chak-Soon intoned fearfully.

Choke understood the Tigon's sentiments. The rats would eat them alive.

More roaring as Rukh threw more Fireballs.

Choke risked another fearful glance behind. The Fireballs hadn't slowed the rats. Just like all the other animals in this cursed city, Death held no fear for them. The vermin chittered as they raced forward, picking up speed, and closing the distance.

"When I say jump, all of you jump; and I mean as high as you can!" Rukh shouted. Choke had no idea what the Human had in mind, but he'd come to trust him. "Jump!"

Choke bunched his muscles and leapt upward as high as he

could, burdened as he was with Chak-Soon. Beneath them passed a wave of fire, white-hot, racing only inches off the ground. A Fire Shower. The air was suddenly crowded with the stench of burning flesh and fur.

"Run!" Rukh said. "There's still more coming!"

Choke didn't need further urging. He picked up speed, kicking aside a stray rat, smoking and dead as he outraced Jessira to the entrance. He burst out into the sunlight where a troop of baboons and a pack of wolves lay in wait. The animals howled with rage upon spotting him.

Choke's heart thudded in his chest. *Devesh save them!*

⸻

Jessira fired off two arrows as soon as she stepped outside. Two baboons went down. The rest held back, but it would only be for a moment. They were working themselves into a killing frenzy. Li-Choke had set the Tigon down. His trident and whip were at the ready. Good. The odds weren't in their favor, but if Rukh would hurry up, they could still make it out of here. She shot off another arrow, putting down a wolf this time. Choke snapped his whip, tearing flesh from a baboon. The animal howled in pain.

Rukh finally exited the library and slammed shut the doors. Without breaking stride, he fired three Fireballs, burning open a temporary path through the area where the baboons were clustered most thickly.

"Stay near me," Jessira ordered Choke. "I'll Blend us." The Bael gave a tight nod and loaded Chak-Soon onto the packhorse, which stood placidly, unworried by the battle about to take place. The baboons and wolves barked in confusion when Jessira and the others suddenly disappeared.

She would have sighed with relief except that Rukh, somehow always forgetting his non-Kumma Talents, ran past them, still in plain sight. Jessira cursed vividly. If she called out to him, she'd give away her own position. Just as she was about to do so, however, inexplicably, first the baboons and then the wolves paused in their pursuit. They glanced around and shook their heads, looking confused. A few wolves still eyed Rukh, but their gazes simply held the measuring assessment of one predator eyeing another. As for the baboons, they hooted to one other and melted away into the ruins of the city. The wolves quickly followed, slipping away in silence through hidden alleys and vacant buildings.

Jessira let go of her Blend and stalked over to Rukh.

"I should have Blended," he said before she could say a word.

"Then why didn't you?" she snapped.

"I didn't want to."

"What!" He had known what to do and had simply chosen not to do it. She was about to let him know just how stupid his decision had been, but understanding came to her. She closed her eyes and prayed for patience. He'd left himself visible for her sake, so the animals would have a target to attack, all in order to save her. Her mouth shut with a snap. She didn't need or want his protection—at least not as much as he seemed to think. What she needed was his respect.

"I respect your courage," he said, reading her thoughts as he so often did. "But I was raised to give myself for those I love. I'd have done the same for Bree or Jaresh."

She sighed in resignation. It was pure Rukh, and it infuriated her. *He* infuriated her, but she loved him, every part of him. She couldn't ask him to go against his nature. "I know," she said, pulling him into an embrace. "I just wish you would let me do the same for you."

He tucked a stray curl of hair behind her ear, and a faint smile creased his lips. "It's who I am."

The last of her irritation left her, leaving her smiling. Sometimes words were like chocolate on his lips, so sweet and wonderful. She would have kissed him, but just then, Li-Choke reminded them of the danger they were still in.

"We should leave before the animals decide to attack us once again."

Jessira glared at the Bael, hard enough for Choke to step back. Even the Tigon seemed to sense her annoyance and wisely kept his muzzle shut. All she wanted was a few hours alone with Rukh. Was that too much to ask?

"I agree," Rukh said. "But I think the animals only attack your kind."

"So it seems," Choke replied.

"Then you should travel with us," Rukh said. Jessira winced. Journeying with Chimeras was *not* something she wanted to do. "We can stay with you long enough until you're safe," Rukh continued. "After that, I suppose you'll go back to the Eastern Plague?"

Choke nodded.

"What about him?" Jessira asked, nodding toward Chak-Soon who glowered at her and Rukh.

Choke shrugged. "He is still new to Hume's ideals. He will learn."

"If you say so," Jessira replied, doubtful the Tigon would learn much of anything. "But if it's all the same to you, I think I'll sleep with my eyes open."

CHAPTER TWENTY-THREE
KNOWLEDGE IN LEDGERS

*If we allowed those who follow Suwraith to speak, they would refuse our invitation
and choose to remain hidden in the shadows. They are cowards.*

~*Our Lives Alone, by Asias Athandra, AF 331*

R ector and Mira were having lunch at a café near Jubilee Hills.
It was a routine debriefing, and they sat outside at a small
table, enjoying the sunlight and the unseasonably fine
weather. While Ashoka's winters were generally mild, even for the
city's warm climate, the past few days had been unusual. It had been
like a blast of summer in the midst of winter, and the entire city felt
more vibrant, more alive, like a need to sing and dance had been
sparked in everyone's blood.

Even Mira must have caught the fever. She had shed her typical
winter's garb of a heavy dress or skirt paired with a full-length blouse
and in their place, wore a green, summer sari that left her arms bare.
Rector thought it looked nice on her. It was a startling notion. When
had he started seeing Mira as an attractive woman?

"Dar'El is still angry with you," Mira said, drawing Rector's
attention back to the conversation at hand.

"Why?" he asked. "I found the man who attacked Bree."

"And gave him an easy death," Mira replied.

Her statement triggered a flash of hurt, and Rector blinked away unbidden tears. He turned away and stared at the passing crowd, his thoughts circling back again and again to Jaciro Temult's workroom and the terrible events there. Those last few seconds just before Rector had taken the Rahail's life had forever been branded into his memory, seared like a moth in candle wax. His knife had slid in smoothly, taking the Rahail in the heart. It had been a clean death, more than the man had deserved. Perhaps it had even been an easy one for him.

But not for Rector.

There were nights when Rector awoke drenched in a cold sweat, his heart thudding and tears springing from his eyes. But it wasn't nightmares that interrupted his sleep. It was something far worse, something real and horrible that he'd witnessed; something he'd authored. It was something he could never forget. He could still see the light fade from the Rahail's eyes like the sun setting on his life. That haunting image and the knowledge that he was responsible for another person's death lingered with him like a curse.

An easy death? If only it were true.

Mira noticed his silence. "What is it?"

Rector turned back to her. "Ask Dar'El if he's ever spilled someone's blood. Ask him if he's ever seen their hope die, their life flee. Ask him then if there is ever such a thing as an easy death."

Mira studied him in silence. "I'm sorry," she finally said.

Rector rubbed at his temples, hoping to soothe his incipient headache even as he sought to set aside thoughts of the Rahail's death. "If given the same choice, I'd do it again," he said.

"I know you would," Mira said. "But I also know how hard it must have been for you." Surprisingly, her voice held a tone of sympathy.

Rector appreciated her sentiment. Her compassion was as touching as it was unexpected. "It wasn't—" he grimaced "—easy."

Mira looked him in the eyes, concern on her face. "Will you be all right?"

"I don't know. But there's nothing to be done about it now." Rector forced a smile. "I guess I'll just have to get past it."

Mira reached across the table and surprised him once again by giving his hand a reassuring squeeze. "At least we know who ordered the attack on Bree and Jaresh. It was this Rahail woman, someone important in the Sil Lor Kum, a MalDin as they call it. She's probably the same one who met with the Kumma on the night Drin Port was murdered."

"We need to find her," Rector said. "When we do, I think we'll also find the Kumma."

"Dar'El believes he might even be the Withering Knife murderer."

"So do I," Rector said. "There's more I learned," he added. "I was able to locate some older records from the warehouse. There were a few journals left in some old, discarded boxes. They indicate more missing poppy seeds and henna and also misplaced shipments of juniper and sourwain."

"Then it was snowblood," Mira breathed. "I never expected...." She trailed off, lost in thought.

Rector scowled. "Meaning you were only guessing before and were prepared to ruin House Wrestiva based on rumors, lies, and innuendo."

"Not *House* Wrestiva," Mira corrected. "Only *Hal'El* Wrestiva. And it turns out our guesses weren't just rumors, lies, or innuendo."

Rector cursed softly. "Sometimes I think it would have been better if I had remained blindly ignorant."

"Blindly ignorant is why you're in this situation," Mira reminded him. "You're a better man for opening your eyes."

"Maybe," Rector said, mulling over Mira's words. Some of what she said was true. He'd learned wisdom, but the cost had been so high; the loss of innocence and exposure to ugly truths he'd never guessed might be real.

"Was there anything else?" Mira asked, breaking into his thoughts.

Rector shook his head. "I just found the boxes a few days ago. Other than what I said, they seem pretty innocuous." He chuckled. "Although the author has poor penmanship."

"What do you mean?"

"Every so often, certain letters are capitalized for no reason."

His words had Mira sitting up straight. "Have you transcribed them?" she asked.

Rector frowned, puzzled by her interest. "What are you thinking?"

"It could be a cipher," she said, going on to remind him of the one Jaresh had solved and by doing so, had confirmed the existence of the Withering Knife.

"It was clever how he figured it out," Rector said. He shifted in his seat, as a troubling thought came to him. "If there is a code, then the Withering Knife murderer *has* to be of House Wrestiva. It might even be Hal'El himself."

Mira chuckled. "That would be too much to hope for," she said.

They fell silent and Rector studied her over the lip of his glass of water, wavering over whether to ask her a question that had long since troubled him.

"What is it?" Mira asked. She smiled at his surprise. "You want to ask me something. It's written on your face."

"Do you think there is any honor left to our Caste?" Rector asked, unsure why her opinion mattered to him. "Or are we just a selfish and greedy shambles of what we were meant to be?"

"We have honor aplenty," Mira said. "Too much in some

instances." She stared him in the eyes, letting him know without words exactly to whom she was referring.

Rector flushed. "How were you able to tolerate me?" he asked. "I was so self-righteous."

Mira laughed. "Well you were most definitely self-righteous," she replied, "but who says I tolerated you?"

Rector rolled his eyes before breaking into a grin. Six months ago, he would have scowled.

"She's doing fine, by the way," Mira said. "Bree," she explained when he didn't respond. "Since you didn't ask, I thought I'd tell you. She should be fully recovered in the next few weeks. I thought you'd like to know."

"So I heard," Rector said, confused. "Was there some other reason you brought this up?"

"You were her friend once," Mira said with a shrug. "That's the only reason I meant."

"Friends." Rector gave a bitter chuckle. "Yes, I suppose so, but I'm sure it's a friendship she regrets and one long since turned to dust. I made sure of that when I offered up her brother to the Wrestivas."

"But knowing what you do now, given the same choice, I'm sure you would have decided otherwise."

Rector nodded. "I would have."

Mira smiled. "Just making sure you haven't changed your mind again."

"I haven't," Rector said. "A few months ago, I told you I would have remained quiet, but back then, I would have done so because it would have been easier on me. Now—" he shrugged. "—I would have remained silent because it would have been the right thing to do. The moral thing. Rukh was…*is* a hero. He should have never been found Unworthy."

"And his relationship with Jessira?"

365

"I don't know," Rector replied, picking at the corner of the table. "Maybe that's a bridge too far for me to cross. I know it's Rukh's business, but somehow, it still affects all of us." He grinned suddenly. "But I don't envy him trying to make peace with a woman like Jessira. Do you remember what she said to us? The quote from *The Book of All Souls: Across the world, the Lord stretched forth His hand and caused Life. And those whom he gave understanding, He named as brothers and sisters.*" He allowed admiration to tinge his voice. "In the heart of our home, the heart of her enemy and she claimed sisterhood. She was utterly fearless."

Rector laughed at Mira's open-mouthed shock at his words.

In a nondescript room in a nondescript building, somewhere to the south of Semaphore Walk, the Council of Rule held a meeting. There were no windows there, and a dim light emanated from several turned-down firefly lamps. It was always thus with the Sil Lor Kum. They were creatures of shadows and deceit.

Or so Ular Sathin believed. The knowledge brought him neither comfort nor guilt. It was simply an unimportant truth, an inconsequential fact to be accepted and forgotten.

He looked at the others seated around the table.

As always, his fellow MalDin wore stylized masks, a means to maintain their anonymity. Despite the precautions, Ular knew the names of nearly everyone here.

Only the SuDin remained unidentified. Ular hated his lack of insight into the Kumma. He had always been an enigma, and in all the years Ular had known him, he had yet to divine the SuDin's true name. It was maddening. In all spheres of life, knowledge was power—even more so amongst the Sil Lor Kum—and to have such a vital piece of information elude his grip for so many years caused Ular no end of grief.

As for the others, at least their names were not a mystery.

There sat the slimy cretin, Moke Urn, the MalDin for Caste Sentya. His skill with numbers and profit made him useful, but his lust for the decadent Mesa Reed made him pathetic. Mesa, the MalDin of Caste Cherid, was a vicious woman, her cruelty masked by her lush beauty and abundant womanly features. Only a fool would bed such a serpent, and such a fool was Yuthero Gaste, the Shiyen MalDin. He was a man rightly lauded for his brilliance—his professorship at Alminius College of Medicine spoke for itself. Nevertheless, Yuthero was a young man with a young man's lusts. Mesa had him by the tenders.

Then there was Varesea Apter, the lovely Rahail MalDin. Ular tapped his chin as he considered her. What had happened to Varesea? She was no longer the quietly competent woman she had once been. She was reticent now, barely speaking a single sentence in the Council meetings. And her eyes—there was a haunted quality to them. Some might assume it was because of her husband's death, but Ular knew better. The man had been a wife-beater. Varesea had little reason to mourn his passing. Why then did Varesea appear so troubled?

Ular didn't know—at least not yet. But he aimed to find out.

The final MalDin, Pera Obbe of Caste Duriah, was a woman Ular wished he could leave unconsidered. She was as unpleasant in demeanor as she was unlovely in appearance, a near incompetent collection of pride and vitriol. And her significance as a MalDin barely merited mention. In fact, her ascension to the Council spoke volumes about the worthlessness of others from her Caste who were also members of the Sil Lor Kum.

Ular Sathin drew back from his speculation and listened more closely as the SuDin began speaking.

"There is a method by which Shiyens can cause an individual to appear dead, but in reality they are merely in a deep slumber."

Ular had never heard of such a drug or method, but it didn't mean such a procedure didn't exist. He noticed Yuthero nodding as the SuDin spoke. Mesa as well. Their expressions of agreement had Ular wondering. Was the drug real, or were the other two somehow involved in a secret plan concocted by the SuDin?

He didn't know, but in his decades as a MalDin, he'd learned to trust his instincts. And he didn't trust the SuDin. Therefore, he couldn't trust Yuthero or Mesa either.

The SuDin continued. "There are Trials scheduled to leave in the coming months. There will be others of our kind, fellow Sil Lor Kum, who will help spirit us away from Ashoka."

"And I suppose you will be the first to leave," Pera said in a sarcastic tone.

The SuDin smiled. "No. It will actually be you," he replied, surprising Pera into silence. "Every arrangement has been made. By next summer, you will be safely ensconced in your new home in Kush."

"Hmm," Pera mused, her eyes hooded in thought. They brightened a moment later. "I like it. Kush. A warm city with a view of the water. Well done." She offered the praise as if she were commending a particularly clever dog.

The SuDin blinked, his only reaction to the insult. He continued on. "Your skills will be sorely missed by the Council," he said, "but another will be raised to take your place and—"

Pera snorted. "There are only four Duriahs in all the Sil Lor Kum," she said. "One of them is competent in his current role, but none of them have the requisite skills to do the job as I have." She grinned evilly. "Good luck replacing me."

Ular mentally groaned. The woman just needed to shut her mouth. What an idiot. She had just let everyone know the strength of her Caste. It was as weak as Pera's intelligence. As for the SuDin's vow to see her settled in another city—if Pera truly believed him, she was an even bigger fool than Ular had taken her for. This *procedure* meant to replicate death would more likely result in Pera's actual demise.

The others watched, rapt as starving dogs offered a steak while the Su Din continued his explanation of what he intended. Ular discounted it all.

What lies.

Hours later, Hal'El finally had an opportunity to break away from House Wrestiva business and see Varesea. It had been weeks since the two of them had found time to be alone, and as such, he had a far different reunion in mind than the one in which they were currently engaged.

Varesea was waiting for him in their Stone Cavern room, *The Tryst Palace*. Her unhappy countenance as she tapped her fingernails on the pine table spoke to a deep-seated annoyance. Hal'El hoped her disquiet wasn't because of her dead husband. She still had episodes when Slathtril's voice would rise in her mind, haranguing her, raging with fury, and promising bitter punishment. Over time, Varesea had learned to shut out her husband's lunatic ravings. She no longer tore at her hair or screamed silently, but by the time her husband's voice finally subsided into silence, she was often left limp and drained.

But right now, she appeared anything but exhausted. She looked angry.

"What is it?" Hal'El asked, taking a seat across from her.

"You're sending Pera to her death," Varesea charged.

Hal'El scowled. Why did she care so much if he sent that pompous, potato-faced Duriah to her well-deserved ending? "No I'm not," he lied.

Varesea took a moment to study his face before she snorted in derision. "You're lying," she accused. "Perhaps by omission, but it's still a lie. If you aren't sending her *to* her death; nevertheless, you will see her dead."

Hal'El sighed. He could never fool Varesea. She was too perceptive. "It is necessary," he said.

"Why?" Varesea challenged.

"Why do you care?"

"Because the others aren't stupid. They'll know death awaits them. Even if Mesa and Yuthero have agreed to lie on your behalf, they'll eventually learn the truth and pull you down."

Hal'El sat back in his chair and worked through his response. He was unprepared for this conversation. The questions were ones to which he didn't have a complete answer. "There truly is a drug and procedure that can do as I promised."

"And Mesa and Yuthero think you'll keep your promise to them?" Varesea scoffed.

Hal'El stiffened in irritation. Varesea's demeanor toward him was no longer gentle and loving. She had changed. Too often, she was curt and disrespectful. Hal'El didn't appreciate it. He had even spoken to her about it on several occasions, and while Varesea would tearfully promise to curb her tongue, thus far, she had not done so. Hal'El suspected she might not be able to, something to do with her dead husband. Varesea had never been the same after Slathtril's murder. He realized she likely never would be…but Hal'El loved her just the same.

"Mesa and Yuthero are too clever to eliminate in such an obvious fashion, but I still plan on ridding myself of that pest, Pera Obbe," Hal'El said.

"Why do you need to get rid of her?" Varesea asked, this time her tone more courteous.

"The Queen wants the Sil Lor Kum pacified," Hal'El explained. "I must do as She demands given how I've defied Her on other matters."

Varesea startled. She leaned forward wearing a look of worried interest. "What aren't you telling me," she said. "In what way have you defied the Queen?"

"I haven't murdered anyone else," he said. "Van Jinnu was the last person either of us killed."

"What about Dr. Verle," Varesea reminded him. "We both know he didn't hang himself."

Hal'El grimaced. "Don't remind me," he said. "If I'd been minutes slower, Bree Shektan might have caught me at the doctor's residence."

It was Varesea's turn to grimace. "Bree Shektan," she spat. "She and that naaja brother of hers need to be ended."

Hal'El smiled at her vindictive tone. Varesea could be generous and patient but not with those whom she deemed an enemy. "All in good time," Hal'El promised.

"You still haven't explained what you mean by 'defying the Queen'," Varesea reminded him.

Hal'El had hoped she'd forgotten, but it was too much to expect. "The Withering Knife," he said. "The Queen demands more deaths."

Varesea's brows knitted in thought. "There has to be a reason why the Queen wants this," she said. "Her claptrap about weakening the Oasis has never made sense."

"I think you're right," Hal'El said. "The Queen said something once—it was in the midst of Her mad ranting, and I was meant to know it—but according to Her own words, the deaths committed with the Knife prime it."

"Prime it?" Varesea's brows remained knitted. "What does *that* mean?"

"I don't know," Hal'El replied, "but I won't do what She wants."

Varesea hissed. "She'll punish you if you don't."

"Let her," Hal'El said, his words sounding bolder than he felt. "I am punished enough as it is. What's one more raving voice in my head?"

"You still hear them?" Varesea asked in a soft, worried tone. She pulled his hands into her own, searching intently into his eyes.

"I hear them," Hal'El answered, not wanting to admit the truth. The murmurings of those he had murdered, Aqua Oilhue, Van Jinnu, and Felt Barnel, continued. At first, he had been able to pretend they were merely his imaginations; but the voices persisted, growing steadily louder and more distinct. At times, he could even hear words amongst the rumbling susurrations. What they vowed was a painful death for Hal'El.

The Withering Knife stole Jivatma, and those so killed never truly died but lingered on in the minds of their murderers. Of this, Hal'El was now certain, just as he was certain that Varesea's ordeals with Slathtril were real. *Slathtril* was real. He lived on, hidden in some dark, deep recess of Varesea's mind; just like Aqua, Van, and Felt hid within Hal'El's. The notion left him cold with terror.

"You think they're real, too, don't you?" Varesea whispered. "The voices."

Hal'El tried to shrug off her worry. "Who can say?" he answered, hoping she didn't hear the lie. "Perhaps we could learn the truth if we had more time to understand the Knife."

"Time is not on our side," Varesea said.

"No it isn't," Hal'El agreed. "The Queen vows to come for Ashoka as soon as She completes the destruction of some place named Craven." He snorted. "She claims it's Ashoka's sister city."

"There is no such place," Varesea said. "She truly is mad."

"Yes, She is," Hal'El said. Unvoiced was the thought: *and all-too soon, we shall be as well.*

———— • ————

A fter an early lunch, Jaresh sat at a table in the sunroom, poring over some financial documents Amma wanted him to audit. She could have had the matter looked into by Magistrate Belt's forensic financial service, but instead she had asked Jaresh to do the work. He couldn't help but feel a swell of pride at her trust. Amma didn't offer false praise.

Jaresh's lips pursed in concentration as he tried to make sense of the sloppy record-keeping and read the crabbed handwriting. He traced numbers across columns and rows, trying to understand what was being recorded. Whoever had kept the records needed a remedial course in handwriting and basic bookkeeping. What a mess. Mistakes were piled upon more mistakes, growing more obvious with every page. Profits were shown where there should have been a loss and vice versa. Finally, there came a quarterly report where the author of the accounts claimed that one of House Shektan's holdings included a negative amount of wheat.

Jaresh groaned at the incompetence. He was wrong about the record-keeper. A remedial course in handwriting or bookkeeping wouldn't have done him any good. The man should simply have been fired. He thumbed through the rest of the thick ledger. It would take him hours to audit it.

And there were three more volumes to go after this one.

With a disappointed shake of his head, he returned to the work. It was going to be a long day.

"What a beautiful day," Bree said, walking into the room. She stood by the windows, basking in the happy sunshine pouring in.

Jaresh looked her way. It was good to see her up and about. For most of the three weeks since the attack in the alley, Bree had been convalescing at home. In fact, she'd only started using stairs a week ago. Until then, she had essentially been a prisoner in her bedroom.

"What are you doing?" Bree asked, walking over to the table and peering over his shoulder.

Jaresh explained his work to her.

"Do you want any help?" she asked.

Jaresh glanced at her in surprise. Bree generally detested anything to do with record-keeping.

She laughed at his reaction. "We both know I hate accounting," she said, unconsciously echoing his thoughts, "but there's only so much sitting around a person can do. I need to be useful." She looked to Jaresh with a hopeful expression.

Silently, he passed her one of the ledgers. She winced as she pulled it toward her.

"Still hurts?" Jaresh asked.

She nodded. "A little less every day," she replied. "I'll be happy when I can take a deep breath without hurting."

They fell into silence, concentrating on the work at hand. Bree's mien grew increasingly irritated. "Who kept these records?" she complained. "Did he understand even the basics of arithmetic?"

"I'm doubting he knew the basics of anything," Jaresh said. "Half the time, it looks like he just puts numbers in columns and rows without any regard for what they're supposed to mean."

Bree grumbled something under breath. Minutes later, she pushed the ledger away. "I take it back," she said with a frustrated huff. "I think I'd rather be bored than try to decipher this illegible scribbling."

"If Amma hadn't specifically asked me to look into this, I'd be right there with you."

"We should be trying to find the people who attacked us," Bree said, staring moodily out the window. "I'd ·like to have a long discussion with them. One with me slicing off parts of their anatomy."

Jaresh understood her desire for vengeance, but it was too late for her to exact it. "Rector already took care of the attacker who got away," he reminded her.

"And let him off too easily," Bree muttered. "They almost killed us. I'd like to have had a chance to kill them back."

"It's better that you didn't," Jaresh said. "If you had just killed them out of hand, we would have never discovered that the person who ordered the attack was probably the same Rahail woman from the Blue Heron," Jaresh said. "Rector's way was better." With a start, he realized, he was defending Rector Bryce. It was an improbable occurrence.

"He never learned this Rahail woman's name, though," Bree replied.

"He can't hand everything to us on a plate of gold," Jaresh answered. He hid a wince. There he went again: defending Rector.

"I suppose not," Bree said with a defeated exhalation. "Our list of suspects for the murderer still stands at twenty-three, doesn't it?"

"Yes," Jaresh admitted.

"There's no other way to bring the number down?"

"If there is, I haven't been able to figure it out."

"Too bad," Bree said. She returned to staring moodily out the windows. "At least Rector learned about the snowblood. It's all the opening Nanna needs to trounce House Wrestiva in the Chamber and bring Rukh home," Bree added.

Something she said sparked an idea. Jaresh quickly followed the line of his thought. "What if we assume the murderer comes from House Wrestiva?" he asked. "We could bring the list of suspects into the single digits if we did."

"A pretty large assumption, though, don't you think?" Bree said with an arch of her eyebrows.

"It's not as large as you might think," Jaresh said. "Who else would produce snowblood other than the Sil Lor Kum?"

Bree's expression cleared. "No one," she said. "And since Rector found the 'lost' ingredients for it within House Wrestiva's records, it stands to reason that someone from that House has to be a member of the Sil Lor Kum." She grinned, the first time Jaresh could recall her smiling since the attack. "Not bad."

Jaresh arched his eyebrows. "Your euphemism for sheer genius could use some work, but I appreciate the sentiment."

Bree laughed. "Try this for 'sheer genius'," she said. "There's also another murder we can follow." He looked at her quizzically. "The murder of Dr. Grasome Verle," she explained.

Jaresh wanted to smack himself in the head. Of course!

Bree wore a predatory expression. "We'll have whoever this Tainted bastard is soon enough," she vowed.

Later, as they spoke of how to proceed with their plans, Nanna intruded on their meeting. His demeanor was as excited as Jaresh could ever recall seeing on him. "We're gathering in the study," Nanna said, breaking into a wide grin. "Farn Arnicep has returned to Ashoka."

CHAPTER TWENTY-FOUR
PRELUDE TO A TRIBUNAL

Have respect for the authority of others or be prepared to challenge their power.
~The Warrior and the Servant (author unknown)

Farn slouched in one of the chairs facing the hearth in Dar'El's study and enjoyed the heat of the crackling fire. The room was comfortable, and he exhaled heavily as he relaxed. The tension left him, and his eyes grew heavy, slowly shuttering as he rested, dozing while he waited for the House Council. The call for their presence had already been sent to them, but it would still take some time for all of them to gather. In the meanwhile, Farn enjoyed the sensation of being warm, something he had sorely missed for the past two months.

It had been a long journey from Stronghold and tired didn't begin to describe how Farn felt. Wrung out and spent with nothing left to give was a better approximation. The last leg of the trip had been especially taxing, with supplies running low and the cold an unrelenting misery. He was lucky to have survived the passage. In fact, he wouldn't have if not for the provisions provided by Cedar's family and Farn's new Talent for Blending. He was grateful for the former, and he had come to accept the latter as simply being a part of who he was now.

He hoped his family would feel the same way. He had yet to see them. Upon entering Ashoka proper, Farn had decided to make his way straight to the House Seat. Duty had weighed heavily on his mind. After all, his family would learn soon enough that he was home, while Rukh's parents would always be desperate for news of their son. Farn judged that a quick debriefing with the House Council was of more pressing import. Afterward, he could see to his own needs.

Farn cracked open his eyes and looked around the empty room. He was surprised his parents hadn't been waiting for him at the House Seat, but somehow he must have outrun the rumors of his return. Farn had arrived unannounced and unexpected. He smiled. They'd probably be here in the next few minutes, Amma, Nanna, and his brothers and sisters. He couldn't wait to see them.

Just then, the door to the study opened, and Farn rose to his feet. Dar'El entered the room, trailed by Satha, Jaresh, and Bree, all of them wearing broad smiles.

"Welcome home," Satha said, pulling Farn into a warm embrace.

"Farn—" was all Jaresh got out before the two of them were hugging.

It was good to see his cousin again. Despite being a Sentya, Farn had always thought of Jaresh as a brother. His Caste had never been an issue between them. Or if it had, Keemo and Rukh must have convinced him that it shouldn't be. And they had been right. It didn't matter. In fact, the most important moments in Farn's life had always been shared with the other three. Jaresh, Keemo, Rukh, and Farn— the four of them had been inseparable. Farn's throat caught. Only he and Jaresh were left of their quartet. Keemo was dead and Rukh was exiled, but Farn would never forgot his friends, his brothers, who were gone; Rukh with his moral compass and forgiving soul, and

Keemo's generous spirit and laughing heart. Farn swallowed heavily, holding back the threatening sobs. Now wasn't the time to break down and blubber like a child.

He wiped away his wet cheeks and moved on to greet Bree. She was as beautiful as he remembered. She had always been reserved in his presence or regal in her cool disregard, but today, even she was teary eyed.

"The rest of the Council should be here eventually," Dar'El said, "but I thought we could get started without them. We can have a more thorough debriefing tomorrow after you've had a chance to see your family and get some rest."

Farn nodded, grateful he wouldn't have to wait for the rest of the Council to arrive.

"Cook Heltin has also been informed," Dar'El continued. "She should have some refreshments prepared in a few minutes." He guided Farn back to his seat before the fireplace. "In the meantime, rest."

"I've sent word to your family," Satha said. "I imagine they'll be here shortly."

"We should get started then," Farn said. "Let me tell you about Rukh."

"How is he doing? Truly?" Dar'El asked, a look of intensity and longing on his face.

Farn considered how to answer. What should he say? Should he explain about Stronghold and how it wasn't an easy place for a Pureblood? Or tell them how Rukh had decided to leave the OutCaste city, determined to recover some mythical book from Hammer? His cousin had chosen a risky path, and it might very well lead to his doom. Farn didn't want to tell Rukh's family all of that. It would be too painful for them to hear.

But then again, how could he lie? Didn't Dar'El, Satha, and the rest of Rukh's family deserve the truth?

"Tell us what happened to our son," Satha said into the intervening silence, a look of pained loss on her face. "Is he—".

"No," Farn interrupted, aghast. "He's alive. He's fine. It's just...." He paused again, thinking again how he should explain Rukh's situation. He decided to just tell them the truth. When he was done, the room was silent.

"Is Stronghold really so terrible?" Jaresh asked, appearing forlorn.

Farn shrugged. "It's not an easy question to answer," he said. "You have to remember: Stronghold was created by the fifty-five survivors of Hammer's Fall. They fled into the Wildness, deep into the Privations where they should have perished. Instead, they somehow eluded death and founded a home for themselves, one that eventually grew to a city of over forty thousand. There is a greatness to what the OutCastes have achieved. It should be honored, even though the means—the mingling of the Castes—might be considered sinful."

"You admire them," Dar'El said sounding surprised.

"I do, but they admire themselves even more," Farn said with a grimace. "The OutCastes are *very* prideful of what they've accomplished and dismissive of everyone else's achievements. They consider themselves a more civilized, ethical people, while the rest of us—Purebloods is the insult they have for us—are culturally degenerate and possibly inferior by birth as well. They aren't shy about saying so, and it's this hypocrisy that makes them so insufferable even as I admire their accomplishments." He shook his head in bemused disgust. "It's strange how their attitude toward us is an exact mirror image of our own toward them."

"*Pride in one's raiment begets an impoverished soul,*" Dar'El said, quoting a line from *The Word and Deed.*

"They don't find that book to be of much use," Farn said. "*The Word and the Deed* I mean. For them, it's essentially meaningless. Their moral compass is derived from an older text."

"*The Book of All Souls*," Bree said.

Farn turned to her in confusion. "How did you know?"

"Jessira," she said. "She lived with us for a number of months. We talked."

"And you're certain she's going to marry this Disbar Merdant? Even though she doesn't love him?" Satha asked.

"As far as I can tell, yes," Farn said. "She's a woman of her word."

"Good," Dar'El said, appearing pleased. "Then there will be one less tie binding Rukh to Stronghold."

"Why is it good?" Jaresh asked with a scowl. "You know what Rukh gave up for Jessira. What he feels for her. How will he ever be happy if he continually sees the woman he loves married to someone else?"

Bree rolled her eyes. "Sometimes I wonder about you," she said. "Remember what Nanna intends."

Jaresh gaped at her wearing a look of mortification. "Never mind what I just said," he muttered. "I'm an idiot."

Farn perked up. There were undercurrents to the conversation he didn't fully fathom, but the implications seemed obvious. Dar'El had a plan to bring Rukh home. "Do you have the votes in the Chamber?" Farn asked, hazarding a guess.

Dar'El turned to him. "How did you know?"

"Law and precedent was always a hobby for him," Jaresh explained, still sounding disgusted with himself.

"I told Rukh what I thought you might try," Farn said. "He wasn't hopeful."

Dar'El smiled. "He should have been. Hopeful, I mean. The Chamber is in flux right now, but the trends are moving in our direction."

"I wish I could reach across time and space and shake some

sense into that boy of ours," Satha said. "He is such a—" She paused, her head tilted. A commotion arose from outside the study, growing steadily louder and closer. Satha smiled. "I think your family is here."

Dar'El stood. "The Council will convene at mid-morning. We'll debrief you then," he said. "In the meantime, enjoy your family."

Farn nodded just as the door to the study was thrown open and his family embraced him with glad shouts of welcome.

———————•●•———————

D ar'El listened closely as Farn once again explained his impressions of Stronghold and her people.

"Rukh said I shouldn't let anyone know I can Blend," Farn began. "Is that still the case?"

"Yes," Sophy answered. "Only the people in this room know what you can do."

"And Rector Bryce?" Dar'El added.

"He won't speak up," Mira vowed.

"You're sure of this?" Sophy asked. "He wasn't loyal to this House in the past."

"I'm certain he'll keep quiet," Mira replied.

"You had better be."

"I can only tell you what I think is the likeliest scenario," Mira said, sounding annoyed. "I don't think I'm misinterpreting him, but if you still have doubts, then you should interview him yourself."

Dar'El sat back, hiding his shock. For the past month, Mira had started standing up for herself, especially in front of her amma. It was good to see. Thus far, Sophy didn't seem to know how to respond, but she'd have to learn. If she persisted in disrespecting Mira, it would eventually lead to a poisoning of their relationship.

"I wish Rukh had taken his own advice," Farn said.

"So do we all," Satha replied.

"Where does the Chamber stand?" Dar'El asked, changing the subject and looking to Durmer for an answer. Habit made him look for Garnet as well, but his old friend wasn't present. He had resigned from the House Council several weeks ago. Garnet had said it was so he could spend more time with his grandchildren, but Dar'El suspected he'd stepped down for some other reason. More likely, Garnet had been forced to confront the awful truth of what was happening to him, how his mind was slowly slipping away. Dar'El couldn't begin to imagine how terrifying such a realization must have been. The situation left Dar'El saddened and depressed.

"We have commitments from a majority of the Houses to vote in our favor," Durmer said, "but we need more. We need sixty percent to overturn Rukh's original verdict."

Jaresh rapped his knuckles on the table. "What if we let the Chamber know that Jessira is engaged to someone else? What if the other 'Els learn that she and Rukh were never a couple?"

Satha nodded. "It's a good idea. Their relationship was a large part of the original reasoning behind Rukh's banishment."

"Should we let the Chamber know about House Wrestiva's likely involvement in the production of snowblood?" Bree asked.

Dar'El shook his head. "Much as I would enjoy doing so, we can't. There simply isn't enough proof. What we have is circumstantial. Plus, if we did, our enemies would know where our investigation stands. We can't do that since we still don't know who they are." He steepled his fingers. "No. When we go after them, we will go after *all* of them. We'll burn them out, root and branch." Dar'El looked to Farn. "None of this information is to leave this room."

Farn nodded. "As long as whatever we do brings Rukh home," he said. "No one has said it, but I feel like I abandoned him."

"No one has said it because it isn't true," Sophy said.

"And if the vote in the Chamber goes our way, you will have a grave decision to make," Satha said. "Only you know Stronghold's location. Will you help lead a Trial to open trade with the OutCastes and bring Rukh home?"

Farn didn't even need to think about the question. "Absolutely."

———●●———

The permanent signs of spring's thaw were evident as winter's grip—never firm to begin with—started to relax. There might be a few remaining weeks of cool weather, but in general, Ashoka's warm days were coming and would soon prevail. Nature knew. Pale, green shoots thrust up through the ground and ready to blossom as the buds on studded tree limbs made ready to unfurl their nascent leaves. And rising through the air were the trilling songs of returned blue jays and robins. Even the sun seemed brighter. As a result, House Shektan's Seat hummed with activity as landscapers and gardeners prepared the grounds.

Bree looked at the activity from the sunroom. The windows were open, and sunshine flooded inside as a warm, steady breeze stirred the tied off curtains and her hair. She breathed in the rich scent of turned earth, loving the heady aroma of loam. It smelled like the promise of new life to be born. Bree smiled. She had always loved the scent of turned earth. It must have been her mother's doing. Amma must have passed on her love of growing things to her daughter.

Bree took another deep breath, grateful as well that her injury no longer pained her. Unconsciously, she rubbed at the scar on her abdomen. It had been six weeks since the attack in the alley, and though the wound no longer caused her discomfort, the memories of that fateful day still lingered. She could have died. The thought filled her less with fear than fury. She was especially angry with her foolish shortsightedness. She should have never been caught in such a compromising situation. Only Jaresh's sword and skill had saved her, and she vowed that she would never again be caught so helpless.

Like all Kumma women, Bree had been taught to fight and educated in the use of her Talents, but she had never given the martial skills the proper attention and devotion they deserved. In her mind, the training had been a bothersome distraction. Why did she need to learn to grapple with someone or learn to use a sword? When would either skill ever prove useful? She had always figured they never would be, and no one had been able to convince her otherwise. Amma had certainly tried; warning Bree about her lax attitude. About how it was her duty to sharpen her fighting Talents as well as her mind, but Bree hadn't listened. She'd been stupid in her ignorant arrogance, and it had nearly cost her everything.

Never again.

Yesterday, Durmer had agreed to start her training over again. This time she would learn what she had once dismissively labeled as being 'a man's warrant'.

"He didn't," Jaresh said, interrupting her thoughts and sounding aghast.

Bree turned around. Her brother and Farn sat at the table. As usual, they were sharing a meal—did young men ever *stop* eating—and getting caught up with one another. It was how they had spent most of the two weeks since Farn's return.

And of course, the object of their conversation was likely to be Rukh. Jaresh was eager to learn every event in their brother's life since his departure from Ashoka. Of course, Bree, like the rest of the family, felt the same way. She was just as desperate to know even the smallest detail about Rukh's life, but even more, she prayed for her brother's safety and happiness. It made her feel like a sinful woman praying for absolution, which, in a way, was the truth. She certainly needed Rukh's forgiveness.

"He didn't what?" Bree asked, joining their conversation.

"Rukh once called Jessira *priya*," Farn explained.

Bree gasped. "To her face?"

Farn nodded.

Bree threw her head back and laughed. "Well, at least he won't let her go without a fight," she said. "And what did she say to him?"

"She called him *priya* first," Farn said, explaining the events leading up to Jessira's declaration. "I think she only said it because she thought he was dying. The pneumothorax and all."

"Does *priya* mean the same thing in Stronghold?" Bree asked.

Farn shrugged. "I'm not sure, but from what I could gather, it might be even more intimate than just 'beloved'. More like 'eternal beloved' or 'only beloved'."

"Why wouldn't 'beloved' be enough?" Jaresh asked, sounding genuinely confused. "There's no such thing as 'only beloved'. It's like saying a person can only ever love one person in their entire life."

Bree shook her head at her brother's lack of imagination and romance. "It's probably not supposed to be taken literally," she explained. "It's figurative; like a hope that the person you love will be someone for whom your life was crafted. In the dramas it's called a 'soulmate'."

Farn and Jaresh both rolled their eyes at her, which only exasperated Bree further. Just as she was about to let loose with a cutting remark, she noticed their twin grins of triumph at her annoyance. She swallowed her words.

They laughed anyway.

Jackholes.

Bree prayed for patience as they only brayed louder. "Anyway," she said, speaking in a loud, long-suffering voice, "it's easy to understand why Rukh would call Jessira '*priya*'. She's wonderful." Bree tilted her head in thought. "A bit scary, but she makes up for it by being beautiful."

Both men looked uncomfortable at her last statement.

"I wouldn't know about that," Jaresh said stiffly.

"She's attractive enough, but a bit too muscular for my taste," Farn added.

Now it was Bree who rolled her eyes. "You're only hedging your bets because she's an OutCaste, and you don't want to admit you find one of them attractive." She wagged a finger at them, knowing it would annoy them, but they deserved it after laughing at her. "But both of you know the same as I: Jessira is beautiful. Rukh was only following his heart."

"And what of morality?" Jaresh asked in a serious tone.

"What about it?" Bree asked. Given how Jaresh had once felt about Mira, his question was either hypocritical, or he had something else in mind.

"Morality is a large part of why Rukh was found Unworthy," Jaresh began. "No matter what *we* think of his feelings toward Jessira, others will feel differently. And the judgment of these others is critical. With tomorrow's meeting of the Chamber, they hold Rukh's future in their hands. Should they learn of his true feelings toward Jessira, their decision becomes easy. They'll never allow us to bring our brother home."

Bree wanted to scoff at Jaresh's worry. Who amongst the three of them would ever expose what Rukh had said to Jessira? However, she also remembered a saying her Nanna liked to quote: *The finest of intentions are ruined in a moment of thoughtlessness.*

"No one else will hear about it," Farn promised as Bree nodded agreement.

———•●•———

Dar'El tried to think past the sudden leaden lump hollowing out his chest. What he'd just been told was a disaster. The Society had gathered at his insistence, meeting in the Hall, and the heptagonal table was full. Everyone was here—Masters, Journeymen, and Apprentices—and everyone had presented their findings. Dar'El had needed a final reckoning of what the Rajans had accomplished. Tomorrow's meeting of the Chamber of the Lords was too important to allow for anything less than a full accounting.

And what his fellow Rajans had to tell him was terrible news indeed.

"We don't have the votes," Dar'El said, trying—and failing—to keep the bitterness from his voice.

Ular Sathin, Master for Caste Muran, cleared his throat. "The influence of those who aren't Kumma is limited in the Chamber of Lords," he explained. "You always knew this was the likely outcome." Polite sympathy suffused his voice.

"Knowing isn't the same as accepting the finality of never again seeing my son," Dar'El growled. He crumpled the pile of papers before him, his fury and despair unmaking his normal control.

"Is there nothing more to be done?" Gren Vos, Master for Caste Shiyen, asked into the silence caused by Dar'El's words. "We are the Society of Rajan. Surely we can do more than this pathetic effort." She glared around the room, looking for answers. She wasn't beaten yet, and Dar'El took heart from her strength.

"The Kummas who voted against Rukh's banishment at his original tribunal were few to begin with," explained Anian Elim, Journeyman Duriah. "We started from a position of weakness." He shrugged. "To have lifted the tally to what it is now is a bit of a miracle."

"I don't need miracles," Gren snapped. "I need effort and achievement. We can do this."

"No we can't," Ular refuted. "The vote is tomorrow. We've all called in every chit and favor owed to us. There's nothing left."

"Some of us have even resorted to not-so-subtle threats about the financial futures of certain Houses," said Chime Plast, Apprentice for Caste Sentya. "The threats have worked on some, but not on all. The more powerful Houses have simply disregarded our urgings. They believe they are too wealthy to fall prey to whatever pressure we might bring against them. They think our threats are toothless, and that if they wait long enough, it will be *we* who will beg for *their* business."

"They may not be wrong," mused Thivel Nonel, Master of Caste Sentya.

"They are wrong," Diffel Larekin, Journeyman for Caste Cherid, said in disagreement. "What happens tomorrow will not be forgotten, at least not by the Society."

"None of which helps Rukh Shektan," said Grain Jola, Master of Caste Rahail.

Dar'El had heard enough. He slapped the table. "The votes aren't there," he repeated. It was time he, along with everyone else, faced the truth. He would never again see his eldest son. His gambit hadn't paid off. Jessira had taken Rukh to Stronghold, but it had been Dar'El who had failed his son. He had been unable to muster the votes needed to bring his boy home.

Silma Thoran, Master for Caste Kumma, was seated next to Dar'El, and she reached across the intervening space between the two of them, gripping Dar'El's forearm. "All is not lost," she said. "The votes aren't in our favor, but they can be."

Dar'El stifled the sudden bloom of hope. He couldn't afford it. Besides, from everything he could reckon, Silma was wrong. There was no way to save Rukh.

"Hear me out," Silma said, likely reading Dar'El's pessimism. "You need a tally of sixty percent of the Chamber in order to rescind Rukh's banishment. Right now, you're at fifty-six." She held up an admonishing finger. "But what you don't know is how many of those who say they will go against you might change their minds if you were to make a direct appeal to them. Instead of using threats and bribes, appeal to their better natures. Many of them lost warriors in the caverns, and many have warriors who survived the expedition entirely due to your son's valiant efforts. In my view, that is your most powerful argument. Use it."

Dar'El closed his eyes and took a deep breath. He exhaled fully and sought to master his pessimism and loss. He needed to think clearly. "How do you propose I proceed?" he asked, still doubtful and unwilling to allow even a thread of optimism into his heart.

"You need to weave the thread of Rukh's accomplishments into a narrative. You need to explain how he came to possess his ill-gotten Talents. And you need to explain more fully his relationship with the ghrina woman. It was this impropriety more than anything else which led to the pronouncement against him."

"It was my fault," Dar'El whispered with a mouth full of guilt. He stared at his crumpled papers, unable to meet anyone's eyes. Outside of his immediate family, he had never told anyone the role he had played in Rukh's banishment. He did so now.

"This changes much," Silma mused after he finished. "I only wish you had discussed this plan with us before executing it."

Gren Vos looked mad enough to chew a plank of ironwood to splinters. "How could you? We might have been able to prevent the initial judgment had we known all the facts. What were you thinking?"

"I was thinking how to save my son," Dar'El said, reining in his rising temper.

"And your actions resulted in him being found Unworthy," Gren snapped back.

"And don't you think I know it?" Dar'El replied, fists clenched. He wanted to hit something, hurt something, especially himself.

Silma held up a hand, calling for silence. "Enough," she said. "The deed is done, and hindsight is always a clear summer day. It is the fog of the present which concerns us. But let us return to the past just this once. In my opinion, given the circumstances at the time and the sentiments against your House, Gren is wrong. Rukh's fate was sealed the moment Ashoka learned of his other Talents. And what you did with the ghrina, convincing her to take him to Stronghold, likely saved your son's life. It kept him alive long enough for us to have tomorrow's vote and hopefully bring him home."

Dar'El let out a breath, one he hadn't realized he'd been holding. Silma's pronouncement relieved much of the guilt he'd carried all these long months, ever since Rukh's exile. He'd told no one how much he blamed himself for his son's fate, not even Satha. "You were saying there's a chance for Rukh tomorrow," Dar'El said, steering the conversation back to what was most important. "What else do you suggest?"

"Tell the Chamber what you did to Rukh and why. Hold nothing back," Silma said. "The 'Els are all fathers first. They'll understand a nanna's fear. Even those who have an acrimonious relationship with your House will be sure to feel pity. Next, speak of Rukh's accomplishments. They are not inconsiderable. Everyone knows of them, but recite them one-by-one, so that all can truly understand what Rukh actually did, all of it. And finally, you must *not* be so controlled in how you talk. You need emotion. You need passion. You need to touch the hearts of your fellow ruling 'Els."

Dar'El nodded. It wouldn't be easy, but it could be done. He wouldn't fail his son again. "You really think it can work?" he asked.

Silma nodded confidently, no uncertainty marring her face. "Absolutely. But much of it depends on your words. And they must be your words. Only you can speak them and make others feel and think as you do."

Afterward, the meeting wound down. Everyone departed, and they offered Dar'El their best wishes. As usual, he was one of the last to leave. He shrugged on his jacket and tucked his hands into the pockets. There was a piece of paper inside one of them. He knew from whom it had likely come even before he pulled it out and read the letter.

Suwraith intends to come against Ashoka this year.

Dar'El glowered. He didn't have time for these games right now.

But when he *did* have time, he'd find out who this MalDin was and wring his fragging neck. One way or another, he'd have the truth.

CHAPTER TWENTY-FIVE
A FINAL OBSTACLE

*Were the battles in the Chamber fought with swords,
they would leave the floor dripping with blood.*

~ From the journal of Hal'El Wrestiva, AF 2059

Satha chewed her lip as Dar'El gathered the papers on his desk and slipped them into his leather satchel. He'd come home from the last night's gathering of the Society and explained what his fellow Rajans had managed in preparation for today's meeting of the Chamber of Lords. The news hadn't been good. Even added to what House Shektan had accomplished on its own, they simply didn't have the votes to bring Rukh home. Satha had almost despaired. They had been so close. If they could have only convinced a handful more Houses to change their votes, then Rukh's judgment would be have overturned.

But it wasn't to be, at least not according to their own polling.

Satha hadn't known whether to cry with fury or weep with sorrow over the news. She might have been able to accept Rukh's death in the Trials—it was a horrid truth every Kumma mother had to face—but this…it was so pointless. Her son was lost to her because of inter-House politics. And she couldn't help feeling that it had been her ambition that had caused it. While her personal aspirations had earned House Shektan great wealth and prestige, it had come at the cost of powerful enemies, and those enemies had stolen the life of her oldest son. It was a bitter pill to swallow.

Only after learning Silma Thoran's assessment of how the Chamber might still be swayed to House Shektan's favor had hope rekindled within Satha's breast. There was still a chance. Silma was a fine reader of inter-House politics, possibly even more so than Garnet. If she said the tally could still go House Shektan's way, than Satha had to believe her. What other choice did she have?

Which meant that only Dar'El's persuasiveness could bring Rukh home. Today's meeting of the Chamber would be decided on the eloquence of her husband's tongue. It wasn't a proposition that filled Satha with a great deal of confidence. Dar'El was brilliant, able to see past the fog of confusion, while others fumbled about in blindness. His was cool, quiet leadership; competent and steady. Unfortunately, those same admirable attributes weren't what was needed today. To sway the Chamber, Dar'El would have to allow his passion free rein. Even though the ruling 'Els were generally older, in their hearts they were still warriors, and their inner fires remained lit. To sway them to House Shektan's purpose, an inspirational call to battle would be needed. Satha wasn't sure it was something Dar'El could manage.

When Dar'El straightened and looked her way, Satha was tempted to question him, ask if he was prepared, but she held her tongue. It would be the least helpful thing she could do. Dar'El needed her unquestioned support. She didn't allow the slightest hint of worry or doubt to mar her features. She made sure to radiate support. Dar'El didn't need second-guessing right now. Today would be difficult enough as it was.

Satha walked across the study, her long gown wisping across the rug. She straightened the collar of Dar'El's shirt. "You'll do well," she said, looking up into his dark eyes. She'd almost said 'fine', but fine wouldn't do. Not today. He needed to hear her confidence as much as his own.

"I'll bring our son home," Dar'El promised. His voice was firm and his eyes clear. There was no hint of doubt in his voice or face.

Satha searched his features. Dar'El was never one to offer false promises. "I believe you," she said, feeling some of her quailing doubts recede like the tide.

Dar'El took her hands in both of his. "Have Cook Heltin prepare a feast. When this is over, we will celebrate." He kissed her fingertips, his face growing somber. "And for all the pain I've caused you, with what I've done to Rukh—I will make amends. I won't fail you."

Satha's eyes softened. He felt the same guilt she did. Somehow it made bearing her own a little easier. They had worked so hard, side-by-side, in building House Shektan; but none of their previous work had ever brought them as close together as they were now. The series of challenges they'd had to face this past year, beginning with Jaresh's killing of Suge Wrestiva, had rekindled their love. It was ironic. "You did what we both thought was best," Satha said. "I agreed with you, remember? So did Silma. If you don't trust my opinion, then trust that of your Kumma Master in the Society."

Dar'El smiled. "It helps to hear you say that, *priya*." He still held her hands, and his head dipped until his forehead was resting against her fingers.

Satha kissed the top of his head. "I love you. Now go and bring back our son."

———————●———————

Sunshine poured through the eastern-facing windows of the Assembly, the amphitheater where the 'Els met. It lit the room in a golden glow and rendered the numerous chandeliers hanging from the coffered muralled ceiling superfluous. As a result, they remained dull and unlit. The wide planks of dark wood, which made up the flooring, also glowed beneath the bright sunshine. They held an inner sheen while fragrant smoke filled the Assembly, rising from the incense candles spaced throughout the room.

The Assembly was large enough to hold over a thousand people, but today it held but a little more than fifty. This was to be a private gathering for the ruling 'Els of Caste Kumma. They were faced with a unique entreaty, one that required intense concentration and thought. As such, the 'Els did not desire the attendance of anyone else other than their own peers. The conference today would be difficult enough without a gathered audience loudly voicing their unneeded opinions or suggestions on the matter at hand. For good reason, those gathered in the Assembly wore serious demeanors. Some even appeared worried.

Despite the singular nature of the convocation, it would still be the Arbiter, Lin'El Kumma, who would lead today's session. The Arbiter entered the Assembly through a door next to the stage, looking vigorous despite his age. Lin'El's white hair and beard contrasted sharply with his Kumma-brown skin and the black robes meant to highlight his status as judge. It was a strictly ceremonial position—his vote was only offered in the event of a tie—but it was the Arbiter who interpreted the various rules and points of etiquette of the Chamber.

Lin'El ascended the dais and gaveled the meeting into session. It only took a few raps of the smooth oval of black onyx against the base of white marble for the room to fall into silence.

Dar'El stood to one side of the stage. He listened as Lin'El explained the nature of today's meeting. It was all pro forma. Everyone knew what was at stake; nonetheless, they listened with polite attention. Once Lin'El was finished, Dar'El took his place behind one of the two lecterns standing on either side of the

Arbiter's dais. As the Supplicant, he had to face the other 'Els and answer any challenges or questions they might have.

Dar'El looked out at the Chamber of Lords and was suddenly struck by the enormity of what he had to do. Many of these men had little love for him or his family. Their minds were already hard against anything that might benefit House Shektan. To persuade them to give him a fair hearing would be difficult. They wouldn't want to. Only something truly rousing and uplifting might change their minds.

Dar'El's heart thudded, all the way into his ears. He wasn't sure he could do it. He was a blunt, plainspoken man, not someone known for his inspirational speech. It was not his forte. Dar'El communicated his opinions with brevity and what some might say was brusqueness. It was who he was, and until now, it had been enough.

But today he had to do more. He would have to rouse passions.

Dar'El's palms grew moist with perspiration, as did his forehead. For a moment, nervousness fluttered through his stomach and chest, nearly stealing his breath. With an almost visible shudder, he pulled his mind back to the task at hand. Inspiring he might not be, but he'd never quit a duty, and he didn't aim to start now. Dar'El *had* to do this. He wasn't here to salvage his own future or that of his House. He was here for Rukh. His son's future relied on Dar'El's ability to inspire.

He would *not* fail.

Dar'El cleared his throat. He spoke in a clear voice, one filled with righteous indignation. "Last summer, while serving in the expeditionary force meant to eradicate the breeding caverns of the Chimeras, my son was judged by this body as being Unworthy. He was never able to speak on his behalf or defend his name and honor. At the time, neither could I." He paused then, as though considering what to say next, although he and Satha had already worked on this speech for weeks. "But now I can, and we meet here today so that we can overturn a terrible injustice. What we decided about my son, Rukh Shektan, those many months ago cannot stand," he continued. "When we learned what Rukh could do, his Talents outside Caste Kumma, we acted in haste and fear. As a result, we banished a young warrior who was amongst the best of us all. Today, we can rectify that mistake. There is information the Chamber must here. I urge you to listen to my testimony with an unbiased ear and an open heart. Only in such a manner can we hope to judge wisely." He looked to Lin'El. "Perhaps in lieu of my ongoing recitation of this new information, we can have someone review the rationale for why my son was found Unworthy. I can then answer each charge."

Lin'El nodded agreement. "Is there anyone who wishes to serve as the Indicter?" he asked.

Several hands shot up, although most of them were hostile to Dar'El's needs. Thankfully, as the Supplicant, he had discretion in who could act as the initial Indicter. He chose Tol'El Suzay, leader of a close House Shektan ally. In fact, Mira had even chosen to apprentice with him for several years, finishing her mentorship just last spring.

"The Supplicant has chosen Tol'El Suzay as the Indicter," Lin'El pronounced. "All in agreement with this choice, signal your assent." Most of the 'Els raised their hands. Lin'El made a show of counting, although it was obvious that those in favor of the motion had the majority. "All opposed?" Fewer hands went up. "By acclamation, Tol'El Suzay will serve as Indicter."

Tol'El approached the lectern, taking his place on the side opposite to where Dar'El stood. Though in his early sixties, Tol'El yet moved with a warrior's fluid grace. His aquiline features were hidden beneath a short beard, and his hooded eyes moved warily as he gazed about the Chamber of Lords. "Your son has Talents not of our Caste," he said to Dar'El, speaking words the two of them had rehearsed over the past few days. "We have heard how this came to be, but it seems a convenient story, one meant to absolve Rukh Shektan of blame. How do we know he did not purposefully seek out these Talents for himself? How do we know he didn't somehow learn these abilities on his own?"

"Think about what a question like that implies," Dar'El said. "If my son learned these Talents by his own device, then all of us should be able to do the same. Such a possibility doesn't bear consideration." He leaned forward, brows furrowed, and hands pressed against the lectern. Dar'El looked at the assembled 'Els, meeting the gaze of those who were against him, staring intently into their eyes. "If all of us can learn the Talents of another Caste, then everyone can. A Duriah could Heal; a Shiyen could Shield, and a Sentya could Cohese. Everything we think we know about our world will have been proven false. It would mean the very Castes themselves are nothing more than an artificial construct with absolutely no basis in morality or holiness. The veracity of *The Book of First Movement* itself would be brought into question. Who here is ready to make such a claim?"

Troubled murmurs met his charge. It seemed most had not thought through the consequences of what it might mean if Rukh's new Talents were self-taught.

Tol'El cleared his throat, regathering the attention of the Chamber. "The implications Dar'El suggests cannot be countenanced. I, for one, will not believe the very basis for our society is built on a monstrous lie. I will not accept that generations of our ancestors lived and died for no reason. It is heresy! I believe any who judged Rukh Unworthy for such a reason should reconsider their decision. I know not all here count Dar'El Shektan an ally, but I say politics must give precedence to morality!"

Dar'El was taken aback by Tol'El's response. It wasn't what they had rehearsed. Tol'El had gone off message, changing what should have been a pithy acknowledgment of Dar'El's testimony into an impassioned defense. It was a surprise, and Dar'El didn't like surprises. His worry lifted somewhat as he studied the Chamber, gauging their response to Tol'El's words. Many 'Els wore troubled expressions as they spoke to those nearby.

"Now. All that said, the more serious charge against your son was his association with a woman not of his Caste," Tol'El said, interrupting the whispered discussions. "In fact, this is a woman not of any Caste, but a ghrina." He looked to Dar'El. "How can you defend such a man? For having relations with a woman not of his Caste, he *should* have been found Unworthy, but for bedding an actual ghrina, an abomination—" Tol'El scowled, appearing as if he wanted to spit out something disgusting. "For such a crime, he should have been marked with the Slash of Iniquity. And rumors state this *thing* with whom he consorted remained at the House Shektan seat for months after Rukh's departure for the Chimera caverns. Why was that? Was it not to care for this ghrina during her pregnancy, a child of your son's infamy?"

Dar'El gritted his teeth. Once again, Tol'El had gone off script. He was *not* to have so forcefully pressed the Indicter's case. He was supposed to have just asked Dar'El to explain Rukh's relationship with Jessira. Instead, Tol'El had gone much further, bringing up a charge so outrageous, so repulsive…How could his friend have done this to him? Suggesting a pregnancy between Rukh and Jessira? Who else would have even considered such a possibility before Tol'El had brought it up?

When he noticed the approving mutterings of the 'Els, he realized many must have already considered just such a possibility. It was a stunning surprise, and Dar'El struggled to control his dismay. How could he have missed something so potentially basic yet potentially devastating to Rukh's future?

A headache began thudding behind Dar'El's eyes. "What you imply bears no resemblance to the truth," he said. "My son and the ghrina—" he mentally scowled at having to call Jessira such a name "—were friends. Nothing more. Any seeming impropriety between them was my doing." In a matter-of-fact tone, Dar'El explained all he'd done to Rukh and Jessira and the reasons why. "Rukh was doomed the moment his Talents became known. He was going to be found Unworthy no matter what I tried to do. The politics of the Chamber demanded his expulsion from Ashoka, but I could still save him. If Jessira took him to Stronghold, at least he would have a chance at a life. I manipulated both of them." Exposing his deceit was painful, but necessary, and Dar'El tried to keep his voice smooth and measured, letting only a hint of his shame to shine through. Ragged penitence wouldn't move these men, but restrained remorse might.

"And what of the pregnancy?" Tol'El persisted.

"There was no pregnancy," Dar'El said. "Jessira remained in Ashoka because I lied to her. I led her to believe that she was the cause for Rukh's banishment. She stayed because of the guilt she bore, and the House Seat was the safest place for her in Ashoka."

Tol'El stroked his beard, seeming both fascinated and repulsed by what he had heard. "It is an ugly story you present," he said. "Cunning treachery and a father's desperate love mixed in with equal measure. How can you prove this is not yet another deception?"

Dar'El glared at the ruling 'El of House Suzay. "I cannot prove a negative, and you know it," he said. "But if you don't believe me, then believe Farn Arnicep. You all know what happened to him. He was there when Rukh and Jessira arrived at Stronghold. From what he saw, they are as I tell you: friends. Nothing more. In fact, Jessira was already engaged to a man of her city prior to meeting Rukh, and this arrangement was unchanged upon her return to Stronghold. It further proves my point: if my son and Jessira had consorted with one another, surely her engagement to this other man would have been dissolved when they made it to Stronghold."

"I believe Farn's testimony has already been provided to the Chamber," Tol'El said. "It confirms Dar'El's claims with regards to his son's relationship with the ghrina." He turned to Dar'El. "Our Houses are allies. All here know it. And I believe you when you say you did what you did to save your son. It is noble, but the means you used to achieve your aims—dissembling to your family, this Chamber, even the ghrina—it is despicable. I would not have it in me to do the same, and I am troubled that you had no such qualms." Tol'El sighed as if in regret. "Nevertheless, it is not you who is faced with our judgment, though in some ways, you should be. Instead, it is your son, Rukh Shektan, who seems to have simply followed the poor guidance you gave him." He turned to the other 'Els. "Based on what we've learned, I believe we should lift the judgment on Rukh Shektan and allow him to return home. He seems to have been nothing more than an innocent dupe in all of this, as much a victim of his nanna's manipulation as we were."

Even before Tol'El finished speaking, satisfied mutterings had arisen throughout the Chamber, including from those most opposed to House Shektan. Dar'El couldn't tell what the pleased nods and conversations might mean. Were his fellow 'Els merely happy to see him humbled, or had they accepted Tol'El's reasoning and were willing to exonerate his son? Perhaps it was a combination of the two. Dar'El could not say, but if it were the latter, he would be grateful. The damage Tol'El's final testimony had done to his reputation would be a small price to pay for Rukh's safe return.

"Does the Supplicant have any response to give?" Lin'El asked.

Dar'El hesitated. None of what had occurred thus far had been planned. The script he and Tol'El had come up with in the past few days, and even last night, had long since been discarded, but if anything, the resultant testimony had ended up being stronger. Rukh's chances of coming home were better because of the risks Tol'El had taken. Dar'El owed his friend a large favor, but right now, he wasn't sure how to proceed. Should he say anything else? Or should he simply allow Tol'El's work to stand on its own? "I have no defense against the findings of the Indicter," Dar'El said, making his decision.

"Does the Indicter have any further questions to ask?" Lin'El asked, turning to Tol'El, who shook his head.

"I have nothing else to offer. My post is relinquished," he said in a formal tone.

"Are there any more challenges to be offered?" Lin'El proposed to the Chamber. A hand shot up. Dar'El groaned. It was Hal'El Wrestiva. "You wish to serve as the Indicter?" Lin'El asked.

Hal'El stood. "I do."

"Are there any objections?" Lin'El asked.

The Assembly remained quiet, and Dar'El gritted his teeth. He wanted to object to Hal'El's choice as Indicter, but he had no further standing to do so.

"Then by acclamation, Hal'El will now serve as the Indicter," Lin'El said. "Take your post and proceed." Lin'El indicated the lectern that Tol'El had given up.

Hal'El limped his way forward. When he was in place, he cleared his throat and began speaking. "The ruling 'El of House Suzay has done a marvelous job interrogating Dar'El Shektan, has he not? His testimony has ruined the reputation of his good friend and close ally. I'm sure all of us were suitably impressed by Tol'El's righteous indignation. I certainly was. Well done." He clapped his hands slowly and derisively. "Nevertheless, this has all been a sham, a charade practiced for weeks prior to today's meeting. And it was executed brilliantly. Even I almost believed it and possibly would have except for one modest fact: Dar'El thinks long and deep on all matters. Tol'El inadvertently reminded me of this truth." He stabbed a finger at his fellow 'Els. "Don't be fooled by this playacting you've heard, this farce. Everything Dar'El and Tol'El told you was rehearsed. It is a means to trick you, to fool you. Their words are like a magician flaunting a handkerchief so we never see when he hides the card under the table. We're so focused on Dar'El's shame, his lies and deceptions, that we never noticed when Tol'El hid Rukh Shektan's infamy under the table. We think him innocent. He is far from it. He was found Unworthy, and the judgment should stand. I've heard nothing to tell me otherwise."

"Then you are as foolish as I always suspected," Dar'El said. He had never liked Hal'El Wrestiva and liked him even less now. "You hear nothing and learn less. It wasn't my testimony alone that the Chamber heard. What of Farn Arnicep? Without coaching or pre-knowledge, he said the same as I regarding Rukh and Jessira's relationship."

"Who is this Jessira?" Hal'El asked in exasperated confusion. "The name of the ghrina? Why not name a pig? They have the same worth."

"As you would know given your son," Dar'El interrupted. His anger was getting the better of him, but he couldn't stop himself.

Hal'El bristled in outrage. "Then let us speak of Farn Arnicep," he growled. "He lived amongst the OutCastes for months. By blood, he is a member of your House, and as such, perhaps *he* is Tainted as well."

Loud hisses of anger arose at his words. It was one thing to insult someone personally, quite another to impugn an entire House. Many had relatives in House Shektan.

Dar'El saw the opening and took it. "Farn Arnicep is tied to seven Houses along his lineage and through marriage. According to the Indicter, all those Kummas are Tainted as well." He stared Hal'El in the eyes, freezing him with a snarl. "Including members of House Wrestiva."

"Obviously, it was not my intent to call into question the honor of your entire House," Hal'El said, appearing chastened. "I simply note the coincidences so prevalent in House Shektan: a Sentya adopted by the ruling 'El and relations between the natural son of the same ruling 'El and a ghrina. Once is an accident. Twice is a coincidence. Thrice is a conspiracy. Farn Arnicep makes thrice."

"If this is your logic, then it is as sloppy as your wisdom," Dar'El said scornfully.

Hal'El rolled his eyes. "Then try this," he challenged. "As it said in *The Word and Deed*: '*Suffer not those who have lineage from two Castes. Know them for the truth. They are Ghrinas, abominations*'. You know this dictate as well as any of us, yet you harbored a ghrina within your home for months."

Dar'El had heard enough. "And also according to *The Word and the Deed*: '*Those who seek wives in a Caste not their own should forever be shunned. They are as the children of their perverse unions: ghrinas, abominations in the eyes of the Lord*'. That verse should hold particular poignancy for you given the life led by your son, Suge Wrestiva. Perhaps if you'd spent more time searching out sin in your own home instead of in mine, your iniquitous son might have amounted to something more than a snowblood addict."

"You dare!"

Dar'El waved aside his anger. "Don't pretend to be shocked. If you're going to speak such vile words about my House and family, don't faint away if I respond in kind. Are there any other questions?"

Hal'El glared at him before turning back to the Chamber. "None of Dar'El's petty insults are important. This is the truth: Tol'El tried to distract us from Rukh Shektan's various sins. He has Talents not of his Caste. For this, he was rightly judged Unworthy. He had a relationship with a woman not of his Caste. For this, he was also correctly found to be Unworthy. Worse, this woman was a ghrina. For this, Rukh Shektan should have been marked with the Slash of Iniquity. He should have been killed and his body left to rot on the Isle of the Crows!" He slammed his fist on the lectern. His words produced shouts and catcalls from the other ruling 'Els, and Hal'El waited for the sounds to die away before continuing on. "Instead, we were merciful. We allowed Rukh Shektan to walk away with his life. But now, months later, we are told that these sins were not of the son but of the father." He shook his head, looking sorrowful. "All-too-well do I know what it means to disregard or explain away the sins of a son. I know the consequences of doing so. Every day I relive them. And I tell you this: everything you've heard from Dar'El Shektan is a nanna's attempt to assuage his guilt. He doesn't want to admit the kind of man he raised. The kind of man *I*, to my everlasting shame, also raised."

Dar'El ground his teeth. Hal'El's last statement had hurt, tying Suge Wrestiva to Rukh. It was a clever ploy. He looked out at his fellow 'Els, too many of whom stared back at him with what appeared to be hostility. Dar'El could feel Rukh's future slipping away. It had been so close, but once again, here came Hal'El Wrestiva to crush all hopes of happiness. Would the man never leave them be? He glanced to the other side of the Arbiter's dais, and Hal'El smirked at him, victory reflected in his eyes.

Dar'El's eyes swam with red and just then, he almost bellowed out what he knew about the Wrestiva warehouse and snowblood. By the barest of margins, he held his tongue. He had to hold onto that secret. It was too important. The city needed Dar'El to find what was really happening with the murders and the Sil Lor Kum, even if the cost was Rukh's future.

Dar'El sought to recapture his poise, taking deep, even breaths to work out his anger. It didn't work. Calmness wouldn't remain. It broke apart like a thought in a room crowded with shouting people. No matter how hard he tried, serenity eluded his grasp. It kept slipping away, so he decided to use the anger instead.

"You have all heard how my son obtained his Talents, and what you have heard is the truth," he began. "Or do you wish to hold false everything we've spent two millennia defending? All the blood spilled cannot be for nothing! Look into you hearts and find where Rukh sinned. Was it because of his unsought Talents? In that case, what would you have him do? What wisdom would you offer? According to *The Warrior and the Servant*, *'A warrior must always choose the path of righteousness, but if one isn't visible, then on his own, he must forge it'.*" Dar'El glared about the room, challenging those he knew might vote against him. "Where was the righteous path my son should have taken? What path would you advise your sons to follow if faced with such a situation?" He glared about a moment more before answering his own question. "There is none!"

Sweat beaded on his brow, and Dar'El wiped it with a handkerchief. "We are told that death is the greatest gift a Kumma warrior can offer to someone in need," he said. "I think this is wrong. The greatest gift is life. We all know what happened to Rukh in the Chimera caverns. He was left to die. It was shamefully done. Even his lieutenant, in the after-action reports, indicated this was true. But I ask you to think of what this means from Rukh's perspective. He carried the burden of his shame. He accepted the abuse and hatred of his brothers. He suffered betrayal, but he fought on. He never quit. Duty demanded no less. Rukh held steadfast, never letting the treason of others defeat his heart, the sin of his unwanted Talents ruin his soul. He *lived*—with all the pain and loneliness that implies— because he is a Kumma. He lived so your sons didn't have to die. Think of the courage it would take to endure in the face of such abuse, and ask yourselves if you possess similar bravery. I do not."

Until this moment, Dar'El had never given full measure to Rukh's accomplishments. Now, hearing the words spoken aloud, he was forced to do so. A tear leaked down the corner of an eye, and he had to take a shuddering breath before he could speak again. "Knowing all this," he began in a quavering voice, "is it really possible that a man of such nobility would desecrate himself in any way, especially with a woman not of his Caste? He would not, and he didn't."

Silence greeted his final statement.

Shortly after, the vote was taken. In the end, eighty-five percent voted in favor of House Shektan's petition.

Rukh was coming home.

CHAPTER TWENTY-SIX
AN UNWRITTEN BOOK

*A willingness to listen to and understand those with whom one
disagrees is not enough. One must also offer acceptance.*

~*Sooths and Small Sayings, by Tramed Billow AF 1387*

"Where go next?" Chak-Soon asked.

Jessira shrugged, worried more about her footing then answering the Tigon's question. Along the eastern edge of the Creosote Plains, the land rose quickly, and the terrain became rough and uneven. Add in the wet, slippery ground—it had rained for the five days since their departure from Hammer—and it wouldn't take much to turn an ankle. Even the packhorse had sense enough to step carefully through the thick, green grass. It made for slow going, but at least this morning the sun had broken through the clouds and brought with it much needed warmth and a return to spring.

Spring.

It wasn't something Jessira could smell so much as sense. There was a vibrancy to the sky and clouds, to the sound of water and birds, even the way the fish ran in the streams. All of it seemed to reflect what she knew: spring was coming. Hopefully, last week's rain and cold would be the last of winter's icy grasp. Then the world could start to come back to life.

Her smile of anticipation faded as she plotted their course.

Soon would come the Soulless River. Passage would be difficult if it was already spring-swollen.

"Where go next?" Chak-Soon repeated.

Jessira shot him an irritated glance. Now he wanted to talk to her? A week after she'd saved his miserable carcass? Not once, had the fragging Tigon offered any kind of acknowledgement of what she'd done for him. She often wondered if Healing the unholy beast had been the right thing to do. Rukh seemed to think so, but Jessira wasn't sure. During their time together, all Chak-Soon had done was keep to himself. He glowered as he watched and listened to the others but offered little in return.

"*We're* going home," she said. "I have no idea where you and Choke are heading." Of course, she wasn't about to tell Chak-Soon where home was. As far as the Tigon was concerned, she and Rukh were on their way back to Ashoka. There was no chance she would trust Chak-Soon with the secret of Stronghold's existence. Not even Li-Choke could know of it. Stronghold survived because no one knew to look for it.

The Tigon grunted. "You Heal. Not thank you. Should say so."

Jessira studied the Tigon. His ears stood erect and faced forward. His eyes were wide open, the pupils narrow slits against the sunlight. But his cat-like features, so like a jaguar's, were indecipherable. Typical. She'd never liked domestic cats either. "Are you saying 'thank you' or are you saying 'you'll never thank me'?"

"Thank you."

If a boulder had fallen on her head, Jessira doubted she would have been more stunned. *Chak-Soon* was thanking her? Even after hearing the words, she struggled to believe that a Tigon was capable of feeling any sense of obligation or gratitude. While Li-Choke had said this Tigon was different, that he was learning to understand about the ideals of brotherhood and peace, even love, Jessira hadn't believed the Bael. Not really. Rukh had been willing to give the creature the benefit of the doubt, but that's because he did so for nearly everyone. Jessira wasn't so generous. Perhaps it was because the Tigon was so quiet and withdrawn. In a Human, such an individual would have been described as being sullen or taciturn, ready to explode at the slightest provocation; and it didn't take much to set off a Tigon. Yet here was Chak-Soon, offering honest appreciation for what she had done for him.

"You're welcome," Jessira replied.

Chak-Soon grunted, and the two of them fell again into silence.

Jessira looked ahead to where Rukh and Li-Choke spoke to one another. The two of them had a genuine affection for one another. It was hard getting used to. While Jessira had come to accept Li-Choke's presence, she still wasn't comfortable around him. Not like Rukh, who seemed to think the Baels were already allies. Again, it was his rare gift: he forgave those he should have hated with every fiber of his being. And if he could forgive Humanity's enemies, then perhaps he could forgive those amongst her kind who had wronged him.

"Mother not right 'bout you," Chak-Soon said, interrupting her thoughts.

She glanced at the tall, powerful Chimera. For once, his inscrutable features were easy to read. The Tigon's ears were wilted, and his gaze was cast downward. Even the way he walked: the droop of his shoulders as he shuffled beside her spoke of an inner turmoil. Chak-Soon was ashamed.

"You think Suwraith is wrong?" Jessira guessed.

Chak-Soon nodded, staring downward, unwilling to look her way. "We kill. Not good. Choke says brothers are we."

Jessira studied the Tigon once more, searching for signs of

deception. He sounded and looked sincere in his statement, and some of the distrust she felt for the big Chimera thawed. Perhaps Li-Choke was right. Maybe Chak-Soon *could* be taught a better path, one in which Humanity was no longer the enemy. It seemed an almost unbelievable change of heart, a miracle really, but it didn't change the fundamentals of the situation. Chak-Soon was but one ordinate—what the Tigons named their commanders—alone in his way of thinking. He was a single green leaf on a tree full of autumn's reds and golds, easily missed and overlooked. What chance did he have of changing the hearts of so many? Of those who held fast to their faith in the Queen and who would leap at the chance to kill those whom She named evil.

Not much. There weren't likely to be many others like Chak-Soon amongst the Tigons.

"What are the two of you talking about?" Rukh asked. He and Li-Choke had slowed down so Jessira and Chak-Soon could catch up with them.

"Chak-Soon was just thanking me for Healing him," Jessira replied. "He was also…." she broke off when she noticed the Tigon's silence.

Once again, he'd separated himself, walking ahead with his head drooping. She understood. Chak-Soon wasn't brooding or being sullen. He was humiliated. All along, the Tigon had been going through a crisis of conscience.

"The rest is for him to say," she added.

———◦———

Chak-Soon was the last to cross to the eastern shore of the Soulless River. Fording the river hadn't been easy—all of them ended up having to swim at least part of the river's breadth—but at least the Creosote Plain was now behind them, and from where they now stood, the Privations soared directly ahead. In reality, the mountains were many miles distant. A thick forest of hardwoods—oak, maple, and elm—arose close by, stretching to the broad shoulders of the mountains.

Rukh turned away from the others as he stripped out of his wet clothes and donned a dry shirt and trousers. Jessira was doing the same. Rukh tried not to stare at her legs. From when they practiced, either with the sword or while wrestling, he knew just how strong her legs could be. How then were they also so soft and warm? He lost himself tracing the elegant lines of their length, the curves where they met....

"This is where we part ways," Li-Choke said.

Rukh broke of his contemplation of Jessira's legs. He hoped he wasn't blushing.

"We'll make our way to the Hunters Flats from here," Choke continued, apparently not noticing Rukh's reaction. "I imagine you'll head for Ashoka."

Rukh grunted, not bothering to correct the Bael. He didn't like lying to Choke—he thought of him as a friend—but Jessira had been insistent that even the most vague sense of Stronghold's location, or even its existence, had to be kept secret from both Chimeras. Rukh didn't blame her. If the Queen ever learned of Jessira's home or worse, its location, the city would be doomed. There was no Oasis to protect it.

"Hate water," Chak-Soon complained, as he wrung out his dripping fur.

Rukh sympathized, an unusual sentiment to hold for a Tigon. In the beginning, he hadn't been sure what to make of Chak-Soon. In fact, there had been many occasions during the early days of their travel together when he had wondered if he'd been wrong to ask Jessira to Heal the Tigon. Eventually, those suspicions had faded as he got to know Chak-Soon. The Tigon was trying to become a better being than nature and the Queen had made him. It couldn't be easy, and Rukh wondered what Chak-Soon would do once he was back amongst his own kind—Tigons who still dreamt of murdering Humans, of rending their flesh in honor of their so-called Mother? What then would Chak-Soon do? Would he fall back into the habits he knew so well? Would he betray Li-Choke?

Rukh didn't know, but he prayed it would be otherwise. He prayed Devesh—or someone—would see the young Tigon through his crisis of conscience. He was surprised by how earnestly he prayed for Chak-Soon.

"The Soulless wasn't so bad," Li-Choke said in response to Chak-Soon's complaint. "You should try fording River Crush. All those rapids and falls." He mock-shuddered. "I hear it can be tense. In fact, it's said that the Western Plague loses more Chimeras to those waters than to any caravan of Humans."

"Where will you go next?" Rukh asked

"To the Eastern Plague. Mother will expect a full report," Li-Choke replied. "She promised to let my brothers live if I obeyed Her will in this matter."

"What will you tell her?" Jessira asked, coming up to join their conversation.

Li-Choke smiled. "Anything to keep me and my kind alive," he said without the faintest hint of irony.

Chak-Soon bared his teeth, exposing sharp fangs. It was an expression Rukh had learned was the Tigon's way of smiling. "Mother think I stupid. She not care what say."

"We'll have to cut south of the Privations," Choke added. "We might pick up some late snow."

"You'll be fine," Jessira said with a smile. "You've got all that fur to keep you warm."

"Not like fur wet," Chak-Soon complained once again.

Jessira chuckled. "So much like a cat."

Rukh was taken aback by Jessira's expression of affection for the Tigon. It set him wondering if it really only required two weeks of travel and an open heart for centuries of hatred to be cleansed? He reckoned it was too simple a solution for such a deep-rooted, complicated problem. But then again, sometimes what everyone knew to be the hardest things in life were, in reality, the easiest. In any case, it was a reason for hope.

"Goodbye, Rukh Shektan," Li-Choke said with a smile. Rukh found his feet dangling off the ground as the Bael hugged him. "Thank you for saving me. Again."

"Travel safe," Chak-Soon said, looking uncertain.

Rukh settled on a handshake with the Tigon.

Their parting words spoken, Rukh and Jessira watched as Li-Choke and Chak-Soon made their way southeast, before they eventually crested a hill and disappeared.

"Time for us to go, too," Jessira said.

Rukh found her staring eastward, toward the soaring Privation Mountains. It was easy to understand why: Jessira wanted to go home. Rukh would have felt the same way if their roles had been reversed. "Stronghold it is," he said.

"Are you sure you want to?" she asked diffidently.

Rukh smiled. "I told you before: my home is with you." He felt the rightness of his words even as he said them.

Jessira's eyes shone. Without a word, she stepped forward and fistfuls of his shirt were caught in her hands. She kissed him. It was hard and passionate, loving and possessive all at once. It was a kiss only she could give, and Rukh didn't want it to end.

The small fire crackled merrily. Rukh and Jessira had set up camp along the banks of a small, spring-fed lake, deep in the thick woodlands that began north of the Privation Mountains and extended all the way down to Samsoul. In the clearing made by the pond, the majesty of the night sky was visible, spread out above them like a shimmering curtain of light. Jessira was cleaning up, wanting privacy while she bathed. The sound of her splashing could be heard, along with the noises of chirping crickets and a nearby owl as it hooted.

Rukh had already bathed, and he sat by the fire, fingering *The Book of First Movement*. It was such a slender book with a soft blue leather cover and the title embossed in gold. Could this really have been written by the First Father? Why didn't he have more to say with his final words?

He glanced toward the pond. Jessira was mostly hidden by a bed of tall rushes that swayed gently in the soft breeze. He couldn't tell, but it seemed as if her back was to him, and little beyond her head and torso was visible. She turned to the side and stretched, arching her back as she ran fingers through her hair. The flash of a pale breast was briefly visible in the moonlight. He sat forward, his interest piqued. He sighed in disappointment when she turned away again.

Jessira looked like she was going to take a while with her bath, so Rukh went back to studying *The Book*. He turned it over in his hands, looking at it from every angle before finally cracking it open. Just as the stories told, the pages were empty. He flipped through *The Book* before coming back to the first page. His eyebrows rose in surprise. A moment earlier, the page had been yellow and blank like all the others; but now there was a single line, written in blue ink with a man's strong hand: '*Believe my song and serve greatness*'.

Rukh pondered the words. Why had no one else been able to read this solitary script until Hume? And surely there had to be more to the First Father's book than this one enigmatic line. He held *The Book* up to the light, looking to see if a faint tracery of words might be visible if the pages were backlit.

Still nothing.

A strange rushing noise filled his ears, a sound of ringing bells, strumming strings, and peeling horns. Rukh felt himself tumbling, down deep toward a gentle blue light.

"Rukh!" the voice was distant. Jessira. He tried to answer, to push against whatever was pulling him downward. Helpless as a leaf on the wind, he fell....

Linder Val Maharj, the Son of the Desert, stood alone within a field of wildflowers at twilight. The sun had already set, and rich reds, yellows, and oranges burnished the sky in jewel-like tones. Autumn was here, and the harvest moon hung above, silver and serene, but the trees lining the field remained clothed in their summer foliage, verdant and green. It was a warm evening.

Linder was a tall, well-built man of middle years with a dark hue. His face was too rugged and worn to be called handsome; the result of early years spent exposed to the heat, the cold, and the rain. His nose was an axe blade that cleaved his acne-scarred face in twain and the dark, forceful eyes of a raptor peered out from beneath heavy brows. Long, black hair, touched with streaks of gray, was tied in the back with a simple leather cord, and an enigmatic smile curved his thin, fierce lips as he held a bouquet of flowers. Though Linder lacked physical beauty, there was a commanding presence to him, an aura most women found attractive.

Not that another woman could have ever tempted him. In the almost three millennia Linder and Cienna, his wife, had been married, he had never once considered sharing the bed of another. His wife was his life and his treasure, his anchor in the world, and he rejoiced every day when he awoke and gazed upon her face. They were immortal, but eternity would not be time enough for their love.

He admonished himself for his distracted thoughts. He was here to arrange a bouquet for tonight's dinner. He already held tulips and hyacinths and yellow roses along with some other flowers that he couldn't name. But, he still needed some sprigs of honeysuckle. Cienna loved the fragrance of honeysuckle, and his wife wanted tonight to be perfect.

After all, their only child, Lienna would be sharing dinner with them.

Linder's smile slipped at the thought of his daughter. She had been such a bright, happy child. So inquisitive. Brilliant in ways few could comprehend. So many secrets she had learned of Jivatma. Only Linder and Cienna exceeded her mastery. How then had she grown into such a distant, distrustful woman? Withdrawn and cold. It had been decades since Linder or Cienna had heard from her.

Occasionally, strange rumors reached them, stories of burnings and terror in the settlements; of a mad woman, running naked, with her hair matted and skin the color of leaves, who capered through small villages on the fringes of the great forest. She would set the buildings alight, screaming that the world, Arisa itself, demanded vengeance for the death of the forests and the murder of small animals. The settlers—whose only crime had been to work their fingers to the bone from sunup to sundown as they tried to make a life for themselves in the wilderness—had been helpless before her. They couldn't stop her madness. Sometimes the killer was given a name: Suwraith: the Bringer of Sorrows. Other times, she was called Lienna.

Cienna had refused to believe the mad woman might be their own daughter, but doubt had often lingered within Linder's breast. He had seen the devastation wrought by this Suwraith, and his people's pain stabbed at his heart. He and Cienna had practically been Nanna and Amma to all of Humanity, and indeed people knew of them as the First Father and First Mother. To see so many slaughtered had left him trembling with rage.

418

But one day a year ago, just as quickly as the killings had begun, they had ended. Since that time, no one again heard the name Suwraith or Lienna.

Then yesterday, their daughter, after an absence of over fifty years, had asked to visit her parents. Cienna was excited, but Linder had reservations. What had their daughter been doing in all these years? Who was she now? How could they know, not having seen or spoken to her in more than half a century?

Linder shook his head, wanting to clear such troublesome thoughts from his mind, unaware that he was frowning. Suddenly, his body whipped around in the direction he knew was home. His pupils dilated and his nostrils flared as though seeking to capture some elusive scent. He focused on some unseen event occurring at the Palace on the Hill, the home he had shared with his wife for over nineteen hundred years. His face grew ashen and seemed to sag as he felt prickles run through his body. A look of horror stole over his face.

Cienna!

He drew on his Well and Voyaged to a plain, small room in the Palace. It was down the hall from the dining room where he had last sensed Cienna's thoughts. Why couldn't he do so anymore? He'd been able to 'feel' Cienna since that day three millennia ago when they had first released the power of the WellStone and brought life to a desolate world. The question raised a fresh terror in his mind.

He raced down the hallway, with no other thought than to reach his wife.

Immediately, he noticed the bodies.

Linder slowed to a stop. These were the people who had chosen to make their lives here at the Palace, as servants to the First Mother and the First Father. They were all good friends. Now, blood pooled beneath their corpses. Knife wounds marred their bodies, some with throats slit. Even in death, their eyes appeared tormented.

Linder barely held down his gorge. He resumed his run, praying and hoping that Cienna had been spared. His fear for her was an illness. His skin was hot and sweaty. His stomach was lead, and he couldn't breathe. He felt as if he'd been mule kicked.

Faster, run faster *was his mantra.*

At last he came to the small dining room. It was an intimate space, square and highlighted by a round cherry wood table polished to a high sheen with seating for four. The light was soft and muted, and the walls were a sky blue. Above the hearth hung a painting of a smiling Linder holding a laughing Cienna. They were by the seashore, looking on as their then three-year-old daughter, Lienna played in the waves.

None of it mattered now.

Where was Cienna?

There!

She lay face up, unmoving on the far side of the table. Just like the servants, centered upon her chest was a gaping wound.

But Cienna's murder had been different. Her clothes hung loose about her once lush and beautiful body, and her skin was pulled tight, her bones prominent. She appeared skeletal, as withered and dry as a roasted cornhusk. Writ large on her face was the torment of betrayal.

With an anguished cry that seemed to shake the room, Linder rushed to her and took her in his arms. His eyes watered as he wept with inconsolable grief. He rocked her back and forth gently, kissing her hair and keening like a stricken animal, crying out his grief and loss.

Time ended. He knew that even if he lived for another thousand years or even ten thousand, he would never recover from the pain of this moment.

His only hope and consolation was that Devesh would shelter Cienna, and he would find her waiting for him across the bridge of life.

"You found her."

Linder startled. That voice. He recognized it.

He looked up. On the other side of table, standing in the entrance to the dining room was his daughter. She was a tall woman, still youthful

420

despite her over-century of life. She was strikingly beautiful by any standards, or would have been had she not been covered in blood. She looked to have bathed in it. Her honey-blonde hair was soaked in it as was her face. And she was naked.

Tears still flowed from his eyes, but Linder no longer sobbed. "Lienna...?" Normally he had a clear, deep voice, a voice accustomed to command and obedience. Now his words came out as a weak croak. He was confused, consumed with misery, his reason for living dead in his arms, and here stood his daughter looking to have been dipped in a vat of blood. "What happened? Who did this? Do you know?" he asked.

Lienna seemed strangely untouched by all the tragedy surrounding her. She wore an indecipherable, confused smile on her face and stepped around the table, seeming to stalk him.

Lienna displayed a foot-long knife dripping with blood. "Whoever killed your wife used this thing." She paused and tilted her head to the side as though confused or listening to an unheard voice. "I think it's called the Withering Knife," she continued, "or at least...I think that's what it...." She trailed off into vacant silence.

A terrible suspicion gripped Linder, one he worked to suppress. His daughter needed him. "Are you hurt?" he asked.

"Of course I'm hurt," Lienna shrieked. "Over and over they cut me!" Her fisted hands slashed at the air. "Over and over with their sharp blades and axes, killing me! Maiming me! Ahh the agony! They kill me over and over again! A thousand times a thousand. Even now, I can feel them stabbing and stabbing! NO! Oh, for the love of mercy! NO! NO! NO!" She clenched her hair in her fists and squeezed her eyes tight, shaking her head back and forth and screaming as if she were tormented by demons only she could see or feel.

Linder stood by, sick with helplessness and unsure what to do.

It seemed Lienna would scream on forever, but with a final shriek, she stopped as suddenly as she had begun. Her eyes snapped open, wild and deranged while her hands slapped to her sides, tearing out fistfuls of hair in the process. She seemed not to notice as she grinned maniacally.

Linder's suspicion deepened. He was beginning to understand who it was who had come to his home like a thief in the night and killed all whom he loved. "It was you," he said softly, horrified that his daughter was the instrument of such evil.

"Yes, it was me," Lienna admitted in a sibilant whisper. "Someone came here and killed everyone you loved," she purred. "And she'll kill you!" Quicker than thought, she threw her knife, burying it in Linder's gut.

Linder reached for a chair to hold himself upright, but it slipped beneath his hand and clattered to the floor alongside him. He lay on his back and gasped with shock. His whole body was weak, boneless. Breathing was a chore, and he felt his life draining away.

Standing above him, Lienna smirked. "The blade withers you away till there's nothing left. It steals your Well. Your Jivatma will be mine." She tittered inanely as she bent and reached for the knife. She paused before taking the hilt and looked into Linder's eyes. "This will hurt."

She grasped the knife.

Earlier Linder had learned the meaning of despair. Now, he learned the meaning of pain. His back arched and a silent scream erupted from his lips. He was on fire. His whole body was aflame. Acid roared through his veins, each beat of his heart seeming to spread it further, making it more intense. The pain seemed to last for days, but in reality, it was only a few short seconds before Lienna released the blade's hilt.

And in the time she held the knife, through the fog of agony, Linder had communion with his daughter, a gross parody of what he and Cienna had once shared. He learned her plans to destroy Humanity, leaving the survivors to live on as nomads, homeless wanderers subsisting on grubs and dirt as they had when Linder was a boy. The reasons were muddled and her thoughts and motivations shifted by the moment, driven by an overpowering anger and hatred. Lienna was insane, but the more fearsome truth was this: she could make real her twisted thoughts and ambitions.

For those with dedication, the Withering Knife could transform the wielder into something else, something never before seen on Arisa, a being like no other. Linder and Cienna had once considered such a transformation for themselves, but had ultimately set it aside. No one should be so powerful.

But Lienna had decided otherwise. She would be the first—and the last.

Linder had to escape. He had to stop her before she made real her hideous vision.

With his strength fading, Linder drew on the last fragment of the WellStone, the smooth, white rock hanging from a strip of leather around his neck. He drew on it for strength and grasped the Withering Knife by its hilt and pulled it from his failing body. He threw it aside, watching as it slid under the table, several feet from his nerveless hands. So much blood on the rug. Cienna would have hated such despoilment.

Lienna gasped and glared at the knife in betrayal. "You said you'd get them all. Especially him," she accused the lifeless dagger. She bent down to retrieve it.

Linder didn't have much time left. He had already tried to Heal himself with the WellStone, but the wound soaked up his attempts like a dry desert absorbed the rain. It would be the death of him, but there was still something he could do. He rolled over onto his side and rocked himself unsteadily to his feet. His daughter had finally retrieved the knife. She looked up as Linder stood.

"No!" she shrieked. "That's impossible! You can't do that!"

"It is possible," he said, his voice weak. He drew more from the WellStone. He couldn't stop his daughter. He lacked the strength, but perhaps he could thwart her will. He knew what she intended, but he knew what might see Humanity safe until others, wiser and stronger than he, found a way to defeat his mad daughter.

Lienna lunged forward, holding the knife before her. She was too late.

Linder Voyaged. He travelled, visiting cities throughout the world and leaving behind something to shelter them from the coming storm. It was a Cohesion of Blend, Shield, and Bow. It was an Oasis.

But there was one final work to be done. Linder Val Maharj, the Son of the Desert poured out all the wisdom he had mastered in his long life as well as his remaining Jivatma. All of it fit into an embarrassingly slim blue volume. He left it upon the doorsteps of the library of his final visitation: a proud, young city named Hammer.

Rukh was lifted upward, away from the shimmering blue disk. The memories of Linder Val Maharj were blurred amongst his own. He couldn't recall his name. What was it? Was he Linder Val Maharj? Or Rukh Shektan? He wasn't sure. Was the Sorrow Bringer His daughter, just as the Baels claimed? No. Or maybe yes. His daughter. Lienna. She'd been mortal once, though clearly mad even then. What of the Withering Blade? Could it really be the same weapon now being used by the Sil Lor Kum in Ashoka? His Wife, Cienna. Dead now. Murdered by Their own Daughter. His heart clutched with sorrow.

Someone shook his shoulder, calling urgently to him. A face peered down at him. He didn't recognize her—he should, but he didn't. Confusion still gripped his mind and memory, but her hair...it was the same color as His Daughter's. Her face was shadowed, but the hair. And She was naked, just like the last time He had seen the thief in the night who had murdered everything He loved and tried to murder the world.

"Lienna!" He screamed.

Jessira was content. She finally had a chance to wash away all the dirt and grime she'd collected during their travels. And this wasn't just a quick pass of a wet towel to wipe away the worst of the filth. No. The pond next to which they had set up camp gave her a chance to take a bath. A real one. She gloried in the simple actions of scrubbing herself clean as she liberally applied soap to skin and nails. She worked until all the grit and grime was scoured away. Her hair also merited special attention, heavy and limp as it was with caked in dirt, sweat, and oil. She sometimes wondered if she should cut it short like how some of her sister warriors wore theirs, but whenever she thought to do so, she would remember why she kept her hair long. Just like her camisole, her hair reminded her of her femininity. And the truth was Jessira *liked* her hair. She liked the feel of the wind rushing through it, waving it about like a banner. She liked the weight of it on her shoulders. She liked running her fingers through it. Or having Rukh do so.

Which was another reason she was taking extra special care tonight. She wanted everything to be perfect.

She glanced back at him. He sat by the fire, holding *The Book of First Movement*. He so wanted to read it. Just then, he looked her away, staring at her, not knowing she could see his features. He wore an expression of intense interest as he watched her. She was mostly hidden by a group of tall rushes, and he could only see her head and shoulders. His attention didn't wane. She smiled and turned to the side, arching her back as she pulled her fingers through the long, wet mass of her hair. She made sure Rukh could see a flash of breast before she turned away.

She could almost hear his sigh of disappointment.

She chuckled. It was nice to know she could have such an effect on the man.

When she was finished with her bath, she dried off and wrapped herself in a towel. She made her way toward the fire and smiled. Just as she'd expected: Rukh had *The Book of First Movement* cracked open on his lap. He stared down at it. Her smile slipped. His expression was vacant and empty. Drool collected at a corner of his gaping mouth.

She ran to him, and shook him, shouting his name.

He didn't answer. His head rolled about listlessly. He fell over on his side. She didn't let fear overwhelm her good sense. She got Rukh back in a sitting position, not caring when her towel slipped off, leaving her naked. Modesty was the least of her concerns. She checked Rukh's pulse, his breathing, his eyes, and put an ear to his chest to listen to his heart even as she conducted *Jivatma*, searching him for injury.

Nothing. He was fine as far as she could tell.

Her heart raced. Was he having some sort of seizure? He hadn't wet himself. Her glance fell upon *The Book*. It glowed, a dim blue light, easily missed against the fire, but it was there. She snatched it from his hands.

He groaned and fell over onto his back.

She stood over him, shaking his shoulder as she urgently called his name.

His eyes fluttered open, full of confusion before an appalled awareness filled them.

"Lienna!"

In a motion that left her breathless, Rukh grasped her arms, scissored his legs between hers and spun her over. He slammed her on her back. Her breath exploded from her lungs. Rukh stared at her, his face intent and searching. He didn't recognize her.

Jessira gasped, struggling to get a word out. Rukh had knocked the wind out of her, but it was quickly returning. She bent her leg, meaning to get it in between the two of them, but he jerked aside, blocking her. She twisted, and got both her feet on his hips. She pushed, and he lifted off the ground. But he was on her again before she could get to her knees.

Rukh held her pinned to the ground. Slowly recognition came to him. "Jessira?" he said, still sounding confused. "What did I...." Memory came to him, and horror came across his face. He scrambled off her. "I'm so sorry," he said. "I didn't know what I was doing."

Jessira cast about, searching desperately for her discarded towel. There. She grabbed it, wrapping it around herself before she turned to face him. Rukh looked anguished. Good. "What in the unholy hells did you think you were doing!" she shouted, not sure whether she was mad because of what he'd done or because of how much he'd scared her.

Rukh looked crestfallen. "I thought you were...I thought I was—"

"You thought what!"

Rukh shook his head. He hesitated. "I thought I was Linder Val Maharj."

Jessira waited a moment for Rukh to say something more, but he remained mulishly silent. He wore a distracted look on his face. She threw her hands in the air. "Fine. Who in the unholy hells is Linder Val Maharj?"

"The Son of the Desert," Rukh said. "We know him as the First Father."

Jessira blinked and settled back on her heels. Her anger was momentarily quenched. Was Rukh losing his mind? He didn't look mad, but his actions certainly had been. She sighed. "Why don't you start at the beginning and just tell me what happened."

Rukh nodded. "It happened when I opened *The Book*. It felt like I was falling into a shimmering blue disk, like a perfectly circular lake." For the next few minutes, he spoke, telling an unbelievable tale, one about the last moments in the lives of the First Father and the First Mother. And of their daughter Lienna who all knew now as Suwraith. "And when you woke me, all I saw was a naked woman with the same color hair as Lienna's. I wasn't sure who I was. I

427

thought I was Linder and...."

"Call him the First Father," Jessira interrupted. "It sounds disrespectful when you call him by his first name."

Rukh nodded. "I thought I was the First Father, and you were Lienna, the daughter who killed everyone I...I mean, *he* loved."

"And so you attacked me? Because you thought you were the First Father, and I was your daughter, Lienna? The one who murdered your wife and became Suwraith?" Jessira asked.

"No! I mean yes. I mean...." Rukh trailed off. He glanced up, finally meeting Jessira's gaze. "You believe me?"

Jessira nodded. A year ago she wouldn't have. But so much had changed in her life since she'd first met Rukh Shektan. In comparison to what she'd been exposed to thus far, believing Rukh had somehow experienced the last moments of the First Father's life seemed a paltry stretch to make.

Jessira stood. "Can I trust you not to read *The Book* while I clean up?" she asked, gesturing to the dirt she was once again covered in.

Rukh nodded, still looking anguished and miserable.

Jessira knew why. She sighed and knelt before him, taking his head in hands and making him look at her. "It wasn't your fault," she said. "And I'm fine. You didn't hurt me." She kissed his forehead. "We'll talk more when I'm finished."

CHAPTER TWENTY-SEVEN
THE PAST NEVER DIES

*After Hume opened my eyes and my heart, when I next beheld the Queen,
I found myself simultaneously saddened and angered. I pitied Her.
How terribly evil and pathetic Mother is.*

~From the journal of SarpanKum Li-Charn, AF 1754

"A nd what of Hume?" Mother asked.

"He is long dead," Li-Choke said, his voice steady, and carrying no hint of the fear coursing through his body.

On the very day he and Chak-Soon had separated from Rukh Shektan and Jessira Grey, Mother had called to them, telling them to prepare for Her arrival. She had come to them at dusk, a twilight visitation from a brooding, malevolent storm. And though She continued to maintain a firmer grip on reality, She still slipped now and again, such as when She had asked about Craven, the supposed sister city to Ashoka. No such place existed. Craven had been the inspired creation of Li-Dirge, used as a means to distract the Queen from carrying forth Her immediate plans to destroy Ashoka. The SarpanKum's wild gambit had worked, but perhaps it had worked too well. Though Jessira Grey did not admit it, there *was* a city in the Privation Mountains, secret and unknown. With Mother's focus upon

Craven, it would be a tragedy if Li-Dirge's lie somehow allowed the Queen to learn of Jessira Grey's hidden home.

However, while Mother was confused about Craven, Li-Choke sensed She was *not* confused about Hume. There had been a probing, questing nature to Her question. She was testing their loyalty.

"And Hammer?" Mother asked.

"Also long gone," Li-Choke announced.

"Is that so?" Mother said. "Then why do you suppose I sent you so far west to search for a man centuries dead in a city dead for equally as long?"

"Loyalty," Chak-Soon growled. "We truth tell."

Li-Choke kept himself from tensing by the barest of margins. Mother would notice his fear.

The Queen turned to the Tigon, who trembled now and then. "You fear Me? You fear your Mother?"

"Yes," Chak-Soon admitted.

Li-Choke gasped, soft and quickly snuffed. He prayed Mother hadn't heard his inadvertent sound of shock.

Either She hadn't or She didn't care. Instead, Mother laughed, a mad swirl of Her clouds. "Finally. I have honesty. Too often the Baels, and even the Tigons lie to Me. It is good to find two of My children who are willing to speak the truth." Thunder rumbled. "For your next task, you will return to the Eastern Plague and report to Li-Shard, the SarpanKum recently reassigned from the West. There you will assist him in the assault on Craven. As soon as I locate the city, I will send word."

Her final words spoke, Mother roared skyward, quickly disappearing.

Chak-Soon stared at the night sky. "Why Mother speak normal?" he asked, once She was long gone.

Li-Choke shrugged. "I don't know, but it can't be good. Not for any of us."

Chak-Soon appeared bewildered. "Why?"

"An insane Mother could be tricked and thwarted. One who is sane—it will be much more difficult."

"Why trick at all?"

"Mother may seem saner, but She is unchanged in this most important aspect: She still wishes to murder all Humanity. And remember, it was a Human woman who Healed you when by rights she should not have done so given what your kind has done to hers over the centuries. Given all that, is Jessira not worthy of life?"

Chak-Soon nodded. "She should live."

———◆———

Lienna soared through the night sky, well pleased with what had just transpired. Li-Choke, of the treacherous Eastern Baels, had held to his word. He had hunted down and slain Hume, just as She had ordered. Or at least had confessed that Hume was long dead. The truth of the matter was irrelevant. The important detail was this: Li-Choke had gone west, discovered a dead Hammer and hadn't lied about it. He had been truthful just as She had hoped he would be. Hammer was extinguished. When it had been killed was of no consequence—years or centuries, Lienna couldn't recall.

She tended to shy away from Her memories. Her recall of events wasn't so clear, and if She focused too much on them, Mother and Father sometimes returned, even Mistress Arisa. It couldn't be allowed, not after Her centuries of confusion and lonely toil.

Her newfound clarity was all because Lienna had finally decided to share Her pain with Her children. For millennia, She had sought to spare them, but She could no longer do so. They would have to share Her burden, which only made sense since it was why She had created them in the first place: to help Her with the execution of Her holy task. Even now, two of the Plagues of Continent Catalyst slumbered, resting as they took on a portion of Her illness. Only Her loyal Baels were unaffected, standing guard over their brethren.

Just then, an essence called to Her from many miles away. It was a trace sensation of sight, sound, and smell; a memory from millennia ago. Lienna recognized it. Lightning flashed in response to Her trembling fear. It was impossible. *He* was dead. She'd seen to it Herself, back when She was mortal. And yet, here was His presence, borne on the air like a pestilential wind. She could taste it. She could never forget it. Or Mother's stench. Could They still live? How? Or had the voices in Her head been real all this time?

Thunder pealed as Lienna screamed in fury. Where was He?

There! She had Him. And this time, She would end Father for all time!

CHAPTER TWENTY-EIGHT
HOUNDING SECRETS

Choices made in the past resonate throughout the years, limiting and expanding options in the future. It is an obvious but often overlooked truism.

~*The Sorrows of Hume, AF 1789*

Farn paused at the entryway to Dar'El's study, surprised to see the House Council waiting for him. He had been called to the Shektan Seat for an afternoon meeting, but he hadn't realized he would face such a formal gathering. Everyone looked so serious. It had Farn wondering if he'd done something wrong, or if something had *gone* wrong.

Sophy Terrell, the Hound, sat perched upon the couch. She had an intense air of concentration about her, and Farn quickly looked away. As a child, he had always tried to avoid the Hound's notice. She was so intimidating, and time had done little to diminish her fearsome presence.

Sharing the couch with Sophy was Satha Shektan, who smiled warmly at him. Farn nodded greeting, smiling in return. He'd grown up in the House Seat as much as he had his own home, and Satha was like a second Amma or a favorite auntie to him.

Seated in a chair next to the hearth was Durmer Volk. The Great

Duriah—an appellation none would dare say in his hearing—
remained the same blocky, stolid man Farn remembered. Even his
thin, shoe-polish black hair and thick, curling mustache drooping past
his perpetually frowning lips were the same.

Of course, Dar'El was also here. He was the one who had called
for the meeting after all.

But where was Garnet Bosde? Since Farn's return to Ashoka, he
had yet to see the old Councilor. Rumor stated Garnet was in
declining health, that his mind wasn't what it had once been. Or so
went the euphemistic description. Farn could read between the lines.
He'd seen something similar happen to his nannamma—his father's
mother. It had been painful for everyone involved; to watch
helplessly as the light of knowledge, love, and laughter faded from
Nannamma's eyes. It had taken a toll on all of them, especially
Nanna.

"Thank you for coming on such short notice," Dar'El said to
Farn, gesturing for him to take a seat. "Now that you're here, we can
begin."

"As you know, we had always hoped the Chamber of Lords
would rescind Rukh's judgment," Satha began. "We never expected
for it to happen, but Fate has decided to grant us her favor." She
smiled wryly. "Which leaves us with a conundrum."

Durmer cleared his throat, and for a wonder he was grinning
broadly. "They—" he gestured to Satha and Dar'El "—never
planned what to do if the Chamber voted in favor of our petition.
For Rukh's sake, for his honor basically, all they cared about was
getting the judgment overturned. Now that it has, they have to figure
out what to do next."

Farn knew what was coming. Dar'El and Satha had already
discussed it with him once before. "I'm the only one who knows
Stronghold's location," he said.

"You would have to go back," Satha confirmed, hesitating a

moment later. "I hate to ask this of you given how recently you returned home, but we need to get word to Rukh as soon as possible and let him know what's transpired."

"Take some time to think it over," Dar'El urged. "Discuss it with your family. This is your decision."

Farn already knew his answer. It was the same as the one he had given the last time he'd been asked. "Of course I'll go," he replied. "You know I'm not going to change my mind on something so important."

Satha stood and drew Farn into a startled embrace. "You have no idea how grateful I am," she said, her eyes tearing.

"I love him, too," Farn said, uncomfortable with Satha's appreciation. "How could I do anything less?"

"There are several other details we need to discuss," Dar'El said. "First, I have proposed the funding of a Trial to Stronghold. Based on what you've told us, it seems we have many items the OutCastes might find useful, and their new firefly lamp designs could prove very valuable to us as well. Second, Jaresh wishes to go with you; and we've given him our blessing. He's yours if you wish."

"I thought the commander of a Trial had full discretion with regard to the compliment," Farn said.

"He does," Dar'El said. "Which leads me to the third item. You will be the one to lead the Trial." He smiled. "Congratulations, Lieutenant. Get used to coming to the House Seat for many meetings in the upcoming weeks. We have a lot to planning to complete. I want to see this Trial ready to depart in a month's time."

———◆———

Dar'El was worn to the nub. For the past three weeks, he had worked from well before sunup to hours after sundown, trying to make sure the caravan to Stronghold was properly provisioned. This would be a Trial unlike any other in Ashoka's history: the first caravan sent to a new city and with no previously established routes or landmarks to follow. Such an expedition hadn't been attempted since the Days of Desolation, and putting it together had required new ways of thinking. The warriors would need food and equipment to take them through everything from a hot spring day to a snowfall in the mountain passes. And since the normal caravan wagons couldn't make it through the Privations, new, smaller versions had to be designed. In the end, though, much of the required gear would still have to be hauled on horses, mules, and donkeys, a far costlier means to haul freight than for other Trials.

The cost of such an approach was staggering. It might have even proven ruinous, except a number of Houses had stepped up and offered to help bear the expenses. Of course, they wanted something in return; likely a discount on whatever items Stronghold was willing to trade, especially any materials and goods that could find a market in Ashoka or elsewhere. It was a grand bargain as far as Dar'El was concerned. House Shektan wouldn't lose money on the Trial, and Rukh would come home.

Right now, however, all those issues were far from his mind. Even the ongoing meeting of the Society of Rajan couldn't hold his attention. He'd barely even registered the many hearty congratulations for his victory in the Chamber or the actual proceedings themselves. All of their warm wishes somehow seemed unimportant. Thankfully, the meeting was soon to adjourn. Thrivel Nonel, the Sentya Master, had a few final words to say before it was over.

And then Dar'El could confront Ular Sathin.

Ular Sathin whose fingertips were faintly stained the orange-brown color of henna.

Dar'El had found the Sil Lor Kum.

The knowledge should have filled him with great satisfaction, but all it did was bring him a churning stomach, one full of upset, betrayal, and heartache. Ular Sathin? How could he? He and Dar'El had been friends for years. Anger and anguish coursed in equal measure through Dar'El as he stared across the table at the Muran Master. The older man had his hand in front of his mouth as he and Anian Elim, the Journeyman Duriah, chuckled over a private joke.

The meeting concluded, and Dar'El made his way toward Ular.

"May I have a word in private?" he asked the Muran Master.

"Of course," Ular said with a friendly smile. A moment later, upon taking in Dar'El's forbidding countenance, his smile faded. "What's happened?" he asked.

"In private," Dar'El said. He glanced meaningfully at the other Rajans.

Ular nodded understanding. "Ah. For my ears only." His expression turned more serious. "You've learned something about one of our fellow Rajans."

Dar'El nodded, unable to say anything more. He was too heartbroken over what he had to do, and a part of him still prayed that there was a more innocuous reason for Ular's stained fingers. In fact, Dar'El had always hoped the traitorous Rajan would turn out to be an Apprentice, someone with whom he didn't have decades of friendship.

The Hall finally emptied and he and Ular were alone. It was time.

He turned to the Muran Master. "The fingertips on your right hand have an unusual color," he noted.

Ular glanced at his hand and chuckled. "You should have seen them before," he said. "I was handling henna and...." He shrugged. "I was clumsy and got some on me. It only started fading a few days ago." He gave a puzzled smile. "Why do you ask?"

It was all smoothly said, a reasonable explanation. It could have happened just as Ular claimed.

But it was a lie. Dar'El knew it.

While he had been speaking, Ular had darted a glance at the closed entrance to the Hall. And right now, though he stared at Dar'El with wide, guileless eyes, a bead of perspiration tracked its way down his forehead. He was nervous.

Dar'El didn't reply. He merely stared flat-eyed at his one-time friend.

Ular licked his lips. "Surely you didn't ask for this private meeting in order to discuss henna," he said, darting another glance at the closed door.

"I know who you are," Dar'El said.

More sweat broke out on Ular's forehead. "What do you mean? Of course you know who I am." His smile became uneasy. "We've known each other for years."

"But until an hour ago, I didn't know you were Sil Lor Kum."

The accusation produced a deathly silence, one eventually broken by a shaky laugh from Ular. "Is this a jest?" he asked. "If so, it's in unbelievably poor taste." He made to stand. "I think I've wasted enough time on your sick humor. Now, if you'll excuse me, I have an important—"

Dar'El snarled. He conducted *Jivatma* and grabbed the Muran Master by the collar, lifting him from his chair and slamming him onto the table.

Ular screamed out in terror. "Don't kill me," he choked out. "I know many things."

Dar'El's hold tightened. He wanted to snap the other man's neck. It would be so easy, and Ular deserved it. But it wouldn't be right. With a cry of disgust, he threw Ular aside. The man didn't deserve an easy death. "I know you know 'things'," Dar'El said. "And you will tell me all of these 'things', especially the name of the Withering Knife murderer."

"He's an older Kumma," Ular blubbered. "A man of wealth. Probably an 'El."

"All this I already know," Dar'El hissed. "Give me his name, or the Isle of the Crows will be your final bed."

"I don't know his name," Ular wailed. He shrieked when Dar'El grabbed him again. "He's the SuDin. Our leader. I've never learned his name," the Muran babbled. "But I know the names of all the other MalDins. I know them all. You'll be able to clear out the Sil Lor Kum, destroy it entirely. All I ask in return is sanctuary."

"You think you should be allowed to live after what you've done?" Dar'El snarled. "It will not happen."

"It has to happen, or you'll learn nothing."

"Or maybe I should break your fingers. One at a time," Dar'El threatened. "We'll see how well you maintain your silence then."

Ular blanched.

Dar'El was equally appalled by his words. What was he saying? Threatening torture? Even someone as degenerate as Ular didn't deserve a fate so terrible. But then again, what about the promised death to which the man would be subjected? Was it not a form of torture? Dar'El growled in frustration. Now wasn't the time for philosophical meanderings.

Ular used Dar'El's momentary distraction to regain a measure of his courage. "You won't do that. I know you too well. You're a man of conviction and honor. Morality is bred into your bones and blood." He swallowed heavily. "You *will* meet my demands, or you will learn nothing."

Dar'El released his grip. "It is not my place to make such a promise. Only the Magisterium can do what you want."

"Then make them see reason!" Ular pleaded.

"If the Magisterium learns your name, they will gut you. You'll be clutching your entrails while the crows peck out your eyes," Dar'El said. "On the other hand, I can give you an easy death."

"An easy death is still a death," Ular said. "I want to live!" He lifted his chin defiantly. "If you tell the Magisterium who I am, my life may end in torment, but it won't help you learn what you want to know."

Dar'El gazed upon the old man in sadness and revulsion. Had there ever been any honor or decency to Ular Sathin? Had it all been a sham? How could someone smile and share friendship with others, all the while lying to them and betraying everything they held dear? "Or I can tell the Magisterium your name, and they can make you the same promise I offer."

"I won't be taken by them," Ular vowed. "You have five hours to save my life. Otherwise, I'll take my secrets to the pyre."

Dar'El moved to seize him. The old man couldn't kill himself if he was tied up.

Ular held up a forestalling hand. "I have a means to end my life even in your custody. Let me walk out of here, and you can go about saving me. Then I'll talk."

Dar'El growled. "Five hours then."

———◆———

There were times when Hal'El was certain he had been marked for glory. How else to explain everything he had accomplished? He was the finest warrior of his generation and had survived more Trials than any man since Hume. From there, he had gone on to become the ruling 'El of one of the oldest, most powerful Houses in Ashoka. And during all this, he'd managed to keep secret his membership in the Sil Lor Kum, even rising to leadership of that hated organization. Then had come the unsought boon of the Withering Knife. With the black blade in his hands, Hal'El had dared hope he now possessed the means by which he could save Ashoka, and defeat Suwraith

Herself. The murders he'd committed with the Knife, the rush of stolen *Jivatma*, it had filled with him heady assuredness. He was more powerful than he had ever been when young and all his injuries, including the damaged knee, had all been miraculously Healed. Devesh, or some being of power, *must* have marked Hal'El for greatness and glory.

But then had arisen the voices in his head, whispering hatred and dire punishment. Aqua Oilhue, Felt Barnel, and Van Jinnu; the names of those he'd murdered; victims who had refused to remain dead. Now, they lingered in his mind like phantasms of revenge; and all his certainty was gone like sandcastles before the tide. His future, like that of Ashoka itself, was uncertain. Would the Sorrow Bringer come against the city this summer as She had vowed? If so, there was nothing Hal'El could do to stop Her. It seemed the future was doomed. They were all going to die.

Once he had thought using the Knife would give him strength enough to challenge Suwraith, but he knew better now. The Knife granted power, but the cost was the wielder's sanity. It wasn't a price Hal'El was willing to pay. He wondered if Suwraith might have once been Human. Had She been faced with a choice similar to his: destruction of all She had loved versus Her sanity? Perhaps She had used the Knife and it had given Her unstoppable power even as it drove Her mad.

With thoughts of loss and death on his mind, he almost didn't recognize Ular Sathin when the old man brushed by him. The Muran was a half a dozen steps past, when Hal'El realized who he was. He had looked upset, his face puffy and his eyes red, as though he'd been crying.

Curious, Hal'El turned to follow. He'd long ago learned to trust his instincts when it came to these type of matters. Something was wrong with Ular, and if so, it might affect the Sil Lor Kum, and through it, Hal'El and Varesea.

Ular walked swiftly back to his home, a row house in Hart's Stand with quiet Rahails living on all sides of his own. Foot traffic dwindled, and Hal'El took the opportunity to duck into a nearby alley and Blend. He'd somehow tortured the knowledge from Van Jinnu and Felt Barnel. He still wasn't sure how he had done so, nor was he particularly proud of his actions, but in the end he wasn't ashamed. If those he'd murdered insisted on staying with him, the least they could be was be useful.

He stepped back onto the street, but by then Ular had already entered his home. All the curtains were drawn, but a light leaked out from around one of them. At least Ular wasn't huddled in total darkness. Just then, the curtain was pulled back a fraction, and Hal'El saw Ular's frightened face peer out into the street.

Even more curious.

Hal'El made his way to the rear of the home. He tested a door half-hidden beneath a clematis-covered pergola. It was unlocked. Hal'El smiled. Ular was spooked, and in his panic, the old fool must have overlooked it. Hal'El eased open the door and stepped inside Ular's home.

He'd never been here before, and he took a moment to get his bearings. He was in a narrow, galley style kitchen that was as neat and tidy as a penitent's mind. A door on the far wall led further into the house, and the room it led to was obviously meant for dining. A rectangular table, four chairs, and white walls were the entirety of the furnishings within it.

It seemed Ular's house was a reflection of his passionless nature.

Movement and sound came from further inside, and Hal'El crept toward it. The next room was a sitting area with a couch, coffee table, and an unlit hearth. A narrow staircase to the side of the front entry led upstairs, and a single firefly lantern on the mantle provided the light.

Ular paced before the fireplace. He was sweating profusely. It was unlike the old man who was known for his cold dispassion.

Hal'El stepped forward. "You seem nervous," he said.

Ular shrieked and darted his gaze about. "Who's there?" he said in a tremulous voice.

"The SuDin," Hal'El said, maintaining his Blend, though it was growing taxing. "Why do you appear so frightened?"

"Who wouldn't be startled when a voice from nowhere suddenly speaks to them?" Ular said. He drew himself up, trying to regain his composure. "Why don't you show yourself?"

Hal'El chuckled. "I think it best if you don't know who I am," he replied. "Although...." He withdrew into the dining room and donned a handkerchief over the lower half of his face. He released the Blend and stepped back into the sitting area. "Better?"

Ular nodded.

"Good. Now you can tell me why you appear as frightened as a gazelle before a Shylow," Hal'El said. "Or is my presence truly so fearsome?"

Ular glanced at the door.

"You're expecting someone?" Hal'El asked. Ular shot another glance. "Or you're wondering if you can get out of this house before I stop you." Ular startled and a look of nervousness took hold over his face. "I've done nothing wrong," Ular said, the panic evident in his voice.

Hal'El knew it was a lie, but the question was, what was the old Muran hiding? He thought about it as he studied Ular. He rocked back when the answer came to him. Ular must have betrayed the Sil Lor Kum. He'd been a member of the organization for decades, and he'd sold them out. It was the only thing that made sense. The only remaining questions were what Ular had been paid for his treachery? And who had he spoken to? Hal'El withdrew the Withering Knife, letting the old man see it. "Who else knows about you?" he demanded.

Ular's eyes grew huge, and he swallowed convulsively. "Kill me and you learn nothing," he vowed.

Ular's death was assured, but not until Hal'El knew who the Muran had been talking to. He had to know. His life and Varesea's might depend on what he learned. "I won't kill you," he said with a chill smile. "I'll cut you. Only once, and you'll feel your *Jivatma* rip apart. You'll feel your soul shred. I can't imagine anything more painful." He took a step forward. "Tell me who you've spoken to!"

Ular darted to the mantle. On it was a clear glass of water. He upended it, pouring the liquid down his throat.

Hal'El cursed, realizing too late what the old man intended. He tore the glass away, but it was already over. Ular frothed at the mouth. His eyes bulged and blood poured from his nose. He would be dead in minutes.

Ular's legs gave way and Hal'El caught him before he fell. "Who did you speak to?" he demanded, shaking the old man in his urgency.

Ular clutched Hal'El's handkerchief and pulled it down. The old Muran smiled at the last. "I always thought it was you, Hal'El Wrestiva."

Despite hurrying as best he could, it turned out Rector was still the last one to arrive for the meeting *he* had requested. Jaresh, Bree, and Mira were already there, waiting at a square table. They spoke quietly amongst themselves, but their conversation ceased when they saw him. Jaresh and Bree gave him wary looks, as if he was an unpredictable dog who might lunge and bite at any moment, while Mira shrugged as if to say it was his own fault for the others' hostility.

Rector mentally sighed.

It was to be expected given what he'd done to them. What he'd done to Rukh. He deserved every ounce of Jaresh and Bree's distrust, even their hatred if it came to it. He just hoped there would come a time when he could make restitution for his offenses and earn their forgiveness. Perhaps it could begin now that Rukh was no longer considered Unworthy. In just a few days, Farn Arnicep would lead the very first Trial to Stronghold. Jaresh was supposed to go with him, too, and if everything went well, they would bring Rukh home. He doubted it would change anything between himself and Dar'El's family, but stranger things had happened.

Rector shook off his thoughts and took the remaining seat at the table. He looked around at the looming walls of bookshelves on all four sides, and shifted uncomfortably. The Cellar, with its poor lighting and claustrophobic spaces, was reminiscent of a dank, dark cave. Rector felt hemmed in, and he wondered how Jaresh and Mira had tolerated the months they'd spent down here during their search for clues about the Withering Knife.

Bree cleared her throat and gave him a pointed look.

Rector took the hint. "Sorry to keep you waiting," he said. "I was finishing up some paperwork, and the time got away from me."

"Why don't you just tell us what you learned?" Mira suggested.

"I've discovered some information which I think might aid our cause," he said. "I was able to make some headway on whoever owns the warehouse I oversee. The bookkeeping made it nearly impossible, but I *think* I might be able to figure it out." He flashed a hesitant smile. "Deciphering accounts and ledgers is not my strong suit, but from what I've ascertained, ownership of the warehouse is held jointly by a company titled Quality Building Divisions and an unnamed silent partner."

"Who's the silent partner?" Bree asked.

"It might be a Rahail," Rector replied. "There was a note inside one of the books I found, and it referred to 'our dear Rahail partner'."

"It's not much to go on," Jaresh mused.

"Which is why I brought the actual ledgers with me," Rector said. "There's something unusual about them. Mira mentioned it I think."

Jaresh nodded. "Letters bolded or capitalized when they need not be."

"I tried applying the code you used on that journal you found, the one from the caravan master who transported the Withering Knife to Rock." He chewed a lip. "It didn't work, so I was hoping you could take a look at them." He passed over a set of bound papers.

Jaresh took the ledgers without comment and flipped through the pages. "How soon do you need these back?" he asked.

"Tonight," Rector replied. "The accountants throw a fuss whenever they see me thumbing through their works," he said. "I'd hate to see their reaction if they discover these books are missing."

Bree looked at him in surprise. "You think the accountants are Sil Lor Kum?" she asked. "Every one of them?"

Rector shook his head. "No. Just someone to whom they answer. *That* person would be of the Sil Lor Kum."

"And you have no idea who it might be?" Mira asked.

Rector gave her a wry expression. "What do you suppose would happen if I did know?"

Mira chuckled. "Probably the same as what happened to the Rahail who attacked Bree and Jaresh."

Bree gave Mira a sour look before turning to Rector. "We never thanked you properly for your help," she said.

Jaresh glanced up from the ledger. "Yes. We owe you a certain debt for what you've done," he said.

"You're welcome," Rector said politely, although the double meaning in Bree and Jaresh's statements was readily evident.

"It *is* a code," Jaresh announced. He didn't look up from the

446

ledger, and his hand groped across the table, seemingly searching for something.

Without comment or having to ask what he needed, Mira passed him a pencil and a clean sheet of paper.

Jaresh nodded his 'thanks', and the paper was soon filled with a trail of letters.

As he worked, Bree and Mira spoke softly of Farn's impending departure while Rector sat ignored.

It was to be expected. The other three here were Shektans, while Rector was nominally a Wrestiva. He was the outsider amongst the four of them, the one who didn't belong. And with the way his life had shaken out, it seemed like there was nowhere he *did* belong. He was a spy, which was the same as a liar and a thief. As a result, Rector found it impossible to join in the laughter and fellowship of his family and friends given how much he detested who he had become.

Choices had consequences, and Rector had made a rather spectacularly poor one many months ago. He should have remained loyal to Dar'El rather than spill everything he knew to House Wrestiva. He had thought he was maintaining the honor of his Caste by exposing Rukh's Talents, but it wasn't the case. He had done as he had because of his arrogant pride.

Now Rector had to work hard in order to keep those same mistakes from defining who he was or what he might become. If he could make amends for what he'd done, Dar'El's heart might soften, especially once Rukh returned. Perhaps then, Rector would be allowed to join a House of his own choosing, and this time, offer it his full loyalty. So much of it was out of his control, and Rector could only do whatever tasks he was assigned to the best of his ability. And while he hated the role he had to play, at least his work on behalf of House Shektan had proven useful.

Rector watched as Jaresh set aside the ledger and focused on the letters he had transcribed. The Sentya's lips moved silently as his brow furrowed in concentration. Sooner than Rector would have imagined possible, he grinned.

"Whoever devised this must not have had much knowledge of codes," Jaresh said. "It's a simple substitution cipher: one letter corresponds to another."

Rector had always known Jaresh was clever, but with this, his estimation of the man rose once more. Jaresh had managed to break the code in less time than it would have taken Rector to read the morning broadsheet.

"The journal hides a conversation between two people," Jaresh continued. "I think one of them is a woman. Her letters are more curved, and she's left-handed."

"Do they say anything important?" Bree asked, leaning forward with an intense, almost lupine expression on her face.

Jaresh grinned. "Nothing except businesses and buildings where these two have dealings. Not all of it is clear-cut, but with time, we should be able to learn who they are."

"We'll have them gutted before the end of the month," Mira said with a cold, deadly smile.

Her attitude was so different from how she usually behaved. Mira could be proud and dismissive when she was made truly angry, but usually she was just matter-of-fact and businesslike. Rector had never seen her display this predatory side before.

Jaresh appeared just as ready for blood. "When we find out who they are, we should,—"

"Not you," Bree interrupted. "You're leaving for Stronghold in a few days."

Jaresh grimaced. "I so wanted to be there when we brought them to justice," he said. "I wanted to see them pay for their crimes."

Rector sympathized with Jaresh's sentiments. He felt the same way. He wouldn't shed a single tear when every member of the Sil Lor Kum was staked out on the Isle of the Crow. In fact, it would be a glad day for everyone involved.

A clock struck the time, and Rector realized he had to go. "I need to get the ledgers back to the warehouse," he said, rising to leave.

⎯⎯⎯•⎯⎯⎯

Bree was the next to depart, which left Mira and Jaresh alone in an uncomfortable silence. The Cellar had never seemed so dark or confining. Jaresh flicked her a sidelong glance, but Mira had her gaze fixed toward the exit. She appeared to be doing her best to avert her eyes from him.

Jaresh realized this might be the last time he saw her. A Trial was always dangerous, especially one that had never before been attempted. There was a real chance he might die, either on the way to Stronghold or on the journey back. If so, this could be the last time he would have to speak with Mira. The realization struck him with a bittersweet longing. His feelings for her might have dulled over the past half-year, but they'd never entirely subsided, and he doubted they ever would.

There was still so much he wanted to say to her, but he wasn't certain if he should. Their kiss might have been nothing more than a momentary loss of judgment on her part, an action she regretted the instant it had occurred. However, he also found he didn't entirely care. Some words had to be spoken, some regrets voiced.

"Jessira once offered to take me with her to Stronghold," Jaresh began. Mira turned to him, a look of mild interest in her eyes. "She knew how I felt about—"

"Don't," Mira interrupted, her eyes closed as if in pain. "Whatever we had was something that should have never happened. It was a mistake we both made."

Her words cut, but Jaresh couldn't fault her for thinking back on their relationship in any other way, especially since he felt the same way. "Yes it was," he agreed softly.

She left off her examination of the exit. "You agree, don't you? *We* could never have been anything other than a disaster for both our families."

"Jessira offered to take you with us as well."

Mira inhaled sharply. A fleeting look of shock stole across her face before her features settled into lines of impassiveness. "You should have told me sooner," she reproached. "As in before Jessira left."

"What would you have done?" Jaresh asked.

"What you didn't. I would have told you of Jessira's offer. We could have chosen our fate together."

Jaresh felt his heart wilting. He'd been too cowardly to allow Mira to make her own decision, and his fear had cost them both. "If I *had* spoken up, would you have gone to Stronghold with me? Even though everyone we love is here?"

Mira didn't say anything. She stared at him, and her hand twitched. Indecision clouded her eyes. She wavered but eventually, she reached for Jaresh's hand. Her touch had once sent a line of fiery longing racing up Jaresh's arm and into his spine. It still did, but now the fire was tame, a memory of heat rather than the burning itself.

A sad acceptance entered Mira's eyes, and she let go of his hand. "We'll never know," she said as she stood to leave.

CHAPTER TWENTY-NINE
RUN THROUGH THE HILLS

Furious reason offers no solution for the simplest of truths:
Death is an irrational Mistress.

~ *The Warrior and the Servant (author unknown)*

essira went back to the pond and washed off the leaves and twigs she'd collected as a result of her brief tussle with Rukh. She felt bad for him—she knew he was eaten up with remorse for what he had done—but she was also annoyed by his actions. Why wouldn't he have just waited for her before reading *The Book of First Movement*? None of this would have happened if he had. They could have gone slowly. He could have slowly read *The Book of First Movement* and learned about—

She inhaled sharply as she realized the enormity of what Rukh had accomplished. Rukh had seen the memories and thoughts of the First Father. Linder Val Maharj. Devesh save them. Once again, almost by accident, Rukh had managed an unfathomable feat. How could one man accomplish so much?

Jessira shook her head in disbelief.

Of course, none of it changed Rukh's underlying stupidity. He was still an idiot, but he was an idiot Devesh seemed to have marked

451

either for greatness or an early death.

The light from the campfire suddenly blinked out.

Now what? She glanced back at their site.

Rukh stood at the edge of the pond. "Get out of the water. Hurry!" he urged. He looked terrified. She wondered for a moment what had him so frightened, but his next words answered her unspoken question. "Suwraith. She's coming." He pointed to the sky where in the distance a madly swirling wall of clouds flew against the winds. The Queen. She crisscrossed the heavens, almost as though She was searching for something. Nevertheless, She would be here soon.

"Fragging unholy hells!" Jessira splashed out of the pond, dried herself off as best she could and got into her clothes in a flash. By the time she was finished, Rukh already had their provisions and bags stowed away on the packhorse.

"We need to get out of here," he said.

"You think it has anything to do with *The Book?*"

Rukh shrugged. "Who cares? We need to go."

"Blend as hard as you can," Jessira said. "Like you've never done before." She took the lead, leading them into the forest, taking a deer trail they'd used to find the pond.

"That hill," Rukh said, pointing to a nearby tor, about a half-mile away. "I want something big to hide behind when the Queen arrives."

Jessira nodded and led them toward the rise as fast as she dared. She had to be careful, though. Footing could be treacherous in the forest's inky blackness. Rukh ran silently on her heels, while the packhorse rumbled along, whoofing with each stride. Its hooves sounded like thunderclaps. Too loud. They needed silence. Jessira reached for Rukh and Linked her Blend with his. For a moment, the world seemed to stretch outward, as if viewed through a concave mirror before snapping back into focus.

Jessira stumbled. She'd never experienced that before while Linking. She risked a look back, but Rukh seemed just as confused as she. He shook his head in answer to her unspoken question.

She grimaced. Whatever had just happened, they'd have to figure it out later, once they were safe.

Rolling toward them from high up in the skies was a rumble of thunder echoing amongst the shallow valleys and rises. It became a hurricane scream of tortured wind with lightning flashing. The ground shook. The Sorrow Bringer was coming.

Jessira picked up speed. The deer track led up the face of the hill. Jessira took a deep breath and sprinted for the top. Rukh was right behind her. He crested the rise just in time. They huddled behind a nearby shelf of rock, hidden by the mass of the low rise. The horse neighed in fear. He had sense enough to understand when mortal danger approached.

Jessira looked up and swallowed back a lump of fear.

Descending from the sky like an avalanche was a wall of cloud, thunder, and coruscating lightning. It was going to be just like on the Hunters Flats when Suwraith had flattened Li-Dirge and his entire command.

"Get down!" Jessira shouted, pressing Rukh against the ground. "Keep your eyes closed!"

They missed what happened next, but a booming quake almost knocked them off their perch. The horse screamed in terror, but maintained his footing. The roaring rumble ground on and on and on.

Jessira opened her eyes.

The Queen had hit the ground with the force of a falling mountain. Roaring upward like an inverted tornado, a spume of water and dirt launched into the air, rising high and forming the shape of a mushroom. It hung suspended for endless minutes before collapsing down on itself, captured in the mad swirl of the Queen's winds and clouds. Mud splattered in all directions, and flattened trees lay like matchsticks for hundreds of yards around. Suwraith hovered over the area before hurling Herself down once more. Jessira ducked her head low. The Sorrow Bringer hammered the land once again, and when She struck, it was with the sound of a thousand anvils ringing. Over and over again, She rose and crashed, rose and crashed, like an unending tide.

Finally, there came a lull when the hellish din of Her hurricane wind and rage was gone.

The Sorrow Bringer had left, or at least Jessira hoped so. She couldn't tell for sure. The world was a soupy fog of dust and debris. The stars themselves were blacked out and the moon lay hidden behind a cloud of dirt. Jessira could hardly see her hand in front of her face. A torrential, muddy rain fell upon them.

Jessira wrapped a protective cloth over her nose and mouth. She was happy to see Rukh do the same for both himself and the packhorse.

"We have to get clear of this dirt-cloud," Rukh said with a cough.

"In a moment," Jessira said, trying to get her emotions under control. She held in a retch as she trembled, a mix of adrenaline and fear as her heart raced as if she'd run ten miles with a full rucksack. Jessira reached for Rukh's hand, clutching it. She needed the warmth of Human contact after what they had just witnessed. Rukh held her hand, gripping it firmly and seeming to need to feel another person's touch as much as she. After a few moments, her breathing steadied, and she nodded. "I'm ready."

Rukh gave her hand a final, reassuring squeeze before he climbed to his feet, helping her rise as well. "Let's go."

They trudged through a mile wide fog of dust, eventually reaching a point where the air grew clean enough to breathe without the filter of a rag over their mouths and noses. By then, the rumbling sound of a mountain of mud raining to the ground had grown distant, but it wasn't forgotten.

——◆◆——

With the coming of dawn, Rukh levered himself to his feet and yawned. Jessira threw off the blanket she'd wrapped around herself and stood as well. She looked as tired as Rukh felt. After the Sorrow Bringer's wrath, neither of them had been able to get much rest. They had stayed up all night, holding to a hard, tight Blend in case the Queen returned.

Rukh looked back the way they'd come where a plume of dust and debris still hung in the air from last night's assault. How had the Sorrow Bringer found them? They'd been Blended. And yet, She'd honed in on their position as if following a compass point.

Jessira spoke. "I think it was *The Book*," she said, answering his unvoiced question as she so often could. "The Chims say the Queen is Daughter to the First Father. Maybe She can sense Her Father's presence. Maybe when you read *The Book of First Movement* and experienced His memories, She could somehow feel a part of Him re-enter the world."

Rukh considered her words as he stared back in the direction from which they'd come. Jessira's explanation made sense. "I guess neither of us should ever open it again," he said.

"Is it even safe to keep?"

Rukh was wondering that exact same question. It might be the safest course to throw it aside, but it wasn't the one he wanted to follow. Rukh didn't want to give up *The Book*, not after working so hard to obtain it. Just as importantly, *The Book* had been lost to Humanity for three hundred years, and if it held the final thoughts of the First Father, it had to be important. They had to find a way to hold onto it.

"For now, I think we should keep it," Rukh replied. "If the Queen found us through it, then She would have chased after us when we left the pond. The fact She didn't suggests She can't track *The Book* unless it's being read."

"I hope you're right," Jessira said, worry tingeing her voice.

Rukh hoped he was right, too.

"We need to get home as fast as possible," Jessira said a moment later.

"We should Blend hard all the way there," he replied.

Jessira nodded. "One of us will have to maintain focus at all times. Even when we're camped for the night"

Rukh blew out an exhalation. "It'll be hard work."

"We've done harder," she said, smiling wanly a moment later. "Our timing certainly is terrible. Looks like we'll have to wait until we reach the city."

"Wait for what?" Rukh asked. A moment later, the answer came to him. "Oh." He sighed in disappointment.

Jessira laughed. "Can you wait?"

"I don't really have a choice, do I?" he asked, smiling half-heartedly. The smile left him. For weeks now, he had wanted to ask Jessira a question. Events had conspired against him, and there had never been a time to bring it up. But after last night, the question had taken on greater urgency. Jessira held his heart in her hands. She could lift him to the clouds if she said 'yes', but how awful if she said 'no.' He had to know one way or the other. "What are we to one another?" Rukh asked, his heart suddenly pounding.

Jessira sobered, sensing the serious nature of his question. "What do you want us to be?" she asked, a fearful, yet hopeful expression on her face.

Jessira deserved wine, music, romantic poetry, and a serenade but Rukh didn't have any of that. All he had was the love in his soul. Nevertheless, he had to do this as properly as possible, as a Kumma should. She stared into his eyes as he took both her hands in his. He kissed her palms and knelt before. He touched her feet. Jessira trembled, and he looked up. "There are many truths in this world, Jessira Viola Grey, but for me, the greatest is this: my love for you. I love you with everything I know. Will you marry me?"

He might have said more, but Jessira pulled him to his feet and kissed him, silencing him. He kissed her back, holding her tight in the circle of his arms.

"Yes," Jessira said with a breathless laugh. "Yes. Now and forever." Her face was wet with tears.

Rukh came to an unexpected stop. He held up a hand for silence and motioned ahead. Jessira read his gestures. Chimeras up the trail. Heading toward them. Three nests of Ur-Fels and a Bael.

Jessira's heart thumped. She had long since learned to trust his more acute senses. In the two weeks since Suwraith had annihilated the area around which she and Rukh had been camping, they'd come across a number of Chims scouting the western foothills of the Privation Mountains. Another group of them approached.

Jessira carefully made her way off the narrow trail they were following. The horse plodded behind her. There was no help for the gelding's heavy steps. Meanwhile, Rukh had already disappeared. Jessira figured he had probably backtracked, wiping out their trail as best he could.

Jessira waited for him to return even as her ears strained for the harsh barking of the Ur-Fels. She sensed movement to the right. With it came the feel of a Blend.

Rukh.

She exhaled in relief and Linked with him. He popped into view.

"We should keep moving," she said the moment he was close enough to hear her whisper. Blended hard as they were, there was little chance their words would carry, but there was no need to take unnecessary risks.

Rukh nodded, and they glanced about, searching their surroundings for a path leading away from the Chims.

They stood along the floor of a deep gully. A stream, heavy with the morning's rain, raced south, carrying a flotsam of wet leaves and small branches. Basalt cliffs with green and orange streaks loomed in sharp relief, merging with the heavy presence of the nearby Privations. The animal track they had been following had seemed like the easiest path up and out of here, but apparently, it was also the easiest way down. They needed another way out of the gap.

A barking sound came to them. An Ur-Fel. Another bark. More. All of them coming from the animal track. The Chims seemed to be gathering, calling loudly as if they had discovered something.

Their trail maybe?

Jessira didn't bother cursing. She uncased her bow, set a string to it, and readied an arrow. Rukh's hands glowed, and a green-hued bubble surrounded him. A Shield.

"It is an unshod horse," a booming bass voice said. Given the depth and clarity of the speech, it had to be the Bael in charge of the nests. "Nothing to it. Leave it be." A moment later. "A boot print you say?" The Bael sounded excited. "There's another. Look."

Jessira and Rukh held still. A fight was best avoided, and perhaps these nests would still somehow overlook them.

The Bael continued. "They likely heard us and cut through the forest to escape our righteous wrath," he said, his voice filled with surety. Jessira tensed, waiting for the moment when flight or fight would become inevitable. "See the scuff marks on the roots of that oak over there. They're making their way south even as we speak. Go! I'll be with you in a moment."

Upon the Bael's shouted order, the Ur-Fels barked with excitement and took off in pursuit of their quarry—in the direction opposite of where Jessira and Rukh stood. They shared wondering looks at their good fortune.

A second later, Jessira tensed.

A crunching sound came from where the Chims had been clustered. A Bael stepped through the clinging branches of a tall lilac bush. He was big, even for one of his kind. White feathers drooped from his horns, dripping wetness. A young commander of the Fan Lor Kum. Despite the cold of the mountain spring, the Bael wore nothing more than a breechcloth and a leather harness. His chained whip was coiled at his hip, and his trident was carelessly held as he seemed to search around.

Jessira swallowed. The Baels claimed to be friends of Humanity, and maybe they were. Li-Choke certainly was, but what about the rest of them? How could they really trust that every Bael believed as Choke did? She readied her bow.

"If you're still here, Li-Choke sends his regards," the Bael said, speaking softly. "I don't have much time. Mother has us hunting for—" he snorted in derision "—a man named Linder and a woman named Cienna. The First Father and the First Mother. Choke thinks She might mean the two of you. We've left a gap in our lines. Make your way north out of this ravine and across the valley on the other side of the cliffs, then head due east. After that, the way is clear. Good luck brothers." With that the Bael disappeared back into the foliage. He raised a ruckus as he burst through the heavy brush, moving south of their position.

"I think that's more than enough excitement for one day," Rukh murmured.

"I'm surprised you didn't want to try and take them all by yourself?" Jessira teased, speaking softly.

"I might have," Rukh said with a grin, "but you'd have just

459

gotten mad at me for stealing all the glory."

Jessira smiled and punched him gently on the arm. "If you *had* tried to fight them alone, I might have killed you just for being stupid."

"Then lucky for me I was wise enough not to go after them."

"You're learning," Jessira said. "Now, let's look for a way out of here."

She scanned north. The trees and undergrowth quickly thinned as the hills soared upward, exposing the heavy, black rock. There appeared to be a thready trail in that direction. The horse might have trouble with it, though.

Jessira pointed out her find. "Look."

Rukh followed the line of her finger and nodded. "Good eyes," he said. His gaze flickered over her. "amongst other things."

She made sure he saw her eye roll.

⚬ ● ⚬

Aia had a hold of Rukh's scent, and this time, she would *not* release it. Well, not exactly his scent. It was more a flavor of his mind. She liked the aroma of his thoughts, and she almost shivered with excitement at the notion that she would soon experience them again.

Aia only wished she was traveling alone to meet her Human, but it wasn't to be. After hearing her tales all winter long about the wonders of Rukh's fingers and hands, several of her younger brothers had decided to accompany her north. Younger brothers were pests at the best of times, but these two could teach a gnat how to be annoying. Shon and Thrum. Idiots. However, since they wished to learn the truth about her tales for themselves—and truth in storytelling was a key facet in the lives the Kesarins—Aia couldn't turn them away.

But if they thought she would share her Human with them, they had better be prepared for bloody noses.

Do not touch anything, Aia warned her brothers as they entered the firelight. *Rukh is very sentimental about his things and creatures. Follow me into the camp and be calm. No growls or snarls or your noses will be bled.*

Shon, a tawny, lean Kesarin, the youngest amongst the three of them, thought himself clever. He yawned.

Aia growled at the disrespect. She unsheathed her claws and Shon's tail curled between his hind legs. His ears drooped.

Better.

Thrum, a rare russet Kesarin, was thicker than Shon and taller. He was only two seasons younger than Aia and still filling out. With his build and intelligence, Nanna thought he might one day challenge for leadership of the Hungrove. That is, if he ever learned wisdom. The fool sat there cross-eyed, staring at a butterfly that had alit on his nose.

Aia watched for a moment before turning aside with a shake of her head. She paid them no more attention. She had more important things to attend to. Such as Rukh. She wanted her Human back.

She stepped into the small clearing where he and his not-mate had stopped for the night. She nervously skirted the fire before stopping before him. She sat down, tail demurely curled before her feet and waited for him to approach.

He grinned, displaying his unfortunate flat teeth. They looked like they belonged in the mouth of a wildebeest. *Aia,* he called out, happiness in his voice. *What are you doing here?*

I missed the flavor of your thoughts.

I missed you, too, he said, *but how did you find me?*

I listened, Aia said with a cock of her head. *How else?* Sometimes her Human could be so obtuse, overlooking that which was obvious.

My mind?

Of course. Aia glanced at the female, who was staring at them

461

with a sense of wonderment. *Your not-mate looks healthy.* She lifted her head and sniffed at Jessira, immediately reconsidering her words. *Or is she your mate now?*

Rukh smiled. *Jessira isn't my mate.*

Aia sniffed. *She smells like your mate.*

Thank you for saving me, the female, Jessira, said approaching slowly. *When I was sick, Rukh told me what you did for me.* Jessira had a pleasant voice, soft but firm. Plus, she had good manners. Aia decided she liked her.

You are welcome.

Rukh smiled, and without being told, he scratched her chin.

Aia's eyes hooded as she stretched out her head, and the line of her mouth became flat. She purred. So good.

He stopped, and she glanced at him, wondering why. She hadn't instructed him to cease. His gaze was focused on the far side of his camp where her brothers were nosing around his packs. Shon, the bottomless pit of hunger, stared at the horse and licked his lips. Aia's tail swished in annoyance. *The small, ugly one is Shon; and the tall, ugly one is Thrum.*

Who are they?

My brothers, Aia said.

They can't eat the horse. The horse is a friend.

Aia blinked and her ears twitched. Laughter bubbled up from her throat. *Your horse dreams of rolling in a field of grass. He thinks you're a devil to keep him from his dream.*

Rukh laughed with her. *You're making that up.*

Aia rubbed her head against Rukh's chest and purred. *How do you know?*

It was a guess, he said, scratching behind her ears.

Aia froze, and her eyes widened. How marvelous. She turned her head to the side so he could more easily reach her ears.

By now, Shon and Thrum had wandered over. Aia straightened

to see what they would do. Thrum sniffed at the top of Rukh's head while Shon stood before Jessira, tail tucked before his feet as he stared at her expectantly.

My chin itches, Shon said, pushing his head against Jessira's chest.

The Human female nearly fell over, but she caught herself. She stepped back, but Shon followed. *What does he want?* Jessira asked sounding panicked.

He just told you. He wants you to scratch his chin, Aia said, speaking patiently as if to a kitten. She turns to Rukh. *Did your mate injure her mind when she was ill?*

Jessira squawked. *My mind is fine. I'm just not used to giant cats wanting a chin rub.*

I thought you said only a few of your kind could speak to those who aren't Kesarin, Rukh said.

Yes, Aia said. *And Shon and Thrum are two of them.* She licked her paw in thoughtful consideration. *Recently, more have been born who are like me.*

Shon thrust his head more insistently into Jessira's chest, eliciting a 'woof'. *Aia says your hands are like magic.* Another thrust. *And my chin itches.*

Fine! Jessira rubbed hard at Shon's chin, a look of annoyed concentration on her face. Soon the tawny cat was lying on his side, head tilted up. His eyes closed as he purred his pleasure. Louder and louder he rumbled. One of his rear legs pawed the air.

Thrum watched all this, his eyes wide with fascination. With a swish of his tail, he shoved his head between Aia and Rukh. *My chin itches, too.*

Rukh knew what Thrum wanted, and he rubbed at the sensitive area directly below the point of Thrum's chin. Soon Thrum was lying on his belly, pushing his head against Rukh's hand, purring like distant thunder.

After a few minutes, Shon stood to his full height. *Truly wondrous,* he said. *Everything Aia claimed. Thrum thought she was lying.* Shon rubbed the corner of his mouth against the top of Jessira's head. She kept her balance with a slight stumble and avoided Shon's attempt to rub the opposite corner of his mouth against her head.

My ears itch, too, Thrum said to Rukh.

I'm not your servant, Rukh informed him.

You're not? Thrum stared at him intently. *My ears are very itchy.* His tail switched. *I think you should rub them.*

He is my Human, Aia said, nosing between the two of them. *Find your own.*

This one is mine, Shon proclaimed.

I think not, Jessira said with a smile.

Quiet, Human, Shon said.

Quiet yourself if you ever want me to rub your chin again.

Shon blinked in astonishment. *You wouldn't.*

I would.

He flopped to his belly and rolled on his back, stretching his legs as far as they would go. He stared at Jessira with his head upside down. *But why?* he cried plaintively.

Jessira's annoyance fell apart. She laughed and rubbed at Shon's chin once again. *Last time,* she said.

Thrum mewed in sadness. *I want a Human.*

I'll rub your ears if you'll stop whining, Rukh offered.

Thrum immediately flopped to the ground.

Although she didn't like Rukh's hands on another Kesarin, Aia felt sorry for Thrum. She allowed her Human to rub her brother's ear, but she soon had enough. She pushed between his hand and Thrum, pressing her forehead against Rukh's chest and rubbing the corners of her mouth against his shoulders. *It is good to hear your voice.*

It's good to see you, too.

She let him rub the side of her face before pulling back. *My *brothers and I wish to explore the mountains. I will visit you again in a few weeks so you can rub my chin once more.** She laughed. **I know how much pleasure it brings you. And next time, bring others of your kind so Thrum can choose his own Human.** She stepped away from Rukh and called to her brothers, a low, brief growl. Shon and Thrum both stood up and joined her. They paced out of the campsite, the two males eyeing the horse hungrily before exiting the light of the fire. **Goodbye, Rukh. Until next time.**

<hr />

Along the western flank of Mount Fort was a scree scattered trail at the base of a steep ravine. Wide columnar rocks loomed to either side with many of the formations slumping down in broken pieces, littering the trail with their debris. The sun stood high at its zenith, but the spring sunshine was wan and distant in the shadowed gorge within which Rukh and Jessira trekked. Their footfalls crunched on the loose rocks, sounding a counterpoint to the fitful wind moaning with a hollow echo through the ravine.

This was the final leg of their journey back. Earlier in the day, they'd come across a squad of scouts and dropped their Blends after both parties became aware of one another. The lieutenant in charge had briefly questioned what they'd seen before sending them on toward the Western Gate. He'd also let them know about the surge of Chimera activity this spring. For the past few weeks, the Fan Lor Kum had been seen working their way deeper into the Privations than had ever been recorded. Their presence so close to Stronghold had everyone concerned, especially since there had even been a few sightings of the Sorrow Bringer as well. But then, two weeks ago, it had all stopped. The Chims had pulled back and returned to their more usual spring encampments.

"It almost seemed like they were searching for someone," the lieutenant in charge of the scouts had said. "They must have found whoever they were looking for. Poor bastards."

Rukh and Jessira had kept silent upon hearing the lieutenant's questioning statement. Who knew how the scouts would have reacted had they learned the truth. They'd merely mumbled a word salad response of dull and bland sentiment, a reaction unlikely to be remembered or raise suspicion.

While it was true that Stronghold needed to know of the Queen's response when Rukh had cracked open *The Book of First Movement* and the events following, such a discussion was one best held before a closed-door meeting of the Home Senate; not before a squad of scouts.

"The Western Gate." Jessira pointed to a narrowing of their trail, a place where large rectangular rocks leaned against one another and formed a tall peaked tunnel, one that was invisible from above.

The sunshine didn't penetrate far into the passageway, and they walked in a chill and murky darkness. After a final turn, the tunnel brightened under the light of a single, dull-red firefly lamp.

From there came the actual gate, a slit in the mountain about the same width as the East Gate: twenty feet with a guardhouse hunched above. The portcullis was up and several warriors stood watch.

Jessira received a cursory glance from the guards while Rukh was favored with a more thorough examination. Some of the scouts eyed him with awe, others with curiosity, and a couple with resentment or even dislike. Overall, it was still a far warmer welcome that he received compared to the last time he had entered the city.

"Word's already come down. Major Pile is expecting your arrival," one of the guards said. "You're to report to him immediately for debriefing."

The lieutenant they'd come across earlier had sent a scout racing back to inform Army West of Rukh and Jessira's return.

Jessira saluted acknowledgment of their orders while Rukh merely nodded. He hadn't yet accepted his commission into the Home Army.

They passed beneath the portcullis, took another sharp turn, and entered the long throat of Hold Passage West. Murder holes abounded along the length of the passageway and dull-red firefly lanterns provided a dim light. After a quarter-mile or so, the tunnel abruptly widened, opening into West Lock. A thick wall separated the fort from Hold Passage West and was defended by a score of warriors who nodded a brief welcome to Rukh and Jessira. They were allowed to pass unchallenged through the stout ironwood gates on into West Lock.

Once inside, the tunnel opened up even further, becoming a large cavern full of training squares and buildings. After unpacking the gelding and leaving him at the stables, Rukh and Jessira made their way to the major's office. Rukh fell in behind her.

"Do we tell the major about *The Book?*" Rukh asked.

"We have to," Jessira replied.

It had been the answer Rukh had expected. He only hoped the people of Stronghold wouldn't expect him to turn *The Book* over to them. He'd been the one who had risked life and limb in order to retrieve it. By his way of thinking, the only other person who had any claim to it was Jessira. Otherwise, he owned it by all the laws of salvage; but there was also a deeper reason for Rukh's reluctance to hand it over. He wanted a chance to read it again, somewhere safe and far from Stronghold. He'd witnessed the last moments in the life of Linder Val Maharj, the First Father; but it seemed like there was so much more he could learn from it. He wanted to study *The Book of First Movement*.

They soon reached Major Pile's office and waited a few minutes before they were shown in to see him.

The major, a graying warrior in his late forties with the softening stomach of someone too accustomed to sitting behind a desk, questioned them at length about their journey. When they had finished, he sighed and rubbed his eyes. His jowls, already sagging, seemed to hang lower. "Rukh Shektan," he began. "For once, could you please enter Stronghold and not overthrow all we know to be true," he entreated, sounding simultaneously disgusted and weary by their account. "Can't you for once just come back and tell us that there's flooding in the hills above River Tame? Or that the pass through Babylin's Hope is snowed in?"

"Sir?" Rukh asked, unsure what he'd done wrong this time.

"Think about it, and I'm sure you'll understand what I mean," he said with another sigh.

The major sounded upset. Good. Rukh hadn't forgotten how Pile had treated his request to join Army West. "I will if it would make the major happier, sir," he replied, unsuccessfully hiding his scorn.

Major Pile chuckled, apparently sensing the sarcasm. "You're a handful." He hesitated a moment. "I am sorry for how I treated you when you came to me. It was wrong of me to have done so. I hope you'll give me—and all of us, really—a chance to earn your forgiveness."

Rukh nodded. He was willing to forgive, but it would take more than a few words for him to do so. He would need actions that matched the major's generous statement.

"I almost feel sorry for the senators if they try to take *The Book* away from you." He must have noticed Rukh's sharpened gaze because his own became penetrating as well. "You know they will. You'll have to fight to keep it." The major turned to Jessira. "The two of you are to report immediately to the Home Senate. If you're right about the Sorrow Bringer and *The Book*, they need to know about it. They should be in session right now. I'll send a runner ahead of you to prepare the way."

"Yes sir," Jessira responded. She snapped off a salute with

military precision, turned on her heel, and left.

Rukh nodded politely before seeing himself out.

Again, Rukh followed Jessira's lead. She took them through Stronghold, heading for Home Croft, although she paused on occasion whenever she ran into friends or family. Rukh tried to make himself as unobtrusive as possible during those reunions. And thankfully, other than a few hooded glances thrown his way, he was generally ignored during those get-togethers.

"Stop scowling so much," Jessira said after one particularly long, dull reunion. "And you are allowed to answer with more than one or two terse words when someone speaks to you."

"I'm not scowling," Rukh protested. "And I'm not saying much so you can have some time to yourself during these reunions."

Jessira shook her head in disgust. "How can he see so well and be so blind?" she muttered. She stopped and turned to face him. "People want to get to know you, Rukh. You're the Trials Champion, the finest anyone has ever seen. Half the people we've met so far are in awe of you, and the rest are worried they've somehow offended you."

"They're in awe of me?" Rukh asked in disbelief. It was one of the more ridiculous notions he'd ever heard.

"Of course they're in awe," Jessira replied.

"And the worry? Why would they care? They didn't last time I was here," he noted, trying to let go of the bitterness the memories provoked.

"They're afraid you might not teach us what you know. They all know you have little reason to love Stronghold, and their own role in that antipathy."

Rukh smirked. So, they weren't afraid of him on a personal level. They were only worried about what he might not give to their precious city. "The famous Stronghold pragmatism." This time the bitterness leaked out.

Jessira heard. She knew him too well. The frown left her face. She stepped forward and took his hands. "You're not a man made to hate, Rukh," she said, staring him in the eyes before kissing the tip of his nose. "Let it go."

Rukh nodded. "I'll do my best," he said, relaxing his posture. Until that moment, he hadn't realized how tense his shoulders were.

"Good," Jessira replied. "We've a meeting to attend. Try to keep up, love." She walked away, her gait loose, relaxed, and confident. Jessira was happy to be home, and no matter how conflicted Rukh had been about coming back to Stronghold, he was glad to see her joy.

Soon, they reached the Hall of Founding where the Home Senate awaited their arrival. Once there, Rukh and Jessira explained all they had seen and encountered. It took hours to relate because the senators kept interrupting every few minutes, wanting clarification on some interaction or observation. They were especially focused—and rightfully so—on the appearance of Suwraith after Rukh's reading of *The Book of First Movement*.

Eventually, the questions trailed off; and they were allowed to depart. Rukh was a bit taken aback that no one had asked him to turn over the Book. But here came the Governor-General, making his way toward them. Now that Mon Peace had them alone, no doubt he would make that very request.

"Stop it," Jessira whispered from behind a smile. "You're scowling again."

Rukh quickly made his expression as bland and unintimidating as possible.

"Now you look constipated."

"I hope you're not getting sick," Mon Peace said. "Just then your expression—are you sure you're feeling well?"

"Yes, sir. I'm fine," Rukh said, not daring to look at Jessira who wore a look of placid innocence, although he noticed her lips twitching from repressed mirth.

"No one has probably told you, but I took it upon myself to find you lodgings during your absence," Mon Peace began. "But don't worry. The money to pay for the lease didn't come from your winnings in the Trials. I paid for it out of my own funds. Consider it a bribe," he said with a wink and a wide grin.

Rukh laughed. Mon Peace was a politician, but he was also just so damn likable. Rukh found himself warming to the man. "And what would you want in return?" he asked.

The Governor-General chuckled. "I'll let you know when I'm more certain you'll do what I ask."

Rukh smiled. "Thank you for your generosity."

The Governor-General waved aside his acknowledgment. "Think nothing of it. I was happy to help. And since you didn't ask, I'll tell you. Your flat is in Crofthold Lucent, Plot Hie, number eight hundred twenty-three. I'm sure you and your bride to be will be most happy there." The Governor-General glanced between Rukh and Jessira, an expectant gleam in his eyes.

After a moment of startled silence, "How did you know?" Jessira blurted out.

The Governor-General chuckled. "I'm old, but I'm not *that* old," he said. "If you haven't already chosen someone to officiate the ceremony, I'd be honored to do so."

Rukh knew the offer was probably just another part of the man's ongoing effort to win him over, but it was still generous. "We'd be grateful," he said.

The Governor-General nodded. "Just make sure my invitation doesn't somehow get lost." Just as he was about to turn away, he snapped his fingers. "The other Senators will also expect invitations."

Rukh's heart sank. "Our wedding is going to be a social event, isn't it?" he asked after the Governor-General left.

"I'm afraid so." Jessira nodded. "My parents are going to be thrilled." She sounded horrified rather than happy.

CHAPTER THIRTY
THOSE WHO ARE HUNTED

The redemption of the fallen man is neither easy nor quick.
It is fraught with hardship and loss, and those who seek to aid
someone traveling this twisted path might do best to
journey ahead and light the way.

~The Word and the Deed

Mira wore a frown of concentration as she studied the documents laid out before her. The papers were important—they had to be—of this, she was certain. A niggling tickle in the back of her mind told her so, but despite spending the better part of three hours trying to tease it out, she had yet to find the elusive answer she sought. The documents were the original death certificates and written testimonies of everyone involved in the Withering Knife murders, and gaining access to them hadn't been easy. In fact, it had required all of Dar'El's considerable pull and a few favors owed. But if Mira couldn't figure out what she was missing, it would all be for naught. And she *was* missing something; something obvious yet important.

Mira glowered, cursing under her breath as the answer refused to come, and her initial hopefulness turned to a growing sense of irritation. What was it? Every time she thought she had it, it slipped free, like the half-heard note of a song begging to be identified. Her scowl deepened as she shoved her way to her feet and pushed the papers away. She glared at the documents, trying to force her treacherous memory to serve up what she was overlooking. Mira stared a moment longer before she turned away with a muttered oath and paced the narrow confines of the walled cubicle in the City Watch Archives.

She was so close. She was sure of it. It was right in front of her, mocking her with its obviousness.

When she had her annoyance under control, Mira turned back to the papers and sorted through them, putting them back in order. Maybe doing something other than forcing the issue would allow her conscious mind to determine what her subconscious seemed to know. The work went quickly, and Mira finished organizing the documents. Once again, she stared down at them, willing them to give up their secrets. It was right there. All she had to do was make the proper association and she'd have it. She stared so hard and....

Still nothing.

With a dejected sigh, Mira gave up. She gathered the documents, ready to slip them back into their binder. Maybe tomorrow she'd figure out what she was missing. She'd start at the very beginning, with the murder of Felt Barnel. She would read every word of every account. No matter how many times it would take, she would find the answer she was seeking.

And at least the papers were easy to read. The handwriting of everyone involved was clear and legible. It would be....

Mira froze. She barely dared to breathe. There was something to what she had just thought. She let her mind play over her words.

Clear and legible...It was the handwriting!

With trembling hands, she sat down and pulled the papers out of the binder. She briefly examined every document, studying the handwriting. She moved faster and faster, each paper passing swiftly beneath her hands. She almost missed what she was looking for, but with an almost physical shock, she saw the missing clue.

The answer was in the documents dealing with the murder of Slathtril Apter, the third Withering Knife victim. There, in her own handwriting, was the witness attestation of Varesea Apter, the man's wife. Mistress Apter wrote with her left hand, and more importantly, Mira had seen an example of her writing before. She'd seen it in the ledgers from Rector's warehouse.

Varesea Apter was the Rahail woman from the Blue Heron. The same one who had tried to have Bree and Jaresh murdered. Mistress Apter was of the Sil Lor Kum. Mira sat down, stunned that the long search was finally over.

To her chagrin, her first thought was to tell Jaresh about her discovery; but he was a week into the Wildness by now. In thinking about him, she was reminded of Jessira's offer to take them to Stronghold. What would she have done had she known about the proposal? Would she have accepted? Mira wasn't sure, which spoke to the depths—

With a grimace, Mira silenced her thoughts. It was too late for regrets and none of it mattered anyway. She had just learned something monumental, and she had to tell someone about it. The next step had to be planned carefully. But who to tell?

Mira wanted to smack herself.

The answer was obvious. It had to be Dar'El. He'd know what to do.

Her decision made, Mira gathered the papers together and dropped them off with the desk clerk of the City Watch Archives.

She stepped outside into the bright sunshine of an early spring day. The weather was chill, and Mira gathered her coat close even as she checked her sword for clearance. After the attack on Bree, all the Shektan women had taken to walking armed through the streets of Ashoka.

Mira took a short alley leading to Martyr Hall, intending to follow the large road to Jubilee Hills and the Shektan House Seat. Halfway through, a shadowed figure, one she didn't notice until it was too late, detached itself from a wall and confronted her.

Hal'El Wrestiva's cold eyes froze her. "I'd like a word with you, Miss Terrell."

———————◆———————

For Rector Bryce, one of the most maddening aspects of working at the warehouse had been his inability to determine ownership of the building he oversaw. House Wrestiva's archives had proven useless in the matter. According to their records, the building was owned by a series of corporations and individuals tied together in an intentionally incomprehensible knot.

Which had led Rector to the City Hall of Records. There, after some painstaking research, he had finally learned what he had been seeking. Titular ownership of the warehouse belonged to Quality Building Divisions and an unknown silent partner. From there, Rector had discovered a rental agreement between Quality Building Divisions and Ashokan Property Investments. This second company had then signed a management agreement with Stole Services, a third corporation. Three companies—one to manage, another to rent, and another as nominal owner of the warehouse.

It was a complicated mess, and it certainly hadn't been easy to disentangle it all. In fact, the diligence and effort required might have even taxed Jaresh's abilities. Rector smiled at the thought. Who would have guessed he would have ever been impressed with the skills of a Sentya?

Now, all that remained was discovering who owned the three corporations in question.

Rector rubbed his forehead, dreading the work ahead of him. It had taken him a week of twelve hour days to get this far, and it would likely take just as long to discover the names of the companies' owners. Rector rolled his shoulders, an unconscious gesture used on the eve of battle. Nothing to do but to get it done. He searched the records for titles of incorporation and was surprised by how quickly he found his answer.

Hal'El Wrestiva. He was the majority partner in all three companies, and the only name to appear on all three companies' manifests of owners. Rector had found the Sil Lor Kum, and he sat back in stunned disbelief.

How could Hal'El Wrestiva be the SuDin of the Sil Lor Kum? The man was a legend. He had survived more Trials than any man since Hume. He was the warrior against whom Rector, and so many others, had measured themselves. He was a hero who nearly everyone admired, but according to the records here, he was also the vilest traitor imaginable. He was a member of the Sil Lor Kum, their leader, and the Withering Knife murderer. Ghrina, an abomination, Tainted, none of it came close to describing the depths of Hal'El's evil.

Rector pinched his brow and shut his eyes. His head hurt, but with a shuddering breath, he firmed his resolve. Hal'El Wrestiva had been a hero, but that was no longer the case. He had to pay his crimes. Mira could help. She could bring this information to Dar'El Shektan, who could then pass it on to the Chamber of Lords. Hal'El would be a feast for crows before tomorrow's sunset.

Rector exited the City Hall of Records. Mira should still be at the City Watch Archives. He could catch her there.

⸺◆⸺

A simple, brown package lay waiting on his desk when Dar'El returned from lunch. It wasn't unusual for those who sought business with House Shektan to send him gifts or tokens of acknowledgment. More rarely, they were simply items he'd forgotten that he'd ordered from months earlier. So it was with an incurious state that Dar'El examined the package. He lifted it up and immediately noticed the heft. Whatever was inside was heavy, and from the shape and feel, it seemed to be a binder of some sort. Dar'El puzzled over the item. Why would anyone send him a stack of papers? He turned the package over, and when he came to the name of the sender, his brows rose in surprise.

Ular Sathin.

It shouldn't have been possible. Ular had died two weeks ago, choosing suicide over honor. Ular Sathin, the Muran Master of the Society of Rajan and secretly a MalDin of the Sil Lor Kum. Ular, the man Dar'El had loved as a friend.

Dar'El's grip on the package tightened. How could Ular have betrayed them as he had? How could he have lied so well and so easily to everyone in his life? Everyone who cared for him? Had Ular secretly laughed at all of them, mocking their trustfulness? All those duplicitous decades of deceit and treachery? Had there ever been anything genuine about the man? Or had every aspect of his life been a sham?

Dar'El set aside the package and waited for his anger to pass. He turned to the wide window offering a view of Mount Bright and the blooming gardens. The day was sunny but suddenly felt cool, and he offered a brief prayer for Jaresh's safety. It was likely futile, but he hoped someone was listening.

With a sigh, he turned about. The anger and hurt were still there, and they always would be. Maybe with time, he would find a way to forgive his old friend; but that day wasn't today.

Dar'El ripped open the package. He'd been right. It was a binder full of paper. There was also a folded letter. It was from Ular.

To those who follow,

If you are reading this, then by now, you have learned the truth about who I am and what I've done. Please understand: it was not my intent to cause you any pain or grief. I never sought to harm you or anyone. I simply lived in accord with my wont. I am the scorpion in the fable. I chose who I became because it seemed to be the most true to my inmost self. Morality and evil have no place in the judgment of my actions. Neither then should friendship and love or good enter into the equation when elucidating my true nature.

I am sure these words bring you no comfort or long-sought answers, and the purpose of this letter is not to provide such. My words are simply to allow you knowledge that I am gone now, off to that great refuge, Death, which for me, has always represented a safe harbor from this dismal world where wretched Fear held an icy guard upon all my Hopes and Dreams. It left me a coward, and a coward's life I led.

You may think I died a coward as well, but it is not the truth. Suicide was not the means to my end. Rather my final act was an act of desperation. I was driven to my death, and it was someone from the Hidden Hand who was the drover.

I hope you learn who it was, and I hope you cause the Sil Lor Kum no end of grief. These documents should allow you fruitful pursuit of such an endeavor.

Warmest Regards,

Ular Sathin

Dar'El re-read the letter again, but it offered no hidden meanings or further insights into who Ular Sathin had truly been. It seemed the man would forever remain an enigma. With a sad exhalation, Dar'El set the letter aside before turning to the packet.

He opened the binder and smiled in triumph. Ular had given away the entirety of the Sil Lor Kum. The first page was titled *Organization of the Sil Lor Kum*. Dar'El's smile fell away an instant later. The rest of the document appeared to be written in a cipher.

He sighed. Where was Jaresh when he needed him?

———◦•◦———

R ector did a double take when he passed by an alley near the City Watch Archives. Exiting the far end had been a man and a woman, and he could have sworn it had been Mira and Hal'El Wrestiva. But when he turned to look again, they were gone.

Rector took a hesitant step into the alley, but the more he thought it through, the more certain he was that it *had* been Mira in the company of Hal'El Wrestiva. But why? What possible reason could she have to talk with that traitor? Surely she wasn't in league with Hal'El. Rector had trouble believing something so outrageous. He wouldn't believe it. There had to be another reason.

And whatever it was, he meant to learn it.

Rector raced to the opposite end of the alley. It opened onto Martyr Hall, and he searched up and down the street. Mira and Hal'El couldn't have gone far, but for some reason, he couldn't find any sign of them. The traffic was too thick.

"Rector!" a voice cried out. "Over here!"

He searched for whoever had called to him. It was Bree and Satha Shektan. They were mounted and bore down on him.

Rector gave a dejected sigh. He'd done his best to avoid Dar'El and his immediate family. Ever since the situation with Rukh, the few times he'd interacted with them, Rector had always been on the receiving end of an angry harangue. He didn't need another such confrontation. Rector had wronged Dar'El's family—he knew it—but he'd had enough of their chastisement. Besides, on most days, he berated himself enough to satisfy anyone's demands.

He tried to mask his disappointment as they approached, but he was obviously unsuccessful based on Satha's frown of annoyance. "I'm sorry our presence causes you so much distress," she said.

"Yes, try to contain your joy," Bree said sarcastically. "Have you seen Mira?"

"That's who I was looking for just before you caught up with me," Rector said. "I could have sworn I saw her a second ago walking with Hal'El Wrestiva." Rector quickly explained what he had learned about Hal'El Wrestiva, and their countenances grew grim.

"Hal'El Wrestiva?" Satha said, her eyes boring into his. "Are you sure?"

Rector nodded.

Satha sat back in her saddle. "What are the odds?" she murmured enigmatically.

"Dar'El received a binder this afternoon," Bree explained. "It supposedly contains information about the Sil Lor Kum, but all the papers are written in code. We were on our way to bring Mira back to the House Seat to work on deciphering the documents."

During all this, Rector had been thinking about what he'd seen with Mira and Hal'El. A sick feeling took hold in the pit of his stomach.

"What is it?" Satha asked.

"Just now, when I thought about what I saw, I realized Mira looked scared," Rector answered.

"You think she's in trouble," Bree said.

"I saw her with Hal'El Wrestiva, the Withering Knife murderer. Of course she's in trouble," Rector snapped, the fear growing stronger. "Can either of you see them from up there?" he asked.

The Shektan women searched up and down Martyr Hall, their frowns deepening.

"She's not here," Bree announced.

"We have to find her," Rector said, feeling the press of time.

"It goes without saying," Satha replied coolly. "Do you have any idea which direction they were going?"

Rector concentrated on what he had seen. "I think northwest."

"Toward Stone Cavern?" Bree asked in surprise. "Not toward Jubilee Hills. I would have thought he would have taken her to House Wrestiva's Seat."

"I think Bree has the right of it," Satha said. "We should—"

Rector was no longer listening. Something Bree had said sparked a memory. He chased after it, searching his mind for a barely remembered scrap of information. What was it…something about Stone—he had it. His shout of triumph silenced the Bree and Satha. "It's Stone Cavern," Rector said.

"How do you know?" Satha asked.

"After Jaresh cracked their cipher, I took another look at the ledgers. It turns out that about six months ago, Quality Building Divisions, the company owned by Hal'El and this partner, the Rahail woman, purchased a building in Stone Cavern."

"You know the address?"

Rector told it to them. "I'll go to the building in Stone Cavern," he announced. "Can the two of you gather some warriors and meet me there?"

"I should go with you," Bree said. "If Mira isn't there, I can act as a messenger and let the warriors know where else we think she might be."

Satha didn't like Bree's plan, but in the end, she relented. "Be careful," she warned.

Bree nodded. "I'll stay out of the fight if it comes to it," she said. "But at least I can protect myself this time." She patted the sword at her hip.

— • —

Hal'El could Blend. Mira had no idea how he had learned such a Talent, but it was true. He'd told her he could do so, but she hadn't believed him until they had stepped out of the alley and onto the busyness of Martyr Hall. Despite the black blade so clearly pressed against her side—and from the cold evil emanating from it, this was most probably the legendary Withering Knife—no one had taken notice. Even when Mira had shouted for help, her pleas had been ignored. There had been a few Rahails and Murans who had glanced their way in suspicion—likely sensing the illegal Blend, which was forbidden within Ashoka—but for some reason, none of them had raised an alarm, either.

How could this be happening? She'd been so close to finishing off the Sil Lor Kum. Mira had discovered the truth about Varesea Apter. She had been about to tell Dar'El Shektan, and afterward, it would have been easy to tear down the Sil Lor Kum and kill all those degenerate bastards.

Now Hal'El Wrestiva, the Withering Knife murderer, was leading her up the stairs of an empty building in Stone Cavern. Mira's heart thudded with fear, but she couldn't think how to save herself. When she tried reaching for her sword, Hal'El had slapped aside her hand, nearly breaking her fingers in the process. His contempt for her skill was evident in how he didn't bother disarming her afterward. However, the rest of the journey, he had maintained in a bruising grasp on her arm the entire time. Now, Hal'El dragged her to the top of the stairs where a single, closed door stood.

Mira swallowed heavily. "What do you intend to do with me?" she asked. She'd asked a variation of the same question many times during the long walk here, but on every occasion, she'd had been met with silence. This time was no different.

Hal'El continued to grip Mira's arm tightly while he unlocked the door and swung it open. The room inside was large but sparsely furnished: a table, several chairs, a couch, and a bed.

"Dar'El sent a sheep to hunt a wolf. His foolishness will cost you your life," Hal'El growled before shoving her unceremoniously inside.

Mira stumbled, almost falling, before she regained her balance.

"Who's this?" a voice asked.

Mira gasped.

On the far side of the room, Varesea Apter lounged upon a bed, wearing nothing more than a breezy chemise.

She and Hal'El were lovers?

The door slammed shut.

⬤ ● ●

Rector crept up the stairs with Bree skulking close on his heels. They'd rushed to the building in Stone Cavern as swiftly as they could manage. Thankfully, Bree's mount had been able to force an opening through the throngs of traffic on Martyr Hall, and Rector had followed right on the horse's hooves. Otherwise, the trip here might have taken twice as long.

When they'd arrived, the building had been darkened. There had been no lights in any of the windows to indicate anyone's presence. The place had appeared empty and abandoned, completely unremarkable except for one oddity. In one corner of the building, on the top floor, the windows had been covered over with plywood, but nowhere else.

In addition, as Rector and Bree had approached the building from the alley in back, he'd noticed what appeared to be a new, wooden fence and gate stretching across the rear yard. From somewhere near it, an unseen woman's tremulous voice had risen in panic before being swiftly muffled.

Rector had conducted *Jivatma*, and the world had grown brighter, sounds sharper, and vision swifter.

The murmured whisper of the building's gate opening caught his attention. Then came a double image: the gate was closed but there was another image superimposed upon it, one of the same gate swinging shut.

Someone was Blended.

He'd passed on the information to Bree, who had nodded, and they had carefully pressed their way through the gate, expecting trouble.

Nothing.

Rector had signaled for Bree to wait outside, but she had shaken her head in negation. He'd tried to press the matter, but she had continued to refuse. Rector had known he couldn't stop and argue the matter. Mira was inside, and she needed help.

With a suppressed growl, he had pressed on, Bree following close behind.

Now, they climbed the final flight of stairs.

"Where do you think—" Bree began.

Rector shushed her to silence.

They approached a single door at the stop of the stairs. Light leaked from beneath it and murmured voices could be heard from the other side of it as well. Then came an angry shout followed by Mira's cry of pain and a loud crashing.

Rector reared back and with all his *Jivatma* enhanced strength, he kicked the door open, ripping it off its hinges.

———●———

For Mira, on a day full of shocks, this one might have been the most stunning.

Hal'El Wrestiva was famous for his fervent beliefs in the strict separation of the Castes. His revulsion with Jaresh's admission into House Shektan was well known. He had even worked to pass a law banning any future such adoption. And it had been Hal'El who had been instrumental in having Rukh declared Unworthy. Again, this was because of Rukh's new Talents and his relationship with Jessira. It was said that Hal'El even frowned upon men and women of different Castes having mere friendships with one another. He opposed any intermingling between those of different Castes on any level.

And yet, here he was with a Rahail lover.

Mira watched in bemused fascination as Varesea uncoiled from the bed and pulled on her clothes. The Rahail woman buttoned up snug britches and slipped on a loose fitting blouse. "We are everything you suspect," Varesea confirmed once she had finished dressing.

"Which is what?" Mira asked, playing for time.

"We are lovers," Varesea replied evenly and without shame. "And you are in no position to judge us, not after your own dalliance with Jaresh Shektan."

Mira didn't bother correcting Varesea's false assumption. Instead, she turned to Hal'El, relieved to see the Withering Knife had been sheathed. "What do you intend to do with me?" she demanded once again, anger lacing her voice. Somewhere in the shock of learning about Hal'El and Varesea's relationship, she had forgotten her fear.

"You will tell us everything House Shektan knows, and then...." Hal'El shrugged, his pregnant silence an all-too clear indication of what he intended.

"You're not really offering me much motive to tell you anything," Mira replied.

"Refuse me, and your fate will be sealed by the Withering Knife," Hal'El said, his face forbidding. "Believe me when I tell you: there is not a more painful death. The Knife steals your *Jivatma*."

So the legends about the Knife were true. Or at least Hal'El wanted her to believe they were.

"House Shektan knows everything," Mira said. "They know you are the SuDin. Even now a troop of warriors are coming to arrest you. Before tomorrow night, you and your lover will be food for the crows. You'll be forever reviled as the worst kind of degenerates."

Varesea laughed. "We are far worse than degenerates, my dear. We are Sil Lor Kum, and we are lovers from different Castes. Surely you can do better with your insults."

"You're right," Mira replied. "You *are* worse. You're ghrinas, both of you." She turned back to Hal'El. "And traitors."

The crushing blow came without warning. Faster than she could follow, Hal'El backhanded her, sending her tumbling. Mira cried out as she crashed into a table, knocking it over. She had the wherewithal to conduct *Jivatma* and Shield. It cushioned her fall.

Mira rose to her feet with her sword leveled and ready to fight. She would die here, but not like a sheep.

She felt brave until Hal'El laughed at her defiance and readied his sword.

Just then, the door burst inward, smacking Hal'El in the head and knocking him to the ground. Rector and Bree charged in.

———— ◆ ————

Despite *Jivatma* flooding into her, the world was quiet and still until the instant Bree stepped into the flat. With a snap, sound and fury raged. It was chaotic, a roar of noise and movement. Images impinged on Bree's senses. Hal'El rose from the ground, looking furious. A Rahail woman—Bree recognized her—Varesea Apter, squared off against Mira, both of them armed with swords.

Bree nearly panicked. She tried to control the surge of adrenaline and fear by taking a deep breath.

Rector and Hal'El needed no such time to gather themselves. They went after one another, a blur of blades. Bree ducked low as Hal'El's sword arched toward her. Rector threw himself in the way, stopping the deadly stroke.

With a start, Bree got her mind working again. She remembered the lessons she'd worked so hard to learn since the attack in the alley.

She attacked Hal'El's flank. He slid aside and then Rector was there. It was tight fighting, a twisting of bodies.

Bree never saw the kick that punched through her Shield and launched her into Mira. The two of them fell to the floor. Varesea loomed over them.

Mira surged to her feet and blocked. From her knees, still wobbly from the kick, Bree aimed a blow at Varesea's legs. The Rahail managed to dart out of the way, but Mira used the distraction. She lanced her sword into Varesea's heart.

Varesea gasped out a final breath. She slid off the blade and fell over dead.

Hal'El cried out.

Bree moved to flank the Wrestiva and Mira did so as well. Rector rose shakily from the ground. Blood flowed freely from a deep cut to his scalp.

"You will die," Hal'El promised, moving toward Mira. At the last instant, he spun about, somehow sensing Bree's thrust. He blocked her, pushing her back. Still spinning, he gut-kicked Rector. His final motion carried him around. His sword punched through Mira's Shield and thrust into her stomach.

With a smile of satisfaction, Hal'El withdrew his blade. An instant later, his face filled with anguish as he looked at Varesea's unmoving body. Without another word, his hand glowed. He threw a Fireball at a plywood-covered window and leapt through the hole he had blasted, disappearing into the night.

Bree crawled to Mira, fear for her friend almost stilling her heart. Rector stumbled over as well.

Mira's eyes darted between the two of them as she gasped in pain. Her pulse fluttered in her neck.

CHAPTER THIRTY-ONE
MIDNIGHT VOWS

Soft as a rose petal is the light of dawn's first blush.
But softer still your wine-kissed lips at midnight,
When fragrant blossoms fall around us like confetti.

~ Midnight's Sunrise, by Maral, AF 702

Jessira settled into the old couch and sighed with comfort. She knew this sofa well. She knew all its lumps, its settled areas, and how best to position herself so she wouldn't sink to the floor. The couch was as familiar as an old friend and had been in her parents' home for as long as Jessira could remember. They had given it to her and Rukh as an early wedding gift, and now, it sat centered on the wall opposite the front door in the hearthspace of their new flat together. It was one of the few pieces of furniture the two of them had managed to scrounge together in the weeks since their return to Stronghold. The other was a bed—hers—the one she'd grown up with and also from her parents' flat. It was another familiar memento to bring to the home she and Rukh would soon share.

Two more days until the wedding. Jessira couldn't wait.

When she'd decided to end her engagement and follow Rukh out of Stronghold, her parents had been deeply upset with her. It wasn't because they wanted Jessira to marry Disbar no matter the cost—in fact, by the time she had left, they had come to dislike her former fiancé as much as she had. However, there might have been a way to end the engagement without so many hard feelings on both sides. But by simply leaving Stronghold with Rukh, Jessira had ended any hope of a graceful termination. Her parents had worried that Jessira's reputation would be irreparably sullied by what she had done.

It should have happened, but it hadn't. Luck or Karma was the reason. It turned out Disbar *did* have something to do with his cousins' attacks on Rukh. There hadn't been definitive evidence, but there was enough to leave a black stain on Disbar's honor. His own reputation was now in tatters.

As a result, Jessira's homecoming—her second in months—had been a joyful occasion without any worries or concerns. Her parents had been more delighted than anyone, especially when they learned Jessira planned to marry Rukh, a man who was suddenly of high standing. And when they learned that the Governor-General himself would officiate the ceremony—in the Home House, no less—with the entire Senate in attendance, they had been beside themselves with joy.

Then had come the wedding preparations. Jessira and her parents had to complete in a few weeks what would normally require a few months. All the details were maddening. Who to invite? Where to seat them? What kind of food to serve? What kind of flowers for Rukh's offertory bouquet? What clothes for the bride and the groom? Who to chaperone Rukh down the aisle since his parents were obviously absent?

Jessira hated every bit of it.

All she wanted was to get married in a small simple ceremony, but it wasn't to be. This morning, Jessira had finally had enough. It was too much. She couldn't stomach any more useless planning, and as a result, she had turned over all decision-making to Amma. Frankly, she was so much better at all of this anyway. As of now, all Jessira had to do was show up. It was a situation both she and her parents were glad of. When she had left the flat this morning, Jessira had heard Nanna mutter something about ornery daughters finally getting out of the way.

By contrast, Rukh had had it easy. Since their return, he'd been politely asked to report to the East Lock and teach the sword to anyone who was willing to learn. It seemed the senior officers didn't want to waste Rukh's Talents on simple scouting where he might be injured or even die. Instead, it had been decided that he could best serve the city by training her warriors. After his demolition of Stronghold's finest, everyone wanted to learn from him; and a special lottery had been held for the ten spaces in Rukh's initial class.

It also turned out that Rukh loved teaching. He enjoyed his work and was finally becoming a part of Stronghold. It was good to see.

Jessira was brought back to the present when Rukh brought her tea.

"What's wrong?" he asked.

Jessira smiled, taking both his hands in hers. "I'm just glad you're happy."

Rukh smiled with her. "I've got a lot to be happy about," he said, kissing her.

Jessira let the kiss deepen before pulling back and settling against Rukh with a purr of contentment. "When did you finally learn wisdom?" she asked. "I mean about how good your life can be," she explained when he looked at her in puzzlement.

"When I took your advice and forgave your people," he replied. "Or at least those who asked."

"I told you before: you're not a man made to hate," she reminded him. "It was eating you up inside."

Rukh answered by kissing the top of her head. "Thank you," he whispered.

Jessira settled against him once more. She took a sip of tea and glanced around the barren flat. "We have a lot of work to do to make this place livable," she remarked.

"We've got time," Rukh said. "After all, everything we really need is already here." He patted the couch on which they sat. "A comfortable sofa and a soft bed on which to sleep. We can pick up the rest as time goes on."

"Sleep? Is that all you think we should do in bed?" Jessira asked.

"What do you have in mind?" Rukh asked, wearing a guileless expression.

He didn't fool her. She could see the sudden intensity in his eyes. "Why don't I give you a demonstration?" Jessira set aside their tea and pulled him forward. She kissed him, softly at first and then deeper. "Does that give you an idea of—"

Her words were cut off when Rukh kissed her again. The kiss lengthened, and Rukh held her close, cupping her face in both his hands. Jessira nestled into the couch as Rukh's weight settled against her. She tugged at his shirt, pulling it from his pants; but even as she struggled to unbutton it, Rukh leaned away. Jessira tried to pull him back, but he refused her urging. He clasped her hands, and gently disentangled them from the fabric of his shirt. He looked as frustrated as she felt.

"What's wrong?" she asked.

Rukh stood and put further distance between the two of them. "In Ashoka, when a man and woman become engaged, according to our traditions, they can no longer share intimacy until the wedding night."

"This isn't Ashoka," Jessira reminded him.

"But I'm still Ashokan. In my heart and soul, it's who I am."

"But you're of Stronghold now," Jessira said. "We don't have those kind of antiquated traditions." She reached for him again only to see him dance away. Jessira sat back in disbelief. "You're serious, aren't you?"

Rukh merely nodded.

"Of all the stupid, Devesh-damned, fragging, backward traditions!" she cried out. "How in the unholy hells...?" She looked at Rukh, wanting to make sure he hadn't changed his mind. He hadn't. He really wasn't going to touch her, not until they were wed.

"I'm sorry," Rukh said, looking miserable

Good. Let him be unhappy. Jessira flopped against the couch and closed her eyes, praying for strength and understanding. First Mother! Why did she have to fall in love with such a maddening man? Her frustration slowly ebbed, and she was able to consider the situation from Rukh's point of view. She opened her eyes. Rukh stood near the hearth, clearly unhappy but just as clearly, still determined to follow through on his promise.

Jessira understood why. Rukh thought he had lost everything: his family, his friends, his honor, his home. He had nothing left except the traditions of Ashoka. She couldn't ask him to give those up as well. The last of her frustration ebbed away and compassion took its place. Jessira stood and approached him slowly so he wouldn't dart away. She took his hands in hers. "I understand why this is so important to you, love," she said. "I can wait."

"You don't mind?" he said, sounding hopeful.

"They're your traditions and you have to honor them. It's who you are: a man of honor."

Rukh smiled in relief. "I love you, Jessira."

"You should," she said. "And I love you, too; but you need to realize that I can't be around you much until the wedding."

"I know."

Jessira kissed him, just briefly and not enough to tempt them to change their minds. "See you at the wedding."

Rukh waited alone in the antechamber, a high-ceilinged, square room with a crystal chandelier to provide a soft light. Warm tapestries of beige and chocolate covered portions of the pale blue plaster walls. An expensive, but uncomfortable, couch took up one side of the room and was faced by high-backed leather chairs and a large, unlit fireplace. A painting—a scene depicting the founding of Stronghold—hung over the hearth. Shadows dappled the ceiling and tall, white double doors with fanciful gilding led into the ballroom.

Rukh paced about in nervousness, occasionally tugging at his collar, trying to loosen it and get some air. It felt like someone was trying to choke him. Unholy hells, but the thing was tight. In fact, his entire outfit was tight like that: stiff, and uncomfortable. It didn't help that it was also as ugly as a Balant's butt. Rukh grimaced. From the thigh-length, starched saffron shirt with its seven buttons—seven being a 'propitious' number—to the overwrought silver filigree vining up the sleeves and collar and down the placket; and the golden pants, billowy like sails and decorated with hundreds of tiny mirrors—it was *not* attractive. This didn't even touch on the pointy saffron shoes also festooned with intricate, over-done silver filigree.

At least it was almost time for the ceremony. Timing was everything to the people of Stronghold. Here, every important event had a supposed 'propitious' moment when it was best for them to occur. For weddings, it was midnight. Even something as private as the consummation of a couple's marriage was said to best occur with dawn's light beaming down on them. A number of small cabins ringing Teardrop Lake had actually been built for just that purpose since very few could afford a flat with an eastern-facing window.

A knock came on the door, and the chamberlain—a tall, spare man in his fifties with a bald pate and a luxuriant, white mustache—

poked his head inside. "It is time," he said in a flat, formal voice.

Rukh took a deep breath. Here it went, the moment he'd been dreading all night when he would have to enter the banquet hall and face several hundred strangers, many of whom were very important here in Stronghold, all while dressed in as ugly a garment as he could recall seeing.

He smiled ruefully. A few months ago, their opinion of him wouldn't have mattered in the slightest.

Rukh nodded to the chamberlain. "I'm ready."

Jessira would already be inside. In Stronghold, the custom held that the bride entered the wedding hall first in order to soak up the admiration of all those in attendance. Rukh hadn't seen her in the two days since his unfortunate decision to adhere to the traditions of Ashoka. He just hoped her dress wasn't as ridiculous as his getup. She deserved to be beautiful on her wedding night.

Of course, he'd thought her beautiful even when she'd been sickened by the poison of a Kesarin's claws, wearing the torn and bloody camouflage clothing of a warrior. He was sure she'd look lovely tonight—even if her wedding dress turned out to be as hideous and gaudy as his own outfit.

Rukh stepped through the tall double doors, and all thoughts flew from his mind.

The ballroom was full, but Rukh hardly noticed. His eyes were only for her.

Jessira stood at the far end of the hall. The glory of her honey-blonde hair was piled high, cascading down her neck and to her shoulders. Large, emerald-studded earrings graced her ears, and a slender, silvery net held up the mass of her hair. Mehndi tattoos covered Jessira's hands, wrists, feet, and ankles and her bare arms rested at her side. Her dress was a soft cream-colored gown with threads of green, the same color as her eyes. It fit her every curve, trailing to the floor and swirling gently with her every movement. On one side, a single slit rose to her knee, exposing a riveting length of leg. Jessira's emerald eyes sparkled with life, energy, and love.

Rukh smiled. The world was fine and wondrous.

———◦———

Jessira smiled when she saw Rukh.

The Governor-General, or whoever had picked out the outfit, had chosen well. Jessira had never seen Rukh look so handsome. His clothes fit him perfectly, and he wore them well. Nevertheless, she understood he wasn't nearly as enamored of his outfit as the tailor who had fashioned them. He looked uncomfortable and self-conscious, but it didn't show in the way he carried himself. He walked with poised self-assurance. He was confident without being arrogant. He was a man whose presence demanded attention.

Rukh stepped forward, moving with an unmatched elegance. His every step was precise and defined and yet somehow languid and unhurried. He could move swiftly without ever seeming to hurry. Sometimes, she thought even his stillness was a dance. He was in all ways a Kumma.

She had to remind herself to breathe when his gaze met hers. His dark eyes soaked in the light like inky pools of blackness, yet glowed with an inner warmth. And his face, so classically handsome with his proud cheeks and full lips, held an expression of love and devotion.

How had they come together? It seemed so unlikely given how often they'd argued, neither willing to give an inch in their beliefs. Time and hard lessons had followed, but she was grateful for all they had endured, even the instances when she had wanted to do nothing but hit him in the mouth. Wisdom had come from their toil and hardships, and now here they were, moments from being wed. Her heart beat a little faster at the thought, and she wondered anew why fortune had seen fit to smile so beneficently upon her.

Rukh paced down the aisle, his gaze focused on her as if there were no one else in the world.

Jessira's eyes welled. Life was so bright and luminous.

———•———

His daughter was to wed tonight. Sateesh struggled to contain his emotions. He was overjoyed for her—Rukh was everything he would have wanted in the man who married Jessira. Still, there was also sorrow. Jessira would be leaving his home, building a new life with Rukh. It was the way of life—Sateesh knew it—but the loss still brought a bittersweet melancholy with it.

He sighed as he glanced at his daughter, marveling anew at how lovely she was. Rukh was a lucky man, and he seemed to understand that. Even a blind man could see the love and devotion the Kumma held for Jessira and she for him. If anyone deserved such happiness, it was the two of them. They had been through so much together, so many tribulations and dangers—enough for several lifetimes—but now they were both home. They were both safe. They should have a long, prosperous life ahead of them.

Sateesh forced himself to pay attention. His part would come soon.

Mon Peace looked ready to speak. The Governor-General wore a simple, unadorned black shirt and pants and stood on a raised dais decorated with rose petals and lilies. "Our world changes, evermore and always, and we with it. What more lovely expression of this truism can we imagine than this wedding between two such wonderful individuals; born of different worlds, yet uniting at the last?" He said more words, chanting the holy mantras from *The Book of All Souls* that bonded a man and woman to one another.

The Governor-General gestured and Sateesh's wife, Crena, dropped her end of the *antarpat*—an embroidered, white, diaphanous curtain—while Sateesh still held his part of it. The gauzy fabric was meant to symbolize the separation of a bride from her groom, and only when her parents had dropped it, could she marry the man they had approved on her behalf. Crena dipped her fingers into the vermillion powder held in the silver chalice Mon Peace offered to her. She turned and applied a bindi, first to Jessira, and then to Rukh. She moved aside, standing behind their daughter.

Mon Peace chanted more mantras before gesturing again.

It was Sateesh's turn. He let the *antarpat* slide to the ground and stepped forward. The Governor-General offered a silver platter. On it, resting on a bed of dried rice stained with turmeric was an unadorned wine-red, ironwood bracelet—Rukh's *kalava*—and a necklace made of small, black beads the size of mustard seeds—Jessira's *thaali*—her hallowed thread. The bracelet represented Rukh's promise to work in all ways to keep Jessira safe and happy. The necklace, which would lie next to her heart, was Jessira's vow to keep her love for Rukh sacred and for him alone.

Sateesh slipped the *thaali* around Jessira's neck before placing the bracelet around Rukh's left wrist. He moved aside.

More chanting while Rukh and Jessira held hands and faced one another.

"I love you," Sateesh heard Rukh whisper to Jessira.

"I love you, too," she whispered to him.

Sateesh blinked back tears as Mon Peace finished the ceremony and shouted his proclamation, announcing that Jessira and Rukh were wed.

Dawn's first blush streamed through the clear panes of the mullioned window, a shimmer of gold highlighting dust motes before it settled upon the four-post bed, covering it with a bright sheen. The light also shone against the glossy cherry finish of the armoire standing on the wall opposite the bed and even the door beside it leading out into a small front room and kitchen. Outside— visible through the window—lay a narrow sward, dewy and bordering Teardrop Lake, which sparkled in the early morning sunshine. The world was quiet within and without.

The wedding ceremony had been brief, but the reception that had followed had seemed to stretch on interminably. Eventually it had wound down, and afterward, Rukh and Jessira had made their way here, to one of the small eastward-facing cabins nestled along the shores of Teardrop Lake made specifically for newlyweds.

Rukh laid his head back, resting it on a pillow as he tried to catch his breath. Jessira lay curled up beside him, breathing heavily as well. A patina of perspiration beaded her forehead as she clutched the thick comforter up to her chest. Just then, Jessira chuckled, soft and low, a fascinating combination of satisfaction and pleasure.

Rukh warmed to the sound with a smug sense of accomplishment. He grinned as he rolled over to face her. "Was it worth the wait?" he asked.

Her expression of disbelief was his first warning. His second was when she clutched the comforter to her mouth, hiding her laughter.

Rukh's face reddened. Jessira stifled her mirth as best she could, but she shook convulsively.

It apparently *hadn't* been worth it. As Jessira laughed, Rukh found himself getting annoyed. It hadn't been *that* bad…had it?

Jessira must have noticed his rising embarrassment. She wiped away tears of laughter and got her hilarity under control. She hiccuped. "I'm sorry," she said, sounding not the least bit apologetic. "It's just your question…Was it worth the wait? Of course not." She grinned, her teeth flashing in the soft light of sunrise. "I love you, but this is something we should have done two days ago. Two months ago."

"So you enjoyed it?" After her laughter in response to his earlier question, Rukh needed to hear her say it.

She put her arms around his neck and pressed herself against him. "Yes," she said. "And if you kiss me again, I'll show how much."

Rukh's worry and embarrassment vanished. Instead, he gloried in the feel of her in his arms, the sparkle of her green eyes, the brilliance of her smile, and the warmth of her soul.

CHAPTER THIRTY-TWO
SECRETS UNEARTHED

Mother's certainty is exceeded only by Her madness.
But sometimes even in Her insanity, She has a means to perceive the truth.
My heart grows fearful on those occasions.

~From the journal of SarpanKum Li-Dirge, AF 2062

Though the wind gusted about him, Li-Choke stood as still as an unmoving boulder. His face was composed, like the morning quiet following a snowfall. He waited, his hooves digging into the soft ground, wet after yesterday's storms. Today looked to be similar. The scent of rain carried on the air, heralded by the gloomy clouds and the blustery wind. A few early blooms—pale, white flowers lying low to the ground—dotted the grass-covered hills. A single blossom lay tucked behind one of Choke's ears.

He listened to his fellow Baels speaking softly to one another. A month ago, the western brothers had arrived, sent by the Queen to take control of the Eastern Plague. By the time of their coming— shortly before Choke and Chak-Soon had returned from their venture to Hammer—the Eastern Plague had almost completed its disintegration, falling into squabbling discord and dissension.

It hadn't been easy, but the newly invested SarpanKum, the

relatively young Li-Shard, and his capable, hard-bitten SarpanKi, Li-Brind, had worked diligently and speedily to gain control of the situation. It had taken all their efforts, as well as those of their western brothers, but eventually, Shard had succeeded. Through regimented and consistent discipline, the Eastern Plague had rounded back into fighting trim with the various Chims overwhelmingly glad to have the Baels once more in command. Even the Tigons had been relieved when the yoke of leadership had been taken from their shoulders.

As for Choke, upon his return, he had reported to his new SarpanKum and explained all he had witnessed since Mother had annihilated Li-Dirge and the other eastern Baels. Some of it, the western brothers had already known, but much was new, such as Rukh Shektan's role in the caverns of the Chimeras; how he had risked everything on behalf of his supposed enemies, going so far as to plan for the Baels' safety in the Hunters Flats. Choke's recitation had raised gasps of disbelief and fervent awe from the assembled Baels, especially when he had been bold enough to name Rukh Shektan a friend. One young brother had even wondered if Hume's heir had finally been found.

It was a question the others had laughed off—Hume was a legend and no Human could ever measure up to the man or his myth—but Choke wasn't so sure. Rukh Shektan was special.

So Choke had remained quiet as the others chuckled over the young Bael's embarrassment. His silence had been noted and he was asked to continue his narration. Choke went on to describe the final destruction of his eastern brothers when Mother had re-discovered them. Then, came the long journey to Hammer and falling in once more with Rukh Shektan and Jessira Grey. He spoke of how the Humans had protected and Healed them, both he and Chak-Soon, a Tigon who had grown to accept the truth of fraternity.

By the end, all the Baels had fallen quiet, shifting about,

unwilling to break what seemed a holy silence.

"His heir *is* found," Li-Shard had declared. "Two of them."

"Three," Li-Brind corrected, looking dumbfounded and amazed. "Chak-Soon as well." The older Bael, so world-weary and cynical, had sounded amazed. He wore the guise of one whose faith—buried beneath heaped up mountains of skepticism—had been unexpectedly redeemed. "Humanity has heard us."

At that moment, Li-Shard had shouted, a sound of pure, unadulterated joy, a cry echoed by their brethren. "Never did I think such a miracle could come to pass. Li-Dirge's sacrifice shall never be forgotten!"

"Through Devesh all things are possible," another Bael intoned prayerfully.

"Perhaps," Brind had said. "Or it may be that a Bael of uncommon courage and decency simply saw the moment and seized it."

"And found a willing heart in Rukh Shektan, and eventually Jessira Grey and Chak-Soon," Li-Choke reminded them. The role of the Humans and the Tigons shouldn't be forgotten or diminished.

"Two Human friends." Li-Shard spoke the words as though tasting them. "It is truly a time of miracles." He turned to Li-Choke. "And you are a Bael of destiny to be able to claim such an attribute."

His brothers had murmured similar sentiments, but Choke found himself troubled by their adulation. He had simply done as he had been taught to believe was right. Was living a moral life really worthy of such praise? Should it not simply be an expectation, rather than an exception? Or perhaps Choke was simply misreading the situation. Perhaps by praising him, his brothers were reaffirming their own faith and teachings; as though Choke's accomplishments were the final expression of everything their ancestors had struggled so mightily to achieve.

Regardless, Choke wasn't sure where the truth lay, but Li-Shard had apparently not suffered as many qualms. The SarpanKum had insisted on elevating Choke from Levner—leader of a Fracture—to Vorsan—commander of a Shatter, fifteen thousand Chimeras. Choke was now a senior commander of the Eastern Plague, but he wasn't sure he was worthy or ready for such a promotion. There were so many details and responsibilities he was now required to manage.

For instance, as a Vorsan, he was expected to attend senior staff meetings, offer his thoughts on the organization of the Eastern Plague, and evaluate the Baels junior to him. And then there were times like this, when the senior staff had to assemble far from the rest of the Fan Lor Kum, in preparation for Mother's arrival. It was a supposed honor Li-Choke would have gladly foregone. His brothers stood in postures of nervous tension, shuffling about restlessly as they spoke to one another, sometimes laughing too loudly. Choke seemed the only one unaffected by anxiety. He stood alone and unmoving. Mother wasn't to be feared. She was to be scorned.

"Has Chak-Soon found any other Tigons worthy of instruction?" Li-Shard asked as he approached.

"Thus far, he's found seven others," Choke replied.

"Impressive. I would never have suspected that so many of the cats would have the wit to understand Hume's instructions," said the SarpanKum.

"Hopefully there will be more, but it isn't easy for them. They are pure carnivores. Their minds are those of a hunter. A predator. It is hard for them to see the world through the eyes of their prey."

The SarpanKum idly stroked one of his horns. "You raise an interesting concept. Is empathy best found amongst those who are herbivores?"

Choke tilted his head in thought. He had never considered the basis of empathy in such a light.

The SarpanKi, standing nearby, laughed. "I find such an idea dubious, at best," he said. "After all, how hard is it to understand the mind of a leaf, or a blade of grass?"

Choke stiffened, disliking the older Bael's derisive tone.

The SarpanKum didn't seem to mind, though, giving no hint he was offended by Li-Brind's mockery. "Omnivores then?" Li-Shard asked.

"More likely," Brind said.

"Humans are omnivores," Choke reminded them.

"And they also understand empathy. Like your friends Jessira Grey and Rukh Shektan," the SarpanKum noted. Shard shook his head in amazement. "No matter how many times I've heard it, I still find myself in awe of Dirge's accomplishments," he said. "We lost a great Bael when the Queen murdered him and the others."

Choke studied Li-Shard askance. In their time together, he had found the SarpanKum to be a strong, kind, and patient leader. It seemed Shard also possessed the mind of a scholar. And while he wasn't as wise as Li-Dirge, he was also much younger. With age, even that might change to Shard's favor.

Li-Choke nodded. "The SarpanKum used to speak of how the Lord often grants us opportunities to understand His will, but it is for us to decipher His intent. Only then, when our footsteps walk the path He intended for us will our hearts be at peace." Choke was glad for the renewal of his faith. Even in the best of times, it wasn't easy to believe in a just God, and following Dirge's death, his faith had worried away like a riverbank before a spring flood. Li-Choke had gone so far as to become indifferent to the proposition of whether Devesh even existed. Into that time of destitution had come Chak-Soon and the holy act of a Human Healing a Tigon. Apparently, Choke's faith had never truly been extinguished, and he found he was the happier for it.

Li-Brind, still cynical, obviously believed otherwise. "I am not as religious as Dirge must have been, nor am I certain Devesh is worthy of our worship. Why has he never done anything about Mother? As far as I am concerned, He should make His *intent* more obvious."

"Or maybe it *is* more obvious and we walk around with blinders. We do have His words from *The Book of All Souls*," the SarpanKum said.

"Li-Dirge believed as you, and so too did Jessira," Li-Choke said.

Li-Brind laughed. "Whether Devesh is real or a fable, why does it matter? We will soon come face-to-storm when Mother arrives. My faith in our Lord would be firmed if He did something about Her."

"Eight Tigons who adhere to tenets of fraternity aren't enough?" Li-Shard asked. He turned to Choke, letting the SarpanKi mull over the question. "And what has become of these eight new brothers?"

Choke smiled. "They've formed a claw. Chak-Soon believes all of them will eventually come to believe as he does." He bowed slightly. "By your leave, I've already moved them into my own Shatter." By tradition, disbursement of various units and warriors of the Fan Lor Kum was generally initiated by one of the Sarpans or even the SarpanKi. While Choke had wide discretion as a Vorsan, by pulling Chak-Soon's newly formed claw into the ranks of his own Shatter, he had bypassed the usual channels of command. He wasn't sure how Li-Shard would take his action. Or even Li-Brand, who was known to be a stickler for rules and protocol

"And from this seed, Chak-Soon hopes to lead others to the truth?" the SarpanKum asked, apparently disregarding Choke's breach of etiquette.

Choke nodded, letting out a soft exhalation of relief; but not daring to look toward Li-Brind, who was probably scowling in anger. "It is what I hope. There are a number of other Tigons in the Eastern Plague who might also come to believe as we do—given time and patient instruction."

Li-Brind snorted in derision. "Patience is not a virtue for which our Tigon brethren have ever been well known."

"Perhaps. But maybe it is one they can be taught," the

SarpanKum answered. "We have never tried to instruct their young, always believing they couldn't learn our lessons."

"It goes against their nature," Brind countered. "They are what they are. Chak-Soon and his cadre of fellow Tigons are an anomaly."

The obdurate edifice of Brind's skepticism had been momentarily cracked when he had heard Li-Choke's account of the events in Hammer, but over time, that firm foundation of cynicism had slowly been rebuilt, brick-by-disbelieving brick.

"You may very well be right," Li-Shard said. "But would you *want* to be right in this matter?"

His question had the SarpanKi discomfited.

Choke found himself impressed by Li-Shard. He hadn't refuted Brind's premise, but he had done something nearly as useful: with a single query, he had challenged the SarpanKi's cynical nature. He had gently urged the older Bael to give up his scornful doubt and embrace hope. Li-Dirge could not have done better.

"Do you know why the Queen has called for us?" Li-Brind asked, turning to Choke as he sought to change the subject. "She demanded your presence in particular."

Choke shook his head. "I don't know," he said. "Whatever it is, I'm sure we'll find it abhorrent."

"She comes," a young Bael said, pointing to the heavens where a wildly swirling cloud the color of an old bruise raced toward them.

"Bend knee and speak the Prayer of Gratitude," Li-Shard commanded. As one, the Baels fell to their knees, foreheads pressed to the wet ground.

Within moments, Mother was there, hovering above them and bearing a soft, spring shower. Thunder rumbled, but it was sporadic and distant, not nearly as frequent or loud as in times past. Choke would have preferred a raging torrent to this gentle rain. Ever since Mother had learned how to pour Her madness down the throats of the Fan Lor Kum, She was so much calmer, and as a result, so much more dangerous. The Plagues of Continent Ember didn't carry the stain of Mother's insanity, so most likely it was being borne by the Chimeras of Continent Catalyst. Regardless, on the few prior occasions when the Queen *had* housed Her madness within Her children on Continent Ember, She had always excluded the Baels. They had often wondered as to why and prayed their brothers on Catalyst had been similarly spared.

But though they did not have to carry even the smallest part of Mother's insanity, they could still sense Her emotions. And right now, Mother was excited, joyful. "My beloved children," She began, "I have need of your assistance."

Choke startled. Never before had She addressed them in such a way, nor had She ever sounded so gentle and caring. Always before, Mother had spoken to the Baels as their distant and cruel Mistress, ordering them about with no regard as to whether they could carry out Her commands. He cast a quick glance upward before returning to a still posture of attentive obedience, head bent low.

"Rise, and hearken unto My words," Mother continued.

With shuffling feet and the groan and creak of leather harnesses, the Baels rose to their feet. Some of the younger brothers shared looks of confusion and concern. It was an uncertainty Li-Choke shared. A young Bael glanced at him, a look of fear on his face. A slight head shake was all Choke could offer, warning the young brother to stillness.

"Miles north there stands a cesspool, a fever-swamp of corruption and evil," Mother said. "We will go to this diseased place and with wind, storm, fire, and blades, we will lance this pus-ridden boil and forever wash away its stench from the sweet soil of our world. Thus, will Li-Choke lead forth a full Shatter of the Fan Lor Kum into the heart of the Privation Mountains. Come forth child, and receive My blessings and My command."

Li-Choke's earlier bravery was abruptly vanished. It was one thing to be present during one of Mother's visits, but it was another to have Her specifically call him forth, to have Her speak directly to him. When the senior commanders of the Fan Lor Kum were gathered together in preparation for one of the Queen's visitations, it had *always* been the case that She spoke only with the SarpanKum.

But the world was changed. Mother was changed—but She remained a dread, fearsome Goddess.

Li-Choke had to swallow down a bitter bolus of bile. His knees trembled, and he locked them in place, stiffening his spine and his resolve. He had to be strong so Mother's wrath wouldn't fall upon his brothers. He made his way forward; moving with what he hoped was a deliberate, confident pace until he stood beside Li-Shard. "What is Your will, my Queen?" he asked in a strong voice.

Thunder rumbled as Mother seemed to laugh. "Though you were once commanded by the traitor, Li-Dirge, your actions in Hammer and afterward have redeemed you in My eyes," She said. Her words held a tinge of mockery. "I trust you have fully grasped My lesson from those many months ago on the Hunters Flats?"

The Queen referred to the murder of his brothers, and Her threat to do the same to the rest of the Baels. Her reminder gave him an opportunity to focus on something other than fear. He gripped tight his anger. In fact, had it been only his life in the balance, he might have spit in the Queen's face and told Her to shove Her commands to the unholy hells. After all, what could She really do to him? Kill him? So what. He was but one soul and he could only die once. But there were all the other Baels to think about. She would murder them if Choke defied Her. He had to do as the Queen commanded, but he would still do his best to thwart Her will. "What am I to do?" Choke asked, grinding out the words past his fury.

"Take a Shatter of My children and follow Me north," Mother commanded. "I will mark your way. You will know when we have arrived. An area south of the Gaunt River is our destination."

Li-Choke nodded, though he was confused. What did Mother intend in some empty part of the world, deep in the Privations? "And when we arrive, what are we to do?"

"Kill any Humans I flush from their venomous lair."

Horror worked its way down Li-Choke's spine. Jessira's home. By the barest of margins, he kept his legs from shaking. "What lair?" he asked.

Mother laughed once more, and lightning streaked the sky. "You will see. Be ready within a fortnight." Her words spoken, the Queen took to the sky and raced off, leaving the Baels to stand about, muttering in confusion.

As soon as She was lost from sight, Li-Shard turned to Choke. "Do you know what She intends?" the SarpanKum demanded.

"I fear She has discovered Jessira Grey's home," Li-Choke replied. "Jessira was always careful never to speak of her city's location, but it seemed most likely to lie hidden somewhere in the Privations."

"The city has no Oasis?" Li-Brind asked.

Choke nodded. "Most likely," he replied. "From what I could ascertain, it is a relatively young city."

"Mother will kill them all," Brind said, sounding appalled despite his hard-bitten cynicism.

"No," Li-Shard said. "She will kill most of them, and we can do nothing to prevent it. But we will do our best to save as many as possible."

"How?" Brind demanded.

"If Jessira had simply trusted me with the location, we could have sent brothers north to warn them," Choke said, furious with the situation.

"Calm yourselves," the SarpanKum said. "The hour is dark, but all is not lost. Take Chak-Soon and his claw. Here is what you must do."

Late into the day, they discussed their plans.

———●———

Mother Lienna waited exactly one fortnight before leading Her children north. She marked out their path, moving slowly so the Fan Lor Kum could more easily follow Her.

While journeying through the mountains, She occasionally came across UnCasted Humans. It had been an unpleasant surprise witnessing so many of them, scurrying about like lice. Once, She would not have seen them. Their means of hiding from Her, their Blends were good, but they no longer sufficed to veil them from Her sight. For millennia Lienna had forgotten the Talents She had once possessed as a Human. She had forgotten Her singular gift: the ability to *feel Jivatma*, like the soft caress of a feather against Her cheek. Her Talent had been one of the reasons Lienna had once been considered the finest Healer in the world. But now Her gift would serve a different calling. If She searched patiently and carefully, She could find any Human anywhere, whether they were Blended or not. And She would kill them all.

So She made Her way through the Privation Mountains, finding caves now and then with UnCasted Humans hiding inside. Their lives were snuffed out and their lairs crushed, buried beneath heaps of rubble. Lienna smiled to Herself with each death. There would be no chance for the vermin to raise an alarm and allow their fellow parasites to flee their hidden city prior to Her arrival.

She travelled on, and eventually came upon a strange rock formation. She chuckled at the sight of it, remembering what it was like to be Human. So phallic. And it so thoughtfully pointed Her children in the direction She intended: toward a large mountain lake shaped like a tear drop. South of the water were fields of grain.

CHAPTER THIRTY-THREE
A DREAM SHATTERED

When we die, will the world notice? It is a hard question to ponder.
I fear we are habitual liars, creatures of self-deceit. I fear we are each
of us a fractured leaf fluttering alone in a cold and empty wind.

~ A Wandering Notion, by Shone Brick, AF 1784

R ukh toyed with the unfamiliar wine-red bracelet—a *kalava*—
circling his left wrist. It was a simple band of ironwood,
plain and unadorned, but it had a glow, a shiny sheen to it
that brightly reflected the early morning sunlight. Rukh had only
received the *kalava* a week ago. Jessira had given it to him on their
wedding night, and he hadn't yet grown used to the feel of it, but
already he enjoyed its heft and what it represented. According to the
customs of Stronghold, the *kalava* signified the bonds by which a
husband was tied to his wife. For her part, Jessira had received a
thaali—a black-beaded necklace worn close to her heart and meant to
symbolize the love she would feel only for her husband. And both
pieces of jewelry had been fashioned from the same plank of
ironwood.

Rukh twirled the bracelet, watching as it spun on his wrist and
glinted in the early morning sunlight as he walked a wide dirt-packed

trail that circled to the east of Stronghold. Following behind were Cedar, Jessira, and Court Deep—the Silversuns—and a few members of Sign's unit, the Shadowcats. Rukh planned on taking them to a field of boulders, a level area where he had done much of his training. It was a wide-open space, perfect for the Ashokan techniques Rukh planned on teaching the Stronghold warriors and far better than the constricting rings of East Lock.

The instruction also gave him an excuse to get out of the city. Too many of Stronghold's warriors viewed him with an unsettling attitude of deference and hero-worship.

The path widened out onto a field littered with boulders and sharp, protruding stones. The area was several hundred feet higher up in elevation than Stronghold itself and had a broad view of the valley encompassing Teardrop Lake and the Croft. It felt private and secluded, yet still a part of the wide world beyond. Farn had been the one to show it to Rukh. The air was cool, but spring had found its grip. The slopes of Mount Frame were covered with green shoots straining to reach the sunshine while fields of pale, yellow wildflowers joyously waved upon their slender stems. There was a feeling in the air, a bubbly sensation demanding a festive celebration.

Spring fever.

Rukh wanted to dance.

"You're not already getting tired of wearing my *kalava*, are you?" Jessira teased, surprising him from behind.

Rukh laughed and by way of answer, he took her in his arms and twirled her about. He didn't care if the Silversuns and Shadowcats—who had straggled up to their position—groaned in disgust upon seeing his display of affection.

"They should go back to the wedding cabin," one of the scouts muttered in mock-revulsion.

Rukh smiled, not embarrassed in the slightest. Spring fever was too wonderful to keep trapped inside.

Jessira punched him in the shoulder. "We should get to work," she said, a warm smile lighting her face.

For the rest of the morning, the Silversuns and the Shadowcats faced off against one another. They sparred while Rukh walked amongst them, correcting forms and postures when necessary. Because of the times he'd trained against Jessira, he already knew what problems to look for. The manner by which Stronghold's warriors were taught was quite different than the instruction Rukh had received in the House of Fire and Mirrors. Here, form and appearance often took precedence over practicality. The Silversuns and Shadowcats flowed through pretty patterns, but their choreographed techniques often left them off balance and poorly prepared to defend against a warrior who might choose to take a different angle than their forms allowed.

"It's not how we were taught," a Shadowcat muttered.

Rukh recognized the warrior. He had been present when Rukh had first entered Stronghold. Tire Cloud was his name. Brother to Wheel Cloud, twice Champion of the Trials of Hume, and the man Rukh had defeated to take the title. "You think I was victorious because I'm faster than the warriors here?" Rukh guessed.

Tire thrust out his chin. "Of course that's why," the young warrior replied. "Even with a Constrainer, your speed was your advantage. If you fought with skill alone and didn't tap your *Jivatma*, how good would you be then?" he challenged.

"Ready your shoke," Rukh said. "We'll find out."

His words drew a buzz of anticipation from the gathered warriors, who began wagering amongst themselves. All of them seemed to be betting on how many strokes it would take for Rukh to defeat Tire. No one was wagering on the opposite occurring.

Tire had initially worn a look of anticipation as he stepped forward, but as he heard the laughter and wagering from those around him, his face fell into a sour grimace. "What an idiot," Sign

Deep said, loud enough for everyone to hear and further humiliating the young Strongholder.

Rukh felt a spike of sympathy for the Shadowcat. No one deserved to be shamed in front of their peers like that. Still, he couldn't take it easy on Tire. The Strongholder would know and would resent the condescension even more than he would the laughter thrown his way by the gathered warriors.

Cedar stepped forward. "On my word," he said. He gave Tire a quick, assessing glance before turning away with a shake of his head.

Rukh studied his opponent, looking for balance and angle of the shoke.

"Begin," Cedar said.

A blocked slash and a hard kick to the gut, and Tire was down. Rukh hadn't even moved from his stance.

Tire lay on the ground and gasped for breath. The kick had knocked the wind out of him.

"I didn't use *Jivatma*," Rukh said. "All I needed was knowledge." He looked the watching warriors in the eyes. "Knowledge and will are the keys to victory in any situation."

"Again," Tire said once he had his breath back.

"Later," Rukh promised. He reached down and helped Tire back to his feet. "We need to finish up here first."

He was about to lead the Silversuns and the Shadowcats through another series of lessons, but from the corner of his eye, he caught movement. To the southeast, trivial as a dust mote but coming their way, a bruise-colored cloud raced the wind.

Rukh's heart clenched.

Jessira followed his gaze, and the color drained from her face. "Devesh save us," she whispered.

The other warriors noticed their fear, but when they followed Rukh and Jessira's gaze, all they saw was a cloud. They turned to one another in confusion.

"We have to get back to the city," Rukh said. "Warn them. If you have a place to hide or a way to evacuate Stronghold, we have to do it. Now!"

"It's just a cloud," Tire said, confused.

Sign was amongst the first to realize what approached. "Devesh save us. It's the Queen. The Sorrow Bringer."

———●———

Lienna surged forward, Her goal was in sight: a large valley, plowed and planted with straight rows of cabbage, wheat, carrots, and barley. Once, She would have taken delight in the growing of crops, but now She saw them for what they truly were: a blight upon the skin of Arisa. The plants and vegetables Humanity used to feed themselves had to be expunged. And this time, Lienna had brought something with Her, something She had never before conceived of using.

And it was all because Her mind was finally clear.

Mother and Father might still mutter now and again, but Their utterances were tolerable. They would always be there—a residual effect of the Withering Blade, which had trapped Their minds—Mother's more than Father's—within the recesses of Lienna's consciousness. But at least Mistress Arisa was gone. Silenced forever.

As for the valley of crops...Lienna smiled. She would smite this infestation and cleanse the land altogether with a sandstorm.

Lienna aimed for the fields, unleashing a scouring tornado wind of shredding sand. All the trees and plants were ripped apart and the soil denuded. Lienna scrubbed the very stones and ground to mirror smoothness.

———●———

Jessira dropped her shoke and anything else that might slow her down. Nothing mattered but alerting Stronghold. The Queen would arrive in minutes. Rukh was already far down the trail, a distant figure outstripping all of them.

A howling wind, full of biting dust and debris, shrieked overhead. Jessira glanced up, her mouth dry with fear.

The Sorrow Bringer.

Jessira stumbled to a halt and watched in horror as Suwraith launched Herself at the Croft. The Queen smashed into the ground, raising a dust cloud that soared skyward. It took on the same mushroom shape as when Suwraith had crunched into the pond, the night Rukh had read *The Book of First Movement*. Seconds later, a dull roar washed over her, building in intensity until it was a howling wail. The Sorrow Bringer traversed the Croft, stripping the ground bare and wrecking the work of generations. In Her wake, She left behind a glassy sheen. The Queen had transformed fertile fields into a dead, crystalline desert.

"Move!" Cedar shouted. "We still have to warn Stronghold."

"There's no time," a warrior said. "She'll be on us in minutes."

"For all we know, She's only discovered the Croft and nothing else," Cedar replied. "We still have to warn Stronghold."

Jessira was no longer listening. She raced off. Need burned within her. Her family—her parents, her brother, Kart—all of them were trapped deep inside the bulk of Mount Fort. She had to try to reach them.

She ran on, heedless of the risks as she piled on the speed. Time slipped away and she cursed how long it was taking to reach the trail's head. Finally, the ground leveled out where the bases of Mounts Fort and Frame blended into the broad valley of Teardrop Lake and the Croft. Not much further to the East Gate.

Before she could enter the narrow cleft leading to the Gate, Rukh stopped her, clutching her arms and spinning her around so she was facing him. She hadn't even noticed him until just now. "I've already warned them," he said. "They're coming. But we have to get clear of the area before the Queen arrives."

Jessira tugged herself free of Rukh's hold. "My family...." She managed three steps before Rukh grabbed hold of her again and held her back.

"You can't," he said. "You'll only make it harder on anyone trying to get out." His face held a look of heartbreak and resolve.

Jessira tugged her arm free of his grip. "They're my family," she cried.

"So are Cedar, Court, and Sign," Rukh answered. "So am I," he added. "If you go inside, you'll be lost to us forever."

Jessira blinked as she took in his words, hating that he was right. She screamed, a raw animal cry of rage, frustration, and fear.

The rest of the Silversuns and Shadowcats arrived.

"I've already warned them," Rukh said before the others entered the cleft. "We should see evacuees coming out any moment."

Cedar breathed heavily, panting, but it seemed more likely from emotion than from the run down the mountain. He took a hesitant step forward. "My wife? My family?"

"It's all in Devesh's hands now," Jessira heard herself say.

"Then we're all doomed," a warrior muttered.

"Clear the area," Rukh said. "Once they come out, we have to lead them to shelter."

Cedar shuddered and he turned away from Stronghold. "We'll head back up the trail," he said, his voice throbbing with suppressed passion. "There's a rallying point no more than a couple miles on the far side of the field we were using."

"It's part of a series of caves we prepared in case something like this ever happened," Jessira explained after seeing Rukh's confusion.

A number of women and children as well as some warriors were making their way through the cleft—a throng, thick and filling the passageway from side-to-side. They were packed in so tight, it was hard for them to make headway. The crowd moved with sluggish speed. Most of them wouldn't make it if the Queen was already heading their way.

"Move it!" Jessira screamed.

"Cedar!" a woman cried out. It was Laya.

Cedar's face cleared into a look of joy and amazement. "Laya!"

"Hurry!" Rukh shouted. "She's coming." He pointed. High in the air, south of them and rapidly heading their way, came the Queen.

Cedar turned to Sign. "Take command of the Shadowcats. Lead our people to safety. Protect them! Chims are likely in the heights."

Sign nodded and with a gesture, she gathered the Shadowcats around her. She led a contingent of folk from Stronghold, the straggling few who had finally managed to exit the cleft.

Cedar turned to Jessira and Court. "We'll stay behind as long as we can; help get out as many as possible."

Jessira knew he would wait until the very end for Laya. Where was she? Jessira scanned the onrushing crowd, which was finally picking up speed. There! Still many yards deep within the passage.

Jessira startled as Rukh launched himself skyward. He landed on an outcropping fifteen feet deep into the cleft and a dozen feet above the crowd before taking off again. He hurdled his way down the throat of the passage, jumping from one spot to another, high above the streaming horde.

"Holy Devesh," Court murmured in awe.

Jessira didn't answer. Her attention was entirely on Rukh. She knew in any other time, she would have been awed by what he was doing: his balance, his grace, his power. Right now she was too afraid to do anything other than pray for him to hurry with whatever he had planned. She glanced skyward and her heart clenched. The Sorrow Bringer was nearly upon them. "Hurry, Rukh," she whispered.

Rukh landed beside Laya. Without missing a beat, he grabbed

her up and hurled himself back in the air. He made his way back through the cleft, bypassing the struggling, seething mass of people below.

Cedar's fists were clenched tight as he wore a look of desperate hope on his face.

Seconds later, Rukh landed beside them. He set Laya on her feet before almost falling to the ground himself, gasping for breath. Jessira reached for him, holding him up. "Thank you," she whispered in his ear.

"We need to get moving," Court said, propping Rukh up from the other side.

Jessira glanced up the trail. The Silversuns were urging their fellow Strongholders to greater speed. But as one, they stumbled to an uncertain halt. Many of them pointed to the sky and screamed in terror as Suwraith circled in a tight spiral. At any moment, She would attack the East Gate.

"Run!" Cedar shouted, getting them moving. Rukh shook himself free of Jessira and Court, staggering toward the path.

Jessira watched him, ready to help if needed. As strong as he was, she knew his vaulting leaps through the cleft couldn't have been easy.

More screams, this time from behind them. The Queen had taken on the shape of an arrowhead, pointed at the heart of their city. Suwraith plunged downward on a rush of wind. Those still in the passageway wouldn't make it.

The Sorrow Bringer seemed to cry out in triumph, a static shout of crackling lightning and booming thunder. She slammed into the narrow, open-ceilinged tunnel leading to the East Gate, folding it over as if were made of soft dough. Stone cracked, boulders tumbled, and the passage was filled with tons of falling debris. Hundreds were crushed.

Lienna, Her work above the fields complete, flew toward the hidden city of UnCasted Humans. They would all die, even the pitiful few who had already begun to scatter like cockroaches scuttling from the light. Let them flee. She'd hunt them down after She had finished off the rest of their wretched brethren, hiding as they were like rats within the nearby mountain. Did they think the mountain's mass would hide them? Protect them?

She smiled to Herself. They were sadly mistaken. She would crush their home, while Her child, Li-Choke, would execute any who managed to escape Her righteous vengeance. And She knew Choke would carry out Her will. He knew the penalty of defiance.

Lienna cried out, a fierce, triumphant scream of lightning and thunder as She arrowed downward. Her goal was the passage from which the miserable Humans poured forth. Her aim was true, and She smashed into the walls, laughing with joy as they collapsed inward, burying hundreds of the Human pests beneath mountains of rubble. Screams of the dying—hundreds, possibly thousands—rose through the wreckage of the passage. The fear of those still trapped smelled sweet like honeysuckle.

Done. No more of the vermin would escape from that route. But to the west, another stream of the parasites sought to escape their tomb.

Pleasure bubbled through Lienna. It had been too long since She had unleashed Her vengeance upon the Human scum. Mistress Arisa would be pleased.

The pleasure slipped away like a fish struggling through Her frantic grasp. Mistress Arisa wasn't real. Even as Lienna thrust aside the hideous memory of the fiend She had once worshipped, questions arose within Her mind. If Mistress Arisa wasn't real, then what was the point of killing the Humans? The answer came fitfully, in unhappy spurts. Had Lienna done as She had over the millennia because She believed Humanity to be a plague on the world? Was there no deeper reason, nothing more rational?

She pushed aside the irritating voice challenging Her beliefs. It sounded too much like Mother, and Mother was long since dead. Besides, She still had work to do. She had no more time for philosophy.

She soared westward, closing off a few smaller exits as She went, killing the few ant-like lines of dismal Humans who had managed to make it to the surface. Her goal, though, was the other main entrance and exit from the UnCasted city. And when She reached it, She smashed the passageway leading inward into heaps of rubble just as She had in the east. But this time, She kept on going, burrowing inside. The dying screams from the swarming mass of maggots lurking within was like music in Her figurative ears. And all throughout, She sent Her scouring sandstorms streaming down tunnels and darkened passageways, shredding and tearing everyone She came across into bloody ribbons.

"Why do You kill them?"

Lienna pulled up short, Her rage momentarily over taken by a needle of fear upon hearing the question. The voice had sounded disquietingly like Mistress Arisa. Lienna paused in Her destruction and listened further, desperate to hear nothing.

And thankfully, there was only blessed quiet.

Lienna moved on and Death rode Her wake. Not even the screams of Her victims could penetrate the cyclone howl of Her raging winds as She murdered the underground city. Splatters of blood, like ink stains, were the only remnants of Her victims. For their sins, they had to die.

"What sins?"

Mother.

"Why do You murder them?"

Father.

"Weakling."

Mistress Arisa.

The prior needle of fear became a thick spar. Lienna paused once again and whimpered. None of them were real. Within Her mind were Mother's memories and possibly some of Father's, but nothing more. Mother and Father were gone, and Mistress Arisa had never existed.

"Then why do You murder in My name?"

The fear blanketed Lienna, and She waited in huddled fear. Her whipping winds became slow, sullen gusts as She tried to still Her racing, terrified thoughts. Arisa wasn't real. She couldn't be. She had merely been a figment of Lienna's insanity. Nothing more. She held tight to the thought as She waited in the darkness and silence. She prayed—to whom She didn't know since either Devesh didn't exist or He was powerless to oppose Her—but She prayed, nonetheless, hoping to never again hear the voice from Her madness, hoping that the angry, ugly, hurtful voice would be silenced forever. She prayed nothing would break the quiet.

"To whom do you pray?" Mistress Arisa asked.

Lienna screamed.

She raced away with a shriek, trying to outrun Mistress' maniacal laughter. It chased after Her, even as She exterminated the hidden city of UnCasted Humans. In some fashion, their screaming deaths helped quiet Lienna's own inner demons.

Sateesh Grey had only heard the warning bells of Stronghold rung once before. It had been years ago, when a fire had broken out in

Crofthold Jonie, consuming several flats on Plot Find. The smoke had carried throughout Stronghold, coating most every hallway and tunnel with a thin layer of fine sooty ash. It had taken weeks to scrub the scent of smoke from the city.

Today, Sateesh had expected something similar: a fire or some other kind of natural disaster. He had rushed from his workroom down in Plot Art of Crofthold Discus. Only after he had run into several friends did he learn the true extent of the disaster facing his home.

Suwraith was coming to Stronghold. It was his people's greatest fear. The Sorrow Bringer would destroy the city.

Evacuation would save a few, but for most there would be little hope, those like Sateesh's family, who were buried too deep within the mountain to reach the surface in time. They would simply be trapped in tunnels full of screaming, terrified people as the Sorrow Bringer brought the ceilings down on their heads. Today, then, would be the end of Sateesh's family and of nearly everyone he loved.

All but maybe Jessira, Cedar, Court, and Sign. They might survive the coming holocaust. The four of them had planned on traveling to a place on Mount Frame where Rukh Shektan trained. Sateesh prayed they were still out there, somewhere safe from the Sorrow Bringer. He added Laya to his prayers. She might be out there as well. She had planned on picnicking with Cedar along the shores of Teardrop Lake and share with him the joy of knowing she was pregnant. It was knowledge that only her own parents, Crena, and Sateesh knew. Another grandchild, and Sateesh would never see the infant born.

So many regrets on this day of doom. Where would the people of Stronghold go? How many would survive, or would this be the end of the OutCastes? It was an unfair world in which they lived. Perhaps the next one—the one on the other side of the bridge of life—would be better.

He prayed it would be so. So many prayers to offer, so many needs. He even voiced a supplication for his new son-in-law, Rukh Shektan, regretting he couldn't have gotten to know the man better. So proud was the Kumma, but he had also taught the OutCastes to be wary of their own arrogance. And that he made Jessira happy was obvious to anyone who saw the two of them together, always seeking one another in a crowded room and sharing a smile whenever their gazes met.

Sateesh climbed the stairs of Crofthold Lucent, wanting to reach his home. His family would have realized the futility of attempted escape and would be there even now, waiting for him at their flat. It was where Sateesh needed to be.

On his way there, he ran into dear friends, and he paused long enough to share a few final words with them. They spoke of regrets and love before embracing a last time. Sateesh knew he would never again see any of those warm, wonderful people.

As Sateesh hurried through the tunnels of Crofthold Lucent, he was struck by the silence of the city. Though the hallways were crowded, the people—usually so boisterous and alive—walked in a stern quiet with heads held high. There was no wailing or crying for salvation. No gnashing of teeth and tearing of clothes. His people were strong, and their bravery, their nobility in the face of annihilation almost unmanned him. These were good people. They didn't deserve to die like this one. No one did: murdered by a mad fiend.

Sateesh approached his flat and struggled to hold back the tears. He ached for his people. What had been the point of Stronghold's existence if it was to be wiped away as if it had never existed? All the generations before, their struggle, their sacrifice—did it mean nothing? He hoped it wasn't the case, prayed that their cries in the wilderness were heard.

Before entering his flat, Sateesh stifled his tears, not wanting his family to see his weakness. They needed his strength in order to face this final day with the grace of their ancestors.

He opened the door. Crena sat on the sofa with their middle grandchild, Lure, in her lap. The child, only nine, looked so much like his namesake uncle, but he would never have a chance to grow up. Jeshni sat alongside Crena with her two youngest, Cearthee and Mahri, both girls, huddled in her arms. Kart stood alongside his wife, a frozen look of mourning on his face. He held tight the hand of his oldest child, Ruhile, who was almost twelve. The boy stood quietly, but terror lurked behind his eyes.

Seeing his grandson's fear, Sateesh collapsed to his knees and finally gave in to his grief. He could no longer hold back the tears, and he sobbed. He gathered his family to him. "It will all be fine," he lied, kissing the heads of Cearthee and Mahri. He clutched Lure, hugging him fiercely, never wanting to let him go. He didn't want to let any of them go. He wanted to see his grandchildren grow up and live wondrous lives of their own, to have all the joy he had been so blessed to experience.

"Are we going to die?" a soft voice asked. It was Ruhile.

Sateesh glanced at Kart, who quietly and almost imperceptibly shook his head. His son didn't want Ruhile to know the truth. So be it. Sateesh mustered a smile. "Devesh will see us through," he said. "We are just afraid of what might happen first."

Lure stroked Sateesh's cheeks. "Amma says it's a sin to lie."

Sateesh's smile faltered. "It is not a lie to say Devesh will see us through, or that He waits for us, one hand always open to bring us home."

"Then we are going to die," Ruhile said, sounded certain. He shuddered but didn't cry. His bravery was beautiful to behold. What a man he would have been.

"Only our bodies," Crena said, speaking into the silence. "Our souls and *Jivatma* will shelter in Devesh's loving embrace. The First

527

Father and Mother will show us the way to our Lord."

A noise of thunder and breaking stone reached them, along with distant, short-lived screams.

Cearthee whimpered and buried her head against Jeshni's leg.

"I love you," Crena said, drawing Mahri to her lap, but speaking to all of them "The Lord loves you. This is not the end. It is just the beginning of a wondrous journey. Remember His promise as it is written in *The Book of All Souls: in all the years of a person's life is there a season. Now is our time for repose and prayer. Seek His light and let the fear pass; for nothing of this world can truly harm you.* Our Lord's promise is real. I know it to be true."

Sateesh's heart swelled with pride. Crena was so quiet and unassuming that others took her to be meek. She was anything but. Crena was the rock, the foundation of everything good in Sateesh's life. She was the shelter and the harbor where he had anchored his soul against the wreaking tides of the world. Crena was everything.

The screams grew closer. Louder. The walls shook. Pebbles and chunks of stone fell to the ground. Larger pieces tumbled to the floor in shards and splinters. Echoing booms carried as tunnels collapsed and ceilings crumbled to dust. All of Plot Discus shuddered.

Sateesh could hear the thudding blows of walls punched open. He pulled his family closer about him, holding tight to them as if they might fly away from his grip in the coming storm. He whispered soft words of encouragement as the youngest among them cried again. He spoke brave words for his brave grandchildren. He cried for them. Their lovely light would be snuffed out before it could truly shine.

Still, he spoke his words of bravery, not caring how they tasted like bitter burnt offerings in his mouth. He would speak them over and over again if they brought even the slightest degree of comfort to his grandchildren.

Closer.

"I love you," Kart said to his family. All of his children were crying now, trembling in fear, even the oldest Ruhile.

"I love you," Sateesh said.

A closer boom. Sateesh looked in the direction from which the sounds were coming. A final echoing thud smashed through his family's home, followed close by a raging wind full of scouring sand.

For an instant only, Sateesh knew terrible pain as his skin was flayed. The screams of his family were mercifully brief. Then all was quiet, except the singing light of Blessed Peace.

Li-Choke stood at the forefront of a single Fracture. He glanced back at the Chimeras strung out along the floor and surrounding ridges of a ravine running north-to-south. Sheer cliff walls—hundreds of feet tall and streaked with green and orange from copper and iron deposits—reared on either side of the canyon, casting much of it in near perpetual gloom. The sun struggled to reach the boulder-strewn floor of the ravine, leaving it cool and untouched by spring's warmth. Long stalactites of ice speared downward from beneath the shadow of rocky overhangs and a wide, shallow stream gurgled in eddies and rapids as it made its way north.

In that direction, the canyon opened out, revealing a tremendous plume of dust blasted into the sky. It lifted heavenward, several miles from where the Fracture stood. A moment later came a sound of thunder. Choke rocked back on his feet, and the echoing boom hurled many Chimeras off their feet. It was a fearful sight, and the Fan Lor Kum watched it in stunned silence. Choke swallowed hard and came to a halt. How many had just been murdered by Mother's hideous will?

Li-Boil, his second in command—his VorsanKi—edged up to

Choke's side. The western Bael was the elder by several seasons, but right now, he seemed the younger. He looked to Choke for guidance. "What evil has She done?" he asked in a fearful whisper.

"A terrible crime. Many of our brothers and sisters died today," Choke answered.

"Humans?"

"Who else?"

"And what of us? Are we to go north and carry out Mother's will? Destroy the survivors?"

Choke turned to him in surprise. "You were present when the SarpanKum and the senior staff decided on how best to deal with this situation," he said. "We'll do our best *not* to engage with any survivors."

"But what of the other Fractures? You've split our forces. What if the Humans survive Mother's wrath in greater numbers than we expect? If even several thousand of them come upon us, we'll be slaughtered like Pheds."

"If several thousand of them were to survive, it would be a wondrous miracle," Choke replied. "I fear it will be far fewer."

"Perhaps. But they would seek our death. And I must know why these strangers are more important than our own brethren?"

Choke was no longer surprised by Boil's lack of commitment to the ideals of fraternity. It was an unexpected failing in far too many of the western Baels. How could so many of his western brothers, the ones Hume had first instructed in the tenets and ideals of fraternity, have lost their way? It was sad to see. Thankfully, the current SarpanKum, Li-Shard, was an exception, and hopefully, he would be able to lead the western Baels back to the righteous path of their ancestors.

"There are times when we must willingly give all we have, even for a stranger," Choke answered. "Death is fearful, but living with the sin of murder is far worse."

"We aren't the ones who killed them," Boil protested.

"Aren't we?" Choke asked. "Simply standing aside when we could have helped those facing Mother's fury does not absolve us, nor can we claim to honor Hume's teachings if we were to act in such a way."

"Then what would you have us do?" Boil asked, settling down into a posture of attentiveness.

"The other Fractures are ranged all along the Privation Mountains. They are miles distant from us and ill-positioned to co-ordinate either with us or with each other."

"We're positioned in such a way that we won't be able to trap any who flee. Is that why you've called a halt to our march?"

"Yes," Choke said. "It is only the first step in our ultimate aim."

"Which is?"

Choke smiled. "As it has been since Hammer's demise: thwart Mother's will."

Boil nodded. "A good plan," he said, not sounding particularly convinced. A moment later, he was called away to settle a problem.

Choke watched his VorsanKi depart, wondering anew how the western Baels had forgotten so much of Hume's teachings.

But it was a question for another time.

Other issues occupied his thoughts. He wished he had a way to know how Chak-Soon was doing. He had tasked the young Tigon and his special claw with a special mission, one only he and the SarpanKum knew about. Chak-Soon had been sent to the Soulless River, separate from the rest of the Fan Lor Kum. He was to prepare for what Choke had hoped wouldn't be needed. But with today's events, it seemed it would be.

Much rested on whether Chak-Soon had completed his mission. If he had, then some small portion of this calamity might still be put to right. Choke hoped so. Thus far, so much had simply gone wrong. For instance, Choke had planned on alerting the warriors and scouts of this hidden mountain city that enemies approached. He had wanted to give as many of them as possible a chance to escape the coming destruction, but Mother had made sure no such warning could be carried. For the past few days, the Fan Lor Kum had come across a number of small caves and well-hidden cabins. They were outposts of the mountain city, and all of them had been obliterated. None of the scouts within had managed to escape, and reports indicated other such redoubts in every other direction had been similarly destroyed.

The city Mother was exterminating had been caught sleeping with no awareness of the death coming their way. The terrible irony of it all was that if not for Li-Dirge's bilgewater story about a city hidden in the mountains—a story meant to save Ashoka—none of this would have come to pass. The Queen would have never discovered this place.

Li-Boil returned. "A nest reports a body of Human warriors— perhaps as many as fifty—traversing the valley just on the other side of the eastern ridge. Blended and with hardly any signs of their passage. The Ur-Fels say they found evidence of their existence purely by accident: a dropped leather glove."

"How far ahead are they?"

"A few hours."

Choke grunted. "If we're lucky, they're warriors Mother missed on Her way here." He considered what to do about the situation. Fifty warriors couldn't do much against the Shatter sent north, but they might be the difference between life and death for a number of their fellow Humans. "Have the Ur-Fels and Braids leave them be. *We* will deal with them."

"We?"

"You and I and eight Baels of my choosing," Choke said. "Command of the Fracture in our absence will be given over to Li-Silt." Choke trusted Silt. The old Bael was someone who was devout in his beliefs regarding Hume's teachings.

"If we aren't careful, Mother will do to all of us as She did to Li-Dirge," Boil warned.

There it was. The older Bael's words only confirmed what Choke had long since suspected. The western brothers were terrified of extinction, and after last summer's events on the Hunters Flats, it was a rational fear. For three hundred years, the Baels had worked to disrupt Mother's plans, but just as diligently, they had hidden their deception. They knew the penalty for betrayal, an instruction vividly explained by the execution of the eastern Baels. And yet, Choke didn't believe Dirge's death and the extermination of his eastern brothers was a reason to abandon the unity of brotherhood. There had to be more to life than simply existing. A being had to have a purpose.

"We will be careful," Choke said. "But we also cannot step aside and say this isn't our fight. We will do all we can without risking that Mother sees our deceit."

Boil didn't appear convinced. "Did Dirge believe as you?" he challenged.

Choke frowned at the not-so-subtle insult. "Dirge lived to see the fulfillment of our deepest dreams: brotherhood with a Human. It was worth his life. And ours. Our SarpanKum—your SarpanKum—affirmed that. You would be wise to heed him."

Boil bowed his head. "As always, I heed those with greater wisdom. I just hope that by doing so, I don't live to see our kind destroyed and our lives stolen from us."

"Our lives belong to Devesh; we simply borrow them. And He will reclaim what is His when the time is right."

The terrain had grown familiar as Farn Arnicep led the Ashokans toward Stronghold. He recognized this long valley, the shallow stream flowing from here to the Croft, where it merged with the River Fled. He even remembered some of the stone outcroppings jutting out from the high granite cliffs and mesas forming the valley's northern and southern border. They were but hours from the Croft.

Of course, the last time he had been through here, the stream had been iced over and the stony ground covered with a fresh layer of snow. Now, patches of tall, soft grass and fields of wildflowers in bloom softened the rocky terrain. Mountain bluebirds and robins trilled their delight in the early morning sunlight and fat bumblebees flitted about, lost in orgiastic delight as they fed on nectar and pollen. The clean scent of pine drifted on the soft breeze as stands of cottonwoods and aspen shaded the Ashokans riding quietly. It was a lovely spring morning.

Farn chewed his lip in worry.

Last time he'd been through here, there had been small outposts set up to monitor every approach to the city. Of course, in the winter, the Home Army of Stronghold didn't man the outposts. Given that Suwraith's creatures *always* waged war in warmer weather, the chance of an attack in heavy snow and cold was exceedingly small.

But it was spring now, and warm.

So where were the warriors? They should have confronted the Ashokans by now. But there was nothing, only a world strangely silent. Worst of all, every one of the outposts the Ashokans had come across had been destroyed by cave-ins.

It stretched credibility. One or even two, Farn could have accepted since earthquakes might be frequent in the mountains. But all of them? It defied logic and chance. Something else had happened. Something bad.

The answer to his unsettling question came a moment later in the form of a titanic cloud exploding skyward from the west. It rose higher and higher. A mile or more it soared. Seconds later, a thunderous boom washed over the Ashokans, the shock wave bending trees, grass, and men alike.

"Holy Devesh," Jaresh said, picking himself off the ground. "What in the unholy hells was that?" Jaresh was a good man. A fine warrior, tough and efficient. He was certainly as skilled as any Muran and Rahail. And he was scared, as well he should be.

Farn certainly was.

He now understood what he and the rest of the Ashokans faced. The strange silence, the absent scouts…all of it made sense now. The grim cloud to the west was in the general direction of the Croft. Something terrible had happened, and something worse was about to happen to Stronghold. Suwraith must have discovered Stronghold.

Farn feared for what was coming next. While he hadn't always been happy during his time amongst the OutCastes, time and distance had given him a new perspective. Fifty-five Humans had hewn a city from the stone heart of a mountain and grown to a multitude. It was the stuff of legends. It was inspirational, and it should be applauded, but Farn understood what that terrible black cloud presaged. Stronghold's existence might end today.

And Rukh might be there. Farn swallowed down his fear. They had to find out what had happened, and save anyone they could.

"Everyone tighten your Blend! Make them as hard as you can!" Farn shouted before turning to Jaresh. "Suwraith. I think the cloud is from Suwraith. She means to destroy Stronghold."

The blood drained from Jaresh's face. "Rukh."

"We have to hurry if we want to do any good here. Stronghold doesn't have an Oasis, and without one, the city stands naked before the Queen. We have to save as many as we can."

With a heavy exhalation, Jaresh seemed to take a hold of his terror. When he next met Farn's gaze, the fear was gone—or at least suppressed—from his eyes. Jaresh nodded. "There's likely to be Chimeras in the hills," he said. "We'll have to be doubly careful."

Farn grunted even as he silently admired Jaresh's courage. He loved his cousin like a brother, but this journey had taught him to respect him as a man. Jaresh would have made a fine Kumma. "Keep your eyes and ears sharp. And no wandering off," he said to the fifty-two warriors under his command. "We need our Blends tight and over-lapping."

If anything, the warriors grew more grim and determined. They loosened scabbarded swords and strung bows, readying for the battle all of them knew was coming. Farn wouldn't have expected anything less. They were Ashokans. They knew their duty.

"Devesh see us through," Jaresh said.

"Right now, no one else can," Farn said.

"What are your orders?" Lieutenant Danslo asked, his face properly stoic.

"We go and learn what's happened to Rukh. And Stronghold. And put the purifying fire to any who need it," Farn answered.

Lienna exulted. The city was broken. Its people were dead and dying. Her work here was all but complete. There were a few Humans left, huddled and terrified in narrow tunnels deep within the heart of the mountain. They would likely die of dehydration, but Lienna saw no need to take any chances. The Human infestation needed uprooting, with no chance for the vermin to re-establish their hold here. Lienna sent out tendrils of Her sandstorm and killed those few people who must have believed themselves safe from Her wrath.

It was done, and She blasted an exit through the side of the mountain. She rained an avalanche of rocks and boulders down below, but She didn't notice. Outside, some of the pests had emerged like locusts, fleeing the destruction of their city. The vermin ranged all over the slopes of the surrounding hills and valleys, but soon, they too would be dead. Her Chims would see to it. They would find and kill the Humans wherever they sought to hide.

"Weakling," a sinister voice whispered to Her in a voice like flaying knives. Mistress Arisa.

Lienna shuddered. She did Her best to ignore the voice. It was a phantasm, a relic of a time of madness. Nevertheless, a lingering fear, a stone of doubt accreted within Her mind. Two other times during the attack today, Mother and Father or Arisa, had spoken to Her. Both times, Lienna had been mocked, treated as though She were dung underfoot.

"It is Your truest nature," the cruel voice whispered. *"Dung eater."*

"Can You not hear the cries of the dying? You were once a beloved Healer," Mother said.

"Your legacy is one of blood, pain, and evil," Father added.

"SILENCE!" Lienna shouted. The cries of the dying *did* bother Her, but worse was Mistress Arisa's derisive laughter, Mother's repetitive questioning, and Father's nattering advice. It was exhausting, and Lienna wanted nothing more than to have all the voices gone from Her mind. They weren't real, and yet here they were, whispering poison into Her mind. This after She had thought She'd found a way to cure Her madness.

"The madness is Your conscience," Father said.

Lienna cried out, spiraling away from the city She had so recently destroyed. She out-stripped the clouds and the wind, seeking to escape the demons in Her mind, knowing all the while that She couldn't. She couldn't even pour more madness into the Fan Lor Kum of Continent Catalyst. If She did, Her children would tear into one another with lethal rage.

No. As She had so many other times, Lienna would have to suffer this pain alone. It was the curse of Her loving spirit.

———————•—————

Chak-Soon growled in annoyance. Fine, powdered soil, like ash, matted his fur and irritated his sensitive nose. His ears lay flat against his head as he tried to keep the dust out. The tremendous cloud of dirt and debris blasted skyward from an hour ago still hung in the air, but it was starting to descend like a hazy brown rain. He couldn't see very well, smell very well, or hear very well. And he didn't like it.

He and his claw stood on the summit of a flat-topped hill. His fellow Tigons ranged in size and coloration from an old, lean, cheetah-spotted cat to a younger, thickly muscled, tabby-striped brute. While Chak-Soon was the ordinate, he didn't consider these Chimeras to be his minions. And unlike other claws, he knew he need not fear being overthrown by those in his command. These Tigons considered themselves brothers.

Chak-Soon set aside his wandering thoughts. He and the claw had climbed this hill to gain their bearings.

The River Gaunt was their destination, and this peak—bald except for a sparse crown of skeletal pine trees—offered a view for miles around, including a south-facing scree slope that was angled toward the wide valley and fields Mother had recently smashed. Even now, despite the sound-deadening dust, he could hear Her at work. She was deep within the bulk of the nearby mountain, likely slaughtering any She came across. Chak-Soon and his Tigons would have to work quickly if they were to help carry out Li-Choke's plan and save as many of the Humans as they could. On the side opposite the scree slope, the Bovars and their precious cargo waited at the bottom of the hill, the means by which to carry out Choke's plan.

"Braids," the young tabby, Chak-Lind grunted.

"Three traps," Chak-Rudd, the old cheetah, stated. He gestured to the south.

Chak-Soon looked to where the other Tigons pointed and saw the snake-like Chimeras, fifteen or twenty of them. They were several hundred yards away, slithering along the base of a nearby ridge. They appeared excited, gesturing about with eager energy. Of course, their enthusiasm was to be expected. A battle awaited, and with Mother's presence, victory was all but assured. The Braids, paused every so often, noses to the air and tongues flicking in and out. Chak-Soon wondered how they could taste or smell anything with all the dust billowing about. His brows furrowed, and a moment later, he realized the reason for their excitement: a Human girl flickered into view halfway in between the Braids and the watching Tigons. The child was unskilled. Her Blend was poorly formed even after she re-established it. The Braids would be upon her in minutes.

Chak-Soon sat back on his heels and considered what to do. Thus far his treason had been confined to his thoughts alone. While he could be accused of spreading dissension, such as the knowledge of fraternity, even then he could simply lie; deny any knowledge of it. So long as Chak-Soon's actions reflected the life he was bred to live, no one need find out what was in his heart. If he saved that girl, though, his future would be set and his past lost. He would be branded a traitor. But only if Mother ever learned of his betrayal.

She wouldn't.

Chak-Soon searched the nearby valley and surrounding hills. Good. No one else was around. It might work, but only if his Tigons were swift and bold. "We save girl."

Chak-Kilt, a young leopard-spotted Tigon growled. "Humans. Why?" he asked, appearing fearful.

"Brothers," Chak-Rudd answered.

Chak-Dred, a snow leopard, nodded. "It why we here."

"Not want," Chak-Kilt said, eyes still filled with fear.

Chak-Soon felt pity for the young Tigon. They all recognized the finality of the step they were about to take. He rested his hand on

Chak-Kilt's shoulder and gave it a gentle squeeze. "We be with you, brother," he said.

In the past, Chak-Soon would have merely demanded obedience to his will, and woe unto any Tigon who failed him. Now he attempted inspiration. It was a form of leadership he would have once labeled as weak. He now understood how wrong he had been. Compassion and empathy weren't a sign of weakness. The truth was, it was far easier to have a hard, unforgiving heart than a soft one. Fraternity opened a being's soul to a much harsher pain. For instance, should one of the Tigons in his claw perish, Chak-Soon knew he would feel a hurt such as he had never felt before when those under his command had died. But then again, fraternity also led to a far deeper joy, such as the bond he shared with these Tigons. He knew they felt the same way about him. Prior to his trip to Hammer, it was a closeness Chak-Soon would have never expected to share with anyone.

Chak-Kilt nodded. "We save."

Chak-Soon gave the leopard a final squeeze on the shoulder before facing down the slope to where the Braids had closed the distance with the Human girl. They would be on her in seconds. "We run. Kill all."

He leapt forward, sprinting downward and screaming at the top of his lungs, not because of bloodlust, but to give the Braids pause. He hoped to halt their progress for even the briefest of moments. It might mean the difference between reaching the child in time or watching as she was cut down.

Luck, or maybe the supposed God, Devesh, was with them. The Braids pulled up short in their pell-mell run, gawking at seeing the claw rushing toward them. But the Tigons didn't pause. They sprinted toward the Braids, all of whom had resumed their chase and likely thought the Tigons wanted to take the kill from them.

Seconds later, yards from the girl—no, there were two others who were Blended with her—Chak-Soon and his claw forked about the child as though she were a rock in their rushing stream. They slammed into the unsuspecting Braids. The battle was brutal and short. The snake-like Chims were taken by surprise and more than half of them were down before the others even realized they were under attack. By the time they rallied to defend themselves, it was too late. The survivors of the initial clash were soon dead as well. Afterward, Chak-Soon was heartened to see that none of his Tigons had thrown aside their swords in favor of tooth and nail. Instead, they had fought with the discipline he had encouraged, using Li-Choke's leadership as an example.

He turned to the cowering child, flickering in and out of view. "You safe now," he told her. "Run north. No Fan Lor Kum there yet. Some Humans." He adjusted his gaze to the others who had chosen to remain Blended. They weren't very good, though. Their fear leaked through their Blends as sharp as a fox's musk. "You all go. We see you safe. Hide your trail."

A Human woman flicked into view as she dropped her Blend. She appeared terrified. "Why are you helping us?" she asked in a quavering voice.

Chak-Soon suppressed a smile. With his assortment of sharp teeth and his blood-splattered fur, it would not have been calming. "You know Jessira? Rukh?" he asked.

Some of the fear in the woman's eyes leaked away, but distrust and confusion persisted. "I know them. They're my family."

"She save me. She and he my brothers," Chak-Soon said. "You my brothers. If see Jessira, tell Chak-Soon save you." This time, he couldn't help it. Her puzzlement was just too funny. He smiled, and a moment later, laughed as she shrank away from him. "You run now," he advised. "Fast."

The woman nodded, still appearing shocked and in disbelief. She Blended and led the other Humans in a sprint to the north, probably wanting to put as much distance as possible between herself and the Tigons who had just saved her life.

———•———

After witnessing the large plume of dust rising from the Croft, Farn had turned the column north. As they rode, the Sorrow Bringer had passed close by, a vile purple-hued thundercloud of lightning and evil. Shortly after Her appearance, several sounds carried to them: a shrieking wind carrying the laughter of a fiend; rocks and stones groaning as they were cracked and pulverized; and screams of terror and pain from of all those poor unfortunates in the Queen's path.

Currently, the Ashokans were due east of Mount Fort, traveling through a narrow pass, along the cleft of a dry stream bed. Jaresh glanced about nervously. No Chims so far, but they had to be out here. South of their position rose the shoulders of Mount Frame. It was a lovely spring day, but despite the beautiful setting, it was impossible to forget the disaster unfolding nearby: the murder of a city.

So much desolation and heartache. When Jaresh had first seen the dust cloud reaching for the heavens, it had seemed like the smoke rising from some awful funeral pyre, signifying the death of innumerable people and the end of all their hopes and dreams. For him, all that mattered was finding Rukh.

"Blends nearby," Plinth Fold, a Rahail said.

Jaresh, riding next to Farn at the head of the column, reined in his horse even before Farn held up his hand and called for a halt.

"The hill directly west of us. Large group of them." Plinth's eyes narrowed. "They're heading our way."

"Hold position," Farn commanded. "Let them make it down the

hill. We'll confront them once they can't run."

"What will we do then?" Jaresh asked.

"Take them in," Farn replied. "It's the right thing to do." He shrugged. "Besides, I don't want them running away from us, which they might. And with Chims out there and the Queen Bitch Herself, all of us—Ashokans and Strongholders alike—will need to lean on one another if we want to make it out of here alive." Another shrug. "And if we're *really* lucky, Rukh might be with them."

"Let's hope so," Jaresh said fervently.

"I don't think those people know we're here," said Query Led, a Muran.

"Their Blends aren't worth a spit," Plinth muttered in disgust.

"It's the best they can do," Farn said. "Considering where they started from, it's not too bad."

"They're coming toward us," Query said. "They're Linked. I still don't think they know we're here."

"Good. When they're in reach, Link with them," Farn ordered. "We'll talk then."

They waited for several minutes.

"I can see their Blends now," Farn said.

"They can see ours, too," Plinth said. "They've stopped."

"Drop me out of the Link, but maintain your Blends. I'm going to let them see me," Farn replied. "I'm a familiar face."

Jaresh couldn't tell if Farn had actually done anything until Plinth spoke again. "They're coming toward us," the Rahail said.

"We're Linked with them," Query said just as a large group of people—men, women, and children—blinked into view.

The Strongholders were unlike anyone Jaresh had ever seen— other than Jessira, of course—and the other Ashokans shifted about in their saddles, unsettled by the discordant appearance of the OutCastes. Every one of them had a masala of features, an inter-mix of Rahail, Muran, Cherid, Duriah, Sentya, and Shiyen. There was no evidence of Kumma heritage.

The silence between the two groups stretched on as they sized up one another. Farn dismounted, and of all things, it was a woman, tall and built like a man, who stepped forward to represent the OutCastes. She was dressed in camouflage and outfitted with a sheathed sword, a cased bow, and a quiver of arrows. Her dark hair was tied back in a braid, and her brown-eyed gaze studied them with a frank, if mistrustful, assessment. She was attractive in a brash, assertive way, much like Jessira, and the two women were similar enough in appearance to have been sisters.

"Sign Deep," Farn said by way of greeting.

"Farn Arnicep," the woman replied. "How is it you return to Stronghold on such an inauspicious day?" Suspicion tinged her voice.

Farn ignored the implied insult. "We were sent by Dar'El Shektan to open trade between your city and ours."

"And you happen to arrive at our doorstep on the same day as the Queen?" She asked. "That doesn't strike you as particularly coincidental?"

"Believe what you wish," Farn said. "We saw Suwraith. She passed overhead. The only reason we're still here rather than on our way back to Ashoka is because we thought we might be able to save some of your people."

"How generous," she said, her voice brittle and on edge.

"Do you know Rukh Shektan?" Jaresh asked, no longer able to keep silent. He had to know what had happened to his brother.

"Who is he to you?" Sign asked.

"My brother. I'm Jaresh."

Her eyes rose. "So. He wasn't lying when he said he had a Sentya brother. Some of us didn't believe him."

"How do you know him?" Jaresh asked.

"She is Jessira's cousin," Farn answered.

Well, that explained the resemblance between the two women.

"Cousin, yes," Sign said, "but our bonds go much deeper. I think of her as my akka, my sister." She turned to Jaresh. "Which means you and I are family."

"What?" Jaresh asked.

"Rukh and Jessira are married," she said. "The last time I saw the two of them—" her voice caught "—they were helping evacuate Stronghold, along with my brother and Cedar. I don't know what happened to them afterward." Toward the end, her voice firmed and her features grew flat and unexpressive. Maybe it was the only way to deal with her pain: shove it deep down and ignore it.

Farn stepped forward until he was no more than a few feet from the OutCaste woman. "We did not bring the Sorrow Bringer to your home," he said, staring her in the eyes. "We came to open trade between our two cities and bring Rukh home. His exile has been lifted by the Chamber of Lords. And now we're here to help save as many of your people as we can. We can Blend better than any of you. Let us help."

Sign considered Farn's words, her face impassive. She turned aside, listening to the words of someone speaking behind her.

"Four more Blends," Plinth said into the silence. "Same hill as the one these came from. Coming fast."

Sign shot a look of disbelief at the Rahail. "We don't feel anything," she said.

"What you do or don't feel doesn't matter," Plinth replied. "They're out there, and they're coming."

Jaresh turned to the hill Plinth indicated, scanning it for signs of movement, but he couldn't see anything.

"Keep your Blends Linked with ours," Farn said to Sign. "We can hide you better that way."

She grimaced in distaste, but heeded Farn's advice—or at least Jaresh assumed she did since the OutCastes didn't pull away.

"They know we're here," Query said. "They're moving to intercept."

"Link them as soon as you can," Farn said. "After that, we need to get moving. I don't like being stopped here out in the open."

A moment later, four individuals, three men and one woman flickered into view, their Blends Linked with those of the Ashokans. It was Rukh, two men Jaresh didn't know, and Jessira.

Jaresh dismounted, grinning widely. His brother was alive. Before he knew it, Rukh was standing before him and pulling him into a firm embrace. Farn was there as well, grinning just as widely as Jaresh.

"What are you two doing here?" Rukh asked, appearing as stunned as Jaresh could ever recall seeing.

"We were sent to bring you home," Farn answered, quickly explaining the commutation of Rukh's sentence. He turned to the two men that Jaresh didn't know. "Court. Cedar," he said in hesitation before embracing them. "I am so sorry for what's happened."

Jaresh briefly wondered who these men were to Farn but other concerns were paramount. "We should get moving," he said, glancing about nervously. "We've been stopped too long as it is."

"Agreed," Farn said.

"Where do you intend to go?" one of the men with Rukh asked—Cedar. He apparently had taken command of the OutCastes from Sign.

"Back to Ashoka," Farn said. "We'll search for any other survivors, and then we're going home."

"Perhaps I will see Ashoka after all," Court said with a half-smile of heartbreak.

Farn squeezed the man's shoulder, his face full of sympathy. "I wish I could have seen you again under better circumstances."

"Another three Blends," Query said. "This time from the south."

"Devesh damn it!" Farn said. "Should we just make camp here and wait for everyone to show up?"

Sign Deep was glad to give over command of the Shadowcats and the other twenty-nine warriors from various units to Cedar. He was the only officer amongst them, and so far she was finding that the crown of leadership was a thorny helm. After the Queen's attack on the East Gate, Sign had been charged with leading those who had escaped the slaughter to safety. Her goal had been a large cavern filled with food, water, and weapons—established for just this kind of emergency.

But soon afterward, Chimeras—Tigons, Braids, and Ur-Fels—had caught their scent. The Strongholders had been forced to flee. But always the Chims were right behind them. A few times, the OutCastes had escaped the traps all around them through the simple expedient of hiding. Luck was on their side, and they always managed to find a place to hole up just before a group of Suwraith's beasts marched by. Sign had kept her people moving and alive, but without any real plan on what to do next.

Hopefully, Cedar could do better, even if it meant relying on the Purebloods. Maybe they would all turn out to be like Rukh: open-minded and humble. It flew in the face of everything she knew about Purebloods and the history of her own kind. But then here was Farn Arnicep. During his time in Stronghold, he had been treated just as poorly as Rukh. He had likely been just as angry about it. But despite it all, Farn was *still* willing to help the OutCastes, going so far as to offer them sanctuary in Ashoka itself. If so, she would bless him to the stars

Of course, she still wondered about his appearance back in Stronghold on the same day as Suwraith's arrival. It was a monumental coincidence, but Cedar trusted Farn. Sign figured she would have to as well—unless she was given a reason not to.

"Sir," an Ashokan said. "Those people from the south…their Blends aren't very good."

Sign grimaced. Prior to Rukh's demonstration in the Trials of Hume, she had never given credence to any of the fables about Pureblood abilities in the use of *Jivatma*. She had been wrong about Kummas, and apparently, she was wrong about Murans and Rahails as well. When the Silversuns had approached, none of the OutCastes had known Cedar and the others were there until long after the Ashokans had detected them. And now, this group from the south….Sign couldn't sense the Blends the Ashokans seemed to so easily feel.

Sign didn't like feeling inferior, and right now, she felt distinctly so. After the horrific tragedies today, it seemed such a petty emotion to hold onto; but she clung to it anyway. It was a way to occupy her mind and help her forget….She choked back a sob. Peddananna and Peddamma, Kart, Jeshni, the children, and so many others—all dead. Her city dead. Her people…a single tear streaked a clean line down her dusty face. The Sorrow Bringer was well-named. Sign felt a sob catch in her throat.

"We'll cry when the time is right," Jessira whispered, squeezing her hand. She must have noticed Sign's grief. "You need to stay strong."

Sign nodded and wiped away the tear. Her cousin was a pillar of strength, and strength is what they all needed. That and courage. She prayed her people—the few who remained—would have enough of both to see them through the terrible days to come. Court stepped to her side. Quiet as he usually was, somehow his presence had always been comforting. He put his arm across her shoulder, drawing her into a brief hug before letting her go. He stayed with her, though, for which she was grateful. She couldn't imagine life without her strong, silent brother.

"Three Blends," Cedar, moving to stand next to them. "I can feel them now."

"So do I," Rukh said. He stood with his family: Jaresh and Farn.

Cedar stepped away from the other Strongholders. "I'll let them know we're here," he said. He dropped his Blend and stood in the midst of the pass, waiting for those approaching to notice him.

A flicker to the south revealed those who were coming, and Sign's mouth dropped. Terror hit her with the force of a hammer, and she gasped in shock.

Standing no more than thirty feet away were three Baels. The fragging bastards could Blend! The world was doomed if Suwraith could give Her demonseed creatures Humanity's Talents.

Rukh and Jessira shouted for the Ashokans to hold off their attack.

"It's Li-Choke," Rukh explained to Farn. "You remember him. He was with us in the Hunters Flats."

Farn appeared as stunned and fearful as Sign. "One of Dirge's Baels?" He sounded doubtful.

"Let them approach," Jessira said. "Choke is a friend. They all are if we allow it."

At a gesture from the brute in the center—the one with the most feathers—the Baels fell to a knee, planting their tridents firmly against the ground. Their chained whips remained coiled at their hips. From behind them came a happy cry.

"Cedar," a voice shouted. A woman dashed out from behind the Baels. Laya! Sign gave a happy shout, as did Jessira and Court. Cedar ran forward, inarticulate in his joy. Tears streamed down Sign's face as she watched them embrace. It was a small enough gesture of hope on a day filled with uncountable tragedy. With Laya came two young girls, both under ten. Her nieces.

"I thought I'd lost you forever when we were separated," Cedar said.

"I tried to get back to you, but there were too many Chimeras in the way, and they kept chasing after us." Laya turned a fond smile to the two girls with her. "At least some good came out of it. I came across these two."

"We were driven away as well," Court said. "Cedar had us circle back to where we last saw you, but by the time we got there, you were gone."

"But we're together now," Cedar said, taking her hands and kissing her fingertips. "That's all that matters."

The Baels remained rooted to the ground. They waited, kneeling as Rukh and several other Ashokans—Farn and Jaresh among them—approached. Cedar held Laya as if he never wished to let her go, and some of Sign's fear ebbed. It hadn't been the Baels who had learned to Blend. It had been Laya and the two girls. Somehow, the horned bastards must have coerced Laya and the others to Blend them.

The lead Bael was talking. Sign wanted to hear what was going on. She walked over to them.

"...she says Chak-Soon saved them from fifty Braids," the Bael said, gesturing to Laya.

"We would have been dead if not for the Tigon and his claw. He said we were brothers. It was surreal, especially when he asked if I knew you and Rukh," Laya said, appearing stunned to find herself amongst her family. "I thought maybe I was having a nightmare, but then we ran into these three." She gestured to the lead Bael. "Li-Choke offered to keep us safe if we Blended them. We didn't have many options, but then *he* also asked if I knew the two of you." She looked to Rukh and Jessira. "I always thought your story about Baels couldn't be true, but it was. All of it. The Chimeras are your friends."

"Not all of them," the one named Li-Choke said, coming to his feet. "Only the Baels and a fistful of Tigons."

"Why are you here?" Rukh asked.

"To exterminate you Humans," Li-Choke said with a grin. Sign did not find him amusing. "Mother commanded that I bring a Shatter north to kill any who escaped Her vengeance. As usual, the Baels have decided to interpret Her wishes in our own fashion."

"What do you intend to do?" Jessira asked.

"Mother visited me just before I ran into Laya Grey," Li-Choke answered. "She claimed to have killed any who had escaped your city from the west. She said a few hundred remain of those who fled to the east."

Sign missed the rest of what the Bael said. A few hundred? Out of forty thousand, that was all that was left? So few. Her eyes welled, and she shared a look of horrified loss with Court. How would they survive? Their people were all but extinct.

"And your suggestion is for us to make for the River Gaunt, where it meets River Heart, and hope some Tigons might save us?" Farn said, his voice a growl of distrust. He stood directly in front of Li-Choke, a hand on the hilt of his sword. "Maybe instead, you can explain why I shouldn't cut you and your 'brothers' down right here and now."

"My suggestion isn't without peril," Choke said, sounding unperturbed by Farn's threat. "There is a Fracture in that area, but only one. The rest of the Shatter will be otherwise occupied. It is your best chance to escape."

"We know him," Jessira said to Farn. "We trust him. You were there when his SarpanKum spared my life and those of my brothers. They weren't lying then. Choke's not lying now."

"I agree. I think we should trust him," Rukh said.

Sign looked to Cedar, waiting on his judgment.

"I don't see how we have much choice," Cedar said with a sigh. "We're going north to the confluence of the River Heart and the River Gaunt."

Sign would have expected Farn to ask the opinion of one of the other Kummas, but surprisingly, he turned to Jaresh. "What do you think?"

"I trust Rukh, and he trusts the Bael," Jaresh replied.

Farn looked like he'd swallowed a lemon. "Fine," he said as he unclenched his hand from his sword. "I don't like it, but I *do* remember this Bael and what Rukh said about him. We'll go north." He turned and pointed a threatening finger at the Baels. "But if anything goes wrong, I'll come back from death's door and take all of you with me."

———◆◆———

They picked up another sixty-nine Strongholders during their journey to where the River Heart emptied into River Gaunt. Adding them to their original sixty-two, perhaps only one hundred thirty-one out of forty thousand of their people had survived this morning's slaughter. It was a loss too terrible to put to words, but Cedar had no time to dwell on his grief. He had to lead his people, save them from the noose of Chims ranged throughout the hills and valleys surrounding Stronghold.

Thus far, they had managed the journey north without coming across any more Chims. It was a minor miracle, even with Li-Choke's promise to keep his forces away from the confluence of the Rivers Heart and Gaunt. Cedar didn't entirely trust the Bael, not after all the terrible events of the day; and he certainly didn't expect their luck to hold out. Only an hour earlier, while pinned against the shore of an oxbow lake, he had been certain they had been discovered. A claw of Tigons—herding Bovars harnessed to a large number of wagons— had passed by close enough to count the cats' teeth.

Even finding the canoes and large rafts Li-Choke had promised ready and waiting along the shoreline of River Heart hadn't settled Cedar's fears. Only when his people were on the water and far from here would he believe they might actually survive this disaster. Several of the watercraft had already been launched, and Cedar silently urged those still boarding to greater speed. The center of his back tingled uncomfortably.

His people were tightly packed on a thin sliver of a beach. Around them loomed the walls of a river canyon, widening where the two waters merged. The cliffs extended east and west along the length of the Gaunt, but along the near eastern shore where they stood, the sandstone bluffs slouched down into the water in a gradual tumble of shale and wagon-sized boulders. To the north, mounded hills marched off into the distance, gradually giving way to scalloped mountains. The light was dying with sunset less than an hour away. Shadows stretched long, but on the ravine's floor, a dismal gloom already held sway. A dull, ceaseless thunder echoed along the canyon's wall from the whitewater rapids as the Gaunt raced downhill, over partially submerged boulders, and through a constriction directly to the east.

Cedar watched as another raft was launched. It raced away, making it through the center of the narrowing channel before being lost to view. None of the Ashokans had yet taken to the water. They stood facing back in the direction from which they had come, bows uncased and arrows nocked.

"Just a few more rafts, and all our people will have boarded," Jessira shouted to him over the rushing roar of the rivers pouring together.

Cedar nodded acknowledgement. Just a little bit longer.

As if in response to his burgeoning hope, from the bluffs to the south rose the hooting cries of Balants. Cedar's gaze snapped in the direction of the sound. Standing atop the mesas, were Balants, Tigons, and Ur-Fels dancing about with excitement.

Cedar's heart sank. Their luck had run out. Down on the floor of the ravine, hundreds of Chims appeared. They had their quarry in sight, and they swarmed down the banks of the Heart; minutes away.

The basso roar of a Bael calling the Fan Lor Kum to battle rumbled on the wind.

"Get the women and children aboard first!" Cedar shouted. "Warriors of Stronghold, form a line. Bows!"

Farn Arnicep was also calling for his Ashokans to battle. Their bows were held in steady hands. The Kummas clustered in groups of two and three, standing eerily silent. "Watch our backs," Farn said to Cedar. "Keep them off the bluffs so they can't get at us from behind. We'll hold the ravine."

"There's too many to fight on your own. You'll be destroyed."

Farn unlimbered his bow. "We'll hold as long as we must," he said with grim determination.

"We can help," Cedar insisted. "We aren't cowards."

"I know," Farn said, "but bravery alone won't win this day. Your warriors would do the most good on the cliffs."

Cedar nodded reluctantly, knowing Farn was right. "We'll keep them off your backs," he promised. He was about to lead his warriors to the slopes of the surrounding bluffs, but he paused and turned back. "Thank you, Farn," he said, staring the Kumma in the eyes and infusing his words with all the gratitude he could muster.

Farn briefly squeezed Cedar's shoulder before turning away.

It had been weeks since Aia and her brothers had found Rukh and Jessira in the wilds to the west of the Privations. After their initial meeting, the Kesarins had left the two Humans, wanting to see the high country where so few of their kind had ever been. Their exploration had been a revelation. The mountains were ominous and powerful, with jagged rocks and swift running water. They could end the life of the unwary as easily as any predator. And while game was plentiful, it was hard to catch. Mountain goats could evade the Kesarins without any effort. Lunging down steep cliffs or climbing ragged hills was not something at which Kesarins excelled. Thankfully, herds of antelope and deer also made their homes along the shoulders and valleys of the high country. They were slow and tasty.

Eventually, Aia had seen enough of the lonely mountains. It was time to go and reclaim her Human.

This morning Aia and her brothers had intended to meet Rukh and Jessira in the hills north of the stifling caverns in which he denned, but those plans had quickly gone awry. Nails had clawed their minds. A howling scream had reverberated over the mountains. The Demon Wind. Aia and her brothers had fled, and she wasn't ashamed to admit her fear. No one challenged the Mistress of the Nobeasts, the Sorrow Bringer as the Humans named Her.

Later, when they felt themselves a safe distance away, Aia had time to worry about Rukh. She searched for his thoughts and found them seething with anger and implacable resolve. Rather than flee from the Demon Wind, her Human had placed himself directly in Her path. For a moment, Aia had wondered if Rukh actually planned on fighting the Sorrow Bringer. Thankfully, he had only worked to save as many of his kind as he could. Eventually, Rukh had retreated along with his mate and several others.

Afterward Aia and her brothers had no time to spare for idle thoughts. The hills crawled with Nobeasts. There were far too many for three Kesarins to handle on their own. Even the entire Hungrove Glaring might not have been able to defeat so many. Once again, Aia, Shon, and Thrum had been forced to flee. It left a bad taste in all their mouths. The Kesarins were hunters. They were *never* hunted, and to behave as prey was to be humiliated.

There finally came a time when the Demon Wind left, and it was then that Thrum had argued with Aia when she suggested they help the Humans by killing any Nobeasts who threatened them. To her brother, it made no sense. What were the Humans to them? They owed them nothing, but Aia was firm in her decision. It was something Rukh would have done, and for some reason, his opinion was important to her.

They will die if we don't help them, Aia said. *The Nobeasts seek to finish what their Mistress started. They will kill all the Humans.*

Shon's ears wilted in sorrow. *Even my Jessira?*

Even she, Aia replied.

They are as numerous as blades of grass, Thrum said. *Choose another. What difference does it make if these two happen to perish?*

Because Jessira is mine, Shon declared. *She will not be eaten.*

And Rukh is mine. So we will help them.

How? Shon said, ignoring Thrum's disgusted snarl.

Aia shrugged, a hooding of her eyes. *We'll know how when the time is right.*

The decision made, the three Kesarins tracked Rukh and Jessira's company, watching from a distance. The Humans were skilled at hiding but a few Nobeasts managed to pick up their trail. These, Aia and her brothers killed. It felt good to go on the attack after spending most of the day running.

Eventually, Rukh and Jessira were joined by a host of other Humans.

Is it another glaring? Thrum asked.

I thought those who lived in the deep, dank hole in the mountain were their glaring, Shon said.

No. These are ones who escaped the Demon Wind, said Aia. *The ones Rukh helped save. He is the finest of them.*

No. The finest of them is Jessira, his mate, Shon noted.

Aia blinked, not sure what her brother was implying.

As his mate, she must be finer since he chose her, Shon explained.

Aia rumbled laughter. *You are wise, Shon. The female is always the finer.*

Thrum whoofed laughter as he thumped Shon on the head. *Simpleton.*

The two males tussled for a bit, ending their play when Shon planted a victorious paw on Thrum's chest.

They're moving, Aia said. Thrum took the opportunity to turn the tables on his brother. Aia hissed, quieting both of them. *Let's go.*

They followed as the Humans made their way to the confluence of two great rivers. The three Kesarins stood on a nearby summit and watched.

The Humans—almost entirely females and young ones—sought to escape the Nobeasts by floating down the frothy water on spindly pieces of wood—an idea of utter insanity. Other Humans—mostly males—stood facing back in the direction from which they had come. They formed a thin wall, defying the countless Nobeasts racing toward them. Some of the Demon Wind's creatures even had the heights. They would indeed finish what their Mistress had begun, and yet the Humans refused to yield.

Fools. Why didn't they flee on their strange, floating, wooden splinters?

And her Human, the greatest lackwit of them all, was scaling the hills with his mate. They planned on fighting. For a moment, Aia wondered what drove the Humans to such foolhardy feats. Was it courage or idiocy? No Kesarin would have risked death on behalf of others the way Rukh and his fellow Humans did.

Once again, Aia sensed his determination. It was like when he had faced the Demon Wind: he wouldn't quit until he was either dead or he had accomplished his goal. Many of the other Humans felt the same way.

Aia wondered at their unwavering selflessness.

They will fight so many? Thrum asked in surprise.

Rukh nearly killed himself caring for his mate, Aia said.

Odd, said Thrum.

Do you think they feel so deeply for us? Shon asked.

No, Aia said, *but they can.* She bounded off to where she saw Rukh ascending the shoulder of a boulder-strewn hill. *We will still defend them!*

R ukh was barely panting when he crested the tumbled down cliff. The Silversuns and Shadowcats and other warriors of Stronghold were right behind him. They had to hold the line here, a thin ridge, no more than fifteen feet wide. There was a steep falloff to either side; into River Heart on one and a rocky, maze-like canyon on the other. Only by descending the incline Rukh had just climbed, could the Chims have a chance to get behind the Ashokans and destroy them. The Strongholders couldn't allow it. They had to defend this position as long as possible; fight off hundreds of Chims with their bare three dozen. Terrible odds, but it was Devesh's way.

As Durmer Volk would have said, 'Life only grows easy when we die.' Rukh smiled in remembrance. The past was a rose-tinted heaven, so much sweeter than today's carnage and pain.

"What a fragging terrible reunion," Jaresh said as he reached the summit.

"Why aren't you with the other Ashokans?" Rukh asked in surprise. He still had trouble believing Jaresh was actually here. Any other time, he would have been overjoyed to see him and hear stories from home. Today was not one of those moments. He was grateful for the presence of his fellow Ashokans—without them, the Strongholders would have long-since perished—but part of him wished they had never come. At least that way, Jaresh, Farn, and all the rest of them would be safe.

"You're my brother. Family should fight alongside one another,"

Jaresh said with a grin. "Besides, Amma and Nanna would kill me if I came home without you."

Rukh smiled. "So now it's you who protects me?"

"It goes without saying," Jaresh said.

Jessira reached the top of the cliff along with the rest of the Stronghold warriors. "Why aren't you with the Ashokans?" she asked of Rukh. "You could Annex with them."

Rukh's heart thudded. Jessira had lost everything, but nothing in her expression revealed her pain. Her eyes and stance were focused and unyielding. She would die here on this ridge if it would see her people survive. Her presence in his life was a precious blessing. "You're my wife. My place is by your side."

Wordlessly, Jessira took his hand and squeezed it in gratitude as she rested her forehead against his.

"We'll make it," he whispered to her, his words a prayer.

Cedar had already set the other warriors in their positions. Only seconds remained before the Chims were within bowshot range. What looked like several hundred of Suwraith's warriors rumbled along the clifftops toward them, the Tigons in the lead. "I need you to hold the center of the line," Cedar said to Rukh.

"I'll stand with him," Jessira said.

"I wish I had one of Durmer's aphorisms right now," Jaresh said. "A moment like this demands one of his pithy warrior phrases."

"There is an old one that should do," Rukh said. He filled his lungs and shouted, "Unto the last breath, wield the wild sword and scream defiance!"

There was a moment's pause before the warriors answered, Jaresh the loudest of them. "Until the sun's demise or Suwraith's death, we war!" they responded.

Rukh conducted *Jivatma*, letting it fill him. Time slowed, the world grew sharper, as the skies reddened with the setting sun. The ominous creaks of bows pulled back to their full length grew louder. He Shielded, and his hands glowed with Fireballs.

"Now!" Cedar shouted.

Rukh hurled Fireballs, incinerating the center of the first two rows of the oncoming Chims. Bows twanged. Arrows took down dozens of the beasts. Many more replaced them. A guttural roar shook the air.

⎯⎯⎯•⎯⎯⎯

It had taken the Kesarins time to skirt the Nobeasts—race downhill to the banks of the larger river, then up the incline of the crumbled cliff. Finally, Aia, Thrum, and Shon arrived upon the slip of stone where Rukh, Jessira, and some of the other Humans battled an endless swarm of the Demon Wind's creatures.

Arrows filled the sky, and the air burned with balls of fire. Rukh.

The Kesarins roared. Their deep-throated cries rose above the battle's din, and for a moment, both sides halted as they sought the cause of the sounds. Aia didn't give the Nobeasts a chance to prepare themselves. She ran full speed. Alongside her was Shon, a tawny blur, and Thrum, a russet shadow. They leapt over the Humans and charged. Tooth and claw ran red with the blood of Nocats, Nodogs, and Nosnakes. Even the horned Kezins died beneath the sudden, vicious attack by Aia and her brothers. The Nobeasts faltered. Their charge broke, and they pulled back.

It bought the Humans precious moments to regroup and retreat. Aia led her brothers back to their line, facing the Nobeasts the entire time. *I couldn't let you fight alone,* she said to Rukh, who appeared stunned to see her.

No one kills my Human, said Shon.

Except for Rukh and Jessira, the rest of the Humans had pulled back from the Kesarins. Fear poured off them like smoke from a fire, but down below where more Humans battled, many of them had minds that were strangely quiet. Aia couldn't understand why their thoughts were silent.

They're Annexed, Rukh said. With a flash of knowledge, he explained what he meant. *It can only be done by Kummas.*

And it makes you better warriors?

Yes.

Reach for your mate. I will show her how.

You can do this? Rukh asked, his mind filled with sudden hope.

Yes. Just as I taught you to Heal.

Rukh nodded. *Give it to every one of them.*

Aia glanced at the Chims. They were readying for another attack. She would have to act quickly. Her brothers could help. She explained what was needed, and they agreed, Thrum less happily than Shon.

Aia reached for the Humans and gave them the knowledge Rukh wished them to have.

They screamed in anguish, but in seconds it was over. The remaining twenty or so Humans stared at her with disturbingly expressionless features. Their minds were silent, and the Chims charged with angry howls.

———————•●•———————

Rukh reached for those around him. He found Jessira, Jaresh, and Cedar. They Annexed and a Quad was born.

The Quad's mission was simple: defend the ridge until the women and children were safe. To best accomplish its task, They all needed one another's Talents. With a twist of Jivatma, knowledge was shared. It was done.

The Quad conducted more Jivatma and Shielded the members. A green glow encompassed each of them. Around it, Triads and Duos readied bows. The Quad conducted more Jivatma and readied a different weapon. The members *hands glowed gold.*

The enemy attacked.

Primary, the most powerful, hurled his Fireballs. The other members were weaker and would have to wait for the enemy to close before the Quad could unleash them. Bowstrings snapped. Arrows flew. Chimeras were killed.

The enemy was in range. Secondary, Tertiary, and Quaternary threw their Fireballs, incinerating the onrushing horde. The Kesarins tore into the Chimeras. They carved a bloody path into the ranks of the Fan Lor Kum. Again and again, the Quad flung Fireballs into the teeth of the enemy.

For a brief period, the Quad and those fighting alongside it held the line, but the weight of the horde turned the tide. The Quad drew swords. It took deep cuts and heavy blows but never quit, contesting every foot it was forced to surrender.

The end was nigh.

"Retreat! The women and children are on the water." The cry came from down below.

A change in plans: survival was now the prime directive. Reach the shores of the river.

The Quad unleashed Primary. His sword was the swiftest. His Jivatma the most suited for battle. Primary pushed yards into the enemy, separated from the rest of the Quad. His Shield brightened, and a Fire Shower burned outward. The enemy died in a perfect circle thirty yards wide, but Primary was left unShielded. He would likely die, but the gambit had accomplished its intended task. The other members could now safely retreat. Three would survive rather than none.

The other members were furious and terrified, but the mission was unchanged.

Primary fought on, surrounded on all sides, taking damage. His Shield flared back to life and was snuffed out almost as quickly under the weight of enemies.

Roars of fury and outrage. The Kesarins, Aia, Shon, and Thrum, slashed an opening for Primary to escape.

The Kesarins also took the moment to run.

As soon as Primary caught up with the others, the Quad raced downhill. It had almost reached the base of the cliff when Quaternary took an arrow in the back. He stumbled before falling the last ten feet.

The Quad dissolved.

———◦———

Jessira shook her head in confusion, trying to make sense of where she was. The world was dark and chaotic. Nightfall. What she'd experienced as part of the Quad...the battle on the ridge...Cedar! Jessira ran to her brother. Not him, too. She couldn't take another loss.

Rukh was by her side.

Farn was already there. "I've got him. Cover us," he ordered Rukh. Farn lifted Cedar and carried him toward a canoe guarded by Jaresh, Court, and Sign. A raft with five or six Ashokans pushed off into the water. Another. Jessira realized with a start that she, Rukh, and the others were the last ones still on the riverbank. They stood alone on a narrow sandbar. Sheltering them overhead was the limestone shoulder of a looming cliff.

Raging forward came a mass of Chims, screaming their hate.

Jessira jumped into the canoe's prow. She readied the oars. Farn boarded, gently lowering Cedar. Rukh, the damn fool, stood alone upon the riverbank, yards in front of the others. His hands glowed, and he threw Fireballs. They exploded into the ranks of the massed Chims, funneled as they were by the narrow sandbar. It slowed them, and they screamed anew, this time in anguish.

Jaresh boarded, followed by Sign and Court.

Jessira shouted. "RUKH!"

He heard her. And just like when he had saved Laya, he bounded along the length of the rock wall. Two jumps, and he was by the canoe. He tumbled inside. Court stood, providing cover with his arrows.

Jessira hauled on the oars.

"Go!" Court shouted. His voice ended in a gurgle.

Jessira saw his head fall forward, clutching a spear that had taken him in the chest. He seemed to sigh before he toppled out of the canoe.

Sign screamed. Jaresh held her back from leaping into the water after her brother. A green glow flickered around them. They were Shielded, and spears and arrows rattled against it. Rukh's face showed the strain but he held onto his *Jivatma*.

Court was gone. Jessira played back the final moments of his life over and over again in her mind, praying she would wake up from this nightmare. Her parents, Kart, Jeshni, Court, her nieces and nephews—all of them were dead. Her people....She bit back a sob. She could grieve when they were safe.

Sign cried softly, hugging herself.

They pushed further into the water, and picked up speed. The rapids were upon them, and it would be almost impossible to traverse in the darkness. But Rukh's hands were lit, providing enough light by which to see. The first stretch would be the most dangerous. According to the maps, a half-mile downriver, the Gaunt smoothed out.

Jessira didn't allow the sorrow hollowing her heart to distract her. She didn't allow the tears to fall. She remained focused on the task at hand. She shuddered with relief when the canoe swept past the rapids and into the deep water where the water flowed smooth and sedate.

Cedar coughed just then, only once, before exhaling heavily and lying still.

THE END

A NOTE FROM THE AUTHOR

Thank you for taking the time to read A *Warrior's Knowledge*, and I hope you've enjoyed the story so far. Also, if you're feeling particularly generous, I hope you'll be kind enough to leave your thoughts about the book with Amazon and Goodreads.

Volume Three of *The Castes and the OutCastes* will be the finale of this tale.

GLOSSARY

Note: Most Arisan scholars use a dating
system based on the fall of the First World. Thus:
BF: Before the Fall of the First World.
AF: After the Fall of the First World.

Adamantine Cliffs: White cliffs, about two hundred feet tall that form the southern border of Dryad Park.

Ahura Temple, the: One of the schools of song in Ashoka. Open only to Sentyas.

Aia: A young Shylow/Kesarin.

Alminius College of Medicine: One of the two Shiyen schools of medicine in Ashoka.

Arbiter, the: The administrative judge of the Chamber of Lords, interpreting the various rules and points of etiquette. Typically, he is an older Kumma chosen by the 'Els for his wisdom and knowledge. Upon his election, he gives up his House name and takes on the surname of 'Kumma'. The position is a largely ceremonial one, and his vote is only offered in the case of a tie. His social standing is that of a ruling 'El. Current Arbiter is Lin'El Kumma.

Ashok: Caste Unknown. Historical figure who is the reputed author of the <u>Compact and Binding</u>, the constitutional basis of all governments in Arisa.

Ashokan Guard, the: A reserve unit of about 25,000 warriors meant to support the High Army in times of crisis. It is composed of veteran Kummas, Murans, and Rahails. A few Duriahs have also joined the Guard over the years.

Baels: The commanders of the Fan Lor Kum. They are feared for their intelligence and unwavering commitment to Humanity's destruction as well as their imposing size, chained whips, and tridents. By convention, they are always given a hyphenated name in which Li- makes the first part.

Book of All Souls, the: Sacred text dating from the First World. Author unknown, but said to be Devesh Himself. Over time since the fall of the First World, it has taken on secondary importance to *The Word and the Deed* in the religious life of most people.

Brand Wall: Caste Rahail. Born AF 2041 to Trudire and Simala Wall. Twenty-one years old at the time of his first Trial.

Bree Shektan: Caste Kumma. House Shektan. Born AF 2044 to Dar'El and Satha Shektan.

Brit Hule: Caste Rahail. Born 2027. He is the youngest Patriarch in living memory as well as the youngest Magistrate in the Magisterium.

Cal Dune: OutCaste. Born AF 2011. Colonel of the Home Army of Stronghold. He is the highest ranking officer in the Army and answerable only to the Governor-General.

Caravan: Trade expedition meant to maintain contact between the cities. Protection of the caravan—a Trial—has come to be seen as a holy duty, for only through the free exchange of knowledge can Humanity hope to survive the Suwraith's unending madness.

Castes, the: The social, moral, and economic organization of all cities on Arisa.

> **Kumma**: The warrior Caste. They are involved in all aspects of defense, supplying the vast majority of warriors to the Ashokan military and the caravans. Their Talents are especially suited for battle.

Sentya: Known for their accounting acumen and their skill with musical instruments and compositions. The finest musicians and composers are always Sentya. They possess the Talent of Lucency, which allows them to think with near utter clarity. In such a state, emotions are distant. They can also project this ability onto others.

Duriah: Born to build, they are thick and stocky. Their Talent is to Cohese: the ability to take various objects and substances, and from them, forge something different and more useful. Rare individuals can DeCohese, which is the ability to break any object down to its basic components. A master craftsman is known as a Cohesor.

Rahail: They maintain the Oasis, sensing where it is growing thin and working to repair and renew it. It is done through their Talent of Sharing wherein they literally give their *Jivatma*, letting it seep into an Oasis and keep it strong. It is an ability they can use but don't really understand, even two thousand years after it first manifested. Their Caste is structured entirely around this Talent, although some join the caravans or the Ashokan Guard.

Muran: Traditionally, they are farmers, although some join the caravans or the Ashokan Guard. Their Talent allows them to bring even a desert to flower. However, the pride of the Caste is their singers.

Cherid: Physically they are the smallest of all the Castes, but Cherids are generally the leaders of a city. It is through their natural intelligence and cunning, as well as their Talent. They possess the ability of Synthesis: they can combine *Jivatmas* and share it out amongst others. Thus, a Rahail can maintain the city's Oasis, not simply with the strength of his own Caste, but that of all Castes if need be.

Shiyen: They all possess the ability to Heal to a certain extent, but only the most gifted amongst them are chosen for one of Ashoka's two medical colleges. The rest are generally craftsmen and merchants.

Cedar Grey: OutCaste. Born AF 2039 to Sateesh and Crena Grey. Lieutenant in the Stronghold Home Guard as a member of the Silversun scouts.

Chamber of Lords: Kumma ruling Council. It consists of all the ruling 'Els and presided over by the Arbiter. It is involved in decision-making that will affect the Caste as a whole. The Chamber also renders judgment for those charged with being Unworthy or thought to be traitors.

Chimeras, the: Suwraith's created forces who comprise the Fan Lor Kum. There are seven species of Chimeras: Baels, Tigons, Braids, Ur-Fels, Bovars, Balants, and Pheds. All species of Chimeras have some degree of intelligence except for Pheds and Bovars. Pheds are simply a meat source, grown only to feed the Fan Lor Kum. Bovars are beasts of burden, much like oxen, but it is from them that the most intelligent of all Chimeras were birthed: the Baels. The Chimeras are marsupial and born in groups of five, what they label a crèche, and mature to full adulthood within a few years, although the Baels take slightly longer.

City Watch, the: Peacekeeping unit of about three hundred warriors, called upon to maintain the peace and investigate crime in Ashoka.

Compact and Binding: The constitution by which all cities on Arisa are organized. Dated to just after the Night of Sorrows.

Conn Mercur: Caste Shiyen. He is the dean of Verchow College of Medicine.

Constrainers: Leather vambraces used in training or tournaments as a means to suppress the expression of an individual's *Jivatma*.

Council of Rule: Ruling Council of the Sil Lor Kum. It is comprised of the SuDin and the six MalDin.

Court Deep: OutCaste. Born AF 2040. Cousin to Cedar and Jessira Grey and brother to Sign Deep.

Crena Grey: OutCaste. Born 2007. Married to Sateesh Grey and amma to Kart, Cedar, Jessira, and Lure. Adopted Court and Sign Deep.

Croft, the: Large fertile valley that provides all of Stronghold's food. It is tightly regulated by the Home Senate.

Crofthold: A neighborhood in Stronghold. Each Crofthold is built vertically, each with ten levels and a large atrium in the center. There are ten Croftholds.

Dar'El Shektan: Caste Kumma. House Shektan. Born AF 2006 as Darjuth Sulle to Jarned and Tune Sulle of House Ranthor. Completed four Trials before retiring at age thirty-one. He transferred to House Shektan upon his return to Ashoka after his fourth and final Trial. Married Satha nee Aybar in AF 2039. Later, in AF 2050, he became the ruling 'El of his House.

Days of Desolation: A period of decades where the light of civilization was almost put out. Suwraith raged unchecked throughout the world, and Humanity lay huddled within its cities, hoping to ride out the storm.

Disbar Merdant: OutCaste. Born 2035. Plumber and engaged to Jessira Grey.

Dos Martel: Caste Muran. Born AF 1998. As well as being the Magistrate representative of her Caste, she is also a singer of great repute.

Dru Barrier: OutCaste. Born AF 2024. Major East of the Home Army of Stronghold. Second highest officer of the Army and answerable only to the Colonel and Governor-General.

Dryad Park: A large, public park known variously as 'the Soul of Ashoka' or 'the green jewel of Ashoka'. It was developed under the auspices of the Magisterium in AF 1363 on an area of boggy, impoverished land full of rundown homes and apartments. The park has gone through several transitions, including a disastrous period of time in the 1600's where the fashion of the day was to return public land to its natural state. The park quickly became a bog once again with swamp gases regularly polluting the air. Thankfully, this idea of 'natural' spaces was swiftly abandoned. In addition, during times of emergency, the park can be converted into arable land.

Durmer Volk: Caste Kumma. House Shektan. Born AF 1990 to Hurum and Kiran Volk. Completed six Trials before retiring at age thirty-five. He is charged with the early training of young Shektans and known as the 'Great Rahail' for how seriously he takes his duties. Member of the House Council.

East Vineyard Steep: An area of relatively rundown homes and buildings, which barely stand erect. However, the main denizens, the Sentyas, prefer it this way. They would rather not waste money to maintain their homes beyond what's absolutely needed.

Fan and the Reed, the: All-female Kumma academy in Ashoka. Founded AF 343.

Fan Lor Kum: The Red Hand of Justice. Suwraith's forces in the Wildness. Their soul purpose is to kill Humans wherever they find them. They are organized into Plagues, and the commander of each

Plague is titled the SarpanKum, a Bael of great cunning and skill. The Fan Lor Kum are sometimes referred to simply as the Chimeras.

Organization of the Fan Lor Kum:

One hundred Chimeras form a Smash and the commander is labeled a Jut

Ten Smashes form a Fracture and the commander is labeled a Levner

Fifteen Fractures form a Shatter and the commander is labeled a Vorsan

Eight Shatters form a Dread and the commander is labeled a Sarpan

Two Dreads form a Plague and the commander is titled the SarpanKum

> *All commanders at every level are Baels. Of note is the SarpanKi, who does not fit into this hierarchy. The SarpanKi is the special adjunct to the SarpanKum, almost always from his crèche, and outranks the Sarpans.

Farn Arnicep: Caste Kumma. House Shektan. Born AF 2041 to Evam and Midre Arnicep. He is twenty-one years old at the time of his first Trial.

Fifty-Five, the: The fifty-five survivors of Hammer's Fall. They went on to found the city of Stronghold in AF 1753.

First Father: Along with the First Mother, He was the ruler of the First World, greatly responsible for the peace and fortune of that time. Legends say that the First Father broke the WellStone and was thereby able to gain entrance to the fortress of the First Mother, and together, they were able to bring life to a dead and desolate land. The Baels claim it was the First Father's own Daughter, Lienna, who murdered both of Her Parents.

First Mother: Along with the First Father, She was the ruler of the First World, greatly responsible for the peace and fortune of that time. The Baels claim it was the First Mother's own Daughter, Lienna, who murdered both of Her Parents.

First World: Legendary time of peace and prosperity prior to the arrival of Suwraith. With the death of the First Mother and the First Father, the First World ended with the Night of Sorrows.

Fol Nacket: Caste Cherid. Born AF 2006. He is the Cherid Magistrate and head of the Magisterium.

Fort and the Sword, the: All-male martial academy in Ashoka. Only open to Kummas. Established AF 121.

Fragrance Wall: An area of manses and estates. It is the home to most Cherids.

Garnet Bosde: Caste Kumma. House Shektan. Born AF 1985 to Reoten and Preema Bosde. Completed five Trials before retiring at age thirty-four. One of Dar'El Shektan's earliest supporters and a member of the House Council.

Gelan Criatus: Caste Shiyen. Born AF 435 in Hammer. Widely considered the Nanna of modern medicine.

Glory Stadium: Ashoka's main stadium where the Tournament of Hume and other citywide events take place.

Gren Vos: Caste Shiyen. Born AF 1975. She was a highly respected physician in her day, and is currently the longest serving Magistrate, having first been elected in AF 2021.

Gris Holianth: Caste Shiyen. Born AF 2011. Owner of the Long Pull, a pub.

Hal'El Wrestiva: Caste Kumma. House Wrestiva. Born AF 2000 as Halthin Bramer to Suge and Bryni Bramer of House Wrestiva. Completed eight Trials before retiring at age 36. Married to Kilwen nee Asthan in AF 2038 and widowed in AF 2049. Became the ruling 'El of his House Wrestiva in 2046. Also is the SuDin of the Sil Lor Kum of Ashoka.

High Army of Ashoka: Professional army of Ashoka made entirely of veterans of the Trials. Most of their ranks are filled out by Kummas, including the post of Liege-Marshall. Currently composed of two legions and a total of approximately 11,000 warriors.

Hold Cavern: A quiet neighborhood of small homes and shops. It is home to many Rahails.

Home Army: The Army of Stronghold.

Home Senate: Highest governmental body in Stronghold with eleven members. There is one senator per Crofthold and the Governor-General.

   Senators:

   Nox Bitter: Represents Crofthold Babylin.
   Mix Ware: Represents Crofthold Primus.
   Brill River: Represents Crofthold Jonie. Oldest senator.
   Gourd Mille: Represents Crofthold Sharing.
   Thistle Rub: Represents Crofthold Lucent.
   Foil Leak: Represents Crofthold Ware.
   Shun Morn: Represents Crofthold Clannad.
   Drape Wilt: Represents Crofthold Cohesed.
   Frame Seek: Represents Crofthold Healed.
   Wheel Cole: Represents Crofthold Synthesis.

Home Watch: Police force of Stronghold. The members are all veterans of the Home Army, with roughly five of them stationed in each of the ten Croftholds.

House of Fire and Mirrors, the: All-male martial academy in Ashoka. Generally for Kummas but open to other Castes. Founded AF 216.

Hume Telrest: Caste Kumma. Born AF 1702. He is universally regarded as the finest warrior in the history of Arisa, having completed twenty Trials. It is in his honor that the Tournament of Hume is held in every city throughout the world.

Hungrove, the: A glaring of Shylows/Kesarin led by Aia's nanna.

Insufi **blade**: The sword given to a warrior during his *upanayana* ceremony.

Ironwood: A fast growing tree known for its lightweight, hardy wood, which has properties similar to iron and is similarly fire resistant.

Isle of the Crows: An island infamous for its black crows in Bar Try Bay. It is where the remains of traitors are left to rot. With the lack of a purifying pyre, such individuals are thought to lose Devesh's grace, and are either punished within the unholy hells or shackled again to the wheel of life to be reborn in a position of impoverishment and suffering.

Jared Randall: Caste Rahail. Born AF 2025. Completed three Trials. Caravan master of the caravan to Nestle. Suspected member of the Sil Lor Kum, although the proof is rather sparse.

Jaresh Shektan: Caste Sentya. House Shektan. Born AF 2042 to Bresh and Shari Konias. His birth parents died in an apartment fire, and he was adopted by Darjuth (later to be Dar'El) and Satha Sulle. He is the only such individual ever adopted into a Kumma House who is himself not a Kumma.

Jaciro Temult: Caste Shiyen. Born AF 2007. A disreputable Shiyen physician whose addiction to opium and alcohol resulted in the loss of his medical license. He is reputed to offer illicit medical services to those for whom discretion is of utmost importance.

Jessira Viola Grey: OutCaste. Born AF 2042 to Sateesh and Crena Grey. Warrior of the Stronghold Home Army and a member of the Silversun scouts.

Jivatma: Some believe this to be the body's soul. It springs from a person's Well like a waterfall and can be made richer and more vibrant through discipline and hard work.

Jone Drent: Caste Duriah. Born AF 2005. He has the rare ability to both Cohese and DeCohese. He is the Duriah Magistrate.

Jubilee Hills: An expansive area of rolling hills. It is home to Kummas.

Kart Grey: OutCaste. Born AF 2028 to Sateesh and Crena Grey. Brother to Jessira Grey and Cedar Grey. Cousin to Court Deep and Sign Deep.

Keemo Chalwin: Caste Kumma. House Dravidia. Born AF 2041 to Loriad and Mishal Chalwin. He is twenty-one years old at the time of his first Trial.

Kesarin, the: See Shylows.

Kezin: See Slayer.

Krain Linshok: Caste Kumma. House Flood. Born AF 2003 to Halsith and Jennis Linshok. He has completed five Trials. He is the Kumma Magistrate.

Kuldige Prayvar: Caste Kumma. Born AF 1825. Originally of House

Trektim, he went on to found House Shektan in AF 1872. He was thereafter known as Kul'El Shektan. He is also a self-confessed member of the Sil Lor Kum, ruling them for a time as the SuDin.

Larina, the: The only school of singing in Ashoka. Open only to Murans.

Laya Grey: OutCaste. Born 2038. Wife of Cedar Grey and vadina to Jessira and Kart Grey and Court and Sign Deep.

Layfind Fish Market: A raucous area of stores and booths near Trell Rue.

Li-Charn: SarpanKum of the Fan Lor Kum at the time of Hammer's Fall.

Li-Dirge: SarpanKum of the Fan Lor Kum during the destruction of the caravan to Nestle.

Li-Reg: SarpanKi to Li-Dirge and his crèche brother.

Lighted Candle, the: Sentya academy given over entirely to the study of finance and accounting.

Lin'El Kumma: Caste Kumma. Born into House Therbal on AF 1980. Completed six Trials and retired at age 34. Elected as the Arbiter of the Chamber of Lords on AF 2051, and thereafter took the surname 'Kumma'.

Lure Grey: OutCaste. Born AF 2044 to Sateesh and Crena Grey. Warrior of the Stronghold Home Army and a member of the Silversun Scouts.

MalDin: The Servants of the Voice. The leaders of the Sil Lor Kum. Along with the SuDin, the six MalDin comprise the Council of Rule.

Mesa Reed: Caste Cherid. Born AF 2017. She is one of the wealthiest women in the city, having earned her money through a combination of inheritance from her deceased husband and her own investments. She is a MalDin of the Sil Lor Kum.

Mira Terrell: Caste Kumma. House Shektan. Born AF 2042 to Janos and Sophy Terrell. She has recently completed her yearlong internship with House Suzay.

Moon Quarter: Area of wharves, docks, and factories. By law, all manufacturing or industry, which might result in malodorous pollution, must be placed in the Moon Quarter. As such, it is an undesirable residential area.

Moke Urn: Caste Sentya. Born AF 2020. He was born in relative poverty and obscurity but is brilliant when it comes to finances. He was given an opportunity to demonstrate his skills as a member of the Sil Lor Kum of which he is now a MalDin.

Mon Peace: OutCaste. Born AF 2000. Governor-General of Stronghold. In his second term.

Nape Pile: OutCaste. Born AF 2014. Major West of the Home Army of Stronghold. Second highest officer of the Army and answerable only to the Colonel and Governor-General.

Night of Sorrows: The night when Suwraith was born and killed nearly half of all people living at the time.

Nine Hills of Ashoka:
                Mount Creolite
                  Mount Walnut
                  Mount Channel
                  Mount Crone
                  Mount Cyan
                  Mount Bright
                  Mount Auburn
                  Mount Equine
                  Mount Style

Oasis: A powerful manifestation, supposedly of *Jivatma*, which appeared suddenly and unexpectedly around certain cities of the First World just prior to Suwraith's arrival. Over the ensuing two millennia, they have proven nearly impervious to Suwraith's power. Rahails maintain the Oasis of a city through their Talent of Sharing, but how they manage this is a mystery even to them.

Peddamma: Aunt as father or mother's older brother's wife or father or mother's older sister.

Peddananna: Uncle as father or mother's older brother or father or mother's older sister's husband.

Plaza of the Martyr: The largest public plaza in Ashoka. Also known as the 'Heart of Ashoka'. It is famous for the Union Fountain.

Plaza of Toll and Toil: The large plaza into which the Magisterium opens. Historically, it was where the contracts of indentured servants were auctioned.

Poque Belt: Caste Sentya. Born AF 2018. He founded a forensic accounting service. Rumor has it he was elected Magistrate for his Caste simply so he could no longer audit the work of other Sentyas.

Rector Bryce: Caste Kumma. House Shektan. Born AF 2029 to Garnet and Maris Bryce. His parents divorced when he was twelve. Completed four Trials before retiring at age thirty-two. Member of Ashokan Guard as a lieutenant of the **Fifth Platoon, Third Company, Second Brigade, Third Legion,** and also a lieutenant in the City Watch.

Ronin: A Kumma warrior expelled from his House. Other than being found Unworthy or given the Slash of Iniquity, nothing is more shameful.

Rose and the Thorn, the: One of the schools of song in Ashoka. Open only to Sentyas.

Rukh Shektan: Caste Kumma. House Shektan. Born AF 2041 to Dar'El and Satha Shektan. He is twenty-one years old at the time of his first Trial. He is the first Virgin to win the Tournament of Hume.

Sarath, the: Rahail academy in Ashoka. Students are instructed in both the maintenance of the Oasis and also trained as warriors.

Sateesh Grey: OutCaste. Born 2008. Married to Crena Grey and nanna to Kart, Cedar, Jessira, and Lure. Adopted Court and Sign Deep.

Satha Shektan: Caste Kumma. House Shektan. Born AF 2019 to Mira and Rukh Aybar of House Shektan. Married Darjuth Sulle (later to be Dar'El) in AF 2039. She is as responsible for House Shektan's rise in wealth and prestige as her husband. She is admired and loathed in equal measure by the other ruling 'Els.

School of Water, the: All-female Kumma academy in Ashoka. Established AF 153.

Semaphore Walk: Ashoka's theater district.

Shield, the: Rahail academy in Ashoka. Focus is on the training of those sufficiently gifted to maintain the Oasis.

Shir'Fen, the: Rahail military academy in Ashoka. Rigorous admission standards and instructors are a mix of Kummas and Rahails.

Shoke: A wooden blade used in training and tournaments. It is blunted and possesses properties that allow it to produce as true a representation as possible of the damage inflicted by an edged weapon without actually causing permanent injury or death.

Shylows: The great cats of the Hunters Flats. They grow to be over seven feet in height and twenty-five feet from nose-to-tail. They are feared for their great speed, power, and ability to see through Blends. The cats are extremely territorial and hunt in glarings, packs of forty-to-fifty. They name themselves the Kesarins.

Sil Lor Kum: The Hidden Hand of Justice. They are the Human agents of Suwraith and are universally hated and despised. Many consider their existence to be a myth, although inexplicable setbacks are often attributed to the Sil Lor Kum.

Sign Deep: OutCaste. Born 2042. Sister to Court Deep and cousin to Kart, Cedar, Jessira Grey.

Slash of Iniquity: A judgment by the Kumma Chamber of Lords in which an individual is found to be deviant and traitorous. Such an individual is either executed with his remains left on the Isle of the Crows or in some instances, merely banished forthwith.

Slayer, the: Leader of a glaring of Shylows. Also known as the Kezin.

Society of Rajan: Legendary society originally founded by Raja, a Cherid, in Hammer who discovered *The Book of First Movement*. The Society has come to believe that *The Book* is the key to defeating Suwraith. Though the Society has failed in its mission of learning the secrets they claim is in *The Book*, nevertheless, they have spread to all the other cities of Arisa, where their influence and reputation is outsized to their actual numbers. The Society in each city is comprised of twenty-one active members: three from each Caste with an Apprentice, Journeyman, and Master. Since the Society members are chosen *after* they have proven their worth as influential and moral members of their Castes, they are generally in their thirties before they are first brought into the Society as Apprentices. Some Rajans do resign or retire, but this is rare, and such individuals are no longer allowed to vote on Society business.

Current members:

Caste Kumma:
Master: Silma Thoran
Journeyman: Dar'El Shektan
Apprentice: Bravun Silan

Caste Sentya:
Master: Thrivel Nonel
Journeyman: Shitha Krane
Apprentice: Chima Plast

Caste Duriah:
Master: Jaka Moth
Journeyman: Anian Elim
Apprentice: Bove Moth

Caste Rahail:
Master: Grain Jola
Journeyman: Lesur Mint
Apprentice: Olin Treave

Caste Shiyen:
Master: Gren Vos
Journeyman: Rassin Chin
Apprentice: Nisin Mercus

Caste Muran:
Master: Ular Sathin
Journeyman: Walid Greenvole
Apprentice: Alms Soildrew

Caste Cherid:
Master: Sim Chilmore

Journeyman: Diffel Karekin

Apprentice: Minet Jorian

Sophy Terrell: Caste Kumma. House Shektan. Born AF 2014 to Kolt and Versana Drathe of House Primase. Married Odonis Terrell of House Shektan in AF 2035. Member of the House Council.

Sorrows of Hume, the: Aphorisms attributed to Hume Telrest.

Spidergrass: A type of plant that grows best in temperate climates. It is used in the fashioning of items once made with metal. Duriah smiths claim it has tensile properties identical to the finest steel.

Stone Cavern: A neighborhood of craft shops and manufacturing. It is where most Duriahs live.

Stronghold: City of OutCastes founded in AF 1753 but the fifty-five survivors of Hammer's Fall. The city is hidden in the Privation Mountains, deep within Mount Fort.

Stronghold Government: The city is divided into ten Croftholds. Each Crofthold has its own Home Council. Within each Crofthold, the Home Councils have wide discretion in governance. The Home Senate is responsible for citywide issues, such as management of the Croft and defense.

Additionally, each Council chooses a Senator to represent their interests in the Home Senate. There are ten Senators.

The Governor-General is the highest elected official, and he elected every five years in a citywide election.

Stryd Bosna: Caste Kumma. House Andthra. Born AF 2032 to Darjuth and Selese Bosna. Completed four Trials. He is the Captain of the caravan to Nestle.

SuDin: The Voice who Commands. The leader of the Sil Lor Kum.

Suge Wrestiva: Caste Kumma. House Wrestiva. Born AF 2040 to Hal'El and Kilwen Wrestiva. He has yet to be chosen for his first Trial. He remains a Virgin at the age of twenty-two. It is somewhat scandalous.

Sunpalm Orchard: A wealthy, quiet neighborhood of stately townhomes and small craft shops. It is home to many Shiyens.

Suwraith: A murderous being of wind and storm who suddenly exploded into existence two thousand years ago. Her only desire seems to be the extinction of Humanity. Her origin is a mystery, although the Baels claim that She was the Daughter of the First Mother and First Father, murdering them on the Night of Sorrows. The Fan Lor Kum name Her Mother Lienna. Humanity also names her the Bringer of Sorrows or the Queen of Madness.

Talents: Skills possessed by individuals of various Castes, each one unique to a Caste.

Tanner's School of Animal Husbandry: Shiyen school of veterinary medicine.

Trial: The holy duty in which warriors leave the safety of an Oasis and enter the Wildness in order to defend a caravan, even if it costs them their lives.

Trell Rue: A fashionable neighborhood of artisan shops and restaurants.

Triumph Court: Plaza surrounding the Glory Stadium.

Ular Sathin: Caste Muran. Clan Balm. Born AF 1989. Completed two Trials before retiring at age twenty-eight. He was a well-to-do farmer before selling his property to other members of his Clan. He is a MalDin of the Sil Lor Kum.

Unworthy: A designation by which a Kumma is felt to be a coward and/or morally compromised. Such an individual is banished from the city.

Upanayana ceremony: Ceremony that consecrates a boy to his duties as a man. It involves two days and two nights of fasting and praying in solitude and silence. In the case of Kummas and other warriors, it is followed by the granting of the *Insufi* blade at dawn.

Vadina: Sister-in-law (brother's wife or husband's sister). In contrast to **maradalu**, which is sister-in-law as a wife's sister.

Varesea Apter: Caste Rahail. Born AF 2019. Married to **Slathtril Apter**. She is a member of the Sil Lor Kum.

Verchow College of Medicine: One of the two Shiyen medical colleges in Ashoka.

Well: The place within an individual wherein *Jivatma* resides. Some believe the Well is simply another word for consciousness, and from consciousness, *Jivatma* springs forth.

Wildness, the: The vast area beyond the borders of the cities and their Oases.

Word and the Deed, the: Author unknown. It is a sacred text written prior to the fall of the First World. Over time, it has supplanted *The Book of All Souls* as the main source of religious scripture within the world.

Yuthero Gaste: Caste Shiyen. Born AF 2025. He is one of the youngest professors of Surgery at Alminius School of Medicine. He is also a MalDin of the Sil Lor Kum.

ABOUT THE AUTHOR

Davis Ashura resides in North Carolina and shares a house with his wonderful wife who somehow overlooked Davis' eccentricities and married him anyway. As proper recompense for her sacrifice, Davis unwittingly turned his wonderful wife into a nerd-girl. To her sad and utter humiliation, she knows *exactly* what is meant by 'Kronos'. Living with them are their two rambunctious boys, both of whom have at various times helped turn Davis' once lustrous, raven-black hair prematurely white. And of course, there are the obligatory strange, strays cats (all authors have cats—it's required by the union). They are fluffy and black with terribly bad breath. When not working—nay laboring—in the creation of his grand works of fiction, Davis practices medicine, but only when the insurance companies tell him he can.

He is the author of the semi-award winning epic fantasy trilogy, *The Castes and the OutCastes*, as well as the YA fantasy, *The Chronicles of William Wilde*. Visit him at www.DavisAshura.com and be appalled by the banality of a writer's life.